Mint Julep

(The Reunion)

As Told to
Gracie Buckhalter

NITA CLARKE

Copyright © 2019 Nita Clarke
All rights reserved
First Edition

PAGE PUBLISHING, INC.
New York, NY

First originally published by Page Publishing, Inc. 2019

ISBN 978-1-64462-699-3 (Paperback)
ISBN 978-1-64462-700-6 (Digital)

Printed in the United States of America

To all my beloved family and faithful friends.
To God be the glory.

Acknowledgments

THE AUTHOR WISHES to acknowledge these great American treasures: Louisiana, Georgia, Kentucky, North and South Carolina, New York, and our friends to the north, Toronto and Montreal, Canada.

New Orleans, Louisiana (the Big Easy); New York, New York (the Big Apple); Savannah, Georgia.

The Atchafalaya River. The mighty Mississippi.

Smooth, delicious Kentucky bourbon and, of course, the gentleman's drink, the nectar of the gods, mint julep.

Foreword

"Laisser Les Bon Temps Rouler, Mon Chère!"

MY FIRST FEW years of life were spent as a military brat, where we moved from base to base, never staying long enough to make any real friends. My family consisted of myself, my older brother, Mom, and Dad. In my early preteens, Mom came to us and said, "Pack your bags, we are moving home." *Home* turned out to be a small town in Louisiana named Opelousas, a big difference from military life. At first, I was a little turned off by the native's funny talk, the food they ate, and the music they listened to. But it wasn't long before I turned into a broken-French-talking, zydeco-dancing, gumbo-eating little Creole girl. I loved the closeness of being in such a small place where you knew everyone and everyone was related. My small family turned into this humongous melting pot of French, African American, Asian, and Native American people, and they all knew me. I couldn't even walk down the street without someone saying, "How you mama doing?" or "Hey, chère, chère!"

Growing up in Louisiana was quite an experience, an experience that my mother, Nita Clarke, is going to share with you in the continuing saga of the LaPierre family, *Mint Julep (the reunion)*. Mint Julep is an excerpt from our lives.

I am so very proud of my mother, of her hard work in achieving her goals of putting Louisiana on the map. Miss. Nita Clarke is an extraordinary writer, mother, and friend. So my advice would be to get her book, because many people don't know the feeling of warmth and love that you can get from a good cup of anything with mint!

Michele Clarke

Foreword

MY NAME IS Michael Clarke, but during the late seventies, I became known as Timothy, the subject of my mother's first children's book, Timothy and the Blanket Fairy.

The book told the world that I sucked my thumb and cuddled a blanket and just how she created the blanket fairy who came one night to take my blanket, and as she put it, I became a big boy who no longer needed to suck my thumb either. Of course, we went to an amusement park to celebrate, but when the book came out, all my personal business was out in the open for the world to know about. How embarrassing was that for a young boy! And if that wasn't bad enough, she would take me with her when she spoke at various schools to promote the book, introducing me as Timothy as I sat, embarrassed, on a stage in an auditorium filled with people.

As I grew older, so did the characters she wrote about, and I became Billy, the main character of her second children's book, The Mystery at Rancho Verde, where I was at least a more mature subject that actually solved a mystery in a setting that was based on her own childhood.

It would not be until years later that I realized that my mother was a writer, and even though she had chosen me to build her characters around, she, in no way, intended to deliberately embarrass me. In fact, I became very proud of her talents, and with my sister, Michele, I am usually one of the first ones through the doors at her book signings, smiling, shaking hands with her fans, and just waiting for someone to ask, "Is that Timothy?"

Mint Julep (The Reunion) has to be her best writings so far, and although I was born in Kentucky, the book captures the essence of the bayou country as I have seen during my visits there. She still celebrates her son, though, but this time as the producer of Mint Julep theme song that opens her website and, as she says, "inspired [her] to finish Mint Julep (the reunion)."

Both my sister and I are still very careful about what we do and what we say when we are in the company of our mother. We have definitely learned that she considers everything when she is writing and we could end up being the subject of her next book.

Congratulations, Maw!

Mike "Gable" Clarke
Lexington, Kentucky

Chapter 1

My name is Alexandra Menard LaPierre, an African European Asian American and heiress to the LaPierre dynasty of manufacturing companies, which provides this fine country of ours with luxurious mint julep cups. I must say that I was very honored and tickled to a delicate and flattering, indeed, shade of pink when Miss. Gracie Buckhalter, fine writer that she is, agreed to let me share this story with her about our family's three-day family reunions, a splendid tradition that began decades ago and is held every five years here in the shadows of the beautiful magnolia trees of the LaPierre-Menard Plantation.

I represent just a single petal in the colorful flower garden of my family; we are delicate daisies, lavish lilies, ravishing roses, viral violets, and most certainly, a few hidden hydrangeas. Even with all our bodacious history and the many secrets that you are about to discover, I am very proud to be a descendant of the LaPierre-Menard family.

If I had to recall the most favorite times of my life, they would most certainly be those times that I spent at the LaPierre-Menard Plantation in the deep recesses of the magnificent magnolia trees of the Bayou Frou-Frous, named after its infamous owner, in the great state of Louisiana, nestled just a few miles from the Atchafalaya River.

Our family reunions brought relatives from all over the entire world, and every year the men would separate from the women to perform the traditional "telling of the family stories" to the next generation of LaPierre-Menard men. Even when I was just a precious child, my time was spent in the company of the older Southern LaPierre-Menard gentlemen, my daddy's strapping brothers, each with their own segment of our family history to tell as they savored their huge cigars after a wickedly delicious meal of Creole cuisine that had been prepared by the women of the family, including my mother and my two portly aunts, who knew very well how to cook, sew, clean, and most assuredly, please their men with their insatiable desires, although none would ever dare to admit to the latter in public. My LaPierre-Menard grandparents actually gave birth to ten boys: my uncles Gaston, Dominique, Simon, Clovis, Batiste, Michel, Rene, Alexandre (after whom I was named), and my own beloved daddy, Jean Pierre, who was named after my great-great-granddaddy. Of course there were the two girls, my aunts Cecile and Sophie. Big families are very common in almost every generation of my family, the result of very big appetites, in more ways than one, if you know what I mean!

My family had been fortunate enough to have inherited this beautiful old place through some shady dealings, some that still make even me blush or cringe at the sheer thought of it all, but nonetheless, they truly are a very important part of our history. The LaPierre-Menard ladies never spoke of it, although it was common knowledge that our family fortune had been made by the kinds of things that proper Southern ladies, with or without color, would never speak of but more than likely experienced in the privacy of their own dreams and acted out in the privacy of their own boudoirs. Just that fact made me even more curious about our history, the stories becoming more fascinating every family reunion as I grew in mind, body, and desire.

I always found it fascinating to hear our men as they carried the stories forth with such great vigor to the delight of every new generation of LaPierre-Menard boys that had accompanied their parents to this place reunion after reunion. I had learned early on that the blood of certain family ancestors truly flowed freely through my veins, leaving me without the least sense of embarrassment or reserve. Therefore, I began to mingle quite openly and easily with the storytellers underneath that big old magnolia tree, to the dismay of the women who simply gazed out of the window of the big house at us while commenting about how unnecessary it was to carry forth such nonsense. The detailed account of our family could make a proper Southern lady swoon in a genteel faint. But I smiled as I envisioned every sensuous moment that the hot breath of the storyteller would recall while my mother, grandmother, and aunts just shook their heads, knowing full well it would come to no avail at all to try to capture my attention with cooking, cleaning, and gossiping. Why, I have to admit, I was more interested in hearing and eventually experiencing the family taboos.

The early recollections of our family's history were always given by my daddy's eldest brother, Gaston Menard LaPierre, as handsome as ever even in aging—the family tease, quite debonair, and still very much the epitome of Southern charm. He and his wife, Kathleen, owned, operated, and retired from a bakery that the two had in Baton Rouge, now managed by their children. It had been a good living for both of them and also afforded Uncle Gaston the opportunity to tell his many stories to the regular clientele. Aunt Kathleen, on the other hand, simply shook her head at his antics and smiled with the customers as she added just a little more powdered sugar to their favorite donut or gave them a second cup of coffee on the house. Our entire family blames the sweet products of Uncle Gaston and Aunt Kathleen's bakery for the rather-enlarged glandular structure of many of the Lapierre-Menard brothers.

Uncle Gaston was probably my favorite throughout my growing-up years, or perhaps it was the content of his portion of the stories that captured my curiosity and caused me to daydream, imagining myself as one of those sultry ancestors of mine. As a sweet young child, I would sit leisurely on Uncle Gaston's knee as he filled the young boys' heads with the knowledge of the family. But as I grew with each passing year, my uncles began to shoo me away, and I found myself sitting leisurely behind one of the nearby trees, where I always thought they could not see me, but I could certainly hear every delightful word.

When I became a young woman in the midst of making my own family history, my uncles began to invite me to join them again for the family ritual as the women peered at me from the windows of the big house. I do declare that there just might have been an occasion or two when I deliberately stuck out my tongue at them to show how well my resistance to their petty occupations was working!

As my memory serves me correctly, the family stories say that my great-great-granddaddy was raised right here on the grounds of this very plantation, but certainly in quite a different capacity than the Southern gentlemen who occupy it now. He had been known as the African with no name as a young boy, said to have been brought to the Gulf of Mexico from the western area of Africa and purchased by the former Master LaPierre because he was capable of speaking and understanding French as well as his own African dialect! As a young man, he was given the name Jean Pierre by the former Master LaPierre, a very proud name that would be given to one male born in every generation of our family, including my own dear daddy, in honorable memory of the first. Or maybe because there were so many children in each generation of the family that the last male automatically had that name to save the trouble of searching for another appropriate name!

My great-granddaddy Jean Pierre was the product of that proud African slave and the beautiful yet devious mistress of the plantation, a European Frenchwoman by the name of Madam Frou-Frous LaPierre. Need I say more about that obvious relationship that was very popular at that time? The hot French blood constantly boiled passionately in Madam Frou-Frous's loins, overpowering Jean Pierre's father when he was going about his duties for the Master LaPierre. Filled with the strength of lust and the desire that throbbed within her loins for the magnificence of the African, the Mistress LaPierre had her way with him, right beneath one of those magnificent magnolia trees. It was the matter of mistress and slave, needless to say, and the power exercised by Madam Frou-Frous most definitely left the African slave powerless with her single command.

Lord only knows how many times Madam Frou-Frous was seen by her servants leaving the big house in the middle of the night while her husband, the Master Philippe LaPierre, lay drunk from the juice of the mimosa vine with which she had calculatingly filled and refilled his cup. When Master LaPierre had conveniently passed out on a brocade divan with his boots still on, Madam Frou-Frous would slip out of the big house to perform her dastardly deed, threatening her servants with a blistering if they ever even hinted to the master about such goings-on.

Threats though they might have been, the rumor still spread throughout the slave quarters that the vocalization of the sensual encounters between the mistress and her black lover could be heard until the early-morning hours, when Madam Frou-Frous could be seen running back to the big house, sweat dripping down the deep crevices of her bosom, never being caught by her seemingly unsuspecting husband.

It was at this portion of the stories that my uncle Gaston would take a mighty big drink of his spiked lemonade, a long draw from his big cigar, and add that the activities occurring between the two produced more sparks than the fireworks on the Fourth of July.

The other men would just laugh, as if it were the very first time they had ever heard him say it, while the young boys would force a laugh as they looked from one to the other, as if they really understood what he meant. Once the laughter had calmed down, Uncle Gaston would continue his story, lowering his voice and setting his eyes in a very sinister manner to create the appropriate ambience for what would come next.

The house slaves could be heard whispering to one another that the mistress would quickly slip into one of her extremely feminine peignoirs that her husband had brought home to her from one of his many overseas travels, and then position herself beside her husband in their huge bed as though the two had shared a truly exciting night together. The servant who brought breakfast to the two the next morning would report back to the other servants, who, in turn, brought the news to the slave quarters that Madam Frou-Frous looked quite satiated as she lay beside the master, grinning from ear to ear as if she had been indeed charmed by her husband. Oh, if only

Madam Frou-Frous could hear the snickering and the laughter that was going on behind her back!

After several years of this fornication, the gossip began to shift toward the amount of weight that Madam Frou-Frous had begun to gain, especially in her bosoms, which now lifted up just below her chin, truly doubled in size as well. Her gal servant told the maid, who told the cook, who told the women in the fields that Madam Frou-Frous appeared to be with child and that the seed growing inside her had to be that from a very dark grapevine since Madam Frou-Frous had been lately complaining to her husband of having a lingering headache while her continuing, lustful activity at the slave quarters was indeed truly ample enough to produce that forbidden fruit.

Madam Frou-Frous was a very wise woman, to say the very least, and wasted no time in convincing her husband to arrange a voyage to Europe for her where she could vacation and nurse herself back to health, complaining of some possible exotic disease that she could very well have caught from one of the many foreigners that visited the plantation, causing her to swell. Surprisingly so, Master LaPierre was quite agreeable in his usual loving manner, consenting and even encouraging her trip abroad. Madam Frou-Frous wept uncontrollably at the thought of having to leave him but assured him that she would be fine, even suggesting that she bring along one of the female slaves to help her throughout the journey. Again, he agreed as he held her tightly in his arms that such a long and dangerous journey could not be made alone, and then he even suggested that she consider bringing a certain slave by the name of Mozelle Castille LaPierre, an African Spanish female that had been brought to their plantation only a few short years before from a farming community close to New Orleans.

Mozelle, a very beautiful young woman with smooth skin the coloring of copper and eyes as black as a Southern night, had been conceived one evening when a Spanish dignitary, who had been traveling throughout the South, sought shelter from a thunderstorm at the home of Master Roderick Castille. After a fulfilling meal, a glass of imported wine, and a gentlemanly smoke, Master Castille offered

Mozelle's mother as a "belly warmer" to the Spaniard, and the rest, as they say, is a part of Southern history.

Years later, Master LaPierre, who became quite smitten with their offspring, had offered a large sum of money to Master Castille as a purchase price to have Mozelle, then at the tender age of seventeen, brought to his plantation to work as a seamstress for both his lovely wife and the other women who lived on the plantation. Appearances were very important to Master LaPierre, so Mozelle became a prize possession to him, and also to the needs of the mistress. Who else would seem most likely to accompany Madam Frou-Frous on such a journey than one who could keep her well-dressed while she continued to swell with the progression of her exotic and unknown swelling disease? Madam Frou-Frous agreed, and Mozelle was charged with accompanying the mistress on her journey.

No one was actually surprised to see the mistress of the LaPierre Plantation sashay into the slave quarters, announcing that she was looking for Mozelle; after all, the plantation as well as the slaves themselves belonged to her and Master LaPierre. The irony, of course, was that it was daylight and she was looking for a slave woman, not Jean Pierre's father! Everyone stood still as if they were frozen in time, with their eyes cast down, as Madam Frou-Frous whipped through the area with her skirts swishing in the breeze that she created. A grown-up Mozelle confidently appeared before the mistress and, while looking her straight in the eyes, announced that she was the woman for whom the mistress was looking. As if inspecting the slave girl for some sort of contagious disease, Madam Frou-Frous walked around her several times and finally said to her, "You'll do."

Both ladies were indeed well-dressed as they boarded the huge ship in New Orleans headed for Europe, a journey that would take just a little over one month to complete. Madam Frou-Frous managed to squeeze out a few tears as she bade farewell to her adoring husband. It was apparent that Mozelle was overwhelmed with the sight of the big ship and found it very difficult not to be terribly afraid but quickly jumped to the mistress's attention when she screamed for Mozelle's help with the baggage.

During that first night at sea, as Mozelle busied herself unpacking the bags and putting away the mistress's things, a well-kept secret was revealed. Madam Frou-Frous confided to Mozelle that she was truly pregnant, and an unfortunate pregnancy it could be, since the child she was carrying either could or could not be that of her husband's. But in the very next breath, Madam Frou-Frous pointed her finger in Mozelle's face and reminded her that she was bound to secrecy for fear of her life and that she should not forget her place as a slave or she would surely regret it. Mozelle struggled to release Madam Frou-Frous from her corset, which had helped hide the truth, agreeing never to tell the secret, and yet at the very moment that the corset snapped open and unleashed the mistress's enormous belly, Mozelle revealed a secret of her own. She, too, was pregnant!

A wise woman always grasps her opportunities as they present themselves, so it would not be long before Madam Frou-Frous seized the situation at hand to create the ideal resolution to the present set of circumstances. The answer was obvious; if the child that Madam Frou-Frous was carrying was indeed a child of a different color than her own husband, the story for all to know would be that Mozelle had given birth to both babies. Yes, twins. And since they would both be fathered by slaves, who would possibly know the difference? Yes. Who would? It would be a truly phenomenal story to be spread throughout the slave quarters, and most assuredly, one that Master LaPierre could not question.

The motion of the great ship whipping against the waves of the sea brought much discomfort to both Madam Frou-Frous and her gal slave Mozelle, as each hung her head over the side of the ship to deposit their morning sickness into the waters. It was convenient enough to complain of seasickness to the various passersby, including the captain, who offered his assistance to the lady and her gal slave. Madam Frou-Frous would graciously thank them for their concern and explain that this was her very first cruise and surely she would eventually become less susceptible to the common travelers' ailment. Mozelle, of course, would keep her eyes cast down in the proper slave manner while following the mistress closely around the mighty ship, serving her needs and simply being there for her beck and call while suffering the very same fate as her mistress.

At mealtime, Madam Frou-Frous would join the captain at his table in the simply lavish dining hall, being served the finest cuisine on extravagant, handmade china plates and sipping imported wines from crystal goblets by the ship's servants, dressed in white jackets and bow ties, while Mozelle would dine with the other slaves traveling with their masters or mistresses belowdecks, on their leftovers. Madam Frou-Frous knew full well that her destiny depended upon Mozelle's faithfulness despite her domestic arrangement, so she would therefore bring bits and pieces of her own meal back to their room for Mozelle to enjoy during the dark hours of the night. After all, if Mozelle was truly going to be of proper assistance to her mistress, she needed to keep up her strength as well. The journey was an extremely long and uncomfortable one for both women because of their delicate conditions, and near its end, both found themselves staying in their room to privately battle morning sickness, seasickness, and the constant need to use the facilities, as the massive ship continued its journey through the sea.

By the time the mighty ship finally docked at the seaside Italian village where the mistress and Mozelle would reside until they were relieved of their delicate conditions, both ladies were indeed quite ready to put their feet on solid ground. Unfortunately, their profound weight gain and sea legs made walking while maintaining a ladylike appearance quite a difficult task.

Arrangements had been made in advance by Master LaPierre for the two ladies to stay in a lovely furnished cottage that was located just outside the tiny city and owned by a local merchant that he had met while on a shopping trip abroad. The two ladies moved in as quickly as they could and began preparing for their upcoming events, a circumstance that truly upholds the belief that strange bedfellows are begotten by common need.

Mozelle used her expert ability to create adorable outfits by hand for the mistress using lovely European fabric that merchants were all too happy to bring to the cottage for her approval; fashions, of course, that in no way resembled maternity clothing. Madam

Frou-Frous demanded that Mozelle look her best in public as well and encouraged her to use whatever leftover fabric to create fashions for herself. Mozelle did just that, creating adorable fashions in a patchwork design for herself that were comfortable, fashionable, but easily distinguished the mistress from the maid.

Before much longer, it was obvious that the delicate Madam Frou-Frous was losing control over her own situation, unable to do much of anything without the help of her capable companion, Mozelle. She was all too happy to relinquish her power over to Mozelle in exchange for the mutual sharing of their delicate conditions since between the two, only Mozelle was truly capable of caring for either one.

Hard to believe, but by the time that the first of the two ladies was just about ready to give birth, Madam Frou-Frous and her gal slave, Mozelle, had actually bonded together as friends, a companionship about which the mistress continually warned Mozelle would be absolutely inappropriate and would most certainly have to end once the two had returned home to the LaPierre Plantation. Of course, Mozelle most definitely had to resume her role as just a slave to the very elite Madam Frou-Frous when the two were in the company of the other residents of the small seaside community, which, due to the circumstances, was not very often indeed. Small necessary trips to the local market were the primary reason to ever leave the cottage, and periodically, the mistress would walk with Mozelle along the water in the cool of the evening, seemingly providing an escort rather than exercising and stretching for her own good.

The mistress kept the secret of her true condition from her new neighbors by openly discussing her unusual illness, citing that her loving husband, Master LaPierre, had been so generous and concerned as to send her on this journey in an attempt to aid in her healing. The mistress would smile between her rosy cheeks, causing them to puff out even more, stretching her nose from cheek to cheek and causing her face to just sort of jump out at anyone standing in front of her.

Both ladies spent lots of time in the cottage just crying their eyes out for no particular reason, and then almost as quickly as they had begun to cry, they would begin to laugh uncontrollably. In between their crying and laughing, the two would fight over who would use the outhouse first, sometimes actually one pushing the other one out of the way in order to get there in time! And of course, there were those lengthy conversations about men, in particular about the men who had impregnated each one, although their true names were never uttered, as both Madam Frou-Frous and Mozelle, still being the tiniest bit cautious of each other, referred to them by other names that would most assuredly be very inappropriate for a true lady to repeat.

It would be difficult for anyone within hearing distance to prove that the screams coming from the cottage were not those of the mistress when the first of the two babies was born. Mozelle stuffed a towel in the mistress's mouth to muffle the sound—after asking permission, of course—while pointing out that the secret would no longer be a secret if Mozelle was still big with child after the neighbors had heard the unmistakable sounds of labor. The mistress agreed, biting down on the towel as Mozelle genuinely cared for her, wiping her sweating face and giving her small sips of cool water while her own child twisted and turned within her as if communicating with the child struggling to come into the world.

Once or twice, the mistress slapped Mozelle across the face as she made an attempt to examine her progress, an action that eventually prompted Mozelle to inform the mistress that she, in her current condition, was in no position to play that tired old master-slave game unless she could deliver her own child. Needless to say, Madam Frou-Frous understood quite well the message, and although reluctantly, she surrendered herself to trusting that Mozelle would not take advantage of the current situation, which required the mistress to rely completely on her gal slave in truly reversed roles.

Madam Frou-Frous moaned and groaned for hours in the agony of childbirth while being extremely careful not to take out her fear and anxiety on the only other human being she had to assist her, a slave girl who was just as pregnant as she was. When the time was right, Mozelle instructed Madam Frou-Frous to "push," but she began to cry like a child instead and uttered in a very low voice that she was too scared to push. Mozelle simply responded with her strong Creole accent as she moved away with arms folded, "Fine, let it stay in there until it can walk, talk, and stand eye to eye with you. Either push now and give birth to a little baby or keep acting silly and give birth to a full-grown man." It was only then that Madam Frou-Frous pushed as hard as she could to bring the life into the world.

When Mozelle announced with great excitement that she could see the baby's head, Madam Frou-Frous was more interested in what color the child was than whether it was a girl or a boy! Only when the sweet baby's shoulders emerged could Mozelle announce that the precious little child would most definitely have a happy home with her, in the slave quarters. Madam Frou-Frous began to cry and refused to even look toward the child as Mozelle sterilized a knife and cut the navel cord. She quickly moved the child to her own bed and began to clean the baby and proudly announced that it was a little boy.

Once the little one had been properly taken care of and was resting quite peacefully, Mozelle began to tend to the sobbing Madam Frou-Frous, cleaning her and the bedclothes while humming a soft lullaby to help her fall asleep. From that moment on, Mozelle never spoke of the fact that this firstborn male child actually belonged to Madam Frou-Frous; she simply claimed him as her own from the very beginning and loved him as though it had been her womb from which he had come.

Both children were born within one week of each other, a boy to Madam Frou-Frous, and a girl to Mozelle. Mozelle, however, cared for the baby boy as if he truly were hers, nursing him and singing him to sleep while holding him as close as could be. When it was time for Mozelle to go into labor with her own child, the sweet baby boy was of first concern to her, especially when Madam Frou-Frous panicked at the idea that she would have to care for that sweet thing while Mozelle labored to bring her own into the world.

As if the sweet child knew exactly what was going on, even in the midst of labor all around him, he slept throughout the entire ordeal. Even while Madam Frou-Frous screamed in sheer horror when she was told by Mozelle that she had to help with the delivery, the sweet baby boy slept peacefully. It was only when Mozelle's darling baby girl caught her first breath of life and released a cry to the world did the sweet baby boy open his eyes to join in the chorus of tiny voices, going completely unnoticed by Madam Frou-Frous, who had nearly fainted when she had to cut the navel cord. There was indeed a bond between the two children, one that would most certainly last their entire lifetimes. That night, an exhausted Mozelle slept comfortably with a tiny sweet baby cradled in each of her arMiss.

Since it was common practice for slaves to name their children after the master of the plantation, the boy was named Jean Pierre LaPierre, and the girl was named Dolice Marie LaPierre, using the only legal name available, which depicted that these children were the property of the LaPierre Plantation and not of Mozelle's former owner, Roderick Castille, or any other master. The plan in place called for Madam Frou-Frous and Mozelle to stay in the small Italian village with the children until all signs of the mistress's pregnancy and birth were indeed impossible to trace. Mozelle buried herself in loving care of the babies, whispering and singing in their tiny ears as she nursed them, seemingly separated from the entire world, while Madam Frou-Frous concentrated her efforts on restructuring her figure.

Indeed, there were several flirtatious indiscretions with extremely handsome Italian men during the following months, but Madam Frou-Frous had evidently learned her lesson well and never went quite as far with any of them as she had with the African on the Bayou Frou-Frous.

Time was quickly passing, and Madam Frou-Frous was beginning to get bored; after all, she had captured yet another milestone in her life and was indeed ready for new discoveries. Even though her friendly disposition with Mozelle continued, she never hesitated to remind Mozelle that she would soon have to resume her birthright as gal slave with never a mention of what had truly happened in that tiny Italian village, or there would, of course, be a punishment deserving of such disobedience. Mozelle paid no nevermind to the chanting of the oversexed mistress, just smiled and resumed the delight of caring for the children.

Sometimes, in the quiet of the evenings, when Madam Frou-Frous had gone for a long walk, Mozelle would watch lovingly as Jean Pierre and Dolice Marie slept peacefully while either holding on to each other or while one sweet child's head lay comfortably upon the other's chest. No matter how far apart the two began in their sleep, eventually they would squirm and roll in an attempt to find each other, finally resting calmly in the spell of Mozelle's soothing lullaby.

It became quite obvious that the younger Dolice Marie had a mind of her own, surpassing Jean Pierre in learning to walk, talk, and the process involved in the use of a chamber pot, while the elder was quite clearly the protector, being the first to offer support when the younger endeavored a new venture. No matter what the role each assumed, it was apparent that the two had truly bonded as brother and sister. And it was certainly apparent that both dearly loved the only parent they knew, their devoted Mama Mozelle.

By the time the two ladies returned to the Bayou Frou-Frous, the "twins" were well over one year old, walking and talking in the fashion of the broken slave rhetoric patterned by their "mother," Mozelle. It was a warm, wonderful homecoming for both ladies prepared by Master LaPierre, complete with music, food, and proper Southern white neighbors from all over the area, who were excited to see the recovered Madam Frou-Frous. She had prepared a tale for her husband as well as the guests about the unknown malady that had plagued her for most of the time that she had been in the lonely Italian village. She spoke of how much she had missed her beloved husband and how just the desire to be with him had been more beneficial to her healing than any of the medicines she had been given by the local physicians. The mistress clung to the master, stroking his arm and allowing him to pamper her with gifts and his undivided attention as she acted the role of the devoted wife.

During the homecoming celebration, Madam Frou-Frous caught Mozelle's eye several times and dared to smile briefly in memory of their friendship in the lovely Italian cottage, but then cast a long stare at her to remind her that to tell the secret would be to suffer severe consequences. Mozelle was much too happy with her children to even give Madam Frou-Frous any concern whatsoever and had no problem with keeping that secret while raising the two children as her own.

The news of the birth of Mozelle's twins had already reached the plantation by messenger, in accordance with the master's instructions, long before they arrived at their new home, Mozelle's home, in the slave quarters. The master had given his orders to ensure that the two children would be properly cared for since Mozelle had been the ever-so-loyal gal slave to his ailing wife and to himself, and to provide for her two children would only be a small token of his appreciation.

Mozelle was indeed grateful, and the laughter of the two sweet children filled her shack and her heart with joy.

The years passed by without much event outside of everyday life on the plantation. Jean Pierre was turning into quite a handsome young man with his silky reddish-brown hair, pecan-colored skin, and hazel eyes that peered through to the very soul of the beholder. Dolice Marie was always by his side, as though she only felt safe while in his company. Her dark hair fell over a mahogany skin tone, with her dark, vixenly eyes that seemed to enchant the beholder. Under Mozelle's scrupulous eye, it was obvious that soon Dolice Marie would mature into a seductress, a trait for which the women of our family have long been famous and infamous as well.

Uncle Gaston would always remark at this point of the stories that although Aunt Kathleen was not a true blood descendant of either the Menard or the LaPierre family, she certainly did fit the bill with the, shall I say, gifts of her adoptive family. This statement, followed by Uncle Gaston's imaginary depiction of Aunt Kathleen's bosom and bustle assets, was always followed by even more laughter and the kind of shenanigans that would be expected more of the young boys than of the older Southern storytellers.

The two children were typically mischievous in their growing up and constantly placing themselves where they had been told countless times not to be, such as near the big house, listening under a window to what was going on inside between the master and the mistress, or running back to the slave quarters from some secret hiding place, giggling while they shared some secret tale. Jean Pierre was quiet and shy, while Dolice Marie was playful and rambunctious, usually the mastermind of some practical joke that would get them both into big trouble. Their fun-loving antics became quite commonplace on the plantation under Mozelle's watchful eye, while the truth about their parentage stayed tucked lovingly away in her memory.

Jean Pierre's father retreated into solitude after the birth of the babies and the return of Madam Frou-Frous. She, sadly, had had her fill of the African, for all intents and purposes, and was probably involved with some other unsuspecting, well-endowed slave right there under her husband's nose. He quietly went about his duties as the master's silversmith, working from early morning to the cool of the evening in the hot, sweaty shop that was known for the stench of the hot coals melting silver. The silver, only the finest that could be purchased by Master LaPierre, of course, was fashioned into the fancy dishes that Madam Frou-Frous loved showing off to her guests and family members when they came to visit. The style was unique to the plantation and was therefore splendid for gift-giving during the Christmas season, although Madam Frou-Frous's exquisite set of dishes was far more elegant than that created for others.

If Jean Pierre's father ever thought of his son, or if Madam Frou-Frous ever wondered what it would be like to hold him in her arms, neither ever let on to anyone, let alone to each other. The children were content to know that Mozelle was there for them, and nothing else was necessary. There was, however, another that captured their interest and would soon raise the epitome of confusion from the pits of the Bayou Frou-Frous to bring havoc and unrest to the peaceful plantation from which there would not, and could not, be relief.

Just outside the confines of the slave quarters was a small shack where Mama Del, thought to be a voodoo priestess, lived and worked her special juju. Whether or not she was born there and had lived there all her life was a great mystery to the other slaves, since she never mingled with anyone, and no one dared to mingle with her. Some say to this day that Mama Del was from Haiti, others claim she's from a distant village in the land of Africa, while still others say that she came directly from the earth, conjured up by some foreigner who had proposed to put a hex on the LaPierre Plantation after some sort of arrangement had fallen through by the workings of some former owner.

One rumor had it that Mama Del had been brought to the plantation directly from a ship that docked in New Orleans from parts unknown. She had enchanted the master's father as he examined the prize cargo, looking for slaves of his own, and found it rather difficult to leave the port without her. Nonetheless, Mama Del was as much a part of LaPierre history as all the former owners are to this day. Mama Del had lived a rich, fulfilling life on the plantation since then, serving both Master LaPierre, and his father before him, as their fortune-teller.

From their innocent early childhood, Jean Pierre and Dolice Marie had shared a deep fascination with Mama Del, who, at the time of their birth, had to have been eighty or ninety years old, by estimation of my uncles. The two were quite comfortable being in the company of the old Gries Gries, and Mozelle knew exactly where to find them when darkness began to set over the plantation and the sweet children had missed getting home by their curfew. Mozelle always showed great respect for Mama Del, the respect deserving of a family matriarch, and of course demanded that the two children do the same. It was always difficult for Jean Pierre and Dolice Marie to leave Mama Del, but they always promised to come back, and Mama Del always encouraged them to do so.

It would be when the two darling children were in their early teens that something sensational happened that would indeed change their destiny and the course of history for everyone on the Bayou Frou-Frous forever. As they approached the old woman's house for one of their anticipated visits, Jean Pierre and Dolice Marie could hear Mama Del repeating the words to one of her voodoo chants combined with the smell of incense burning their nostrils. They felt a strong desire to come even closer. It was a strange occurrence, one that the children had never experienced before, but in their curiosity and youthful trust, they went forward to the familiar confines of the old woman's shack.

Mama Del was sitting at a table in one of the back rooms of the shack, from where she called out to the children, leading the way toward her with the sound of her voice. The children continued through a door toward a dim light at the back of the house, searching for the voice. Suddenly, as if in a dream, a vision of a woman appeared seated at a table, a scarf draped several times and then tied tightly around her head just above her eyes, completely covering her hair. The old woman slowly raised her eyes to meet those of the children, and when she smiled broadly, she showed that familiar sight of a mouth absent of any teeth at all. Smoke curled around her from a corncob pipe that hung from her mouth. The children had never seen Mama Del in that manner before, and certainly any other children would have run screaming away from the sight of it all. But not Jean Pierre and Dolice Marie—they approached the scene without the slightest reserve!

The room was filled with an eerie presence, strange figures were lined on the tables, and thick black smoke circled throughout as Mama Del continued with the strange chants. There were bones, feathers, tea leaves, and various other related objects that were evidently essential to the earthly practice of the old woman. She beckoned the children to come closer and see what wonders lay ahead for them as she shook a small leather purse and threw its contents onto the table. Without a moment's hesitation, the children approached, their eyes wide and their mouths open in excitement and anticipation as Mama Del performed her wondrous deed.

Mama Del cackled in delight as she scanned the contents of the bag, seemingly seeing the delightful news that she had been searching for and had evidently expected. What the children were told exactly that day, no one truly knows, but Uncle Gaston's account of the rest of the story would indeed imply that it was such news that gave both Jean Pierre and Dolice Marie the knowledge that their fortune would indeed be good fortune.

You see, Mama Del knew everything, or so she could certainly find out with all her tricks and incantations, and she told the children that soon they would be recognized for whom they really were, the true owners of the LaPierre Plantation. Yes, the true owners. If the children did exactly as the old woman said. She pointed at the pattern of the objects that lay on the table, explaining that the days ahead would be filled with much change and that the two should be ready to do just as they were told without hesitation or question. Jean Pierre and Dolice Marie quickly agreed to the terms that Mama Del had laid out before them, and although they were absolutely confused as to how this could be possible for two young slave children, they giggled and squealed at the thought of it all.

Mama Del also told the children that although Mozelle was always most certainly "mother" to both of them, she was actually only Dolice Marie's mother by the process of birth. Jean Pierre's mother, on the other hand, was not Mozelle by the process of birth, but by the fulfillment of her tremendous love for the sweet boy. The children looked at each other and began to ask Mama Del the kind of questions that one might expect from such shocking news. Jean Pierre never thought of asking who his father was, but now he wanted to know who his mother was, if not Mozelle. Dolice Marie knew that Mozelle was her mother, but then who was her father? Both children began to cling to each other and well up with tears. Mama Del cackled again in delight as she scanned the bones, feathers, tea leaves, and various other objects that lay on the table to bring forth the truth to the bewildered children.

Smoke exploded all over the place, creating an even more intense moment, and when Mama Del opened her mouth to tell the truth, she waved her hands and suddenly the smoke disappeared.

"He who is the master is the true father of one child. She who is the mistress is the true mother who once ran wild. That which was once a great secret now can unfold, on this day and forward, this truth shall be told!"

Uncle Gaston lit another huge cigar and let the smoke float eerily in circles as he continued. The truth was simply that Jean Pierre's true mother was indeed none other than the sex-crazed Madam Frou-Frous, who had given birth to him in that seaside Italian village, and Dolice Marie's father was none other than Master Philippe LaPierre himself! Of course, the master and mistress had no idea that one had been unfaithful to the other. Or did they?

Mama Del continued by telling the sweet children that Mozelle and Jean Pierre's father were actually brother and sister (Mozelle had chosen to name him after her brother), and this, of course, would make Jean Pierre and Dolice Marie first cousins rather than brother and sister, as they had been led to believe, Mozelle actually being Jean Pierre's aunt. In all this confusion, Mama Del continued the story.

Jean Pierre's father and mother had been brought to the shores of this land together from their village in Western Africa while his mother was still carrying him safely in her womb. Master Roderick Castille's father had actually purchased the two adult slaves on the coast of the Gulf of Mexico and brought them to his plantation located on the far side of the LaPierre Plantation, where their child was born.

One night, while some of the plantation masters were enjoying a leisurely game of cards, Master LaPierre's father actually asked if they could play for one of the Castille slaves instead of money, since all the men were rich by the standards of that day and age. Why, he agreed and dealt the cards. It finally came down to the owners of the LaPierre and the Castille Plantations, and a single flip of a card that brought Jean Pierre's father to the LaPierre Plantation, where he grew to be a very strong, handsome young man that eventually ignited the passion inside and the resulting lustful behavior that consumed Madam LaPierre.

Jean Pierre and Dolice Marie paused, looking at each other, and although they were quite confused and appeared extremely disappointed, Mama Del assured them that such concerns were not theirs and that they still belonged to Mozelle, Jean Pierre's father, and most of all, to each other. The young boys also paused, looking at each other, and although they were quite confused, Uncle Gaston assured them that family history does not always have to make sense!

Now, the question was, Were the two LaPierre children willing to do whatever was necessary to fulfill a destiny in which they had an entire plantation to inherit, once the present master and mistress were eliminated? Without even a second thought, Jean Pierre and Dolice Marie agreed, and so began the Great Hoax of 1856!

Mama Del prepared some powerful juju, gave it to the children, and told Jean Pierre and Dolice Marie to slip some into Madam Frou-Frous's lemonade while she was sunning herself on a blanket in the backyard and then do the same to the master as he sat near the madam, reading from a large book of literature. Oh my goodness! What happened next is probably the most excitement that the plantation had ever experienced in its entire history.

Jean Pierre managed to get madam's attention by taking her off guard to wildly describe some story about one of the slaves catching a wild boar. Of course, she resisted, casting him aside as just another slave boy looking for a treat from the madam of the great plantation. While the madam was trying desperately to shoo Jean Pierre away with every threat possible, Dolice Marie slipped the wickedly potent potion into her refreshing lemonade, and thus the wait began. Within just a few moments, Madam Frou-Frous took a few sips from the lemonade and, soon after a few more moments, began to show signs of discomfort, scratching herself in the most excessively polite manner that she could, considering the circumstances. Jean Pierre continued to talk about the wild boar, with his hands flying in the air, while Madam Frou-Frous tried desperately to get away from him so that she could address her discomfort in the privacy of her home, but soon it became apparent that the juju was getting the best of her. She began to scratch herself violently while tearing at her clothes, screaming and shedding tears like raindrops during a summer storm as the master tried fruitlessly to assist her, even asking if perhaps her exotic disease was reoccurring.

Jean Pierre continued his story, ignoring the madam's antics and the master's insistence that he go back to the slave quarters, deliberately taunting and following her around the yard as she tried desperately to walk toward the house yet keep her pride intact. Dolice Marie followed the scene at a close distance, hiding behind the trees that lined the walkway to the big house, laughing and covering her mouth to not be heard. Suddenly, to the shock of the master, Madam Frou-Frous began to rip her clothes off—first, her lovely, tailor-made, originally designed dress that her husband had shipped from Europe, then down to her petticoat and corset, twirling and arching her back, trying to reach every area that was itching to find some relief. The master was truly helpless as he watched the scene in sheer bewilderment from what he surely considered to be a safe distance. It was then that the madam turned to the master and began to talk, and oh my goodness, talk she did!

She said quite loudly, as the scene of insanity continued, that she was surely being punished for her wicked ways, ways that had led her to succumb to the demon lust for the silversmith that produced the child called Jean Pierre. She continued, telling the master that she had threatened Mozelle with sure death if she ever told anyone that the children were not really twins but actually one child for herself and one for Madam Frou-Frous.

Dolice Marie emerged from behind a tree with a sinister-looking glass of lemonade in her hand, which she politely handed to the master. The master finally reached for the glass of lemonade and gulped it down in an attempt to rid himself of the pesky little girl. It is truly a glorious sight when the truth raises its mighty head to devour the evil that man can create! In a matter of minutes, Master LaPierre began to laugh hysterically; in fact, he laughed so hard that tears began to flow down both cheeks like the flowing waters of a Louisiana waterfall. Why, it was such an embarrassing sight to see, Madam Frou-Frous virtually naked, scratching profusely, and the master giggling like a schoolgirl. But the icing on the cake was indeed what he said to Madam Frou-Frous in front of Jean Pierre, Dolice Marie, and the many slaves that dared to come close enough to hear.

In between his laughter, he could be heard to say the most shocking words that anyone on the plantation would ever hear again. The slave girl named Dolice Marie was his daughter, the child created between himself and Mozelle, the child that was born while the madam and Mozelle had gone off to Europe so that the madam allegedly could heal herself of her many infirmities. He added that he had known all along that she was slipping out to meet the silversmith and that he had only faked being drunk so as to sneak out himself to meet Mozelle! He laughed hysterically as he told how brilliant a plan Mama Del had developed and how he had agreed that Mozelle herself should accompany Madam Frou-Frous to Europe. Imagine, the two of them assisting each other with the delivery of each other's lover's child! Priceless! Priceless! Suddenly, everything stopped, no itching and no laughing, as the surprise confessions shocked both the madam and the master of the LaPierre Plantation, who now glared deeply into each other's eyes as they stood face-to-face. Within the blink of an eye, Madam Frou-Frous balled up her fist and swung, slamming it into the master's jaw; he fell slightly back and returned the punch with power that seemed to come from the bottom of his imported Italian slip-ons. The fury flung back and forth as the two began to duke it out like two professional boxers, exchanging punches and screaming nasty names at each other.

The slaves were now quietly coming out of their shacks to observe the outrageous fight, pretending to be going about their daily business on the plantation, while Mama Del laughed hysterically in the quiet of her own shack. Jean Pierre and Dolice Marie, followed closely by Jean Pierre's father, ran to meet Mozelle, who hurried them into her own shack and quickly closed the door.

The secrets were out, and the scene outside the slave quarters continued as the master and the mistress of the LaPierre Plantation beat at and on each other all the way into the bayou and were never seen on the premises again. In fact, as the story goes, that was how the area became known as the Bayou Frou-Frous.

It would be three months before anyone truly trusted that the LaPierres were gone forever, and so work continued without fail for fear of being exposed as a plantation without a master and being run by the likes of slaves. A scout was sent into the bayou every day to make sure that there would never again be signs of the two, and when all were fully assured that the coast was truly clear, there were shouts of joy and the dancing of the "La La" with fiddle and washtub for an equal number of days.

Jean Pierre and Dolice Marie moved Mozelle and her brother, the African, into the big house, where they all politely set up housekeeping in the twelve-bedroom, four-outhouse dwelling, dividing some of the mistress's clothes among the other slave women and the master's clothes among the other slave men.

Many of the furnishings in the big house were transferred to the slave quarters after dark, making each shack a quite-comfortable dwelling, including crystal chandeliers, silver serving sets, Victorian chairs, and silk sheets. Outside the shacks were just as they had been before, shacks with broken-down front porches, with splintered wood under tin roofs that barely kept the rain out, and broken windows covered with rotting wood.

Mama Del was given the four-poster bed that was discovered in the attic of the big house, where it had been for years, probably since the death of the former master's father, himself having been afraid to sleep in the bed where his daddy had died. Rumor had it that he was plagued severely by nightmares of the old man each time he tried to sleep in the bed.

Of course, there could be no renovation to the outside of the shacks, not now, of course, but there would come a time. Imagine! An entire family of common slaves now the clandestine owners of one of the largest plantations on the Bayou Frou-Frous, a reality that had to be kept a guarded secret for fear that some other master would realize that the slaves were alone. It was a dangerous time, but a time of silent rejoicing, a time of running buck wild, a time like no other any of them had ever experienced or could have ever imagined.

Chapter 2

THE YEARS PASSED by slowly and pleasantly while life on the plantation was thriving for everyone that lived there, although none of the masters and mistresses from the neighboring plantations had the slightest idea that these slaves no longer had a master or a mistress. In fact, it seemed as though the neighbors did not miss the pretentious Madam Frou-Frous or the seemingly henpecked Master LaPierre at all. No one had ever come just to visit with them, anyway, only the regular people that had always conducted business with the plantation hands. Whatever the plantation had always provided was truly in abundance now, because the residents were working for themselves and for one another.

During the daylight hours, the former slaves of the former Master LaPierre and his wife, Madam Frou-Frous, continued their clever charade, going on about the business of being slaves by working and sweating in the fields, in the silversmith shop, and in all the other familiar spots they had once been worked under harsh plantation rule. The cows now produced an enormous amount of milk for drinking, as well as to churn into butter, while providing substantial amounts of choice beef; the chickens laid enough eggs for the residents to enjoy themselves and to sell to the merchants in the local shops that had always done business with the master.

The fields, too, were absolutely bountiful, heartily producing enough vegetables, sugarcane, and sweet potatoes to feed the residents of the entire plantation until their stomachs were full, with even enough left over to sell to local passersby on their way to or from some other town. (A welcomed contradiction to the previous arrangement under plantation rules!)

To avoid too many proper Southern white people from roaming and snooping around the plantation, several tables from the big house were strategically placed along the road in front of the main entrance to the plantation, which was now hidden from the public by several lovely flower bushes, where such products could be sold. Because these people assumed that the money was still going to Master LaPierre, the purchase prices remained the same, as if still set by the rich, proper Southern white owner of the plantation. Because of this, Jean Pierre made it essential for those who were in the area of selling to learn to count money so as not to be cheated by the proper Southern white people who might accidentally make a bad judgment in their own counting.

Mozelle began serving her cool lemonade, sweetened with the sugarcane from the plantation, in the silver cups that were being hand-made by Jean Pierre's father, to those who were thirsty as well. If a passerby began to admire the silver cup, Mozelle would offer it to them for a very small price, money that would certainly be given to their "master," of course, who was up at the big house, ailing from some fictional affliction while being cared for by the "mistress."

Money was being made so fast that whatever was not being used to purchase the regular supplies had to be hidden in secret places all over the plantation. Uncle Gaston always added that our family history also included the rumor that some of that money was surely still stashed away in secret places around the former plantation, perhaps buried in the gardens, or even underneath one of the graves, and no doubt between the bricks of the many additions to the big house or the former slave quarters. It was quite charming to watch the young boys try desperately not to seem too interested in the hidden money, and yet none could control the discreet movement of their searching eyes that gave away their secret thoughts about someday searching for such hidden treasures.

Jean Pierre, now openly known among the residents of the plantation as the son of the former mistress, put himself in charge of keeping track of the everyday money since he now bore the title of master of the plantation. He was one of the very few residents that already knew how to count money, having learned such from both carefully watching others while an exchange was being made and from Mozelle, who had learned when she accompanied the former mistress into town to purchase supplies. It was Jean Pierre who made certain that the money from everyone's hard work was divided equally among all the residents after the weekly visits from the outside shoppers, while operational money was locked away in a place he felt was appropriate for only him to know. To use the money would certainly draw unwanted attention from nosy, proper Southern white people, so most of the residents also hid their separate shares until time would allow them to buy freely and openly without being questioned about the manner in which the money had been acquired. Besides, everything that anyone could ever want, from food and clothing to decent places to live, came to everyone without any cost at all. He also knew that there would surely come a time when some of, if not all, the residents would want a place of their own, so Jean Pierre, thinking ahead to such a time, wanted everyone to have a proper share. After all, they were all family, bearing the name of their former lives, LaPierre.

Jean Pierre's responsibilities to the residents and to the plantation itself became so overwhelming that he soon began teaching several of the other young men exactly how to master the silversmith business and actually expanded the shop into one of the other adjacent shacks to accommodate the growing business, all very quietly and secretively, of course. Jean Pierre taught them how to melt down the silver dishes that Madam Frou-Frous loved to give as gifts, as well as her personal sets, to create the silver cups that were now Jean Pierre's trademark and which, by the way, had become very popular with those proper Southern white people who came to do business, keeping cool in the hot Louisiana sun while sipping Mozelle's cool lemonade sweetened with sugarcane.

The residents were taught to always be aware that someone could be watching them, and definitely to be careful to keep their heads bowed and their eyes cast down with an appropriate *sir* or *ma'am* when addressing the proper Southern white people as they journeyed to or past the plantation. It was such a game and always fun for them to plaster a silly grin on their faces in sheer servitude for the benefit of the master or mistress when called a "good ole boy," "an obedient gal," "uncle," "wench," or just plain "nigger."

Uncle Gaston made it very clear that it was surely easy to comply to such outrageous demands and insults when one knew that it was just that, a game, and one that was certainly making a fool out of the one that seemingly had the upper hand!

Of course, that was all during the daylight hours, but at the setting of the sun, during the darkness of night, there was a profound change over the entire plantation and its residents.

The women dashed up to the big house and dressed up in the mistress's finest clothing, most of which had been sewn for her by Mozelle herself, peering at themselves in the floor-length mirrors and pretending to be her or mocking some other proper Southern white woman that had come to visit. They kicked up their heels in the mistress's imported shoes and lifted their hair high above their heads with her lavish European combs. The smell of Madam Frou-Frous's expensive French perfume in its various scents blended together and filled the entire house with a tantalizing odor.

The men, too, dashed up to the big house and dressed up in the master's finest clothing and tall hats, mocking the pretentious proper Southern white men they had seen and using the master's language to talk about the "lazy slaves" and the "hot-blooded wenches." It was during these times that they laughed hysterically while teasing and mocking one another's slave mannerisms while they had been in the presence of the masters or the mistresses. All the while, Jean Pierre's father, the old African, watched Jean Pierre with loving eyes, the son that he could now openly admire and give his affection to.

There was always plenty of music from old African drums that had been left by the early slaves that had gone on to the other world, or from several tin tubs that provided a lively beat blended with fiddles and washboards that added a unique sound when scraped with spoons, plenty of delicious food, corn liquor, and apple wine served in those beautiful silver cups that adorned the huge and expensive dining room table in the big house. They ate until they were quite full, danced until their feet began to ache, and laughed hysterically at how shrewd they all were for tricking the supposedly intelligent, proper Southern white people of the area!

The festivities always went on for several hours after dark—that is, until their fun gave way to exhaustion and the realization that the next day was soon approaching and it would be life as usual, that is, to the spectator's eye.

Life on the plantation was surely pleasant now, but regrettably, there was a storm brewing in the states of the south, the likes of which no man, neither black nor white, free or slave, had ever experienced before, and it was coming to the great state of Louisiana, and more specifically for my family's sake, to the Bayou Frou-Frous as well.

One afternoon, as Mozelle and Dolice Marie were selling the vegetables from one of the gardens that they had situated on one of the tables on the dusty road in front of the plantation, there approached a handsome young stranger traveling down the highway. The stranger tipped his dusty hat as he asked for a cup of Mozelle's cool lemonade, reaching deep into his pocket for a coin to reciprocate the kind gesture. Mozelle pushed the money away from her and accommodated the stranger with a smile, dipping a silver cup full of her cool, sweet lemonade and, of course, keeping her eyes cast down all the while.

Dolice Marie, on the other hand, had grown into a beautiful young woman, small in stature but abundant in all the right places, and she had absolutely no problem showing the confidence of her nature as well as her budding body to any man, be he black or white, and therefore she stared the stranger straight in the eye, lapsing into one of her coy smiles. The stranger could hardly keep his eyes off her as he drank the lemonade, his hands shaking while his eyes were scanning her from head to toe.

Dolice Marie had discovered at her early age that she had the knack for charming men. Mozelle asked the stranger if he would like yet another cup of lemonade, and he nodded in agreement, gulping it down with his eyes still glued to Dolice Marie, sweat from his lusty thoughts mixed with the dirt from the road dripping down his face.

He tipped his hat again and turned toward the highway to continue his journey. Just a short way down the road, the stranger paused, turned around, and walked back to Mozelle and Dolice Marie.

The stranger began to talk about things that were just as strange to Mozelle and Dolice Marie as he himself was strange. He said that he had heard talk in many of the small towns he'd been through about a war that was coming between the Northern and the Southern states, a war that would most likely put an end to slavery altogether and an end to the pain and suffering that the slaves had long endured. He spoke of many sympathetic proper Northern white people and even a few proper Southern white people who were against slavery and were true followers of President Abraham Lincoln, willing to do whatever was necessary to help the slaves gain their freedom. He smiled at Mozelle and Dolice Marie as he proclaimed that he was very proud to be one of them.

Mozelle and Dolice Marie looked quite inquisitively at each other and then at the stranger. Well, why would Mozelle and Dolice Marie, or any of the other residents on the LaPierre Plantation, as a matter of fact, care about some silly war between the Northern and Southern states or this Mr. Lincoln? They were already quite free, and had been so for some time, even though no one else could know that, nor could Mozelle or Dolice Marie tell the stranger such a secret. They were probably all living a much better life now than the stranger himself could possibly ever hope to live, but both Mozelle and Dolice Marie were still very gracious for his conversation, and as they thanked the stranger for his concern, he, after tipping his hat a third time, disappeared down the road, looking back every now and then to catch yet another glimpse of the tantalizing Dolice Marie. The shameful little heifer enjoyed every single minute of it!

Mozelle contemplated while smiling to herself and replaying the sensuous exchange between Dolice Marie and the stranger over and over in her head but never voiced an opinion to anyone as she continued her quiet life of clandestine freedom and dressmaking. All the while she was scheming in her head about an idea that she had that could possibly involve her own Dolice Marie and several others among the young women on the plantation. What a scheme it would be, and goodness, how her scheme could turn the course of history forever! She smiled to herself, keeping the scheme to herself until the time would be just right.

The old storytellers, my daddy's sweet brothers, loved the look of contemplation and excitement on the faces of the young boys as each proudly told their portion of the stories of our family tree while pausing only to refreshen their cool, spiked lemonade and perhaps light another big cigar. Of course, the stories became a little louder with much more laughter and a lot more detail as they drank their cool, spiked lemonade a little quicker! The young boys sat quite proudly under the magnolia trees during their summer of initiation as they were experiencing this rite of passage into LaPierre-Menard manhood, a place that would prove both stranger and more tantalizing than any fiction could ever be. Now, where were we?

Oh, yes.

A young man by the name of Jubilation, Jubil for short, had been given the job as the livery stable attendant by the former Master LaPierre along with the responsibility of taking care of the horses on the plantation, but now that Jean Pierre was the master, Jubil became his right-hand man as well as his best friend and was also put in charge of running the errands in town. Jubil was maybe a year or two older than Jean Pierre, and probably a full head taller. Even though the two had played together as slave children, Jubil was still certainly eager to please the new plantation master in whatever way he could.

He was an extremely loyal, hardworking young man, smart with a ready smile and always ready to discuss one of his many creative ideas or listen to one of Jean Pierre's.

On one particular trip to the city to buy supplies, on behalf of the master, of course—oh, for sure—Jubil overheard some proper Southern white men in the general store talking about a war that had been declared between the Northern and Southern states, and about the Southern soldiers called Confederates that were taking over entire plantations, stealing and selling expensive family heirlooms for money to fund their rebel army as well as taking food and personal belongings for themselves. They were also known to take the women for themselves, doing the kind of things that a proper Southern lady would not allow even her husband to do to her even in peacetime. My goodness! What an absolutely horrifying thought! And of course, Jubil emphasized, they wanted to keep their slaves and their lives just the way it had always been, exactly as it had always been, and gave no never mind to sympathetic, proper white people who thought otherwise.

Jubil explained that he had begun to attract a little more attention than was necessary by the owner of the general store as he was lazily shopping and trying to eavesdrop just a little more of the conversation and decided that it was best that he just smile and back out of the door to ensure his own safety. Jubil also spoke of the other army that was heading directly from the North toward the Southern states to fight on behalf of the slaves. He'd heard one of the men call it Abraham Lincoln's army, the liberal army that he supposed only wanted the slaves for themselves. One of the men had shouted, "No Southerner had better get caught dead supporting the Union Army!" Well, that sounded mighty challenging to the new owners of the LaPierre Plantation; after all, they had been living the life of luxury right under the noses of the other masters as well as these confederate soldiers and were not about to allow anyone to take or destroy what was now rightfully theirs. Whether the soldiers were Southern or Northern, the residents of the LaPierre Plantation couldn't have cared less about their war, but between the two armies, they were leaning more toward helping the Northern Army, if they had to choose, while liberating themselves of as many slave-loving Southerners as was possible.

Jubil was sweating and out of breath as he drove the horse and wagon loaded with supplies to the front door of the big house. Everyone ran out to hear the story, and everyone had a different idea about handling the situation, but all agreed on one thing that was for sure: not one of them would be leaving their homes, and not one home would be taken away. Jean Pierre quieted everyone down and asked for each person to speak one at a time. It was at this time that Mozelle remembered how Dolice Marie had enchanted the stranger on the highway that day and told Jean Pierre that she had a plan that just might save them all from the impending visitors of the rebel army, but she needed a few days to gather her thoughts together.

Plans were made for everyone to meet in the living room of the big house sometime during the following weekend.

For several days, Mozelle just walked throughout the LaPierre Plantation, observing, planning, and designing a plan that would benefit the residents as well as eliminate the bother. Finally, she went from house to house as she gathered eleven of the young women living in the former slave quarters who were at least sixteen years old—Dolice Marie would make number 12—and gave each one of them a room of their very own in the big house. When everyone met together in the living room, Mozelle began to announce the details of her plan.

First of all, the young women, if they accepted the job, would, from then on, live and work in the big house and were instructed to keep their rooms perfectly clean, especially their beds, and each would be given her choice of Madam Frou-Frous's clothing and shoes, as well as her lavish nightgowns made out of pure silk that had been imported from the Orient. Mozelle continued with the plan by telling the residents that the young women would have to be ready at a moment's notice, if the rebel soldiers were seen coming toward the plantation, to run to their rooms, put on a fancy dress, and meet downstairs in the parlor, sitting on one of the brocade divans. Their very important job would be to provide comfort for the weary soldiers in whatever way they could, feeding them, helping them to bathe, and of course, entertaining them, each in the privacy of their own rooMiss. The ladies giggled while the residents listened intently as Mozelle went on to explain that she would ask Mama Del to create one of her elaborate concoctions that the ladies would administer to the soldiers as they lay satiated from the lavish attention given to them by the young women.

While the devil rebel soldiers would be sleeping soundly, and in the suit in which they were born, the young women would rob them of all their possessions, especially the precious ores of gold and silver from the decorations on their uniforMiss. These ores would then be given to Jean Pierre and his father, who would fashion them into the shape of bullets that would fit the weapons carried by the Union soldiers. The money, if there was any to be had, would be put into a common fund for all the ladies, to divide for their personal choice after the war had ended. Uncle Gaston was eager to add that he was most assured that some of those exquisite silver cups that our ancestors were making in those days could possibly have been created with Confederate silver!

Mozelle explained to the residents that she was getting a bit too old to be an active part of the plan that she wanted to implement and was therefore putting Dolice Marie in charge. After all, Dolice Marie was the daughter of the former plantation master and therefore deserved the title madam of the LaPierre Plantation and all the proper respect that went along with that position and title, even as young as she was at that point. Dolice Marie would now be known as Madam LaPierre, and the other young women were to be known as her ladies, titles that would soon prove themselves quite fascinating and extremely productive.

The idea was rather pleasing to everyone; after all, all the "ladies" had certainly been called far worse and most definitely done worse during their lives as slaves. Dolice Marie accepted her title and the responsibility with great pride and with an air of just sheer vanity as she eluded that this was the position she had been born to accept. Of course!

Mozelle then cautioned everyone that there could be absolutely no trace of the rebel soldiers' stay anywhere on the plantation for fear of the residents being executed themselves by proper Southern white people, so the soldiers would be planted in the botanical gardens behind the big house; after all, what better fertilizer than that created by the waste of the earth? Just enough ground would be turned to accommodate the number of soldiers visiting the big house at any given time, and upon hearing a signal from the ladies in the big house, when their jobs had been completed, several strong men would be needed to remove the soldiers and put their naked bodies in the ground and cover their naked bodies with the loose dirt and flowers.

Their boots would be given to the men of the plantation, and their clothes burned daily during the routine burning of the garbage so as not to draw any unnecessary attention to themselves. The horses would be simply added to the property of the plantation, carefully cared for by Jubil and his men at the livery stables, and offered to the Union soldiers on their journey throughout the South. It was all a very splendid idea, and after several minutes of silent contemplation, the residents began to nod in agreement with Mozelle. She smiled contentedly, closing her eyes as she was hugged by Dolice Marie and her ladies.

All this scheming and preparation, but nothing was happening in the way of a war going on, and certainly no soldiers, neither Confederate nor Union, were anywhere to be seen near the LaPierre Plantation. Dolice Marie began to have unannounced practice drills for the ladies and stationed several of the young men at both ends of the road leading up to the plantation as scouts, reporting anything that would bear any resemblance to a soldier with any color uniform. She would count the seconds that it would take for the ladies to dress up and be sitting in the parlor when the soldiers came calling.

She even taught them what to say should a rebel soldier not be especially fascinated by a bunch of colored women dressed up and sitting prettily on a divan, questioning the whereabouts of their mistress.

"Why, sir, my mistress has provided me with these beautiful clothes to tempt your eyes and has ordered me to provide you with every desire of your heart to give you comfort and rest before you continue on your journey to fight in this terrible old war. She herself is busy tending to the affairs of the plantation while the master is protecting what is his by fighting in the war, on the side of the South, of course."

Dolice Marie would then make her daring entrance, proclaiming her position on the plantation as mistress as she would sashay around the room while her eyes cast a spell all their own.

Dolice Marie and the ladies would then laugh uncontrollably even after they had enacted the scene over and over. Mozelle would just shake her head at their antics as her nimble fingers worked rapidly to create more gowns for the ladies.

It would not be until a lazy summer day that the plan would actually have its opportunity to manifest itself. Jean Pierre first noticed a burst of dust flying from quite a distance up the highway, calling his father and the other men from the silversmith's shops to witness the event. The men cupped their hands over their eyes to block the glaring sun as they stared toward the dust. Finally, two of Jubil's men could be seen riding in the wagon, horses running as though something truly frightening was running behind them. Everyone came running from the fields and the big house to see just what was coming their way. The wagon stopped abruptly in front of Jean Pierre and his father, who had, by now, been joined by Dolice Marie, Mozelle, and the eleven ladies. Breathing heavily from exhaustion and excitement, the men in the wagon began to tell everyone about a group of men they had seen in the town, while they were getting the supplies for the plantation, who were talking about the war. The strangers were wearing uniforms, and at first, they were not sure if these men were Union or rebel, but as they passed a bottle of corn liquor from one to the other, they began to curse Mr. Lincoln and called him a nigger lover. The strangers raised their glasses of corn liquor to the sky, toasted the South, and vowed to win the war and bring honor back to their homes and their families. Uncle Gaston sounded so brilliant when he said at this point, "I'm sure it would be safe to say that these strangers were most assuredly rebels belonging to the Confederate Army of the South and that it was most certainly…showtime."

As sure as the sun rose that next morning, the Confederate soldiers were crossing the bridge at the Atchafalaya River when the scouts came running back to the plantation. Once the signal was given, Dolice Marie readied the nervous ladies and quickly had them sitting on the brocade divans while Mozelle assisted the cook with a tempting breakfast slightly laced with one of Mama Del's special, very potent potions. Everything was in order as it should be, including the former slaves attending to the business of the plantation, as though it should be, while Jean Pierre and his father busied themselves pressing out the cups with the hot, melting silver, as they should be. The field hands were sweating in the blazing, hot sun, women carrying their precious little babies in sacks tied to their backs, moaning and groaning the sounds of their slave days, speaking to one another in the way of the old religion that had been brought from Africa the generation before. It looked as though nothing had changed!

As the rebel soldiers approached the plantation, Jubil, who was mounted on his favorite horse, suddenly appeared on the dirt road in front of them. He removed his hat, jumped down from the horse, and in the most splendid reenactment of his former self as a slave, cast his eyes to the ground and asked for permission to speak. The soldiers, of course, laughed as they enjoyed the moment and beckoned him to say whatever it was that he had to say.

"Quickly, boy."

Jubil smiled and responded with a "Ya'suh." He then said, "I'm sho' my mass'r would be pleased if you would stop fo' a cup of cool water befo' you go back to fiten the war. He be jest up the road in his house. Ya'll can folla' me, suh, if ya'll have a mind to."

"Is that all your master has to offer, boy, water?"

"No, suh," Jubil answered, smiling with a silly grin. "I'm sho' the mass'r has plenty corn liqa to wet yo' whissle."

Jubil led the soldiers down the dusty road and through the secret entrance to the plantation, a certainly safe thing to do; after all, they would certainly not be coming out to tell anyone where the secret entrance was. Jubil whistled, and within seconds, several men from the plantation came running from the livery stable, heads down, eyes down as they quickly attended to the soldiers' horses, leading them away to be groomed and fed.

Moments later, Dolice Marie could hear one of the soldiers on the porch of the big house asking Mozelle just where he could find the master and the mistress. The door to the big house slowly opened as Mozelle exposed the lovely ladies and explained that they were there to accommodate the soldiers' every desire, as ordered by the master and the mistress. Of course, Mozelle was very careful to keep her eyes cast down as she spoke with the utmost respect, an act that was obviously pleasing to the soldiers, because they smiled. Mozelle opened the door wider in order for the soldiers to see Dolice Marie, looking quite provocative in her tight-fitting gown, which revealed a great deal of her bosoms, which were straining against the fabric. She held a silk fan to her face, slowly bringing it down as she fanned down herself quite seductively, the soldiers' eyes following her every movement. She waved the fan to invite the soldiers inside as she curtsied in respect, addressing them as "sir" and "master" to gain their trust.

The air within the big house was electrifying, mesmerizing the soldiers under some strange spell. There were probably twenty of them, and as they entered the house, Dolice Marie instructed her ladies to make the soldiers comfortable, giving true meaning to the "South rising again!" They began to remove some soldiers' boots and jackets, and some were led to the dining room as Mozelle and the cook quickly began serving food and beverage before the men could utter another word. It was a difficult task for the soldiers to resist the attention of Madam Dolice Marie and her ladies, and they soon succumbed helplessly.

Jean Pierre and several young men from the plantation were hiding under the back porch of the big house, listening for any sounds of any unnecessary roughness toward the ladies that might require their immediate attention while patiently waiting for the signal to remove the limp bodies of the soldiers from the rooms, to strip them, lift them, and plant them in the garden. Several hours later, Dolice Marie quietly stood at the back porch in a satin robe that the former madam had purchased on one of her shopping trips to the great city of New York, motioning for the men to come in to remove the soldiers. After listening to each soldier's chest to be sure that there truly was not a breath left in his body, Jean Pierre and his men went about their duties. Not a word was spoken as everyone assumed their responsibility to dispose of any sign that rebel soldiers had been anywhere near the plantation.

Cleanup took very little time since the plan had been ready to be executed by the time the soldiers had finally shown up. Fresh flowers were planted atop the garden graves of the soldiers as the field hands went about their regular daily duties. Rebel uniforms were burned with the evening trash, and by sunset that evening, there was not a single sign that the rebel soldiers had ever been there, and the stage was set for when yet another opportunity would present itself. Not a single word was ever spoken about that first night, but everyone knew that it was most certainly successful.

During the next four years, rebel soldiers checked in to Madam Dolice Marie's bordello, but they never checked out. There must have been hundreds of rebel soldiers literally "pushing up daisies" in the gardens of the plantation, as well as roses, gardenias, and oddly enough, mint, all growing gloriously in the LaPierre gardens, which stretched as far as the eye could see. Mozelle, Madam Dolice Marie, and the ladies were given plenty of experience in providing the very best comfort available in the South and had certainly done their share to direct the course of the great Civil War even though their contribution might never have been recorded in American history.

As for Jean Pierre and his father, along with the other men to whom they had given knowledge of the trade, the production of enough silver bullets under the guise of manufacturing silver cups kept the Union Army in ammunition throughout the entire war. Word swiftly spread to many of the regiments of the Union Army that sympathetic Southerners were providing their soldiers with solid silver bullets as well as boots and horses; however, Union soldiers were shocked, and quite impressed, when they learned that the sympathetic Southerners were actually black!

By the end of the Civil War, major improvements had been made to the plantation and to the business that was keeping it thriving. First and most importantly, the fact that the former slaves of the LaPierre Plantation were now forced to be recognized as the true owners because of the Emancipation Proclamation, even though no one actually questioned the fact anymore, plus the fact that no one had any idea as to where the European LaPierres were!

It was rumored by someone who claimed to have seen them that they were eaten by several alligators as they continued their fistfight while going deeper and deeper into the bayou. Someone else had sworn that the two were allegedly seen in a town near Baton Rouge, delirious, half-dressed, dirty, and begging for food while claiming to be the master and mistress of the very well-to-do LaPierre Plantation.

Whatever the truth was, it didn't matter, since the LaPierres were still in business.

Second, there was no one left who could legally take the plantation away from its present residents, and so they were left alone and allowed to openly live the life that had been a fabulous secret for so long, without even having to answer any questions. In fact, many of the freed slaves from other plantations around the area asked to become a part of the success of the LaPierre Plantation, bringing their own special talents or their knowledge of a trade with them, which certainly added even more revenue. Several offered their knowledge of logging and turning trees into wood for construction, adding an entire new wing with several more rooms to the big house in order to accommodate more young ladies for Madam Dolice Marie's bordello, an extremely successful business all by itself, openly operating now and enjoying the added patronage from the local towns, including the sheriff, the deputies, and the proper Southern gentlemen who served as members of the Southern legislature.

There was so much money that the ladies were now themselves ordering gowns, hats, stylish shoes, and silky, sexy lingerie, a necessity, considering the trade, if you know what I mean, from the great city of New York and even from Europe itself, and from the very distributors that the former LaPierres had used to purchase the very same!

There was beautiful fabric that Mozelle used to create gowns for the ladies and dresses for the other female residents as well as fabric for curtains and other little tidbits of beauty for the plantation, and that meant every resident's home.

Other newcomers, burly, muscular, sweaty men with raggedy clothes, big hands, and a deep desire and willingness to do something valuable and special for themselves, joined Jean Pierre and his father in the silversmith's shop, hoping to learn the trade. In fact, the shop had now expanded to at least twice its original size, with brand-new furnaces to heat up the metal and water troughs to cool it down so the men could fashion it into the very popular cups. Jean Pierre now openly made his orders for the silver from the very distributor that the former master had used, his business welcomed, of course, since money has no color when it comes to greed.

The former slave shacks were reconstructed into right, proper one-family homes with the help of the new residents, complete with genuine floors, windows with real glass, and an outhouse in the backyard of every single house. Mozelle made sure that each home had adorable new curtains and fancy napkins to dress up the dinner table, a table that always had at least one set of silver cups to boast of, compliments of Master Jean Pierre. It would most certainly be safe to say that the former slave shacks, which were at one time not even fitting for a mangy dog, were now a comfortable neighborhood with everything that a proper suburban area family could want. In fact, there were probably twenty-five or thirty lovely little houses all grouped together and creating a very nice neighborhood, quite a far cry from what had been in the not-too-distant past.

The entrance to the LaPierre Plantation itself was now hidden by an abundance of trees and huge bushes that the men had planted and cared for properly to create a wall of nature's protection from those that might still seek to harm the residents if they found out the truth. Only those outsiders that were considered "customers" or "friendlies," as the residents called them, knew exactly where the true entrance was located, and from time to time, the entrance was moved just to make sure there was no trouble from people who proved themselves to be untrustworthy.

Mozelle also helped many of the little girls on the plantation to learn the simple art of fine-sewing, crocheting, and knitting, which they could put to good use in keeping themselves and their homes looking quite impressive, while some of their creations were displayed for purchase by the many shoppers that were quite interested in such divine-looking needlework.

The little boys were taught to fish, paint fences, hunt, run errands, and do anything else that would help them learn a trade that could benefit the day-to-day operation of the plantation. They could be heard all over the neighborhood screaming while their moms scrubbed them down from head to toe after a long day of dirt and sweat, little boys pretending to be little men. It was for sure that all that screaming would certainly subside later when the girls began to look for the boys who looked and smelled quite clean.

The vegetable gardens and the fields were producing faster than anyone could have ever anticipated, filling the kitchen cupboards with jar after jar of canned nutrition saved for the winter months. And of course, the flower gardens were thriving, interspersed with the wild growing mint that was surely taking over the weeds and generating a delightful aroma that could be smelled throughout the entire plantation. Jubil had several times expressed to Jean Pierre that there was a strong need for someone, anyone, to do something, anything, about the abundance of mint growing insanely in the garden that might prove useful to the plantation. Master Jean Pierre agreed but had no ideas, and since the aroma was so pleasing to everyone, it was just left to grow wild amid the flowers and whatever else there might be there in the garden.

But it wasn't always just work. Absolutely not! The residents knew how to throw a party, and the "La Las" were truly commonplace, on the spur of the moment, complete with music, dancing, good food, and plenty of sordid activity that went on in the livery stable, keeping the amount of procreation on the plantation at its peak. There was something for everyone, and everyone had something that they could be proud of—surely the most important reason of all to celebrate. Usually, the parties were held in the new neighborhood directly under the glow of moonlight, where everyone could be together and come just as they were, whether just out of the fields or out of one of those lavish rooms in the big house. At least for the moment, no one bothered the community of former slaves, that place where the local proper white Southern people were able to cheaply purchase anything from flowers, fruits and vegetables, lemonade sweetened with sugarcane and served in silver cups, and the kind of purchases that could only be found at Madam Dolice Marie's house of pleasure.

During the La Las, Mozelle was happy just to sit on the porch of one of the houses with her brother, that proud old African, surrounded by a multitude of children while sipping on a silver cup of pure corn liquor and watching everyone else having fun. Mama Del was content in the confines of her comfortable new home that had virtually been reconstructed from floor to ceiling, orders from Master Jean Pierre, who instructed several men to make sure Mama Del was always happy and always properly taken care of. The wise old woman was invaluable to both himself and Dolice Marie, and both were devoted to her.

Jean Pierre and a select group of men kept a careful watch over the festivities as well as the entire operation of the plantation, while several young women in the neighborhood kept a careful watch over him. He was not amused, and as they giggled in his presence, he kept his stately stare directly ahead, his mind alert to anything out of the ordinary, completely giving no attention to their silliness. The master was far too busy to acknowledge their childish flirtations, and when finally tired of their advances, he would wave them away with the threat of a spanking. As the story goes, there were always those who thought that particular threat sounded quite tempting! Of course, Uncle Gaston was the first to acknowledge such a thought.

Dolice Marie, on the other hand, was always the center of attention at the festivities, and everywhere else, for that matter; that place she loved and always expected to be, kicking her heels up high and lifting her skirt tails so that the men could see everything that they could otherwise only imagine. She was most definitely at home in the middle of excitement, and if there was none going on, Dolice Marie was just the lady who could, and did, make it happen. By now, I'm sure you know what I mean. Far too busy with the operation of the bordello and making money to keep it a thriving business on the plantation, Dolice Marie had not had the time to pursue a truly loving relationship, although there were plenty of customers who had fallen madly in love with her and expressed their desire to become her suitor. She would simply tease, toss her head back, and flash those eyes that melted the ice in their glass of cool, sweet lemonade.

And as for Jean Pierre's father, the African, now older and probably now much wiser, he was happy and very content to just sit on the back porch of the big house, just smoking his pipe and gazing out over the prosperous land that he and the other residents now owned. No one ever knew what was in his head, what memories he had learned and tucked away about his homeland or about the carryings-on with Mistress Frou-Frous. It was obvious that he loved his son, Jean Pierre, but he also loved to be alone in the quiet of his thoughts.

Uncle Gaston always leaned back in his chair at this point of the stories as he told the young boys that there is a tale that some years later the old African had been found dead in just that place, on the back porch of the big house. It could have most probably been that he had been dead for several days before he was discovered by some of the plantation children as they were playing. The children said that they were accustomed to seeing him every day, just peacefully sitting there with a smile on his face, but had no indication that he was no longer breathing; they simply thought he was just sleeping.

The Master Jean Pierre's father was lavishly laid to rest at the far end of the plantation, underneath a lovely magnolia tree, where he could continue to oversee the land that he so loved, with a ceremony that included the singing of the songs of the faraway country, special words to the god of their homeland, dancing, and a long procession all around the plantation. Loving words as well were said by Mozelle, and a grieving Jean Pierre shed tears that flowed at the graveside, all remembering his life.

Chapter 3

SEVERAL BLISSFUL YEARS had now passed quite peacefully since the days of slavery and that great Civil War, and financially quite successfully for the residents of the LaPierre Plantation, where children were constantly being born and the elderly laid to rest beside the old African in the plantation cemetery, under the beauty of the magnolia trees. The residents on the plantation numbered more than one hundred now, creating the sense of a separate city altogether from those on the other side of the Bayou Frou-Frous and those that lay on the other side of the Atchafalaya River.

Money was coming in from the many businesses that operated on the plantation, from the silversmith shop to the bordello, which now had twenty-seven young women making money, although most of them now owned their own little home and only came to the big house to "work." Money was still being hidden in various places around the plantation while Mama Del cast her magical mojos that taught the residents to make sure everything was running fairly, smoothly, and safely. The former slave plantation was now owned, operated, and enjoyed by a family that was working and playing together, the likes of which had never been seen in these parts before.

Jubil now had business from the other plantations coming to the livery stables, offering his expertise and advice for the care of their horses as well as providing shoes and boarding when necessary. Jubil and several other men that he handpicked and personally trained had worked hard to build absolutely wonderful stables that could accommodate quite a number of horses at one time. He had become quite familiar with the various maladies that could afflict horses and had even begun to produce his own remedies. Jubil seemed to be most happy when he was with the horses, and many of the locals were all too happy to pay his small price for such knowledge, and therefore, Jubil stayed quite busy and brought a great share of money to the plantation. Jubil had also built a small cottage beside the stables, where he lived, so he could be near the horses in case they needed him or someone else needed a horse on the spur of the moment.

None of the other plantations, including that of Roderick Castille, Mozelle's former master, were thriving like the LaPierre's, because many of their former slaves were now working and enjoying life as LaPierre's. Of course, some former slaves had traveled North to enjoy their freedom, all the way to that great country of Canada, where they could find work while others joined the army of the North, and still others, although very few, stayed on their former master's plantations to sharecrop.

Jubil devised a plan to learn to read and write for himself and many of the children on the plantation by exchanging free livery stable services from those proper Southern white people who just could not afford the small price of his knowledge. In fact, some of those proper Southern white people even volunteered to help Jubil and the men that worked with him at the stables to build a proper school building where the lessons could be taught in the presence of educational privacy. It was an extremely fair proposition, even considering that these poor could, and did, afford the delicacies afforded them at Madam Dolice Marie's bordello.

The offspring of the former Master and Mistress LaPierre, Jean Pierre and Dolice Marie, were now twenty-four years old and well respected as Mr. and Miss LaPierre because of their devotion and fairness to the residents of the plantation. They considered themselves master and mistress over the plantation operations, not the residents, who were free to come and go as they pleased.

Although many of the young women in the neighborhood were all still eagerly vying for Jean Pierre's attention, a spirited young teenager named Evelina LaPierre had stolen his heart. Evelina worked in the kitchen at the big house with the cook, learning all about preparing and storing food as well as helping Miss Dolice Marie in decorating and caring for the big house, as well as learning to sew under the watchful eye of Mama Mozelle, as she was now called by everyone.

Evelina lived with her mother in the new neighborhood and was not easily tormented by the neighborhood boys who loved to tease her, but she could hold her own, even at a height no taller than four and one-half feet! Her curly brownish hair, dark and glistening eyes, and sharp European features presented a lovely but stern face that commanded authority or that could put her tormentor at risk from her powerful fist. It was just those qualities that had stolen Jean Pierre's heart and made him swell with desire for Evelina, although it was a difficult task for him to conquer since assuming the role of Mr. LaPierre and taking responsibility for the entire plantation and all its residents. With all his vast responsibility and wise decision-making abilities, Jean Pierre was extremely shy with the ladies, especially this one that stayed on his mind. It was obvious to everyone that the two had been exchanging glances, and Jean Pierre was definitely spending more time in the big house, whether looking for a cup of Mama Mozelle's cool, sweet lemonade or pretending to inspect the house for any necessary repairs.

It would be at least another few months of stealing glances and sweet smiles between the two, and the constant urging from Jubil, before Jean Pierre mustered up enough courage to approach Evelina at her mother's house to ask if she would be so kind as to take a walk with him in the gardens; in fact, by the time he made up his mind to do so, even Evelina's mother was standing at the doorway, waiting to ask him what had taken him so long. Surely, any of the mothers on the LaPierre Plantation would have wanted their daughter to be the bride of such a man with such a reputation, and such a fortune.

Uncle Gaston continued his portion of the stories by telling the young boys that it was rumored that Evelina's mother had been born and raised on the LaPierre Plantation, the child of two Haitians or two West Indians. He was certainly not quite sure which one as he continued telling the story of our family history. The former master had hired an Irishman whose name was O-something, Uncle Gaston continued, to serve as his foreman, a friendly overseer whose job it was to make sure that all the work was done in a timely manner. A fair and honest man, O-Something was very kind to the master's slaves, as long as they did their share of the work and did not cause him to have to lose his temper.

During his time at the LaPierre Plantation, O-Something had developed quite a passion for colored women and most certainly, as well as quite openly, favored Evelina's mother, making visits to her shack occasionally to enjoy her cooking and to stir up a little heat of their own, if you know what I mean. O-Something was on the LaPierre property for several years but had moved on with a group of men who had come through the area looking for strong young men to work on the railroad up North. Evelina had been conceived by then, and although it was not common practice for a proper white man of any nationality to feel or openly display his affection for a slave, O-Something walked right up to Evelina's mother's shack and bade his farewell to her, never to return. Uncle Gaston would always shake his head sadly as he described their parting, O-Something staring back at Evelina's mother as he rode farther and farther away from the LaPierre Plantation with the other young men in a wagon, while she waved on and on until she could no longer see him. The other slaves knew better than to comment to Evelina's mother on her behavior, and they knew better than to comment as she began to grow larger and larger, blossoming with child during the next few months. Evelina brought great joy to her mother, but there would be no other man in her life that could replace the Irishman who had left her so long ago.

Jean Pierre, too, marched up to the front door of Evelina and her mother's home, awkwardly carrying an impressive bunch of flowers from the gardens in back of the big house. That fresh scent of mint seemed to intertwine between the various scents of the flowers to create an intoxicating aroma that simply swept Evelina off her feet—truly love at first sight fulfilled for both of them. That first awkward walk in the gardens opened the door to many such encounters and the simple verbal commitment to each other.

Dolice Marie, on the other hand, had become quite jealous of Jean Pierre's relationship with Evelina, a relationship that sometimes completely excluded her. After all, the two of them had been raised as brother and sister, although they were actually first cousins, and shared the dual responsibility as owners of the LaPierre Plantation. Although she admitted it to no one, including her beloved Jean Pierre and Mama Mozelle, Dolice Marie had begun to long for the excitement and security of a real relationship, like that of Jean Pierre and Evelina, one that was not dependent upon her physical attributes or her financial status, which was unbelievable for a woman of that day—a woman of color and, most assuredly, a former slave.

Dolice Marie's business suitors ranged from the sheriff of the town just outside the Atchafalaya River, several of his deputies, several plantation owners from around the area, the mayor, several members of the great state of Louisiana legislature, and even a couple of good ole boys from Texas who enjoyed "hoopin' and hollerin'" while they were getting their money's worth. You do know what I mean.

Dolice Marie was also feeling the need to mother someone, a child or two, maybe even more, children that would love her unconditionally and learn from her just how to enjoy the finer things in life, like fancy clothes, big houses, flirtatious glances with seductive eyes, and of course, lavish silver cups to drink from. In all her years, she had never looked at any of the young men on the plantation as a possible suitor, a husband, and a father to her children; no one on the plantation fit the description of the ideal man in her eyes, and she found herself daydreaming of something more, something just out of reach.

Even as she totally ignored the advances of the neighborhood men, Dolice Marie was beginning to realize that the only way she could possibly find what she truly needed in her life was to leave the plantation, which she had never had the occasion to do so during all those years.

Even the thought of leaving home frightened her terribly, but she could not escape the possibilities that could be outside the confines of the plantation. The plantation was always home, even as a slave, and she had everything anyone could want now, and everything on the plantation was worth something to her, until this moment. Dolice Marie was suddenly unhappy, and her mind was consumed with dreams of a day when she would leave her home, her family, and the only life she had ever known. But to go where? And more importantly, would she find what she was looking for beyond the confines of the plantation? It became both a time of love and a time of longing for the two children of the notorious former slave masters, the infamous Monsieur and Madam LaPierre.

Southern summers are desperately hot, with a hazy sun that beats down upon the earth and all its inhabitants like a sledgehammer, draining the very energy and life out of absolutely everything in its path. Uncle Gaston always wiped his brow with his handkerchief to dramatize just how hot it can get and then twisted it, as if wringing perspiration out of it. The only relief from the heat seems to come after a Southern thunderstorm that cuts into the humidity and brings a temporary breeze that soothes the Southern soul and cools the body down. It was during one such night that the residents of the LaPierre Plantation were prompted to open their windows to allow the breeze to enter and give them somewhat of a comfortable, restful sleep. Suddenly, as if everyone had been awakened by the exact same bad dream, a dream that the earth was shaking and quivering under their feet, the sound of loud thunder began to pound in their ears. Everyone began to run out of their homes, clutching their children and looking around for some sign of what was happening. Some could be seen rushing from their outhouses while still pulling up their britches to find out where and why the loud noise was coming. A flash of light passed in the distance like fire rising to the sky, moving up and down and frightening the living daylights out of everyone that was seeing it. Jubil quickly mounted a horse and sped past his neighbors toward the sight, while Jean Pierre instructed everyone to get back to their homes until Jubil returned.

Dolice Marie and her ladies ran to the neighborhood from the big house and found shelter with Mama Mozelle on the porches of several of the homes, each clutching one another, while Jean Pierre ran to Mama Del's home, where he, of course, found her sound asleep. Hours later, Jubil returned with a look of sheer astonishment; his eyes were nearly bulging out of their sockets as he described a large number of horses with riders dressed all in white, even the covering on their faces, and all were carrying large torches. Jubil described how he had followed the riders from a safe distance until they reached an open field on the other side of the Bayou Frou-Frous, where he witnessed them having some sort of ceremony under a huge burning cross.

Jubil was trying to catch his breath when Jean Pierre instructed everyone to go back to bed since the sun would soon be up, the fields would be waiting to be tended, and at that moment, there was no immediate concern. Jean Pierre told Jubil to rest up and go early the next morning to town for supplies and listen for any talk about the strange occurrence that he could bring back to the plantation. He also told Dolice Marie to listen carefully to her customers during the next few days and encourage them, in her very special way, to reveal any knowledge of these riders that could, in any way, be a threat to their lives on the plantation, or the lives of anyone on any plantation.

The LaPierre Plantation was very quiet the next day as the residents went about their duties cautiously while waiting for any news about the riders. When the hot sun finally set and the residents were gathering together in the newly constructed schoolhouse to discuss the situation at hand, the sound of thunder and the vibration of the earth began again; the riders were passing by, dressed in their white garments and carrying their large torches. It was obvious to the residents that the riders were certainly a situation to be reckoned with, and all were anxious to hear what Jubil and Dolice Marie had to say about what they had learned.

Jubil began by telling everyone what he had heard while he was in town. It seemed that the riders had come to the great state of Louisiana from another Southern state to bring danger, havoc, and destruction, not to mention those horrible headdresses and secondhand clothing in drab colors, to all the former slaves who considered themselves "free," and to any sympathetic proper Southern white people who might be helping them. Jubil added that it was possible that the riders were too far away from the plantation to even notice it since it was now nestled under those huge magnolia trees, with the main entrance situated a distance from the road, which was a blessing all in itself.

Dolice Marie shared what information she had obtained from one of her customers, who promised that the residents of the LaPierre Plantation would be safe from what he called the Night Riders; after all, the plantation contributed quite a bit of valuable commodities to the local townspeople—if you know what I mean!

The residents were horrified at such talk, threats against the very life they had come to know, and they began to huddle together and looked at Jean Pierre to bring the answers that would solve the problem. Jean Pierre asked all the residents to be patient until he and Jubil could find out just what kind of threat these Night Riders posed, if any, at the present time. He promised that he would figure out something and let everyone know as soon as he did.

Several more nights went by with the same disturbance from the Night Riders, but by now the residents felt slightly safer knowing that Jean Pierre and Jubil were putting their heads together to come up with a suitable solution. On several occasions, Jean Pierre rode with Jubil behind the intruders to their ceremonial place and observed the goings-on for himself. Jean Pierre commented that he felt certain that he recognized a few of the voices that seemed quite familiar to him, but caution, of course, kept him from going any closer to be sure.

On another occasion, Jean Pierre and Jubil even visited the site of the big cross burning during the daylight hours and saw the ashes and felt the danger. Even though the entire situation seemed considerably odd to both of them, they knew that eventually the Night Riders would have to be dealt with. But how?

One particular evening, Jean Pierre and Jubil gathered together a large group of the men on the plantation to conduct a meeting to discuss possible resolutions to the situation, while the other residents were instructed to stay in their homes, assured that no one and nothing was going to disturb their peaceful way of life. The meeting went on through the night, but when the other residents were awakening to their daily activities, there came a sudden roar of thunder, this time corning from the back of the LaPierre Plantation itself, beyond the flower gardens, and this time during the daylight hours. Everyone began to run, grabbing their children on their way, toward the sound and the quivering of the earth, only to be stopped dead in their tracks as they witnessed a most horrible, frightening sight. The Night Riders were on the plantation, and they were indeed riding directly toward them, dressed all in white, just as Jubil had said, with their faces covered in the white as well and carrying torches. Everyone began to scream and run in the opposite direction when, just as abruptly as the thunder and the quivering had begun, it stopped.

As the residents stopped to look behind them, the Night Riders dismounted from their horses, laughing hysterically and pulling the white covers off their faces to reveal Jean Pierre, Jubil, and several of the other men from the plantation that had been in the secret meeting, not the white faces they had expected to see.

Uncle Gaston slapped his knee and laughed just as hysterically as our ancestors probably did as he told the story. Even though it was a sight to behold, the residents were not quite so sure what it meant until Jean Pierre began to tell them that this masquerade was the perfect way to confuse the Night Riders into assuring that they would be leaving them and the plantation alone.

The plan was to outsmart the Night Riders by pretending to be them, staging a ceremony like the one Jubil had witnessed under the big burning cross the first night that the ground had quivered and the sound of thunder woke them all up. Jubil continued to explain the plan by stating that the Night Riders were sure to keep going if they happened upon the LaPierre Plantation and saw that other Night Riders were already there. Of course, it was obvious that if the real Night Riders came too terribly close to the fake ones, the color of their hands would surely give them away. But as usual, Mama Mozelle had the perfect solution to that dilemma, reminding everyone that there were plenty of gloves taken from Confederate soldiers and hidden deeply under the front porch of the big house. It was yet another perfect idea!

I do recall all my uncles laughing wildly with Uncle Gaston when telling the young boys that it was indeed our family that was responsible for that old saying "If you can't beat them, join them."

The plan would be put to the test just a few nights later, when the familiar sound of many horses passing by gave the signal to suit and saddle up. All the white sheets from the big house and many from the neighborhood houses had been fashioned by Mama Mozelle to outfit the rest of the men that had been chosen to be a part of the plan, and they quickly donned their costumes, pulled on the Confederate soldiers' gloves, mounted their horses, lit the torches, and took their places right outside the confines of the plantation on the dusty road, standing perfectly still as if someone would actually hear them from that distance. The real Night Riders rode past as usual, without even a single glance their way.

Disappointed and eager to show off their magnificent plan, Jubil came up with a worthy revision: Why not ride out a little more, a little distance from the plantation entrance, to greet the real Night Riders as they passed by the plantation? After a brief moment of contemplation, Jean Pierre and the pretenders agreed it would be worth the try. Again the thunder came, again the earth quivered, again the men suited and saddled up, but this time they headed off a little farther down the road. They were poised quite arrogantly when the real Night Riders approached them, stopping directly in front of their unknown counterparts, coming face-to-face with the very thing they despised. Suddenly, Jubil raised his torch high in the air, perhaps a sign of solidarity, one he had witnessed that fateful night under the big burning cross. There was a loud cry of brotherhood as both the fake and real Night Riders raised and lowered their torches, yelling praises to the South and destruction to the niggers, an occurrence that lasted several exciting minutes. Finally, the real Night Riders rode off, most certainly to their secret ceremony under the big burning cross. The residents of the LaPierre Plantation sat motionless for several more minutes, assuring that the detestable Night Riders were truly out of sight and far away from their families. They rode back to the plantation silently still yet certainly proud of what they had accomplished that historical night.

This silly business went on for several more occasions, but the men of the plantation were beginning to tire of the only pleasure they seemed to be getting from it all, humiliating the Night Riders night after night after night. Jean Pierre went to Mama Del for advice and the kind of assistance that only she could contribute to ending the charade. Her plan was to lure the Night Riders directly into the plantation and allow them to see just whom they had been keeping company with, explaining that once they had completed the secret ceremony under a big burning cross, the fake Night Riders could lift the coverings off their faces and put an end to the nuisances once and for all. And then she smiled, laughed, and cackled loudly, assuring Jean Pierre that the results would be most pleasing to him and his fellow impostors.

Jean Pierre never doubted Mama Del for an instance, and Evelina never doubted him either as everyone prepared for the event of his or her lives, to that date, anyway.

Just as the many times before, the Night Riders appeared on the road, only this time their fake counterparts led the way down a brand-new, unknown path to the plantation, beckoning them to follow. The Night Riders followed hesitantly at first but quite confidently as they began to ride past the residents who were playing their familiar part of dirt-poor sharecroppers walking along the path leading behind the plantation big house, past the gardens, to the clearing where the secret ceremony would be held.

The sound of laughter and the acknowledgment of some sort of brotherhood filled the smoky atmosphere beneath a big burning cross that was highly visible as they neared several other fake Night Riders already there with their big torches held high. The men began to dismount their horses with ease and to create a human circle all around the cross, shouting their superlatives about their very hosts, who were now offering each a silver cup filled with Mama Mozelle's cool, sweet lemonade laced with Mama Del's unique concoction.

The ceremony went on and on until it was obvious that the Night Riders were beginning to get a little woozy in the head from the mixture. The fake Night Riders signaled one another that it was indeed time to begin to disrobe themselves to show their true identities to their monster guests, who would surely have died from heart attacks alone from the sheer shock of their own ignorance. As each fell to the ground, looking straight into the eyes of their captors, Jean

Pierre and Jubil, along with the other men who were part of the plan, stripped them, lifted them, and planted them in the garden between the mint leaves and with their Confederate heroes, a fair resolution to a tumultuous annoyance.

Of course, all the white-sheet disguises were burned with the afternoon trash, along with the remains of the big cross.

Days later, Jubil brought back the latest gossip from the city to the plantation after one of his trips there for supplies. Several locals were missing, he heard, and the story from the proper Southern white men at the general store stated that they had heard the men were grabbed by some ghosts of the people of color that had actually lifted the missing from their horses and beat them to death and their bodies were absorbed into the ground. The proper Southern white men were extremely frightened as they spoke, Jubil told the residents of the LaPierre Plantation, but Jean Pierre simply shook his head and smiled. He was satisfied just knowing that he had recognized some of those voices.

"That…was that!" Uncle Gaston would add as my uncles laughed uncontrollably, their bellies shaking as they stomped their feet and clapped their hands in total approval. The young boys were fascinated and, probably at that moment, just as frightened as the locals at that general store so long ago, which was surely an added reason for my uncles to cut up as they always did.

Although history tells us that the Night Riders in their white disguises continued throughout the South, and still continue in various places today, there would never again be rumors or any evidence that they ever made it back to the terrain of the Bayou Frou-Frous.

Everything and everyone finally settled down again to life as usual on the LaPierre Plantation. Jean Pierre spent much of his time building a new house at the very far end of the bayou, closer to Mama Del's house. Rumor had it that he was actually building it for himself and Evelina, preparing a perfect place for his new bride to live with him along with precious little children that he talked about with Jubil. Jean Pierre would smile and blush all at the same time as he shared his plans with Jubil but, as yet, had not done so with Evelina.

Occasionally, Dolice Marie would catch a glance of the two of them as Jean Pierre and Evelina stood together holding hands in the big house or stealing a quick kiss in the fields, or even while walking toward the site of the new house. Evelina had a suspicion that Jean Pierre would eventually ask her to marry him, but until he did, she had no intentions of making it easy on him.

But all the loving attention that Jean Pierre and Evelina had for each other was causing Dolice Marie to be even more unhappy and even more convinced that it was time for her to leave. She knew what that feeling of jealousy was now and that empty feeling of loneliness, a kind of a hole in the heart that only a member of the opposite sex could fill, the kind of relationship that Jean Pierre and Evelina had begun to develop right there in front of her, a relationship that certainly did not include her.

With Jubil's never-ending support, Jean Pierre finally had the courage and the nerve to ask Evelina's mother for her daughter's hand in marriage. It was right in the middle of a Louisiana thunderstorm, when Jean Pierre was helping Jubil to get the horses in the stables, that Jubil began to tease him about being a coward, one that had faced life as a slave, the Confederate soldiers, and even the Night Riders but did not have the courage to face a little girl that barely came up to his shoulders. Jubil added that Jean Pierre would eventually lose the love of his life to some other man who would be brave enough to ask for Evelina's hand in marriage if he did not move faster.

The more Jubil talked, the more Jean Pierre became angry with him, ranting and raving with such language that would embarrass any decent folk and asking Jubil to stop teasing. All of a sudden, he abruptly stopped what he was doing, and after pointing his finger in Jubil's face, Jean Pierre made his way soaking wet through the rain puddles to Evelina's house and asked her mother for her hand before he even bade the good woman a good evening! After staring at him for several minutes, she again asked him what had taken him so long! Evelina was so proud of Jean Pierre that she could not wait for him to ask her; she simply squealed "Yes" to a thrilled Jean Pierre at least one hundred times.

Jean Pierre planned a La La for the following evening after work, with plenty of food, drink, and music made with the old fiddle, the squeeze-box, the washboard with spoons, and anything else that would make noise to announce that he and Evelina would be "jumping the broom" at harvesttime into a new life together as husband and wife and that they would be moving into the new house that had just been built near Mama Del's house.

Although the announcement was truly exciting to the residents of the LaPierre Plantation, it was certainly no surprise to anyone as they hugged and kissed the two, celebrating with dancing while drinking corn liquor and apple wine. Dolice Marie kept a distance from the celebration, saddened by it all, and made a quiet announcement to herself; it would be when Jean Pierre and Evelina became husband and wife that she would leave. Where she would go would be settled in her mind by then, so while the entire plantation accepted the news with joy, Dolice Marie planned her own future with sorrow.

Harvesttime would be just about another month or so away, so Mama Mozelle and Evelina's mother busied themselves creating the most wonderful wedding gown that anyone could possibly imagine for Evelina, while Jubil and Jean Pierre picked through the former master's dress shirts and suits. Of course, everyone would have something wonderful to wear to share the moment, and even though Dolice Marie went through the motions of being fitted for her new gown, she remained quiet and subdued. It was obvious to Mama Mozelle that something was very wrong, and in her heart she suspected the worst but dared not say anything to her daughter for fear of making the situation far greater than it already was.

Harvesttime came, and all the preparation for Jean Pierre and Evelina's wedding came together quite nicely, especially Evelina's gown. She was beautiful from head to toe, a LaPierre trait that Uncle Gaston was all too proud to point out to the young boys. I had actually seen him "strut" back and forth like a seductive woman at this point of the story when he was a lot younger, but age did not keep him from making suggestive movements in the air with his hands to emphasize that particular reality, if I must agree with him myself.

Jean Pierre was dashing in his wedding suit as he walked outside to greet his beautiful bride, while Mama Mozelle cried her heart out and Dolice Marie hid herself away from everyone to watch from a distance. Tears flooded her face and streamed down her cleavage into her dress as she witnessed the union of her beloved Jean Pierre and Evelina, a union that she knew had taken him away from her forever. Besides, this was actually the first time any celebration had been held on the LaPierre Plantation where she was not the center of attention. Even though she had not heard anyone ask for her, Mama Mozelle knew full well what was going on; many of the tears she shed in happiness for Jean Pierre and Evelina were actually tears of sadness, knowing full well that her daughter would be leaving her and all that she had known all her life.

While everyone was busy celebrating, Dolice Marie suddenly decided that now was the time to leave and quickly ran to the big house to gather the things that would fit into the former mistress's train cases to take with her. Throughout the month prior to the harvest, while everyone was planning Jean Pierre and Evelina's wedding, she had heard how exciting the great city of New Orleans was from many of her customers. In fact, she had even been invited to leave with several of them who were simply enchanted by her beauty. But for now she would simply leave alone, and she would find her own happiness alone, and she would not stop until she, too, knew the kind of happiness that Jean Pierre and Evelina had found between the two of them.

As everyone danced and celebrated the marriage of Jean Pierre and Evelina, Dolice Marie gathered her things and walked down the path leading away from the big house, looking back only once to bid farewell. And for a brief moment, both Mama Mozelle and Jean Pierre felt the division as they knew full well that today was the day that Dolice Marie would leave them.

It was the year 1868. Dolice Marie and Jean Pierre were now twenty-five years old.

Chapter 4

THIS PART OF the stories of our family was of particular interest to Uncle Dominique Eduard Lapierre-Menard, Dommie for short, a nickname given to him by a Creole queen during his younger days in the great city of New Orleans, where he was born. There is always a colorful tale to tell about every one of our ancestors, and Uncle Dommie is certainly no exception. This precious uncle followed in the chubby footsteps of our ancestors, whose great passion was food, actually the art of creating something spectacular to eat out of virtually nothing, as the slaves once did after the masters gave them the leftovers from what had been their healthy meals.

Uncle Dommie made his way from a Southern university only to become a dishwasher in one of New Orleans's finest restaurants, and finally, after he married a lovely waitress named Philamena employed at that same restaurant, the two opened their own mom-and-pop café by the great river, where everyone is still welcome and the food is still the best in the city, and at prices everyone can afford. The aroma of gumbo, étouffée, jambalaya, and the tastiest sauces found anywhere in the entire world, served with fish or chicken and, of course, rice—lots and lots of rice—can still be inhaled for at least a mile down the mighty river! In fact, during my youth, I can still remember that it was always Uncle Dommie and Aunt Philamena that planned and did all the cooking for our family reunions here under the huge magnolia trees. Much of the old silversmith's shops had been turned into an outdoor kitchen and dining room by then, where food could be prepared and served in the sanitary manner that it should be! And just like Uncle Gaston's, Uncle Dommie's café by the great Mississippi River is run by his and Aunt Philamena's children, who will one day hand it down to theirs, proof that the LaPierre-Menard family still looks after its own.

Now back to the stories!

Uncle Dommie always grabbed a big slurp from his cool, spiked, sweet lemonade, swished it around in his mouth as if he were using mouthwash, and then after swallowing, slowly wiped the sweat from his balding head with an embroidered handkerchief trimmed with lace (no doubt a souvenir from his shameless youth), prior to the telling of our family's triumphant entry into the great city of New Orleans. The other storytellers would laugh a mischievous laugh as if they were all sharing some secret that only they could laugh about, frustrating the young boys as they just looked from one to the other in ignorance, yet anticipation as well, as they continued their rite of initiation.

It was the year 1868, three years after the great Civil War had ended and twelve years since the great hoax that had made Dolice Marie one-half of the two owners of the LaPierre Plantation. That and much more was on her mind as she settled herself on the uncomfortable seat afforded to her on the monstrous iron-and-steel mechanical horse that would take her to the great city of New Orleans, surrounded by others of color that were not allowed to sit in the cars reserved for the proper Southern white people. That was certainly no matter to Dolice Marie since she had always been surrounded by people of color and the only proper Southern white people she ever had any real dealings with, other than the former LaPierre master and mistress, were either planted in the gardens of the LaPierre Plantation or those who had shared a bed in the LaPierre bordello. It was quite evident that these men and women of color did not have her polish or her style, since their clothing was not fit for even the field hands during their workday on her plantation. She gathered herself together with her belongings on the hard seat with an outward suggestion that she would certainly not have anything to do with any of these mere commoners, brushing away bits and pieces of trash that were also commonplace in the last car reserved for the people of color.

Alone in the privacy of the hard seat, Dolice Marie felt mixed emotions, saddened at leaving her beloved home; her mother, Mozelle; Mama Del; and that secret part of herself that was only completely safe and secure when she was with her beloved Jean Pierre, coupled with that overwhelming feeling of excitement at the thought of striking out on her own, especially in a place that was truly known for its guiltless excitement. She wondered if anyone had even missed her yet as they celebrated that wonderful marriage that she hoped would be hers one day as well. She felt the tears swell inside but refused to let them fall from her eyes. She was a woman now, on her own, and it was indeed time for her to begin to present herself as one.

Dolice Marie had no idea what she would do once she reached the great city of New Orleans, but she did know that she was determined to succeed at something, and no one would or could stop her. The train sped along the tracks at a remarkable speed, causing the trees and houses along the way to whiz past even faster, yet going in the opposite direction, as the train whistle blew so loudly that nothing else could be heard, not even the sound of one's own thoughts. The smell of the steam filled Dolice Marie's nostrils, lightly burned her eyes, and she found herself becoming dizzy as she peered out of the window and nearly choked on her own breath at the sight of the only thing that she knew to be greater than herself, the mighty Mississippi River!

As far as the eye could see, there was glistening water! Dolice Marie had never seen such a sight and turned to share her discovery with the others in the train car, but everyone else was either sound asleep or simply not enchanted at all by the awesome sight. She breathed deeply and inhaled the thick humidity and the ocean scents, which were foreign to her senses, as she realized that her new life was just outside her reach. It would be just a matter of hours now before the train pulled into the station in the great city of New Orleans, and Dolice Marie would embark on a brand-new life. Dolice Marie felt her heart jump then flutter with sheer joy.

The train pulled into the station, stopping with a sudden jolt.

Dolice Marie adjusted her hat as she stood with the others, pretending as if she knew exactly what she was doing and where she was going, still ignoring the others in the train car with whom she had just made the long trip. She tried desperately not to show the other people how truly excited she was, for fear of certainly appearing to be just short of a country bumpkin, not a woman experienced with the self-assurance and nuance of a city slicker. Once she was outside the train, it would not be long before reality set in, and Dolice Marie would have to take action if she was to succeed in a city the size and with the legend of New Orleans.

At first, Dolice Marie began to gleefully follow the other people of color that had shared her train car as they traveled with confidence to some familiar place, but once surrounded by the despicable conditions with which they had certainly and obviously chosen to live, she realized that she needed to explore her other options in the opposite direction. She walked awkwardly, juggling her train cases to balance their weight, passing people who gawked at her, whispered to one another as though taken by surprise, and who surely and undoubtedly were captivated by her unusual, extraordinary beauty. She ignored them, however, and continued her journey, all the while absorbing the beauty and charm of the great city, not to mention the heat and humidity that was beginning to drain her of her energy. It was time for Dolice Marie to find a place to stay for the night.

There seemed to be a boardinghouse on every corner, giving Dolice Marie the idea that she truly had several to choose from, and as she confidently approached the first door, she again adjusted her hat and the train cases that she had been carrying. After knocking several times on the big wooden door of the first boardinghouse she came upon, Dolice Marie looked around as she waited patiently for someone to answer, but no one did, and so she knocked again. This time, she noticed the window curtain open and close as if someone was watching her from the inside, but still no one answered. Thinking that certainly the other boardinghouses along the way would be somewhat more accommodating, if not more friendly, Dolice Marie continued on to the next one, commenting out loud as she scurried away that it was surely this owner's loss not to have her business. She tossed her head up in the air and continued her journey throughout the streets of New Orleans in search of a place to lay her head and her train cases down, even if just for the night.

She made her way to the city's famous French Quarter and continued on to the first boardinghouse in view, and someone did answer the door, although he or she did not open it. A man's voice just shouted back at Dolice Marie through the thick wood, "All the rooms are full." Of course, Dolice Marie thought he was extremely rude to yell at her through the door, but she was still very enthusiastic and optimistic as she approached yet another boardinghouse, and experienced yet another disappointment in her quest to find a decent place to stay. In fact, she had probably knocked on ten doors along the street and found every boardinghouse to be either full or no one answered, someone just peering at her through the curtains or the proprietor slamming the door in her face after shouting rude things to her. She certainly did not understand, but she knew that she was tired now, aggravated, hungry, not a person to be tampered with, and the train cases had become extremely heavy and awkward.

Uncle Dommie stated that the story goes that it was right then and there that Dolice Marie, in her most desperate hour to date, stood in the middle of a New Orleans City street, dropped the train cases from under her arms, and without any regard to the many people who snickered at her as they passed her by, cried her eyes out, clenching her fists as she stomped her feet. Well, Mama Mozelle would have surely slapped her plump behind good at the sight of such a tantrum!

Proper Southern white people ran about in all directions from the horrifying scene of this extremely well-dressed woman of color throwing what they most assuredly thought was some ritual dance to call the powers of evil down upon them all.

Dolice Marie's antics did call down a power, the familiar power that was always there for her, the loving power of Mama Del, who calmed her down and actually spoke to her heart from across all those miles, telling her about all the evil Southern goings-on when it came to the treatment of the people of color even though Mr. Lincoln had freed the slaves. Mama Del told her to briefly remember those days of slavery that she and all the people that lived on the LaPierre Plantation had experienced, and even though fate had truly been good to Dolice Marie, that in her youth she had been protected from any further mean and evil doings by a master or mistress, not everyone had been that fortunate. In fact, she was truly more well-bred and properly trained than the likes of the very people who were being so cruel and shameful to her and the other people of color.

Mama Del concluded by telling Dolice Marie that unfortunately, many of the proper Southern white people of the great city of New Orleans still considered her a darky, an ignorant yet well-dressed slave who deserved only to cook in their kitchens, clean their homes, and keep a quiet lip while accomplishing both.

Perhaps it was only then that Dolice Marie began to calm down and began to understand that there was one separate place for the proper Southern white people and another separate place for the people of color to live and that she truly should be on the opposite side of the great city with the other people that she thought had actually chosen to live as such. Mama Del offered to send some of her magical juju to bring instant pain and suffering upon the people who had rejected her, but Dolice Marie told her no—this she could truly handle all by herself. She gathered her pride, wiped the tears from her face, and picked up her train cases and all the courage she could muster, reminding herself that she was a LaPierre, one-half owner of the LaPierre Plantation. And besides that, she was truly dressed better than any proper Southern white lady that she had seen on the streets of New Orleans since her arrival, and thus she again headed on down the narrow street of the French Quarter.

Dolice Marie approached the very next boardinghouse that she came upon, fully prepared this time to stand her ground. The proprietor had watched her having her fit in the middle of the street and was shaking with fear when he saw her approach his door. Dolice Marie knocked and knocked, determined not to move until someone finally came to the door, as the proprietor and his wife clung to each other on the other side for fear of being turned into some sort of animal or inanimate object by this seemingly crazed voodoo priestess.

Dolice Marie could hear a man's voice yell loudly through the wooden door for her to go away, but she stood her ground, responding that she would surely sleep on his doorstep if he didn't open the door at that very minute, a sight she was certain would keep the kind of clientele he preferred forever away from his doorstep. The proprietor opened the door just enough for his face to appear through, pleading quietly for her to go away and not harm him, his wife, or their boarders, but before he could slam the door on her, Dolice Marie placed her tiny foot between the door and the doorframe, pulled out a roll of money, slapped the owner on the cheek several times with it, and made an offer to him that he surely could not refuse; she bought the boardinghouse for more money than the proprietor had probably ever had in his entire lifetime and removed the former owner and all his boarders (who fled to the streets without their belongings, screaming as if they were being chased by ghosts) in far less time than it had taken her to arrive in the great city of New Orleans on the train.

In fact, within a matter of another two hours, Dolice Marie had prepared herself a welcome meal in her new kitchen, bathed in the hot, bubbly waters in her new bathroom, and changed the linen on a bed in what appeared to be her new master bedroom.

Uncle Dommie laughed hysterically as he demonstrated the action our ancestor had made with the roll of money that sealed our family's victorious entrance into the great city of New Orleans.

By nightfall, Dolice Marie was truly content, breathing a sigh of relief as she stood on the beautiful French-laced wrought iron balcony of her brand-new boardinghouse that faced a narrow street of the French Quarter in the middle of New Orleans. She gave little or no concern to the proper Southern white people who stood below shouting obscenities at her, throwing food objects at her and threatening to do her bodily harm. Neither did she give any concern at all to the sheriff, who seemed to be quite amused by the sight of so many proper Southern white people being outwitted by the likes of the tiny former slave. He gazed up at her with his hands on his hips, smiling and shaking his head as he instructed the almost-riotous congregation of proper Southern white people to go home and let him handle the situation.

Dolice Marie suddenly gazed at the scene with her vixenly eyes, planning her next move and the manner in which she would handle the sheriff if he dared to ascend the stairway to her balcony. She smiled one of those impish smiles of hers, turned around and backed up to the balcony railing, lifted her skirt, pulled down her imported, fashionable bloomers, and exposed her very round and plump derriere to those below in a fashion that was hardly becoming of a lady, while proper Southern white ladies languished in outrage and proper Southern white gentlemen stared lustfully with their mouths open.

The sheriff, himself already quite charmed by the antics of the outrageous Dolice Marie, tipped his hat, and again commanded the crowd to leave the premises before he would begin to remove them himself. Dolice Marie smiled, tossed her head in the air again, and disappeared through the lovely doors, knowing full well that there would be more trouble to come, but for now, the message had truly been sent loud and clear on that balcony that night in the middle of the great city of New Orleans: Dolice Marie LaPierre was there to stay!

Many miles down the railroad track, across the mighty Mississippi River, the residents of the LaPierre Plantation were still celebrating the marriage of Jean Pierre and Evelina, while Dolice Marie was claiming her territory in the great city of New Orleans. It was Mama Mozelle that acknowledged first that her child had escaped while everyone else was dancing and having a wonderful time. Her tearful eyes met with Jean Pierre's as he, too, acknowledged that Dolice Marie was indeed gone to create a life of her own. No words were spoken at that time, and soon the celebrating would give way to the kind of celebrating that newlyweds do in their privacy.

Jean Pierre and Evelina nestled themselves in their new house away from the residents who were either still celebrating or finding their own way home to rest before the responsibilities of the coming new day. Jean Pierre wanted a son to continue his legacy and to oversee the LaPierre Plantation, and with Dolice Marie gone somewhere to pursue her own life, it was now his task as well as his pleasure to bring forth yet another generation of LaPierres.

Jean Pierre could hear Evelina's steady breathing as she lay next to him and would do so for the rest of their lives. He stared out of the window at the brilliant full moon, feeling more content and peaceful than he had ever felt before and yet wondering if Dolice Marie was all right and if she was at peace now as well as she slept somewhere for the first time in their lives away from each other, on the other side of that moon. His heart was torn between their separation and his new connection to the woman he loved in that way that he had never known for any other. Somewhere along the night, nestled in the warmth of the body that lay next to him, Jean Pierre fell asleep.

Mama Mozelle sat rocking in a wooden rocker on the front porch of the big house, wondering the same thing about Dolice Marie while contemplating her task at hand, finding a new madam to replace Dolice Marie at the bordello. She was far too old and far too feeble to accept such a challenge herself, but she was still the expert at choosing the most capable of the ladies, who were now asleep inside, to head her small family of working girls at the LaPierre bordello. Perhaps it should be Annabelle, the eldest daughter of Polain and Enith LaPierre, two truly faithful workers on the plantation who were the first to start work in the fields each morning and the last to climb in their beds at night. Surely, Annabelle was very beautiful, there was no doubt about that, and she could certainly draw the customers, but even though she was two years older than Dolice Marie, Annabelle did not have Dolice Marie's business savvy or her eye for fine fashion. Mozelle thought deeply as she rocked slowly. Perhaps Annabelle could learn the business end once she realized that she would bear the title Madam Annabelle, responsible for the entire business being conducted at the big house, and of course, she would have Mama Mozelle there to help her along the way. That was that then, Mozelle thought, and as she continued her rocking well into the morning sun, much like a mother bird protecting her young in the nest, she thought of the one that had flown away as a single tear escaped down her cheek and into the wind.

Jubil was making one more check of the horses as he, too, headed toward his house to rest for the night that would soon give way to the morning. He yawned and stretched as he checked each stall, bidding each horse a good night and allowing his own jealousy of Jean Pierre and Evelina, and the little girl Dolice Marie that had grown into a woman able to command her own destiny, to freely flow as tears in the privacy of the barn. Surely, Jubil could leave anytime he wanted as well; after all, he was as old as Jean Pierre and Dolice Marie, had been learning to read, could count money, and was capable of running the plantation all by himself if he had to. But where would he go?

Plantation life was all that he had ever known even though he had mastered every trade on the plantation, except what to do with the enormous amount of mint that was growing wild all over the gardens and much of the land behind the big house into the Bayou Frou-Frous. Mama Mozelle had had him pick plenty of it for her cool, sweet lemonade to sell to customers who liked that extra freshness in their lemonade, but that much and even more had grown in its place. Jubil felt lonely, and for some reason, tonight he felt as though he had lost his best friend, Jean Pierre, as he imagined him in Evelina's arms in their brand-new house. Jubil entered his own house, fell on his bed, and promised himself that he would ask Mama Del in the morning about a potion that could make his life more complete, but for now, it was time for him to try to sleep.

Dolice Marie, too, wondered about Jean Pierre, Mama Mozelle, and all her family back home at the LaPierre Plantation as she gazed at the moon from her huge bed lavishly dressed with sheets of cool silk, fluffy pillows with fancy casings, and the smell of an exotic aroma. Although she was extremely tired from the day's events, she found it very hard to fall asleep in the midst of the new surroundings, which seemed to creak and pop and make all kinds of strange noises to which she was not yet accustomed. And although she was absolutely beautiful in her imported, eggshell-colored silk pajamas that she had found in one of the armoires in another bedroom, she felt lost in the middle of the big four-poster bed that lay in the middle of the huge bedroom that she had claimed as her very own when she had taken over the boardinghouse. She, too, felt lonely, even though she couldn't bring herself to admit it to herself or even believe such. Dolice Marie was also afraid and overwhelmed with thoughts of what she was going to do with herself in the great city of New Orleans and how much more she might have to fight to protect this new possession. She stared at the moon until, sometime during the dark hours of the night, Dolice Marie fell asleep.

Just down the narrow streets of New Orleans, near the mighty Mississippi River, the widow Beatrice Carson Declouette admired herself in front of her floor-length mirror, adjusting her large silk hat just so, then slipping on her lace gloves while keeping an admiring eye on herself in the mirror. Such a routine for just a simple walk in the park! Miss BB, as she was known to everyone on her end of town, grasped her tiny brass bell from the dresser and rang it ever so ladylike. Moments later, a tall man of color named Obadiah appeared in the room, carrying two small poodle dogs, one black and one white. She smiled quite broadly when she saw her "children."

At this point, Uncle Dommie explained to the young boys that although Miss BB was not a blood relative of our family, old stories say that she was very instrumental in assisting in its development and thus deserves ample recognition.

Madam Declouette had left her home in Savannah, Georgia, when her heart and good sense had been stolen by a proper Southern gentleman from the great state of North Carolina, Monsieur Daniel Declouette, a French Canadian and first-generation American who had become a member of Southern society when he had taken over the family import-and-export business when the elder Monsieur Declouette had become disabled when bitten by a poisonous snake that was hidden in a lovely vase from Ethiopia. It was this twist of fate and brave business venture that brought the younger Monsieur Declouette to the river and to the Carson import-and-export business of Savannah, subsequently to the arms of the lovely Beatrice Carson.

Harrison Carson was not only known as a shrewd businessman, but he also had a brilliant political mind as well, and it would be at such a political function for a certain Southern candidate campaigning for a Savannah office that the young Declouette met and fell in love with Harrison Carson's only daughter, Miss. BB, a nickname that had been given to her by a family member when she was very young.

The two courted but a short while before the adventurous Monsieur Declouette asked Harrison Carson for the hand of his beloved daughter in marriage, explaining that he would be moving his business to the shores of the Mississippi River in the great city of New Orleans and could not imagine leaving without this wonderful woman that had captured his heart and thrilled his spirit. Harrison Carson's love for his daughter was far greater than his desire to selfishly keep her near to him, and the merging of the Carson-Declouette import-and-export businesses was a far greater avenue than a spinster at home with a doting father!

After a truly extravagant wedding, Miss BB bade a tearful farewell to her father and mother as well as the city of Savannah to begin a new life with her husband near the Mississippi River in New Orleans. After many years of financial success and social status, Miss BB's husband, the Monsieur Daniel Declouette, also met with an unfortunate and untimely catastrophe when his ship lost its course in thick fog and rammed into an island where rumor had it that both he and his crew members became dinner for some island natives who later had been seen by other sailors wearing lovely jewelry from the Orient.

Although she and Monsieur Declouette had been married for many years at the time of the tragedy, the lovely Miss BB had no children to carry on the Declouette name, only the company of her two "children," poodles named FiFi and GiGi, which her beloved husband had given her as an anniversary gift. Upon her beloved father's death, Miss BB also inherited her father's personal slave, Obadiah, who had chosen to remain with her when slavery was abolished. Miss BB then hired Obadiah with a good salary to be her personal assistant, having him well-educated as well as handsomely dressed in the finest tradition of the Carson-Declouette families.

It was most obvious that Miss BB loved Obadiah and cherished him as her closest confidant, trusting him with the money left to her by her husband, eventually her father and father-in-law, when they passed on to the next life, as well as her own life. She, too, developed an adventurous spirit after their deaths that oftentimes found her in the midst of social upheaval and the subject of social gossip, both very much to her enjoyment, I might add!

Miss BB frequently found herself laughing hysterically while reading about herself in the local newspaper over her morning coffee with Obadiah. Seems the newspaper's claims were that Miss BB was either being associated with some crazy cause she allegedly supported or had been seen in the company of characters with less social status than herself, even being allegedly seen smoking a cigar. Whether these allegations were true or not, they did indeed bring great pleasure to the charming and eccentric widow.

Uncle Dommie told the young boys that rumor had it that the lovely, sophisticated Miss BB's family was actually related to the former president of these United States, why, Mr. Thomas Jefferson. Of course, being related to Mr. Jefferson meant being related to everyone that was related to him. Whether or not it was common knowledge at that time, it was still common truth that Mr. Jefferson had fathered several children with a certain woman of color named Sally, an indiscretion yet historical by nature, making those offspring well in the bloodline of Miss Beatrice Carson forever. Strangely enough, particularly during that time in history, Miss BB was proud of being related to Mr. Jefferson and, most certainly, to all his relations. Another one of those allegations that heightened her adventurous nature and gave the newspapers even more to talk about.

Obadiah opened the doors to the house for Miss BB and her children, and as she strolled through the narrow streets of the great city of New Orleans, she was greeted with conversation by her neighbors. The conversation that was on everybody's lips on this beautiful day was about a certain woman of color who had manipulated her way into a boardinghouse in the French Quarter, forcing the owner and his guests to leave while she herself refused to leave the boardinghouse with a claim that she had purchased the property. The nerve of her! Oh, there were words like *heifer*, *trash*, and yes, the N-word as the neighbors continued to tell their version of the story.

Miss BB simply shook her head with disgust, uttered words of sheer surprise, raised her embroidered handkerchief to her throat as if she were about to swoon into a faint, and as she did so, bade her farewells while guiding the dog leashes away from the neighborhood.

Once out of eyesight of her nosy neighbors, Miss BB grabbed both babies in her arms and began a quick trek to the French Quarter, where she found, there in front of God and many of the good citizens of the great city of New Orleans, a young woman of color hanging her naked derriere over the balcony of a boardinghouse. Shameful! Once she felt it had hung there long enough, the girl turned around, stuck her tongue out at the crowd below, and after tossing her head in the air, disappeared through the beautiful French doors.

Miss BB could not contain her laughter as she stared at the sight while her heart was immediately captivated by the ill-bred, uneducated, yet noticeably well-dressed woman of color. She stared at the closed French doors long after Dolice Marie had disappeared, contemplating what she had just witnessed and finding herself truly captivated by what she had seen. Encouraging FiFi and GiGi to quickly eliminate themselves in the park on the way home and avoiding the gossiping of the neighborhood snobs, it would be quite obvious to anyone in her path that Miss BB was on a mission, one that kept her from sleeping at all that fateful night.

It would be early the next morning that Miss BB would make her first contact with the wild and fearless young woman known as Dolice Marie. A hard knock on the front door caused Dolice Marie to be startled, and she sneaked down the stairs until she could see the front door out of the window, but she herself could not be seen. There, on her front porch, was a tall man of color dressed in a tall hat, a dazzling white shirt, and a black suit with tails. At first, Dolice Marie could not believe what she was seeing, but after another hard knock on the door, she acknowledged that she was at least hearing this stranger's knock. She had never seen a man of color dressed so fine at the LaPierre Plantation and certainly not anywhere else. Dolice Marie greeted the man and asked what his business was with her. He simply replied in perfect English by saying that he had a message for her, and not knowing if the message was from one of her family members at the LaPierre Plantation, she was forced to open the door just a little. The man removed his hat, smiled to expose a mouthful of perfect white teeth, and asked if he could come in. Since he was a man of color, Dolice Marie felt that perhaps she could trust him, and even though he might try to harm her, she was also very ready to take him down in a flash, so she opened the door all the way and beckoned the man to enter.

The man explained that his name was Obadiah Carson and that his employer was requesting a meeting with her at her earliest convenience, for tea at her home, the home of Miss Beatrice Carson Declouette. Dolice Marie was confused, and certainly not impressed, so she asked the man to repeat what he had said, adding that she would also like him to tell her why this Miss Beatrice, whatever her name was, would want to invite her for tea. After several times repeating the same thing, the man grew impatient and concluded the conversation by telling Dolice Marie that he would be by to pick her up on Sunday, when the sun was highest in the sky, that would be noon, if by chance she knew how to tell time. He bade her adieu, tipped his tall hat again, and mounted the seat on a very large carriage drawn by an equally large horse that was parked out in front of the boardinghouse. Within seconds, he was gone.

Dolice Marie was not quite sure what to think of the strange encounter of the day before but was quite prepared when Obadiah returned the next day, just as he had said, when the sun was highest in the sky. So as not to seem too terribly anxious, Dolice Marie gave the impatient Obadiah the opportunity to knock several times before she answered the door, addressing him finally as if she had truly not given any thought to the invitation given the day before, but quickly gave way to her curiosity when Obadiah called her bluff and turned to walk away. After grabbing her lovely chapeau and parasol that had been strategically placed just within the doorway, Dolice Marie tossed her head in the air as she accepted Obadiah's hand to assist her into the carriage.

The drive to Miss BB's was quite pleasant, and while Dolice Marie thought deeply about her family at the LaPierre Plantation, especially Jean Pierre and Mama Mozelle, she could easily ignore the usual antics of the proper Southern white people along the way while covered slightly by her fashionable parasol. Just outside the great city, quite near the mighty Mississippi River, Obadiah turned the carriage down a beautifully landscaped pathway lined with white azalea bushes leading to an exquisite Southern home framed with flowing lavender wisteria seemingly waving at them. Dolice Marie was not the least bit impressed, of course, since her own home on the Bayou Frou-Frous was just as dazzling, if not more.

Obadiah pulled the carriage up to the house and assisted Dolice Marie from the seat to the front door of the house, where Miss BB was standing, smiling, and extending her hand to welcome Dolice Marie to her home. Although Dolice Marie was certainly still truly confused as to the visit, she felt a certain connection to the woman, whose apparent early beauty was only charmed by the lines of age and experience, and so she accepted her hand. Amid a huge collection of antiques, family heirlooms, and lovely imports that were most assuredly memoirs from her own family as well as her husband's occupational treasures appeared a small table with a delicate lace cloth and well-polished sterling silver tea accessories, perfectly aligned and set for two. Miss BB motioned for Dolice Marie to sit, and within minutes, it was truly obvious that Dolice Marie had an ally in the great city of New Orleans.

"But the question was," Uncle Dommie would say as he scanned each young boy's eyes, "What was Miss BB's plan for the unsuspecting Dolice Marie?"

Meanwhile, Jean Pierre found it quite difficult to leave his beautiful, new wife, but the chores of the day were indeed calling him from the warmth of her arms, and he kissed her gently so as not to awaken her as he escaped from their bedroom to head out to the fields. Jubil was the first to comment about his "silly grin," and for that moment, the two were boys again, razzing each other about the kinds of things that would cause children to blush. Arm in arm, Jean Pierre and Jubil made their way to the fields to greet the morning sun and the other residents of the LaPierre Plantation.

Evelina reached for her new husband and realized that the morning had already come and he had already awakened to his responsibilities. She smiled and closed her eyes as she placed both hands on her stomach, acknowledging the fact that she had indeed conceived their first child the night before, a child that she already knew would be healthy, strong, and a blessing to a doting father. Evelina rolled over on her other side and fell back to sleep.

Mozelle walked to Polain and Enith's home to discuss the decision she had made the night before about employing Annabelle as the new head of the LaPierre bordello. She found the young woman and her mother on their front porch scrubbing clothes on a washboard in a large tin tub. Both welcomed Mozelle, but it was apparent that both were lost as to why the mother of the mistress and the master of the LaPierre Plantation would be visiting them, and at such an early hour of the morning.

Mozelle quickly explained the decision that she had made the night before and presented the idea to Enith, even before asking Annabelle. Unfortunately, Enith was not as excited as the other parents had been during the great Civil War at the idea of their daughters sharing their womanhood with strangers. Mozelle assured Enith that she understood but that, surely, together they could come up with some conclusion that would benefit both the bordello and Annabelle's family. The two women continued their discussion on the front porch of Polain and Enith's home for several hours as Annabelle continued her washing, with one ear finely tuned to the conversation at hand.

Finally, an agreement was made: Annabelle would serve as the madam of the LaPierre bordello only in the business sense of the title but would not partake in the physical end of the business. Mozelle would work with her daily to help her develop her skills as overseer of the LaPierre bordello, and yes, Annabelle would have access to the fine garments just as the other ladies who did participate in the physical end of the business, as well as an equal share of the money brought in, and of course, the opportunity to change her mind about participating in the business at hand if ever or whenever she so chose to do so.

Uncle Dommie would cast a long wink as he scanned each young boy's eyes to bring even more mystery and intrigue to our family's history. After leaning back in his chair, he would skip back in a flash to Miss BB's house.

After a delightful cup of tea and a fresh French pastry, Miss BB began to recognize the restlessness of her guest and quickly changed her conversation to the reason she had invited Dolice Marie for tea. After a brief pause, Miss BB came straight to the point.

"You remind me of myself when I was your age," she said in an appealing, long, and drawn-out Southern accent unlike that of the natives of the great city of New Orleans. "Spunky and determined to make my mark on the world one way or another. I, too, commanded an audience with my antics but gained my fortune when I began to present myself as a lady with all the proprieties that accompany such a title. It was as a lady that I met and married my beloved husband, and I dare say that it will be as a lady that you meet yours! There will always be time for fun, I assure you. Just read the morning newspaper!"

Dolice Marie stared deeply into the charming lady's eyes and asked, What did any of that have to do with her? Miss BB explained that she had never had the blessings of a child in all her years, just her husband's sweet niece that lived in France, but had made a vow to herself after his death that she would give her assistance wherever possible. And although Dolice Marie was a truly lovely, well-dressed young woman, she was not yet a lady. And until she became a lady, the proper Southerners of the great city of New Orleans would continue to treat her like a commoner, a darky, a freed slave, with little regard for everything else she was.

"Besides," Miss BB concluded, "it would do this old heart of mine quite good to see the wrinkled, old, pretentious bitches of New Orleans shaken up a bit by the very thing their equally old, tired, henpecked husbands lust after in the quiet of the night!" She sipped her tea while giving a wink to Dolice Marie.

"My dearly departed husband's niece will be coming here within the next few weeks from France looking for the chance to finish up her education in dance and theater. She, too, will need a friend. Yes, the two of you could take New Orleans by storm!"

Miss BB began to stare into space while seriously thinking and then finally told Dolice Marie that both girls would certainly need a good friend at this time, one that would be easily accepted by the proper white Southerners of the great city of New Orleans, she said, turning over one hand. And one who had the temperament and the courage to hand-wrestle an alligator single-handedly, she said, turning over the other hand.

The two began to laugh out loud as both realized that they were indeed on the same page, while a genuine bond between the two was being developed, one that could lead to fascinating times. Just before nightfall, Miss BB summoned Obadiah and asked that he take the Lady Dolice Marie back to her home. Accompanying her were two large boxes that Miss BB had already asked one of her servants to pack and tie with cord.

"One, my dear, is filled with food that you will probably need before Obadiah can get out and shop for your necessities, and the other is filled with personal items that you will enjoy, some silk, some fragrance, some feathers, and some fur!" She laughed again, kissed Dolice Marie softly on her forehead, and stood waving as Obadiah turned the large house and carriage back toward the city. Upon his arrival back to the mansion, Obadiah found his dearest Miss BB sound asleep on a divan in the parlor. Carefully picking her up, he carried her up to her bedroom, where he placed her on her bed, called for her servant to prepare her for bed, extinguished the candles on the bedroom walls, and softly closed the door to prepare himself for bed. Miss BB slept comfortably as even in her sleep her plans were still being created.

Just as Miss BB had said, her niece arrived in the great city of New Orleans several weeks later and, not long after, was brought to Dolice Marie's boardinghouse by Obadiah. Dolice Marie was awakened from a nap suddenly by the sound of someone knocking loudly on the front door to the boardinghouse, thrusting her back into awakeness and the torrid heat of the day. At her door was a tiny specimen of a girl, seemingly no taller than a child, but truly developed like a woman. Her golden-red hair hung down over her eyes, down over her shoulders, and was topped by a lovely plumed hat that immediately caught Dolice Marie's eye. The stranger's extremely white freckled skin paled even more in contrast to her piercing green eyes, which were squinting from the bright sun as she struggled to see inside the parlor window. Her tiny lips quivered as though she had just been chastised by a parent for being bad. Obadiah placed her train cases on the steps of the boardinghouse and waited for Dolice Marie to reply. Dolice Marie, hiding behind the heavy brocade curtains, was truly confused at the sight of this visitor and wondered why a proper Southern white lady would be knocking on her door, so she gathered her courage, politely opened the door, and asked her.

"Miss BB has sent me here, but I am not a proper Southern white lady, madam. I am French!" the lady answered in a language that sounded like a blend of broken English, French, and the strong Southern drawl of Savannah, all rolled up into one, but was strangely understandable to Dolice Marie.

Dolice Marie opened the heavy curtain a little more to see Obadiah sitting upon the carriage led by the large horse. She quickly opened the door, and the two young women embraced as though they had known each other forever. It was a true moment of sisterhood, a union destined to be. Dolice Marie was truly excited to have a friend in the great city of New Orleans, and besides, she was extremely impressed by the girl's fashion sense and that adorable little purse that she was carrying.

Chapter 5

IT WAS VERY obvious that the young boys enjoyed hearing the stories about their sensuous ancestor, Dolice Marie LaPierre, and about all her adventures, and surely one could write an entire novel dedicated to just her, but there were those that made as equal a great mark on future generations as Dolice Marie LaPierre. And the next generation was on its way!

The LaPierre Plantation was thriving, providing a prosperous life for the nearly two hundred residents that lived and made their living within its confines, from the silversmith's shop that had expanded into three buildings, now with the ability to obtain and melt down more silver than ever before; the livery stables, which could boast of having the majority of the business from the entire area, thanks to Jubil; Mama Mozelle's thriving fruit and vegetable stands, which served more than one purpose; not to mention that cool, sweet lemonade sweetened with sugarcane and served up in those beautiful silver cups, to the temptations of the LaPierre bordello, which truly needed absolutely no further explanation, and everything else in between. Life was good.

Jean Pierre now spent much of his time with his new role as husband to Evelina, serving more in the Master LaPierre role of approving or delegating rather than himself strenuously working in the fields or the shops. Evelina was proudly and quite big with child now, spending much of her time with Mama Mozelle, learning to sew and cook, and all the other duties she would have to perform as the wife of the master of the LaPierre Plantation.

Annabelle had proudly accepted her new role as madam of the LaPierre bordello and was eagerly demonstrating just why Mama Mozelle had chosen her to serve as Dolice Marie's quite successful administrator. She was genuinely accepted by the other ladies that worked in the bordello and found it quite easy to slip into Dolice Marie's former role, and her shoes, since both wore the same size and Dolice Marie had left several pairs in her closet, having run out of room in her train cases.

With all this going on, Jubil found his role expanding with Jean Pierre's direction to serve as the plantation overseer, responsible for making sure everything was going as it should, and always with the master's permission, of course. Mama Del had given Jubil hope by telling him that he did not need one of her concoctions to provide a good life for himself; that was on its way even without her help. The news had given him more of a sense of confidence, and it showed as he proudly rode his horse throughout the living quarters, the fields, and the shops, fulfilling his duties as overseer.

The plantation that was once home to broken-down slave quarters, equally broken-down bodies, minds, and dusty fields, was now a city in its own right, one that would and could now be known as Mon Village du LaPierre en Bayou Frou-Frous, which is what it is known as to this very day.

The heat and the humidity of the summer months gave way to the cool of fall and the nippy air of the winter months in the great state of Louisiana, and it would be sometime in that transitional season of spring in the year 1869 that the residents of Mon Village du LaPierre en Bayou Frou-Frous were awakened by screams coming from Jean Pierre and Evelina's home, the kind of screams that foretold the birth of their first baby and the beginning of another generation in the line of our family.

Jean Pierre frantically ran to the home of the midwife, Miss Penelope, who was already dressing herself when he knocked nervously on her door to give her the news that she, of course, already knew. Miss Penelope looked strangely at Jean Pierre as he stood in her doorway with his pants and shirt in hands instead of on his body. She simply shook her head and moved past him toward the house.

For the next several hours, well into the next day, Evelina labored in the process of giving birth, sweating and clinging to the midwife during her contractions while promising in rather-profuse language to never bear another child and threatening to actually kill a very pathetically confused Jean Pierre if he dared ever to touch her again in between. Mama Mozelle ran into the house just in time to pry Evelina off Jean Pierre and send him out of the house until the women's work was done. Jubil ran to comfort his good friend Jean Pierre, who had hidden in the fields, where they both stayed until finally a very weary Mama Mozelle announced that Evelina had given birth to a beautiful baby girl and that it was now safe for Jean Pierre to come back into his house to meet the sweet baby girl because Evelina was sound asleep.

There is truly no sweeter scene than a brand-new father and his baby girl, a scene that can make a grown man cry like the days when he was just a baby as well. That was the scene as Jean Pierre accepted this child into his arms, dropping tears of joy onto her tiny cheek and smiling all at the same time, guided gently by Miss Penelope, who was standing quite near to assure that the new father properly held his new child, a baby girl, and as Evelina slept, Jean Pierre welcomed Mon Claire LaPierre into their world. After placing another beautiful silver cup on the shelf next to Jean Pierre's and Evelina's, Mama Mozelle led Jean Pierre with the baby to Mama Del's house, where the secret birth ritual was performed, a ritual that still to this day is kept a secret from everyone except those who are chosen to serve as Mama Del's confidant.

Uncle Dommie smiled and settled back in his chair, shaking his head, along with my other uncles, with such great pride that the young boys could feel it even in their youth.

In the great city of New Orleans, Dolice Marie LaPierre was suddenly exhilarated by the breath of new life that swept through her as it entered the world far away down the railroad tracks at Mon Village du LaPierre en Bayou Frou-Frous. She gasped for her own breath and smiled sweetly as she explained to her new friend that a child had been born, the child of her beloved Jean Pierre. The two hugged again as Dolice Marie brought her up the steep staircase to the sleeping quarters, where Angeline chose the bedroom down the hallway from the master bedroom, the room that was decorated all in bright colors that also faced the narrow street of the French Quarter. Angeline Toussaint-Marie was her name, brand-new to the city of New Orleans, from Dijon, France, where her parents owned a farm, much like Dolice Marie's plantation at the Bayou Frou-Frous. The twenty-three-year-old had sailed across the ocean all by herself at the urging of Grandmama Declouette, a well-to-do Parisian businesswoman who had financed the trip with the urging of Angeline's beloved aunt Miss BB in order for Angeline to pursue her career as a carousel dancer, what the Westerners called the cancan, in the legendary city of New Orleans.

Her granmama had introduced Angeline to the finer things of the French life during summer visits from Dijon, including art, classical music, the opera, the ballet, literature, and occasionally, how to "strut her stuff," which her granmama could still do with little effort. Dolice Marie listened excitedly, with no idea as to what this new friend was referring to, but so happy to have someone that accepted her as that, a friend.

It was obvious that Dolice Marie and Angeline had quickly forged a friendly alliance, by the curious means of Miss BB Carson Declouette, which made being away from home much easier for both of them, but as yet, they were both strangers with lots to learn about each other, Dolice Marie being especially curious about where Angeline had found that darling little purse.

After preparing and sharing a meal together in the large formal dining room, the two discussed their former lives and plans for their futures while sitting on Dolice Marie's big bed in just their undergarments. Angeline spoke quite fondly of her very kind granmama, her sweet and deceased uncle Gordon Declouette's mama, who lived in an extremely large chateau in downtown Paris, in the shadows of the Eiffel Tower, where she conducted her business and provided room and board for at least one dozen young women at a time, each who came to her to learn a particular trade. Angeline explained that

Granmama was extremely intelligent, a member of the great Parisian society and did her charitable work for no self-gratification, just the look of satisfaction on the young women's faces at the end of each day.

Angeline went on to tell Dolice Marie how all the young women loved her granmama so and even called her Madam Declouette in respect for providing them with shelter, food, and the most beautiful gowns in all of France. Granmama would not let Angeline go upstairs to the young women's living quarters in all those years growing up, and she simply assumed that it was because the young women needed their privacy and quiet as they studied their lessons. Angeline admired the good name of her granmama and was truly impressed at the very important men that visited her regularly, including those that appeared to be members of great dignity, and how they showed their devotion to her by sending her and the young women such wonderful gifts. The gifts were always brought by handsome young messengers that were allowed to bring the gifts to the women's quarters, from where she could then hear laughter as the women opened their gifts and graciously thanked the handsome messengers.

Money was never a problem for Angeline's granmama either; there always seemed to be more than enough for the women to eat the very best foods, have gowns made from the purest silks, and of course, their knowledge of worldly things made them an even more precious commodity.

Dolice Marie sat quietly while listening to Angeline proudly tell her story that slowly began to sound very much like the goings-on at the LaPierre bordello, until finally, almost astonished, she could no longer contain herself and began to laugh loudly and uncontrollably. Well, Angeline was quite perplexed and became extremely angry at the idea that Dolice Marie, who knew nothing about her family, would be laughing at her wonderful granmama. Dolice Marie apologized profusely with both tears of laughter and those of deep regret, trying to explain to Angeline why she was laughing, describing the goings-on at the LaPierre Plantation from that short period when she lived as a slave, how she and Jean Pierre became the master and mistress of the plantation, and how Mama Mozelle helped the LaPierre bordello come into existence with Dolice Marie as the madam over eleven other young women.

Dolice Marie began to quiet down as she suddenly paused, realizing that Angeline had absolutely no idea what kind of business Granmama had truly been conducting in that large chateau in the city of Paris, and felt as though she had perhaps exposed a terrible secret. Both were very quiet as Angeline, although taken aback and a tiny bit embarrassed, listened intently to Dolice Marie's story as she realized that Granmama and her newfound friend, Dolice Marie, had truly both been expert businesswomen in that common profession, even though each was many miles away from the other, separated only by an ocean. And could it be that Miss BB had known all along about the business dealings conducted by both her deceased husband's mama in Paris as well as Dolice Marie's Mama Mozelle on the Bayou Frou-Frous in the great state of Louisiana and that all the preparation of the two young women had been for more than one reason? One never knows the entire story until one has lived it, does one?

"Well," Angeline finally commented in her thick accent as she leaned against the headboard of the big bed, a look of deep thought on her face, "so Granmama was really Granmadam! And all that time the women upstairs were…getting rich!"

Dolice Marie answered yes in a quiet whisper, as if she were just a little child that had just told the truth about some awful affair, apologizing for having been so careless as to reveal such a secret about Angeline's beloved granmama.

"No, no, no!" Angeline said. "There is no need to apologize! Here we are, two young women with the opportunity of a lifetime and so many successful examples to follow! Perhaps we should be happy that we can create a legacy all our own!"

"What a legacy, indeed," Uncle Dommie would say as he scanned the young boys' eyes, and the Southern gentlemen would howl with laughter!

Life for Jean Pierre and Evelina seemed complete now with the birth of their first child, Mon Claire, and like any other father, Jean Pierre generously showered her with his love and with the kinds of things that other children of color were not so fortunate to possess. Jean Pierre and Jubil made wooden toys for her to play with while Mama Mozelle made cloth dolls for her and sewed the finest dresses that anyone of any color would have loved to wear.

Days turned into weeks, and weeks into months, as Dolice Marie and Angeline divided their time between the boardinghouse and long stays at Miss BB's mansion. Having agreed to the direction that the boardinghouse should go, all three now had a common goal, making the hard work a little more bearable, particularly when contemplating the vast amount of money that could be coming their way.

Obadiah carried the two ladies back and forth in the carriage with the large horse, smiling to himself as he secretly listened to them as they giggled together in back of the carriage. He was as protective of them as a proud father would be of his own children, but as nosy as any man could be about the secrets of a woman.

While at Miss BB's house, Dolice Marie was learning to become a lady, how to properly walk, talk, and respond to the advances of a respectable gentleman who showed his interest. It was not always an easy task; Dolice Marie would tire easily of walking with books on her head or, believe it or not, trying on hats and clothing with the seamstress. She would often throw such things around the room and yell that the sort of things she was learning surely had nothing to do with her as she lay flat on her back to make her contributions to the business. Miss BB, ever the caretaker, would demand her attention and reminded her that she did not necessarily have to be flat on her back if she cooperated!

Dolice Marie was especially troublesome when Miss BB would ask one of the male servants to play the part of an overly anxious suitor to the always-temperamental Dolice Marie, the pretend suitor who, several times, narrowly escaped a blow from Dolice Marie's fist as she raised her lovely new skirts and went after him with an extremely threatening balled-up fist. Miss BB was always ready to intervene, reminding Dolice Marie that there were many ways other than a fistfight to ward off a suitor!

Indeed, there were constant fittings by special dressmakers that were hired by Miss BB and special coaches to teach her how to sit, eat, and even flirt, if the occasion called for it.

Angeline, on the other hand, spent her time learning to play the piano and to dance from musicians and fine dance instructors that Miss BB had hired. There were many times that Dolice Marie was invited to join in as Angeline's dance partner, giving both girls the experience they would eventually need. But the noise of an inexperienced piano player ran jolts of frustration through ears of the people who at least knew what good music should sound like.

Everyone was paid well to provide their service and cautioned equally as well to keep their mouths shut about what was going on at the Declouette Mansion and at the boardinghouse in the French Quarter of the great city of New Orleans.

There would be plenty of time for the hungry newspaper reporters to get their hands on the story.

The local gossipers, old bitties, as Miss BB liked to call them, were anxious to ask questions when they would find her walking the children toward the park, always curious about Obadiah traveling so much and asking who her guests were. If she could not avoid her nosy neighbors, Miss BB would feign complete shock, as always, holding her handkerchief to her nose as though she were near a faint, and respond that Obadiah most definitely had a fine talking-to coming his way if she ever found out that there were indeed shenanigans going on! She would then, of course, quickly excuse herself, informing her neighbors that she must hurry in order to find Obadiah and do just that.

Months went by as Dolice Marie and Angeline's friendship blossomed into kinship, the ladies exchanging their secrets as sisters would. Dolice Marie and Angeline shared everything, with the exception of certain fashion articles that were almost guarded, certainly hidden, to maintain some sort of individualism, even competition, where it counted the most to the two of them.

When alone at the boardinghouse after a full day at Miss BB's, Angeline taught Dolice Marie about those things that she loved, the opera and classical music, the ballet, and what was expected, as Miss

BB always said, from a true lady when in the company of a true gentlemen—when to blush, when and how to laugh, especially at something witty that the gentleman might say.

Dolice Marie, in turn, taught Angeline how to use all her feminine attributes to assure that the true gentleman would certainly be lured by her charm, seduced by her eyes, beckoned by her bosoms, and mesmerized by the manner in which she commanded every situation by the mere movement of her voluptuous body parts, and in between they would laugh so loud that the walls of the boardinghouse would shake.

Angeline also assisted Miss BB in teaching Dolice Marie how to read and to speak and understand the more common European French language that was spoken in the great city of New Orleans, as opposed to the Creole that was spoken on the plantations and in the smaller villages by the people of color. There was always a lesson to be learned, a lesson to be taught, whether in the boardinghouse or at Miss BB's. But it was Dolice Marie that taught Angeline the language that everyone understood, the language that required no movement of the lips to utter a sound, the language that would assure the two of them a truly healthy income in the coming months and years.

Evelina was as content as any woman could be, spending her days caring for their home, for their sweet little baby girl, and spending her nights eagerly caring for her man! Oh, how fortunate it is for men that their women do forget the pains and the struggle of childbirth once their precious bundle of joy arrives, or there would surely be only one child per family on this earth, especially in Jean Pierre's family.

And so it was with Evelina, Jean Pierre's beloved wife, who welcomed the fact that she was with child again when Mon Claire was at the tender age of six months old. Jean Pierre stood frozen in the front door to their house as a smiling, almost-giddy Evelina lovingly shared the news that they were to have another child. As she reached to put her arms around him, Jean Pierre nearly jumped out of the door, explaining to her that he was not sure if he should be happy or scared to death that Evelina would surely kill him this time. Evelina laughed as though she had absolutely no idea as to what he was talking about and smiled as she hugged him lovingly.

For all the residents of Mon Village du LaPierre en Bayou Frou-Frous, another child for Jean Pierre and Evelina would certainly be a welcomed addition to not only their own personal family but also to the extended family of the village. But everyone had experienced Evelina's carryings-on and heard her screams during the birth of Mon Claire and had already begun to extend their congratulations as well as their condolences to the Master Jean Pierre! Many of the women often stopped Jean Pierre as he went about his duties to cheerfully give their words of advice while all the while laughing as they went about their way. Jean Pierre had just learned to take it all in stride when Evelina began her ritual of announcing to the entire population that she was about to give birth again, only this time it was during the brightness of day, while everyone was still at work.

Miss Penelope and Mama Mozelle felt it coming and immediately began their separate rituals of gathering all the necessary supplies together and running to Evelina's side while Jubil ran toward Jean Pierre's house also, just in time to intercept Evelina's extremely powerful right hook. Just as the year before, Evelina screamed, cursed, and promised she would never again give birth because, this time, if Jean Pierre ever came near her again, she was surely going to kill him—that is, if she could ever get her hands on him, so he'd better run!

Jubil and Jean Pierre did just that, ran fearfully toward the gardens, where they fell on the hard ground amid an enormous growth of mint, where they stayed until well into the night, breathless from their vigorous flight. Totally exhausted and breathing laboriously, Jean Pierre grabbed a handful of the vines and scanned the vast area where mint had virtually taken over the gardens. The two searched the area with disbelief—mint was everywhere. But the question was as it had been for quite some time: What to do with it?

It would be hours later before Jean Pierre heard Mama Mozelle yelling his name. Jean Pierre was again a father, but this time a father to twin boys, who were waiting to be held by their father, and she assured him that it was now safe to enter his home because Evelina was once again sound asleep and posed no danger to him. Still not completely convinced, Jean Pierre quietly entered his house, where Miss Penelope was sitting on the bed beside a sleeping Evelina, holding and rocking both babies. He smiled proudly as he reached to hold them in his arms, putting a kiss on each of their foreheads, then proudly whispering what a man he was to now have two boys! He would call them Petois and Pecous, names he had heard the former master of the plantation, Philippe LaPierre, mention while speaking about his family far away in France.

As he stood enjoying the first moments of his sons' new life, Evelina moved just a tad to comfort herself on the bed, and Jean Pierre jumped so high that Mama Mozelle and Miss Penelope had to grab the boys before he dropped them on the floor, the two ladies commenting that men could be so silly and that no wonder women were given the job of bringing the children into the world.

Mon Claire LaPierre, their firstborn, was sound asleep in her nursery, where she had been since early evening, undisturbed by the frantic escapades of her mother giving birth to her baby brothers in the very next bedroom. Perhaps even she had thought it best to be sound asleep rather than to be any further cause for her mother to scream.

After placing two more beautiful silver cups on the shelf next to Mon Claire's, Jean Pierre's, and Evelina's, Jean Pierre looked in upon the sleeping Mon Claire and again quietly followed Mama Mozelle away from his home, this time with his twin sons, to Mama Del's house for the secret birth ritual.

Again, in the great city of New Orleans, Dolice Marie felt the breath of life in her spirit as she stood solemnly on her beautiful French-laced wrought iron balcony, dressed in her sensuous silk lavender nightgown, with adorable pink satin slippers that adorned her tiny feet. She smiled for a brief moment and closed her eyes to enjoy the great revelation once again, although her heart was breaking and her spirit shaken again at the reality that she was totally alone. And now Jean Pierre not only had Evelina; he also had children to carry on his name and the work of her family back home. She let the tears flow down her cheeks this time, giving in to the pain that swelled in her heart. Her tears were interrupted by the sound of Angeline almost successfully playing the piano downstairs in the parlor of the boardinghouse. She wiped the tears away and forced herself to bring herself back into her own world and the business ahead.

The time had finally come, time to find the women who would staff the boardinghouse and create the new business in the French Quarter of the great city of New Orleans. This would be Miss BB's foremost contribution, she told Dolice Marie and Angeline, since she felt she had proven that she had such great taste in choosing just the right people for just the right job! It was decided that she and Obadiah would begin to inconspicuously search the city streets of New Orleans in anticipation of gathering together several lovely ladies of diverse persuasions to join Miss Dolice Marie and her faithful assistant, Angeline, in building their business. Besides, it would most assuredly be a much easier and more acceptable task for Miss BB to ride in that carriage driven by a man of color and drawn by the huge horse than Miss Dolice Marie having to avoid the glaring looks and evil words from proper Southern white ladies who probably already had an idea what was beginning to happen in that boardinghouse. Of course, their proper Southern white husbands walked throughout the city with smirks on their faces, coming together themselves as that secret society of men who always seemed to know just where such houses were located and just how to make themselves extremely welcomed by such charming ladies.

And so it was for that purpose that Miss BB and Obadiah rode throughout the great city, visiting the various neighborhoods that had developed around that magnificent river, searching for women who found it difficult to earn a decent living or that had come to the great city from another country only to be disappointed at not finding their dreaMiss. The problem was not finding the women who might be interested in joining Miss Dolice Marie's staff at the boardinghouse, but convincing them to trust the very rich, very white, very aristocratic Miss BB and the large man of color who was driving her.

As he had done with Dolice Marie the first occasion he had met her, Obadiah repeated to the young women with utmost courtesy that he would be back to pick up anyone who desired to go with him the very next day, at noon, when the sun was highest in the sky, to the boardinghouse, where each would find an abundance of food to eat, more-than-adequate shelter, friendship, and an exquisite collection of the finest fashions available.

And just as he had promised, Obadiah made that same trip around the great river at noon the next day and, driving four women at a time back to the boardinghouse, brought eight quite hesitant yet curious young women, some with dirty faces and filthy clothing, others with horrendous appetites, to the parlor of the boardinghouse, where they came face-to-face with Miss BB, Madam Dolice Marie, and her faithful assistant, Angeline.

There was a sweet, delicate Filipino child named Nila and a lovely young woman from Japan that Angeline called Mei Ling because she could not pronounce her real name and thought the name she chose sounded quite exotic; there were two Irish lassies, or perhaps they were Scottish—hard to tell without obvious characteristics—Katie and Chelsea, who actually found Obadiah as he was driving throughout the neighborhood populated by people who had just come to the city looking for work and a better way of life, and of course, there were the ladies of color, Georgia and Shirley, two sisters that lived in that part of the city that Dolice Marie had once upon a time found herself quickly leaving. And lastly, there were the two that had just arrived in the country from either Italy or Spain, Maria and Isabella, proving that variety is the spice of life!

Although there were language barriers, as well as many other issues yet to conquer, these first young women were delighted to have a roof over their heads, a steady supply of food, a warm bath, and a comfortable bed in which to sleep, alone for now.

Miss BB was pleasantly surprised when they arrived and, quite surprising to the young women, found herself greeting each one with a big hug. Not completely understanding exactly what was going on, the women were very unresponsive to her, but Miss BB continued as their welcoming committee, reminding the new ladies as well as Dolice Marie and Angeline that there would be work to do to get these young women ready, but the good news was that Miss BB now had the newly prepared Dolice Marie and Angeline to assist her. But for now, a warm bubble bath, a delightful meal, comfortable clothing, and a good night's sleep for all of them was the first task at hand.

There would be great discussions between the three trained ladies (Miss BB, Dolice Marie, and Angeline) over tea and delicious French pastry with the new ladies, describing with language, hand gestures, and playacting the purpose of their investiture. Eventually, the message became clear and there were lots of giggles as the world's oldest profession came together in one tiny spot.

Again Obadiah began to drive the carriage led by the huge horse back and forth from the boardinghouse to Miss BB's mansion, either filled with four young women at a time who were virtually covered by several parasols while he listened intently as they giggled about something that only they were eager about or a carriage filled with supplies from Miss BB's that he would deliver to the boardinghouse.

Again, there were lessons to be taught and lessons to be learned as instructors of every kind came in and out of Miss BB's mansion. Again, everyone was paid well to provide their services and cautioned equally as well to keep their mouths shut about what was going on at the Declouette Mansion and at the boardinghouse in the French Quarter of the great city of New Orleans.

There were major renovations to the boardinghouse as well, going on from dusk until dawn, by hired help instructed that, by keeping their knowledge to themselves, great rewards would be given to them. The neighbors between the boardinghouse and Miss BB's mansion whispered among themselves, and sometimes even to Miss BB, as she walked her babies to the park, citing that that darky probably had something to do with all the refurbishing going on. Miss BB simply shook her head in disbelief and held her handkerchief close to her mouth as she listened while trying to keep from laughing out loud as she went about her way. Once back home with Obadiah and her new family, she would repeat what she had heard and everyone would laugh hysterically.

Just prior to the city's preparation for the New Year's celebration in the French Quarter, Miss BB was very proud to introduce to Obadiah and her staff the finished product, what she secretly called the mystery eight ladies of the New Orleans House. They were absolutely exquisite as they processioned one by one down the lavish stairway of the Declouette Mansion as if in their own private cotillion. Oh, how they smiled as they were applauded for their beauty as well as their ladylike mannerisMiss.

Dolice Marie and Angeline applauded the young ladies, too, and praised them for their devotion and the completion of their hard work. Miss BB was so excited that she announced right then and there that she was going to throw a party—no, a celebration—there in the Declouette Mansion, to introduce the lovely ladies to people of great stature from great distances, great influence, and with great amounts of money.

Miss BB explained to everyone as she thought out loud that these would not be potential clientele; no, these guests would be her personal friends that would bring their business savvy, would spread the word in their business world, and would provide a link for tired, weary businessmen who found themselves alone in the great city of New Orleans. She chuckled as she whispered to Obadiah that there would surely be gossip now from her nosy neighbors and enough hanky-panky for the reporters to fill an entire newspaper! Again, there were the language, hand gestures, and playacting to be sure that this very important message was understood and, of course, accepted by everyone.

As the night finally wound down and everyone had gone their separate ways, Obadiah once again found the charming Miss BB sound asleep in her very flattering white silk dress from the activity of the day, her two babies, GiGi and FiFi, curled peacefully on her lap. He once again lifted her from her spot and carried her up the stairway to her bed, where he was met by her servant, who dressed her for bed, where she would sleep until the light of early morning. Once he extinguished the candles in her room, Obadiah made his way down the stairway and to the kitchen, where he and the servants of the Declouette Mansion gathered to eat, drink, and make merry all their own.

Dolice Marie left the cheerful ladies downstairs in the boardinghouse, where Angeline was playing a delightful tune on the piano, to spend a few moments alone on the balcony. The cool of the evening felt comforting, and as she turned away from the balcony to return to her bedroom, she caught a quick glimpse of one of the sheriff's deputies standing just below her on the other side of the street, as one seemed to always be, smoking a long cigar and blowing smoke in her direction. She walked back to the railing in a confrontational move that laid claim to whatever it was that the deputy evidently was seeking in this contact with the lovely Dolice Marie. The standoff lasted three or four minutes as the deputy confidently smoked his cigar with an occasional grin on his face while Dolice Marie held a stationary stare straight in his eyes, hands on her hips, her head tossed in that familiar fashion of hers.

Suddenly, as if the two had actually just had a satisfying conversation that had led them both to a mutual agreement about something that only the two of them knew about—or could it be that Dolice Marie was putting into practice the art of being a lady?—both turned around and pursued their separate directions. Little did Dolice Marie know that once she was safely inside her room and had closed and locked her balcony door, the deputy resumed his protective guard from across the street, as one had been commanded to do since the day Dolice Marie became the proprietor of the boardinghouse.

Chapter 6

JEAN PIERRE AND Evelina LaPierre now had three wonderful children to further the LaPierre family line and test their temperament, as all children do: Mon Claire LaPierre, now nearly one and one-half years old, and twin boys named Petois and Pecous LaPierre, now three months old. Evelina was once again back to normal and tempting Jean Pierre with the marital antics that seemed to always eventually find Jean Pierre on the other end of Evelina's rage once their bliss created another life. It was not unusual for her to slap or grab him on his muscular behind when he was unsuspecting such, or sneaking into his bath while she was totally naked, covered in nothing more than a smile.

"The poor child," Uncle Dommie said, as he always called Jean Pierre, "didn't know which end was up at any given time with Evelina!"

Annabelle was successfully supervising the events at the bordello by now, and always dressed quite nicely, I might add, with the ever-present and welcomed assistance from Mama Mozelle, while Jubil found himself more and more in charge of even making major decisions on his own with regard to the operations of Mon Village, the newly acquired nickname for the area once known as the LaPierre Plantation. Mon Village was now totally self-sufficient, creating a great life for all that lived there, although completely shut off from the community outside, with only the exception of clientele who came with pockets filled with money or the occasional trips to the nearby town for essentials not found at Mon Village, at least not yet.

Production of the silver cups was now at its peak, with orders and silver actually coming in from the local clientele as well as from the great city of New Orleans and, all in between, clients who would settle for nothing less to accompany their fancy parties and dinner get-togethers. Jean Pierre had even designed a family crest that consisted of a drawing of the big house where the initial of the customer could fit quite nicely below it and that also commanded quite a nice price. That crest is still a valuable asset to the silver cups still being manufactured today, I am so very proud to say!

Of course, the customers could have their horses groomed, fed, and shoed, if necessary, while the proper Southern white gentlemen and their ladies shopped throughout the many shops that now had their own area of Mon Village. More often than not, a proper Southern white gentleman could lose his direction and find himself at the steps of the bordello while his unsuspecting wife enjoyed a silver cup full of Mama Mozelle's cool, sweet lemonade and a tour of the lovely gardens from which they could fill their baskets with the variety of beautiful flowers, that is, those in between the mint, whose growth was now overwhelming.

Many of the residents and their children could now read and write, thanks to Jubil's smart dealings that gave education in trade for services, and of course, everyone had learned to count money, and several of the young women who chose not to work in the bordello or in service to Mama Mozelle in keeping the big house in top shape became teachers in the schoolhouse, holding regular classes for the children while their parents worked in the fields or in the shops that were filled with fresh vegetables, eggs, sugarcane, and many other items that Mon Village now produced.

Monsieur Jubilation, as the residents now called him, could be seen every day riding his horse with several other young men that he had assigned to work with him in order to keep order and peace as well as protection from the unknown throughout Mon Village. Having been assured by Mama Del that he would soon find the right woman for himself by his own doings, he was confident that all was as it should be in both his business as well as his personal life.

One particular evening, after making his final rounds for the day and just as he was about to turn in for the night, Jubil caught sight of a dim light shining from the direction of the gardens. Many of the residents had claimed to have seen shadows in that very area before, the area where the rebel soldiers and Night Riders had found their final resting place, right there in the midst of the very things they abhorred on the earth. Out of paralyzing fear of ghosts and goblins, no one that lived at Mon Village ever went near that area during the night hours, so Jubil was particularly cautious himself and kept a close eye out before approaching. After watching for a few more seconds, he grabbed a sharp knife that he used for skinning rabbits, from the livery stable, and slowly, quietly began to walk toward the light that was by now just off in the distance. As he neared the site and the light became brighter, he noticed a figure holding a lantern and, while walking through the gardens, occasionally stooping and then standing back up again. Extremely hesitant to approach for fear that the figure could actually be the ghost of one of the bodies secretly buried there in the gardens, Jubil peered at the sight more than he approached it while his heart felt like it was surely coming out of his chest! But the figure itself came nearer to Jubil, and soon he recognized that it was just one of the young women that worked at the schoolhouse, helping those ladies that were teaching the younger ones to read and write. The young woman was tall, but not as tall as Jubil, and thin, with beautiful skin the color of deep midnight, her hair completely covered by the familiar wrap that most of the women still wore when working at some task during the day.

As he approached a little closer, he noticed that the young woman was picking mint vines from the ground and putting them in a basket that she was carrying on her arm. Jubil was fascinated and equally inquisitive as to why this young woman was gathering the mint leaves, since he had never known anyone who had ever shown any interest before and so had not been able to find a way to rid Mon Village of the pesky weed, other than using it in Mama Mozelle's cool, sweet lemonade when certain customers asked for it.

The young woman continued diligently at her task without noticing that Jubil was getting closer and closer to her, until he suddenly stepped upon a piece of dried wood that crackled so loud it caused her to stop, scream, and look around, startled at the possible intrusion. Jubil took the opportunity to carefully approach, assuring her that he was not going to hurt her, that he was just interested in what she could possibly be thinking of doing with all that mint. Once she regained her composure, she recognized that the intruder was indeed Monsieur Jubilation, and she began to smile.

"Why, for medicinal purposes, of course, sir," she answered with all due respect.

Jubil was fascinated, his eyes glued to the beauty of her perfectly round face while his heart pounded so loud he was actually afraid she might truly hear it. When he finally realized that she was staring back at him with an inquisitive look all her own, he quickly regained his composure and asked her name and offered his cloak as well to shelter her from the cool of the evening. She accepted his generosity with a smile, and the two sat down on the hard ground while the young woman explained that her name was Sylvia, the daughter of Lalone and Essie LaPierre, adding that because there was so much mint growing in the gardens, she did not think that anyone would mind if she took some of it to use for medicinal purposes, as she had already mentioned.

Jubil replied, "No, of course not," shaking his head, absolutely intrigued with Miss Sylvia and what medicinal purposes she referred to, and so he politely asked her to explain.

"Well, Monsieur Jubil," she said while staring into space, as if trying to recollect, "my mother makes a tea with it." The young woman responded as if everyone knew that. "With both the mint leaves and stalks, hot water, and sweetened with honey, or sugarcane as I prefer it. It soothes an aching stomach and helps us fall asleep and sleep peacefully. Smelling it opens up the nose when it's all stopped up so you can breathe better. The leaves are good for chewing, makes the breath feel and smell fresh, and helps make a sore throat a lot better too. We also wrap it in a cloth, beat it with a hammer, and mix it with that harsh soap to take a bath with, to wash our hair, and to wash the clothes or to clean the house. We sometimes even put a little in when we're making pralines, too, just for a little different taste. And we even have some mint growing behind our house, near our outhouse, to keep down the odor," she whispered and demonstrated by pinching her nose with two fingers.

Miss Sylvia added with a giggle that her father sometimes washed it really good, soaked it in his corn liquor, and let it sit for days and days before he sat down on the back porch with some of his friends after a hard day's work and they drank until they felt no pain at all! The two laughed while the wheels were turning in Jubil's head as he pondered some way in which this new knowledge of the mint could answer two needs: just what to do with it and just how much to charge the new customers for such knowledge. He could hardly wait to talk to Jean Pierre.

Jubil and Miss Sylvia chatted for several more minutes until Miss Sylvia finally announced that she should probably be getting home before her parents began to worry. Jubil volunteered eagerly to walk the young woman home and then skipped on to his own home like a child with a crush on his teacher after he had done such.

"Yes, Jubil slept quite well that night," Uncle Dommie would add. "Quite well, indeed!"

When the sun came up the next morning, an elated Jubil ran straight to Jean Pierre's house to tell him the good news about how to solve the mystery of what to do with the mint. Jubil found Jean Pierre sitting on the steps of the front porch with his head in his hands, as if he had truly lost his best friend. As Jubil approached him, it was obvious that he was extremely happy to see his old friend, almost grateful as he began to smile quite broadly. Jubil was dismayed and sat down near his friend on the step and placed a caring arm around him. Jean Pierre looked behind him, toward the inside his house, as if making sure no one was listening, and began to explain to Jubil that Evelina, who was cheerfully humming inside the house, had begun to sleep more, longer, and anywhere she was at the time. Jean Pierre said that she had begun to eat strange combinations of foods again and could either begin to laugh or cry at the drop of a hat, without a warning or reason, just like she did both times she had been pregnant, a condition that scared poor Jean Pierre to death.

Jean Pierre was trembling as he continued to explain that he truly loved their children and would be absolutely pleased to have an entire house full of children if he could only figure out a way to avoid the birth process. He continued to confide to Jubil that his heart and his body just could not take it again. Jubil began to laugh and explained to Jean Pierre that there was absolutely only one way to avoid the entire situation, and that was to stay far, far away from Evelina at all times. Jean Pierre agreed he could *never* do that!

But Uncle Dommie added that keeping away from any woman would be impossible for any LaPierre man since the men in our family are the closest thing to "a mangy dog in season" when it comes to the fulfillment of certainly the strongest urge there is—their passion.

"But oh, my," he would add, "what a phenomenal trait and treat it is for the women in their path!"

Eventually, the conversation did shift to Jubil's encounter with Miss Sylvia the night before and what the two had discussed regarding the various uses for mint, and Jubil's desire to capitalize on such knowledge. Although Jean Pierre was still toying with his own situation with Evelina, the idea of ridding Mon Village of the pesky vines and the possibility of making more money for its inhabitants did help snap him back to the reality of the moment. Theirs was a conversation of great planning as they walked together through the gardens while a monumental structuring of an entirely new phase of development at Mon Village was beginning to give birth, a phase that would surely put our family's mark on the history of the great state of Louisiana, if not just on its flawless silver cups.

Within days, the residents of Mon Village became witnesses to a brand-new building being constructed along the line of shops that were situated in an unintentional and unplanned commercial area located directly across the residential area of Mon Village. Several men worked together with such motivation and uncanny skill to construct the building, while another group consisting of several youth from the schoolhouse was picking and processing the mint for the various uses outlined and supervised by none other than Miss Sylvia.

The decision had been made that Miss Sylvia would be the overseer of this project, and once the shop was completed and stocked as it should be, a blushing Miss Sylvia would be its proprietor. The plan would call for the sale of mint for those many uses to the customers that shopped at Mon Village, but it was, as always, free to the residents who lived there; all they had to do was either pick it as they needed it or simply throw a few handful out of their back door and start their own field. Since every resident was indeed a limb on the branches of the mammoth design of Mon Village as well as the LaPierre family, each would, of course, be expected to pull their own weight and pull their own mint for their own personal use as well.

Our early family believed in such sharing of its wealth, and although there are those who still believe in and practice such, there are indeed those who, somehow along the line, have either misplaced or just completely lost what our early ancestors taught and believe in.

Before long, the doors to the new shop were opened and proper Southern white customers lined up to learn about and purchase their own supply of this new beneficial and popular commodity. Miss Sylvia blossomed in her new role as proprietor of the shop and enjoyed explaining its many uses to both residents and customers as Monsieur Jubilation enjoyed watching her do so. Yes. There was truly an obvious infatuation brewing between the two, but whether or not Miss Sylvia had any desire in furthering her interest in Monsieur Jubilation would remain to be seen as the young woman exhausted herself in the valuable new shop.

Mama Mozelle, in her ever-expanding role as the Mon Village matriarch, began to soak mint leaves in corn liquor according to Miss Sylvia's instructions from her father's favorite beverage, bottling it in a jug and making sure there would always be enough for herself and Mama Del's own "medicinal purposes."

Of course, it wasn't very long before Annabelle decided to introduce that same process to her customers and the drink became a favorite addition to the refreshments served at the bordello, offering Mama Mozelle's cool, sweet lemonade as well as the spiked, mint-flavored corn liquor served in a beautiful silver cup, suitable for purchase, of course. Annabelle instructed her ladies not to indulge in the beverage during working hours for fear of a lady being cheated by a customer, or vice versa, but after hours was certainly suitable to wind down from the day's work.

Uncle Dommie would wink at the young boys, insinuating that the beverage caused quite a party away from the bordello after hours, when the ladies went about their own personal indulgences.

In the great city of New Orleans, equally great preparations were being made for a gala, a grande bal masque, at Miss BB Declouette's mansion to celebrate a brand-new business that would soon be opening in the French Quarter and to celebrate great and old friendships.

Miss BB personally addressed each invitation on lovely linen notecards with the Declouette seal that would not only find their way throughout the great states of Louisiana, North and South Carolina, the noble Commonwealth of Kentucky, and her beloved home in Georgia, but even outside the boundaries of these United States, to the French territory and English territory of Canada, that blessed friend that had hidden and housed so many slaves that were led there by Miss Harriet Tubman during the Civil War. Undeniably, Canada could always boast of its many descendants with intertwined bloodlines that resulted from such kindness.

Miss BB requested an RSVP by messenger, if possible, as soon as possible so that adequate food, beverage, and fun could be provided for the guests. Those that would be staying overnight would also have the pleasure of restful as well as beautiful accommodations for as long as they cared to visit with Miss BB, an exciting thought for her as well to have her friends stay a while. Obadiah had the task of delivering the invitations to the few locals that Miss BB entrusted with her friendship, those in whom she confided and those who had provided their services and who were paid to keep their mouths shut.

Uncle Dommie commented that Obadiah looked quite distinguished in his suit and top hat, not to mention his white gloves, as he drove the carriage from residence to residence, delivering the invitations, repeating at each door that Miss BB requested that everyone wear a mask to her grande bal masque as he tipped his hat and carried his message to the next place. Yes, Miss. BB was most certainly having the time of her life!

Within only a few short weeks, Miss BB had received RSVPs from virtually everyone she had invited; after all, who could possibly want to miss such an event with such a socialite as the charming lady? Of course, Miss BB had actually purposely neglected to invite her nosy neighbors for the sheer pleasure of it all and the fact that they would enjoy themselves without invitation anyway, and most assuredly she would hear about it during one of those walks with her children to the park. Fascinating. And of course, she knew that the newspaper reporters would most assuredly find a way to stick their noses where they were not invited and write about it anyway.

Large packages with international postage were arriving almost daily to the Declouette Mansion and almost immediately delivered to Madam Dolice Marie's boardinghouse by the ever-faithful Obadiah. Uncle Dommie commented that our family history declares that some of the nosy neighbors were actually spying on the events with their opera glasses, of all things, in order to get as close a look as possible. Can you imagine?

The mansion itself was being spruced up as well with lovely decorations and Miss BB's stored-away antiques that Obadiah carried up from the cellar and down from the attic, joining in with the servants to beautify the mansion for such a great event. Candles of various bright colors were strategically placed throughout to create just the appropriate ambience as well as to light the way into and throughout the mansion. Only the very best musicians were hired to provide their most beautiful music, either to dance by or to simply listen to while enjoying an enjoyable conversation. It was a wonderful time of preparation, and Miss BB proudly told everyone that she had not had such fun since before the loss of her beloved husband, but she still remembered how.

Miss BB's personal servants were placed in charge of arranging the food and beverage tables in the exact manner that she preferred. Special uniforms had been created for all of them, including delightful masks for them to wear, which allowed them to discreetly peek at the guests without being noticed and bring the information back to Miss BB.

The cook could be heard throughout the mansion giving orders to her staff as delicacies from around the world were being prepared by the finest chefs in all of Louisiana, from seafood delights to fresh fruit and vegetables, delicate pastries, and pots and pots of steamy white rice.

Times were just as exciting for the ladies of the boardinghouse in the French Quarter as all prepared themselves for the upcoming affair. There were boxes to be opened, exquisite ball gowns in the most beautiful of colors to decide upon, masks to try on, eloquent corsets and bustles to choose from, and an abundance of silky, slinky stockings that felt absolutely divine as they stretched to stimulate a pair of anticipating legs!

Midmorning of the day of the grande bal masqué, while Miss BB was enjoying her brunch with her children on the screened-in back porch, a messenger from the noble Commonwealth of Kentucky was announced to her by Obadiah, carrying a letter of introduction handwritten by her husband's dear friend Mr. Samuels.

> *This here letter is to introduce to you my trusted messenger, Monte Leonard, who hails from Kentucky, the land of God's most precious gifts to us all: our beloved horses and our ability to make the finest bourbon in all his great earth.*

Miss BB was thrilled to engage Mr. Leonard, who, unlike the stiff, proper Southern white gentlemen that she had been surrounded by for ages, was quite relaxed in casual attire, with a quick wit, to say the least, and thus she invited him to join her for a cup of Louisiana's finest beverage, its splendid coffee with chicory, of course. The two had a chuckle as Mr. Leonard accepted her invitation and leaned over to kiss the sweet widow on her cheek rather than on her hand, which was absolutely permissible to the playful Miss BB.

Mr. Leonard had come to deliver the message that Mr. Samuels would not be able to attend Miss BB's grande bal masqué due to a conflicting appointment that same evening and was indeed regretful not to be able to enjoy her company and the entertainment of the affair. He was, however, sending forth several bottles of his most cherished commodity, his smooth Kentucky bourbon, for her guests to enjoy, noting that any affair without the presence of Kentucky bourbon was like the wonder of a woman perfectly dressed without the presence of her seductive smile. Both laughed loudly as Mr. Leonard added that there were also a few bottles for Miss BB to put away for her own special moments alone.

At that very moment, Obadiah and some of Miss BB's personal servants brought the heavy boxes of Kentucky bourbon onto the screened-in back porch. She squealed in the sheer delight of it all, and Mr. Leonard knew exactly what message to bring back home.

After a very lovely visit together, Miss BB and Mr. Leonard bade their fond farewells until another time as he climbed aboard the seat of his wagon, tipped his leather wide-brimmed hat, and headed off down the path from the Declouette Mansion. Miss BB waved until she could not see him any longer and hurried to finish the preparations for the grande bal masqué. Under Miss BB's instructions, Obadiah and several of the servants prepared a beautiful Queen Anne table covered with a delicate lace cloth, lined with lovely crystal glasses, especially for the savoring of Kentucky bourbon on the opposite side of the table with champagne. Now it was truly perfect!

On the night of the grande bal masqué, Obadiah began driving the ladies from the boardinghouse to the Declouette Mansion several hours before the guests began to arrive. Miss BB was very excited about being able to spend time with her old friends and introduce them to her new ones. Because the expectation was so tremendous, she had to sit down and catch her breath several times, so Obadiah situated her on the front porch, with GiGi and FiFi beside her, where she could view everything that was going on and exactly as it was happening, all while discreetly sipping on a crystal glass filled with the finest Kentucky bourbon, Obadiah occasionally filling it when necessary.

The food was deliciously prepared by the cook and her staff and strategically placed throughout the ballroom, the beverages were sparkling, the decorations were simply engaging, the music resounded throughout the entire mansion, the servants were primed, and without a doubt, the mystery ladies of the New Orleans House were just utterly radiant by anyone's standards as they cascaded themselves throughout the Declouette Mansion, their faces mysteriously covered by a haunting mask, their gowns shimmering in the candlelight, and their conduct befitting of the true ladies they had been taught to be.

Miss BB herself was stunning in her white lace ball gown with delicate pink silk trimmings, certainly an absolutely gracious hostess as well as she greeted her guests with a hug and a kiss from her position on the front porch. It was a wondrous affair with so many impressive carriages drawn by equally impressive horses yielding to a simply divine driver sitting on the top seat, appropriately dressed with white gloves and top hats just like Obadiah. Since Miss BB had no notion of exactly how to be discriminatory, everyone was invited to her grande bal masqué—absolutely everyone!

The mansion was completely surrounded by carriages and people walking around the grounds, wonderfully attired for the most prestigious grande bal masqué in that great city of New Orleans. It would not be long before the inside the mansion was filled with the murmur of jubilant voices, all extremely polite and discussing some fascinating topic that captured the ear of another. Other than Miss BB and those that had traveled together to the grande bal masqué, no one really knew who the other was, and they would not until the bewitching hour of midnight.

Miss BB's eight favorite guests were truly having the time of their lives as well as they mingled throughout the crowd as though they had belonged there all along. Angeline, in a soft lilac ball gown that clearly spoke of her genteel, ladylike qualities, found herself spending the evening dancing with several different gentlemen, all of whom seemed to have stolen her from the rest of the guests, not that Angeline seemed to have any mind at all. The other ladies as well were spending their time dancing and enjoying conversations with the unknown gentlemen, adding more mystery to themselves, with their faces covered as they enjoyed the bliss of the grande bal masqué.

But the belle of the ball was truly the lovely Mademoiselle Dolice Marie LaPierre, dressed divinely in an absolutely exquisite, slinky, form-fitting sea-foam-green satin gown that had been created especially for her by Miss BB's personal seamstress, who made an entrance, I declare, that caught the eye of every man in the Declouette Mansion, virtually stopping time in its movement as she floated throughout the great hall with the confidence of any proper Southern white woman. It was a moment that Miss BB had counted on, a moment that was, without a doubt, unforgettable. Miss BB had to congratulate the beautiful young woman when Dolice Marie finally found her way to greet her with a kiss on the hand and a whisper in the ear.

Without a doubt, there were those ladies whose escorts sometimes stayed away from them a bit too long while spending time with some other lovely lady, completely forgetting with whom they had traveled to attend the grande bal masqué. It was not too terribly odd, indeed, to find a lady politely interrupting her escort and leading him away only to remind him with whom he had come and with whom he would leave. It would most certainly be a magical night to remember, for sure, for all those that accepted the invitation to the Declouette Mansion.

As the night progressed toward midnight, Dolice Marie, who had been having the time of her life as she flirted and teased with the many gentlemen that had been personally introduced by Miss BB herself, that were entranced with her very being, caught the eye of a tall gentleman with beautiful reddish hair escaping on either side of his mask, who had been staring at her from across the large ballroom through his golden mask while following her every move—oh, most discreetly, I might add. Or so he thought. Realizing that she now knew that he was looking at her, the gentleman began to walk quite proudly toward the provocative Dolice Marie, stopping briefly to scoop up two glasses of French champagne in lovely crystal glasses and carry them to her, bowing as he offered one glass to her.

The gentleman introduced himself in a thick English accent as Mr. Bernard Menard, a second-generation import-export dealer from Toronto, Canada, with American shops in both Boston and New York City as well. Dolice Marie accepted the champagne and listened while slightly fanning herself with a simply gorgeous Oriental fan that she had snatched from one of the other ladies while they were all trying on gowns in the boardinghouse. She responded in near-perfect European French, with a slight remnant of Creole, that she was indeed Mademoiselle Dolice Marie LaPierre, the proprietor of a boardinghouse located in the French Quarter of the great city of New Orleans. It was most probably that very moment that Mr. Bernard Menard lost his heart to the enchanting Dolice Marie, or could it have been those hourglass hips and healthy bosoms?

From the opposite end of the great ballroom of the Declouette Mansion, Miss BB smiled approvingly with Obadiah as they carefully watched Dolice Marie with the striking son of her good friend, peeking from beneath her own mask. It would not be long before the gentleman politely took Dolice Marie's champagne glass to set both his and hers down on a nearby lovely Victorian table, gathered the tiny Dolice Marie into his arms, and twirled her onto the dance floor for a waltz, where the other ladies of the night as well as the invited guests from near and far were also enjoying themselves.

Gazing across the room, Miss BB and Obadiah also noticed that Angeline had seemingly found the man of her choice, since she would not let anyone else dance with her while the gentleman, too, seemed to be smitten by her girlish looks and her charming personality. Again, they smiled approvingly. Miss BB was having a wonderful time trying to keep up with everything and, at one point in the evening, when she found herself squinting in order to see, once or twice, gave serious consideration to using her own opera glasses to spy on everyone and everything! Ah, but she was still wickedly enchanted at just the sight of everyone mixing and mingling there before her very eyes, poor that they might be, anyway.

Amid the laughter and the crowded dance floor, Mr. Bernard Menard could be seen extending his arm to the lovely Mademoiselle LaPierre and leading her outside to the terrace, where other couples, including those who would soon be in the business, could be seen sharing private moments together. The two walked slowly together throughout the gardens until they found a quiet gazebo, where Mr. Bernard Menard asked Mademoiselle LaPierre to sit with him for a while, offering his cloak to shield her from the night air, which she accepted with a smile, and sat down on one of the benches.

Dolice Marie sat, listening with sound attention as she heard the charming Mr. Bernard Menard speak for more than an hour about his work, his devotion to his family, and his plans for the future, until they were interrupted by a rise of laughter coming from the Declouette Mansion. It was midnight, and Mr. Bernard Menard gently removed Dolice Marie's mask to expose the beautiful, tantalizing young woman of color, and he could be heard telling Dolice Marie, "How beautiful you are!" as he removed his own.

Dolice Marie smiled curiously, blushing as she thanked the gentleman, fanning herself again as he again could be heard asking her, "Mademoiselle, would you please join me for a walk along the river?"

Without saying a word, Dolice Marie, curiously blushing again, accepted his arm, to the delight of Miss BB and Obadiah, who had found their way to the gazebo.

"Yes," Uncle Dommie would say, "it is for this reason that we became known as the LaPierre-Menard descendants, that very moment when Mr. Bernard Menard lost his heart to Mademoiselle Dolice Marie LaPierre."

It was indeed a magical night for everyone! Miss BB could not have been more proud than if she indeed had been Dolice Marie and Angeline's mother as she watched Dolice Marie disappear from the mansion with Mr. Bernard Menard. Dolice Marie glanced ever so slowly over her shoulder to meet Miss BB's eyes with a smile that spoke more than words could have at that moment.

Angeline found herself infatuated with the likes of an older gentleman, a Monsieur Henri de Marquis, Miss BB's valued friend from Montreal, Canada. It would be Henri that would escort Angeline and the other ladies back to the boardinghouse at the end of the evening, requesting his own driver and carriage, as well as Obadiah and his carriage, to make the trip back to the French Quarter. Miss BB positioned herself in a swing on the front porch, with GiGi and FiFi curled in her lap, to await Obadiah as she bade farewell to her guests while those guests that were staying the night continued to enjoy the remnants of the grande bal masqué.

Dolice Marie and Mr. Bernard Menard, on the other hand, strolled slowly to the mighty Mississippi River, mesmerized by each other's company as they gazed at the glistening waters that seemed never-ending. The night was pleasantly cool, with a lazy breeze rising from the rolling river. There were very few words spoken between the two, only the kind of language that the heart could hear or even understand while time had no meaning.

Mr. Bernard Menard paused to brush his palm across Dolice Marie's cheek, and as her dark eyes opened wide to meet his, the glistening from the river could be seen sparkling in them. Mr. Bernard Menard slowly brought his lips closer to hers, and she stood still to accept them, the two gradually committing to an embrace that seemed to last forever.

The two resumed their walk, this time with arms wrapped about each other, and before long, what seemed like just a few minutes, Dolice Marie and Mr. Bernard Menard were standing in front of Miss BB's mansion. The music was still playing as the two entered the great ballroom, where the last few remaining guests were bidding good night to Miss BB, while Obadiah was giving instructions for the night to the servants that had been having the time of their lives as well. What few bottles of fine Kentucky bourbon that were left were given away as a present to Miss BB's most cherished friends to enjoy in their own privacy—that is, with the exception of those bottles that she still had stored away for her own.

Mr. Bernard Menard swept Dolice Marie off her feet and carried her to the dance floor, where he again enjoyed one final waltz. As the two filled the dance floor with the obvious mutual affection and passion that they had for each other, Mr. Bernard Menard whispered the question that Dolice Marie already had in her heart. "Mademoiselle, come to bed with me?"

Dolice Marie was absolutely captivated beyond words as she smiled and said yes, not too quickly, of course, as to give the kind gentleman the idea that she was truly, already captivated or simply easy to take to bed. Suddenly, the music seemed to become much louder, much faster, as the two twirled around and around the great ballroom. Mr. Bernard Menard's strong arms felt comforting and safe as Dolice Marie allowed herself to be swept away as he carried her up the spiral staircase to the awaiting bedroom suite.

At the boardinghouse, Angeline and the other ladies were alone in the parlor, giggling from a bit too much of the bubbly champagne while discussing the events of the evening. Needless to say, there were ball gowns, shoes, gloves, and corsets all over the place! Angeline could not wait to tell Dolice Marie about the handsome gentleman that she had met at the grande bal masqué, but Dolice Marie was nowhere to be found amid the piles of clothing and people in the parlor. Angeline simply smiled as she climbed the stairway up to her room, reliving every exciting and enchanting moment of the grande bal masqué.

Within the solitude of desire in a suite at the Declouette Mansion, a secret unfolded as the two hearts came together, embracing love. Dolice Marie LaPierre wept as she confessed the truth to Mr. Bernard Menard that she, although the madam of the LaPierre bordello on the Bayou Frou-Frous, and now the proprietor of a New Orleans boardinghouse soon to open with the sole purpose of providing entertainment for gentlemen in the area, a vixenly girl with seductive eyes and knowledge of the ways of a man, was still, yes, a virgin!

Why, the first time I heard Uncle Dommie explain that very first moment of passion between my ancestors, I nearly swooned with sheer disbelief but, as he continued…

Mama Mozelle had been very cautious of keeping her daughter from the actual business of the big house at the LaPierre Plantation even though it was Dolice Marie's intriguing looks that had actually brought in the business. Mama Del had long before told Mama Mozelle that there would be a man in Dolice Marie's future that would love her forever with all his might, a man who would be gentle, would be understanding, and would teach her the art of lovemaking in his own special way. For that reason, she was not to be touched in that particular manner by a swarm of proper or improper white Southern men who would only take advantage of what she had to offer.

"Dolice Marie was not for sale!"

The story goes that Dolice Marie had long played the part but had no dealings in the actual role of the business. Just like Annabelle's parents, Mama Mozelle had protected her for just this special moment of her life. But again, I digress.

Dolice Marie was so concerned that Mr. Bernard Menard would certainly shoo her away from him for not being experienced in the ways of passion, or not be as gentle as he would need to be, but it would be just the contrary. Mr. Bernard Menard held her tightly that night, confirming that this tiny girl was truly the love of his life, and as the night progressed, the two created that sweet, gentle fire that can only sweep through bodies consumed in genuine passion. And oh, my, what a night it was! And when both awakened in the middle of the night, Dolice Marie herself confidently reached over to embrace Mr. Bernard Menard, and he responded by quietly asking her, "Are you awake?" And she, no longer shy, replied, "Yes." My, my, my!

The distinct sounds of a rainstorm awakened Dolice Marie in that unfamiliar bed in the suite of the Declouette Mansion, and as her eyes became fully opened, she turned quickly to find that the bed was completely empty other than herself—Mr. Bernard Menard was gone! There on the lovely embroidered pillow beside her was a linen notecard with the House of Menard seal, explaining that he had to leave quickly for personal business's sake but would again be in her arms as soon as would be possible. Why, Dolice Marie was absolutely furious, brokenhearted, and indeed most embarrassed that she had chosen this man to give her precious womanhood to.

She quickly dressed and ran down the stairs to meet Miss BB and Obadiah, who were having their morning coffee and reading the morning newspaper's description of the events of the night before, and, without as much as a "Hello," grabbed her cloak and ran from the mansion into the rain while shouting the various superlatives of her former self. Without second thought, Miss BB gestured in agreement with Obadiah, who was already standing, to find the child and bring her home. Some things never change! Obadiah had to actually pick up the soaking-wet Dolice Marie, who was throwing a fit in the middle of the street, place her in the carriage, drive her to the boardinghouse, and make sure that she was safely inside and into the arms of her friend, sister, and confidante Angeline.

The rain intensified her disappointment, but even though Dolice Marie cried, fussed, cussed, and cried again, no one, not even Angeline, could convince her that if it was truly meant to be between herself and Mr. Bernard Menard, he would indeed come back to her. No one, not even Miss BB herself, could convince the saddened, crushed woman that had weathered the pangs of slavery as well as the sting of not being accepted in her beloved great city of New Orleans, and so without further thought, Dolice Marie suddenly stopped crying and announced that she was going to completely throw herself into the preparation of the business at hand. Love was just a silly waste of time, and she would have no part of it ever again.

It was on one particular Saturday afternoon several weeks after Miss BB's grande bal masqué that a stranger from the great city of New Orleans visited the shops at Mon Village while on a trip to the Atchafalaya River area in search of valuable furs and Armadillo skin. His name was Monsieur Henri de Marquis, a fur trapper, who had been told by the people around the area that he could find a proper present at Mon Village for a young Frenchwoman by the name of Angeline Toussaint-Marie that he had met and would soon announce his love to.

The stranger spoke quite openly of this woman that he had met at a recent grande bal masqué that had been given by a dear friend of his, Madam Beatrice Carson Declouette. As he searched throughout the shops for just the proper gift, Monsieur de Marquis repeated to anyone who would listen, as well as an unsuspecting Mama Mozelle, all about the story of the woman who had stolen his heart and who, together with another woman (of color), owned a boardinghouse right there in the center of the great city of New Orleans and whose name, as you might expect, was Mademoiselle Dolice Marie LaPierre. The stranger was wondering if perhaps there could be some connection between the family name there at Mon Village and the lovely lady who shared the premises with the woman he would soon tell that he loved.

Mama Mozelle's heart was pounding with excitement as she poured the stranger a silver cup full of her now-famous cool lemonade sweetened with sugarcane as she listened to the stranger discussing such with one of the residents who worked in the silver shop. She slyly and cautiously asked all the right questions until it became apparent to her that this truly was her very own daughter that had brought the family trade to the great city of New Orleans and was, by the description of the stranger, doing quite well for herself. She motioned to one of the many children there at Mon Village to find Jean Pierre, and within just a few minutes, Jean Pierre and Jubil joined Mama Mozelle, and they, too, asked more of the right questions and happily concluded that there most certainly could only be one Dolice Marie Marie LaPierre. Tears began to flow down the cheeks of Dolice Marie's cherished family, an acknowledgement to the stranger that they were indeed related in the most special way there could ever be.

While the stranger enjoyed his refreshment and browsed through the collection of beautiful silver cups, Mama Mozelle, Jean Pierre, and Jubil gathered a basketful of items for him to bring back to the boardinghouse, for their very much loved and very missed Dolice Marie, which included several beautiful silver cups and several jars of the corn liquor and mint delight for her enjoyment.

Monsieur Henri de Marquis delightfully purchased several sets of the silver cups for his own private use for trading while trapping, as well as several jars of the corn liquor and mint concoction, which he sampled and had set quite pleasingly with his own personal taste for spirits. He was also quite pleased to bring the basket of gifts and the special good wishes from the family at Mon Village to the lady in the great city of New Orleans.

After enjoying a meal and good conversation with the residents of Mon Village, the stranger, no longer a stranger, bade his farewell. It was indeed a very bittersweet goodbye as Monsieur Henri de Marquis mounted his horse, tipped his hat, and rode off, leaving the family to deal with their own recollections of the time when Dolice Marie was the mistress of the LaPierre Plantation. I must admit that

I still get a bit misty myself even today when listening to this part of the story.

Perhaps it was the recent talk of love that stimulated the passions at Mon Village or the tender longings from the nostalgia of "family" that prompted Jubil to lay claim to his own lady love, but it would take more than that to stimulate the courage he needed to tell her so.

Jubil did everything he could to impress Miss Sylvia—riding his horse to and fro throughout the day, especially in front of her shop while she was tending to her business with teaching about and processing the mint, which was now considered priceless to those that shopped at Mon Village. Jubil never failed to tip his hat to her; in fact, he tipped his hat every single time he passed the shop, so much so that Miss Sylvia had to actually close her door in order to give the proper attention to her job, which was necessary, instead of continuously acknowledging Monsieur Jubilation's presence. Whether or not there was a mutual attraction still remained to be seen, since Miss Sylvia constantly remained totally focused on her job and gave no credibility to the antics of the likes of Monsieur Jubilation, at least not at the moment.

It was in the year of 1870. Jean Pierre and Dolice Marie LaPierre were now twenty-seven years old.

Chapter 7

IN SPITE OF the seemingly unyielding odds, everyone and everything managed to come together right at the New Year's Eve celebration in 1871 without the assistance of any newspaper advertising or door-to-door fliers, only the business savvy of Miss BB's good and friendly connections that came from here, there, and everywhere. The swift gossip of the neighborhood tongues that were all too ablaze with tales of the "whorehouse opening in the French Quarter" gave monumental curiosity to the opened doors of the New Orleans House as well, that bewitching locale that was reserved for gentlemen that had deep pockets and a deep desire for entertainment with the secret company of a lovely lady, which was located right there under their noses in the center of the great city of New Orleans. In fact, all the skyrockets blasting in the sky and the loud celebrating in the middle of the narrow streets of the French Quarter, just beneath Mademoiselle Dolice Marie's balconies, could very well have been for the gentlemen that happened to have found their way to the New Orleans House that night.

Every single room of the New Orleans House was filled, more than once, I might add, during the inaugural night, while Angeline played the piano and danced with the "guests" with complete allegiance to her new beaux, Henri de Marquis, who had gone out of town on a business trip shortly after their first meeting.

Dolice Marie busied herself as the proud madam, still handling only the administrative side of the business, knowing full well that she was not in the proper attitude to partake of the activities but also knowing full well that money had to be made for herself and for those that had agreed to work with her. She had no time for a broken heart either, but she used her sad disposition as a source of strength that would allow her to serve in the business capacity of surveillance over the ladies and the property, keeping both from any harm, but should it ever arise, an ever-ready fist and a sharp tongue were both available in case of any altercation.

Uncle Dommie quite proudly told the young boys that there was probably enough money made that opening night alone to open at least two more houses and hire ten more ladies, while my other uncles happily agreed. All was beginning to come together for Dolice Marie, Angeline, and their collection of lovely ladies, a time when everyone should have been delighted and celebrating, but for Dolice Marie, it was just another year and the thought of celebrating it all alone even in the midst of so many new friends was almost unbearable.

Occasionally, Miss BB would send Obadiah to fetch Dolice Marie and bring her over to chat about the business, all in the guise of chatting about how the poor dear was really feeling. Miss BB continued to encourage Dolice Marie to not give up on Mr. Bernard Menard, a man of true substance and honest to his word.

"If his message said he would be back, my darling, trust that he will!" was her constant message to Dolice Marie in that long, slow Southern drawl that simply added to her charm.

Dolice Marie would, over and over, toss her head up in the air and refuse to discuss the subject, although her heart was simply bursting in pain and wonder about the man who had won her heart.

Nothing can compare to that special sense of family, whether it is your own family through blood or those people that bring us the special kind of joy and security that only family can bring. Finally, after many, many lonely months, Dolice Marie received her first taste of her bona fide home since leaving the LaPierre Plantation more than three long years before.

Angeline was certainly excited as she recognized a grinning Monsieur Henri de Marquis knocking early one morning at the front door of the New Orleans House, packages and baskets in both of his hands, surely for her, since he had proclaimed his love for her just before embarking on his trip, to where she had not known.

Angeline ran down the stairs in her white silk nightgown trimmed with tiny white satin flowers, with Dolice Marie following close behind, opening the door so quickly that she nearly fell upon him as she scurried to greet the monsieur. It was truly a wonderful greeting! Angeline and Henri stood embracing in the doorway as Dolice Marie, wearing a dazzling hot-pink satin robe with matching delicate slippers, approached the two. As she helped Henri with his packages and welcomed several men who were accompanying him, she stared with great wonder as she recognized the design of the silver cups and grabbed for the basket that they were in, excited as well as she closed her eyes and held a cup tightly against her voluptuous breasts. Who else's hand could create such beauty and craftsmanship than her own Jean Pierre?

Monsieur Henri de Marquis kissed Dolice Marie softly on her cheek and began to tell her just how he had happened upon her family and the truly amazing Mon Village du LaPierre en Bayou Frou-Frous and the beautiful silver cups. He spoke of Mama Mozelle, Jubil, Evelina and their children, and her beloved Jean Pierre, which truly caught her attention and brought her to tears.

Although she asked many questions with tears of homesickness in her eyes, Dolice Marie, however, expressed her confusion as to the name the monsieur had called her beautiful home, since she had only known it as the LaPierre Plantation, over which she was the mistress, whether or not she was there in her person or in the great city of New Orleans. (The little vixen was truly taken aback by the news of the name change without her permission and began to pout like a little child, folding her arms and actually throwing a very ugly tantrum.) How disappointing life was to her! Not only was she alone without family or a love in her heart, but she was also forgotten by her family, who would do such a thing without asking her. It was a sad time for her, a time that seemed to be the worst she had ever experienced.

Angeline tried her best to comfort Dolice Marie, hugging her around the shoulders and leading her to one of the divans in the parlor while assuring her that no matter what the name, the plantation was still there, still hers, and all the people she loved were most assuredly as well. The monsieur began to quickly show her the beautiful gifts that he had purchased from the various shops with which to shower Angeline, hoping to prove to Dolice Marie that her home was certainly thriving. He grabbed for a jar of the mint-and-corn-liquor mixture, poured a silver cup full of the beverage, and offered it to Dolice Marie, assuring her that this was created on her land by the hands of the very people she so loved. She sipped it hesitantly, twisted her face to demonstrate its intensity, then smiled to show her approval, and then she gulped the remainder in the cup, only to fill it up again. Henri cautioned her to sip only, and sip slowly, since the mixture carried quite a kick to it.

Angeline and the monsieur joined her in a toast that led to another, and another, and still another, until it was obvious that the New Orleans House would surely be closed for business that day due to circumstances that had most certainly become out of the control of the proprietor's hands! Why, the other ladies could hear them laughing from their rooms upstairs and peeked downstairs to see what the commotion was all about. Dolice Marie beckoned the ladies to join them, assuring them that this day there would be no work, only celebration, if only for the fact that today a small portion of her home had come to be with her in the form of the cherished silver cups, now filled with the hypnotic mint mixture that had everyone in its spell.

Angeline began to play the piano while the Irish (or Scottish) lassies began to dance a jig, soon joined by the other ladies, creating a large circle while kicking their legs up high into the air to the sound of the music. Then in her inebriated state of drunken ecstasy, Angeline began to dance, kicking her heels up, lifting her gown in the center of the circle, and spinning around and around and around to the rhythm of the others' hands clapping and feet stomping, which encouraged her to do more. Monsieur Henri de Marquis was quite surprised and extremely impressed at his lady love's talent, and he began to clap his hands faster and stomp his feet harder, until Angeline was spinning so fast she nearly collapsed into his arms and began to laugh and squeal, causing the ladies to do the same.

Their laughter could be heard all around the neighborhood! Imagine what the other people must have been thinking. But then again, there was always some sort of carryings-on going on at the New Orleans House!

The mixture of the very potent mint beverage coupled with the motion of Angeline's twirling made Dolice Marie quite dizzy, causing her to suspect that last night's supper just might be coming back to haunt her, so she struggled to stop either herself or the room from spinning around so uncontrollably. As she neared the stairway to the bedroom quarters, Dolice Marie was unexpectedly confused at the sight of several stairways, all willowing as if underwater, causing her to be certainly unsure as to which one was truly real. She grabbed ahold of a banister and, holding on for dear life, began to hoist herself from one step to another until she finally reached the destination of her bedroom. Once inside, she fell upon her huge bed and again struggled to stop either herself or the room from spinning. The noise of the good times downstairs throbbed in her head and actually kept time with the hand clapping and foot stomping that was going on. Just as Dolice Marie was about to fall into an intoxicated sleep, she heard the sound of something hitting against the window of her French wrought iron balcony doors, a sound that seemed to be coming from a great distance. Almost as if in a dream, she began to drag herself from the bed toward the direction of the balcony, all the while determined to get there to meet her great nemesis, the sheriff. Or so she thought.

The bed was spinning, the room was spinning, and both were spinning in different directions, but Dolice Marie's stubborn nature gave her the strength and the resolve to make it to the balcony, where she came face-to-face with not the sheriff as she imagined, but Mr. Bernard Menard, sitting—quite eloquently, I might add—upon the driver's seat of a horse-driven buggy! As he tipped his hat to her beneath the balcony and asked her to kindly meet him at the front door, Dolice Marie, in a state of complete and utter shock, swooned into a very ladylike faint that left her crumpled on the floor of the lovely French-laced wrought iron balcony!

Well, Mr. Bernard Menard ran to the front door of the New Orleans House, tipped his hat as he ran hurriedly past the drunken gathering in the parlor that had been unable to open the door, up the stairs to the balcony in a flash, gathered the stunned Dolice Marie into his arms, and laid her gently on her bed, stroking her head and calling her name quite softly. Dolice Marie opened her eyes briefly, closed them quickly, and then opened them again before she could absolutely accept the fact that the strong arms that were surrounding her truly belonged to, yes, Mr. Bernard Menard! Dolice Marie sighed in contentment, cuddling closer to his chest, where, within just a matter of moments, both were peacefully and soundly asleep! Several hours later, after the sun had already set over the great city of New Orleans, Dolice Marie was awakened by the sweet breath of life, and she smiled, knowing in her heart that Jean Pierre and Evelina had brought yet another child into the world. She looked happily at Mr. Bernard Menard as he lay sleeping and quietly found the same spot in his arms to gently lie back down. Suddenly she sat up as she began to feel yet another breath of life, only this one was surely not the sweet breath of birth but the labored breath of eternal life.

As she quickly sat up, she awakened Mr. Bernard Menard, who immediately reached to draw her closer to him again, but she pulled away, telling him that it was time for her to go home to Mon Village du LaPierre en Bayou Frou-Frous, and although she loved him deeply, indeed, she must go home as soon as possible because something was going to happen and she truly needed to be there when it did. Mr. Bernard Menard assured her that he would personally see to it that she did just that, go home, but that nothing could be done in the middle of the night, that she needed to simply calm down and wait for the morning sun and the break of day.

After several minutes of coaxing, Dolice Marie finally yet reluctantly agreed and resumed her position in Mr. Bernard Menard arms, and as she allowed herself to relax, she felt his heart beating against her own and both succumbed to their own hour of passion.

And back home, yes, it was true. Evelina had given birth to another little girl and named her Jelee. Jean Pierre was again hiding in the fields, where Mama Mozelle found him with Jubil after

Evelina did her usual war dance, which scared poor Jean Pierre to death. Jubil, who had been trying desperately to charm Miss Sylvia, was now absolutely confused as to whether or not he wanted a family and if it would be worth it to have to hide in the fields to avoid being murdered when it was time to bring a child into the world. But as usual, Evelina settled down and became her old self after a while, pursuing a bewildered Jean Pierre with her seductive charms while Jubil resumed his continued daily pursuit of the lovely Miss Sylvia.

"Oh, how quickly we can forget all about the bad and remember just the good," Uncle Dommie would always say while the other storytellers would nod in agreement, as if remembering their own moments.

Dolice Marie was awakened again by the presence of labored breath that swept through her heart, causing her to lose her own, and she quickly succumbed to being held tightly by Mr. Bernard Menard, he who had captured her heart and taught her what true love felt like. Dolice Marie had never before awakened in the arms of any man, and most certainly not with the pounding headache that was surely the demon residue from the intoxication of the night before. For the very first time in her life, Dolice Marie felt completely out of her own control, but when Mr. Bernard Menard, who sensed such, assured her without saying a word that she was just where she needed to be. Dolice Marie knew that she was safe there in his arms, where she wanted and so needed to be.

Dolice Marie quietly repeated that she needed to go home as soon as possible before anything horrible happened while she was not there. Mr. Bernard Menard assured her that he, too, felt such a need for her to go and added that he knew exactly what it felt like since even though he had been bewitched by her and could not bear to be away from her, he knew that he had to leave her when the proper time came.

Raising himself up to lean on one elbow, he explained to Dolice Marie that the long period away from her was truly not by choice but by dire necessity, the same kind of necessity that she was now feeling. He had been summoned to London by a courier from the House of Menard of Toronto, in the middle of that fateful night, that informed him that both of his parents had been injured and that both were then in the Royal Hospital. Mr. Bernard Menard expressed that his deep concern for and obligation to his parents caused him to drop everything and hurry to be at his parents' side. He added that he was sure that she would understand and wait for him after reading his note without hesitation, but if he had caused her any undue worry, for that he did indeed apologize.

Dolice Marie assured him with a broad smile that she did not worry a bit about him for she believed in him and that it was his love that had kept her absolutely joyful while he had been away. Indeed!

Mr. Bernard Menard kissed her on her forehead as he continued, stating that he was very anxious because of the uncertainty of the condition of his family and thus had set sail immediately, arriving to find both parents with broken limbs, bandages, and bruises everywhere and each confined helplessly in separate small hospital beds in separate rooms.

Once the initial shock of the state of his parents had subsided and both were assured that he was there to care for them, Mr. Bernard Menard retired to a waiting room, where he was surprisingly greeted by his distraught aunt, Minnie Menard, younger sister to his own distinguished father, who began to tell him the sad story of his parents' fate.

It seemed that his mother and father had just made their grand entrance at a state dinner in London when his mother accidentally tripped on something, perhaps a grape, which was carelessly situated under her fashionable slipper, as she was smiling and waving royally at the other guests while descending the stairs, taking his father with her as she tried to stable herself, reaching to save herself by grasping his arm. Both began to roll uncontrollably throughout the whole affair, just missing Her Highness, the queen, pray tell, and finding themselves embarrassingly plopped in the middle of the stringed quartet that, I might add, was playing a lovely Mozart piece at that time, after knocking down several other heads of state and their spouses, a table filled with gourmet food, and several waiters who were delivering drinks to other guests!

"It was a shocking sight," Aunt Minnie Menard told her royal nephew with tears dropping down from her eyes onto her linen and lace handkerchief. "Simply shocking!" She continued by telling Mr. Bernard Menard that despite his parents' numerous injuries, the elder Menards were also quite embarrassed by the whole ordeal and were indeed the talk of the entire city of Toronto and virtually all of Europe by the time the younger Menard had arrived. So not only would Mr. Bernard Menard be responsible for tending to his ailing parents, he would also have to make restitution for the damage from the accident as well as to help soothe his parents' damaged dispositions.

Aunt Minnie Menard continued to catch her tears with her handkerchief as Mr. Bernard Menard reached to comfort her in his arms, realizing finally that she truly was not crying at all but indeed overwhelmed with hysterical laughter. Mr. Bernard Menard was quite taken aback, offended that she would be so disrespectful as to laugh at the ailing elder Menards, until he, too, could no longer hold back his laughter, citing the buffoonery of it all.

Well, the two filled the waiting room with their laughter, which was so loud that both were asked to immediately leave the premises by a hefty nurse who pointed a pudgy finger toward the exit. Mr. Bernard Menard assured Dolice Marie that as soon as his parents as well as his aunt Minnie Menard were able to show themselves in public again, for more reasons than one, he immediately traveled to be with her, leaving firm instructions for his parents' journey back to Toronto. It had been an extremely delicate time, and he could not tell Dolice Marie enough how he had thought of her day after day, after day.

It was obvious that the previous story was of no consequence to the high-strung, vixenly little girl from the bayous of the great state of Louisiana as she swooned with absolute love for the stately gentleman, Mr. Bernard Menard, swelling with an unfamiliar pool of tears that filled her eyes as she struggled to hold them back.

As she reached to hold him closer to her, she backed away quickly, letting out a resounding belch, and, while covering her mouth with both hands, began to choke in quite an unsightly, unladylike manner. Mr. Bernard Menard looked at her quite curiously as she ran past him toward the lovely French-laced wrought iron balcony doors, desperately trying to open them before the spirits of the night before came back up to haunt her.

Without a second thought, Mr. Bernard Menard grabbed a spittoon and towel and rushed to the balcony just as Dolice Marie disposed of the demon that had been causing her grief in the form of a hangover! It was a truly embarrassing sight for Dolice Marie, who could not stop apologizing for her uncontrolled disposition, explaining that she had indulged a tad too much in celebration with Angeline and Monsieur de Marquis the night before, having had no idea that she would, or even could, be so sick. Mr. Bernard Menard assisted her in cleaning herself up, repeating over and over that it was all right and that she should not be the least bit embarrassed, while Dolice Marie dragged herself back to her bed.

Mr. Bernard Menard lay softly beside Dolice Marie, holding her and seeking to give her comfort in whatever manner he could as Dolice Marie fell back into a deep sleep in the succor and the safety of his arMiss. As he stared lovingly at her in her peaceful sleep, breathing quietly and steadily, Dolice Marie suddenly inhaled quite deeply and snored so loudly, in a very unladylike manner, I have to say, into Mr. Bernard Menard's ear, that it startled him, causing him to quickly push her away from him at the exact same moment that she awoke, having snored so loudly that she had indeed awakened her own self! Well, you can just imagine how shocked and embarrassed she must have been, pushing herself away from Mr. Bernard Menard and covering her face with her hands. Of course, the kindly Mr. Bernard Menard tried his very best to assure her that she had nothing about which to be embarrassed, as poor Dolice Marie apologized and explained that she was indeed afflicted with an extremely troublesome time with asthma and therefore could sometimes snore terribly loud.

Uncle Dommie added that the LaPierre-Menard men still have the knack for choosing women that can saw lumber in their sleep! It was always a hoot to see him throw his head back and pretend to be snoring loudly as he mocked Aunt Philamena, all the while complaining about her terrible time with asthma. Of course, the young boys were just absolutely tickled at all of Uncle Dommie's antics.

Several hours later, it was the brightness of the Louisiana sun shining through the curtains of the New Orleans House that woke Dolice Marie and Mr. Bernard Menard from their satiated sleep and reminded Dolice Marie that she was late getting home. She quickly prepared for the journey, gathering her things together and rushing down the stairs, past the drunken gathering that was still asleep in the parlor, and out the front door of the New Orleans House and into the muggy Louisiana humidity, Mr. Bernard Menard following close behind. Suddenly, Dolice Marie stopped in her tracks, realizing that no one would know where she was, where she was going, and how long she would be gone. Mr. Bernard Menard calmed her down quickly, ran to his carriage, where he found a quill and notepad to leave a message, and scribbling something on the notepad, placed it on the piano, where he was certain that Angeline would indeed notice it when she awakened. All was well again.

Mr. Bernard Menard assisted Dolice Marie into his carriage, positioned himself on the driver's seat, and gave his horse the command to begin their journey to the railroad station. As they rode through the great city of New Orleans while being gawked at by people who were walking along the street, Dolice Marie shared what she had experienced as she made her journey in the dark, dirty last car of the train, her experiences after her arrival in the city, and just how the New Orleans House had come about. What she had learned about people, about herself, and how to ignore those who were just plain ugly and were not worthy of even a rude comment. Mr. Bernard Menard commanded his horse to halt and, there, in the middle of the city street, tenderly kissed Dolice Marie to reassure her that she was most certainly the most beautiful woman in the entire world and that he could only be pleased that she should care for him but a tiny bit of what he cared for her. Dolice Marie smiled and relaxed in the carriage. And reach the train station they did, with Dolice Marie sitting in the carriage, with an assumed-proper Southern white gentleman escorting a woman of color! The astonished proper Southern white passengers who were waiting for a train were shocked, as well as the ticket agent, who nearly had a heart attack when he saw that the two of them were actually approaching him together.

There were several proper Southern white people there who appeared to be most insulted at the sight, whispering under their breath the kinds of slanderous things that were commonplace for the day. There was also a handful of people of color, quietly standing off at a distance from the proper white Southerners, as would be expected. No one could possibly have been prepared for what was about to happen, but even the birds, the mosquitoes, and the crickets silenced themselves in order to not miss even one sigh.

Dolice Marie adjusted her adorable, tight-fighting gray jacket, which topped a matching full skirt over layers of underskirts flowing beneath as she stepped down from the carriage, Mr. Bernard Menard lending his hand to assist her. She positioned herself just a short distance from the ticket office and opened her parasol with a tiny white-eyelet-lace-gloved hand, all the while keeping a close eye on the agent and Mr. Bernard Menard from beneath her plume-adorned hat, which was tilted ever so slightly to her right side.

"One ticket to the Atchafalaya station, please, in your best car," he happily and innocently requested from the ticket agent, casting a smile toward Dolice Marie.

The agent seemed to be in a state of shock, seemingly incapable of speaking, much to the chagrin of dear Mr. Bernard Menard, who immediately knew the reason but attempted to dismiss such rudeness regarding a person's color as sheer and blatant ignorance, a trait he absolutely had no time for. He cleared his throat and repeated the request, staring with a serious eye upon the ticket agent. "One ticket to the Atchafalaya station, please…and in your most comfortable car."

"Mister, it would be my pleasure to do just that," the agent began in a low whisper, "but the laws of the great state of Louisiana require that I ask if the passenger will be yourself or"—he coughed—"the *lady*."

"Does it matter?" Mr. Bernard Menard interrupted. "Pray tell, my good man, does it matter?"

Uncle Dommie truly loved this part of the story, and I can remember mouthing those exact words with him as he proudly spoke the words of our celebrated ancestor. But again, I digress.

It was apparent that both the crowd of proper Southern white people as well as the few people of color who were waiting at the train station were curious as to what would happen next, becoming extremely quiet, with all eyes on the scene directly in front of the ticket office, while inching closer to be able to hear every word. Most certainly, the crowd of proper Southern white people would have stormed the lovely Dolice Marie, were it not for the dashing, handsome, brave, protective—but again, I digress.

The ticket agent peered back and forth from Mr. Bernard Menard to the crowd of people, apparently appealing for some sort of assistance from someone, but instead, Mr. Bernard Menard raised his voice and began to repeat his request for the third time, when he was suddenly interrupted by the ticket agent, who, shaking with fear and sweating profusely, explained the law of the land, citing that he needed to know which would be the passenger in order to know which car to put said passenger in.

The ticket agent continued by stating that Mr. Bernard Menard would have his choice of cars that were not already full of proper Southern white passengers and there was a car at the very end of the train that was reserved for people of color. The ticket agent concluded by saying that perhaps Mr. Bernard Menard should be most happy that he was a proper white person with such privilege during that time in history, causing Mr. Bernard Menard to straighten up and stare the ticket agent directly in the eye to inform him that he was absolutely happy to say that he was not a proper Southern white person at all; he was a proud Canadian with absolutely no reservations about a person's skin color. He continued that he had heard all about the conditions of the car reserved for the people of color and would not dare think of his lady traveling all the way to the Atchafalaya River station in such horrible surroundings, nor could he dare think of himself traveling in such suitable conditions because his skin was white, knowing that the former was true.

"Sir, the train will be approaching this station shortly, and it would be most unfortunate if either of you were to miss it. Perhaps if you prefer not to answer me, you can purchase the ticket from the conductor when the train arrives."

"Splendid!" Mr. Bernard Menard retorted loudly with a hand thrown high up in the air, as if performing in a Shakespearean play. Mr. Bernard Menard proudly walked over to the place where Dolice Marie was standing, placing his arm in hers again, and the two proceeded to walk together to the track to await the train and its conductor, completely ignoring anyone but themselves. It would be the better part of half an hour before the train whistle sounded as it came around a bend, smoke circling in the air as if announcing the arrival of the president himself.

By this time, of course, there were more people in the area around the train station, all waiting for the train that was slowing to a complete stop in front of the station, and most probably waiting also for the fury they expected when Mr. Bernard Menard attempted to purchase a train ticket for the precocious little woman of color that could not be ignored.

The proper Southern white people began to board the train, giving their tickets to the conductor and rushing to a window, where they could hang out and still get a clear view of the activity outside. The people of color stood back, waiting their turn to approach the conductor and take their place in the very last car of the train, that is, if there was any room after everyone else had been boarded. At this moment, Mr. Bernard Menard made his way to the conductor, suggesting that Dolice Marie stay her distance until he could straighten the situation out with as much peace and calm as possible. When the conductor asked him for his ticket, he kindly explained that the ticket agent had refused to sell one ticket to the Atchafalaya station to him without knowing for which one, either himself or the lady, the lovely Mademoiselle LaPierre, because of some silly law that made absolutely no sense at all. The conductor looked toward Mr. Bernard Menard's hand, his eyes following it all the way to Dolice Marie, who smiled and even had the audacity to wink her eye.

An extremely intense yet quiet conversation followed between Mr. Bernard Menard and the train's conductor, the sound of their voices barely audible as Dolice Marie and everyone else strained to hear even an iota of what was being said.

Suddenly, the conductor, quite intrigued indeed, boarded the train; the proper Southern white people who were now seated quite comfortably and spread out in the train cars were instructed to move forward to occupy the cars farther to the front. Mr. Bernard Menard motioned for Dolice Marie to board the train and seat herself farther up front from the cars located farther to the rear of the train, where trash was stored during the journeys, where the people of color were ordained to travel. Dolice Marie cocked her head to the side in her familiar victorious pose, twisting her parasol slightly, and as she boarded the train, Uncle Dommie moved closer to the young Southern boys and whispered, "Some say that she actually lifted her bustle and pointed mischievously to her plump derriere, giving all who were in full view the opportunity to plant a kiss."

My great big uncles laughed uncontrollably at the statement, while the young Southern boys blushed, not quite sure yet just how to process all the strange goings-on in the LaPierre-Menard family.

But then, in an unprecedented turn of events, Mr. Bernard Menard turned toward the remaining people of color who were standing at their proper distance from the train and motioned for them to join him. Well, you can imagine how terribly confused they were, knowing the full extent of the law and its resulting punishment, but Mr. Bernard Menard motioned for them to join him again, this time smiling and pointing the way to the car that was nearer the front of the train, the one that would be most comfortable for their journey, the one where his sweet Dolice Marie was already seated on a padded seat.

One by one—and quite hesitantly, I might add—the dear people of color boarded the train, bypassing the evil eye of the conductor, and to the disbelief of the proper Southern white people as they passed through the now-crowded train cars up front to find their seats!

Just before the great train began to speed down the track in the direction of the Atchafalaya River station, away from the great city of New Orleans, Mr. Bernard Menard kissed his lady love goodbye. Dolice Marie whispered in his ear the question that was probably on everyone's mind: "What happened that could have allowed such a conclusion to such an impossible situation?"

Mr. Bernard Menard quietly explained that even though he was truly a man of peace, insulted by laws that said a person's place on a train was dictated by that person's skin color, he knew that he was just one man fighting a useless cause, until suddenly he remembered that the strongest weapon in any battle is wit, the uncanny ability to outwit the opponent. And thus, he did.

Actually, Mr. Bernard Menard essentially wanted only to make sure that his lovely Dolice Marie would be assured a comfortable and clean place on the train throughout her journey home, but the ticket agent had made such an enormous task of making sure the law was protected that Mr. Bernard Menard felt he should at least have a little fun as well.

Mr. Bernard Menard had assured the conductor that he would find a personal gift awaiting him at the Atchafalaya River station upon his arrival, a gift that was worthy of such a gentleman, an intelligent gentleman who realized that the number of passengers his train was carrying and the mathematical hazards of such passengers being spread sporadically throughout the cars would most assuredly cause the train to need to produce more steam in order to pull the train around the Louisiana curves toward the Atchafalaya River station! But with everyone moved up toward the front, the back end of the train would be free to flow faster without the use of steam, actually causing the train to run faster while using less steam, as the back cars, in speeding up, would give a boost to the cars in front.

Mr. Bernard Menard also explained that the gift he would leave at the Atchafalaya River Station would be a letter from himself to the conductor's superior, citing how very smart it was of him to recognize such an ingenious plan, one for certain deserving of a reward for saving money for the company. Of course, Mr. Bernard Menard would put a few dollars in the letter to let the company know how much it was personally worth to him and his beautiful lady. Mr. Bernard Menard told the conductor to be sure to observe him at the ticket office as he was sending the wire ahead of him.

Of course, no one in that particular car at least had any idea whether or not Mr. Bernard Menard was telling the truth about some mathematical hazard, but for whatever reason, everyone in the car would now enjoy a comfortable journey. Everyone smiled and thanked Mr. Bernard Menard as he gave one more goodbye kiss to his Dolice Marie and disappeared off the train. Dolice Marie peered out of the window until the mighty iron horse began its slow motion from the New Orleans station. Mr. Bernard Menard tipped his hat at Dolice Marie, and she blew him a kiss until she could no longer see him.

Just as before, Dolice Marie was captivated by the presence of the only thing she knew to be greater than herself, the mighty Mississippi River. She quickly pressed her face and hands up against the window of the train car like a child peering through the window of a candy shop, seemingly inhaling the awesome sight, while the other passengers were more impressed with their comfortable, padded seats. Dolice Marie remembered from her previous experience in the car at the rear of the train that it would be fruitless to draw anyone's attention to the sight of the mighty river, so she savored it all by herself, giving in as well to her excitement as she squealed with delight. Surely, anyone else would be screaming with the joy of a comfortable journey, a nostalgic journey home, and the love of a real gentleman, but Dolice Marie was far too mesmerized by the rolling waters of the mighty Mississippi River to think of anything else, at least for now.

At Mon Village, Jean Pierre stopped dead in his tracks as he walked with Mon Claire back toward his and Evelina's house from the outhouse in the backyard. For a brief moment, everything seemed to still; there was not a sound from the birds, the crickets, or the other people who were in the housing area. Suddenly, a burst of hot, humid wind shot past Jean Pierre, and he held Mon Claire tightly to his chest, covering her tiny face from flying debris while struggling to catch his breath. And suddenly again, it was still. Jean Pierre, realizing what it all meant, dashed into his house, depositing Mon Claire into a confused Evelina's arms as he immediately dashed right back out of the house, running toward Mama Mozelle's house with all the speed he could muster.

"She's coming, Mama," Uncle Dommie said, mimicking Jean Pierre. "Dolice Marie is coming!"

Uncle Dommie laughed a haughty laugh as he added, "Nothing but a hot, humid wind was capable of announcing that Dolice Marie was on her way home."

Mama Mozelle was busy putting the finishing touches on a lovely family quilt that she had been making from tiny scraps of personal items from everyone in the family's personal belongings when Jean Pierre ran into her house.

"Yes," she replied with great excitement to Jean Pierre, confirming what he had said, "and I've just finished this quilt, just in time."

It was true, Dolice Marie was coming, but she was even closer than Jean Pierre or Mama Mozelle could have ever imagined.

Upon arrival at the Atchafalaya River train station, Dolice Marie sat herself and her train cases on a bench that was clearly reserved for proper Southern white people, quite oblivious to the rude comments and threats being thrown her way by angry passengers. She was certain, beyond a doubt, that her family knew that she was home, and she knew that someone would most assuredly be at the Atchafalaya River train station shortly to pick her up and carry her home to Mon Village. Strangely enough, the proper Southern white people chose to stand, sweating in the hot sun, while Dolice Marie sat comfortably on a station bench shaded by a cool tree. Home was just a few miles away now, and Dolice Marie was determined not to let any Jim Crow lovers rob her of the joy of her homecoming.

It would not be long before Dolice Marie saw a man of color leading a horse and wagon headed straight toward her. She cupped her hand over her eyes to shade the sun, dropped her parasol, and ran toward the sight. It was Jubil, covered with the dust of the road and leading the horse directly in front of her.

Jubil jumped down from the wagon to welcome her with a hug, and although Dolice Marie was so excited that she could burst, she calmly turned to the proper Southern white people who were still gawking at her, picked up her parasol while Jubil loaded the wagon with her train cases, and smiled sweetly while batting her intriguing eyes. Suddenly, she tossed that head of hers again and accepted Jubil's hand as he assisted her into the wagon.

Once on the open road to Mon Village, Dolice Marie and Jubil began to laugh hysterically just as they had always done with Jean Pierre. It was truly obvious that Dolice Marie might have appeared the epitome of culture at the train station, but she was still able to bring the worst out of the proper white Southern ladies and gentlemen who could not help but be drawn into her antics.

Dolice Marie excitedly began to point out familiar landmarks, an old cemetery now covered in weeds, a fork in the road that led to the Castille Plantation by one path and the Bayou Frou-Frous by the other, and finally, the strong smell of fresh mint in the air that she inhaled with her eyes closed, and of course the huge magnolia trees that hid the path that led to the walkway of the big house. Dolice Marie fanned herself in the heat and humidity with a dainty handkerchief that had been doused in Angeline's fine French *parfum*, overwhelmed with the reality that she was indeed home after three long years. She inhaled another deep breath as the horse led the way down the path and toward the big house, smiling broadly and peering in all directions to catch a glimpse of someone, anyone who would be coming to greet her, but the entire area appeared to be a ghost town.

Mama Mozelle was not sitting on the front porch of the big house as she expected, and the doors were closed shut, an indication that it was not open for business. There were no workers in the fields, no one in the flower gardens, the livery stable, or even the silversmith shop. In fact, the unfamiliar shops that lined the area near the residential area were also closed shut.

Dolice Marie climbed down from the wagon, absolutely horrified at the thought that there was no one there to greet her after such a long time being away from home, even if they didn't know she had been on her way. She began to spin around and around, as if desperately trying to scan all directions at one time, tears beginning to flow down her cheeks, alarming the empathetic nature of Jubil, who jumped from the wagon and grabbed Dolice Marie to hold her tightly in his arms as she wept with disappointment, all the while calling out for Mama Mozelle and Jean Pierre.

Out of the corner of his eye, Jubil could see everyone beginning to slowly emerge from their hiding places and approach them while Dolice Marie buried her head in his chest, sobbing ever so loudly. Dolice Marie suddenly raised her head up and began to smile as she realized that she was now being surrounded by a multitude of the residents, who were being led by her beloved Mama Mozelle, with Jean Pierre and his family. Dolice Marie reached out to hug them all at one time as everyone's tears flowed freely and the music of a La La began to play.

Some of the ladies began to bring an enormous amount of food to the scene, while the men brought wooden tables to set it all on. Dolice Marie was ecstatic as she went from person to person, hugging them while seemingly drinking in every inch of them with her glowing eyes.

There were children everywhere, faces she had never seen before, and the matured faces of those who had been mere babies when she left, but it was Jean Pierre and Evelina's four children that immediately captured her heart.

Mon Claire was almost four, a darling little girl with curly hair that Jean Pierre described as "a handful," with no interest in learning the work of the women at all. In fact, Mon Claire spent much of her time with Jubil at the livery stable, learning the business of the horses, or with the boys, playing rough-and-tumble games. Evelina simply left her alone to be who she was evidently intended to be, assuring Jean Pierre that some little boy would eventually catch her eye and she would grab for the chance to please him as only a woman could.

Jean Pierre took the chubby twins, Petois and Pecous, with him when surveying the day-to-day operations of Mon Village, all the while hoping that they would grow up to follow in his footsteps as Master LaPierre, and at almost three years old, the two were already eager to please their father. Both boys had a healthy appetite for food, and Evelina had no trouble at all getting them to eat either vegetable, fruit, fish, or meat. Of course, they enjoyed their rice, and lots of it!

It would be the youngest, Jelee, named after my own great-grandmother, that stole Dolice Marie's heart and made her smile broadly. The tiny newborn was the image of a younger Dolice Marie, and the two bonded immediately. Jelee smiled at Dolice Marie as she grabbed for her, almost falling out of Evelina's arms in an effort to be held by her in the process. Evelina leaned over to give the baby to Dolice Marie, and suddenly, Dolice Marie felt a true connection to Evelina as Jean Pierre's wife, as family, and she smiled lovingly at her, no longer feeling that she had stolen Jean Pierre away from her. Evelina felt the same and simply nodded in acknowledgment.

It was a wonderful homecoming with family and friends, and even though she was tired from the journey on the train, Dolice Marie was much too excited to rest. She and Mama Mozelle walked throughout what now appeared to be a city all its own, the latter explaining to her why it was now called Mon Village and all the rest of the long title. With Jelee happily in her arms, Dolice Marie could not have felt any happier. In her deepest Creole accent, personified even more now that she was surrounded by those who spoke with the thick combination of French and African dialects, Dolice Marie thanked everyone for having made all this possible.

The music, dancing, and feast continued well into the cool of the evening. It was apparent that the children were beginning to tire, and so was Mama Mozelle, but there was yet one stop to be made before Dolice Marie could turn in for the night. At the very moment that Dolice Marie felt the familiar tug, Jean Pierre felt it also. He quickly brought the children and Evelina home from the gathering as others began to clean up the area and say good night. Again there were hugs and kisses that seemingly never ended, everyone holding one another as though they were afraid it would all end again at that very moment.

Dolice Marie accompanied Mama Mozelle to the big house, where Annabelle and her girls had already returned and were seated on the front porch. In respect for the former madam of the house and the mistress of all of Mon Village, the ladies stood and lowered their heads in the presence of Dolice Marie and Mama Mozelle. Yes, it was quite a sight to be seen.

Dolice Marie met Jean Pierre as both were heading to Mama Del's house, Jean Pierre carrying a plate filled with the delights of the day and a jar filled with the mint concoction that had become extremely popular with everyone at Mon Village. The two held hands as they entered the house, both remembering that moment many years earlier when their fate had been sealed by this old woman and her very special juju. The old woman was smoking her corncob pipe, as she had been all those years before, and she smiled that toothless smile, opening her arms to embrace them both.

Uncle Dommie moved closer to the young boys and assured them that what happened in Mama Del's house with Dolice Marie and Jean Pierre was the family secret that they, too, would experience when the time came and they were both ripe. After the more than two-hour ritual with Mama Del, Dolice Marie and Jean Pierre walked exhaustedly arm-in-arm toward their respective destinations, Dolice Marie to the familiar resting place in the big house, and Jean Pierre to the ever-loving and open arms of his bride, Evelina, that is, until it was time to give birth to their next child.

Jean Pierre and Dolice Marie found it hard to part, even for just the night, and began a game of walking each other halfway home over and over, which only found each right back at the same point they had begun. There was so much for the two of them to talk about, and all the time in the world was at their disposal, so they agreed to make that time sometime during the next day, a time for just the two of them and Mama Mozelle to laugh and reminisce, to plan for the future of Mon Village, and to discuss the first love that Dolice Marie had ever felt in her entire life. That in itself was reason for each to share an embrace good night and run hurriedly home.

Dolice Marie slept comfortably in the master bedroom, where she had slept so many nights before, dreaming about Mr. Bernard Menard and longing for him to be there with her. She smiled as she turned over on her side to peer at the moon outside her window, and before long, she was asleep, a child again, with her beloved Jean

Pierre and her Mama Mozelle just beyond the walls of the big house, not miles away and not just in her thoughts.

Time alone came during the afternoon of the very next day, while Evelina was going about her daily duties with the children, that is, all except Mon Claire, who proudly rode behind Jubil in the saddle on his favorite steed, Garçon. With a jug of Mama Mozelle's sweet, cool lemonade and a jug of the increasingly popular mint concoction, Dolice Marie, Jean Pierre, and Mama Mozelle slowly headed toward the huge magnolia trees that led the way to where the old African lay in rest, wishing their good day to everyone that was happily working their familiar day.

Uncle Dommie pointed out that the young boys were, at that very moment, indeed very close to that exact spot, and he pointed to the African's grave a few feet away, which now rested beneath a tall stone covering upon which the names Menard and LaPierre were engraved. Since absolutely no one seemed to have ever known the African's name, he was given the full respect of being the head of the entire family on both sides of the two children that made it possible for the wealthy future of the LaPierre-Menard descendants, a privilege that these young boys are now privy to every year.

Under the spell of the intoxicating mint concoction and the sheer joy of just being together, the three laughed until they cried, tears of joy streaming down each face as they recalled that infamous final chapter in the lives of Madam Frou-Frous and Master Philippe LaPierre when Dolice Marie and Jean Pierre were just children, the opening of the big house after Mama Mozelle began to see its potential as Dolice Marie began to blossom and mature, the Night Riders and, of course, the Confederate soldiers buried just a few yards away from where they were now seated, deep within the gardens where mint now dominated uncontrollably. Their laughter echoed into the Bayou Frou-Frous.

Uncle Dommie intensified the moment by telling the young boys that their laughter can sometimes still be heard during the quiet of night, when all lay asleep and dreaming. It was apparent that these boys were indeed fighting to resist their fears and perhaps appear to be incapable of handling such talk in front of their peers. There were always sheepish grins at this point of the story and forced gestures of disbelief as the older gentlemen again burst into a gala of laughter.

It was then that Dolice Marie told Mama Mozelle and Jean Pierre about the dashing, charming Mr. Bernard Menard, the Canadian with skin the color of cotton, hair as red as the beauty of sunset, but with a truly gentle and tender heart like the old African, the kind of man that she had never known before, the man that had taught her things of wonder and amazement. She closed her eyes as she told the two that she was surely, deeply in love. Jean Pierre was ecstatic for his sister, who was actually his cousin and not his sister at all; Mama Mozelle was equally ecstatic as Jean Pierre, but not the least surprised.

Dolice Marie expressed her excitement and approval over the changes all around the former slave plantation and expressed her sorrow like a tiny child that she was not there to help with its growth, a far cry from the feisty little spitfire that had made her dramatic claim to the great city of New Orleans. Mama Mozelle comforted her as Dolice Marie lay on one of her arms, Jean Pierre in her other, just as they did when the two were very young.

Mama Mozelle kissed Dolice Marie gently on her head as she explained that her leaving was the right thing to do since her growth was destined to be while she was away from the safety of home, and besides, how would she have ever met the dashing young man? Dolice Marie rose up on her elbow to peer into Mama Mozelle's eyes as she listened to her speak of Mr. Bernard Menard as the man she knew would truly make Dolice Marie extremely happy for as long as they both lived, even though she had not met him yet. This truly was the man that Mama Del had foretold, the one she said would love Dolice Marie, and then added that she believed that he would give Dolice Marie a good life, and many children, children like the precious little one already growing inside her.

An astonished Dolice Marie gently rubbed her stomach and smiled broadly while tears filled her eyes, asking over and over, "A precious little baby, Mama?" knowing full well that it was certainly Mama Mozelle who would know about such things and she need not question any further.

Well, Jean Pierre just beamed at the news and added that it was about time she did her part to populate the family since he had already brought four children into their world, with probably more on the way. He also seriously made it known that he hoped that Dolice Marie would not make bringing children into the world as hard as Evelina had with each of their four. Mama Mozelle just shook her head and looked at him for the silly boy she remembered he could be when his babies were born.

As Mama Mozelle lay comfortably with her children under that beautiful big magnolia tree, she suddenly began to gaze far into the distance, thinking deeply about something that had now come to her mind. Jean Pierre and Dolice Marie became very quiet, like children again, as they waited for her to tell them what was bearing so heavily on her mind.

Mama Mozelle began to explain that everyone on the Bayou Frou-Frous carried the name LaPierre as their last name due to the events of the former plantation days where the slaves were considered property of the master and the plantation, only three-fifths human, as a matter of fact, and had never known any other name but LaPierre. Those were very dreadful days that could only bring back horrible memories even in the midst of the love of family.

Uncle Dommie told the young boys quite seriously that suddenly Mama Mozelle had something that was weighing quite heavily on her heart, especially now that Dolice Marie was living away from the familiar surroundings of those who knew themselves as LaPierres, but what about her offspring and Jean Pierre's offspring that might one day leave Mon Village, that would bear the name of their loved ones in lands possibly far away from Mon Village? The chance that family members could fall in love with one another without knowing that they shared the same bloodline was quite displeasing as well as disturbing to Mama Mozelle.

The slave masters had had healthy sexual appetites that created the children of the plantations in their various shades of color, children whose bloodline was impossible to know since the masters, and in some cases, the mistresses, never claimed many, if any, of them publicly. And now that Dolice Marie had ventured out into the world outside the confines of the bayou area, her offspring, that precious child she was carrying, would truly need to know exactly who blood relatives were at all times to avoid the possibility of finding themselves in an impossible relationship.

Mama Mozelle had seen many years behind her and experienced many different things, enough to let her know that the love of family is far different from the love given to those outside of family. Dolice Marie and Jean Pierre agreed. Mama Mozelle then added with a look of supposition that such a reunion, just as they were enjoying at that moment, should be instituted from then forth in order to avoid such an unfortunate situation by introducing blood relatives to one another and in order to pass on the stories of the very colorful family. Mama Mozelle made both Jean Pierre and Dolice Marie promise that they would come back to Mon Village, at that very spot, ever so often at an appointed time to share the stories with the next generation.

Uncle Dommie proudly confirmed that promise by telling the young boys, "And that's why we're all here, at this time, at the very spot where Mama Mozelle made our ancestors, Jean Pierre and Dolice Marie, promise to come back to do just what we're doing!"

Sometime during that special moment that the three had shared under the huge magnolia trees and under the spell of the Bayou Frou-Frous, Mama Mozelle's spirit peacefully slipped away from Jean Pierre and Dolice Marie to join the resting spirit of her brother, the old African, in the afterworld. In the midst of their celebration, the three had fallen asleep in one another's arms, and only Jean Pierre and Dolice Marie would awaken.

Mama Del had sensed it hours before and had already begun her ritual of incense and incantations for the dead in an attempt to purify the soul before it crossed over into the afterworld to meet the ancestors. It was Mama Mozelle's final labored breath that had awakened the two children, who had known no other parent but the wise and loving Mozelle. Mama Del moaned and groaned in sorrow as she continued the ritual, smoke from the incense as well as from her corncob pipe filling the room, blinding her to the outside world, connecting her with the spiritual.

Jean Pierre and Dolice Marie, realizing that Mama Mozelle was not still sleeping but no longer had the breath of life, began to wail with the great pain of their loss, tossing their hands in the air and straining their muscles in great sorrow. Mama Del wailed alone, her hands reaching to the sky and her face turned toward the heavens. Their moans of agony echoed throughout the bayou, creating the eerie sounds of a seemingly entire people grieving with tremendous anguish.

There would be no comfort for Jean Pierre and Dolice Marie, no human force that could relieve the sudden void that now ripped through their hearts. They began to weep, sobbing with ceaseless tears that clouded the reality that Mama Mozelle was indeed gone, and they must now make that sad announcement to the other residents of Mon Village.

Jean Pierre carefully picked Mama Mozelle up into his arms, her head and arms falling lifelessly as he and Dolice Marie began their solemn journey back to Mon Village, as if simply replaying the scenes from a horrible dream. Dolice Marie was extremely weak and found it difficult to walk, leaning on Jean Pierre and grasping Mama Mozelle for support.

As they neared Mon Village, several of the residents caught sight of them and cupped their hands over their eyes to block the glare of the sun to be able to see clearly. But after a brief moment of wonder, they realized that Jean Pierre was carrying the lifeless body of their beloved Mama Mozelle. The chorus of wails, moans, and words of bereavement became louder and stronger as more residents became aware of Mama Mozelle's passing. The grief was overwhelming.

Evelina spied her husband as she peered out of the window of their house to see what was happening and quickly ran out of the house, instructing the children to stay on the front porch until she came back. She ran, almost fell several times on the dusty pathway, with tears streaming down both cheeks to offer her assistance to her beloved husband, Jean Pierre, and her sister-in-law, Dolice Marie. As she came close to the three, she screamed as well, kissing Mama Mozelle and allowing her tears to fall on her face.

Field hands came in from their daily tasks, shopkeepers ran out from their shops, the silver shop was suddenly stilled, the children ran from the schoolhouse, and Annabelle and her ladies from the big house, some still dressed in their work clothing, ran, too, all toward Jean Pierre and Dolice Marie.

Jubil was just riding back into Mon Village when he heard the unmistakable sounds of mourning as he dismounted his horse and began running toward the scene, not knowing exactly what was going on but knowing in his heart that Jean Pierre somehow needed him. In her weakened condition, Dolice Marie gathered her strength and began to call for Jubil, leading him to the residential area, to Mama Mozelle's house, where Jean Pierre would lay Mama Mozelle's body until the burial arrangements had been made.

It was truly the saddest of times for the entire population of Mon Village, and they allowed themselves that special privilege of mourning, grieving, and encouraged one another to do the same. For two days, Mama Mozelle's body lay peacefully resting in her bed, dressed in her finest dress, with her hair done neatly, courtesy of Annabelle and her ladies of the big house. The residents of Mon Village filed past Mama Mozelle's body to give their farewells and shed their tears as they moaned and swayed with grief. The sounds of Mother Africa came and filled Mon Village with the moans and groans that had once been commonplace while one of the older residents who still remembered how to pound the skins of an old African drum. Jean Pierre and Dolice Marie were comforted by those around them who freely showered one another with hugs and words of sorrow.

Jubil found Miss Sylvia at his side throughout that time of anguish and consented to her witnessing the depth of his bereavement, most grateful to her for being there for him. During the two days of mourning, Jubil and some of the other men from Mon Village worked painfully, tearfully, but diligently to build the wooden box that would hold Mama Mozelle's body and to prepare the grave for their matriarch, and when the time had come to lay her to rest beside the old African, there seemed to be that noticeable silence again, silence where even the birds and the crickets were stilled, all in honor of Mama Mozelle.

MINT JULEP

The long procession of family, friends, and neighbors began at early morning, with everyone parading around and around the grave site under the magnolia trees for at least two hours. The clapping of their hands and the swaying of their heads to the subtle beat accompanied the eerie moans from the bereaved, a procession that lived deep within their souls and was guided by the ancestors with whom Mama Mozelle, and her brother, the African, now lived again. It was grief in its greatest and final hour. The scene continued until the hot Louisiana sun signaled that it was time to lower the body into the grave. Mama Mozelle's body was laid to rest beside her brother's body for their eternal sleep, while their spirits assumed their righteous place to watch over their earthly family. In her house, Mama Del now slept peacefully and soundly.

I always felt quite sad at this part of the story. Uncle Dommie would always pause for a few minutes while all my other uncles bowed their heads and seemingly said a prayer, while Uncle Simon would always let tears flow down both of his cheeks. Surely, it was an awkward moment for the young boys, not truly knowing what they should do but eventually all bowing their heads by the time Uncle Dommie would clear his throat and ask his familiar, "Now, where was I?"

The procession back to the residential area of Mon Village was quite a different event for everyone. The sounds of silence or the moans of grief gave way to joyful clapping and utterings filled with glee. Jubil and his men would come back another day to cover the homemade casket with the surrounding dirt and plant flowers all around. But for now it was time to celebrate Mama Mozelle's life, and that they all did.

The celebration of Mama Mozelle's life went on for hours in the hot Louisiana sun, with food everywhere, music of the La La echoing all over the place, and plenty of the mint concoction circulating among the men, secretly to some of the women as well, while Dolice Marie sat alone on Mama Mozelle's former porch.

Evelina assured her that it was most likely the combination of grief, the hot sun, and not sleeping at all for two nights prior that was now causing the poor girl to be unable to keep anything down, not even Mama Mozelle's cool, sweet lemonade, which she had prepared for the ailing child. Jean Pierre and Dolice Marie as well knew perfectly well what the cause of the sudden illness really was, but Jean Pierre would keep quiet until Dolice Marie would be first to make the big announcement that she was, indeed, with child.

Chapter 8

UNCLE SIMON WAS still wiping tears away from his eyes when Uncle Dommie cleared his throat, catching his attention and reminding him that it was his turn to continue the story. Uncle Simon wiped his face with a plain white handkerchief, blew his nose quite profusely, and prepared himself to carry on the tale of our family's infiltration into the great city of New York. Just as my other wonderful uncles, Uncle Simon had a story all his own, although much of it is completely unknown. He was born and raised right here at Mon Village, just like my entire family, it seemed, but just like our ancestor Dolice Marie LaPierre, Uncle Simon always had that secret call for the big-city life. From what they tell me, he gave into that desire when just a young man after finishing his education at one of the all-black Southern schools with a major in education, his passion since childhood.

New York's Harlem was like a magnet that simply drew young men as well as young women into its nightlife, and when it drew Uncle Simon, it seemed his entire life skipped ten years. Nobody in the family knew exactly what Uncle Simon was doing in his early years in the great city of New York, and quite frankly, no one dared to ask or even cared to know. (Some things truly are better off not knowing!) Anyway, when he did come back home to Mon Village for family reunion, he brought along his lady love, my aunt Stella, a schoolteacher who most certainly had put a damper in Uncle Simon's shenanigans and an arrow straight through his heart. The two settled down in a small brownstone where they lived and loved, every day walking to and from the local elementary school, where Aunt Stella as well as Uncle Simon were employed, and to the local nightclubs a little farther down the street on the weekends. Uncle Simon and Aunt Stella raised six lovely children; two of them followed in their parents' footsteps and became teachers in one of the Southern schools in Baton Rouge, the other four staying in the great city of New York with careers ranging from accounting to joining the family members who enjoyed the craft of preparing food.

Uncle Simon told the young boys that the unexpected and devastating loss of Mama Mozelle alone was truly going to make leaving Mon Village an even more difficult task for Dolice Marie, but she knew that she had a business to run in the great city of New Orleans, a business that included others who depended upon her to succeed.

She also knew that Mr. Bernard Menard surely needed to know about their precious little child that was growing inside her, a child that would bear the name LaPierre but Menard as well. Or would it? Would such a refined gentleman like Mr. Bernard Menard ever even consider making a life with her, a woman of color, like Mama Mozelle had said under the big magnolia tree? Would his family in Toronto accept her as their son's wife, or even as a total human being at all? Even though Mama Del had always been right about her knowledge of the future, did she know about such challenges of the heart? All of it together was just too much to think about, so Dolice Marie decided not to think about anything of that nature for just a couple more days, and then she would consider seriously contemplating what would come next for herself, the precious little baby she was carrying in her womb, and the discussion with Jean Pierre about the continued success of Mon Village.

Being the mistress of this wonderful area gave her full authority over everything, of course, along with her beloved Jean Pierre, but now it would be a task she must endeavor upon without the presence and wise counsel from Mama Mozelle. She had been the center of everything for everyone, and everyone looked to her for their answers as well as their strength and guidance. She would not be on the porch of her house anymore, or on the porch of the big house, for anyone and everyone to just freely stop by to talk to about anything.

Being mistress seemed so unimportant now in the great depth of the current events, so empty and useless a title. It was obvious that Dolice Marie could easily just give Jean Pierre and Evelina sole rights to the entire place and never give Mon Village a second thought, but she also knew that Mama Mozelle had intended the legacy to be created by both of them from the very beginning. She was the mistress, and Jean Pierre was the master, and she realized that that should never change. But even so, Dolice Marie felt extremely torn and guilty for wanting and needing to be self-absorbed with her grief and with her own life rather than having to worry about the success of Mon Village. Besides, this early stage of her pregnancy was creating such a disruption in her daily routine that she truly felt physically incapable at that time of handling anything other than her morning, afternoon, and evening sickness.

And again, what about Mr. Bernard Menard? Dolice Marie was convinced that he would never live at such a place as Mon Village when he was so accustomed to the likes of Toronto, the great city of New Orleans, New York City, and the many other cities in Europe where he could enjoy the finer things that made up his life. But again, Dolice Marie raised her hands to the sky as if crying to the ancestors for their advice and again contended that it was all just too much to think about at one time, especially when her thoughts kept reaching back toward her beloved Mama Mozelle. Dolice Marie decided that she would do now what she always did whenever she had been in a quandary about something: she would discuss it all with Jean Pierre. But not now. Now she would just take a little nap on the cool ground under that big magnolia tree.

Jean Pierre, too, was feeling the need to just close himself and his family off from the rest of the hustle and bustle of Mon Village, and from whatever else lay outside the confines of the peaceful and safe place that had always been his home. His grief was overwhelming, filling his head with the sights and sounds of Mama Mozelle from the time when he was a little boy until now, when he should be handling this situation like the man she expected him to be. He felt so alone and lonely.

As he walked around the property with his chubby little twin boys, Petois and Pecous, he surveyed the vastness of the responsibility that came with being the master of such a boundless area. While feeling a mixture of pride and despair, Jean Pierre certainly didn't feel comfortable at the thought of just giving that sole responsibility to his sister, especially now that she was experiencing a brand-new life away from Mon Village and a future that would never find her alone again—at least that was his greatest desire for her.

He was also quite convinced that Dolice Marie was truly incapable of maintaining the day-to-day operations of Mon Village all by herself. Jean Pierre knew that proposition could and would only be a disaster, and he shook his head to clear his mind of such an outrageous thought.

Mon Claire, the twins, and Jelee were each greatly loved and cherished, but, admittedly, an added responsibility for himself and Evelina, so he was quite aware of what Dolice Marie would be facing with the birth of her first child. Jean Pierre even thought about just giving his rights to Mon Village to Jubil, his faithful friend and confidant. Jubil was now trying very hard to build a life with Miss Sylvia, a combination that would certainly be good leadership for everyone. But what about the next generation of LaPierres?

Jean Pierre had never gone any farther than the surrounding areas of the Bayou Frou-Frous as a young man, and no farther than some of the other plantations located quite near when he was just a boy, so he knew that his children would probably only know this place as well and would, of course, inherit it when Jean Pierre passed on to the after world to be with the ancestors. Perhaps that was the deciding factor; both his and Dolice Marie's children should at least be given the same opportunity to make their own decisions about whether or not they would want the responsibility of becoming the master or the mistress of the former slave plantation. Of course, none of their children would have a choice if he gave up his ownership, and he certainly did not want to appear to be weak in front of Evelina or Dolice Marie, so Jean Pierre decided that today was not the day to be thinking so hard. He, too, decided that he would take care of everything in a day or two. Perhaps he would even ask Dolice Marie for her opinion; after all, she appeared to have matured quite a bit in the more than three years that she had been gone. But for now, he was suddenly brought back to the present day and the situation at hand by Evelina's voice calling in the distance for him to bring the boys back home to eat. Once in the comfort and security of his home, Jean Pierre found himself suddenly overwhelmed with sleep and barely made it to his bed before he could be heard snoring by Evelina and the children, who quietly laughed about it with one another.

Hours later, as Dolice Marie lay sleeping on the cool ground under the big magnolia tree, and Jean Pierre slept soundly in his warm, comfortable bed, a cold breeze suddenly ran chills through their bodies and awakened them both with a start. As if they were being directed toward the same place, Dolice Marie and Jean Pierre began to run toward each other until they collapsed in each other's arms, hugging tightly as if they had not seen each other for decades. Both Dolice Marie and Jean Pierre wept as they realized that they had shared the same dream in which Mama Mozelle, along with her brother, the African, the first Jean Pierre LaPierre, had appeared to each one of them, consoling both of them and encouraging both of them down their own separate path that had been decided for each many years before. Mama Mozelle had given both the answers to their questions and the comfort in knowing that she and all the ancestors would be with both Jean Pierre and Dolice Marie as each pursued their destiny, Dolice Marie with her beloved Mr. Bernard Menard in the places he was waiting to take her, and Jean Pierre with his beloved family at Mon Village.

With their direction and their future course seemingly laid out for both of them, Jean Pierre and Dolice Marie felt weak indeed from the relief of their fears and from the burden of their own stressful thoughts about their future. They gained their strength from each other, holding on to each as they walked back toward Jean Pierre and Evelina's house, where she and the children were waiting for them on the front porch.

Uncle Simon's tender heart was ever present during this portion of the telling of the story as he described how lovingly Evelina placed her arms around her husband. As tiny a woman as she was, Evelina truly seemed the stronger of the two, at least for that moment, drawing from her husband his need for her and giving back her power to hold him up.

Dolice Marie no longer felt that terrible jealousy that she once had for the relationship between her beloved Jean Pierre and his Evelina; now she knew that she wanted the exact kind of relationship with Mr. Bernard Menard that the two were sharing, and just the thought caused Dolice Marie to begin to cry and then laugh and then cry again, a sure sign indeed that her condition was progressing along quite normally. It was a truly wonderful moment, a moment that no one wanted to ever end.

After a wonderful dinner with family and friends, a dinner that seemingly never, ever ended with the chubby little twins, Dolice Marie realized how very tired she was and retired in one of the back bedrooms at Jean Pierre and Evelina's house, directly across the nursery, where Mon Claire and baby Jelee were asleep. Looking in on the two girls, Dolice Marie was again brought to tears as she lovingly kissed each precious girl and then, all at once, Jelee began to squirm. Dolice Marie lifted the infant Jelee from her cradle, holding her gently yet firmly against her even more-voluptuous bosoms as she escaped into her bedroom and laid the precious child down beside her. Dolice Marie whispered softly, "Labelle Jelee," into the infant's ear, and both were fast and peacefully asleep within minutes.

Uncle Simon again teared up as he repeated "Labelle Jelee" to the young boys, while my other wonderful uncles, quite irritated, I might add, encouraged him to just get on with the story.

Enraptured by welcomed surrender to total slumber as she was, Dolice Marie began to dream. There, before her very eyes, was the vision of a precious little girl, one whose hair was parted deeply down the middle and again across the head from ear to ear, each parted area fashioned in the familiar African qwets of her own ancestors.

Dolice Marie began to squirm uncomfortably in the bed as she struggled to clearly see the precious child's face, but the entire oval area of the face was engulfed in pure, brilliant light. Why, it seemed that the more she struggled, the more brilliant the light became, until she finally succumbed to the fact that perhaps she was only permitted to know the gender of the precious child and not its features. As she began to relax again, she heard the tender voice of Mama Mozelle in her heart whispering to her, "You will fill her with all that she will need to know, and then you will see her clearly with little regard for her features."

Somewhere along the night, as she drifted between deep slumber and the drifting between the two worlds, Dolice Marie could be heard calling her sweet little daughter by name, Monique Aimee Elizabeth LaPierre-Menard. *Monique Aimee* in honor and to celebrate the only culture that she was truly familiar with, the culture of the slave master who had named her and her beloved family members, and *Elizabeth* in honor and to celebrate Mr. Bernard Menard's culture, the only other name she had ever heard that resembled that of his culture.

Jean Pierre and Evelina ran into the room, where they found Jelee lying safely beside Dolice Marie while looking up at her with those beautiful big eyes, while their rest had been disturbed from the conversation Dolice Marie was having with no one in sight. Wiping the sleep from her eyes and smiling sweetly, Dolice Marie welcomed the early morning, Jean Pierre, and Evelina and questioned why everyone was awake so early. Realizing that Dolice Marie was just having a very graphic dream, Evelina lifted Jelee from the bed and assured Dolice Marie that the sweet child was probably ready to nurse anyway.

"The baby is a girl," Dolice Marie said shyly to Jean Pierre and Evelina, "a mademoiselle."

There was silence for a moment as Evelina realized that Dolice Marie was speaking of herself, that she was indeed carrying a child, and somehow knew that it would be a precious little girl. And before either Jean Pierre or Evelina could ask the question, Dolice Marie proudly told them that it had been in a dream that Mama Mozelle told her that the cherished child inside her womb was truly a girl.

Well, you can just imagine the joy that filled the house at that very moment, joy that brought tears again, laughter, and just as Dolice Marie stood up from the bed to again embrace Jean Pierre and Evelina, she was again troubled by the bubbling of the demon morning sickness. Evelina could be heard as she assisted Dolice Marie to the outhouse. "Yeah, chère, precious baby girls make you have the morning sickness much more than the boys do. Ask me, child, I know!"

My sweet uncles laughed themselves silly as they mocked our dear ancestor Evelina, but she indeed knew all about childbearing since she already had given birth to four precious children, and my own dear grandfather, Jean Pierre, had not even been born yet!

Once Dolice Marie began to feel a little better, she decided to go for a walk around the grounds of Mon Village, a visit to Mama Mozelle's house that would now be just an empty house without her. All her belongings would stay just as they were for now, until Jean Pierre and Dolice Marie could decide upon just what to do with that sweet cottage that Mama Mozelle had taken so much time to make sure was decorated exactly the way she wanted. Dolice Marie found it hard to even be on her porch without seeing her going about her daily routine with so many of the children of Mon Village surrounding her while she taught them the kinds of things that they would never forget.

When Dolice Marie finally tore herself away from Mama Mozelle's house, she began to walk toward the big house to visit Annabelle and the ladies, if they were not too busy to share a hello. Stepping upon the large porch, Dolice Marie noticed something hanging across the back of Mama Mozelle's favorite rocking chair, the chair from where she had mourned Dolice Marie's leaving, the chair from where she had made so many of the decisions that kept Mon Village thriving as it was even at that time.

As Dolice Marie neared the chair, she realized that it was a beautiful quilt, one that had been created with odds and ends from the many years that had already gone by. There were pieces of scrap from Dolice Marie's first dresses and Jean Pierre's first pants; there were even pieces familiar to Dolice Marie that had come from Madam

Frou-Frous's and Master Philippe's closet. As she searched the quilt with her eyes filling with tears, she also noticed pieces of scrap from the old African and patches of scrap made from Jean Pierre and Evelina's clothing when they jumped the broom, as well as the beautiful fabric that Mama Mozelle had to create clothing for Mon Claire and the chubby little twins, Petois and Pecous. Dolice Marie held the quilt close to her, smelling the fragrance of her Mama Mozelle and fully knowing that she had indeed created this masterpiece of their lives for her, a family treasure that would be handed down to her child and for generations to come.

It was only then that Dolice Marie realized that she somehow needed to send a message to Mr. Bernard Menard to let him know what had happened while she had been away, and to Angeline and to Madam BB, letting then know when she would be coming home. As she approached the door to the big house, Dolice Marie suddenly turned away and began to walk back toward Jean Pierre and Evelina's house. She was certain that she did not care to run into any of her former customers, nor did she feel comfortable being in Annabelle's territory now. After all, all this would now be Jean Pierre's responsibility as Mama Mozelle and the ancestors had explained to both of them in the dream. Dolice Marie felt relieved and clung even tighter to the quilt as she turned again to descend the stairs of the big house in her quest to join Jean Pierre and Evelina at their home to get a message to the great city of New Orleans. Jubil suggested that Dolice Marie send a telegraph message to Mr. Bernard Menard, Angeline, and Miss BB in the great city of New Orleans. He explained how he had seen proper Southern white people sending these kinds of messages while he was at the general store, getting supplies for Mon Village, and contemplated that it had to be easy enough for them to do. In fact, Jubil was more than happy to volunteer to go to the general store and ask the man to send Dolice Marie's message.

Jubil explained that he had seen proper Southern white people just giving their messages to the man behind iron bars in the general store who did something with that telegraph machine that evidently made the message go where it was supposed to go. Dolice Marie was fascinated and agreed that the telegraph machine sounded like the very best idea, and thus began a lengthy message for Jubil to take with him, so lengthy, in fact, that the impatient Jubil threw up his hands and began to walk way. Well, by now every one of the young boys had figured out that Dolice Marie was still a force to be reckoned with, and before Jubil could take another step, Dolice Marie had poor Jubil by his collar, as she did when they were just precious little children, bringing him down to his knees as she twisted his ear.

"You just tell your old telegraph man that I said to tell Miss BB in the great city of New Orleans that I will be home in two weeks on the afternoon train to the Atchafalaya River station and that I would be most grateful if Obadiah could pick me up there. I would also be obliged if she would tell her niece, Angeline, as well as Mr. Bernard Menard that I am just fine and will see them in two weeks. Now," Dolice Marie said as she released Jubil's ear and began to iron his shirt with her hand, "you just get going before I throw you out there with those mangy old dogs in the fields!"

As serious as the conversation and the threat to Jubil's being had momentarily been, Dolice Marie and Jubil laughed so loud and so hard that the tears began to fall from both of their eyes.

It would not be too terribly long at all before the telegraph message reached Miss BB in the great city of New Orleans, alleviating the worry that she had for her delightful Dolice Marie since she had escaped from everyone by train to visit her family and friends at Mon Village. Miss BB sat back in her comfortable chair on the back screened-in porch, with her babies FiFi and GiGi on the floor beside her, fanning herself in sheer delight that Dolice Marie would be coming home soon. Obadiah was relieved as well, and comforted Miss BB and himself with a lovely shot glass filled with the smooth, delicious Kentucky bourbon that Mr. Samuels had been all too gracious as to send several bottles to her for her personal use as well as to entertain her guests at the grande bal masqué, by his messenger Mr. Monte Leonard. Madam BB and Obadiah clicked their glasses in a toast, quickly downed the enchanting drink, and smiled as she read through her evening newspaper, wondering if she had indeed made the headlines again, and he went about the duty of informing Angeline that Dolice Marie would indeed be home soon.

Dear God, Uncle Simon would never fail to tear up once again, to the despair of my other sweet uncles, as he prepared himself to begin to describe what happened next. Anyone would certainly think that by now Uncle Simon would have surely expressed all the emotion he had, particularly since he had remembered this portion of the family story over and over and over, but I declare, it never failed!

It seems that while Dolice Marie was on her visit to Mon Village with her family and friends, Mr. Bernard Menard had taken the opportunity to visit his own family in Toronto before going to the great city of New York to welcome a brand-new shipment of simply divine imports and exports from Europe that were being delivered by ship to his own import-export company. Unfortunately, Madam BB and Angeline were unsure as to where the charming gentleman might be at the time that Miss BB had received the message from Dolice Marie, so neither was sure as to where to even begin trying to reach him with the news.

In the meantime, Dolice Marie, Jean Pierre, and his family were enjoying the time that they were spending together. During the day, Dolice Marie could be found chasing after Jean Pierre and Jubil as she did when they were all children, laughing and frolicking through the gardens and the fields until Mama Mozelle could be heard telling them that it was time to come in. There was no Mama Mozelle to yell for them, but Evelina was indeed capable of sending her voice far enough for the three of them to hear.

In the evenings, Dolice Marie would spend her time just being with the children, either in the nursery or on the front porch of Jean Pierre and Evelina's house. Mon Claire was a very active child who never seemed to run out of energy, always wanting to spend her time with Jubil and his horses. Jubil, of course, did not mind the child being with him at all; besides, she was the first child of his best friend, Jean Pierre, and he protected her as if she were his own. Mon Claire could be found anywhere in the house or on the porch sound asleep, where she had just dropped wherever she was from sheer exhaustion.

Now the chubby little twins, Petois and Pecous, never seemed to leave the dinner table—that is, unless Jean Pierre just insisted that they accompany him to tend to men's work. On the other hand,

Evelina thought that her sweet baby boys' chubby little hands and feet were just so cute. Even in their youth, Petois and Pecous enjoyed mixing foods together and spent more time with Evelina, watching her prepare meals, than Mon Claire ever would.

But Dolice Marie's favorite of her nieces and nephews, if we are ever permitted to have favorites in the family, was most certainly Jelee, the precious child that she had named Labelle Jelee. Evelina noticed how the sweet infant child's beautiful big eyes would follow Dolice Marie all around the house and how she would cry when Dolice Marie was out of her sight.

One particular evening after dinner, while Dolice Marie, Jean Pierre, Evelina, Jubil, and Miss Sylvia were resting in the rocking chairs on the front porch, Evelina suddenly remembered something that her own mother had said to her when she was carrying the chubby little twins.

It seemed as though Mon Claire suddenly wanted nothing to do with her own mother the entire time she was with child. Only Jean Pierre could fix her food, take her to the outhouse, or put her to bed without having to hear the child scream and yell. Why, Evelina was so upset, believing that her firstborn just had no more love for her or desire to be with her own mother that she simply cried herself silly—that is, until her mother predicted that she was indeed carrying a boy. Evelina's mother explained to her that when a woman is carrying a precious baby boy, little girls want nothing to do with them, just as Mon Claire wanted nothing to do with Evelina when she was carrying the chubby little twins, and vice versa. Because Jelee was so attached to Dolice Marie at such a tender age, Evelina was absolutely convinced that the child growing inside Dolice Marie's womb was indeed a precious little girl. Well, the old wives' tale did make a lot of sense since the chubby little twins had truly been keeping their distance from their aunt Dolice Marie.

On several occasions, Dolice Marie found herself facing the direction of the big house but still could not force herself to enter. Annabelle was certainly doing an excellent job; so many customers were coming in and out that the doors were constantly swinging one direction and swinging the other direction, if you know what I mean. It would just be too sorrowful and painful for her to visit the big house without Mama Mozelle sitting there on the porch as she always was, looking out for everyone inside and outside.

Still in the great city of New Orleans, there was no word from or about Mr. Bernard Menard. Miss BB and Angeline were so afraid that he and Dolice Marie would again be apart for another long period, and Miss BB and Angeline knew how uncomfortable that situation would be for the both of them. Word had been sent to Toronto and the great city of New York by telegraph, but no word had yet been returned. Even Hemi de Marquis volunteered to set out with some of the trappers in his company to search for him, but Angeline refused to be away from him again, even for her best friend and confidante.

As the time came closer for Dolice Marie to return to her business and her new life in the great city of New Orleans, she began to despair and became indeed melancholy. How long would it be before she would be back with her beloved Jean Pierre and his wonderful family? The tears began to swell inside as Dolice Marie began to gather her things together to pack into the train cases, all but the beautiful quilt that she knew Mama Mozelle had left for her, embracing it as if the quilt were indeed her own mother.

As she stood in the room in Jean Pierre and Evelina's house, Dolice Marie began to hear the faint sounds of music, the kind of music that was played during a celebration with fiddles, drums, violins, and the washboard with spoons. It was a La La, and surely it had to be a La La in honor of her own self.

Dolice Marie ran outside the house and toward the music, smiling as she saw her family and friends coming together in the middle of the residential area, the area where the La Las had been held all her life. There was food everywhere, music coming from everywhere, and all the people she had known all her life. Yes, this was her going-away party, and she was the center of attention, that place where Dolice Marie loved to be.

Miss Sylvia had prepared plenty of freshly crushed mint for the corn liquor concoction, served in silver cups, of course, that had truly become a special commodity at Mon Village. The residents of Mon

Village enjoyed their La La until the very dark of night, when everyone said their goodbyes to Dolice Marie. It was extremely difficult for anyone to hold back the tears while hugs were shared and special gifts were given to the vixenly little girl that had indeed grown up, but not so much as not to miss her home and these wonderful people. With her arms filled with wonderful remembrances, Dolice Marie solemnly walked back to the house with Jean Pierre and his family.

Uncle Simon had to pause several times during this portion of the story to blow his nose, in such a manly sort of manner, if you can imagine, tears flowing freely down his cheeks. My other sweet uncles would offer to complete the telling of Dolice Marie's departure from Mon Village, but Uncle Simon would shoo them away with his hand, compose himself, and dig right back in.

Their last night together was indeed the saddest time for Dolice Marie and Jean Pierre as they walked through Mon Village, discussing the different directions that their lives were now going to take. Since having discovered the telegraph machine, Dolice Marie promised to stay in touch with Jean Pierre, and hopefully one day he and Evelina and the children could plan to visit her in the great city of New Orleans.

Near the end of the evening on that last night, Dolice Marie and Jean Pierre made their round to Mama Del's house for Dolice Marie's farewell to that special person in both of their lives, bringing along with them another jug of the mint with corn liquor concoction that she enjoyed so very much. Mama Del was always quite happy to see the both of them smiling in that toothless manner that always seemed to cheer the two up, no matter what the problem might have been. Mama Del placed her hand upon Dolice Marie's stomach and smiled again, acknowledging that precious little baby who was most certainly smiling back at her from the womb.

The walk back to Jean Pierre and Evelina's house was one with great somber and sadness as Jean Pierre and Dolice Marie allowed their tears to flow freely as they remembered all the good times and the not-so-good times that they had shared together. They agreed to stay in touch this time and planned to visit each other often, not only Dolice Marie corning home to Mon Village, but also Jean Pierre considering bringing his family to New Orleans.

The night passed by quickly, and the morning light reminded Dolice Marie that today was the day that she must leave home again and return to her new life. Had she slept at all during the night? Well, who would under such circumstances? The goodbyes were painful, as everyone would expect from a family that truly loved one another as this one did, and truly still does. Dolice Marie was overwhelmed with the gifts from her loved ones, especially the quilt made from Mama Mozelle's own hands and a basket filled with beautiful silver cups made from her own Jean Pierre's hands.

It was decided that Jubil alone would drive Dolice Marie in the wagon to the Atchafalaya River train station, where they would say goodbye. Tears were just everywhere, in the past and in the present, as Uncle Simon fought hard not to shed any further tears as he continued to describe the solemn goodbye. I do remember times when more than just Uncle Simon would be crying, but of course, no one else would ever admit it.

Dolice Marie cried all the way to the Atchafalaya River station, catching her tears with one of Mama Mozelle's handkerchiefs, which she had found when she and Jean Pierre were gathering her things together in her home. Jubil was simply without words to comfort Dolice Marie, so he continued his drive without saying more than "That's it, chère, just get it all out. You'll feel better!"

When the train made the final curve toward the Atchafalaya River station, Dolice Marie, still crying, asked Jubil to leave before her so that she could see him going back toward Mon Village. She was truly in no mood to play games with the proper Southern white people there at the station, standing back away from them but ready at a moment's notice to show her other side should the need arise. Why, the story goes that Dolice Marie simply went back to the train car reserved for the people of color. (Although it was still the car before the very last car, where the seats were padded and much cleaner than the last car had been.) It was truly the saddest portion of our family history. Even the mighty Mississippi had lost its special effect on Dolice Marie, and before long, she found herself fast asleep with her head against the window of the huge iron monster.

Dolice Marie was awakened by the engineer of the huge train, who was yelling out the next stop, the great city of New Orleans. There was no real excitement as it had been the very first time she had made this journey as she wiped her face with the handkerchief and prepared herself and her train cases to get off the train, adjusting her hat and trying to adjust her attitude before she met with Obadiah, who would take her home to the New Orleans House. She was beginning to become truly anxious to see Miss BB and, of course, her best friend and confidante, Angeline, but most of all, she was beginning to become extremely excited about eventually seeing Mr. Bernard Menard.

As Dolice Marie stumbled down the stairs of the train, trying desperately to carry all that she had with her, she took notice of Obadiah descending from the seat of Miss BB's buggy a few yards away, to assist her with her belongings. She smiled broadly as she began to walk toward him when, suddenly, without any mind at all, Mr. Bernard Menard jumped out of the back of the buggy, tipped his hat, and smiled at her. She, of course, swooned into a very ladylike faint, falling to the ground before he could catch her. When she awakened moments later in the buggy, comfortable in Mr. Bernard Menard's arms, she swooned again as he kissed her gently on her lips.

It was always at this portion of the telling of the family stories on the first day of our family reunion that one of the women, either my own sweet mama or one of my aunts, either from the big house or the outside kitchen, would begin to call out to my sweet uncles that it was indeed time for the young boys to rest. There was always their fussing that would demand the men to leave the young boys alone with their silly stories so that they could all go to bed, while my sweet uncles simply laughed themselves silly one more time.

There would be much for the young boys to think about in their private dreams as they each contemplated what they had heard this first day from the old storytellers at our family reunion and what they might hear tomorrow. It was always fun to watch as the storytellers found themselves being urged to go to bed themselves by the women of the family, who had just had enough for the day. And even though I have heard the stories time and again, I find myself being just as excited and anxious to hear what the next uncle would have to say tomorrow. But for now, I think I, too, will join the family as we rest up for the remainder of the family history.

    Good night, Miss Gracie!

Chapter 9

Miss Gracie Buckhalter, fine writer that she is, had agreed the night before to meet with me in the kitchen of the big house for some stimulating Louisiana coffee and Cook's finest beignets. And that we did, at 6:00 a.m., both ready to get back to the work of discussing my family's fascinating stories.

It is indeed an obvious fact that the LaPierre family could never boast of any famous, beloved Civil War heroes on our family tree, no General Beauregard, no Rhett Butler or Scarlett O'Hara, but we truly had our share of infamous proper Southern white people in the bloodline, many who did not know it, those who tried to ignore it, and most assuredly, those who took advantage of it in more ways than one. If you know what I mean!

The former Master and Mistress LaPierre, Philippe and Frou-Frous, never did find their way back to Mon Village, although rumors still made their way back to the residents like the abundance of mint growing wild in the flower gardens. Jubil always overheard some story about the two while he went about his duties in the small town near the Atchafalaya River, whether he was listening for them or just overheating them. If Jubil knew the truth concerning the LaPierre disappearance or not, that information stayed tucked away in his memory, and not a word was ever spoken by him or to him regarding such information.

Well, wherever the two of them were truly remained a mystery to the locals throughout the years that passed since their delightful disappearance, and eventually, the LaPierres became infamous antiheroes whose legacy was captured by cult followings that had their own stories about them. Of course, these stories always had an eerie twist to them, an eerie twist that kept everyone interested, speculating, while Mama Del, the ever-present overseer of Mon Village, just laughed hysterically. One would certainly think that the spiritual matriarch of the family might have had something to do with their disappearance, would one not?

My uncle Simon always crossed his knee with his other leg before he proudly proclaimed to the young boys that Mama Del had made sure that no matter what, those two would never, ever set foot on Mon Village soil ever again.

My other dear, sweet uncles laughed fervently while slapping their own knee in amusement while the young boys pondered the true meaning of it all.

I must admit that I could feel myself becoming just a little nostalgic when discussing day 2 with Miss Gracie Buckhalter, the stories told on the Saturdays of our family reunions. Fridays were always such a short time together, a time when everyone was either driving their cars to Mon Village from some distant place or just opening the doors to their homes right here in the residential area for incoming family members. There always seemed to be only time for a quick kiss on the jaw, a hug, and the simple act of settling in for the fun and nostalgia of what the next two days would surely bring.

Of course, Fridays brought the family together for the evening dinner and the commencement of the traditional telling of the family stories as offered by my sweet uncles Gaston, Dominick, and Simon to the young boys who were being initiated into LaPierre manhood. Oh, how I loved listening to the family stories as they were being shared by my precious uncles, my grandfather's flock, that is, my own daddy's older brothers, with whom I have spent my lifetime, and oh, how we have watched one another grow older! I have often thought what it must have been like while they themselves were being initiated by my great-granddaddy's flock, their own sweet uncles who have gone on now to meet the great and wise ancestors in the other world.

And then there was Sunday. Sunday always began in solemnity, as it was the day that the entire family devoted itself to the memory of our loved ones with a religious ceremony that brought tears to everyone's eyes.

Sunday afternoon was the time that everyone toasted the spirits of those long gone with plenty of spirits of their own, if you know what I mean!

I explained to Miss Gracie Buckhalter as we enjoyed yet another one of Cook's delicious and most assuredly fattening beignets that day 2 of our family reunions always seemed to begin with that perpetual threat of a Southern rainstorm, causing just about everyone from wherever they were to begin to peer toward the heavens, all the while sending their prayers toward heaven that the sky would not open and send a torrential downpour on the activities of the members of the LaPierre-Menard family. Strange as it may seem, however, I can truly say that in all those years of my youth, as I peered toward the heavens with my own anticipation, I do not recall a single time that the threat ever became a reality.

When it was finally agreed upon by at least the majority of the adults that the day would indeed be dry, the rhythmic sounds of zydeco music would begin, the coals would be lit on the pits for some fine-tasting barbecue, crawfish would be prepared for the boiling, fresh fish would be prepared for the frying, while conversations and family laughter could again be heard throughout Mon Village.

Even the multitude of egrets that roamed the bayous considered themselves welcomed and walked throughout Mon Village as if they, too, were visiting with their family and ancestors.

My family was always excited about touring the ever-growing and ever-changing grounds of Mon Village, walking in the footsteps where our beloved ancestors had once walked, worked, and created this wondrous place under the huge magnolia trees. Every single person seemed to have their own personal memory, perhaps a favorite area of the vastness of the former slave plantation that brought a sort of ghostly memory, a vision that they eagerly shared with everyone else. One person's memory would become another person's memory during future reunions, assuring the fact that our family was truly the very essence of what these family reunions were all about.

It would be sometime during this second day of the reunion that the women of the LaPierre-Menard family found themselves gathering in one side of the huge outdoor kitchen to begin their beauty ritual in preparation for the Sunday service and the remembrance of those that had passed on into the other world to meet the ancestors. It was not unusual for everyone to hear their laughter rising every once in a while, the whole time the men just dismissed their antics as ridiculous, but all the while truly hoping that the women's conversations were not being shared about any of them.

I do believe that I had heard in one of the stories that this very kitchen was where the very first manufacturing company had been operated, the place where the son of the very first Jean Pierre LaPierre had created his beautiful silver cups for the notorious mistress Madam Frou-Frous.

And just as I did so long ago, and indeed my ancestors before me and the girls of today still do, I did try to spy on my mother and my sweet aunts as they gathered together with their hair, nail, and body paraphernalia to share with one another their individual beauty secrets, cackling and gossiping all the while under the warm Louisiana breeze being generated by several electric box fans during the modern days. After making my own choice to hear the family stories as they were being told by my sweet uncles, it became a simple matter of fact that my place and my preference was without question with the men of the family, so the usual response from my female relatives when they would catch me sneaking about their womanly business was always "Shoo, girl!"

My sweet aunties Cecile and Sophia (nicknamed Cee Cee and Fee Fee), fraternal twins who truly looked absolutely nothing alike, were nestled in the chronology of my grandfather's children between my uncles Simon and Clovis. Day 1 of our reunions, which was already introduced, was always monopolized by the antics of my older uncles, Gaston and Dominique, followed by the first portion of my uncle Simon's portion of the telling of the family stories. My sweet aunties were not the least bit offended that they had been eliminated from that perfect order of storytellers, nor were their feelings hurt that they were not invited to join in the listening to the family stories, but they had their own stories that they were content in sharing, if only with one another.

Both Aunt Cecile and Aunt Sophia married men who lived and worked on Mon Village, one a LaPierre from the order of the LaPierre plantation and master ownership during the infamous slave days, and the other a Castille, an offspring of one of those big, burly men whose family members had chosen to join the LaPierre family when freedom came their way.

Aunt Cee Cee's husband, Uncle Dobb, worked very hard in the family silversmith business, following in my great-granddaddy's footsteps, which was where he was working when the two of them fell in love.

Uncle Dobb was perhaps five or more years older than Aunt Cee Cee and would place himself in her path as she was returning home from school, just to say hello. When she finally became of age, Uncle Dobb gave my granddaddy, Jean Pierre, the required respect of asking for Aunt Cee Cee's hand in marriage but was almost rejected due to his mistake in preparing for the event with a full bottle of corn liquor, flavored, of course, with the ever-popular, and ever-present, mint.

Aunt Fee Fee's husband, on the other hand, worked as a carpenter on Mon Village, building new houses in the residential area and new shops in the business area and providing renovations to both whenever necessary, all being a seemingly ongoing job. He name was Tomas, and his family carried the name Castille from their former life, just like Mama Mozelle's name, as their middle name after choosing to become LaPierres.

Uncle Tomas was a very quiet man with a deep love for Aunt Fee Fee and had asked for her hand in marriage several years after Aunt Cee Cee and Uncle Dobb had married. Theirs was a long romance that was calmly and clearly precipitated by Aunt Fee Fee as she switched herself in front of him as he was going about his workday, flexing his muscles as he lifted a panel of wood or hammered a nail to secure it. I do declare that Aunt Fee Fee was "as fast as hell," as the old people might say about her, if you will excuse my French, presenting herself as a true LaPierre woman, and just as so many men before him, Uncle Tomas became caught up in her LaPierre mystique.

During the building of the great railways, the great World Wars, and the other great events when all the men, both men of color and those who were white, had gone off to find work or fight the enemy overseas, my dear aunts did their part here at home by providing the brilliance of Madam C. J. Walker's ingenuity for black hair by pressing it with a hot comb and creating fashionable curls, as well as showing women how to enhance their own natural beauty with voluptuous red lips and matching red fingernails and toenails.

Even though employment outside the proper Southern white people's homes for women of color was rare in those days, my aunts still believed, as Madam C. J. Walker did, that every woman should look and feel her very best even if her duties were just working premises, that is, cleaning houses, ironing clothes, or raising children for proper Southern white people.

My aunts' services became so popular, and, indeed, quite necessary, for so many Southern women of color there at Mon Village and at the surrounding former plantations that it eventually became necessary for them to open a special place, all their own, for these women to meet. Their tiny beauty shop became a refuge for the Southern women of color, a place where they could find a sense of pride and respectability while the tiny financial recompense they provided in return kept my sweet aunts from the chores of the Southern white people's homes.

It was because of these two women that the women of the family would predictably find that spot during the family reunions, where they could pursue that same mission while catching up on the latest gossip, which seemed to get louder and louder, and, I might add, all at the same time. Every time they were together. I do declare! I do believe that is the exact reason the women of my family begin all their conversations quite loudly in an attempt to get their personal point across before everyone else joins in with theirs.

Aunt Cee Cee, Aunt Fee Fee, and Uncle Clovis were the last children born to the union between my dear grandfather, Jean Pierre, and my first grandmother, God rest her beloved soul, Ma-Elsie, as she was called. Sweet thing went on to meet the ancestors after being stung repeatedly by a swarm of bees that chased her all around the gardens, followed by my granddaddy and a long line of residents who were trying desperately to catch her before the bees caught her. Unfortunately, the bees finally caught her before they did. Some say the trouble began with her bonnet, perhaps the color, the texture, or even the smell of it that had attracted the bees, but whatever it was, our dear Ma-Elsie truly did die with a bee in her bonnet.

Yes, my granddaddy did marry again. LaPierre men were never known to stay alone for very long. In fact, it was shortly after meeting my own beloved grandmother, Momo-Belle, who had captured his heart when she stopped by to console him, carrying a steaming hot pot of gumbo after reading Ma-Elsie's obituary in the newspaper, that my granddaddy felt the notion to become one with someone else. Their union produced my sweet uncles Michele, Rene, Alexandre (after whom I am named), and my own dear daddy, Jean Pierre, of course.

These wonderful family reunions provided all of them the perfect opportunity for everyone to be together again, smiling and clowning around underneath those big magnolia trees as if they were all still children themselves. Right here on the Bayou Frou-Frous.

My granddaddy and Momo-Belle also had one daughter, who might have been recognized as the tenth son of the combined children of the LaPierre-Menard grandparents, which I have truly never understood, my dear sweet aunt Marie.

Aunt Marie, the youngest of all of my grandparents' children, was nicknamed Aimee because of her sweet, pleasing way of asking my granddaddy to "pick up ah-me," "hold ah-me," or carry ah-me." When Aunt Marie, or Aunt Aimee, was twelve or so, she announced to the family that she was not to be known as Marie any longer; in fact, she stated that she was to be known as Ingrid and assured everyone that her real parents were from Sweden. Well, everybody laughed and simply contended that the poor child was quite creative, to say the very least.

During her midteens, Aunt Aimee began to answer only when she was addressed as Consuela, whom she claimed was from a small town in South America and incapable of speaking any English at all—that is, with the exception of an occasional *yes* or *no*.

Of course, my grandparents were now beginning to weather a bit and were quite anxious for Aunt Aimee to find herself. But it would be when Aunt Aimee announced that she was truly a gambling man from the great state of Mississippi whose name was Charlie Watson, on the run from the law after getting caught cheating during a high-spirited game of poker, I might add, that my grandparents finally realized that Aunt Aimee or Aunt Marie was truly not herself.

When she was ultimately diagnosed with multiple personality disorder, my family agreed that the family history would state that my grandparents did indeed have a daughter named Marie.

Marie, on the other hand, was given a limb all to herself on the family tree, a limb that she had undeniably been out on for some time, anyway, to share with those personalities of herself that she had introduced to the family throughout the years—oh, and for their ancestors as well, I might add.

One story has it that Aunt Marie moved into one of the sweet houses in the residential area at Mon Village and had lived quite happily for a very long time. Some say she married a drifter and moved to parts unknown to any of the family, while others say that she married one of her own personalities and could often be seen actually beating herself up while having what could have been two people engaged in a brutal conversation. *Tsk! Tsk!* Nonetheless, the entire family was truly content just knowing that Aunt Marie was, at the very least, never alone.

My grandparents happily spent the remainder of their lives together here at Mon Village on the Bayou Frou-Frous just tending to the family businesses until they passed on into the other world. They are buried right here in the family cemetery with Ma-Elsie and Momo-Belle, on either side of my dear granddaddy, if you can just imagine, as the cemetery now began to consume more space than the living quarters.

Well, I have truly gotten ahead of myself by reminiscing about that portion of the family that I grew up knowing, and I truly do apologize for running on and on.

Once everyone had finally meandered to his or her designated place under the big magnolia trees at Mon Village, the traditional telling of the family stories would commence again. It was not uncommon to find one or more of my sweet uncles helping a precious little child, perhaps a great-grandchild or a second- or third-generation niece or nephew, to climb upon a comfortable knee. I must admit, I still feel somewhat jealous that I am far too grown now to take my own familiar spot on a knee, where I had often heard the stories.

Uncle Simon always opened the second day of the reunion stories directly after the family breakfast by asking the young boys and my other wonderful uncles to join hands as he led them in prayer. Prayer was probably the very last spark of civilization that came to the Bayou Frou-Frous on its own, and strangely enough, it would be my dear great-great-granddaddy's firstborn child, our beloved Mon Claire, that would make truly monumental changes to Mon Village on behalf of prayer. But again, that story is still yet to be told.

Now, where were we? Oh, yes! Back to the ancestors…

Chapter 10

IT WAS APPROXIMATELY 1874 or 1875, and the flower garden of residents at Mon Village, the former slaves of the LaPierre Plantation, and those from several other surrounding plantations that had chosen to become LaPierres when freedom came found themselves living quite prosperously. Mon Village had become a real city all to itself with a peaceful residential area and a thriving business district that was being created by the needs of the many and the talents of the few, a city all to itself, complete with the pleasures of the big house. If you know what I mean!

Jean Pierre had finally accepted his destiny as the master of it all, gently and lovingly managing the great dynasty with the pride of a king with his beautiful queen, Evelina, and their children, along with great expectations for the child growing quickly inside Evelina's womb.

Jean Pierre was indeed ready for this child's birth, having already learned from the previous births that he had to be ready at a moment's notice to take flight toward the flower gardens at Evelina's first whimper of labor. I do declare, there must have been a path dug deep by his previous flights from their house directly to the gardens as he escaped Evelina's threats, and always with Jubil mightily leading the way.

Now, I do recollect that my sweet uncle Simon had ended the Friday night's traditional telling of the family stories to all the young boys by describing how my naughty, petite ancestor Dolice

Marie LaPierre had swooned into a genteel faint at the sight of her beloved Mr. Bernard Menard at the Atchafalaya River train station upon returning from her visit with her family here on the Bayou Frou-Frous.

Upon finally awakening in her own bed with Angeline, Miss BB, cuddling GiGi and FiFi, Obadiah, as well as Mr. Bernard Menard all standing over her, Dolice Marie sat up straight after realizing where she was, began to sweat profusely, burped loudly—and quite unladylike, I might add—and then proceeded to resume her vigil of morning, noon, and evening sickness in response to her delicate condition, which, at that time, was still unknown to any of them, or so she thought.

The ladies of the New Orleans House peeped in and out of the master bedroom, paying their respect to Mademoiselle Dolice Marie upon her return and offering their assistance before they quickly continued on with their daily duties, indeed. Dolice Marie showed her appreciation to each one by extending her hand in pretense that she might have some malady that they could "catch" and render them incapacitated and therefore perhaps causing the New Orleans House to lose unnecessary money. Of course, each one was eager to please the Mademoiselle Dolice Marie and blew kisses to her from a distance as they backed out of the room.

Angeline gasped, almost regurgitating at the sight that lay there on the plump comforter that covered the big bed and then ran for a cold towel. Mr. Bernard Menard yelped and then ran frantically for a spittoon while the dear Miss BB and Obadiah, quite cool and unequivocally still in their places, I might add, turned ever so slightly to face each other with a smirk and an upward-raised brow that said quite convincingly to each other that the lady could possibly be, as they both agreed, with child.

It was obvious to Dolice Marie, too, that the two of them were, at the very least, considering the real reason she had been so sick, and therefore she lifted herself up on her elbows, glaring at them both with a look that seemed to say, and quite pathetically, I might add, "Shhhhh! Please do not say anything yet!"

When quite convinced that she could indeed trust her two friends, Dolice Marie fell backward on her bed, drained of all her energy.

Angeline appeared first with one of the employees of the New Orleans House that began quickly cleaning the debris on the bed while Angeline approached with a damp washcloth to wipe poor Dolice Marie's face, all the while whispering in her ear how very sorry she was that her dear best friend had come home with such a malady. As Angeline continued her sweet care for Dolice Marie, she suddenly backed away, eyes fixed on Dolice Marie, her mouth dropped wide open, quivering as she dropped the washcloth on the bed. Just as she was about to bring out the whole truth, and certainly nothing but the truth, for all to hear, Miss BB quickly grabbed her by the shoulders, covered her mouth with a well-dressed, lace-covered hand, and began to escort her out of the room at the exact moment that Mr. Bernard Menard began to reenter the room lovingly carrying a spittoon, which Dolice Marie politely excused herself for using and then began to cry.

Obadiah, along with one of the employees of the New Orleans House, excused himself to join the ladies in the kitchen of the New Orleans House as the loving man with the long red hair knelt beside Dolice Marie's bed and gently stroked her forehead. Mr. Bernard Menard comforted her with a soft kiss upon her cheek, and she responded by reaching toward his cheek with her own lips, but reached farther, toward his ear. After a moment or two, Mr. Bernard Menard's face turned as red as his hair, and then as white as a ghost, and then was highlighted by a beaming smile as bright as a full moon on a star-filled night. Once again the gentle man gathered Dolice Marie into his arms and embraced her as if she would surely slip away from him, and within just a few more moments, Dolice Marie began to snore so loudly that the kind gentleman felt it would indeed be quite proper now to move into the kitchen with Angeline, Obadiah, and Miss BB while leaving Dolice Marie alone with her…*asthma*!

Miss BB was quietly brewing tea when Mr. Bernard Menard joined her, Angeline, and Obadiah in the kitchen of the New Orleans House, quietly slipping onto one of the padded chairs around the kitchen table. No one spoke for several minutes as each prepared his or her own cup of tea to his or her own special taste requirements, and with the utmost politeness toward one another.

The room was completely silent for an amount of time that soon became awkward for everyone, and just at the very moment that Angeline was about to speak, Mr. Bernard Menard stood abruptly and, while running his fingers through his long red hair, smiled broadly, took a deep breath, and said, "I am so overwhelmed with joy and great anticipation, my dear friends, that I can hardly contain myself!"

Mr. Bernard Menard began to walk around the table with a colossal and glowing grin upon his face as everyone's eyes followed his every step while he actually almost inspired to dance a jig.

"The lovely Mademoiselle Dolice Marie has done an extraordinary thing, a most remarkable thing," he whispered as he leaned over the table and scanned their eyes while searching for some sort of response, seemingly hypnotizing his small audience.

"She has conceived a child…she has conceived *my* child!" he shouted, standing straight up, with his hands held high in the air.

Obadiah took a big gulp of his tea while silence again filled the room as everyone attempted a smile. At this time, it was Miss BB who attempted to make a comment just as Mr. Bernard Menard began again to fill the room with his professions of joy.

"I love her!" he retorted with hands flying in the air. "Yes! I absolutely adore her! I want to marry her!"

All eyes were on the dashing Mr. Bernard Menard as he continued his parade throughout the kitchen of the New Orleans House, both his actions and verbiage being so loud that he awakened the sleeping Dolice Marie, who suddenly appeared in the doorway with the appearance of a small waif from the great streets of the great city of New Orleans. Mr. Bernard Menard rushed to her assistance as Dolice Marie attempted to seat herself in one of the chairs around the kitchen table, maneuvering her with a most delicate of touches, as if she were a fragile gem.

Uncle Simon always asked the young boys if any of them thought that Dolice Marie had overheard Mr. Bernard Menard as he was carrying on about his love for her while she was standing at the door to the kitchen of the New Orleans House, if it was then and there that he proposed marriage. If so, what was her answer? And the story would indeed always change in accordance with their outweighing response.

If more young boys replied yes in agreement that she had overheard everything that Mr. Bernard Menard had said, Uncle Simon would agree with their decision and laugh hysterically with my other uncles, describing a truly loving moment between Dolice Marie and Mr. Bernard Menard, a moment that included many hugs and tears in the kitchen of the New Orleans House as Mr. Bernard Menard asked his lady love, the Mademoiselle Dolice Marie, to marry him, and of course, she shouted to the heavens an undeniable "Yes, Monsieur Menard," while tears streamed down her face.

However, if the majority of the young boys disagreed, that Dolice Marie had not heard anything that Mr. Bernard Menard had said, the story would invariably include some other time when Mr. Bernard Menard, kneeling down on one knee, and quite nervously, I might add, would profess his undying love to his lady love, Dolice Marie, and then ask her to be his wife, while Miss BB, Angeline, and Obadiah dabbed away the tears from their own eyes with delicate cloth napkins, along with my sweet uncle Simon, several other uncles, and even though unlikely, several of the young boys being initiated who desperately tried to obscure the fact that tears were swelling up in their own eyes as well.

No matter what the outcome of the conversation was, the dashing, handsome, suave, sophisticated—well, by now you know what I mean—Mr. Bernard Menard was indeed quite captured by the tiny former-slave girl and could not foresee a future without her as his wife.

Of course, there were many other stories throughout the years that my dear uncles would thread into the family stories about how Mr. Bernard Menard actually proposed to his lady love, Dolice Marie, but my especially favorite one speaks of the dear man's incessant and tender care of his impregnated loved one as Dolice Marie endured those ugly early days of carrying his child. It seemed as though the kind man had purchased an exquisitely beautiful yet simplistic in design and far less-complicated than their controversial relationship had been, I might add, engagement ring that he was prepared to shower upon Dolice Marie at any given time. Well, one "given time" truly did happen.

Always considering the needs of his lady love, the Mademoiselle Dolice Marie, before anything else, Mr. Bernard Menard had volunteered to massage her tiny swollen feet, actually positioning himself on the floor to avoid any further inconvenience for her even though she tried her very best to dissuade his attempts. Once kneeling down on the hard, cold floor of the New Orleans House, Mr. Bernard Menard slipped the precious gem on her tiny big toe while all the while uttering the words, "Marry me, my darling. I cannot and will not live without you!"

The story continued that Mr. Bernard Menard had then smiled that ingratiating smile of his, and the lovely Mademoiselle Dolice Marie—why, yes, she did, she did indeed—swooned into a genteel faint, but not before whispering yes to the question at hand.

Even before my sweet uncle Simon could swell with tears of joy in his eyes, my other uncles began to peer at him with tears in their own. Uncle Simon would always catch his tears in his handkerchief with one hand, and with his head down, he would motion with his other hand that it was indeed time for the next brother, my uncle Clovis, to take over with his portion of the traditional telling of the family stories. It was also a moment that everyone seemed to take to compose themselves as yet another chapter, and yet still another uncle in the LaPierre-Menard family line began to evolve.

Uncle Clovis was just as precious to me as any of my other uncles, my sweet daddy's brothers, and he was also the uncle that was truly gifted as a natural-born musician. Although many of the family members and the long line of residents of Mon Village had that special natural knack for putting rhythm together with anything they could find to create the sound of zydeco music, what had once been known as the La La, Uncle Clovis seemed to have a true talent for both the instrument and the voice, whether during the traditional telling of the family stories or as the chosen head of the family choir on Sunday, day 3 of our family reunions.

My heart would always become zealous with joy as I anticipated the opening of his portion of the traditional telling of the family stories, and undoubtedly, Uncle Clovis's older and younger brothers, including my own dear daddy, were just as excited as I was to hear whatever musical gift he was about to give to us.

To encourage Uncle Clovis, my other dear uncles would always set the pulse for him by humming softly, tapping their feet to create a rhythm, and then swaying to the rhythm they were creating. It was always quite charming to watch him as he kept refusing ever so sweetly over and over until he was absolutely forced by their continual persuasion to give in and to join his voice to the rhythm they were creating.

> *Just another day on the bayou:*
> *High humidity with the morning light,*
> *Glistening with the sweat from some afternoon delight,*
> *But after working like a slave from morning till night,*
> *I need a cool mint julep, in a silver cup, just to make life right.*

Uh-uh-uh! Everyone, including the young boys, would throw their hands up in the air and just laugh on and on with pride. Oh, my uncle Clovis! The dear man was always making music and always had a song to offer, a song that gave the listener a brief glimpse into the affairs of the LaPierre-Menard family offered in the manner in which its members had always lived it, with plenty of true commotion, rhythm, and rhyme.

My lovable uncle Clovis was one of those ancestors that had remained at Mon Village for all his life, dedicated to its continuing progress and, after having fallen in love with the daughter of one of the descendants of slaves that was born and raised right here under the iron hands of the former masters and mistresses, became quite content to stay right here with her. Tall and built out of pure, lean muscle with a ready smile and that familiar bulge in his belly that had only come with age and as a result of the common family traits, my uncle Clovis still represented the physical strength of our ancestors, yet he housed a heart of sheer sugar and just plain tenderness.

My aunt Gertrude, "Gertie," as we all knew her, had always been best friends with my aunts Cee Cee and Fee Fee while they were all growing up, and to hear them tell it, Uncle Clovis was always underfoot when the girls were playing their girlie-girl games and had even tried to sneak in their room once or twice while they were enjoying a slumber party, just to be near his Gertie, as he called her.

Short and rather "roly-poly" all her adult life, Aunt Gertie was as faithful as could be to my dear uncle, and their union produced four children of their very own while they raised several others that had just popped up during dinner one day and stayed until they became adults, not to mention the number of dogs, cats, birds, squirrels, and other animals that Uncle Clovis and the children would frequently bring home. These family reunions were just as important for bringing family together as it was to reunite Uncle Clovis and Aunt Gertie with the many children that had crossed the threshold of their home here in the shadows of those big magnolia trees.

Uncle Clovis had attended the school right here at Mon Village when he was a child, catching what little education he could while working hard in the fields and humming out the music that seemed to always be in his head. Eventually, Uncle Clovis had his own turn at heading up the construction crew that was continually making repairs and changes to the residential areas, a job that he has cherished even until today, but he also had his time working with the men at the silver shop. Since this was the family business, it was not uncommon for most of the men to learn that business as well while learning about the job they were truly interested in doing for the rest of their working lives.

Aunt Gertie volunteered her hands to all the womanly things necessary to keep the former plantation thriving and producing richly for all who lived there, whether cooking, sewing, and ironing, teaching the younger women to do so, or assisting her very best friends, my sweets aunts, in their beauty shop, Aunt Gertie was always there to help.

Although all my dear uncles and their beloved spouses knew full well the feelings of true love, devotion, and responsibility, no one could possibly have had a more agreeable and pleasing personality or was more easy to love than my own uncle Clovis. Out of all the brothers of my father's generation, it was this uncle that was the first to show up to assist in a crisis, fully prepared and yet far too humble to accept even a simple thank-you. So the more I listened to the traditional telling of the family stories, the more I realized that Uncle Clovis was indeed the very best choice for the job of recreating that wedding and early marriage of our feisty little ancestor Dolice Marie LaPierre, and Uncle Clovis always did so with such pride, with humility, and of course, with lots of music.

Well, as it has indeed already been established, Dolice Marie most certainly did accept Mr. Bernard Menard's loving proposal of marriage without the least hesitation about those nasty little concerns that the ladies of the New Orleans House brought to his attention, such as, "What would people say?" and citing that he would never be able to locate a man of the cloth to perform such a wedding ceremony, one between a proper white man from any country and a woman of color, particularly a feisty little woman of color who already had developed such a questionable reputation in the great city of New Orleans that had preceded her wherever she went or whatever she attempted to do. Why, what would people think of such a thing?

That question caused the young boys to search one another's eyes as Uncle Clovis hesitated for a moment to allow them to ponder just as Mr. Bernard Menard had scanned Miss BB's, Angeline's, and Obadiah's eyes, as well as the eyes of the working ladies of the New Orleans House, who had found a comfortable spot in the kitchen after hearing the loud proclamations of the love-struck Menard, I might add, for several minutes in his very own preponderance over the subject, and he finally blurted out, "Why, I never noticed that Mademoiselle Dolice Marie was a woman of color." He said this quite seriously and quite innocently as well as he held his beloved Dolice Marie in his arMiss. "And actually, I am quite positive that there is at least one Canadian priest that would find it nothing less than divine supplication to perform such a ceremony, and without giving such nonsense as the color of one's skin even a twitter of thought!"

Miss BB simply sipped her tea, smiling and offering her comfort to her sweet Dolice Marie without response or even notice to the ladies' statements while quietly listening to the conversation between them and Mr. Bernard Menard, the wheels of sheer sinister plotting spinning around and around in the dear lady's head.

When it finally became apparent that Mr. Bernard Menard simply refused to give in to their fears or concerns about his desired marriage to his lady love, the ladies of the New Orleans House peered upward toward the ceiling in deep momentary contemplation, shrugged their shoulders in agreement that all was truly and absolutely sensational, and slipped away to resume their own duties.

"A wedding!" Angeline finally said as the ladies cleared the room, with her eyes bright and with apparent excitement in her voice. "Ooh, la la!"

Other than the fact that Jean Pierre and Evelina had "jumped the broom," Dolice and Mr. Bernard Menard would truly be the first members of our family to actually have a wedding, and what a wedding it would be! In less than one minute, Miss BB had the entire situation all figured out, as she usually did, and had come up with the ideal solution to the current set of circumstances at hand. After all, these were truly the kinds of circumstances that tickled the great lady's imagination and stirred her creative thinking.

"What a delightfully enchanting opportunity to dabble in a little mischief as well as celebrate such a wondrous occasion!" she said with a sly smirk on her mouth and a faraway look in her eyes.

Everyone around the charming Miss BB had long before learned to trust her wisdom, her judgment, and her ability to get any job done with the most pleasant of means and, whenever necessary, with the most devious of techniques. Without an iota of further thought, the entire plan was laid out with perfect detail before Mr. Bernard Menard could utter even a single suggestion.

First, the wedding ceremony would be held right in the backyard of the Declouette Mansion, at the edge of the gardens, eliminating the need to travel to New York or to Toronto. Miss BB suggested that the tasteful gazebo just to the right of the flower gardens would serve as the perfect altar, where the facilitator would conduct the ceremony.

There was already a natural pathway from the back of the Declouette Mansion to the gazebo that would be beautifully decorated with the many varieties of flowers that were already growing in the gardens. Chairs would be strategically placed on either side of the gazebo to accommodate the scores of guests that would be invited. Tables would be placed on one side of the pathway for the reception that would immediately follow the nuptials.

And food, of course, there would be plenty of delicious food, including an exquisitely decorated wedding cake, an abundance of music as well, this time including the rhythms of the old La Las as well as the rhythms of the great city of New Orleans, and of course, there would be plenty of good old-fashioned gossip for the old bitties of the neighborhood with which to amuse themselves and, hopefully, more than enough gossip to fill the pages of the New Orleans newspapers. Miss BB just smiled with delight as she sipped her tea.

The wheels were spinning indeed, just as they had been when preparations were being made for the grande bal masqué just prior to the grand opening of the New Orleans House only a few short years ago. It was truly another exciting time for the sweet Miss BB, who was determined to make it so for everyone.

Due to the prevailing situation, that is, the lovely Mademoiselle Dolice Marie's delicate condition, there would unfortunately be far too little time to invite the previous list of guests that had been invited to the grande bal masqué, with there being such short notice, that is, but it was certainly worth, as Miss BB said, one good try.

And family, family would always find a way, indeed. Family from those mosquito-laden swamps of the Bayou Frou-Frous to the truly very sophisticated land to the north in Canada. Family would be there without a doubt.

My precious uncle Clovis would always nod in agreement with my other uncles that family could always be depended upon to be there when needed and sealed that conclusion by ensuring the young boys that since they were the next limb on the family tree, it would soon be their responsibility to ensure that they, too, could always be depended upon to be there, especially when it became their turn to pass on the stories of the family.

Because Mr. Bernard Menard was indeed a religious man of great conviction, as was his entire family, the wedding ceremony would most assuredly have to be conducted by a man of the cloth, and being that the wedding would take place in the Deep South, which Catholicism had long before claimed by its presence, Miss BB concluded that a priest would do just fine, a priest from the great city of New Orleans and nowhere else. "Yes," she stated aloud, "a Jesuit! Ha! And I know a couple of them that owe me a favor or two!"

Mr. Bernard Menard agreed with contentment at the idea of a priest presiding over the ceremony and, without a doubt, left the finding of a Jesuit priest to Miss BB while the uncles pretended to be lending themselves to an imaginary list of things to do.

Now, to notify both of the families, the LaPierres at Mon Village and the Menards in Canada, Angeline and Miss BB would assist Dolice Marie in preparing the proper words for a wire to be sent to her beloved Jean Pierre while Mr. Bernard Menard prepared a wire to be sent to his beloved parents in Toronto, both of which Obadiah would deliver to the telegraph office in the great city of New Orleans when they both had, indeed, been completed.

The date was set for just short of a month from the day that they had all put their heads together in the kitchen of the New Orleans House, just ahead of the blistering summers of the great state of Louisiana, but just before the finale of Louisiana's most wonderful season of spring. Just how much the bride-to-be would have begun to protrude was also taken into consideration by the great planners, who concluded that Dolice Marie would not have begun to show quite obviously within that period.

Now, as far as what everyone would wear, it was decided among everyone that all the lovely ladies of the New Orleans House would serve the wedding party as Dolice Marie's bridesmaids—Angeline would be her maid of honor, of course. The beautiful ladies of the New Orleans House would be all too happy to share this unforgettable moment with Mademoiselle Dolice Marie, who stated that she wanted to be the person to tell them. Miss BB retorted that the lovely ladies of the New Orleans House would surely have to wear much more than they were accustomed to on a daily basis, and then everyone laughed, of course, including my own dear uncles.

Angeline also thought it would be quite appropriate to include Dolice Marie's beloved sister-in-law, Evelina, in the wedding party, to procession down the aisle to the gazebo directly in front of Angeline, since Evelina would need much more room in the front of her, indeed, for her ever-bulging belly. Everyone agreed and watched as Dolice and Angeline began to giggle just like schoolgirls as they held hands, shaking them up and down then suddenly exploding into tears.

"What a sight that must have been!" my uncle Clovis concluded as he faked tears streaming down his own cheeks.

Miss BB announced that to provide the entire wedding party with the clothing they needed would be her personal honor, a wedding gift to the bride and groom, if they would accept it, of course. She also reminded everyone of the quite-capable seamstress that was in her employment, the same one that had dressed everyone so beautifully for the grande bal masqué.

Mr. Bernard Menard also announced at this point that he had an excellent idea. He was going to ask his best friend from Toronto, Willem, to be his best man but would truly appreciate it if Obadiah would also serve as his only groomsman, something he had already considered once or twice since recognizing the fact that Obadiah had always been so kind to both himself and his bride-to-be.

Goodness! The planning went on for hours! All this thrilling preparation was truly just a tad too much for the bride-to-be, who had fallen sound asleep in the arms of her beloved, Mr. Bernard Menard, comfortably snuggled up in his arms in the kitchen of the New Orleans House, content with all that lay ahead of her and occasionally reminding everyone that she was still in their presence with one of her loud asthmatic snores!

Chapter 11

AT THE PEACEFUL Mon Village, Jean Pierre opened a wire that Jubil had just brought to him from the local town where he had been shopping for those necessities not readily available in the shops or the fields of the former plantation. Struggling through the words of the wire with Jubil's assistance, Jean Pierre became truly delighted, indeed almost giddy, when he realized that the message was from his Dolice Marie, a message bringing the announcement of her upcoming nuptials to a Mr. Bernard Menard, with the invitation for himself and Evelina to join them at the home of a Miss Beatrice Carson Declouette in the great city of New Orleans, where arrangements had already been made for their overnight accommodations, with proper wedding attire provided for them as well.

The wire also stated that the wedding celebration would be held in less than one month from the date that the wire had been sent, hardly enough time, indeed, to prepare for such an event. Jean Pierre was truly overwhelmed by the words of the wire and most definitely pleased at the news that his Dolice Marie would soon be married, allowing the tears that had swelled in his eyes while reading the wire to flow freely down his cheeks.

Jubil hugged his best friend, Jean Pierre, who immediately informed him that he would most definitely need to attend the wedding celebration as well since he had always been so close to Dolice Marie while they were all growing up, like another big brother, and how much she would certainly want him there. Jean Pierre stated that he would ask Miss Sylvia and Miss Penelope to care for the children while he, Evelina and Jubil, made the trip to the great city of New Orleans for this very special event. Jean Pierre's mind was racing with thoughts as he paced back and forth, with Jubil following closely behind like his personal assistant.

But the current children were truly not Jean Pierre's biggest concern at all; it was Evelina who was already quite big with their next child, and although he felt that the time was still sometime ahead, he was quite concerned that the trip itself would be difficult for her. Jean Pierre shared his concern with Evelina after the two had danced around on the front porch for a spell after he had shared the wire with her. Sweet Evelina assured Jean Pierre that she was already in his good hands, and besides, she would not miss the opportunity to witness Dolice Marie LaPierre finally "jump the broom." And thus it was agreed upon that Jubil would respond to the wire that Jean Pierre and Evelina LaPierre, along with Jubilation LaPierre, would be proud, and most honored, indeed, to be Dolice Marie's and Mr. Bernard Menard's guests for this very auspicious event.

Back home in Toronto, Canada, Lord and Lady Menard received the wire from their beloved son, Bernard, and eagerly awaited their secretary of incoming correspondence to read it to them. Both properly positioned themselves on a hefty chesterfield in the library and checked each other to be sure that they were indeed properly dressed for such an event. Once they had properly acknowledged that each was indeed properly attired, Lord Menard motioned to the secretary of incoming correspondence to begin.

"Dearest Mum and Dad," the wire began. "It gives me great pleasure to notify both of you that I have fallen madly in love with a wonderful woman by the name of Dolice Marie LaPierre, a charming lady of means that I had the honor to have met at a grande bal masqué here in the great city of New Orleans. My precious Dolice Marie has won over a heart that has been all too preoccupied with work over these past years, and I have asked her to marry me before she slips through my fingers and falls for another. We hope to be married soon, here in New Orleans, which is more readily available to her family, who own and operate a plantation near the Atchafalaya River."

Lord and Lady Menard smiled with approval, commenting that their son was blessed to have stumbled upon such an enchanting lady with both money and social position, and again motioned to the secretary of incoming correspondence to continue.

"I am certain that you will be able to attend, and I shall send word of the details in time for you to prepare for the journey. Please ask my best friend, Willem, to be ready to travel here with you since I would be most honored if he would stand as my best man and would indeed appreciate him traveling with you throughout the long distance. Oh, and I do hope that you have finally forgiven my beloved aunt Minnie Menard for not being able to control her good senses and giving in to laughing so hysterically about your horrible accident while in England and causing us both to be thrown out of the Royal Hospital. If you have not forgiven her, I would surely appreciate you giving that a thought as I would love for her to attend as well."

The two smiled quite courteously with each other while adjusting themselves on the chesterfield, promising to discuss that matter a little later.

"I must tell you that it has been called to my attention on several occasions that my lady love is, as many have called her, a woman of color," the wire continued.

Lord and Lady Menard looked quite curiously at each other. "Why, I wonder what color she is," commented Lady Menard.

After another several moments of peering out of the window in contemplation, Lord and Lady Menard agreed that color was an absolutely fabulous addition to the House of Menard that had indeed been dreadfully too white for far too many generations!

Once again, the secretary of incoming correspondence began to read the words of the wire.

"Finally, dearest Mum and Dad," Mr. Bernard Menard wrote, "my beloved has done a most wonderful thing; she has conceived my child and will honor me with a boy or a girl within just a few short months after our wedding. Just think, dear ones, you will be a grandmom and granddad before the end of the year."

Lord Menard looked quite befuddled at Lady Menard and whispered, "How could that be possible? I had no idea that a child could be conceived before marriage! I told you that our son was quite brilliant!"

Both smiled with pride and delight.

After reading the final goodbyes of Mr. Bernard Menard's wire, the secretary of incoming correspondence graciously bade adieu to Lord and Lady Menard, leaving them to ponder happily over the news of their son's good fortune.

And back in the great city of New Orleans, there were preparations for a truly splendid wedding underway at the Declouette Mansion, with the same vigor and resolve that was adopted while everyone was preparing for the grande bal masqué, with the same professionals assigned to decorate the mansion, the same cooks preparing some delicious cuisine prepared from here, there, and everywhere, the same seamstress, with her dressmakers, attained to be in charge of attending to the honors of dressing the blushing yet ever-so-expanding bride-to-be, along with her beloved sister-in-law, who was essentially almost about to pop herself, and all the lovely ladies who would be in attendance, including those lovely ladies of the New Orleans House.

Even though Miss BB had already hired the same musicians to provide music for both the wedding march and the reception, she had most assuredly made provisions for the addition of the music of the La La as well, the music Dolice Marie and her family were indeed much more familiar with, along with some plantation blues and, of course, some good old New Orleans jazz, just as she had promised.

Of course, there were those same, ever-present nosy neighbors who were looking for any avenue to catch a glimpse as to what was going on at the widow Declouette's mansion, but this event would not be anything like the grande bal masqué, especially when it came to the publicity and the juicy particulars that were being created at every twist and turn.

Miss BB was having a ball, another time of her life. As she walked throughout the grounds of the Declouette Mansion, cuddling FiFi and GiGi, she giggled when she spotted al photographer or a journalist or two from the local newspapers who thought they were sneaking around the azalea bushes while Miss BB smiled that naughty little smile of hers as she lifted just one of her eyebrows in such genuine contentment, giving them just a little bit more to write about as she actually led the way to everything that was going on.

Obadiah, dressed in his familiar black coat with tails, white gloves, and the top hat that could be spotted towering above just about everyone and everything, was given strict orders from Miss BB to make himself and everyone else quite visible to all the nosy neighbors and to any and all the photographers and journalists that he might find sneaking around. Miss BB suggested that perhaps Obadiah should smile broadly, and perhaps even tip his hat as he passed by, just to add a little more spice to the occasion with his antics. Obadiah laughed in agreement as he loaded the familiar carriage pulled by the huge horse with supplies from the shops in the great city of New Orleans during several trips and then filled it again with the lovely ladies of the New Orleans House as they giggled and wiggled during several more trips, strategically completing all his tasks to put people and things in their proper places, but this time not hiding anything that he or any of his passengers were doing. Can you just imagine?

Just two weeks prior to their wedding day, a messenger from the great city of New York came to the New Orleans House with a wire for Mr. Bernard Menard that had great importance, indeed, importance about certain activities concerning his import-export business, he confided to Dolice. After reading the wire, Mr. Bernard Menard thanked and tipped the messenger then proceeded to scowl as he peered into space, one eyebrow quivering and lips pouting, as though he were truly in deep thought.

After a few moments, Mr. Bernard Menard embraced an anxiously curious Dolice Marie and announced that it was truly beyond his control but that he must quickly depart and return to the great city of New York to tend to the affairs of his business, a business that would belong to his beloved Dolice Marie as well once they were married, and a task that simply could not wait until after their wedding.

Well, it became quite obvious that the Mademoiselle Dolice Marie was extremely upset about this announcement, and soon her eyebrow began to quiver, her lips began to pout, and when she folded her arms and began to roll her eyes, Mr. Bernard Menard's eyes grew quite large and he quickly began to explain that his presence was truly needed, and immediately, but that nothing could or would ever keep him away from his lady love and the ceremony that would forever join them together as one.

Dolice Marie stared deeply into his eyes and then began to cry, and quite loudly, I might add, causing Angeline and the ladies of the New Orleans House to come to her aid as she stood in the center of the parlor wailing away as if she were already laboring to bring their child into the world.

After an entire afternoon of trying desperately hard to settle the anger festering within his lady love, and listening to her wail, I might also add, Mr. Bernard Menard decided that it was much more important to soothe her aching and to spoil the surprise that he had for her than to risk the impending explosion that was seemingly about to occur at any minute. After exhaling an extremely large breath, Mr. Bernard Menard unhappily made known the true importance of this short visit.

The messenger's wire had actually been from Mr. Bernard Menard's contractor in the great city of New York, who had explained to him quietly that the lovely and quite lavish cottage, I might add, again, that Mr. Bernard Menard had had built and furnished for the three of them had been flooded by the sudden waters that had rolled onto the shore from the Atlantic Ocean to the coastline of the Eastern Seaboard. Everything had been ruined, and the question now at hand was, Would it be possible for Mr. Bernard Menard to come quickly in order to survey the damage and make orders for reparations in order to prepare the home for them once the wedding was over and that time when he would be bringing his new bride to their new home?

Mr. Bernard Menard explained that he had truly wanted this to be a surprise for his sweet Dolice Marie, a lovely new home with a fairy-tale nursery for their firstborn, and now that the damage had virtually destroyed all his plans, there was no way that the three of them would have this wonderful place in which to live if he did not quickly take care of the problem at hand. He held her tightly as he assured her again that nothing would keep him away from her, adding how very much he loved her and that he was truly looking forward to spending the rest of his life with her and their child.

It was truly a tearful goodbye, and one that was quite loud, I might add, Dolice Marie wailing as she watched Mr. Bernard Menard drive his carriage down the narrow streets, the two blowing kisses to each other until they could no longer see each other, Dolice Marie being comforted only by the presence of her precious best friend, Angeline, and her beloved Miss BB.

I remember my dear uncles' faces as they seemed to express the pain that our petite ancestor surely and most clearly must have felt as she bade a tearful goodbye to the man who had stolen her heart.

Throughout those sad days that slowly passed, Dolice Marie spent her time with Angeline, Miss BB, and the ladies of the New Orleans House at the Declouette Mansion being fitted for their gowns and shoes, choosing colors and flowers, and helping design the decorations for the wedding. Although it should have been an extremely delightful and joyous occasion for everyone, especially for Dolice Marie, she could be heard sobbing herself to sleep every night in her bedroom at the New Orleans House. And even though everyone tried desperately to help Dolice Marie through her sadness, everyone also knew that only the sights and sounds of her beloved Mr. Bernard Menard would truly bring her genuine happiness back to her and also to those around her.

It was also quite obvious, and indeed a topic for discussion about her, that Dolice just might have been a little concerned as to whether or not Mr. Bernard Menard would truly ever come back, as if, and I dare to say, he had chosen this very separation as an opportunity to eliminate himself from the very commitment that he had made to marry her.

My sweet uncles would shake their heads in sorrowful contemplation, as if they truly did not already know the answer; they would sigh and even attempt to wipe away an imaginary tear, just for further accentuation. And I might also add that they were always successful. I can honestly say that I have never, ever known any group of young boys over the years that did not appear to be just as sad as my uncles appeared to be during this portion of the stories. Truly!

Whether or not there would be a groom at the wedding, there was still a wedding on the way, and when the time finally came to travel to that wedding, Jean Pierre, Evelina, and Jubil bade their farewells to the children as well as to Miss Sylvia and Miss Penelope before cautiously climbing aboard the huge iron monster that blew steam into the air and whose enormous whistle vibrated throughout their chests, startling them and causing every one of them to jump while their eyes bulged with great fear, while all the while following the lead of the other people of color who were also boarding the train bound for the great city of New Orleans.

Little did they know that their own Dolice Marie LaPierre and her intended groom, Mr. Bernard Menard, had previously created Louisiana history on that very train and that it was because of his allegiance to the equal treatment of all human beings and Dolice Marie's desire to flaunt his goodness and kindness smack-dab in the faces of those who were not being so caring about the equal treatment of all human beings, I might add, that Jean Pierre, his loving wife, Evelina, and their lifelong friend, Jubil, with all the other people of color who were just ahead of them, could now choose a comfortable seat in the train car just ahead of the train car that had previously been reserved for the people of color, the train car that now simply carried excess luggage, small animals being transported with their human masters, and some leftover garbage.

Evelina clung fearfully to her husband's arm while Jubil sat in the seat across them, holding on to anything he could find while inspecting all that was going on as the train slowly began its journey down the tracks between the Atchafalaya River station and the station in the great city of New Orleans. Evelina closed her eyes and smiled as she described to Jean Pierre how her stomach truly seemed to turn over several times when the train began to move. Jean Pierre agreed that he, too, had felt the same sensation once the huge train began to move and tried desperately to comfort her with a smile that he hoped would show her that he was still in complete control.

Slowly, as the train picked up speed and the thick steam rose even higher in the sky, Evelina, Jean Pierre, and Jubil began to cautiously relax and enjoy the experience. Evelina, however, still held on quite tightly to her husband's arm, with no apparent intention of letting go.

Just like with Dolice Marie, the appearance of the great and mighty Mississippi River was an overwhelmingly invigorating adventure for the three, but they proudly proclaimed their joy by laughing loudly, pointing to the window at the direction of the great river, and clapping their hands like children.

The other passengers of color were seemingly not the least bit enthused at the sight of the celebrated river but smiled sheepishly anyway just to be kind to the three who could have cared less if they indeed appeared to be country bumpkins.

By the time the train had reached its top speed, the three residents of Mon Village, out on their first excursion away from their home, were truly enjoying themselves as they peered through the windows, watching what appeared to be the whole world speeding by. It was only when the train began to slow down as it approached the New Orleans train station that Jean Pierre, Evelina, and Jubil began to connect with the fact that they were truly away, far away from home, and about to embark on the greatest adventures of their lives.

The two very exciting days before the wedding found an impatient Dolice Marie sitting, standing, pacing, and sitting again in the parlor of the New Orleans House, with Miss BB and her two constant companions, FiFi and GiGi, waiting for Obadiah to return from the train station with her beloved Jean Pierre, Evelina, and Jubil.

Business was going on as usual upstairs in the left wing of the New Orleans House, with soft piano music being played, courtesy of the finally talented Angeline. There was the constant sound of the upstairs doors being opened and slammed shut by happy customers who tipped their hats when they entered the parlor and who exited with smiles on their faces and deep, empty pockets, I might also add.

On the other hand, the entire right wing of the New Orleans House had been closed off from the business at hand to accommodate Dolice Marie's beloved family, to ensure that they would be comfortable yet away from such goings-on while visiting and attending the LaPierre-Menard wedding.

With all this preparation in place, the only thing left to do, the hardest part of all, was to wait. When Obadiah finally did arrive at the New Orleans House in the big carriage pulled by that equally large horse, Dolice Marie was truly overwhelmed with joy and truly excited about being with her beloved family from Mon Village. Obadiah hopped clown from the bench of the large carriage and paraded himself around to the other side to assist a truly pregnant Evelina to the ground as she squealed in absolute joy at seeing Dolice Marie, reaching her arms outward and running toward her until they fell into each other's arms, or as close as they could get, of course. Oh, what a sight it was! The only thing that even dared to take Dolice Marie away from Evelina was the sight of her beloved Jean Pierre being so close to her, close enough to hold tightly and feel the feeling of his skin next to hers as the two held on to each other as if they would never let go of each other again. And there were those tears, many tears, as they peered deeply into each other's eyes, almost expecting one to disappear or to awaken and realize that it was all just a dream.

But it wasn't a dream! The Mistress Dolice Marie and the Master Jean Pierre were truly standing face-to-face, hand in hand.

And of course there was Jubil, who just stood there with his hat in his hand, smiling at the sight, wiping away a few tears of his own as they fell from his eyes, until Dolice Marie pulled herself away from Jean Pierre for just a moment to hug him as well while Miss BB and Obadiah watched with such happiness for their Dolice Marie, and yes, with tears in their own eyes.

Once inside the New Orleans House, Dolice Marie proudly introduced her family from Mon Village to her best friend, Angeline, who was equally happy to meet all the people that she felt she already knew from her many conversations about them with Dolice Marie. Needless to say, everyone was also anxious indeed to meet Dolice

Marie's husband-to-be, Mr. Bernard Menard, a desire that Dolice Marie knew she would eventually have to address, but before she could do so, she began to cry, and quite loudly, I might also add! It was such a sad occurrence to see Dolice Marie surrounded by the people that she loved so dearly, and who deeply loved her, facing the most wonderful day of her life, perhaps without the groom!

When Dolice Marie could finally calm herself down enough to explain to the family where Mr. Bernard Menard was at that very moment, just two days before the scheduled wedding, everyone, in their attempt to comfort the poor child, agreed that there was still plenty of time for him to get back and that get back he truly would, indeed!

While Obadiah led Jean Pierre and Jubil on a tour of the New Orleans House and then to their individual rooms upstairs, Dolice Marie, Angeline, Evelina, and Miss BB settled themselves in the comfort of the kitchen of the New Orleans House for coffee, conversations, and plenty of tears that lasted well into the evening while each tried to give their own brand of comfort to poor Dolice Marie, which seemed to be absolutely fruitless.

Jean Pierre and Jubil, quite impressed by the sights and sounds of the New Orleans House, eventually joined everyone else in the kitchen, where they prepared themselves for dinner. Not even the presence and the aroma of her favorite foods that would ordinarily satisfy her hormonal cravings, lovingly prepared by Cook, could ease Dolice Marie's pain (although Evelina found enormous satisfaction in not only her own portion but Dolice Marie's as well).

As the sun slowly set and darkness began to cover the great city of New Orleans with the appearance of a warn woolen blanket of many colors, Miss BB announced that it was truly well past the time for FiFi and GiGi to be away from home and asked Obadiah if he would be so kind as to take them all home. She gently kissed Dolice Marie on her forehead and again assured her that Mr. Bernard Menard was probably on his way home at that very minute, encouraging her to make herself beautiful for his homecoming. After a sweet good night to Jean Pierre, Evelina, and Jubil, Miss BB gathered her babies and disappeared through the front door to join Obadiah, who was standing on the side of the big carriage, waiting to assist her.

Uncle Clovis always mentioned at this part of the story that he had heard once or twice throughout the years that Miss BB had quietly asked Obadiah whether or not he thought Mr. Bernard Menard would ever come home to Dolice Marie. And just as he did at this portion of the family stories each and every time he told it to the young boys, he would look straight into their eyes and ask, "What do you think?"

Uncle Clovis would ask in a sinister sort of way as he scanned their eyes. "Do you think Mr. Bernard Menard will ever come back to Dolice Marie?"

Poor, sweet boys! Why, what were they to say? After just a few moments of waiting time, Uncle Clovis would quickly continue his portion of the family stories before any of the young boys could answer. Oh, how very shrewd he was, indeed.

Dolice Marie finally gave way to total exhaustion and announced that she was truly ready to rest, although she was positively overjoyed and content to have her family there with her, especially at this time of uncertainty. Evelina agreed that she, too, was ready to lie down and put her feet up for a while. After exchanging loving hugs and kisses in the hallway that divided the bedrooms on the left from the bedrooms on the right, Dolice, Jean Pierre and Evelina, and Jubil went their separate ways to their own bedrooms, leaving Dolice Marie alone with her own thoughts.

Again, Uncle Clovis would pause to mention to the young boys yet another story that he had heard once or twice as he was growing up, a story that finds Evelina as well quietly asking Jean Pierre in the privacy of their own room in the New Orleans House if he thought Mr. Bernard Menard would ever come home to Dolice Marie.

Once alone in her own master bed in the master bedroom, Dolice Marie tossed and turned until she finally sobbed herself to sleep. Jean Pierre found it difficult to fall asleep as he contemplated the pain his sweet sister—er, cousin—was certainly feeling just across the hall, and he, too, tossed and turned.

In a bedroom down the hall from Jean Pierre and Evelina's, Jubil was restless as well, tossing and turning in his bed while planning the manner in which Mr. Bernard Menard would certainly pay for any malice against his dear friend Dolice Marie and for causing such tension within the family.

Evelina, on the other hand, found it quite easy to fall fast asleep with a smile on her face within the matter of minutes in the comfort of her own dreams and the warmth of the comforters and silk sheets, caressing that sweet baby within while nestled under the strong arm of her husband.

Truly, the question on everyone's mind, from the Declouette Mansion to the New Orleans House, and everything in between, was whether or not Mr. Bernard Menard would find his way back home to Dolice Marie and in time for the wedding that was now less than two days away.

Sometime during the deep darkness of the night, as Dolice Marie drifted in and out of a truly restless sleep, a thunderstorm suddenly landed over the great city of New Orleans, bringing with it heavy rains, extremely loud claps of thunder, and incessant bolts of lightning. The storm was so very loud and unwavering that the wind slammed over and over against the beautiful French doors from the wrought iron balcony that led to Dolice Marie's bedroom, causing them to tremble and quiver as the sound of the wind became deafening. Dolice Marie sat straight up in her bed, confused and startled by the noise, her eyes already sore from the constant crying and now wide with the fear of the unknown.

She hastily grabbed a lovely peach-colored silk robe that was hanging on the back of the door to the master bedroom and, after covering herself, dashed toward the doors to the balcony to make sure that they were locked and incapable of opening to bring the stormy weather into her room.

Suddenly, the doors began to rattle as if a tornado had surely touched down right there on the balcony of the master bedroom of the New Orleans House. Then, after another deafening clap of thunder, a shriek of lightning lit up the entire balcony and revealed what appeared to be the form of a man in a long cape with a hat on his head standing there, just outside of Dolice Marie's bedroom doors. Dolice Marie screamed with terror, and as she turned to run out of the bedroom door into the hallway, she was met by Jean Pierre and Jubil, who were on their way to save her from whatever was terrorizing her.

Jean Pierre hastened Dolice Marie to the back of the bedroom, near the door that led to the master bedroom, away from the balcony doors, while he and Jubil carefully approached the balcony doors, each man grasping a fireplace poker with which they had armed themselves for protection against the unknown assailant.

Just as Jean Pierre cautiously sneaked upon the balcony doors to see just what he could see, the balcony doors began to tremble again and the lightning lit up the entire balcony to again reveal what appeared to be the figure of a man wearing a cloak and a hat. Dolice Marie screamed. The scene continued over and over several times until the noise of it all awakened Angeline, who peered through the door that led to the master bedroom and was greeted by Dolice Marie, who grabbed her and held on to her as if she were a sturdy tree.

Jean Pierre carefully approached the doors again and, this time, tapped rather hard on the glass in an attempt to frighten the figure away from the New Orleans House. All of a sudden, there was a loud, muffled sound, perhaps even one familiar to Dolice Marie, that came from beyond the balcony doors, which caused Dolice Marie, still wrapped around Angeline, to move carefully toward the sound.

"Hallo," Dolice Marie said in her well-mixed tonality, and with all due precautions, I might add. "Monsieur Menard?" she asked.

The muffled noise sounded again, and Dolice Marie suddenly recognized the muffled sound coming from her balcony as, yes, yes, that of her beloved Mr. Bernard Menard standing in the cold rain, soaking wet, with the wind whirling all about him, trying desperately to open the locked doors.

As Dolice Marie drew closer and yelled out another "Hallo" to be sure that it was indeed Mr. Bernard Menard before opening the balcony doors, the lightning lit up the balcony once again, startling Jean Pierre and Jubil, who positioned themselves right in front of the doors, with their trusty fireplace pokers aimed toward the intruder, once again ready for whatever was ahead of them, and suddenly, the figure called out Dolice Marie's name.

"Mademoiselle Dolice Marie, my love, it is I, Monsieur Bernard Menard!" he responded, tipping his soaking-wet hat and smiling through the raindrops when he knew she could finally see him, causing Dolice Marie to rush past Jean Pierre and Jubil to open the balcony doors in order to allow her beloved to enter the master bedroom.

"Monsieur, I had no idea that it was you!" Dolice Marie retorted as she gave him a fond embrace. "How can I tell you how very sorry I am?"

"Think nothing of it, my love," he answered, struggling to remove the cold, wet clothing. "I am just so very happy to be home with you."

"But why did you climb up to the balcony, monsieur? Why did you not just knock on the front door?" Dolice Marie inquired with a sweetness that she could feel only for her beloved Mr. Bernard Menard.

"Why, I had intended to surprise you, my love," Mr. Bernard Menard began to explain, "by climbing up the outside stairway onto the balcony, through the opened doors, and into your arms, but alas, it had not occurred to me that there would be a storm and the doors would be locked! I remembered how very much you love the smell of the rain."

Angeline exhaled quite deeply in relief, while Jean Pierre and Jubil appeared to be dumbfounded as they stared at the scene between the two, until Dolice Marie finally released her tight grip on Mr. Bernard Menard to happily introduce him to her family. What had been days of tears and despair had quickly been converted to huge smiles and giddy, girlish antics in the presence of her beloved.

Angeline quickly hugged Mr. Bernard Menard and serenely exited the master bedroom to return to her own. Jean Pierre and Jubil stood in the midst of the scene, speechless, with eyes wide and curiously staring at Mr. Bernard Menard until they began to feel quite awkward and immediately began to express their good nights, adding how very pleased they both were to meet the man their beautiful Dolice Marie had chosen, and eagerly began to back out of the master bedroom.

"Good night and thank you for protecting my lovely bride-to-be!" Mr. Bernard Menard said, briskly shaking hands with Jean Pierre and Jubil, who continued to stare at the kindly gentleman even as they tried desperately to smile politely.

As the two quietly walked back to their respective bedrooms, Jean Pierre paused and turned to Jubil and said quite directly, "I had no idea that Dolice Marie's husband-to-be was not a man of color!"

Jubil agreed and added that Mr. Bernard Menard was very white, indeed, and Jean Pierre agreed that Mr. Bernard Menard was truly the whitest white man they had ever seen!

Chapter 12

MORNING CAME ALL too quickly for the soon-to-be bride and groom, who lay closely together and fully clad, I might also add, on the huge bed in the master bedroom of the New Orleans House after a night of storms and homecoming. Mr. Bernard Menard had fallen asleep in his wet clothing, which, apparently, had dried on him and was, for certain, still damp in places, causing him to have a chill and to shiver enough to awaken himself and the lovely Mademoiselle Dolice Marie beside him from their peaceful sleep. Of course, it took several moments for the two of them to become fully awakened enough to realize that they were together again, in the security of each other's arms, but when both had their eyes fully opened and their minds fully prepared for what they were seeing, Mr. Bernard Menard and the Mademoiselle Dolice Marie embraced each other so tightly that his clothing seemed to wring out and drip drops of water onto the bedsheets. But who cared? They were together again, and there was to be a wedding, their wedding, just a day away that would joyfully bind them together forever.

In the midst of all the wonderment of the moment, a soft knock sounded from the outside the master bedroom door, followed by Angeline's tiny voice calling for Dolice Marie. Ignoring the knock and accrediting the sounds to a dream, Mr. Bernard Menard and Dolice adjusted themselves on the bed to gather just a little more comfort, smiling all the while as though there were no one else in the entire world but themselves. Angeline, however, was persistent and knocked again, a little louder this time, and called for Dolice Marie just a little louder.

"Dolice Marie, my friend, I apologize for disturbing you, but there are people in the parlor here who say that they are here to see Monsieur Menard."

"Oh, no, Angeline, please tell them that we are resting," Dolice answered, positioning herself again to get just a little more comfortable in the arms of her beloved.

"That is all well and good, Ami, but the people downstairs in the parlor are the Lord and Lady Menard, Monsieur Menard's mother and father, and his friend Willem, here from Toronto. They say they are expected."

Dolice Marie and Mr. Bernard Menard suddenly sat straight up as though someone had just jabbed them both with a hat pin, mouths wide open and eyes bulging equally as wide.

"Oh no!" Mr. Bernard Menard squealed. "Today is Saturday, is it not? The morning before our wedding. Was I not supposed to pick them up at the train station?'"

"Oui, monsieur," Dolice Marie answered as she rose up as quickly as she could, considering her present set of circumstances, from the warmth and comfort of Mr. Bernard Menard's arms "It is truly Saturday, monsieur," she continued, "the day before our wedding, something that your parents did not forget, and it is apparent that they have found their own way here and they are downstairs in the parlor at this very minute!"

Angeline quietly knocked on the door again, reminding Dolice Marie and Mr. Bernard Menard that Lord and Lady Menard, and Willem, were not going to go away, and the problem of the business of the lovely ladies of the New Orleans House was just about to be exposed as soon as Cook rang the bell for breakfast.

"You must visit with them, Angeline," Mr. Bernard Menard said softly, "until we can get dressed and come down at separate times."

"As you wish," Angeline whispered, "but hurry!"

Dolice Marie and Mr. Bernard Menard could hear the sounds of Angeline scurrying away from the door from within the confines of the master bedroom. And meanwhile, downstairs in the parlor,

Lord and Lady Menard stared at the ceiling above their heads quite quizzically as a *thump-thump-thumping* sounded from the upstairs where Dolice Marie and Mr. Bernard Menard were "creating major changes to the master bedroom and one of the guest bedrooms just down the hall." Mr. Bernard Menard moved his clothing, as damp as they were, and his travel bags that contained his belongings, and anything else that could have connected himself to the master bedroom, away from the master bedroom and into one of the guest rooms, where Jubil was still comfortably sleeping.

"I do apologize," Mr. Bernard Menard said to the woozy Jubil as he quietly plopped his things into one of the corners of the room, "but I am afraid that you and I are going to have to room together until the wedding. I truly hope you do not have any objections, my dear friend."

Jubil simply glanced over toward the kind man and mentally reminded himself that Mr. Bernard Menard was indeed the whitest white man he had ever encountered in all his years at Mon Village. He could not help but stare at him, certainly appearing to be rather ridiculous even to himself, but soon shook his head in an attempt to clear the scene from his brain and to become capable of responding to the question.

"Of course not," Jubil responded. "I am certain that we can manage for at least another day."

Dolice Marie, huffing and puffing, cleared any remaining remnants of her beloved's visit to her bedroom and quietly proceeded to the bathroom to prepare herself to meet her future mother- and father-in-law and Mr. Bernard Menard's best friend, Willem. In all the commotion of the early-morning activity and the suddenness of Mr. Bernard Menard's knowledge of his family's presence just beneath them, Dolice Marie paused happily to smile as she realized that she had not been plagued with her bouts of morning, noon, and evening sickness.

Angeline forced a smile and cleared her throat as she approached Willem and the Menards to begin an extensive explanation that was designed to buy just a little more time for the love bugs that were just upstairs, preparing themselves for what was already downstairs.

"And wouldn't you know that it would be Mr. Bernard Menard that would have to face the music first," Uncle Clovis said as he crossed one knee with the other leg while leaning back in his chair, sparking more laughter from my other uncles.

"Mum, Dad, Willem, how very good to see you all," Mr. Bernard Menard said as he hugged his loved ones all at once.

"I do apologize for not being at the train station to meet you this morning. Time has most certainly gotten away from me! But how is it that you were able to find your way here?"

With an extremely curious look on his face, Lord Menard began to explain, "Strangely enough, an impressively dressed very large man of color driving a lovely carriage led by an equally large horse met us at the train station, walked directly up to us as if he had known us for some time, and announced that he had come to pick us up and take us to where you and your bride-to-be were staying. We, of course, were expecting you."

"Oh! That would be my aunt's chauffeur, Obadiah," Angeline interrupted. "You will meet her tonight at the rehearsal dinner."

A bit of a surprise to Mr. Bernard Menard, indeed, Obadiah having been at the train station just in time to pick up the family from Toronto and then the unexpected news of a rehearsal dinner. Having not been around for several weeks, Mr. Bernard Menard quickly decided that it would be best if he simply smiled as if he had known all along that there would be a rehearsal dinner and sighed as he prepared himself for any other surprises that might come his way. It was obvious that the impressively dressed very large black man was Obadiah, but how in the world he knew to be there at the train station was quite the mystery, one that Mr. Bernard Menard was sure would have a mystical answer.

Smiles were everywhere, and Lady Menard was profoundly impressed that Angeline had actually curtsied in her presence, and so was Willem, who could not seem to keep his eyes off the lovely little French girl. Angeline smiled very innocently, and as soon as she could connect her eyes with Mr. Bernard Menard's eyes, she seemed to be coaching him to follow her lead. He, in turn, was pleased, indeed, to do just that, follow, not lead, especially in this situation.

Although they were truly happy to see Mr. Bernard Menard, it became quite apparent within a few moments that the Lord and Lady Menard were becoming a little anxious to meet their future daughter-in-law, and their eyes grew quite large when one of the lovely ladies of the New Orleans House, Georgia, to be exact, sashayed nonchalantly in front of them on her way to the kitchen.

"Struttin' her stuff is more like what she was doing," as Uncle Clovis would say, "wearing a bright-red silk robe that only barely covered the necessary parts, if you know what I mean!"

Just another excuse for my silly uncles to laugh themselves even sillier for the moment as they punched one another and mimicked Georgia's sultry strut in front of the unsuspecting Menards and Willem, while the young boys were indeed visualizing every curve of the lovely lady of the New Orleans House.

It was also quite apparent that Lady Menard, suddenly grasping at her chest while sweating profusely and inhaling quite deeply, as if she were truly experiencing a heart attack, while Lord Menard's jaw dropped nearly down to the floor, had mistaken the curvaceous Georgia for their son's beloved Dolice Marie. Well, needless to say, all eyes had fallen directly on Georgia, who, knowing full well how to capture an audience under her spell and work it, was just about to introduce herself to the family when Dolice Marie saw her from where she was standing at the top of the stairs and let out a loud gasp herself that caught the attention of everyone in the parlor. Georgia glanced toward the stairs as Dolice Marie descended the stairs and thus entered the parlor, Georgia quickly detoured and circled back around to pass Dolice Marie as she headed back toward the stairs, head in the air, hand on her hip, struttin' out as she had just strutted in.

The scene that my sweet uncles most assuredly created in their own minds must have truly been one that tickled their fancies, because there would always be a thunder of laughter at this portion of the stories. I was never quite sure if it was because the young boys would sit under the shade of the big magnolia trees almost hypnotized by the legends that my sweet uncles would tell, or perhaps the fact that the lady Georgia had just made her entrance into the LaPierre-Menard history. But that story is yet to be told, indeed!

And now where were we? Oh! Yes, in the parlor of the New Orleans House…

Mr. Bernard Menard gathered the tiny Dolice Marie closer to him as she approached, wrapped her in his long arms, and kissed her softly on the top of her head. Oh, how beautiful my pregnant young ancestor looked, dressed in a dazzling dark-blue silk gown with short puffed sleeves that curved into a gathered neckline trimmed in glorious white that matched the empire line just under her extremely abundant bosoms that truly appeared to be quite ready to accommodate the child, or even two, developing inside her.

Dolice Marie had twisted her hair upward, away from her face, and braided lovely little white flowers throughout. It was truly obvious that the dear Mr. Bernard Menard was deeply in love with her and quite honored to introduce Dolice Marie to his family.

"This is my beloved Dolice Marie," he said, beaming as he introduced her to his parents and his best friend, Willem. Dolice Marie smiled quite confidently as only she could have in such a situation, with an upturned eyebrow, and then extended her tiny hand toward the Menards. Lord and Lady Menard looked at each other and quietly breathed a sigh of joy as they both reached out to grasp Dolice Marie's hands and, in their sheer thanksgiving that the curvaceous Georgia was truly not their future daughter-in-law, actually reached out to hug her. It was just as though the entire scenario with Georgia had been well orchestrated by someone in order to soften that first encounter with the Menards, but who knew? Who would ever know?

Jean Pierre and Jubil, finally awakened, strolled past Georgia and several of the other ladies of the New Orleans House (exchanging glances with one another, just like a man, I might add!), who had now gathered at the top of the stairs, while exchanging hugs and tears of their own for the successful meeting between their beloved Dolice Marie and her new family, just the way it should have been, I would say.

Dolice Marie's face radiated as she saw her Jean Pierre approaching and reached out with one of her hands as she held on to Mr.

Bernard Menard's hand with the other. The introductions were quite pleasant, during which Jean Pierre explained that his lovely wife, Evelina, was still comfortably sleeping and would surely be down to meet everyone as soon as she was well rested.

Lord and Lady Menard agreed again with each other as they quickly glanced toward each that *color* was truly going to be an absolutely delightful addition to the House of Menard, which had indeed been dreadfully too white for far too many generations.

Uncle Clovis always added that it appeared as if everyone had suddenly felt like, "What the hell!" and went on with the business of celebrating the fact that two people were in love and would soon be joined together.

Willem, on the other hand, found it necessary to extend yet another hug or two to the little French girl Angeline, and each one with just a little more power in his arms than the one before. Whether or not Angeline was interested in Willem's subtle advances, she kept herself quite focused on the business at hand, that is, keeping Lord and Lady Menard away from the fact that they were now being wined and dined in a, uh-uh, whorehouse in the middle of the French Quarter of the great city of New Orleans.

When Dolice Marie announced that Lord and Lady Menard would have the comfort of the master bedroom while they were in the great city of New Orleans, Angeline suddenly interrupted again to announce that her beloved aunt, Miss BB, had already made arrangements for the two of them to stay with her at the Declouette Mansion; in fact, other than the small train case that carried the personal effects for the Lord and Lady Menard, their belongings had already been taken to the Declouette Mansion.

Dolice Marie and Mr. Bernard Menard, who were suddenly taken aback by all the unsuspected news, realized indeed what Angeline was doing when she winked her eye at them several times as she led Lord and Lady Menard, along with Jean Pierre and Jubil, toward the formal dining room, where Cook had prepared a wonderful lunch of Creole delicacies, French desserts, and topped it all off with the finest Italian wine that could be found in all of the South.

MINT JULEP

Lord and Lady Menard, and Willem, were truly captivated and apparently having the time of their lives and soon were filled with questions, first about the origin of Creole foods, which Cook was more than happy to loudly proclaim, "All 'dis fuss about some leftover food from the master's house, chère!"

Good Creole cooks were also great storytellers, with an abundance of stories about their own good cooking as well as an abundant waistline to prove that the quality of their food was truly second to none, and Cook at the New Orleans House (as she was always called) was no different. When invited to tell her story about the origin of Creole foods, Cook continued to serve the guests seated at the dining room table and politely pulled a chair back and seated herself when everyone else was served, to the delight of Lord and Lady Menard, who were truly fascinated with Cook's stories and whose noses were truly being tickled by the delicious Italian wine, glass after glass.

My uncles always loved to mimic their favorite characters from the past, and it was always a sure wager that Uncle Clovis's mimicking of Cook from the New Orleans House was one of his most exciting moments during his portion of the traditional telling of the family stories.

"No, chère," he would say, "whil' de master and his mistress was feedin' off of de tender meat and fresh vegetables that was prepared by one of the house niggers, the slaves created their own dinners from the scraps in the master's pots...and dat was called Creole!"

Uncle Clovis would put his hand on his hip as he mimicked what he imagined Cook would do as she told her stories, speaking with an obviously broken English accent with traces of the Creole dialect that raised the level of laughter among my uncles even louder.

"A fresh pot of steamed rice," Uncle Clovis would continue, mimicking Cook. "Every meal in the slave quarters always was sho to have a fresh pot of steamed rice if he didn't have nothin' else!"

Cook continued her story by telling the Menards that "mixin'" was the secret.

"Chère, the slaves would mix a little tomato, chicken, sausage, maybe a little okrey dey got from the master's pots to the rice and call it dinner."

"Nowadays, you have to pay a hefty price for a meal like that," one of my old uncles would add, causing all the other uncles to nod in agreement.

"Yeah, you right!"

Another uncle would add his comment to my other uncles' comments, citing the fact that in these modern times, the Creole dishes that originated from the scraps of the former master's table are now being sold in major restaurants as Cajun food by shrewd chefs who make a huge profit by selling a cheap recipe to the public! My, my, my!

Once Cook had finished telling her stories and the guests had finished with their meal, Lord and Lady Menard began to ask those questions of a more personal nature, if you know what I mean. Leaning over the dining room table, Lord Menard whispered quietly to his son with reference to the lovely ladies of the New Orleans House who had joined them one by one for the meal.

"I am sure that it is most probably none of my business, my dear son, since we are mere guests in the establishment of your bride-to-be, but who are these other lovely ladies?"

The Lady Menard, who had frantically searched for and had finally located a fashionable pair of opera glasses from her purse, stared shamelessly through the magnified glasses and continued the speculation by citing that the ladies were most assuredly "quite beautiful, courteous, most definitely friendly, and...well-dressed in very little clothing, indeed!"

Mr. Bernard Menard gently removed the opera glasses from his mother's hand and reminded her with a whisper to her ear that she might appear to be a snob to the gentle ladies who were, at that time, staring back at the Lady Menard and acting as if they were having their pictures taken. Everyone had a good laugh at the Lady Menard's expense and toasted their playfulness with another glass of wine, while Lord Menard and Willem blushed.

"The generosity of Mademoiselle Dolice Marie has made it possible for several young women to have a home here at the New Orleans House and to receive an education in this great city of ours," Angeline said in her thick French accent, applying the same description that she had once given to Dolice Marie about her own grandmama's delicate work under the shadow of the Eifel Tower in Paris.

"Several of them have just recently arrived in the United States on big ships from lands far, far away from here." Angeline continued talking as Dolice Marie giggled, remembering how the two of them, in their nightclothes, had once sat in the big bed in the master bedroom, planning their future in the great city of New Orleans.

"How very wonderful," Lady Menard said proudly, "and how very kind of you." She then continued, "Especially taking in the poor pregnant waifs!"

She was, of course, speaking of Jean Pierre's sweet Evelina, who had finally awakened and found her way downstairs to the parlor. Jean Pierre quickly popped up from his chair in the dining room when he realized just who the Lady Menard was speaking of and scurried toward the quite-addled Evelina, who seemed to be just as confused at the scene as the Menards were.

"No, madam," Jean Pierre said quite proudly as he seated Evelina in his chair at the dining room table. "This is my wife, Evelina, who is expecting our fourth child."

"Oh! More relatives, I see!" Lady Menard stated, raising her glass of wine. "Well, the more, the merrier, as they say!

By the end of the afternoon, Lord and Lady Menard had become great friends with all the lovely ladies of the New Orleans House, as well as Jean Pierre, Evelina, and Jubil, and had become quite comfortable with the idea that their future daughter-in-law had such a huge heart that she could so easily open her home to the homeless women who came to the great city of New Orleans.

Between the generous glasses of superb Italian wine, coupled with her natural curiosity, Lady Menard at one point had actually seated herself as close as she could be to Dolice Marie and had placed a lovely crystal wine goblet upon her stomach and clapped her hands when she announced to everyone that she had indeed heard her grandbaby's heartbeat! Lord Menard was far too modest to indulge himself in such issues but found himself blowing kisses at Dolice Marie's stomach as he made smiley faces at the imaginary grandchild-to-be.

Mr. Bernard Menard thought it all quite wonderful, but it was obvious that his attention and his devotion were directed toward his beloved Dolice Marie. Willem, too, had found a fancy, the sweet little lady from France, Angeline, who felt it best not to lead the poor gentleman on a desperate path to heartbreak since her own poor heart had not yet given up on Monsieur Henri de Marquis, although she had not heard from him since he had visited the New Orleans House with news from Dolice Marie's family at Mon Village. Only news of him had come to Angeline via a wire telling her that Monsieur de Marquis had joined a wagon train headed west to help open a path for others who would want to follow, which led her to believe that his travels were far greater on his mind than anything else, but she had not yet been able to convince her own poor heart of such. Angeline did, however, give herself permission to enjoy the excitement and the presence of all those wonderful people that she had been hearing of for so long.

Well, it was either the powers of Mama Del from down the railroad tracks at Mon Village or perhaps just the universe performing one of those great mysteries that brought Obadiah to the front door of the New Orleans House, dressed in his usual attire and fully prepared with orders from Miss BB to bring Lord and Lady Menard to the Declouette Mansion. Obadiah also stated that he would return later that evening to also bring the remaining members of the wedding party to the Declouette Mansion for the rehearsal dinner. He excused himself as he reached for Lord and Lady Menard's personal train cases and, after placing them in the huge carriage, positioned himself at the door, awaiting his passengers, where Mr. Bernard Menard formally introduced him to his family and friend.

"Well, there he is again! I wonder if he's a relative too."

Lady Menard whispered to Lord Menard as they walked through the door of the New Orleans House and toward the carriage.

As Obadiah assisted the Lady Menard into the carriage, the poor thing tripped on her own foot as she was waving goodbye to the family standing in the doorway, a consequence that revealed indeed that Lady Menard was just a tad tipsy! Both she and Lord Menard began to giggle as both tried to assist each other into the carriage, while Mr. Bernard Menard and Willem raced to lend a helping hand.

"Mum, Dad," Mr. Bernard Menard called out, "are you all right?"

"Well, of course we are," Lord Menard answered. "Tallyho, big man!" Lord Menard said as he waved his hand to give Obadiah the orders to take off toward the Declouette Mansion.

"Off we go now!"

Obadiah clicked his tongue against his teeth twice and gently snapped the reins to cause the proud horse to move forward, and just as it did, Obadiah jerked the reins so tightly and so fast that the huge horse reared, causing the carriage to stand on just its back wheels, thrusting Lord and Lady Menard back and forth in the back seat of the carriage.

Screams could be heard from the inside the carriage and from everyone as they ran from the New Orleans House and out into the street. Within a matter of seconds, the huge horse was under control again, dropping its front legs to the ground and causing the carriage to also drop to the ground with a loud thud, thrusting Lord and Lady Menard's head up and down against the roof of the carriage several times as they screamed again. When all the action abruptly stopped, Obadiah calmly turned toward the family with a sternly professional expression on his face, tipped his hat, raised an eyebrow, and smiled so broadly that he exposed every single tooth he had in his mouth.

"Tallyho, big man! Off we go now!" My crazy uncles would yell in unison then explode into yet another thunder of laughter.

And now that the lovely ladies of the New Orleans House, Jean Pierre and Evelina, Jubil, Willem, Angeline, as well as Mr. Bernard Menard and, of course, Dolice Marie LaPierre were alone and away from ear range of the Lord and Lady Menard, everyone began to laugh hysterically as each began to describe the scene that had just happened, just outside as the quiet, reserved Obadiah had enjoyed his one sweet moment of retaliation.

Chapter 13

Miss BB was quite comfortable sitting on her front porch swing, cuddled up on the overstuffed floral-covered pillows with tiny eyelet ruffles sewn all around, sipping on a tall glass of honey-sweetened ice tea with Father Michael Dubois, the Jesuit priest who owed her a favor or two and who had agreed to perform the wedding ceremony, which was now just a few short hours away, when the two carriages approached the Declouette Mansion. Obadiah led the way, with the Declouette carriage filled with the lovely ladies of the New Orleans House, followed closely by Mr. Bernard Menard's carriage, which carried Willem, Angeline, Jean Pierre and Evelina, Jubil, and of course, Dolice Marie.

At a careful distance behind them, careful not to be seen, that is, were several photographers from the local newspapers, sneaking around and hot on the trail of a juicy story that was truly being offered to them by the charming gentlewoman of the Declouette Mansion. Miss BB was aware of where every sneaky reporter and every sneaky photographer was hidden around the mansion, each being carefully watched by one of the mansion's employees, who had already been assigned to follow their every move. Miss BB also encouraged all her guests to enjoy themselves by giving the nosy media, and her nosy neighbors as well, something juicy to see and something juicy to write about.

Lord and Lady Menard were resting peacefully upstairs in their room when everyone finally arrived for the wedding rehearsal and for a taste of that delicious gumbo that was simmering on the stove. Miss BB had assured them that one of the employees would awaken them at the first sign of the arrival of the wedding party and that one of the staff most certainly did make sure they were made aware as soon as the first carriage could be seen coming through the gates of the Declouette Mansion, which was absolutely beautifully decorated and fully prepared for the events that would lead up to the next day's ceremonies. With everyone there in place and fully prepared to get the show on the road, the wedding rehearsal was absolutely perfect, a premonition of the following day's success, with a fine dinner as a well-deserved reward. There was plenty of getting to know one another over deep bowls of gumbo and steaming rice as well as long crystal glasses filled with sparkling champagne, giving the wedding party a heads-up with regard to the coming celebration.

As the sun began to set, Mr. Bernard Menard announced that it was indeed time to get some rest since the morning would surely arrive soon and there were still things left to be done. Everyone agreed, until Miss BB announced that the men, and that meant *all* of the men, were to spend the night at the Declouette Mansion, while the ladies, and that meant *all* the ladies, were to be transported back to the New Orleans House. She quickly explained that it was tradition for the bride and the groom to be separated the night before their wedding, and therefore the fact that she was including everyone in the traditional scenario would ensure that everyone did truly rest, indeed.

Once home again at the New Orleans House, Dolice Marie and Angeline relaxed in the master bedroom, giggling and talking together on the big bed just as they had done years before while getting to know each other and making their plans for the future. Both were entirely too excited to sleep yet too tired to begin their preparation ritual for the wedding. Evelina, on the other hand, had curled herself up on the foot of the big bed and had already fallen off to sleep, with her hand cuddling the baby in her oversize belly, before Dolice Marie and Angeline could get completely comfortable. Even the giggling and jumping on the big bed did not disturb Evelina, and sometime during the night, Dolice Marie and Angeline finally fell asleep, completely dressed!

Miss BB found her comfortable spot again on the front porch swing to watch the sun set along with her babies, GiGi and FiFi, where she would wait for Obadiah and think joyously about the next day. Suddenly, she caught sight of a very familiar silhouette resting on a slow-moving horse just over the horizon. Miss BB cupped her aging hand over her squinting eyes as if she were shading them from the sun high up in the sky when, all of a sudden, she beamed, smiling from ear to ear as she recognized her new old friend from the noble Commonwealth of Kentucky, Mr. Monte Leonard.

Within minutes, Monte Leonard smiled broadly himself as he was greeted by several employees of the Declouette Mansion, prepared and eager to assist him with his horse and with that special gift that he was bringing to his new old friend, Miss BB, from his employer, Mr. Samuels, several bottles of smooth Kentucky bourbon, of course! Miss BB jumped up from the swing on the front porch, clapping her hands as she greeted Monte Leonard with an embrace, obviously enchanted with his presence, truly grateful for his special company.

"Well, Miss BB," he said after their long embrace, removing his hat and running his fingers through his long brown hair. "What a pleasure it is to see you again. I trust that you will accept this here gift from my employer, Mr. Samuels, who sends his best to you and also to the wedding party."

After a short while, Obadiah returned, and once handing over the horse and carriage to one of the Declouette Mansion staff, he bade his good night to Miss BB and Monte Leonard, who, shortly thereafter, made their escape into the Declouette Mansion, arm in arm and smiling broadly.

Monte Leonard asked Miss BB about the possibilities of securing a veterinarian for his ailing horse, who had shown some serious signs of a damaged front leg during the last few miles of the trip from the noble Commonwealth of Kentucky, which had caused an entire day's delay in reaching their destination. Monte Leonard seemed quite concerned about this favorite horse of his, one that had been groomed from birth on one of the capable Kentucky farms, explaining that he was just not prepared to say goodbye to it as yet. Miss BB assured him that she would have Obadiah look into the possibilities of securing the very finest veterinarian available in the great city of New Orleans as soon as the sun raised its head, and then after a deep bowl of gumbo and steaming rice, she led him to his room and bade him a good night.

Early the next morning, the morning of the LaPierre-Menard wedding, as Monte Leonard strolled through the grounds of the beautiful Declouette Mansion for his morning smoke, he caught sight of a figure leading a horse near the stables, where the guests' horses were being boarded. As he neared the scene, Monte Leonard realized that the horse was indeed his own horse, now with wrappings around his damaged leg and being led by a man of color down a dusty path. Monte Leonard had never heard of a man of color being a veterinarian in that day and age (but then again, this was the great city of New Orleans), so he carefully approached the man to inquire just who he was and just what he was doing with this ailing horse.

Well, lo and behold, the man introduced himself to Monte Leonard as "Jubilation LaPierre, suh, Jubil for short, from Mon Village in the great state of Louisiana, the best friend of the bride's brother, or cousin, or whatever!"

With his eyes cast down in the familiar manner of a former slave when addressing a proper Southern white man of the Deep South, Jubil explained that he had carefully watched the veterinarian as he tried to heal the horse's malady but unfortunately could not, as he had already explained to Obadiah. The veterinarian had told Obadiah to tell Mr. Leonard that his horse was no longer capable of carrying a passenger and would be better off being put down, out of his misery.

Monte Leonard, still cautious, of course, leaned down to inspect his horse's ailing leg with one eye still on Jubil, and as he did, the horse freely lifted the leg as if it were perfectly natural, not the least bit injured. Monte Leonard looked at Jubil with complete astonishment and finally asked, "Where is the veterinarian?"

"Gone, suh," Jubil answered.

"Gone!" Monte Leonard repeated.

There was a long moment of silence as Monte Leonard continued to inspect the horse's leg.

"You can ride him, suh," Jubil finally said. "He be all right now. No need to be puttin' him down now."

"Really?" Monte Leonard asked, and Jubil simply nodded, with his eyes still cast down.

Monte Leonard again pondered the situation and then hopped aboard the horse and took him for a slow walk around the same dusty path where he had first encountered Jubil. Each time around the path, Monte Leonard sped up a bit until the horse was now at a near-galloping speed without the least bit of strain to the leg, which caused Monte Leonard to stop, dismount, and ask Jubil just how he had healed the horse's leg.

Jubil explained that this was his job at Mon Village and that he and horses, well, just seemed to understand one another, much better than he and human beings understood one another. Jubil explained that he had created his own medicines out of natural herbs, roots, and of course, the abundance of mint (which seemed to never stop growing at Mon Village) for curing whatever seemed to be ailing the animals that he cared for back home at Mon Village and for those that had been brought to him by the people outside Mon Village that had begun to trust his care for their horses.

Monte Leonard's eyes twinkled under the long hair that hung down over them, as if they were seeing far into the future, then he smiled and proceeded to reach inside his pocket to pull out several gold coins that he attempted to give to Jubil, who refused to accept the money, telling Monte Leonard that this was just a favor he had done for a horse who needed his attention. Well, Monte Leonard insisted that Jubil take the coins, and oh, he also insisted that Jubil immediately stop calling him "suh" and hanging his head down in his presence.

"I'm not one of these here proper Southern white people from this here city of New Orleans. I'm a proud native of the noble Commonwealth of Kentucky, and I think we just may be able to help each other out. I mean, your love and knowledge for the care of horses and my need for your knowledge and the kind of care you give to horses! We'll talk about some serious possibilities after these here proceedings. And thank you, Jubil," he said, extending his hand to shake it. "Thank you, thank you."

Jubil quickly corrected himself and shook Monte Leonard's hand and raised his head to look him straight in his eyes. Both smiled.

Why, it was a proud moment from our family's past that my dear uncles truly cherished, and I can remember their chests swelling out just a little bit more as they pondered the sheer joy and importance of it all.

The day of the wedding was just as busy as, if not more than, the previous weeks of planning had been and found everyone busily tending to their own particular chores in preparation for that precious moment that was just that, simply moments away.

Mr. Bernard Menard, his best friend, Willem, from Toronto, Obadiah, Jean Pierre, and Jubil were all tucked away in one of the downstairs rooms of the Declouette Mansion, where they were opening boxes and attempting to match tuxedos, fancy dress shirts, cummerbunds, gloves, and top hats, not to mention socks and shoes!

A slightly pregnant Dolice Marie, a very pregnant Evelina, Angeline, and the lovely ladies of the New Orleans House had arrived early and were greeted by Miss BB at the back door of the Declouette Mansion and were immediately tucked away in one of the upstairs rooms of the mansion, where they also began opening boxes and attempted to match evening gowns, gloves, stockings, and shoes that had been delivered early that morning for them to wear at the wedding.

The beautiful and equally devoted Angeline, Dolice Marie's best friend and confidante, who would stand with her as her maid of honor, was truly bedazzled at the beauty of her own gown, dusty pink in color and created with delicate yet whimsical silk cloth, distinguished only from the gowns being worn by Evelina and the lovely ladies of the New Orleans House by the thick ivory silk sash that hugged her waistline and was then fashioned into a large bow just above the bustle in the back. Strikingly beautiful!

The girls just giggled as they searched through all the boxes to find their own gowns, which had been especially created in each individual size, their matching stockings and high-top buttoned shoes, and of course, their pearls—there were pearls everywhere for everyone to wear, a wedding gift that had been delivered that morning as well, an extremely thoughtful gift from the great city of New York for everyone, from the groom himself, the ever-suave and sophisticated Mr. Bernard Menard.

Miss BB was again having the time of her life as she went from lady to lady clasping the string of beautiful pearls around each neck and leaving each with a smile and a sincere word of praise. Utterly enchanting!

In another section of the upstairs room of the Declouette Mansion, all alone, the blushing bride-to-be, who had escaped the commotion of the other women preparing for her wedding, slowly lifted the top of the box that contained her own wedding gown, uncharacteristically quiet and shy as she fingered the gown. It was apparent that the former slave girl from the LaPierre Plantation, the little girl who accepted her place as mistress, that saucy young woman who stole her place in the New Orleans society, was, yes, at a complete loss for words; in fact, she was simply scared to death!

"Unfortunately, my dear," Miss BB's voice sounded, bringing Dolice Marie back to the reality at hand, "you cannot walk down the aisle in your corset, although, I might add, you do wear it well!"

Dolice Marie herself was amused at the comment and smiled like a shy little girl, casting her eyes upward at the kindly lady that had become her earthly mother.

"Before you even concern yourself with it, my darling, let me assure you that every woman is the least bit nervous on her wedding day. Why, it would not even be a wedding day without a little nervousness!" Miss BB said as she touched Dolice Marie's hand with such apparent love. "But I am truly afraid that if you do not prepare yourself now for your wedding day, one of these other lovely ladies," she said, motioning to the lovely ladies of the New Orleans House, who had now entered the room, "will be glad to take your place!" She laughed out loud, amused at her own clever comment.

Dolice Marie LaPierre was simply the epitome of Southern charm and beauty that day, wrapped in a rather-flattering yet modest and simplistic, believe it or not, wedding gown that Miss BB had chosen for her from a fashion catalog of exquisite gowns for all occasions from one of those fine stores in Europe. As she slipped into the lace-covered off-white long-sleeved sheath with foot after foot of flowing lace train behind her, even Dolice Marie felt the atmosphere change suddenly into a fairy-tale scene where everyone lives happily ever after. It was also apparent that there could be absolutely no postponement of this wedding day since the beautiful wedding gown was already just a tad snug and could not possibly accept yet another inch of baby fat!

Angeline smiled with great admiration for what she was witnessing, clapping her hands like a small child, with eyes wide and cheeks pink with delight.

"Look, Aunt BB," Angeline said with glee and with her thick French accent, "is she not the most beautiful bride you have ever seen?"

There were many "Oohs" and "Aahs" as well as tears as everyone in the room admired Dolice Marie's beauty and grace that seemed to engulf her from every fiber of the dress and flowed down to the very tip of the rippling train that traveled well into the better half of the upstairs room in the Declouette Mansion.

Then suddenly there was a hush that fell throughout the room as the lovely ladies of the New Orleans House began to look toward Madam Dolice Marie, who now stood in front of the floor-length mirror, admiring what she, too, was witnessing. Miss BB wept as she ceremonially placed the tiara with the veil upon Dolice Marie's head, stepping back a foot or two, surrounded by Angeline and the lovely ladies of the New Orleans House, to admire the young woman as though Dolice Marie were the painting that the artist had just completed.

But Dolice Marie was completely oblivious to all that was going on around her now, oblivious to the sounds and sights of the human world, because now she had been drawn into the netherworld to be with her beloved Mama Mozelle, there in the full-length mirror, smiling and blowing kisses to her in true maternal acquiesce. And although Dolice Marie was smiling for all to see, her smiles were truly meant for her beloved Mama Mozelle and that old African-with-No-Name, who stood happily and proudly beside his sister, there in the mirror. Hmmmmmm, now, what was that old African's name?

Again, my sweet uncles, led by my uncle Clovis, pondered that question as they wrinkled their brows, squinted their eyes, and looked without direction, still seeking that age-old question, "What was that old African's name?"

"Oh," Uncle Clovis would finally say, "Jean Pierre I."

Those old codgers! Always ready to add just a little more theatrics to the traditional telling of the family stories, while the young boys inhaled every syllable of every word.

When Obadiah finally knocked softly on the door to the room in the Declouette Mansion being occupied by the ladies of the wedding party to announce to everyone that the very special moment was indeed almost upon them, a sudden hush seemed to suck the very air out of the room, an implosion of sorts, if you know what I mean. All the ladies seemed to be frozen in time, until Miss BB opened the door and motioned for Obadiah to come in quickly.

"Dahlin', I need you to do me a favor," she whispered. "Get some money out of the ginger jar and grab that bothersome photographer hiding behind the white azalea bush that thinks no one knows he's there and tell him to get his hind parts in here, with his camera. Why, we, ladies, look far too good not to be captured in a photograph, and since the wedding photographer is probably already being overworked out there, this might be the perfect time to expose the sneaky little twit."

Everyone laughed at the charming Miss BB as she smoothed her upswept hair under the smashingly exquisite wide floppy-brimmed straw hat with a delicate pure silk ribbon (pink, of course) weaved throughout.

"Oh, and, Obadiah," she continued, "there should be no need to offer him any more money than what's in the ginger jar for this private undertaking. Simply tell him if he doesn't want the job, you have the liberty of offering it to the other photographer who is hiding among the wisteria."

While Obadiah was out searching for the photographer, Miss BB was leading the ladies of the wedding party to the balcony outside the room, where everyone began to giggle and strike silly poses. When Obadiah returned just a few moments later with the photographer (the one that had been hiding behind the white azalea bush) in tow, the beautiful bride and all the ladies began to take their places where Miss BB had already assigned them.

"Snap away," she said, "and make it good! You may end up with an exclusive story!"

The photographer was indeed overwhelmed by such interweaving of colors, not to mention pregnant bellies, on the balcony and appeared to be frozen, with eyes bulging—that is, until Obadiah slightly nudged him with his elbow on the fellow's back to remind him that he was there to do a job, and a hasty one at that, since the wedding hour was now directly upon them.

What a lovely portrait it turned out to be! Dolice Marie seated in a white lace wrought iron chair in her beautiful wedding gown without the veil, her head resting on the shoulder of Miss BB, who was seated beside her on one side, protecting her from the brilliance of the watchful sun high in the sky by her fashionable chapeau; Evelina on the other side in a twin chair, holding Dolice Marie's hand with one of her own and her other caressing her resting abdomen; and of course, Angeline standing just behind the three, with her head to one side, while the lovely ladies of the New Orleans House, all dressed in their exquisite wedding garments, with the appearance of sheer pride, stood posing in their own individual way while surrounding the scene in the presence of the fluffy white clouds in the background appeared as a divine gift from the heavens, perfectly positioned and framing forever those captured in the wedding-day portrait.

The photographer's eye had captured the very essence of the story of our early ancestors in the great city of New Orleans, and the very portrait hangs now where it has hung ever since being brought to Mon Village decades later, in the parlor of the big house, for all generations to admire.

Obadiah escaped with the photographer when the shoot was over but returned just a few moments later to inform everyone that it was truly time to begin the wedding procession. There was the sound of silence coming from the room where the women had been dressing, but no one answered as Obadiah knocked the first time.

Yet another knock on the door, this one harder, indeed, than the first, followed by Obadiah verbally expressing the fact that it was indeed time for the wedding procession; in fact, the beautiful, soft music had already begun.

"Chile, yo' man is waiting," Georgia said with her hand on her hip, a flip of her head, and a coquettish look about herself, which brought everyone back to the moment. One more look in the mirror, one more hug for one another, and one more tear wiped away, and then finally the door was opened to the hallway.

Georgia led the way through the door and down the hallway to the staircase, while the other ladies of the New Orleans House followed closely behind her, adjusting themselves just one final time and choosing their bouquets from one of the employees of the mansion on their way. Miss BB made the final adjustments to herself and to Dolice Marie as well, then once the two reached the top of the stairs, Miss BB was greeted by Obadiah, who extended his arm to escort her to her seat situated right next to an extremely anxious Jubil.

Oh, it was quite obvious that the press had found superior hiding places to cover such a controversial event being held at the Declouette Mansion, places where they could see every person and hear every word. How smart they all thought they were, hiding behind azalea bushes and pretending to be inauspiciously walking past the mansion, even tipping their hats when eyed by Obadiah or one of the many guests of various skin colors that had truly caught their eye. But it was Dolice Marie's old friend the sheriff that seemed to have the biggest eye of all, that protective eye that seemed to have followed Dolice Marie since she first came to the great city of New Orleans. The sheriff, too, seemed to know exactly where the media intruders were hiding, and after finding his own comfortable spot where everything was in his full vision, he leaned against a wall with his fat cigar and did what he did best, watched out for Dolice Marie.

Once everyone was in their proper place, Miss BB gave the subtle signal, and the soft music from the stringed quartet could be heard again, the signal for the guests to turn their attention to the wedding party as it soon began its slow march down the pathway and up to the gazebo. There, within the colonnade of an exquisitely decorated gazebo, in the middle of the Declouette Mansion backyard, stood the even more handsome Mr. Bernard Menard, his best man, Willem, and finally, once everything was properly unfolding as it should, an anxious Obadiah.

A very pregnant Evelina adjusted the front of the skirt of her lovely gown, which kept rising uncomfortably, before she began to lead the procession of beautiful women toward the gazebo. She blushed, smiling quite girlishly as she breathed a deep breath, raised her head, and began the procession down the path, dropping soft rose pedals as she slowly and methodically led the way.

And of course, there were those lovely ladies of the New Orleans House that followed Evelina, led by the sultry Georgia, hips freely moving from side to side, heads bobbing all around as they greeted every guest seated along the way. I do declare it would not surprise me one bit if the ladies of the New Orleans House had been switching themselves down that pathway to the gazebo as if they were openly soliciting for some future business for themselves! (If you know what I mean!)

It was an extraordinary Louisiana day with plenty of sunshine, fluffy clouds, with birds singing their own special song mingled with the "Oohs," "Aahs," and sweet conversations of compliments softly rising from the guests. Miss BB was completely overwhelmed with emotion and dabbed the tears away from her eyes with a sweet cotton handkerchief that she took from her evening bag. Monte Leonard, seated behind her, reached over the chair to pat her on the shoulder. Lord Menard, seated with a very giggly Lady Menard on the other side of the pathway, with Mr. Bernard Menard's family, captured and savored every moment with his opera glasses while beaming just like the proud father that he truly was. It was an incredibly wonderful sight, with not a dry eye in the crowd, as the members of the wedding party moved slowly toward their places in and around the gazebo.

Angeline was the last in the procession, and once everyone was exactly where they were supposed to be, all the guests now properly standing, the stringed quartet paused for a moment to again prepare for the next segment of the wedding, the bride's entrance. I still get excited just thinking about hearing about it!

Red and pink rose petals now covered the pathway to the gazebo, where an apparently shy Jean Pierre extended his arm to his beautiful sister—er, cousin—Dolice Marie, with tears swelling in his eyes as he waited for the wedding march to begin. Oh, I can just imagine how simply debonair my ancestor looked on that day—handsome, of course, and as proud as a Southern peacock.

In unison the guests turned slightly, in customary honor and respect, toward Jean Pierre and Dolice Marie as the two slowly floated down the pathway to the gazebo while the sound of "Oohs" and "Aahs" still sounded from each row.

Miss BB was overcome with emotion, just as any true mother would be at this special time in her daughter's life. Angeline could be seen wiping her eyes several times as she stood in the gazebo beside the Jesuit priest. Evelina, the poor darling, truly looked uncomfortable but still very beautiful, and because of her present condition, Miss BB had already instructed one of her employees to secure a midwife just in case Evelina would decide to pop while she and Jean Pierre were guests at the Declouette Mansion.

By the time Jean Pierre had escorted Dolice Marie to the top of the gazebo stairs and put her hand on Mr. Bernard Menard's hand to "give her away," Dolice Marie could be heard quietly crying at first yet progressing steadily into a loud sob; in fact, it became quite difficult to hear the Jesuit priest reciting the words of the wedding ceremony over the wails of the blushing bride.

Through the vows of love, obedience, and "Until death do we part," through the exchanging of the rings and the traditional "jumping of the broom," Dolice Marie sobbed tears of joy and, most assuredly, from the tug of the raging hormones of her own pregnancy. It would not be until the Jesuit priest finally pronounced them man and wife, Mr. Bernard Menard kissed his bride, and the guests extended a standing ovation of applause that Dolice Marie could finally calm herself down and realize that she was, indeed, truly married.

In the midst of cheerful applause, there was another whose moans and groans could be heard now as the Jesuit priest introduced Mr. and Mrs. Bernard Menard to family and guests; moans and groans that Jean Pierre immediately recognized as that of his own Evelina beginning her labor and birth ritual.

Jean Pierre, with Jubil closely behind him, ran up the gazebo steps and reached for Evelina just as she was about to let out one enormous scream, lifted her into the air so high that her feet touched the clouds and her head barely missed scraping along the ground as he ran down the pathway, past the guests, who were reacting with sheer shock and unbelievable excitement, and straight to the Declouette Mansion, where the midwife was waiting.

As usual, Evelina was restricting Jean Pierre from ever touching her again, threatening him with his very life if he dared even consider another relation with her, while the poor man simply searched for a place to run, as he and Jubil had run so many times before. But this was all happening in the great city of New Orleans, among the many strangers that had come to be a part of such a wonderful event, and so after gently laying an extremely unhappy Evelina on the bed in the Declouette Mansion to be cared for by the capable midwife, Jean Pierre and Jubil leaned against the door in the hallway and simply waited.

Well, as fate would have it, a sweet baby boy was born, and in a fraction of the time that his other children had taken to come into the world. The midwife peeked out of the door and quietly beckoned Jean Pierre to come in, assuring him that it would be safe now since Evelina was fast asleep. As usual, Jubil accompanied him just to be sure.

Once inside the room, a very proud and happy Jean Pierre knelt down beside the bed and kissed his beloved Evelina on her forehead and then lifted his sweet son from her arms and caressed him gently while allowing his own tears to flow quite freely. Jubil smiled broadly and, after planting his own kiss on Jean Pierre's sweet baby boy, announced that he would return to the wedding reception and let everyone know, but it would be Dolice Marie that had already made that announcement.

It seems that the family story states that the newly wedded Madam Dolice Marie felt a powerful and warm breath of new life sweep through her very being at the exact moment that Evelina had given birth to her sweet baby boy while standing in the receiving line. In fact, as my dear uncle Clovis stated, "And the good thing about it was that Dolice Marie had finally stopped all that howling!"

Oh, and as usual, my other wonderful uncles would just laugh and laugh, giving Uncle Clovis just a moment to catch his breath and sip some cool, sweet lemonade, which he, too, had probably spiked with a little corn liquor.

So while the wedding party and the guests were enjoying themselves tremendously at the reception, another life had entered the line of the LaPierre family. Jubil quietly closed the door to the bedroom to allow Jean Pierre and Evelina to welcome their new son into the world with privacy. He slowly found his way back to the wedding reception to share the good news of the birth of the baby with the delighted guests, a moment that caused Jubil to again reflect on his own life and a future with Miss Sylvia that he knew was either now or never.

Monte Leonard found Jubil sitting alone at the wedding reception while the other guests mingled among themselves and while Dolice Marie and Mr. Bernard Menard enjoyed a few moments being with Jean Pierre and the new baby, while Evelina, who had labored to give birth to her fifth child, rested peacefully. Monte Leonard, who was celebrating the wedding by keeping company with a glass of smooth Kentucky bourbon and a big cigar, pulled a chair away from the table and seated himself near Jubil.

It was obvious that Monte Leonard had something on his mind and that he was truly ready to discuss it with Jubil, that is, if Jubil was ready to give an attentive mind and a listening ear, but before Monte Leonard could put his glass of smooth Kentucky bourbon down on the table, Jubil had already taken the lead.

"How's your horse, Mr. Leonard?" Jubil asked with an apparent air of complete sincerity.

"Very well, thanks to you," Monte Leonard answered. "Very well, indeed!"

There was silence for a while as the two men turned their attention to a lovely waltz that was now being played by the musicians that had been hired by Miss BB and toward the guests who were spinning around the grounds of the Declouette Mansion to the same sounds. Once the music had subsided and the applause had died down, Monte Leonard turned to Jubil and reminded him that he had mentioned earlier that he would like to talk with him after the wedding and felt that this was truly an ideal time and place, if Jubil would accommodate him.

Jubil nodded in agreement, although he was quite perplexed as to just why the kind Kentuckian would seek him out, but agreed, and so the two men pulled their chairs a little closer together. Monte Leonard freshened his glass of smooth Kentucky bourbon and poured one for Jubil as well. It was obvious that Jubil was having a bit of a difficult time feeling "social" with the proper white Kentuckian, so Monte Leonard tipped Jubil's glass of smooth Kentucky bourbon with his own and then raised it in a toast to their "newfound friendship." Jubil responded by lifting his glass in agreement with Monte Leonard, coupled with a broad smile that most probably said more than Jubil could have possibly verbalized.

"Well, Jubil, I told you that I was looking forward to talking with you about some possibilities that may be coming up in my home in the noble Commonwealth of Kentucky," Monte Leonard proudly said.

"You see, we Kentuckians are horse-racing fanatics and very proud of our sport. Shoot, I can remember horse races ever since I was a little boy over by the Commons Park and on Race Street in Lexington, and I never tire of it either. It's like a passion, you know what I mean?"

Jubil might not have really known what Monte Leonard was talking about, but he nodded as if he did and listened carefully to see if he eventually could figure it all out.

"Now, my work with Mr. Samuels in delivering this here fine, smooth Kentucky bourbon is very important to me, very important!"

he said, lifting his drink again in absolute admiration. "'Cause it puts money in my pocket and a kick in my spirit. But my real hankering is for horse racing, just like any Kentuckian with a right mind!" Monte Leonard laughed and slapped Jubil on his leg. "Kentucky is God's country, the land he put here for breeding horses, and we lost far too many of them during the Civil War, so many that the horse industry began to suffer and people sadly began to look for other ways to bring money back into the commonwealth."

Monte Leonard leaned back in the chair, crossed his leg, and made himself quite comfortable as he continued to relay a story that made absolutely no sense to Jubil, who was still hoping to find out just what Monte Leonard wanted from him.

"Well, there's this here young feller, Colonel Meriwether Lewis Clark Jr., the proud grandson of some explorer named William Clark, who decided that he was going to bring the horse industry back to life in Kentucky, so he visited the racetracks in Europe, and especially the Epsom Derby in England, talked to all their big-shot racing leaders, and learned a lot about the sport. Well, when he came back to Kentucky, he had his mind all made up to create a racetrack just like the one in England, only this race would be only for Kentucky-bred horses. I heard he convinced over three hundred people to invest one hundred bucks each to open up the Louisville Jockey Club and then leased the land for a racetrack, and a grandstand from his two uncles, John and Henry Churchill, I declare, a whole bunch of other people, and I had hoped that the racetrack would be built in Lexington, but the railroad company had another idea. The railroad company decided to run its tracks through Louisville instead of Lexington, and that was the end of that! Well, wherever it's at, pretty soon Kentuckians will be able to show off their breeding abilities again and make a little money for themselves, and for the commonwealth, of course. I hear they want to call it the Kentucky Derby. Now, don't that sound like something that might need a good veterinarian?"

He took another big draw from his big cigar and continued.

"Well, with all that big-time stuff going on, I'm afraid that someone is going to lose track of the most important thing in that race, and that's the horse! We have good trainers, good groomers, and good jockeys, that's for sure, but most importantly, we will need a decent veterinarian, a horse doctor, one who can keep our horses in the best shape they can be for racing. And perish the thought, to heal 'em up quickly after the race, if there is ever that need."

Jubil was finally able to nod in agreement with something that Monte Leonard had said to him. Being a good horse doctor—he could easily understand that! Jubil laughed and took another big drink of his smooth Kentucky bourbon, and this time, Monte Leonard slapped his own knee. Jubil smiled, and although he was still not quite sure if he would ever be sure about the rest of the conversation, he was at least sure that he was needed to care for horses, and at that moment, that was all that was necessary.

Jubil explained to Monte Leonard that he already had a job, one that he truly loved at the only place that he had known all his life, a place where many people depended upon him for much more than just the care of their animals. Jubil told Monte Leonard that he was indeed the overseer of Mon Village, and with him gone from his many duties, surely something would be lacking.

But Monte Leonard had an agenda that he was indeed working with, and a ready answer for any concern that Jubil could have possibly raised.

"I'm only talking about two months out of each year," he said, "one month during the spring season and one month during the fall. The way I see it, time before racing season to properly prepare the horses and time after to properly prepare them for breeding and some for selling. Why, there can't be any racing in the snow and ice of a Kentucky winter, and surely not when its blistering hot in the summer."

Although it all had begun to make perfect sense to Jubil, he also felt that the decision was dependent upon more than just him alone, and so he told Monte Leonard.

"No need for a direct answer right now," Monte Leonard told Jubil. "Just don't be forgetting about this conversation."

Jubil nodded in agreement again and clicked his glass of smooth Kentucky bourbon with that of Monte Leonard's, and the two again turned their attention to the celebration at hand.

Chapter 14

MY UNCLE MICHELE was a military man who was truly devoted to God, to family, and to country in ways that began quite early in his life, as was demonstrated by his closeness and devotion to my grandparents and his siblings as well as his decision to volunteer to join the Army at the tender age of seventeen. Yes, my grandparents did have their proverbial "fit" when he announced his intentions, but it was apparent that Uncle Michele would not be satisfied earning his living while working at Mon Village in any of the many production companies.

Unlike the vast majority of my other uncles who went not much farther than the perimeter of the great state of Louisiana, my uncle Michele traveled the world and, from the many rumors about his incredible life, had his share of experiences, if you know what I mean!

Uncle Michele's military history included the common cleaning of latrines that had been reserved for military men of color in those days to the most prestigious contributions to the country as a paratrooper and, in his latter days, as a soldier of top secret clearance distinction. Even though he served this country well and traveled the world, Uncle Michele found love and family right here at home, at Mon Village, where he fell in love with the tempestuous Mercedes, pronounced in the Deep South as "Mercy-dees," while on a furlough at home from a tour of duty in France just after the big war.

By the time Uncle Michele finally had the opportunity to come home, Mon Village had its own "juke joint," where the men could find a cold beer, the most current music played on the "jukebox" (or some spirited zydeco sounds played on a squeeze-box, a fiddle, a tin tub, and a washboard with two spoons played live by some of my other uncles and their buddies), a good poker game, and most assuredly, a place to wind down after a long, hard day of work on the bayou. It would be there, at the Mon Village "juke joint" that my uncle Michele met and fell in love with Aunt Mercedes, who was working there as a waitress at that time.

I had always heard from my other uncles that Aunt Mercedes was a tiny little spitfire with long black hair who always walked around the Bayou Frou-Frous with no shoes on when she was a young girl, despite the warnings from her parents that she could get worms or red bugs.

I had also heard quite often that Aunt Mercedes had never run from a good fight but was often the one that instigated the fights that she had ever had the cause to be in.

Aunt Mercedes had often bragged, or should I say threatened, as the case may be, that she would pour boiling-hot water into the ear of any sleeping man that was brave enough to do her wrong, and rumor had it that she had actually bitten one boyfriend's arm straight through a winter's coat and had indeed drawn blood! With such a reputation, it was truly a wonder that so many of the young boys at Mon Village were still infatuated with Aunt Mercedes, who eventually said yes to a marriage proposal and moved away with her new husband, leaving many broken hearts and her tough reputation behind her.

Mercedes eventually divorced that first husband and then returned to her parents' home at Mon Village with her infant daughter after some extremely inconsolable and irreconcilable events that evidently occurred between herself and her husband, wherever they had gone to create that new life with each other. Evidently, all they truly created together was some great animosity and the tiny little daughter that she brought home, Eva, who became the joy of my sweet uncle Michele's life, accepting, protecting, and loving her as his very own.

Since divorce was an uncommon circumstance, truly never heard of in the confines of Mon Village prior to that time, the two decided to elope and come home already married to avoid any criticism. Strangely enough, and quite curious to Uncle Michele and Aunt Mercedes, no one at Mon Village seemed to give second thoughts to what the two of them had done or even what they would do in the future since everyone was swept up in their own lives—indeed, the manner in which everyone should live their lives. There was, however, that grand celebration in their honor when they did come home from wherever they had been, attending to their wedding business.

The three became a loving family and traveled the distance between the stars during my sweet uncle Michele's military career, courageously weathering the storms of homesickness, discrimination, wars, foreign assignments, and everything else in between. After thirteen years together, the two were truly blessed with a precious baby boy of their own, a boy they named Emile, who would grow up to bring them great joy, and as my uncle Michele once explained to Eva, "No matter how many sons me and your momma may have in the future, you will always be my firstborn, my first love." After thirty years in the military, Uncle Michele and Aunt Mercedes came back to Mon Village to finish out their days in the peace, tranquility, and family of Mon Village, building a beautiful yet unpretentious home on a small slope in the very back of the residential area, where they could have their privacy, or so they thought at first. My aunt Mercedes and my uncle Michele were quite passionate, and powerfully so, whether engaged in some sort of disagreement or the truly passionate and powerful manner in which the two would make up. Why, my other sweet uncles would just laugh as they teased Uncle Michele about the times, even now, that they could be heard yelling from their house all the way to the Bayou Frou-Frous about something that had raised the feathers on Aunt Mercedes's lovely neck and gotten her going about something that only she knew about. (Rumor had it that Aunt Mercedes would become especially uncontrollable when Uncle Michele would innocently pull out a salt-and-pepper shaker to season his food before tasting it!) But then, just moments later, she would ever-so-charmingly ask him, and just as calmly as she had been ruffled, if he would care for more corn bread or if he needed another cold drink, and he would answer sweetly with a loving "No" or "Yes, honey, but I'll get it. Thank you."

Those two, I tell you, created more conversation on the Bayou Frou-Frous than anyone or anything else ever did! My uncles would just grin and tease Uncle Michele, and he would just grin back with them, shaking his head and agreeing with a "Yeah, you right!"

Because of his measureless experience with passion and all that he had experienced in his life, it was no wonder that my uncle Michele's portion of the telling of the family stories would be about the following extremely emotional and passionate events in the lives of the Menards and the LaPierres. Shall we continue?

Jean Pierre was indeed truly delighted at the birth of his newest child, his sweet little baby boy, but the idea of going through that labor and birth dance with Evelina again, at their ages, seemed too difficult a task to ever repeat anymore. As he stared hopelessly at his beautiful Evelina, who was now resting calmly and peacefully with the sweet little baby boy in her arms, a cloud of smoke suddenly entered the room, completely engulfing Jean Pierre, causing him to jump fearfully and quickly away from the bed, trying desperately to protect himself from the unknown. A quiet, familiar voice spoke in his ear the words that would forever be the reckoning of Jean Pierre and his wife, Evelina.

"Name the sweet baby boy Jean Pierre, after his father, and in honor of your father, the African-with-No-Name [the first Jean Pierre], and Evelina will no longer conceive, but you must first be positive that you truly want no more babies, 'cause there will be no way to reverse the decision...ever!"

Jean Pierre fell backward against a wall with his arms high in the air in great fear, not knowing who or where the voice was coming from, but it was when the voice laughed that familiar laugh that Jean Pierre had heard throughout his youth that he realized that he was hearing the voice of his beloved Mama Del. Jean Pierre looked around the room, searching for Mama Del, but she was not there in the great city of New Orleans; the voice was coming from far down the railroad tracks, from his home at Mon Village.

"You must think, think carefully, and be very sure of your decision, Jean Pierre, before you seal the fate of your family with this name."

Jean Pierre closed his eyes, nodding in agreement with the voice, and thought deeply about the other children that he cherished so much, his firstborn child, Mon Claire; the chubby little twin boys, Petois and Pecous; as well as the baby girl, LaBelle Jelee. As he leaned over Evelina to kiss the newborn baby boy, she squirmed to readjust herself, causing Jean Pierre to panic and jump away again, covering his head with his hands. Well, that most certainly convinced Jean Pierre that he was truly and completely convinced that enough was truly enough.

Feeling quite confident and truly at ease now, Jean Pierre lifted his sweet baby boy from the safe arms of his mother and whispered in his ear, "You, my sweet, precious baby boy, will be known now and forever as the third Jean Pierre, after your father, and in honor of my father, your grandfather, the African-with-No-Name who became known as Jean Pierre!"

Jean Pierre sighed with contentment and placed the child back on the bed with Evelina and, after kissing both on their foreheads, escaped from the birth room to inform the experienced midwife that he was going back to join Dolice Marie at the wedding party.

And thus ends the story of the first LaPierre who was born away from Mon Village, indeed born in the great city of New Orleans, who would be the last child conceived by Jean Pierre and Evelina LaPierre. Indeed, my own great-granddaddy!

Oh, what a grand night it was for the Menard wedding! Even the stars danced with the planets as the music rose above the earth to join them in the heavens. It was a wonderful and memorable time for everyone, a glorious memory to be enveloped within the heart and cherished throughout time. It was a night filled with explosive music, delicious food, and plenty of bubbly champagne or smooth Kentucky bourbon, if that fit your fancy. It was a night of love, a night of passion, a night of joyous laughter, and a night filled with plenty of giggles, giggles, as the lovely ladies of the New Orleans House, led by the sensuous Georgia, attempted to teach the Lady

Menard how to "strut her stuff," while the Lord Menard attempted to mimic her, and quite stiffly, I might add! Angeline and Willem clapped their hands as they swayed with the music, certainly hearing the loud thumping of their own hearts as their thoughts for and of each other dominated and questioned their brains to know whether or not they should even be thinking of each other in that passionate manner.

Miss BB and Obadiah rejoined the festivities after spending a little time with Evelina and the newest member of the LaPierre family, inviting the journalists and the photographers to join them as guests as they proceeded toward the bride and groom, citing the fact that they had surely acquired enough scoop and gossip to fill their tabloids. To assure that the point had been driven home, indeed, the sheriff followed, collecting notepads and cameras along the way, with a promise to return them when the party was over. Both the journalists and the photographers seemed extremely surprised as they were exposed, assuming that they had been successful in hiding themselves and their tasks at hand.

Monte Leonard and Jubil both sat at the table where they had been throughout the entire reception, except for the time that Jubil had spent assisting Jean Pierre in the labor room, churning the ideas within their heads that they had discussed previously about the need for a good veterinarian for the horse races in the noble Commonwealth of Kentucky. Monte Leonard's thoughts were exciting and hopeful, while Jubil's thoughts were confusing and conflicting. Both avoided another conversation about it for the moment, but the thought was very close to both of them.

After the throwing of the bride's bouquet, which was caught by the lovely lassie Chelsea of the New Orleans House (who had the dickens of a time jerking it out of another lady's hands), the opening of the gifts, which could have filled one of the carriages (including a beautiful set of six handmade pure silver cups with the LaPierre crest on one side and the letter *M* on the other side, from Dolice Marie's own beloved Jean Pierre), the reception finally began to wind down and the guests began to depart. After many hugs and kisses, the bride and groom found themselves alone with just the familiar family and the friends that were staying at the Declouette Mansion, like Monte Leonard. As well as Lord and Lady Menard, who would stay for one more night. With their journey to the great state of New York planned to begin the next afternoon, the tug of separation from the ones Dolice Marie had grown to love and the family she adored became reality, and her eyes began to fill with tears as she looked from one to the other.

"Congratulations, mon bébé," Miss BB said as she kissed Dolice Marie on her forehead. "It is time for rest now, beloved. There will be plenty of time for goodbyes when the day arrives. For now, rest and enjoy this man of yours!"

Everyone laughed with Miss BB for just a moment, and then the lovely ladies of the New Orleans House bade their farewells to join a tear-filled Obadiah at the front door of the Declouette Mansion to begin their journey across town. It was a difficult moment, indeed, for those ladies that had actually been discovered by Dolice Marie and Angeline those many years ago to bid their farewells to Madam Dolice Marie and for her to bid her farewell to each of them. Dolice Marie met them at the door to exchange hugs and kisses with each of them, finding it truly difficult to hold back the tears that were again swelling in her eyes.

"There were probably enough tears from those people to fill the other carriage," Uncle Michele would say. "Lord, now you know that's love!"

My other uncles, of course, would always nod in agreement.

Angeline bade her good night to Willem at the door with a slight curtsey after he kissed her ever so tenderly on her tiny hand. It was obvious by the fleeting glimpses that the two exchanged at the door that this would not be the last moments they would share.

"Until tomorrow, then, Mademoiselle Angeline," Willem said with a hidden grin that could be seen by just the two of them.

Angeline simply answered him with a hidden grin of her own, and the fluttering of her eyelashes, and then she disappeared through the door.

When Angeline and the last of the ladies had slipped through the front door, Madam Dolice Marie and Mr. Bernard Menard bade their good nights and disappeared up the stairs of the Declouette Mansion to the wedding quarters that had been prepared for their first night as man and wife. As the two began to enter the room, Mr. Bernard Menard lifted his tiny new wife, with their child inside, to carry her over the threshold and closed the door behind them with the tap of his foot.

And thus a new name had been added to the long line of LaPierres, the name of Menard.

"Monsieur Menard," Madam Dolice Marie said as he laid her gently on their marriage bed, "promise me one thing on this special night, please."

"Of course, beloved," he responded. "Anything!"

"Promise me that our sweet bébé will be born at Mon Village, please, promise me that one thing!"

Without a single thought as to just how that would be accomplished, Mr. Bernard Menard promised with all his heart that their child would be born at Mon Village, no matter what it would take to make that happen.

Jean Pierre slipped in between the sheets and as close as he could be to his beautiful newborn son, who was now resting close to his mother, Evelina. He could not take his eyes off the child, staring at him with a loving glare and with that familiar wonder in his mind about all creation. He thought again for a moment about his decision to name the sweet boy Jean Pierre III and sealing the fate of his marriage to Evelina with just the children the two of them now had, with no opportunity for any more children in the future. The thought dominated his mind as he stared from Evelina to the beautiful newborn baby, and somewhere along the night, with his head resting on the side of his Evelina's head, Jean Pierre fell into a deep, peaceful, and content sleep.

Dolice Marie's beloved Miss BB was the first to break down into a flood of tears as Mr. and Mrs. Bernard Menard began their descent down the steep stairs of the New Orleans House, with him carrying their train cases, catching a smiling Madam Dolice Marie off guard and causing her to begin to tear up. Angeline glanced sadly from Miss BB to Madam Dolice Marie and back again before she, too, began to cry, leading another flood of tears up and down the steep stairs and throughout the parlor, where the lovely ladies of the New Orleans House were standing with their ever-present, ever-faithful Obadiah. Of course, Lord and Lady Menard would be able to see the newlywed Menards as much as possible since they would be in Upstate New York and the elder Menards in Toronto, but it was a bittersweet and solemn event for them nonetheless.

But it was that goodbye between Dolice Marie and her precious Jean Pierre that caused her to truly weep with a broken heart as she cuddled Evelina with the newborn baby in one arm and Jean Pierre in the other. Jean Pierre and Evelina wept as well as each tried desperately to console the other.

"I would ask you not to come to the train station," Dolice Marie said between tearful gasps for air. "I could not bear saying goodbye to you there! I will see you soon. Monsieur Bernard Menard has promised me that our sweet bébé will be born at Mon Village!"

Jean Pierre quickly glanced toward Mr. Bernard Menard's direction for confirmation of Dolice Marie's statement, which he received with a nod. Jean Pierre was satisfied now and hugged Dolice Marie one more time before letting her go.

Of course, my sweet uncles, especially my uncle Simon, would always tear up as well as if they were actually experiencing their own solemn goodbyes to our glorious ancestors.

And oh, dear, the goodbyes were indeed terribly long and extremely hard for everyone as each person said their own goodbye to the Menards in their own way. But there was, however, enough tears to fill the New Orleans House. Mr. Bernard Menard was the first to exit the New Orleans House, placing the train cases in the carriage while everyone else followed slowly behind him. It would not be until Obadiah reminded everyone that the train would be leaving soon that they were able to release their embraces and encourage Madam Dolice Marie LaPierre-Menard to go forth into her new life, a brand-new life that was just a few days down the railroad tracks.

Once Mr. and Mrs. Bernard Menard were comfortably in the huge carriage, Obadiah gave the command for the huge horse to proceed, and as it did, Dolice Marie began to cry quite loudly, waving to Miss BB and Angeline, who were now embracing each other and crying uncontrollably indeed. The lovely ladies of the New Orleans House stood in the doorway, bidding their goodbyes as well to the former slave girl, the now Madam Dolice Marie LaPierre-Menard, who had now disappeared from their sight while Mr. Bernard Menard held her tightly.

The solemn goodbye between Madam Dolice Marie LaPierre-Menard and Obadiah was just as painful as it had been to say goodbye to her beloved Miss BB and her best friend and confidante, Angeline. Obadiah shook Mr. Bernard Menard's hand quite strongly, stiffly embraced his sweet Dolice Marie, tipped his hat, and hopped aboard the seat of the huge carriage, and after one more glance at the two, he commanded the huge horse to turn around and follow the same way back home as Dolice Marie continued to cry, and quite loudly, at that. It was quite obvious to Dolice Marie that the goodbye was just as painful for Obadiah as well, and although her heart urged her to plead with him to stay until the train pulled away from the New Orleans station, she bade him farewell and turned her back, smothering her face in Mr. Bernard Menard's lapel in order not to see him leave her.

And as Dolice Marie opened an eye, she noticed the sheriff standing not too far away, that seemingly ever-present entity that had been a clandestine companion throughout her entire life in the great city of New Orleans. He tipped his hat, smiled briefly, turned his back, and walked away.

And on the trail back to the Declouette Mansion, Obadiah allowed himself that hidden release of tears that fell from his eyes as though they were coming from deep within his heart.

Chapter 15

THE SEEMINGLY NEVER-ENDING train trip toward the great state of New York was long and tiring, indeed, but the farther north the newlywed Menards journeyed, the more Madam Dolice Marie LaPierre-Menard was recognized as the legal wife of the tall redheaded Canadian man from Toronto, with all the service and respect given to the proper white people aboard that or any other train.

From the depths of the South, always traveling north and toward the east, the Menards journeyed, the unfamiliar sights occasionally bringing a faint smile to Madam Menard's lips, but a smile that would quickly dissipate as she remembered the loved ones that she was leaving behind, farther and farther away.

Mr. Bernard Menard, the ever-attending and ever-adoring husband, tried with all his might and knowledge to make his beautiful wife happy, but his attempts were all failures. Dolice Marie, however, never failed to let him know that her unhappiness was truly not because of him; it was because she missed her family and friends so very much and that she truly loved him with all her heart. It was truly useless for him to try to convince Dolice Marie that she would meet new friends and that he was indeed a part of her family now, so the kindly man simply held her as tight as he could and hoped that, eventually, that message would become a reality for her as well.

My beloved Uncle Rene would always mention to my other uncles and to the young boys during their initiation at this point of the traditional telling of the family stories that he knew exactly how

Dolice felt since he had journeyed from Mon Village to the great state of New York many times when he was just a young man seeking a higher education at one of the colleges there. Uncle Rene would always come home after each semester and during the holidays, but it was always so difficult for him to leave his beloved home again.

Uncle Rene, who was the third youngest brother behind my own dear daddy, had the height of the tallest LaPierre and the weight of the smallest LaPierre down the line of our family, making him quite tall and very skinny. It was remarkable that he was as strong as he was and how he was able to lift heavy items, such as his own adoring wife, Lucia, who was not very large herself, but indeed larger than Uncle Rene.

Uncle Rene had skin the color of caramel oozing over a juicy green apple on a stick, with wavy dark-brown hair that was always cut short atop his head. His hazel eyes could pierce the soul of the person he was looking at, seeming to be able to read the mind of another person straight through their own eyes.

Uncle Rene was as kind and as gentle as all my other uncles, with the same humorous nature, capable of a great practical joke and a warm shoulder when either one was truly necessary. It was always Uncle Rene, Uncle Alexandre, and my own dear daddy that caused havoc for their older brothers all around Mon Village when they were all very young, but it was obvious that they truly loved one another and that they would protect one another each time that time would come around, and for boys, that time seemed to be always.

Uncle Rene's wife, Lucia, which means "light" in English, was a student at the same college that Uncle Rene attended in the great state of New York, the first naturalized American born in her family with an Italian heritage. Lucia Giovanni truly became the light of Uncle Rene's life, helping him with his studies as well as helping him with plans for his future, neither one even realizing that they had already fallen in love with each other until their graduation and the parting of their ways to pursue their separate futures. Uncle Rene traveled back to live at Mon Village, teaching school to the children there, while Lucia went back to her parents' home on one of the New York islands to continue her study of music, particularly the cello, or, actually, any stringed instrument. Her dream was to play the cello or the violin in a famous symphony, a dream that she had excitedly shared with Uncle Rene.

During the months that followed, both Uncle Rene and my soon-to-be aunt Lucia missed each other so very much that they began to exchange wires and letters back and forth. Eventually, they began to visit each other, Uncle Rene back and forth to the great state of New York, and Aunt Lucia back and forth to Mon Village.

"Burning up the roads," as my crazy uncles would say, laughing all the while.

Needless to say, it would not be very long before Uncle Rene asked Aunt Lucia to marry him and move to Mon Village with him, where he would build a fine home for her with everything she could ever want. Aunt Lucia said yes, of course, and seemed to be quite happy at first. But as tempting as all that seemed, Aunt Lucia also reminded Uncle Rene that she, too, had a dream, and why would he not consider moving to the great state of New York, where they could find a beautiful home together and live there forever after? Besides, good teachers were always needed everywhere in America.

The situation seemed to be so desperate, and try as they might, one could not convince the other that his or her dream was the most important dream of the two. But just when it seemed as though there was no way to please both of those stubborn people, Mama Del gave them both a dream that they could pursue together.

Mama Del slipped into one of the dreams of both Uncle Rene and Aunt Lucia as they slept unhappily away from each other in separate states, both yearning for the other one but incapable of coming to a peaceful resolution to their present set of circumstances. Mama Del's dream was a simple one, a dream that would make the most of both Uncle Rene's and Aunt Lucia's education and personal dreams for their futures. Why not encourage Lucia to teach music classes to the children at Mon Village during the school year, and during the summer break, Rene could travel with Lucia back to the great state of New York to pursue her dreams of becoming a professional cellist or violinist in a famous symphony orchestra?

MINT JULEP

"After all," Mama Del concluded, "marriage should always be a give-and-take situation, and neither man nor woman should ever have the complete say-so!"

Well, as usual, Mama Del had come up with the perfect solution. It would not be long before Uncle Rene made that train trip to the great state of New York to woo and wed his dearly loved Lucia. And what a *woo* it was! Uncle Rene promised to build an auditorium at Mon Village where Aunt Lucia could teach music to the children plus have great symphonies of her very own during the school year with students that she had taught and encouraged to be great musicians as well. He also explained that even though music was quite popular at Mon Village, it was primarily the folk music of the great state of Louisiana, both French and zydeco, with not much recognition of the beautiful music of the classical composers. Teaching at Mon Village would give her the perfect opportunity to introduce the children to this music as well as create great musicians, right there in her own backyard. Plus, Uncle Rene promised to always be there for her if and when she wanted to travel back to the great state of New York to pursue one of those professional symphonies.

Well, Mama Del was right, as always. Uncle Rene built that beautiful home for the two of them at Mon Village just as he had promised, with an auditorium directly behind the schoolhouse that any professional musician could appreciate and enjoy. Before long, Uncle Rene and Aunt Lucia were married, and not long after that, the children at Mon Village were introduced to the music that Aunt Lucia loved so very much.

Over the years, there would be concerts at Mon Village for everyone to enjoy, with proud parents and proud students, some students that actually lived Aunt Lucia's dream of playing beautiful music in a professional symphony in the great state of New York. Of course, there were those older residents of Mon Village that couldn't have cared less about this type of music and simply turned up their radios or hummed just a little louder when the concerts were being held.

And for years, Uncle Rene kept another promise as well; he traveled to the great state of New York every summer to experience

Aunt Lucia's dream as she played her cello or violin with a professional orchestra. It would not be long before Uncle Rene and Aunt Lucia realized that simply being together was the greatest dream of all, so when their sweet baby girl Gina was born, it was quite easy to put an end to those trips to the great state of New York, except to visit with Lucia's parents and just concentrate on home.

At this point of the stories, it was not uncommon for one of my older uncles to "noogie" Uncle Rene on top of his head with a knuckle, which led to a roar of laughter from the other brothers and, of course, the young boys!

The nearness of the upstate portion of New York, the brand-new home to the newlywed Menards, could be felt in the air as it progressively changed from the moist humidity of the Southern states to the crispness of the cool mountain air. Mr. Bernard Menard reached into the train case that was under his seat to bring forth one of Lady Menard's anticipated wedding gifts, a thick shawl that had been knitted by one of the Menard employees. Dolice Marie faked a smile with a genuine thank-you to her husband, who wrapped her in the shawl and in his arms as the train began slowing down near the station in their new home. Mr. Bernard Menard began to describe to Dolice Marie what she was seeing in an attempt to not give in to her sadness and hopefully draw her attention to the beauty of her new home.

As the train slowed to a complete stop, Mr. Bernard Menard pointed through the window at a well-dressed Canadian man sitting atop a seat on a beautiful carriage being pulled by a well-groomed white horse. The man was wearing a brown derby hat on his head, with a bow tie adorning his tweed suit. Mr. Bernard Menard waved at the man through the train window, and he immediately waved back to him with a beaming smile. The man jumped down from the seat atop the beautiful carriage, opened the carriage door, and stood there as if he were waiting for something—that something, of course, were the newlywed Menards.

"This is Edward," Mr. Bernard Menard said eagerly as he fervently shook the man's hand.

The man tipped his hat and quickly bowed his head. "It is indeed my pleasure, Madam Menard," he said as he assisted Madam Dolice Marie into the carriage.

"We have all been waiting for you to arrive."

Dolice Marie smiled that fake smile again but genuinely thanked Edward for being so very kind as she reached out of the carriage window to shake his hand. She felt deep down inside that she and Edward were going to be great friends.

When the newlywed Menards and Edward finally reached the lovely little cottage that Mr. Bernard Menard had put his heart and soul into, lovingly creating a home for his beloved Dolice Marie, there were several other employees of that Menard household to meet, beginning with Wilhelmina the Cook, who had been in the Menard household in Toronto for over twenty years, now very happy to be employed in the younger Menard household. There were other employees as well. All the men dressed in handsome suits. Another man, known as Horatio, and the ladies with crisp white aprons over light-blue dresses, one tiny lady known as Maggie. Every one of them shook Madam Dolice Marie's hand, curtsied quickly, and welcomed her to her new home with a warm smile. By the time the introductions were all done, Madam Dolice Marie's smiles were becoming less fake, indeed.

Mr. Bernard Menard felt quite hopeful now as he led his beautiful wife on a delightful tour of their cottage, from the kitchen to the master bedroom and guest rooms to the carriage house and the well-groomed gardens all around the house. Dolice Marie said not a word as she pulled the shawl tighter around her but acknowledged with a small smile that Mr. Bernard Menard had, indeed, done a most wonderful job in creating this new home for the two of them.

In the great city of New Orleans, the Declouette Mansion appeared to be much larger, much more quiet, and indeed, quite lonely now that all the guests were either back at their homes or on their way back to their homes. I remember Uncle Rene telling the young boys that he always felt that way, quite empty, when Aunt Lucia had gone back to her parents' home in the great state of New York while they were courting. All my other uncles seemed to agree with that sentiment and had their own story to tell the young boys about being alone again after being separated from a loved one.

It was certainly apparent that Miss BB was feeling quite lonely as she walked the grounds of the Declouette Mansion with her sweet babies, FiFi and GiGi, reliving all the good times that she had just a few days ago. She missed her sweet Dolice Marie and all the activity that had gone on while Dolice Marie had been in the great city of New Orleans. Not even her treasured Obadiah could bring a smile to Miss BB's face, a task that was truly difficult to bring to his own.

Angeline, the new madam of the New Orleans House (certainly by chance and not by choice), was evidently feeling that same sense of loneliness and emptiness as she walked out onto the balcony from her own room that faced the narrow streets of that great city. She, too, missed Dolice Marie tremendously and tried to convince herself that she was truly happy for her best friend, who was now married to a truly wonderful man, with opportunities for a most wonderful future, but she was also sad for herself. Angeline thought of Henri de Marquis, who had promised to come back for her one day but had never even written a single letter or sent a single wire to her, and then she thought of Willem, who had spoken to her with his eyes just a few days ago. Would he be the one to pursue a relationship with her? Would she ever see him again as well?

There seemed to be nothing but sadness in that great city of New Orleans even though life and business went on as usual. But not for her, not on this day. Angeline quickly bathed, dressed, passed the lovely ladies of the New Orleans House, and was running down the stairs to find a carriage driver to take her to the Declouette Mansion when she ran into none other than, you guessed it, Obadiah, dressed in his entire familiar garb and sitting atop the Declouette carriage drawn by that extremely large horse. Obadiah tipped his hat at Angeline and explained that Miss BB was feeling quite blue and had sent him to the New Orleans House to ask her for the pleasure of her company for a day or even more at the Declouette Mansion. Angeline laughed out loud and shook her head in disbelief because of the irony of it all but quickly remembered that since she had met Dolice Marie and her family, anything was possible, indeed! Angeline hopped into the carriage and headed toward the Declouette Mansion, where Aunt BB was waiting with plenty of gumbo, steaming white rice, and two bottles of smooth Kentucky bourbon.

"Now that's how you get over the blues," Uncle Rene would always add.

Need I mention that there was a loud roar of laughter, as usual, right after Uncle Rene would add his two cents' worth?

Down the tracks, farther away from the great city of New Orleans, Jean Pierre brought his son Jean Pierre III to Mama Del's house, but this time for more than just that secret ceremony performed for all the newborn LaPierre children. He felt completely alone and lost but was not quite sure exactly why. Of course, he missed his Dolice Marie, but he was so very happy for her that she had found real love with someone who would always love and protect her, just as he loved and protected his own Evelina. He loved and cherished his children, all of them, but still there was something missing in his world now, and he hoped that it would be Mama Del that would lead him to his truth, whatever that might be.

"Chile, now, don't you go asking me what the matter is with you!" Mama Del said, giving the sweet child back to his father immediately after performing the secret ceremony on Jean Pierre III. And even before Jean Pierre could ask her, she said, "Boy, you got a wife, you got chirren, and you is the massa' of all you can see around you! You should be nuttin' but happy. So what you think is the matta?"

Jean Pierre was simply confused. He had gone to Mama Del to ask her for help, and now she was asking him what he thought was wrong. Jean Pierre had learned at a very early age that Mama Del truly packed a wallop, and the wrong answer from him could find him suffering from one of her old-fashioned licks upon his head, so he thought and thought about the answer that Mama Del might be hoping to hear from him.

"I don't know, Mama Del," Jean Pierre finally answered. "Maybe I just don't appreciate all that I do have."

Mama Del smiled from ear to ear, allowing her aged gums to show around the old corncob pipe that she always kept in her mouth, evidently approving of Jean Pierre's answer.

"Nah, was that so hard, boy?" Mama Del asked, and then she cackled so loud that Jean Pierre could actually feel his insides vibrating! "Maybe you need to go out and work in the fields for a while so you can 'member jest where it is you come from, boy!"

Jean Pierre nodded in agreement with the old Greis Greis woman as he walked slowly out of her house, knowing full well that he had done just what Mama Del had said, lost track of where he had come from. When he finally made it home that evening, Jean Pierre gave Evelina and each of their children an even bigger hug than usual, listened a little more attentively than usual, and made sure that he said "I love you" just a little bit more meaningfully than he had ever said it to each of them before.

As the sun began to set on yet another event-filled day for the residents of Mon Village, Jubil climbed into his bed and brought it all back to his memory—the train trip to the great city of New Orleans and seeing sights he had never, ever seen, meeting all the wonderful new people in their lives, the wedding of his sweet Dolice Marie and her beloved Monsieur Bernard Menard, the birth of Jean Pierre and Evelina's new baby boy, all reminding him of just how very lonely he really was. He could almost smell all the smells from that glorious time and hear all the music playing in his ear. And he realized that it was truly far past time for him to ask Miss Sylvia's hand in marriage and, even more, far past time for him to make the decision of whether or not he would take Monte Leonard up on his job offer to work with the horses in the noble Commonwealth of Kentucky and just how his decision would affect his pursuit of a relationship with Miss Sylvia. Jubil tossed and turned throughout the entire night, even though he reminded himself that Mama Del had already assured him that a bright future was truly already planned for him, indeed. But when would that be? And how would he recognize it when it did happen? And what was he supposed to do when it happened? And oh my, what would *it* be?

With that much going on in his head, sometime during the night, Jubil was finally able to fall into a deep sleep.

Chapter 16

WHEN THE MORNING sun finally appeared over the vastness of Mon Village, adding a warmth, a light, and moving strategically as if it were actually moving the darkness out of the way to give life and breath to the day, Jubil awakened with a determination that even caused his muscles to jump and throb, seemingly moving ahead of the rest of his body. He inhaled the morning air and, just as he did every morning, dressed quickly to survey the Mon Village property.

Today, Jubil also had something, someone, heavily on his mind, the same someone that was always on his mind, and as usual, he had to find the courage to match his determination to approach Miss Sylvia to let her know just how much he cared about her. His heart thumped even louder this day as he neared her shop, and he even slowed his horse down to make himself jump off the trusty steed to land right in the front door, but instead he found himself circling Miss Sylvia's shop, his usual game of hide-and-seek, hoping that Miss Sylvia was watching.

Oh, yes, Miss Sylvia was watching, all right, straight out of the corner of her eye, as Jubil pretended that he had "bid'ness" right there in the shop area and, in particular, around and around, or near Miss Sylvia's shop, just as he always did. Well, today Miss Sylvia had a plan as well. In fact, today Miss Sylvia had created a scenario in her own mind, indeed, a scenario of circumstance, a plan with a mental alternative that was truly about to evolve, if you know what I mean!

It was certainly not a secret that the lovely Miss Sylvia had been approached by several suitors but had not succumbed to any of their designs or flirtations since she truly had Jubil tucked safely away in her heart, but the time had come for the relationship to either come about or fade into the darkness just as the aroma of a delicious gumbo fades away when the pot is finally empty, washed, and put away. She had watched Jubil in his many antics since they had met in the middle of the mint growing in the fields and had felt herself become truly anxious for him to approach her with those feelings that she was sure he had for her as well. But today she had become frustrated when realizing that this was yet another day that he would continue without saying a single word to her about any future together.

Today was different for Miss Sylvia, because she had created a mental deadline for Jubil, a deadline that had truly reached its completion that very day. As she watched Jubil ride his horse around and around the shop area, she sent the mental message to him that this day was his final opportunity to empty his heart and tell her what she already knew about the two of them, or she would surely choose to accept the advances of one of her other suitors.

The birth of Jean Pierre and Evelina's sweet baby boy Jean Pierre III had caused Miss Sylvia to realize her own maternal needs and to realize even more importantly how much longer she had as a young woman to fulfill those needs. Miss Sylvia was truly convinced that Jubil was the man that she hoped and longed for, but today she also realized that hoping and longing for someone would not make it happen, and it was certainly time for some kind of action.

Evidently and unfortunately, Jubil did not receive that mental message, and Miss Sylvia watched and rolled her eyes as Jubil tipped his hat and continued his morning routine, riding his horse away from the shop area.

All my sweet uncles would shake their heads in empathetic despair for Jubil and Miss Sylvia. Uncle Rene would always point his finger at the young boys as he would tell them that they need always remember the story of Jubil and Miss Sylvia when they found themselves in such a situation. But then he would smile and say,

"And always remember that things are not always the way they seem to be either!"

Perhaps Jubil did receive Miss Sylvia's mental message for him, because he soon found himself at Jean Pierre and Evelina's house, where he found Jean Pierre sitting in one of the rocking chairs on the front porch, holding Jean Pierre III and spending time with his chubby little twin boys, Petois and Pecous. Jean Pierre had a good idea why Jubil had come for the visit and quickly shooed the chubby little twins into the house and beckoned Jubil toward one of the rocking chairs on the porch. For ten or fifteen minutes, Jubil gave Jean Pierre every single reason he could conjure to explain his present set of thoughts about the offer from Mr. Monte Leonard that would lead him to the noble Commonwealth of Kentucky for the spring and fall racing meets. When Jubil had finally run out of wind, Jean Pierre simply stared at him for a few moments and then responded, "So…you let Miss Sylvia slip right through your fingers, eh?"

Without another pretense, Jubil surrendered to the truth while staring at the porch floor, shaking his head, as if he were truly glad that the truth had finally come out. Jean Pierre leaned over ever so slightly to pat his old friend on his back, being ever so careful as not to remind his dear friend Jubil that he had once pushed him hard, very hard indeed, to expose his true feelings to his beloved Evelina.

By the time their conversation had ended, the sun was beginning to set behind the big house, and it would be with a simple handshake that Jean Pierre gave his blessing to his best friend, wishing him well and a safe and speedy return to the only family Jubil had ever known.

Perhaps it was time for a change, Jubil thought as he slipped between the sheets on his bed; perhaps spending time in the noble Commonwealth of Kentucky would help him clear his mind and even help him find the courage he needed to let Miss Sylvia know that he was truly in love with her. Time away would also give Miss Sylvia a chance to miss him, Jubil thought, and realize just how important and perfect they were for each other. And so that was it, Jubil had just made up his mind to travel to the noble Commonwealth of Kentucky, just in time for the fall meet.

Jubil found himself awake even before the sun arose that very next morning. After pushing himself out of bed, he packed a few of his belongings in his saddlebags and, after hopping aboard the saddle, led his horse toward the fields, toward the middle of the mint, where he had first met Miss Sylvia. Reaching down from the horse, Jubil grabbed several handfuls of the mint that grew wild in the massive fields of Mon Village, tucked some safely away in his coat pocket, and began to drop pieces of the leaves on the ground as he led his horse away from Mon Village, leaving for the very first time in his life, watering the mint leaves with his tears as he created a mint-laden path toward the noble Commonwealth of Kentucky that would direct and lead him safely home again.

Meanwhile, life in the Menard household of Upstate New York had become much more bearable for all involved, or concerned, that is, since the time that Madam Dolice Marie had become daily a little more accustomed to her new home and new friends in the great state of New York. Although Madam Dolice Marie had become a little more comfortable about being away from her home, her family, and those that she had adopted as her loved ones, there was, indeed, still the matter of the pregnancy.

My dear uncles could probably share their own separate stories of such matters to the young boys for days on end, but one thing that would be a matter of total agreement for sure in all their stories: "If you don't have a job, then get a hobby," Uncle Rene would say while my other uncles just went way overboard with laughter.

"A man's gotta find something constructive to do with his time away from home 'cause women can be really crazy when they're pregnant!"

I, personally, was always just so grateful that none of my beloved aunts could hear any of their nonsense.

Mr. Bernard Menard approached the front door of the lovely Menard cottage after a busy day at his import-export business, virtually clueless as to how he would find his precious wife on this particular day, the thought that was constantly on his mind, expecting either the loud sobs emitting from Madam Dolice Marie or a radiantly glowing smile from ear to ear. Today there was a strange silence throughout the entire cottage; there were no sobs, no employees running throughout the rooms, searching for some way to comfort the extremely largely pregnant and quite uncomfortable madam of the Menard house, nor was there that rare but extremely delightful chorus of giggles as Madam Dolice Marie and Maggie and/or Edward joined her in unpacking the humongous assortment of packages that they had brought home from a shopping excursion in the city.

There was, however, the aroma of some delectable dish being created, leading Mr. Bernard Menard toward the kitchen, where he found Wilhelmina the Cook, preparing a fancy feast and found the entire household staff gathered together, smiling while staring out of the kitchen window onto the screened-in patio.

Mr. Bernard Menard acknowledged everyone with a curious smile and, looking out onto the patio as well, beamed with such a smile of his own that it could have lit up the entire Menard cottage. There, lying still, and very quietly, I might also add, in a comfortable lounge chair was his beloved Madam Dolice Marie, relaxing with both hands cuddling her stomach as though she were cuddling the anticipated sweet child within, with her eyes closed, and with a beautiful smile on her face, while being softly and strategically massaged by the gardener's wife, Kip Salmas (given the sweet nickname Kip by one missionary who named her after his favorite writer, Rudyard Kipling, after failing repeatedly to correctly pronounce her true Filipino name). Mr. Bernard Menard turned to look approvingly yet quizzically at the Menard cottage staff of employees, who smiled happily back with him but immediately encouraged him not to disturb the scene, at least not just yet.

Across the screened-in patio where the beautiful gardens were now being taken care of solely by Kip's husband, Kuya, Mr. Bernard Menard caught sight of the small Filipino man who was trying desperately to get his attention. When he was finally able to do so, Kuya began to point toward the side of the house, asking with his actions for Mr. Bernard Menard to meet him there, which a smiling Mr. Bernard Menard was indeed happy to do so.

Kuya had been referred to the Menard household by one of Mr. Bernard Menard's business associates who had been using Kuya's gardening expertise for more than five years, since the time he had come to the United States from the Philippine islands with his aged mother and his tiny wife, Kip. Missionaries who had made it possible for him and his family to come to America had given him the name Kuya, the name traditionally given to the eldest son of the Filipino family and one that was much easier for everyone to pronounce.

Kuya began immediately apologizing to Mr. Bernard Menard for interrupting him while speaking in a very broken Filipino accent but with a message that was extremely pleasing to Madam Dolice Marie's very baffled husband. It seemed as though Kuya felt that he had been discourteous to take it upon himself to ask his wife, Kip, to bring some of their ancient world to assist Madam Dolice Marie through her last months of pregnancy as well as to comfort her in her loneliness, and all without ever asking Mr. Bernard Menard's permission. Their own sweet baby girl, Patima, was being cared for by Kuya's mother for the day, the wise Filipino grandmother who had brought the ancient wisdom and the know-how to calm the mind and the body with her from their home on the Philippine islands.

Mr. Bernard Menard made it quite plain, over and over (and over) that he was indeed eternally grateful and most assuredly pleased with Kuya's thoughtfulness and quietly invited him in for a cup of tea while his wife continued her magic, explaining that he had not heard that kind of peace and quiet in this Menard household—why, never, as a matter of fact.

By the time Kuya and Mr. Bernard Menard had settled themselves in the kitchen with their cups of tea, the Madam Dolice Marie was sound asleep and snoring quite loudly, as usual, while stretched out on the lounge chair on the screened-in patio, which was surrounded by the aroma of beautiful flowers and the faint yet provocative smoke from a nearby jasmine incense that Kip had lit in the midst of smooth rocks in a ceramic bowl. The scene was unbelievable to Mr. Bernard Menard, who could not turn his eyes away until he noticed that Kip was standing quietly and patiently at the kitchen door. Kuya stood quickly to introduce Kip to Mr. Bernard Menard, who happily extended his arms toward her, surrounding her with a strong hug and thanking her abundantly for bringing peace to his beloved Madam Dolice Marie, indeed to his entire Menard household. He explained that he had almost entirely given up hope of ever finding a solution to the present set of circumstances and believed that it was truly nothing less than a miracle that the dear lady had brought this wonderful peace to his household.

Kuya and Kip both humbly smiled as they exited the Menard cottage, followed closely by Mr. Bernard Menard, who was still offering his gratitude as he walked with them even farther down the street. Kip quietly began to speak in the native Filipino language to her husband, who answered her in the language and, finally, turned to Mr. Bernard Menard.

"My wife would like me to ask you if you would want her to come again another day to spend time with Madam Dolice Marie—"

But before the dear man could even finish the question, Mr. Bernard Menard had already said, "Yes, please!"

Well, that truly became the beginning of a lifelong friendship between Kuya and Kip Salmas and the entire LaPierre-Menard family; in fact, one could say it became a family affair, if you know what I mean! But that story is still to be told.

There would actually be one more incident that called for desperate measures that our family seemed to always encounter, this one just prior to the excitement of the birth of the Menard child, an event that was always relayed to the young boys by my wacky uncles with a certain degree of pride. In fact, Uncle Rene would always begin making sure that everything was particularly quiet before he even began to relay this story. As he would always begin, Uncle Rene would say, "Well, once again it seems that poor Mr. Bernard Menard was finding himself in yet another one of those…shall we say, Madam Dolice Marie moments!"

Uncle Rene would say it quite seriously as he seemed to prepare the young boys for another story that involved my event-filled ancestor, the explosive petite Madam Dolice Marie LaPierre-Menard!

Yes, it is true…

Mr. Bernard Menard was awakened in the middle of the night by strange groaning and moaning that seemed to be emitting from his lady love, the Madam Dolice Marie, in her sleep, but not the usual asthma snoring that she had used so many times to explain those dreadful noises coming directly from her, but another sound, one as though something quite painful was truly happening to her.

Mr. Bernard Menard quickly gathered Madam Dolice Marie closer to himself and gently shook her until she was finally awake. The poor dear began to frown as though she truly was experiencing some sort of dreadful pain while Mr. Bernard Menard did everything possible to discover just where the pain was coming from. Well, eventually it was discovered that the lovely Madam Dolice Marie was indeed experiencing a truly devastating toothache! It was then and only then that Mr. Bernard Menard realized that his Dolice Marie had never been to a dentist and, blinded by his great love for her, had actually never noticed that her teeth were quite overdue for some devastating pain.

Explaining to his lady love that he indeed had to locate a reputable dentist to relieve her of her excruciating pain, Mr. Bernard Menard gently laid Madam Dolice Marie back down on her pillow and quickly ran from their bedroom toward the staff quarters, until he came face-to-face with Edward's door. As if reacting to a dream, poor Edward opened the door to his bedroom just as Mr. Bernard Menard was about to knock. By this time, Mr. Bernard Menard and Edward were joined by Wilhelmina the Cook and Maggie. Quickly explaining the situation to Edward while all the while apologizing to everyone for having to awaken them, Mr. Bernard Menard gave his instructions before he ran quickly back to the arms of his ailing Madam Dolice Marie.

"I will accept none less than the finest dentist in all these eastern states," Mr. Bernard Menard stated while raising his clenched fist in the air, "and I charge you with finding him, or her, and as quickly as you can, most assuredly, before the child attempts to be born!"

My uncles truly had a good time acting out just how Mr. Bernard Menard probably looked at that moment and just how much louder Madam Dolice Marie would be if she had to indeed deal with both her painful tooth ailment and the pangs of labor all at the same time.

Unfortunately for everyone involved, this particular incident would be over only after one and one-half weeks after it began, bringing relief for everyone in the household, I might also add. The constant ails from the Madam Dolice Marie made it impossible for her to sleep, although everyone truly tried in many ways, indeed, to help her, but her wails continuously rang throughout the house, landing directly in the staff quarters. Not even her trusted friend Kip could help her as she had in the past, but the faithful Kip continued to try with all her resources nonetheless.

Edward, truly exhausted yet successful in his journey, knocked on the Menard bedroom door on a miserably cold New York evening and happily informed Mr. Bernard Menard that he had indeed found the finest dentist on the East Coast, a highly experienced dentist that came with many qualified references and who had been practicing the medical art of dentistry since 1872.

Edward stated that it was imperative that the good dentist care for the Madam Dolice as soon as possible since he had recently discovered that he himself was ailing from a dreadful disease that required him to be in a drier climate and hence would be heading westward for his own health as soon as he had performed the healing on the ailing Madam Dolice Marie. Edward then concluded that the good dentist was sitting in the parlor at that very moment and that it might do everyone well to quickly bring the Madam Dolice Marie to his care, as his temperament was as popular as his medical reputation.

And sure enough, there, standing in the middle of the Menard parlor, admiring the Menards' exquisite taste in paintings, timepieces, and furniture, was a tall extremely thin man dressed in a black suit with a thin black tie around the collar of a white shirt, a thick handlebar mustache, and a holster with a gun hanging on his hip, a leather strap tied at the thigh. The man turned to face Mr. Bernard Menard, quickly reached to shake his hand, and quickly introduced himself. There was truly an apparent and, indeed, an obvious hurriedness about his persona.

"My pleasure to meet you, suh," he said with a charmingly Southern accent. "I am truly captivated by your unmistakably good taste in the fineries of life that I myself also truly appreciate. I am John Henry, John Henry Holliday, at your service, suh, originally from Griffin, Georgia, but my practice of the medical art of dentistry has led me to Atlanta, Georgia. Most of the people who know me, especially all my former patients, just call me Doc, Doc Holliday, that is. Now, what can I do for you that would have your butler actually hunt me down and drag me all the way from Atlanta to New York?"

Despite his aggressive nature and a tremendously annoying, hacking cough that seemed to go on forever, Doc Holliday proved himself to be just what Mr. Bernard Menard had requested, the very best dentist on the East Coast, alleviating the lovely Madam Dolice Marie's tooth pain in little or no time as well as bringing quiet and calm back to the entire household.

With Madam Dolice Marie now sound asleep in the Menard bedroom, the entire Menard staff took advantage of the opportunity to settle themselves in for a long (and welcomed) winter's nap.

The story says that Doc Holliday refused to accept even a dime for the services that he had given to Madam Dolice Marie, but he did invite Mr. Bernard Menard to a game of poker with the high stakes being a spunky pinto colt that he had seen in one of the Menard stables. Not being a gambling man at all, Mr. Bernard Menard gratefully offered to give the horse to the good dentist, but alas, Doc Holliday refused his generosity, himself being quite the gambler who did not see the excitement of simply accepting what he truly wanted. So shortly after sipping a few glasses of Menard imported brandy, the gentlemanly Doc Holliday tipped his hat, bade his farewells to the Menard household, and headed on down the highway.

According to LaPierre-Menard history, certainly not spoken about in certain circles, to say the least, there was a gentleman's gentleman who visited Mon Village several times and actually stayed for extended periods on occasion until he finally passed away. The whisper was that he could always find his way there when time required and most definitely when he needed a trusted yet discreet place to, shall we say, hide from the outside world for a bit of time. I might also add that the story has it that there was never a resident at Mon Village that didn't have impeccable teeth as well during the days of ole Doc Holliday.

MINT JULEP

I was given the lovely name Alexandra by my beloved parents after and in honor of my second-to-the-youngest uncle, Alexandre, the brother born right before my own dear daddy. Uncle Alexandre was also my godfather, that special title that gave him full custody of me should something dreadful had ever happened to my own dear daddy and mama, which meant the right to raise me until I was of the legal age to take my own life into my own hands.

Because my uncle Alexandre was so very close in age to my uncle Rene, he chose to follow in the footsteps of his elder sibling, and he, too, pursued his higher education in the great state of New York, at the very same college, but seeking a degree in theater, much to the chagrin of my grandparents, who thought his decision to become an actor was, at the least, a horrible one and encouraged him to "keep a day job at all times" during the pursuit of his pseudo-illustrious career. And that he did, indeed, working small jobs, sometimes two or three at a time, jobs from A–Z, just to keep food on his table, I might add, and certainly to keep his parents off his back throughout his college years.

I truly adored my uncle Alexandre, and it was apparent while we were all at our family reunions that he, too, adored me even when all his children were there as well—and there were many children, if you know what I mean!

Uncle Alexandre was medium height, medium muscular weight, with a cap of wiry curls that sat atop his head, with freckles that dotted his mulatto-toned skin and soft, sweet lips that were barely seen under his thin, youthful mustache. To the many girls that were touched by his truly good looks and the fact that he did become a popular off-Broadway actor, he was truly a handsome man, indeed a very quiet boy that became a very quiet young man, and once convinced that he had the ability to capture any of the lovely girls that caught his eye, he began to add his contributions to the population explosion.

Perhaps it was because Uncle Alexandre had never, ever been away from Mon Village when he finally experienced what true freedom was like while in the great state of New York, or perhaps it was because there were so many more temptations at the end of my uncles' generation than during the time my dear uncles Gaston, Simon, and Clovis were growing up, whichever, but my uncle Alexandre would have given Casanova a run for his money and his title.

After sweeping through Harlem with his first love, Joyce, with whom he fathered three children, Uncle Alexandre moved uptown to Manhattan and fathered at least one more with each of several other lovely ladies, and a set of twin girls with Marissa in the village as well, all before he completed his undergraduate studies in theater. My grandparents were not amused, to say the least, when Uncle Alexandre introduced not only a brand-new girlfriend just about every semester but a new grandchild at least every other year as well. Being the sweet and gentle people that they were, none of Uncle Alexandre's children were ever left out of anything, including love and an equal share of the pickins at Mon Village!

Needless to say, indeed, Uncle Alexandre never married but spent the greater portion of his adult life concentrating on his acting career and his responsibility to his many children. My other uncles always said he never married because "he had broken the hearts of too many women and the word had spread violently through the ranks that Alexandre LaPierre was indeed off-limits!"

And now, back to another unmarried man with a purpose!

Jubil was not quite sure if he was still in the South or had reached the North, or whatever places that might lie in between the two, poor darling, having absolutely no knowledge of an east or a west either at that point in time. He did know, however, that the noble Commonwealth of Kentucky was truly the most beautiful land that he had ever seen in his entire life, having really only seen Mon Village, the small town by the Atchafalaya River, and the great city of New Orleans briefly during Dolice Marie and Menard's wedding.

The air smelled so different—none of that faint smell of mint that seemed to sit atop the Louisiana air at Mon Village. The grass seemed to grow different, not the parched patches caused by the hot Louisiana sun. And the horses, which were truly everywhere, seemed to claim ownership over the entire place, and all the people he watched seemed to be quite agreeable with that fact.

MINT JULEP

Jubil felt as though he had been riding his horse for at least decades when he finally reached the place that Monte Leonard had told him all about, Lexington, and it was just as he had said, quiet and beautiful. Jubil was extremely tired and dirty as he slowly led the horse to the main workhouse of the farm that he had been instructed to find if he had ever made up his mind to come to the noble Commonwealth of Kentucky. And now he was there.

At that very moment, Jubil felt a little more excitement than he felt homesickness, but he knew that would be short-lived and as he tied his horse to the wooden bar in front of the workhouse, his knees beginning to tremble as he realized that he was actually about to knock on the front door of a place where he had never been to meet people, more likely than not, Caucasian people, who would more than likely not be extremely happy to meet with him.

As he knocked on the door the first time, someone came up behind him, a cowboy with a big hat, who startled Jubil, but the man opened the door and, with a smile, signaled him to go in first. Jubil slowly walked in, acknowledging the cowboy with a quick nod, and then found himself as the center of attention among about fifteen men, all dressed like cowboys, all Caucasian men at that. Suddenly, from across the room, Jubil heard a familiar voice.

"Well, I never!"

It was Monte Leonard, quickly walking across the room, beaming as though he had just won that horse race he had spoken of so frequently in the great city of New Orleans, his hand extended toward Jubil.

"So you decided to come after all!" Monte Leonard said. "I couldn't be more happy!"

After a few moments of small talk, Monte Leonard turned around to introduce Jubil to the other men in the room.

"This here's Jubil, everybody," he said, apparently quite pleased about that fact, "the man from Louisiana I was tellin' ya'll about. Jubil, you remember? The veterinarian."

After a short time of introductions, Jubil began to feel just a little more comfortable, indeed, about himself standing in the middle of a group of Caucasians where he was the center of attention. After a quick jigger of smooth Kentucky bourbon, Monte Leonard called it a night for both himself and his friend Jubil, leading the way toward Jubil's new but temporary home, in the bunkhouse with the other workers, who would be spending their time during the spring and the fall racing seasons using their special talents to care for the horses. During the brief walk from the main workhouse to the bunkhouse, Monte Leonard assured Jubil that he had indeed made the right decision to come to the noble Commonwealth of Kentucky and that he would certainly have no regrets.

It would be just a few moments after the two reached the bunkhouse that Monte Leonard announced that he was tired and bade his good nights, heading for the place that he called home, away from the farm, with his own house, horse, and family. Jubil dropped his satchel on the floor of the empty bunkhouse where Monte Leonard had instructed him to, near a bunk bed that appeared to have been reserved for him, and walked onto the porch to sit down on a rocking chair that seemed to be calling his name. Tired, of course, and most assuredly homesick, but truly excited and eager to pursue this, the greatest adventure of his entire life thus far, Jubil sank down in the rocking chair and let his mind wander as he watched the Kentucky sun sink as well behind the Kentucky horizon.

Jubil noticed that there seemed to be some sort of activity continually going on all over the place, even at this late hour, and Jubil could see the silhouettes of both men and horses either going to or coming from somewhere as his eyes began to open and close, serenely fighting that need for sleep, at least until he could meet all his roommates who would share the bunkhouse with him. Jubil closed his eyes and wished upon a shooting star that this incoming group of men would be as cordial to him as those that he had met in the workhouse just a little while ago.

Well, it would not be too terribly long before Jubil would find out if his dream had indeed come true, as he was awakened by the sound of someone walking up the steps to the porch of the bunkhouse. He quickly opened his eyes and straightened up in the rocking chair to come face-to-face with not the group of Caucasian men that he was expecting, not men at all, in fact—they were, however, boys. They were boys of color, eight or nine of them! Young boys probably no older than twelve, thirteen, or fourteen years of age, probably not even going through puberty as yet, none with facial hair, but their arms were very muscular and their faces wore the signs of the manhood about to explode within them.

Jubil stood up, completely engulfed in sheer shock as he watched each of the young boys take their shoes of at the porch and, one by one, walk over to introduce themselves to him. It was quite obvious that these young boys were expecting him; they knew his name and welcomed him as though they already knew him.

"Could it be that these young boys, some even younger than yourselves, were indeed the horse experts on this Kentucky farm?"

My sweet uncle Alexandre would always ask this question to our young boys at the family reunions as he began to describe Jubil's first experience in the noble Commonwealth of Kentucky. It was truly obvious that our young boys just beamed with pride as they listened to the stories of young boys of color, boys their own ages, and just how important they all were in creating the horse races of today.

Uncle Alexandre would also tell our young boys that Jubil must truly have been confused when he learned that the trainers, exercise boys, the groomers, the jockeys, and even some of the owners of the horses that are written about in the pages of history were actually young boys of color, those that Jubilation LaPierre actually had the pleasure of meeting, working with, and sharing a bed with in the bunkhouse on a farm in Lexington, Kentucky. But for now, Jubil was simply amazed.

Perhaps the oldest of the young boys at the time of Jubil's first encounter in the noble Commonwealth of Kentucky was a young boy by the name of Isaac, thirteen or fourteen years of age, an exercise boy at the Lexington stables who was truly determined to win a Kentucky Derby. There was a boy called Billy, Walker being his surname, who also claimed his fame to a Kentucky Derby. Jubil was most impressed with this young boy who told him that he had been a slave as well and, at the tender age of thirteen years old, had already been successfully riding for two years.

Some were born in the noble Commonwealth of Kentucky, while others were brought there from other parts of the country to join forces, and join forces they most definitely did. Throughout the young boys' introductions and their challenges against one another for the title of winner of the Kentucky Derby, Jubil knew that within the walls of the bunkhouse, he was truly the one with the least amount of knowledge about the subject, but he was sure he would not leave the noble Commonwealth of Kentucky the same; in fact, he knew already that he would never be the same ever again.

Sleep came only after the young boys had finally settled down in the bunkhouse, their antics ranging from the mature talk of the horse farmwork to the silliness of the children they were, indeed. Jubil found himself feeling as though he had been hired to be their father instead of their equal, but their youth only required a few hours of sleep, so when the morning came, even with the darkness of the moon still present, while the sun still slept, it was Jubil who found himself last to roll out of bed while the young boys laughed at him for being so late and so old.

The first trip of the day was to the dining hall, located on the far side of the main workhouse of the farm, where all the workers, both Caucasian men and men of color, were served a very hearty meal that would last them through the early morning hours as they performed their work tasks until the sun was high in the noon sky, when they would meet again for lunch.

All the young boys were there, enjoying their breakfast as if it were either the first food they had eaten in some time or as though it might be their last. There was not much conversation during the meals, just the exception of the work instructions that would send all the workers to their various locations to all reach the same goal, which, of course, would be the training and well-being of the pride of the Kentucky farm, its horses.

Just as Jubil was finishing his breakfast and the last drops of his coffee, Monte Leonard appeared at the table with the owner of the farm, one of the men that he had met the night before. Both men were smiling while both extended their hand to Jubil and informed him that a formal tour of the farm would be a great place to start the day, the perfect idea for someone who was just as raw as tobacco about the workings of an authentic horse farm. He was most interested in viewing the horses, wondering if there was a noticeable difference between a horse raised in the great state of Louisiana and one raised in the noble Commonwealth of Kentucky.

Jubil was impressed, indeed, at the truly professional precision of the Kentucky farm, which seemed to roll as far as the eye could see, from the water troughs that continually fed the clean, fresh water supply to the fields and the horses, to the many people who maintained the food supply for both the humans and the horses. There were people and barns everywhere, some where the hay was kept, and some fancy barns painted white, where Jubil assumed the horses were bred or where they just lived. It was a truly beautiful experience for Jubil, and his eyes stored up some of those ideas to bring back to his home at Mon Village.

As the three men neared one of those fancy barns, Jubil could feel the excitement as he began to smell that familiar odor of the horses that came from his own stables at Mon Village, and he could hardly wait to touch one of those beautiful creatures. The young boys were there, each taking care of their own personal task at hand, grooming the horses, exercising the horses, or out on the track, training the horses. They all waved at Jubil as he continued the tour with Monte Leonard and the owner of the farm, and he felt good, needed, and truly welcomed.

Jubil's eyes were drawn immediately toward a small chestnut horse with a white star and two socks, one on each of his hind legs, rather frisky as he was being brushed by the young boy named Oliver, Ollie for short. Jubil felt quite comfortable as he walked over to the horse to acquaint himself and to examine him, of course. As Jubil was examining the horse's legs, the owner of the farm began to tell him about the horse, which was just a couple of years old at that time.

The farm owner explained that the horse was called Aristides, and although he came from a very good bloodline, a thoroughbred bloodline, in fact, he was truly not expected to do very well at any of the races, especially not expected to win the Kentucky Derby. Aristides was only about fifteen hands high and appeared to have a more pleasant, childlike demeanor, not like his half-brother, the aggressive bay Chesapeake, a few months older and the favorite of the farm. Jubil listened carefully to the experts as he watched the entire goings-on all around him, particularly Ollie, the young boy grooming Aristides, who winked at him when the farm owner was speaking.

Once the tour of the farm was completed, Jubil headed back to the bunkhouse to gather his special roots and herbs from his saddlebags to begin an initial examination of all the horses at the stables. While reaching into the saddlebags, Jubil unwittingly grabbed a handful of the mint that he had stuffed into one of his saddlebags as he was leaving his beloved home in Mon Village, and of course, his homesickness struck him in the broadness of his heart, causing Jubil to fight back his tears and his thoughts of Miss Sylvia. Jubil wiped his tears away with a handkerchief and calmed his loneliness with the thought that this first trip to the noble Commonwealth of Kentucky would only be for just two short weeks.

While Jubil was in the noble Commonwealth of Kentucky for his very first time, Mr. Bernard Menard, in the great state of New York, was approached by Kip, his gardener's wife, who had become quite a necessity in her own right to the needs of the Madam Dolice Marie in her time of expectancy, with her concerns that the madam was indeed very close to her time. Kip also reminded Mr. Bernard Menard that he had indeed promised Madam Dolice Marie that she could give birth to the child in her own native home at Mon Village. Kip explained that this had been the topic of Madam Dolice Marie's conversations for weeks now and she was indeed expecting to be at Mon Village and tended to by her family and loved ones as the baby was being born.

Well, Mr. Bernard Menard, always aware of always keeping his word, thanked Kip many times over and began to think of the easiest and best way for his beloved wife to travel that distance, discussing the matter at great length with Edward and the other members of his household staff. For days they had their heads together until it became obvious that Kip's concerns were becoming a little more frantic with each passing day and the plan had to be nailed down immediately.

With a little help from his own import-export business, Mr. Bernard Menard was able to have a brand-new, fancy carriage from France delivered to the Atchafalaya River railroad station in Louisiana, just a few miles away from Mon Village, where he could drive his lady love directly into her native home in as much comfort as would be truly possible. He also had a lovely riding hat ordered for her as well to keep the lovely Madam Dolice Marie's head protected from the weather during her carriage ride to her native home. Of course, the Menards would have to travel by train from the Upstate New York railroad station to the Atchafalaya River railroad station, a journey in itself, and one that needed to begin now!

Chapter 17

Jubil's very first experience in the noble Commonwealth of Kentucky in his new capacity as horse doctor could hardly be compared to anything he had ever experienced in his entire life, up to date, and the local races were even more exciting than Monte Leonard had described them to be. People came from places all over the noble Commonwealth of Kentucky, from many other parts of the United States of America, and farther, even from other countries outside the country's borders, to witness the riders, the young men of color, challenging one another atop well-bred, well-groomed, and professionally trained horses. And there in the middle of the entire goings-on about him was Jubil, keeping a careful eye on the disposition of every horse in the racing lineups, attending to each of them as he would tend to his very own horses, a feeling that he had already begun to feel about each and every horse around him.

Jubil was especially impressed with the manner in which the people who attended the local races were dressed, and most impressively with their hats, the fashionable derby hats that the men wore and the feathery, colorful hats worn by the ladies. Jubil had already made up his mind after seeing the very first derby hat sitting atop the head of a gentleman adorned in a tweed suit that he, too, most definitely needed one and decided that he would also bring one of the ladies' hats home to Miss Sylvia—yes, a bright-red one with long willowing feathers! How could she possibly resist that?

MINT JULEP

Those local races were simply overwhelming to Jubil, to say the least, and to everyone that attended or participated, but none would be quite as exciting as the race that was now being prepared for, that one race that would be forever known as the Kentucky Derby.

Jubil's two-week stay in the noble Commonwealth of Kentucky with the young boys of color passed quickly, and after receiving more money in his hand than he had ever held before, and after purchasing one gentlemen's derby hat and one ladies' hat in bright red with long willowing feathers, Jubil bade his farewells to Monte Leonard and to the young men of color and steered his horse down the path toward Mon Village. He was not the least bit surprised to see how much that annoying mint had grown in just two short weeks, but he was grateful to see that the path he had sewn was indeed leading his way, all the way home.

Mama Del paused in the middle of tending to her garden of mysterious herbs and spices growing alongside her house, wrinkled even more her already deeply wrinkled brow, raced toward her mystical table of spells and incantations, and then, after performing one of her most mystical, magical rituals, came to a startling conclusion, which she announced quite loudly in the quiet that was of her own voice: Dolice Marie was on her way home to Mon Village.

Evelina paused right in the middle of stirring a pot of delicious sausage étouffée and, without a word, slowly turned toward the door to the house that she and Jean Pierre shared with their children, as if she were truly in some sort of a trance.

Jean Pierre was in the outhouse in the backyard of their home when he, too, paused and became as still as a zombie.

Jubil, who had just returned home from the noble Commonwealth of Kentucky, was brushing his horse while daydreaming of Miss Sylvia and how happy she would be about the gift he had brought to her when he also became mystified, suddenly turning in that same direction and beginning a slow pace toward the same direction as Evelina and Jean Pierre were heading.

Miss Penelope, who was sitting comfortably in her rocking chair on the front porch of her home while crocheting a lovely shawl, suddenly stopped rocking and stood facing toward that same direction, cupping her hand to shield her eyes from the sun.

The lovely ladies of the big house suddenly stopped doing whatever they were doing (if you know what I mean), offered their apologies (and credit) to their, uh hum…guests, and quickly met with one another downstairs in the parlor clad in their lovely silk robes and bolted for the front door, heading toward that same place.

In just the time it took for Jean Pierre to pull up his trousers, everyone found himself or herself standing together in the middle of the residential area. A hot wind swept through, stirring up the dust and causing everyone to lose their breath as the birds and the insects stilled their voices. In the midst of the sudden quiet, Jean Pierre suddenly shouted out with great confidence and with great joy, "Dolice Marie is coming!"

And indeed she was, but she was certainly not alone, and most assuredly not in the very best of spirits. Yes, Madam Dolice Marie's child was also on the way, and everyone knew that it was time to make the way as easy and as quiet as possible.

And oh, were they ever right, and oh, if everyone could have possibly known just what condition she was in at that particular time! Just as if someone had given them the permission to move, Evelina, Jean Pierre, Jubil, Miss Penelope, and the lovely ladies of the big house began to run in different directions to some undisclosed location to perform some task known only to each of them in preparation for Madam Dolice Marie's visit.

Mama Del quickly made her way to prepare herself for that secret ritual that only she ever performed on all the LaPierre children.

It was a busy time, indeed, but a time that definitely required everyone to be fully prepared and adequately prepared for what was just up the road.

Not too terribly far down the dusty, bumpy roads that led to Mon Village, Mr. Bernard Menard could be seen sitting atop the seat of the fancy French carriage led by an equally fancy white horse, trying desperately to adjust its direction toward his destination while his fair lady, the Madam Dolice Marie LaPierre-Menard, held her lovely riding hat quite tightly with one hand to keep it from flying away while trying desperately to keep her composure with the other hand as she bounced up and down and side to side on one of the padded seats on the inside.

Mr. Bernard Menard seemed to be steering the disobedient horse in the appropriate direction, but it seemed to be dragging the fancy carriage into every pothole along the dusty road while causing Madam Dolice Marie to fly up and down from the seat several times as if she had just been catapulted. She suddenly screamed for Mr. Bernard Menard to pull the bucking carriage over to the side of the road as she had accidentally, uh-hum, eliminated on herself! Mr. Bernard Menard tried desperately to accommodate her and, after several minutes of trying to guide the horse by its reins, eventually slowed the carriage down and directed the horse to the side of the road with a jolt. Madam Dolice Marie began to cry when she realized that it was actually not an elimination of that sort but that, indeed, her water had broken and the child within her was insisting upon entering the world!

Meanwhile, back at Jean Pierre and Evelina's house, preparations were already being made for Madam Dolice Marie, who was just about to pop in on them, if you know what I mean. Clean sheets had already been placed upon the spare bed in their spare bedroom, where plenty of candlelight would make the delivery just a little brighter. The windows had been opened to create a cross-current of cool breeze throughout the room, and Miss Penelope already had a huge sterilized gumbo pot on the wood-burning stove just about ready to boil while everything else that she would need was placed just in her reach, including clean towels and a sterilized knife for Mr. Bernard Menard to cut the navel cord. Everyone worked quickly and quietly with a precision that seemed to have all been rehearsed time and time before.

Back down the dusty road, Mr. Bernard Menard had finally brought the feisty horse and fancy carriage to a screeching halt on the side of the dusty road, where it became apparent to both himself and Dolice that their child was very eager to come into the world. After a moment of smiles, laughter, and tears, reality finally set in and both also realized that they needed to hurry if they were going to get to Mon Village before the blessed event happened in the carriage on the side of that road. Madam Dolice Marie sucked in her breath and pointed her finger toward home.

The journey continued for at least another mile until Madam Dolice Marie suddenly yelled from the inside of the fancy carriage to Mr. Bernard Menard and pointed ahead of them. There, in the midst of a huge cloud of dust, was Jean Pierre and Jubil atop the seat of that familiar old wagon being drawn by a swift horse with a mission in his eyes.

Once the wagon reached the fancy carriage, Jean Pierre and Jubil assisted Madam Dolice Marie into the back of the wagon, which had been fully prepared with blankets and sheets to make a soft bed for the remainder of the trip. With just a tip of their hats, Mr. Bernard Menard, Jean Pierre, and Jubil exchanged their hellos while Madam Dolice Marie screamed in the pain of labor while the Mon Village horse-driven wagon headed toward Jean Pierre's house, where Evelina and Miss Penelope were waiting and fully prepared, indeed, for the task at hand.

While Mr. Bernard Menard hopped upon the horse that was leading the fancy carriage to follow the wagon, Jean Pierre and Jubil appeared to be extremely impressed at the sight of the fancy carriage and decided that they would accompany Mr. Bernard Menard back to this site to bring the fancy thing to Mon Village once the baby was born and Madam Dolice Marie was finally resting.

After gently bringing Madam Dolice Marie to the labor bed in Jean Pierre and Evelina's house, Jean Pierre and Jubil began to escort Mr. Bernard Menard out of the house and to the gardens, where it would be safe for him to wait until the birth of their baby. Mr. Bernard Menard resisted and insisted that his place was to be at the side of his lady love throughout the entire labor and birth process; Jean Pierre and Jubil simply looked at each other, shrugged their shoulders in a temporary agreement, and began the brief wait on the porch. Mr. Bernard Menard ran to Madam Dolice Marie's side just in time to hear her scream a tremendous scream directly into his ear and pop him up against his forehead with her hand. In her accent, which was now a combination of Creole, European French, and the swank of Upstate New York, Madam Dolice Marie bellowed, "Monsieur Bernard Menard, you have had your last relation with me! Should you make the sad mistake to approach me ever again, surely you shall die!"

Well, Mr. Bernard Menard was taken aback by such a change in the personality of his lady love and thus dismissed the statement as hysteria and again moved toward her to hold her in his arms when, again, Dolice popped him up against his forehead with her hand.

The yelling and screaming began again, all directed at the poor Mr. Bernard Menard, who was now completely in shock, having lost all direction when, suddenly, the front screen door of Jean Pierre and Evelina's house opened to reveal Jean Pierre and Jubil waiting just as Madam Dolice Marie threw a pitcher of water toward the unsuspecting father-to-be. Mr. Bernard Menard ducked and began to run, his long red hair flying in the wind, led by Jean Pierre and Jubil, who had made that trek to the gardens several times before.

It was always so wonderful to anticipate and watch my sweet uncles as they all pointed in the same direction at the exact same time, shouting in unison, "They went that a-way," and then burst into one of their thunder of laughter!

Once safely hidden in the midst of the gardens, the three men caught their breath as Jean Pierre took the opportunity to share with Mr. Bernard Menard all about the disease that the LaPierre women seemed to have once they were in labor to bring forth their children, but also assuring him that Madam Dolice Marie would snap back immediately after the child was born. Jean Pierre also quietly whispered to Mr. Bernard Menard that he should beware in the future when Dolice began to require more attention than normal, when her face became enlightened with a seductive smile and her hands seemed to be everywhere on his person.

As strange as it truly must have been for the dear Mr. Bernard Menard to hear such talk, he did listen quite intently and followed the lead of his brother-in-law, who most certainly should have known what he was speaking about, having five children of his own now and evidently having survived the LaPierre women's disease.

Madam Dolice Marie labored for many hours to bring forth the first LaPierre-Menard to the line of generations that had preceded her, reaching out to Evelina and Miss Penelope, who were standing beside her, attending to her every need. And of course to the ancestors that surrounded her, who touched the earth just one more time to bring their ancient wisdom—that is, in the midst of Madam Dolice Marie's yelling and screaming!

Well, somewhere in the midst of that great experience that only a woman can completely know, Madam Dolice Marie LaPierre-Menard gave life to the beginnings of yet another generation with one big push, as instructed by Miss Penelope and assisted by Evelina. Everyone began to smile, with tears of joy streaming down their faces as well, when the precious child took its first breath and let out a cry that resonated throughout Jean Pierre and Evelina's house, leading the three ladies to conclude that this was truly Madam Dolice Marie's offspring. Once the navel cord was cut and Miss Penelope tended to the new mother, Evelina cleaned the sweet child and placed it lovingly next to its mother, who held it and cuddled it with all the love that had truly been given to her when Mama Mozelle had given her life.

Throughout the quiet confines of Mama Del's house arose that familiar smoke as she gave her special and familiar assistance, as she had throughout Dolice Marie's entire life and that of many of the ancestors before Dolice. At the very moment that the precious child entered the world, Mama Del's laughter arose like smoke accompanying the ancestors as they rose to the heavens, leaving Dolice Marie in peace, smiling as she caressed her precious baby girl, and then both were off to sleep.

By the time Miss Penelope yelled out that familiar signal that it was indeed safe to go back into the house, the three men were fast asleep on the hard ground in the gardens of Mon Village, surrounded appropriately by rows of beautiful flowers and as many, if not even more, rows of that pesky mint. Mr. Bernard Menard jumped up first and began to run toward the house, followed closely by Jean Pierre and Jubil, stopping just short of the porch, where Evelina was standing with a glowing grin on her face. He smiled at her as he walked through the opened screen door to the house. Once he was inside, Miss Penelope led the way with her extended hand where Mr. Bernard Menard could find the tiny sweet little girl lying beside a sleeping Madam Dolice Marie. His lady love seemed at peace now, but the signs of the long labor of love were apparent: her hair was matted with hot sweat, and her breathing was quick and deep, as though she had just run a long foot race. Mr. Bernard Menard leaned over the baby and kissed his beloved wife on the forehead.

"Thank you," he whispered in her ear. "Monique Aimee Elizabeth LaPierre-Menard," Mr. Bernard Menard said as he lifted the precious little child into his arms, cradling it and gently rocking from side to side while smiling from ear to ear, just like the proud father that he truly was. And just as Jean Pierre and Jubil had said, the LaPierre women's disease indeed had ended when the baby was born.

There was yet one more trip that the three men now needed to make together, that trip taken many times by Jean Pierre immediately after the birth of each of his children. Even though the kindly Mr. Bernard Menard was truly lost as to the exact reason that Jean Pierre led him away again from the house and his sweet lady love, he had indeed learned to trust his brother-in-law and followed Jean Pierre without any hesitation, with his precious baby girl in his arms, over to Mama Del's house, for that secret ceremony that every LaPierre child would experience.

Although neither Uncle Alexandre nor any of my other beloved uncles ever disclosed any of the secret details of that secret ceremony always held in Mama Del's house after a LaPierre baby was born, he did describe our precious Mr. Bernard Menard upon his return to Jean Pierre and Evelina's house from Mama Del's house as: "Quite pale, even more white than when he went into Mama Del's house. In fact, he was the whitest white man that anyone would ever see around Mon Village!"

Why, yes, my uncles had the laugh of their lives as they shared that moment with the young boys and, most definitely, among themselves!

Chapter 18

WITH THE MADAM Dolice LaPierre-Menard still resting peacefully with the newly born Monique Aimee Elizabeth LaPierre-Menard in her arms, Mr. Bernard Menard, Jean Pierre, and Jubil rode horses back down the dusty road in the hot, humid Louisiana sun to where they had left the fancy French carriage. Both Jean Pierre and Jubil were fascinated with the beautiful carriage, and after hooking that equally fancy horse that Mr. Bernard Menard was riding to the fancy carriage, Jubil hooked his and Jean Pierre's horses to the back of the carriage and hopped inside while Mr. Bernard Menard hopped atop the seat above the carriage and grabbed ahold of and then snapped the horse's reins to make him rear and then gallop. Jean Pierre and Jubil laughed hysterically like little children as they both bounced around from seat to seat in the fancy carriage.

The curious residents of Mon Village came running to inspect the fancy French carriage being pulled by the equally fancy horse as it bobbed and weaved through the dusty paths toward its final destination. Mr. Bernard Menard tipped his hat and waved at everyone as he listened for the directions given to him by Jean Pierre, who was smiling and waving at the residents as well from the inside of the fancy carriage. While Madam Dolice Marie LaPierre-Menard continued to rest peacefully with the sweet baby girl, Mr. Bernard Menard parked the fancy French carriage in front of Jean Pierre and Evelina's house and was greeted by their children, Mon Claire; the chubby twins, Petois and Pecous; LaBelle Jelee; and Jean Pierre III, who was being held in his mother's arMiss. After some well-needed refreshments and another quick look at his new baby girl and his beautiful wife, Madam Dolice Marie, Mr. Bernard Menard accepted the invitation from Jean Pierre and Jubil to tour the grounds of Mon Village on foot.

Mr. Bernard Menard was shocked, indeed, to learn—and the hard way, I might also add—that the facilities were located outside each house in the residential area, a fact that he unfortunately had to experience firsthand after not being able to hold himself a second longer and after making that very uncomfortable discovery. After returning from the outhouse in back of Jean Pierre and Evelina's house, Mr. Bernard Menard decided to make a list of improvements that could easily be made to his wife's beloved home, improvements that could most certainly be merchandise-funneled through his own import-export business and most assuredly beneficial to all the residents. With his cheeks quite pink—facial cheeks, I might clarify—Mr. Bernard Menard began to survey the Mon Village property with pen and paper in hand, being accompanied by Jean Pierre and Jubil every step of the way.

Even before the topic of making the much-needed improvements to Mon Village was introduced to the many young boys who would visit Mon Village during our family reunions, my daffy uncles began to laugh with one another, which, of course, caused the young boys to feel just a tad uncomfortable as they awaited yet another tale in the long list of traditional stories being told to them. After they had finally gathered their wits about themselves, Uncle Alexandre would clear his throat and begin again.

Mr. Bernard Menard explained to Jean Pierre and Jubil that there was a brand-new porcelain device that had been invented for the inside of a house and could easily be imported from England, a device with a flushing action that was complete with a bidet, should anyone choose to have such installed with the device—no more outhouses and no more nighttime chamber pots! Jean Pierre and Jubil just looked at each other with sheer and utter confusion since they had no idea what Mr. Bernard Menard was talking about.

Just as confusing to the two was Mr. Bernard Menard's description of an incandescent light bulb, which had been invented by a Mr. Thomas Alva Edison, which would bring light to each of the houses and shops, without candles! Well, it must have been apparent to Mr. Bernard Menard that neither Jean Pierre nor Jubil had any idea of what he was talking about and so, after a quick smile, a quick run of his fingers through his long red hair, and a quick turn toward the vastness of Mon Village, he made a simple request.

"My dear brother-in-law," he began, "may I please have your permission to make some improvements to this beautiful place? Some improvements, sir, that I know will certainly be appreciated by everyone who lives or visits here? This will be a gift to you from my beloved bride, and myself."

Strangely enough, until that very moment, neither Jean Pierre nor Jubil had ever seen the necessity to change anything about Mon Village, a home that had never been less than perfect to them and to all those who lived in the peace-filled confines. But neither did they want to deny to anyone a modernized version of what was already there, and so Jean Pierre smiled and extended his hand to his brother-in-law to seal the agreement that Mr. Bernard Menard did indeed have his permission to do whatever he felt was necessary to make Mon Village even better than ever before.

Throughout the years, it would be Mr. Bernard Menard and his quite capable import-export business that would keep Mon Village thoroughly modern in every respect, as noted by my dear uncles, which meant that Mon Village received all the latest and most innovative inventions that would give the residents an exceptional capability of getting the job done, whatever that job was.

Due to the continuing efforts of Mr. Bernard Menard and his booming import-export business, the residents of Mon Village were able to perform even the most menial of tasks in a timely and, most assuredly, with much less effort than ever before, farm equipment, household appliances, construction devices, personal hygiene gadgets, fabric, shoes, and eventually the radio, which would bring both good and bad news of the outside world a little closer to the confines of Mon Village.

One of those stories told at our family reunions by my beloved uncles describes yet another situation, this one with an employee working for the Menard import-export business who discovered a large can on the Mon Village property one day while digging to make improvements—a large can, one filled with lots of money.

Mr. Bernard Menard always made sure that his employees were as honest as himself, so indeed the employee brought the money to him and, in turn, Mr. Bernard Menard brought the money to Jean Pierre. It was true that lots of money had been hidden all over Mon Village by the residents as well as Jean Pierre and Dolice Marie when money was being made but times were not quite as free as they had become. This certainly perplexed Mr. Bernard Menard, and he kindly insisted that all monies be dug up and kept in the private homes until he could help everyone create a mutual banking system where all money would be safe and all residents would be able to deposit their personal money in an individual account as well as make their own personal withdrawals without question.

The residents were certainly not as trusting of Mr. Bernard Menard as Jean Pierre and Jubil were, but after witnessing Jean Pierre digging up his cans of money and putting it in a safe place in his own home to wait for the new Mon Village bank, each soon began to do the same.

Within a day, Jubil had chosen a group of men from the Mon Village construction crew to plan and build a new shop in the business district, a shop that would eventually become known as the Residents Bank of Mon Village, and before Mr. and Mrs. Bernard Menard returned to their home in the great state of New York, several trusted residents had been chosen to learn bow to maintain the day-to-day operations of the bank.

Uncle Alexandre would always point out that the entire fortune of hidden money was probably never completely found, and that rumor had it that money was probably still hidden on the grounds of Mon Village at that very moment.

By the time the Menards, with their newborn baby girl, Monique Aimee Elizabeth LaPierre-Menard, made their own plans to return to their home in the great state of New York, plans to make Mon Village virtually a city in itself in every respect were well on the way.

With all this celebration, one thing became incredibly obvious to both Mr. Bernard Menard and his flourishing import-export business: nothing or no one would ever free the grounds of Mon Village from that pesky mint, which had survived both the steam of hot Louisiana weather and the floods of stormy weather. It also became quite obvious that as long as there was just one man or one woman alive who had formerly lived life as a slave, the entrance to Mon Village would remain a secret and hidden from the outside world, unless one was invited, that is.

With Madam Dolice Marie preoccupied with her new husband and newborn baby and Jean Pierre spending more time with his own family, Jubil began to feel those old feelings of loneliness creeping upon him while his mind floated away from him to seemingly being with Miss Sylvia. Jubil could actually picture Miss Sylvia in her fancy new red racing bonnet that he had brought to her from the noble Commonwealth of Kentucky, wearing a huge smile because he had come to court while all the while she would just be waiting to say yes whenever he actually popped that crucial question. But when would that be? Jubil was just as afraid of Miss Sylvia now as he had been of the "ghost" that he thought the mysterious light was in the fields that special night he met Miss Sylvia so long ago, the night that she had been picking the mint from the gardens.

After tossing and turning and turning and tossing again throughout the entire night, Jubil made up his mind that today was the day that he would try again to let Miss Sylvia know his true feelings, that he would give her the fancy red racing hat as a gesture of his love and ask her to spend the rest of her life with him. He realized that he could no longer spend another restless night fully awake, thinking about her. Jubil knew that he needed his rest, so he knew that he had to face Miss Sylvia or simply die from exhaustion.

Hopefully, facing her could not possibly be as bad as what he had already been experiencing, and so without giving himself another chance to chicken out of the situation, Jubil prepared himself both mentally and physically to face his greatest demon, that tiny little woman in the mint shop.

First, he would walk to the business area instead of riding his horse; walking would give him less of an opportunity to get away quickly if he indeed decided to chicken out again. Second, he would give her the fancy red riding hat with a big smile, and after she returned his smile with a smile of her own, Jubil would ask Miss Sylvia to take a walk with him, where he could begin to discuss his feelings for her.

Well, that was that, and after cleaning himself up and putting his own fancy derby hat atop his head, Jubil set out walking with the hatbox under his arm, fully confident and fully committed to this task at hand.

Within minutes, Jubil found himself standing in front of Miss Sylvia's mint shop, and he grabbed the doorknob and, without even thinking, opened the door to walk in. There were people in the shop, familiar people, of course, from the residential area, all talking about the many uses of mint that Miss Sylvia had discovered and passed along to each of them.

The people in the shop said hello, and everyone there commented on Jubil's "fine hat," and they asked questions about his trip to the noble Commonwealth of Kentucky. Jubil was extremely proud that his neighbors were so very kind as to remark about his recent trip and about his hat most definitely, most of all.

As Jubil maneuvered himself toward the front of the store, where Miss Sylvia was helping one of her customers, he straightened himself out just one more time to be sure that he looked his very best even though his heart was beating so hard that he was afraid she would see it beating from the outside his clothes! Miss Sylvia was smiling sweetly with her customer, so Jubil naturally assumed that she would maintain that smile once she noticed that he was in the shop and waiting to see her; however, when she noticed that he was behind her customer, the smile on her mouth turned to a very sour expression. Once the customer finally moved on, Jubil moved closer to Miss Sylvia and cleared his throat to capture her attention. And that he did!

"Why, Mr. Jubilation LaPierre, back from his very important trip, I see," she said as she continued to stock shelves and busy herself with anything but looking him straight in the eye.

"Why, yes, I am," Jubil responded to her comment. "I brought you somethin'," Jubil continued as he followed her around the mint shop. "I hope you'll like it."

A very surprised Miss Sylvia turned to look directly at Jubil. "For me?" Miss Sylvia asked in a manner that was beginning to sound a tad like both affection rising and sarcasm falling all at the same time. "Now, why did you go and do that, sir?"

Oh, what a perfect question for her to ask, and oh, what a perfect time for Jubil to answer her by telling her everything that was in his heart! But he simply stood there for a few moments, cleared his throat, and finally forced himself to give to her the answer he had prepared himself to give her for so very long.

"'Well, Miss Sylvia…I think you are…just as…well…just as beautiful as any of those fancy ladies that I saw at the races over the past two weeks…so I thought, well…that you would look just as beautiful as they do in one of their fancy hats," Jubil mumbled. "So I bought you this," he added as he shyly and with head hanging gave the hatbox to Miss Sylvia.

"Oh my!" she replied as she stared at the hatbox.

"Gon' nah, take it, it's yours!" Jubil responded, seemingly gaining his composure.

"Why, Mr. Jubil, I just don't know what to say!"

"No need to say anythin', Miss Sylvia," Jubil said, encouraging her to take the hatbox. "Jess take it."

Miss Sylvia slowly and shyly took the hatbox from Jubil, her eyes nearly bulging from her head when she reached in the hatbox to remove the fancy red racing hat.

"Oh, my, my, my…it is a beautiful hat indeed!"

"Gon'! Try it on!" Jubil said to Miss Sylvia, quite comfortable now, as he coaxed her to try the hat on and look at herself in the mirror that hung on the wall in the little mint shop. The young woman complied and was just as surprised as Jubil at how truly beautiful she did look in her new, fancy red racing hat.

"Well, Mr. Jubil," Miss Sylvia said as she turned to face him, "this is truly a beautiful hat, a wonderful hat, indeed, and I do declare...I do believe that even I think that I look quite beautiful in this hat...but a gift as expensive as this...from a man...may require some sort of, well, return favor...if you please...and if that is your intention, Mr. Jubilation LaPierre, then you can just have it back!"

Miss Sylvia tossed her head, put one hand on her hip, and held the hat out toward Jubil. Jubil was completely surprised, indeed, with Miss Sylvia's response, but also very determined to make his true intentions known before he walked out of the shop this very day.

"No return favor expected," Jubil said, finding himself much less shy and more frustrated than anything. "No favor of any kind expected, Miss Sylvia. Just a gift to someone that I care for."

"Care for?"

"Yes...care for," Jubil answered with a shy smile. "A lot!"

"Oh my!" Miss Sylvia answered, realizing that this was truly the very moment that she had longed for, and she had already given up the idea that she would ever hear those words from the man that she, too, cared for.

"Miss Sylvia, I more than jess care for you." Jubil sighed and pressed on with the long-anticipated conversation. "I already know we could be good together, 'cause I take you with me in my head everywhere I go, all the time...and we get along good, too...in my head!"

Miss Sylvia just had to laugh, but after noticing the expression of embarrassment on Jubil's face, she quickly apologized and encouraged him to go on with his conversation.

"I wasn't laughing at you, Mr. Jubil, I was laughing with you," Miss Sylvia said in her most genteel manner, sealing the explanation with a little girlie-girl smile.

"Now you would think that a man who has had such difficulty with his pursuit of the woman he loves would truly know better," my uncle Michele would say to the young boys as he prepared them for what was about to come next. "Know better, that is, than to speak before he gave a whole lot of thought about just how far back he was going to put his pursuit if he opened his mouth too far!"

The young boys were not quite so sure what that meant, but Uncle Michele was truly eager to let them know: Jubil was about to put his pursuit straight down his throat, along with his foot.

"I'm so glad to know that, Miss Sylvia," Jubil replied, feeling very relaxed now, indeed, and ready to jump in with both feet. "I would like you to give some thought to spending some time with me, Miss Sylvia," Jubil said. "Maybe go for a walk so we can talk about our future."

"Our future," she answered.

"Uh-huh," Jubil replied. "I'll be going back to the horses in Kentucky in a few months, and I was hoping we could reach some sort of conclusions about us before I had to go again. It's for sho' we ain't getting any younger, Miss Sylvia, and well, everybody knows that a woman needs a good man."

"Oooohh!"

My uncles would laugh, and so hard that I often thought for sure that one day one of them was going to have a heart attack at this part of the telling of the family stories.

"Young men," Uncle Michele would tell the young boys, "Remember this: never speak of a woman's age, especially never remind her of how old she's getting, and for goodness's sake, never, never, never tell her what she needs!"

Well, it was certainly too bad that Jubil did not have that lesson before he opened his mouth to Miss Sylvia that day in her shop so very long ago. Story has it that Miss Sylvia threw the fancy red racing hat at Jubil, hatbox and all, in front of all the people in the shop and then chased him out of the shop with both of her fists balled up. Jubil ran and ran all around Mon Village until he finally found Jean Pierre as he was heading back to his house from the silversmith's shop. After explaining to his friend what he had said, word for word, Jean Pierre had just one word of advice for Jubil.

"Beg!"

Chapter 19

BEING BORN AND raised in the Deep South of this most wonderful country of ours should certainly make it quite understandable, and not in the least bit a surprise, that I called my own dear daddy Big Daddy, for more reasons than one. My daddy, the youngest in the line of children that were the generation to which my beloved uncles and aunts belonged, was named Jean Pierre V, Quincy for short, the nickname that my sweet mother gave to him when they were dating, that little name that stayed with him until the time he went on to meet the ancestors in the other world.

Big Daddy was a great big man, standing over six feet tall, with huge muscles that bulged thick through his shirt, which his body had probably gained as he performed his duties in masonry for the Mon Village construction crew, a job he held and loved for many years. Whether it was stonework, brickwork, granite, sandstone, or just plain ole stone, Big Daddy knew how to do it all, and his signature was on virtually every modern improvement in either the business or residential areas of Mon Village.

Everyone that knew Big Daddy knew him to be a very happy man with a great big smile, great big hands with great big calluses that showed just how hard he worked, and a great big heart that was filled with love for his family, and for my mama all those years that they spent together.

Big Daddy was very much like the other Jean Pierres that preceded him and those of his brothers and sisters that chose to grow up and build their futures at Mon Village—no desire to see the world or capture a dream somewhere else away from home. He found his home, his peace, and the love of his life right at Mon Village and never felt the need to leave.

My mama was truly well educated in the standards provided by the schoolhouse at Mon Village at that time and became a teacher herself, dedicated to teaching those that would come after her. Mama believed that education was just as important as any of the other jobs at Mon Village and insisted that even those residents who chose to work in the silver shops or on the construction crews at least learn to read, write, and count money. She always told all her students, "No one can cheat you out of what is yours if you know how to read, write, and count money."

And that would be the manner in which Big Daddy and my mama met each other, while she was teaching him to read and write. The story says that after my mama taught my daddy to read and write, he wrote a lovely note to her stating how very much he loved her, and yes, she answered him back. My mama sent Big Daddy a lovely poem by Elizabeth Barrett Browning, and at the end of the poem, she wrote to him that she would tell him just how she felt about him—after he read the poem to her.

My uncles said that it might have taken him a while to learn all those words, but he finally did, and she did, and then…well, the rest is family history!

My mama's name was Zothra, but everyone called her Zoe, probably resembling the Spanish side of our family more than the French side with her darker-brown skin, dark eyes, and lovely long straight hair, which she always wore in some sort of upsweep that allowed her beautiful eyes to truly express themselves.

Mama was of medium height, medium build, with a smile that always said, "It's okay," when she hugged me after I ran to her with one of my boo-boos that I had gotten while trying to keep up with my boy cousins during one of their excursions. I was the only child that Big Daddy and my mama had, but I was certainly not alone: my childhood was filled with plenty of cousins who shared their love, their never-ending thirst for excitement, and provided plenty of activity with me.

Just like all my modern-day relatives, Big Daddy had a deep-seated faith for the Lord, and it was Big Daddy who volunteered to tell the stories about how religion finally came to be at Mon Village, and when it was his turn to tell his part of the family stories, all my other uncles became very quiet and listened to his every word.

My mama always told me that Big Daddy felt the calling to the cloth while they were both still young and that, after learning to read and write, Big Daddy began to read an old Bible, a family treasure that had been handed down from one generation to another generation after the family began to practice religion, or "'ligion," as Big Daddy always mocked the early language of our ancestors.

Eventually, Big Daddy took over the church duties of his older brothers and began preaching in the old church house, filling it up to the point that a new one soon had to be built. Mama always said that the women who actually chose to attend church were really more interested in catching Big Daddy's eye than saving their own souls.

Uncle Clovis would burst into laughter when he would pretend he was one of the women strutting into Big Daddy's church. "Here they come!" he would tease, walking around with his hand on his hip, pretending to be one of those women. "With hats the size of Texas on their heads and candy-apple-red lips and fingernails, carrying patent leather purses and fighting over a seat in the pew in the direct line of the podium and the preacher!"

Silly men would just explode into laughter, while the young boys laughed along with them while covering their mouths and looking at one another like they had just seen their first naked woman.

Big Daddy always began his portion of the telling of the traditional family stories with not only a prayer but also a sermon, the same sermon that he would deliver the next morning at the beginning of the Sunday services, of which he was always in charge. Many of my other uncles commented quite openly that Big Daddy took that opportunity to actually practice his sermon on captured ears, but Big Daddy gave his brothers no never mind and proudly stood to give his prayer, his practice sermon, and his portion of the traditional telling of the family stories.

The child of Mama Mozelle created with the former Master LaPierre and the child of the old African-with-No-Name, later known as Jean Pierre, created with the former Mistress LaPierre had truly lifted themselves up from the depths of slavery to the heights of master and mistress over a thriving plantation, now a self-sufficient city all to itself.

Madam Dolice Marie LaPierre-Menard was now residing quite comfortably in a lovely cottage in Upstate New York, settled quite happily with her beloved husband, Mr. Bernard Menard, and both enjoying their pride and joy, Monique Aimee Elizabeth LaPierre-Menard, as she grew into a lovely young lady. The memories that never faded and her thoughts of Mon Village were still never too far from her heart even though she had finally accepted her place with her beloved family in the great state of New York.

Back in the great city of New Orleans, Angeline was now the madam of the New Orleans House—that is, with the assistance of her beloved aunt and Madam Dolice Marie's beloved foster mother, Miss BB Carson Declouette—and yes, business was truly booming! Angeline concentrated on the administrative and financial end of the business, while Georgia tended to the real business at hand (if you know what I mean), leading the lovely ladies of the New Orleans House in every other way.

Angeline was now hearing from Mr. Bernard Menard's best friend, Willem, regularly, although she had not yet made up her mind if she should allow that relationship to move further.

The New Orleans House now had a full-time pianist as well, Madeleine Dubois-Chachere, from the great city of Baton Rouge, who came in every weekend to play music for the lovely ladies and their, well, guests!

Yes, Jubil begged and begged until Miss Sylvia finally said yes and was happily making adjustments to the house that had formerly been just Jubil's house, adding that feminine touch to each room: new curtains, bright colors, and of course, lots of silver dishes and cups from the silversmith's shop. Jubil was truly pleased with every little modification because it meant that Miss Sylvia would soon be moving in. Both Jubil and Miss Sylvia had agreed that it was best to go straight to "jumping the broom" instead of having a long courting period for fear of more misunderstandings like the one that had occurred in her shop.

Jean Pierre LaPierre was now master of all that the eye could see along the edge of the Bayou Frou-Frous, also living quite comfortably and settled quite happily with his devoted wife, Evelina, and their five children, Mon Claire; the chubby twins, Petois and Pecous; LaBelle Jelee; and of course, Jean Pierre III, all growing in body and mind. There was no need, nor would there ever be again, for the fear of Evelina carrying another LaPierre child and putting Jean Pierre through the nightmare he had gone through for all his children, after naming the last child Jean Pierre III. That binding agreement between Jean Pierre and Mama Del allowed Jean Pierre to truly enjoy his life with his beloved wife, Evelina.

Mon Claire LaPierre, Jean Pierre and Evelina's beloved firstborn, had a curiosity that often found her in places that could indeed cause her great harm, but for reasons far beyond anyone's meager thoughts, the sweet child always found her way back home safely, but she never quite understood why her parents were so pleased to see her when she finally did return home.

Although she was quite petite, Mon Claire was said to have had very long legs that seemed to be longer than her whole body, beautiful hazel-brown eyes, with long brown hair that hung over smooth skin the color of the sand that served as a beach at all the edges of the Bayou Frou-Frous. The muscles of her arms and long legs bulged as a sure sign that the child could handle both heavy work and heavy play without so much as a whimper, while her smile could capture the heart of anyone in its path.

Quite the tomboy, Mon Claire spent the larger part of her day with Jubil in the stables, eagerly assisting him with the care of the horses and learning at a truly outrageously young age how to ride the massive steed. Jubil had actually held her in his arms while he rode one of his trusty steeds, Garçon, throughout the vast areas of Mon Village since she was barely three years old. While other children might have been just a tad hesitant to even get near such a giant animal, Mon Claire always held her own with an apparent determination that she could indeed master all that came in her path.

By the time Mon Claire was probably just ten years old, she could ride any horse at the stables, with or without a saddle, as well as any boy or man on Mon Village, as a matter of fact. Jubil entrusted her with a horse of her own, one sired by his beloved Garçon, which Mon Claire named Ti-Garçon, or "little boy." Strict rules were set down by Jean Pierre and Evelina that included Mon Claire finishing all her chores around the house before she could go off exploring, and curfew meant being home before the sun set behind their house.

Mon Claire could often be seen soaring through the residential area on Ti-Garçon, with her hair flying across her face. Evelina had long given up trying to catch her firstborn child and would run to the porch to just get a glimpse of the sweet young thing as she rode past her house with a look of sheer delight on her face. Although Mon Claire was an obedient child with great love for her parents and her uncle Jubil, her love for horses often clouded her good judgment and found her in the deepest of trouble with Jean Pierre.

It would be one of those particularly beautiful evenings on the shores of the Bayou Frou-Frous that would lead Mon Claire to one of her most memorable experiences, one that would indeed shape the future of the entire family. Just as the sun showed its need to set on Mon Village in order to rise in another part of the Earth, Mon Claire caught sight of a glimmer of light in the woods just off in the distance and in the opposite direction of home.

Without even a second thought about the repercussions that would follow for being late getting home, the precocious Mon Claire bravely guided her beloved Ti-Garçon toward the light, slowly approaching it between the tall trees, over the shallow, muddy waters of the bayou, until she reached a huge canvas tent. The candlelight within the tent cast shadows of the people that were inside, and she could hear the sound of musical instruments being played, some she recognized as the instruments played during the La Las; some instruments sounded as strange as the voices of the people who were inside.

She dismounted Ti-Garçon and was leading him by the reins as she walked closer to the inexplicable event going on inside the tent when suddenly the voices and the music stopped. Mon Claire leaned closer toward the tent and could hear a man's voice muttering at first and then becoming progressively louder, with the people in the tent shouting, "Amen!" every now and then. The scene and the sounds were all too strange to Mon Claire, but that same curiosity that killed the cat stirred deep within her, and Mon Claire decided to stay, come what may.

The voices became loud again, and the music played as the people inside the tent actually began to dance, bumping into one another, crying and shaking all over. Mon Claire could not see clearly through the tent material, and while still leading Ti-Garçon by his rein, she began to walk slowly around the tent in search of an opening, which she found on the opposite side of the tent. There she observed the man that she had been hearing through the tent material putting his hands on the top of a person's head while speaking in some sort of gibberish, while others were clapping their hands, dancing, and speaking in the same kind of gibberish.

It was all Greek to Mon Claire, but as she continued her observation, she began to tremble, her eyes beginning to water and bulge out of their sockets while she uncontrollably began to bat her eyelashes. The rein she held in her hand began to tremble as well, and as she looked up to Ti-Garçon, she realized that he, too, was trembling and looked as though he was feeling the same woozy feeling that she was feeling. That feeling became more intense, so intense that neither Mon Claire nor Ti-Garçon could move their legs to run away.

Without warning, both Mon Claire and Ti-Garçon were, as they say, slain in the spirit and fell forward into the tent and into the people inside, causing mass confusion, although neither one had any idea at all what was happening all around them. Moments later, both Mon Claire and Ti-Garçon awakened to find themselves lying on the ground inside the tent, surrounded by the people, proper Southern white people, all of them, hovering over the two of them while speaking in that strange language, arms raised to the sky, some of them crying.

The strange man that had his hands on the head of one of the people had his face directly in Mon Claire's face and was clenching his fist while angrily telling something, "Come on out of her!"

Afraid and dazed, Mon Claire jumped up and, with Ti-Garçon's rein still in her hand, quickly ran away from the scene, both hers and Ti-Garçon's feet barely touching the ground, with the proper Southern white people still shouting and dancing in the tent.

Mon Claire rode like the wind all the way back to the stables of Mon Village, frightened yet curious still as to what had happened to her and to her best friend, Ti-Garçon. Jubil was going about his evening chores and barely said a word to her, so she quickly kissed Ti-Garçon on his nose and ran through the residential area until she reached her home.

It was truly amazing that Mon Claire did not seem to be late, although she felt that she had been away from home for hours and hours, expecting Jean Pierre to be waiting on the front porch with his arms folded, just ready to punish her for being tardy, but instead, the house was quiet and peaceful, just the usual sounds of the other children playing. Evelina greeted her with an unexpected smile, just like she always did when Mon Claire was truly on time from one of her great adventures.

Still very dazed and quite confused, Mon Claire slipped into her bed and tried hard to recollect the events of that evening, the sounds, the sights, and most assuredly, what happened when both she and Ti-Garçon had fallen to the ground. As she dozed off to sleep, she felt herself being swept away, a sort of floating feeling that she had never before felt, while a voice inside her head spoke to her of things she had never thought of before. Somewhere deep inside herself, Mon Claire knew what she had to do; she had to go back to the great tent the next night, even if it meant being punished by her father, Jean Pierre.

And so that she did: night after night, Mon Claire rode the mighty Ti-Garçon to the secret place across the Bayou Frou-Frous, where she joined with the people inside the tent as they spoke the strange language, danced, and listened to the man who, night after night, placed his hands upon the heads of the people, who fell out on the floor, just as she and Ti-Garçon had done that fateful first night. And still night after night, Mon Claire was greeted by Jean Pierre and Evelina as if she was not late at all, although inside herself she knew that she just absolutely had to be.

One particular night, the voice inside her head instructed Mon Claire to extend an invitation to the man in the tent to come to Mon Village with all his people and teach Jean Pierre, Evelina, Jubil, and all the residents all about what she was learning, about God and his son, Jesus, and his special 'ligion, as she called it. With bravery so typical of the young Mon Claire, she walked right up to the man and presented her suggestion that everyone go to Mon Village. A thunder of music and shouts of "Amen" rang throughout the tent, with an apparent answer to the question of the delighted Mon Claire, who again rode from the scene on her trusted steed, Ti-Garçon, both flying like the wind to bring the news to Jean Pierre and Evelina.

Unfortunately, however, Jean Pierre and Evelina were not as eager to invite any more strangers to their home at Mon Village than was absolutely necessary, especially proper Southern white folk, who just might bring more trouble than good to their peaceful existence. Mon Claire begged and pleaded with her parents until she wore their resistance down and Jean Pierre finally agreed to at least meet with the strange man and his group before allowing them to come to Mon Village. "Jubil and I will go to them," he told his daughter, who would be just as excited either way.

Not knowing exactly what to expect, Jean Pierre and Jubil armed themselves with heavy sticks, weapons that could protect them but not cause permanent bodily harm to anyone. Mon Claire rode in the saddle with Jean Pierre, who demanded that she hold him tightly around the waist and, if anything went wrong, ride hard back to Mon Village to gather more men to assist in the situation.

Once on the other side of the Bayou Frou-Frous, Jean Pierre could see the tent and hear the carryings-on that had hypnotized his firstborn child, and he cautiously crept a little closer to get a first-hand look. Just as Mon Claire had said, there was music and people speaking in strange languages, the man who put his hands on other people's heads, and those people who would fall on the ground. It was a curious sight that mesmerized Jean Pierre, and just as he turned to ask Jubil's opinion about such things, Jubil himself fell on the ground, slain in the spirit, right off his horse, at Jean Pierre's feet.

When the news began to spread throughout Mon Village that 'ligion services would be held regularly beginning the first day that the residents would not be scheduled to work, rumors began to spread like cow manure rolling down a hill. Some said this was the working of the proper Southern white people who were trying to infiltrate Mon Village and bring back the hate-filled days of slavery, some said it was the evil work of other plantation owners who were jealous of the progress being made at Mon Village, and yet others believed it could be the remnants of the ancient African beliefs that had seemingly died with the old African-with-No-Name that would later be known as Jean Pierre I.

Whatever the general consensus was at that time, every single adult resident at Mon Village was indeed prepared to analyze the situation and draw his or her own conclusion.

When the school bell began to ring on that Sunday morning, the residents of Mon Village began their trek into the unknown as they walked from their homes and found a place to sit or just stand. Preacher Bubba McKnight and his lady singers, dressed just alike in their long flowing gowns, slowly marched into the schoolhouse while clapping their hands, singing, and shaking their tambourines, with Mon Claire leading the way.

Everyone was quiet, with their eyes staring directly at the preacher as he found his way to the front of the schoolhouse, right in front where the teachers would be teaching during the school day. The ladies, in their long flowing gowns, found their places behind the preacher, and when everything was absolutely quiet, the preacher began to speak quite loudly about "hellfire and damnation" to all those who disobeyed the laws of God and how the gates of heaven would swing open mighty wide for those who follow the path of righteousness.

The ladies began to shake their tambourines, clap their hands, and speak those strange words that were truly unfamiliar to the residents who were attending the services. As each began to peer from one to the other for some sort of explanation, one of the preacher's ladies fell out on the floor. The other ladies began to raise their hands up to the ceiling, with their eyes nearly bulging out. Many of the residents stood to run in great fear of such going-on, but Mon Claire pleaded with them to stay, explaining that she, too, had fallen under the spell of the preacher's words and that it was truly nothing to fear.

Preacher Bubba McKnight continued with his words while the ladies continued with their music for what seemed an eternity, successfully gaining the attention of everyone within listening range of his powerful voice! At times the preacher would suddenly stop talking at all, as if he were listening to some voice way out in the distance, but then he would suddenly raise his voice again, causing the residents to jump straight up in their places.

Finally, the preacher looked out among the crowd and asked those who believed that they were sinners and needed prayer to come forward to receive God's forgiveness. No one moved at all, just looked around to see if anyone else would stand to go up to the man and let him place his hands on their heads.

Preacher Bubba McKnight began preaching again about just what sin is, raising his voice and his hands as he preached about stealing from your neighbor.

The residents nodded in agreement, acknowledging that no one at Mon Village had ever, or would ever, steal from his or her neighbor, and therefore no one needed to go forth to let the preacher place his hands on their heads to receive God's forgiveness and possibly fall on the floor.

Next, Preacher Bubba McKnight preached against jealousy, anger, drunkenness, and disrespect of women and parents.

While the residents agreed a little louder, they still did not feel the need to go forth to let Preacher Bubba McKnight place his hands on their heads to receive God's forgiveness, and possibly fall on the floor.

Preacher Bubba McKnight reached in his coat pocket to pull out a handkerchief to wipe his sweating brow and then began to speak about killing your fellow man, your brother in the eyes of the Lord.

And again the residents nodded in agreement even louder than before, acknowledging that everyone at Mon Village was family and would never kill (of course, there were those little indiscretions during the Civil War that no one ever spoke about anymore, the ones resting quite nicely in the gardens, but that was self-protection, surely not the kind of killing that Preacher Bubba McKnight was talking about). But still the residents felt no need at all to go forth to let him place his hands on their heads to receive God's forgiveness, and possibly fall on the floor.

Oh, but it was when Preacher Bubba McKnight preached his loudest about.

"Lustful thoughts, adultery, fornication, and sex for money."

It was at this moment that the residents in the schoolhouse truly became a congregation, one that quietly looked from one to another, speaking not one single word as they slowly rose one by one to walk with their heads down all the way to the front, where Preacher Bubba McKnight placed his hands on each one, even the ladies of the big house, Miss Annabelle's ladies, and yes, as you would imagine, each one fell out on the floor as they received God's forgiveness. Chile! It truly was a sight to behold!

Well, it would not be too very long before the residents at the local town, those proper Southern white folk who spent their money on the various commodities being offered by the residents at Mon Village, began to hear about Bubba McKnight and his ladies' recent visit, and not long after that, indeed, letters began to arrive at Mon Village, letters that came from the various denominations of worship in the surrounding towns requesting equal opportunity (oh my!) for the same kind of time that had been given to Preacher Bubba McKnight in order to teach their own particular form of 'ligion. It was a perplexing time for Jean Pierre, but after careful thought and discussion with, well, who else but his own sweet Mon Claire, Jean Pierre was able to offer a very fair proposition to everyone who had written requesting equal time at the Mon Village schoolhouse.

Over the next few weeks, Jean Pierre, with Jubil and Mon Claire, stood at the dirt road to Mon Village, just a short distance from where Mama Mozelle and Dolice Marie had once stood to sell their vegetables, flowers, and that sweet, cool lemonade, greeting preachers, pastors, priests, and even a rabbi who actually came to Mon Village from as far as the great city of Lake Charles.

Whenever possible, some of the other residents of Mon Village joined the three on the dirt road to offer their own opinions, what times and what places the various services could be held, but it was extremely important, indeed, when Annabelle showed up with her lovely ladies (now dressed in ordinary clothing, with no makeup, no fineries, and no fancy shoes) and actually offered the big house with its many rooms as the perfect place to accommodate everyone's preference.

And what would that mean to the business that had brought in solid, continuous income for so many years?

"Well," my own Big Daddy would say, "goes to show you that the knowledge of the good things of life brings with it the knowledge of what sin is, wouldn't you say?"

Big Daddy searched the young boys' faces as he drove his point home to them.

"Sounds to me like it meant the end to the business of the big house as the residents of Mon Village and the patrons from the surrounding cities had known, for now, anyway. But for how long?"

How long indeed!

Chapter 20

SEVERAL YEARS HAD passed, and it was now the year 1875 for everyone, whether in the great states of Louisiana or New York, in the great city of New Orleans, or in the noble Commonwealth of Kentucky; it was a year that was truly destined to be a significant one for everyone, but not so significant as it would be for Mr. Jubilation LaPierre.

The addition of religion in the everyday lives of the residents of Mon Village was truly as significant as significant could get, indeed. The big house was now a temporary boardinghouse for many of the ladies that had worked there previously, and the parlor was now being used for the various religious services, which included Catholic Masses, Protestant services, and many other services that the residents chose to attend.

One story has it that the preacher Bubba McKnight felt the need for and then insisted upon a "cleansing" of the big house before any services could be held. Seemed he had felt the presence of "unclean spirits" coming from the big house while he had been preaching in the schoolhouse that needed to be expelled, so he and the ladies that traveled with him spent several days and nights in the big house in constant prayer.

The residents of Mon Village were instructed to stay away, but the sound of the tambourines and the strange language could be heard throughout the former plantation both day and night for several days and nights as Preacher Bubba McKnight, as my crazy uncles would say in unison, "sent up some industrial-strength prayers!"

All of a sudden, as the story continued, the prayers and the music finally stopped abruptly, causing the residents to approach the big house and stand at a safe distance to observe what would happen next. Preacher Bubba McKnight and the traveling ladies slowly emerged through the front door and onto the porch, appearing quite weathered and exhausted from the task, but Bubba McKnight, in an extremely hoarse voice, only had one thing to say to everyone: "This house is clean."

And then the group simply (and quite quickly, I might add) continued walking toward the flower gardens with the look of sheer shock on their faces. The story says that Preacher Bubba McKnight and his traveling ladies never returned to Mon Village, but rumor had it that they put up a mighty fight to rid the big house of its unclean spirits. Indeed!

With that taken care of, Jean Pierre instructed the construction crew to build single houses in areas to the left and right of the big house for the ladies, while the transformation into a regular church house could be made of the former big house, which would allow several different religious services to be held at the same time.

In order for them to still be able to make a living, Jean Pierre employed Annabelle and the other ladies to keep the church house both clean and operational. Even Petois and Pecous, Jean Pierre and Evelina's chubby little twins, were allowed to go inside now to observe Cook in her kitchen, to the delight of both, who loved to eat and loved to cook as well.

It was beginning to look like a banner year for Angeline and the lovely ladies of the New Orleans House as well; they were raking in more money than ever before with the addition of Madeleine Dubois-Chachere, who was beginning to bring in a crowd all her own with her piano playing. No one knew exactly why Madeleine had brought her talents to the great city of New Orleans, and especially why she had come to the New Orleans House, but no one was complaining either. One of the lovely ladies of the New Orleans House thought that maybe Madeleine was running away from the law, while another thought that she might have escaped from some lover that wanted to keep her just for himself. No one knew where she lived or where she went to during the week in the great city of New Orleans, but ever since that first day that she knocked on the door of the New Orleans House to offer her talent for a small fee, there had been plenty of festive music, dancing, and lively conversation. Besides, Miss BB truly enjoyed Madeleine's company and gave no second thought to her personal business.

Madeleine Dubois-Chachere was very tall and thin, with silky skin the color of midnight, with cheekbones so high that they seemed to make her black eyes slant and her cheeks hollow out. Her hair was extremely short, decorated with beautiful, bright flowers on those Saturday evenings, and always hanging from her ears were long earrings that resembled ivory elephant tusks that nearly touched her shoulders; her clothes, created from very light gauze, wrapped around her several times and draped down over the piano bench and tipped down to touch her sandals. She was a live painting, a live person that could easily be matted, framed, and hung in a gallery, where everyone could feast their eyes on her beauty, but there she was in all her mystery, in the parlor of the New Orleans House, giving more people more things to gossip about than they had had in a very long time.

Saturday nights were now the weekly party night for the ladies of the New Orleans House as well as for their regular customers and some new outsiders who only came out for a snifter of brandy, an unprofessional but truly entertaining show of beautiful dancing girls (Angeline's opportunity to express her love for the high-kicking dance) and plates piled high with some Creole delicacy that was prepared by Cook in her steamy and pleasantly odorous kitchen, all offered for a small pittance, a fraction of what it would cost to climb the stairs with one or the lovelies.

Obadiah always had the pleasure of escorting his beloved Miss BB to the festivities each and every Saturday evening, and it was for sure, indeed, that Miss BB not only enjoyed the music and the company but was also quite pleased to see the direction in which the New Orleans House had begun to transition; all in all, it was truly nice to see the New Orleans House still make money while the girls had themselves a good time, indeed, while standing on their feet for a change.

Every Saturday, Miss BB would proudly walk into the New Orleans House, arm in arm with Obadiah, dressed in one of her most fashionable outfits, with matching gloves and a wide-brimmed hat that either had brightly colored feathers or ribbons twisted and tied into lovely bows all around. Then Obadiah, who had lately revealed a secret to Miss BB that he had a notion for the lovely Shirley of the New Orleans House, would trade in his all-black attire for a bright-red or vivid-green bow tie for the Saturday occasions in hopes that Miss Shirley would make some sort of a sweet comment, and most of the Saturdays, she did, indeed.

Angeline would always have a special chair or room for one on a divan in the parlor for Miss BB, but no brandy for her, absolutely not. Obadiah always put Miss BB's eloquent silver flask in his jacket pocket filled to the brim with smooth Kentucky bourbon, where it could be easily retrieved whenever she became a tad, uh-uh, thirsty.

Yes, the year of our Lord 1875 was definitely proving itself to be a year of great changes, great discoveries, and most assuredly, just plain old greatness, and for Jubil and Miss Sylvia, it meant their long-awaited-for wedding with the promise of a wonderful future together and unforgettable experiences that would truly become family history.

Big Daddy always said, "Jubil and Miss Sylvia's wedding had to be planned and celebrated as quickly as possible while the bride and groom were still speaking to each other." And so it was, a very quickly planned wedding, and everything planned with the expert assistance of Evelina, Annabelle, and Miss Penelope, without a moment wasted, which allowed the bride-to-be and her groom to simply show up, and that they did, to the delight of every single resident at Mon Village.

Jubil and Miss Sylvia "jumped the broom" at a most beautiful wedding, followed by an extremely festive reception smack-dab in the middle of the residential area, with something for everyone to fill their stomach with delicious food and lift their spirits with everyone's favorite liquid spirit. By the time Jubil and Miss Sylvia left their reception for their newly decorated house, both were so happy that no one at Mon Village saw them for over a week, and once they emerged, the two were never seen or heard in an argumentative moment ever again.

Jubil had journeyed to the noble Commonwealth of Kentucky several times by the time 1875 came around and had developed quite a camaraderie with the young men that he virtually lived with in the bunkhouse twice per year, sometimes for just two weeks, and sometimes, depending upon the status of an injured horse, Jubil could find himself on the Kentucky farm for up to one month at a time.

Jubil was always homesick as he rode his trusty steed toward the trail of mint that led him to his destination in the noble Commonwealth of Kentucky and always extremely amazed at just how much the mint had grown and spread out both left and right of the trail that he and his horse had dug straight down the middle in between the two trips he made each year.

Traveling down that mint trail gave Jubil a small taste of Mon Village all the way to the farm and the bunkhouse, where the young men were always waiting and anxious to see him. Being so much older than these younger boys gave Jubil a sort of permission to look upon each one of them as one of his own sons, and none of them seemed to mind, that is, until it came to the discussion of that one topic that anyone of them could run circles around Jubil, and that would be how to race a horse.

Jubil had received word from Monte Leonard via a wire asking him to be at the farm either on or before May 1, 1875, because there would be so much to be done on the farm before making that journey to the great city of Louisville, where the very first Kentucky Derby would be held just two weeks later. Jubil had no idea what he should expect, but the excitement that everyone else had became truly contagious when he rode up to the bunkhouse, where the young boys were just finishing their day. They were all smiles and handshakes as each one welcomed Jubil back to the world of horse racing, and as usual, the conversation that night was how each one was going to win the race and go down in history as the first Kentucky Derby winner.

It was a very busy time for everyone, indeed, that first May of the first Kentucky Derby, from grooming the horses, exercising them, and the local races being run on Race Street in the great city of Lexington, all just rehearsal and preparation for that big race that would be held on May 17.

Jubil was extremely busy as well, which was a welcomed substitute for the longing he had in his heart for his beloved bride, Miss Sylvia, since he had to leave shortly after their wedding. Working so hard kept his mind busy during the day, but after the young boys fell asleep in the bunkhouse, Jubil no longer had control of his mind or his heart and would find himself back at home at Mon Village in Miss Sylvia's arMiss.

Most of Jubil's time was spent in the fancy barns, inspecting and reinspecting the legs and hooves of the racehorses for any major damage as well as any simple cuts or bruises that could become major if left untreated, and his work was always complimented by the farm and horse owners for the good job he was doing.

The favorite to win the Kentucky Derby as far as the farmhands were concerned was still the aggressive bay Chesapeake, who did not particularly like his hooves being touched by anyone, but Jubil would sternly forge ahead anyway and always bring lots of apples.

Jubil had formed a good relationship with all the horses, but he was still pretty partial to the chestnut horse Aristides, the little horse, the one with the white star and what looked to be socks on his two hind legs, the horse that everyone thought was least likely to win, but if Jubil had been a betting man, his money would have certainly gone on Aristides.

Jubil loved the local races with the crowds of people who came to bet for their favorite horse and watch them either win or lose, but either way, someone always seemed to be having a good time, but everyone always looked their very best. Jubil would pop his derby hat on his head and stand with Monte Leonard and the owners while the races were going on, but at the end of the day, it was the young boys who had turned into professional jockeys, for the moment, that had all his attention and his respect.

Just prior to hitting the highway and boarding the horses on the train to travel to the great city of Louisville for the biggest horse race ever held, there was a special local race that caught everyone's attention and made a celebrity out of an exercise boy from the Lexington stables, and Jubil had the pleasure of being there when it happened.

It would be when Jubil was conversing with Monte Leonard between races that one of the trainers approached one of the owners to tell him that one of the jockeys would be unable to participate in the upcoming local race because of a health problem. The owner was quite concerned, and after discussing the present situation at hand with the trainer, the fourteen-year-old stableboy by the name of Isaac was called upon to mount his first racehorse. All the young jockeys were taken by surprise as Isaac mounted the horse to participate in the race, but no one was as surprised as he was.

Big Daddy said, "No one in the family ever knew if the young jockey known as Isaac Burns Murphy had won that first race or not, but it was a sure thing that there would be plenty more races for him to choose from!"

When the day before the first Kentucky Derby finally came about, everything and everyone was moving quite fast, including the time, from loading the horses onto one of the train cars along with their special feed and grooming brushes to making sure that all the jockeys were present with all that they needed, including their racing hats and silks. The train would leave that day, taking with it the horses, the men, and the young boys that were trained to care for them when they waited for everyone else to reach the destination. The owners, trainers, and their guests would travel in their fancy carriages pulled by horses that were decorated with the special colors chosen for the jockeys who were riding their horses in the race. My, my, I do declare, everything was color-coordinated!

It was quite a long ride to the great city of Louisville, in comparison to today's travel, and arrangements had been made for everyone to spend the night prior to the day of the race. Jubil, of course, would bunk with his buddies from the Lexington farm in the Louisville Jockey Club bunkhouse, while the owners and trainers would have a warm bed in the clubhouse, where they could meet other owners and trainers of horses that came from other great cities and states.

Jubil and Monte Leonard followed in back of everyone else, riding their own horses and appreciating the time that the two of them had to chat about the business of horse racing while Monte Leonard shared a sip or two of his smooth Kentucky bourbon with Jubil, who still kept a steady eye on virtually everything along the way to the great city of Louisville, inhaling the beauty of the perfect weather—sun shining, warm with just that tinge of that brisk, icy Kentucky air, fluffy white clouds lazily floating by—and slowly exhaling his excitement so as not to appear to be so excited that he appeared to be a country bumpkin to the city folk while in the midst of the most important experience in his life, that is, other than his passionate and everlasting love for his new bride, Miss Sylvia.

As the entourage neared the Louisville Jockey Club on the outskirts of the great city of Louisville, it became quite apparent to everyone on that road that day that this was more than just another horse race; this was truly an international affair.

Jubil could see the field of colorful hats that the ladies were wearing moving toward the stands and decided at just that moment that he was going to purchase another fancy racing hat for Miss Sylvia, perhaps yellow this time.

It was also quite apparent that Monte Leonard was just as amazed as Jubil was at what they were seeing with their own eyes as he smiled a hefty smile, took his hat off, and ran his fingers through his hair. After a quick sip of his smooth Kentucky bourbon that Jubil was just too excited to sip with him, Monte Leonard told Jubil that they had better ride if they were ahead of the entourage to make sure that everyone and everything was where they were supposed to be, and as they did, Jubil had a much better view of people going about the business of preparing for the race. Just as he and Monte Leonard were, there were thousands of men and women in the stands already waiting for the races. Horses were being brought to the stables, where they would stay and made ready, all sorts of farmhands were doing their jobs, there was chatter and electricity in the air, and Jubil could barely catch his breath.

Finally, as Monte Leonard accompanied Jubil to check on the horses, Jubil saw the young jockeys, those that he shared the bunkhouse with and several that were completely unfamiliar to him, who would ride horses that he was truly unfamiliar with. Jubil barely recognized Ollie Lewis in his jockey hat, wearing green and orange silks to represent the Lexington farm, appearing to be much older than his real age, but it would be when several of the other young boys caught sight of Jubil and gave him their youthful smiles that he finally recognized his buddies. Not all would be as fortunate as Ollie to ride in that first Kentucky Derby, but it was apparent, indeed, that even if just one rode across that winning line, it would be for all of them.

Big Daddy said he really did not know how which jockey was chosen to ride which horse, but the story has it that Ollie Lewis rode the teeny tiny Aristides that day, the horse thought least likely to win the race.

The excitement and anticipation heightened as the trainers began to lead the horses with their riders from the stables toward the area where they would stay before reaching the starting line for the big race. There were fifteen horses, fifteen riders, all paraded past Jubil, who only then noticed that there were actually fourteen jockeys of color, and the only white jockey, Bobby Swim was his name, was already a well-known jockey, sitting atop Chesapeake.

As the horses were being led out, Ollie Lewis stopped to talk to the owner of Chesapeake and Aristides; the jockey seemed to be listening quite intensely to the owner while nodding in agreement with his final instructions, and then he, too, followed the lead.

Moments later, several officials from the Louisville Jockey Club began giving directions to those who would be participating, and it became apparent that it was time for the first race of the day to be run, the derby being run as the second race. Jubil decided that the first race was more than likely a sort of practice run for the derby, a race that would give everyone a good look at the condition of the track and perhaps even to stir up just a little more excitement, as if any more excitement could be or needed to be stirred up.

As Jubil emerged onto the area surrounding the track, just below the stands, he caught sight of Monte Leonard and several other people leaning on the fence that separated the track from the stands, and for the first time, Jubil was truly able to experience the enormity of the whole event; it was breathtaking, so much so that his heart seemed to skip a beat.

The track itself was spectacular, smooth dirt all around, not even one rock or a stone to be seen; two huge turns, one at either end of the track; and people everywhere, men in their derby hats and, of course, the women well-dressed with gloves and wide-brimmed, flowing hats on their heads.

And of course, there were horses, and more horses everywhere. Monte Leonard called Jubil by name, bringing him back down to earth, where he had surely escaped from, and waved him over to where he was standing with several other men that he had either already met or not met at all, Caucasian men and men of color, who were the owners and trainers of the horses either on the track for that first race or waiting for their turn at the Kentucky Derby. After several handshakes and many introductions, Jubil quietly resumed his great fascination with all that he could see, smell, and hear.

There was a loud sound emitting from an extremely longhorn being blown by a man dressed in a suit with a long coat and a pair of dress knickers, a gentlemen's hat on his head; perhaps he was the man in charge, because while he was blowing the notes from the longhorn, everyone immediately became quiet, so very quiet that Jubil became afraid that anyone standing near him could hear his heart thumping through his shirt.

The horses were now standing across the track in a long line, some moving around and snorting while the jockey tried to hold them still, probably as many as fifteen running in that race, and more than likely, a few of Jubil's young buddies from the bunkhouse at the Lexington farm were jockeys as well.

Just when everyone and everything was at its quietest and the horses were standing as still as they possibly could stand, there was the sound of a loud gunshot that scared Jubil, echoing and resonating throughout the entire setting to tell the horses to begin their challenging race around the track, and they did, moving so swiftly that the dirt on the track jumped up from under their hooves, their speed creating a swift wind that whooshed past Jubil and the people he was standing with. The crowd roared, yelling out the name of their favorite horses in unison, standing and cheering louder and louder as the horses passed them in the stands. Jubil leaned on the fence and followed the horses with his eyes all around the track, past the turns, down the home stretch, and finally, across the finish line. The people in the stands clapped their hands. Whether they had won or not, everyone was yelling. It was a remarkable feeling indeed.

At the end of the race, a man with a tall ladder moved toward a large board that was posted in an area where just about everyone could see the results from the first race, pinning large numbers on the board to show the crowd the number of the horses that officially showed, placed, or won. The crowd roared again, and Jubil could see people leaving their seats to go to the betting windows to collect their money, while those that had not been as fortunate as to win that first race tore up their tickets and dropped them on the ground. Jubil and Monte Leonard looked at each other and just shook their heads; seemed that Monte Leonard had placed a bet as well but unfortunately did not bet on the right horse.

Some time was allotted for the huge crowd to move back and forth from the stands, officials carefully observing so as to prepare for the big race of the day that would be run momentarily. The results from the previous race were removed from the big board, while men slowly walked around the track with rakes to make it even again, to smooth out the dirt that had been broken and spread over the track by the high-speeding horses who kicked the dirt up with their hooves, and finally, Jubil could see the horses of the inaugural Kentucky Derby moving toward the starting line. A man's voice echoed throughout the racetrack: "Welcome to the first running of the Kentucky Derby!"

The crowd roared on and on for what sounded like a good ten minutes, until the man's voice sounded again, this time to call out the names of the horses that would be running in the race as the jockeys walked them slowly around the track for everyone to see. The people in the stands stood and clapped again and again at the sound of each name, much louder, of course, for their chosen victor.

The members of the Louisville Jockey Club introduced themselves and each gave a brief speech about who they were and what would be going on that day, and after the last man had finished his speech, the man with the longhorn could be seen standing at one end of the starting line, getting in position to blow those same notes that he had blown at the beginning of the first race.

As soon as all the horses were lined up on the starting line and as still as they could possibly be, a hush fell over the stands—not a sound to be heard. The man lifted his horn and began to blow the same notes he had blown at the beginning of the first race. Suddenly, there was the piercing sound of a single gunshot fired in the air, followed by the sound of shrieking or quick gasps of air from spectators, who were completely caught off guard, and then finally the sound of another man who yelled out in a strong voice as soon as the first of the fifteen horses bolted through the starting line: "And they're off!"

Aristides immediately shot out from the starting line, with his jockey, Ollie Lewis, leaning over him and quickly guiding him to gallop to the lead of the fifteen-horse competition, with several other horses quickly pursuing him for the top position. As Big Daddy would always say, "As if to say, 'Oh no, you don't!'" And of course, my crazy uncles would just laugh on and on, give one another high fives, and tap a few of the young boys on their backs.

While the crowd of people began to roar with sheer excitement when a horse named McCreery galloped beside Aristides just as they neared the end of the first quarter, Aristides soon met that challenge and grabbed the lead again. Being trailed by McCreery, Ten Broeck, Volcano, and Verdigris, with the colt's big brother, Chesapeake, slipping farther back down the track.

Ollie Lewis seemed to drive Aristides hard to take over the lead but then slowed down to fall back behind several of the other horses and began to run neck and neck with Chesapeake, which truly perplexed Jubil, who just could not understand why Ollie would have fallen back behind so many of the horses after such a brilliant start, unless there was something medically wrong with one of them, but even before Jubil could catch his own breath, Aristides exploded again to take over the lead as the little fireball of a horse, being challenged again, glided over the track as if his hooves were barely touching the dirt.

The horses sounded like thunder as they bolted down the back stretch, swiftly galloping past Jubil and Monte Leonard, who were standing with the trainers and owners, the sound of the jockeys' whips sounding like lightning crackling down from the heavens, while the magnificent animals generated a sweaty breeze that swept across the human faces and penetrated their nostrils; the sound of horse and jockey communicating with each other was almost spiritual indeed, even if no human words were spoken.

The massive crowd of people in the stands was simply thrilled with the spectacular showing of power and precision, watching the little horse that was considered least likely to win such a prestigious race seeming to be playing tag with his big brother, Chesapeake. Aristides would run neck and neck with Chesapeake for a tad and then spring forward to capture the lead, over and over, around that first stretch and then, with plenty of strength and courage, around the first turn of the one-mile-and-one-half race.

By this time Jubil was finally beginning to understand that Ollie was having Aristides taunt his big brother to make him run faster in an attempt to make Chesapeake take the lead and win the race, but unfortunately, the older horse was not able to keep up with the pace of the big race and began falling farther and farther behind.

And there they went, around the second turn, and onto the home stretch, they galloped with Aristides still full of energy and vigor, Ollie Lewis pulling him ahead of the horses but then trailing them again to encourage Chesapeake to run faster, over and over. The two horses seemed to play the game, but it would be when horse and jockey ran past where Jubil and Monte Leonard were standing with the owners and trainers for the final time that something quite different than anyone anticipated happened. Ollie Lewis quickly glanced toward the owner, who apparently gave him some sort of a signal that changed the entire course of the events of that first Kentucky Derby. Ollie leaned forward, and suddenly, Aristides darted from behind the other horses where he had fallen, and the game changed from tag to catch-me-if-you-can!

By the time Oliver Lewis led Aristides down the home stretch toward the finish line, the little horse that could was a long length ahead of the horse behind him that would cross the finish line in second place. The crowd yelled, as if their very voices could push Aristides toward the finish line, but as the horse could be seen crossing it over to win the Kentucky Derby, every one of the people in the stands went wild, standing up and waving their hats, gloves, and handkerchiefs (or their win-or-lose betting slip)! Oliver Lewis threw his hands up in the air as a sign of victory, releasing the reins so that Aristides could continue to slow down and then parade around the track once more, this time as a champion.

The favorite that day, the bay Chesapeake, came in eighth place, while Ten Broeck took fifth place but would surely make his own history in those derbies to come. There were two fillies that ran that day, and there were other horses that might not have won the first big race either but they, too, would soon go down in horse racing history as champions in their own right, winning races, setting records, and being immortalized in stone for the entire world to see and know who they and their riders were.

Big Daddy told the young boys, "A young man of color, Oliver Lewis, won the very first Kentucky Derby." Then he would say as he sat back in his chair, crossed his leg over the other, and held his head up high with pride, "And set the standard for American horse racing with a record of two minutes and thirty-seven seconds and three-quarters, with a winning purse for the Lexington farm of $2,850!" Monumental, to say the least.

My other uncles would begin to applaud for several minutes, just like all the people in the stands did that day in May 1875, when a little horse beat the odds and stepped to win his place in history.

Monte Leonard slapped Jubil on his back and grabbed him by his arm to lead him to the finish line, where the owners, trainers, and so very many of the fans were, reaching out to touch Aristides and shake hands with Oliver Lewis.

While Ollie was still sitting on the horse who now and forever would be known as a champion, he leaned over to hug Aristides and placed a congratulatory kiss on his neck, patting him several times, and in what truly appeared to be a gesture reciprocated, Aristides swung his long neck around as if to look the young jockey in his eye.

"What a pair!" Monte Leonard said, referring to both horse and young jockey. "Be back, Jubil. Gotta go claim mah winnins!"

Jubil looked at Monte Leonard inquisitively.

"Well, you said you weren't a gamblin' man, so I did the honors for both you and me!" Monte Leonard laughed and quickly disappeared; Jubil just shook his head in amazement and grinned back at him.

Jubil used his reputation as the horse doctor to quickly make his way through the crowd of people and over to the horse and jockey to, first, make sure that Aristides's legs and hooves had not been damaged during the race and, second, congratulate and hug the young man that was his roommate at the bunkhouse at the Lexington farm. When Jubil reached up to hug Ollie Lewis, he could see the tears in his eyes, certainly tears of joy and, most assuredly, tears of pride.

The story goes that over the next twenty-five years, Jubil would make that journey through the middle of a path of mint showing him the way to and from the noble Commonwealth of Kentucky to care for the horses during the spring and fall meets and would be witness to many more moments like that very first Kentucky Derby day, all documented in an old diary that has been kept in a cedar chest in the big house along with other memorabilia from the era of Jean Pierre, Jubil, and Dolice Marie LaPierre.

Jubil's old diary made record of all the young jockeys that he had either bunked with or met when jockeys would come to the great Kentucky Derby. He also kept record of other races that he had attended over the years and of all the horses that he had either had the privilege to treat or just inspect for injury during his long career. The reading of the excerpt from the old diary was always extremely exciting to both the young boys, and even to my sweet old uncles, who never seemed to tire of hearing it.

It would be at this portion of the traditional telling of the family stories that Big Daddy would reach under his chair to bring forth Jubil's old diary, pretend to blow dust off its cover, and open it where he had placed a red velvet bookmarker with overwhelming pride!

MINT JULEP

From Jubilation LaPierre

I was scared, mighty scared, when I first made that trip to Kentucky. Many times on the way, I wanted to just turn my horse around and go back home to Mon Village. I was riding into a new place and going to meet people that might have even changed their mind about meeting me. Now that I look around at the many faces of the people that I have come to know and respect, I am mighty glad that I came. I am most happy about meeting these young jockeys who have raised themselves from some of the most terrible situations, some from this time in history, unfortunately, some knowing what it felt like to be owned by another person or just those situations that we bring on ourselves. I often asked myself when I looked in their young faces, "Where are your parents? Your mama?" But I never did, maybe because I really didn't want to hear their answers. I always loved horses, but this opportunity was more than I ever could dream about. And the mint from Mon Village followed me all the way there. I think some of the people on the farm have been picking it and using it for something, but I'm not sure what it is yet. What a way to bring two great places together! Lord knows there's enough of it growing between Mon Village and the noble Commonwealth off Kentucky!

I called William Walker Willie and probably spent more time with him because we both knew what living as slaves was all about. Such a young face to have such old sorrows. Willie won the fall 1875 Kentucky Derby, right after Ollie did, and then in the 1876 Kentucky Derby. Willie also won the 1877 Kentucky Derby, riding Baden-Baden. and the 1878 spring running of the Kentucky Derby. He rode Ten Broeck on July 4, 1878, the same horse that challenged Ollie in that first Kentucky Derby in 1875, for a full four miles against a mare named Molly McCarthy, and she came all the way from California. Boy was like a son to me! Miss Sylvia said they all had a special place in my heart, and she was right.

I met a whole lot of Lewis boys over those first few years, and I often wondered if they were maybe all related. George Garret Lewis won the derby on a horse named Fonso in 1880, although the officials said something about there being a foul. I never really understood any of that. Poor George died on July 5 in Hutchinson station, the same year after a race in Missouri. We were told that he had some really bad injuries inside himself that killed him. He was only eighteen years old. I know he would have been a real champion if he had lived longer. That was the first time Miss Sylvia came with me to Kentucky. We used one of those fancy carriages from Mon Village that Mr. Bernard Menard brought to us, and she cried all the way back home. It was so sad.

Then there was Babe Hurd, who rode Apollo to win the 1882 Kentucky Derby. Erskine Henderson finished ninth in that same Kentucky Derby. Babe went on to become a steeplechaser, or so we were told. The boy was really good!

In 1885, Erskine Henderson became the sixth jockey of color to win the Kentucky Derby. He won in 1885 riding on Joe Cotton. It was a close win for Erskine and his final ride in the derby since he only finished seventh in the 1883 Kentucky Derby. Erskine did ride Joe Cotton in the Tennessee and Coney Island Derbies in 1883. I did not see him anymore after that, but I am sure he was still working with horses. He was too good not to be.

Isaac Lewis was another one of those Lewis boys, strong and scared of nothing on the racetrack. He won four Kentucky Derbies from 1886 to 1889, riding Montrose in 1887. I think he was only about seventeen at that time. If he was not related to Ollie Lewis, he sure got some racing tips from him! Just like Ollie, Isaac was really fast to get his horse from the starting line. He would dart out there on whatever horse he was riding like he was either chasing something or running away from something. He once told me that he had started riding at just eleven years old.

One of the nicest young men I have ever met was Isaac Murphy, born Isaac Burns. Now, here was a jockey! Yessir! Isaac won three Kentucky Derbies riding Buchanan in 1884, Riley in 1890, and Kingman in 1891. After winning the 1884 Kentucky Derby, he went on to win the Oaks and the Clark Handicap. Don't know that any other jockey, either a jockey of color or a white jockey, ever did that much before. He once told me that his father had served in the Union Army during the Civil War. Isaac said his dad was even a prisoner of war and had died at Camp Nelson. He said his family moved here to Lexington after that and lived with his granddaddy. He added the "Murphy" to his name after that to honor his granddaddy. When I met him, he had been a jockey since he was fourteen years old. That sweet boy died in 1896. He was only thirty-five. Everyone was told that it was pneumonia. There had been lots of rumors about him, but I paid no never mind to any of them and encouraged the others to do the same. Sad thing, too, that Miss Sylvia always seemed to come to the farm to attend a funeral.

Shelby Barnes became a hero to many of the young jockeys after winning more than two hundred races in one year, 1888. He was national riding champion in 1889. His nickname was Pike, but to me, he was just great!

Soup Perkins—that's how I knew him, but his first name was James. I tell you that boy could eat some soup! He was young, really young, and won the Kentucky Derby in 1895 riding Hanna, only fifteen years old. He and Alonzo Clayton were the youngest of the whole bunch of young jockeys. I heard he started riding in 1891 at about eleven years old and won his first race at the Latonia racetrack. Soup was fun to be around. He was also a real horseman.

Speaking of young, the very youngest Kentucky Derby winner was a jockey by the name of Alonzo Clayton, nicknamed Lonnie. In 1892, Lonnie rode on Azra and won in one of those really close victories, by a nose or a neck, but he won nonetheless. Lonnie was a traveling mall, riding and racing horses in Chicago and as far as New Jersey, but he raced in four Kentucky Derbies, winning two seconds and a third. He also competed and won the Kentucky Oaks twice riding Selika in 1894 and Voladora in 1895. I believe there were just three jockeys of color that rode in the Preakness, and Lonnie was one of them, finishing third in 1896. One of his other great moments was getting the 1893 Churchill Downs jockey crown. It was the fall meet. We were all so very proud of him.

In 1896, Willie Simms won the Kentucky Derby riding Ben Brush, and again in 1898 riding Plaudit. He also could brag about winning all the Triple Crown events, the Preakness in 1898 riding Sly Fox, and the Belmont twice, once on Comanche in 1893 and again in 1894 on Henry of Navaree.

Simms had the chance to race in England riding an American horse. Willie Simms brought so much to horse racing, and horse racing gave so much to him, as it did to all the jockeys of color, something special that they could do better than anyone else.

I was only around for a while when Jimmy Winkfield started his career in 1898. He was blamed for causing a four-horse spill in his very first race and then put on suspension for a year. By the time Jimmy began winning every race in sight, I was retired from being a horse doctor. But in the coming years after that, Jimmy Winkfield won four Kentucky Derbies. In 1900 he took third place riding Thrive. In 1901, Jimmy came in first place riding His Eminence, first place in 1902 riding Alan-a-Dale, and second place in 1903 riding Early. I even heard that Jimmy even went to Russia and rode for the Czar I.

I heard people say he was just a horse, but to me Aristides was a champion, even fifteen years after the very first Kentucky Derby. I cried for Aristides just as much as I cried for Isaac Murphy and George Garrett Lewis, and so did Miss Sylvia and all the young jockeys, and so did many others at the Lexington farm, maybe even around the world.

Aristides died on June 21, 1893, at eighteen years old, just like George Garrett Lewis had died at eighteen.

Big Daddy would pause for just a brief minute after reading the excerpt from Jubil's old diary, then close its pages and place it back under his chair. I never failed to shed my own tears after hearing the writings of that dear boy Jubil. In fact, all my uncles shed tears as well and had to take just a moment to compose themselves.

My, my, my! What a day the Saturdays would be each and every one of our family reunions for my beloved uncles, my own dear daddy, the women of the family, including my own sweet mother, and of course, those young boys who would be telling these stories to the other young boys of our family someday.

It would be just about this time every Saturday that somebody would yell out to my uncles that it was truly time for the boys to get to bed, but not in those exact words, I might add. So I told Miss Gracie that I would think that this would be a good place for us to stop for the night as well; after all, a good night's sleep would be quite appropriate and necessary to cover the events of the last day of our family reunions, the finishing of the traditional telling of the family stories, our family's remembrance and celebration of our ancestors that have gone on to glory, and the final family dinner together.

Oh, yes, and there is still so very much to tell, but for now…

Good night, Miss Gracie!

Chapter 21

I MUST ADMIT THAT I was extremely embarrassed, to say the very least, and even blushed to a deep, delicate shade of pink when I arrived late at the big house to find Miss Gracie, fine writer that she is, already there enjoying breakfast with Cook! I dare say that I have always taken great pride in myself for never being late for an engagement or an appointment, but this morning, I found myself perhaps enjoying my sleep just a bit too much and had to rush in order to meet Miss Gracie for this last meeting with her to discuss the stories about my beloved family.

Only moments after arriving at the big house did I truly realize just how much information was still remaining to be discussed and just how very little time we had for such profound discussions.

Well, if I remember correctly, we left off last night with my own dear Big Daddy reading the words of Jubilation LaPierre's old diary about his own personal experiences in the noble Commonwealth of Kentucky while working with the horses. Oh! How I do love that portion of the traditional telling of the family stories!

My family had said their good nights, and everyone had scurried off to either sleep or to continue the personal preparation of themselves for the Sunday services and the celebration of our beloved ancestors—nothing more than the usual Saturday-evening rituals that always took precedence over sleep while we were celebrating our family reunions.

Sunday-morning proceedings were absolutely wonderful and certainly filled with those family memories that just cause me to feel even better each time I would hear about them from those dear uncles of mine, and even now when I simply think of them. I never tired of hearing the stories through all these years, not once, and I remember them today as if they were happening all around me.

I remember that the female members of the family—that would be my own beloved mother, along with all my sweet aunts that so much enjoyed these moments together—would gather together in their hair curlers partially covered by lovely hair scarves, with their beautiful, full red lips and red fingernails prepared the day before, even before the sun began to rise lazily over the LaPierre homestead, to make their trek throughout the Mon Village gardens to gather flowers to adorn the entire church house.

Their sweet giggles could be heard all throughout the Bayou Frou-Frous, while their smiles glowed brightly in the dawning of the sun. Now and then, they would hug one another or poke fun with one another about something that only they knew about. Their sweet antics left imprints in my own memories of each one of them, that is, until they could be replaced by new memories of them at the next family reunion.

When I was younger, and always while I was sneaking around to spy on the activities of my sweet uncles and my own dear daddy as they gathered to gossip about their women, I remember that this was also one of those affordable moments that the women of our family used to gossip about their husbands. While the loud laughs were emitting from the gardens as the women performed the task of choosing just the right flowers, in between all that pesky mint, that is, the loud thumps of my uncles' hearts echoed throughout the Bayou Frou-Frous as each one tried desperately to assure the other ones that they were not the least bit concerned about what their woman was saying to the other women about them!

For the young boys being initiated into our family's manhood, an early Sunday-morning breakfast with the old storytellers before our Sunday services was a treat, and almost as exciting as listening to their stories about the voluptuous women of the family with their scantily clad bodies, if you know what I mean!

I can remember many times spying on them through the window of the outside kitchen that had just the day before served as the beauty parlor for my sweet aunts and my own beloved mother, and now the men feasted on a breakfast of thick bacon, runny, soft-fried eggs, grits with red-eye gravy, fresh-baked biscuits, and strong, dark coffee for the older men and just a taste of "coffee-milk" for the young boys. Of course, the conversations during breakfast were always the same year after year, the traditional stories about our family as told by my sweet old uncles.

Uncle Batiste LaPierre

As I grew older and began to understand more about life, I watched sadly while the torch of life was passed from one LaPierre brother to another and as the labored breath of life overshadowed them, one after the other, taking them from the earth to the dwelling place of the ancestors. Age does not always dictate the order in which life escapes from us, so even though my dear uncle Gaston was the firstborn, it was actually my uncle Batiste, whom I never met, that was taken away first.

My uncle Batiste, who was so lovingly tucked between my uncles Michele and Alexandre, the latter being my beloved godfather as well, and my namesake, had already gone on to where the ancestors lived even before my own dear daddy was born. When Uncle Batiste was just a little boy, my own dear granddaddy (my beloved Big Daddy's daddy) built a tree house for his younger boys within the safety of the strong limbs of a beautiful magnolia tree, and he even fashioned a swing on the other side of the tree for all the boys to enjoy.

Not to be considered partial to his sons, my granddaddy also built a lovely dollhouse for his girls when they were younger, where they could actually walk in, stand, and pretend to be taking care of a dolly home. How precious!

My beloved granddaddy always warned his sons about the rules: "Never swing too high, always swing with your backs away from the Bayou Frou-Frous, and swing only when one of your other brothers, or sisters, is present."

My granddaddy also threatened each one of them individually with a whooping if he ever caught any of them breaking any one of those rules that he had made for them. But as they say, boys will be boys.

It would be on a sizzling, hot summer day, when all the children of the time were helping my dear granddaddy with their chores around Mon Village, that Uncle Batiste would decide to steal a quick swing to make a cool breeze to cool himself down. Breaking all the rules, Uncle Batiste ran to the tree house, hopped upon the swing without paying any attention as to which direction he was facing, and began to create the coolest breeze of all.

Well, that cool breeze began to feel exceptionally good to Uncle Batiste, so he stretched his legs out even farther to "pump" his ride in the sky even higher, even faster and, unknowingly to him, with his eyes closed and his mind flying high, dangerously close to disaster.

Suddenly, Uncle Batiste began to hear my granddaddy, his own daddy, calling out for him at a distance, yelling out his name and coming even closer to him with each yell. Uncle Batiste was certainly aware now that he would be in big trouble if he was caught breaking the rules of the swing, so he reached his pump even higher in the sky, just one more time, and as my granddaddy's yell came right upon him, Uncle Batiste jumped, flew in the sky for a quick moment, and then landed—yes, he did. Uncle Batiste jumped directly into the Bayou Frou-Frous, just as my granddaddy yelled at him to *stop*!

Everything seemed to be frozen for an instant, except for the swing that continued its flight through the air, uncontrollable without its passenger, and just as suddenly, my granddaddy, joined now by his sons that had been working with him, ran to the bayou and jumped in without a second thought.

The dirty waters of the Bayou Frou-Frous splashed all around my granddaddy as he dived deep into the muck and slime whose DNA would surely expose the remains of the hundreds of slaves who found their own death by thinking the waters could be their escape route to freedom. In and out my granddaddy dived into the waters, desperately searching for his beloved son, each time rising out of the waters with empty hands and being closer yet to his lifetime of being brokenhearted for the loss of his child.

Momo Belle came running toward the bayou after hearing the screams of her sons, one hand caressing her heart and the other waving back and forth as if it had no bone at all, serving to balance her as she maneuvered from the big house to the Bayou Frou-Frous. She stopped abruptly at the edge of the bayou and had fallen to her knees, with one hand on either side of her head, when she saw my granddaddy emerge from the water dragging a pile of moss with him. He held his hands out to the grieving mother as she began to scream out to her son.

"Batiste!" she screamed. "Batiste, mon ti bébé!"

Oh my goodness, it truly was a very sad time, a very, very terrible time. There, beside the Bayou Frou-Frous in the great state of Louisiana, my poor granddaddy and my grandmama both trying so desperately to understand just what had happened and why so quickly.

My grandparents were soon joined by the remainder of the family—everyone weeping, wailing, holding on to one another, and stomping their feet in agony at the loss of this child, a son, a brother, a loved one. How could anyone survive such a loss, indeed?

Gradually, one by one, my sweet granddaddy, Momo Belle, and all the children that were present began to quiet down and slowly turn their attention toward the Bayou Frou-Frous, where a sound was radiating. Why, a voice, I must clarify, calling out each of their names. A familiar voice that no one ever expected to hear ever again, the voice of—yes, it was—my own uncle Batiste, who had just flown into the murky waters of the Bayou Frou-Frous, presumed gone forever.

Well, everyone, as you can imagine, was quite frightened by the sound and was too afraid to believe that Batiste had survived such an accident. But he had.

Batiste had somehow survived the flight into the Bayou Frou-Frous and could now be seen waving, soaking wet, covered in moss and who could possibly know what else, standing on the other side of the waters where the distance from shore to shore narrowed. My granddaddy screamed out to him, "Batiste, Batiste, mon ti garçon, stay there! Papa is coming to get you!"

And that he did. My granddaddy swam across the murky waters of the Bayou Frou-Frous where Batiste stood patiently waiting for him, smiling as he stretched out his hands toward his father, who returned the smile as he grabbed him and held him in the safety of his arMiss. It was a wonderful reunion for everyone there on the shore of the Bayou Frou-Frous, where my uncle Batiste had soared into the air and had dropped, allegedly, to his death.

After carrying him home, drying him off, and soothing his aches and bruises, my granddaddy gave my uncle Batiste the whooping that he had promised to any of his sons that broke any of the rules of the swing.

Several years later, when Batiste was a young man searching for his place in life, a circus came to town, and as did many of the other parents around the area, my granddaddy took his family to see the animals, the clowns, and the sheer excitement that accompanies such an event.

Batiste was especially enchanted by the trapeze artists and all the acts where the performers would fly through the air, and he eventually told his parents that he wanted to join the circus.

After trying desperately to change their son's mind without success, my granddaddy and Momo Belle finally said goodbye to their precious son and sent him off with plenty of hugs, kisses, and big wishes for great times.

Batiste eventually was rewarded for his courage and his talent and was soon given the circus act of a lifetime as the man shot from a canon and entertained both adults and children for years to come, never tiring of his opportunity to fly in the air and enjoying life to the fullest. Batiste always pursued new ways to fly higher, faster, and ever farther as he perfected his circus act.

One particular evening, with all the seats in the big tent filled to capacity, Batiste decided to put absolutely everything that he had ever learned into his act, and to thrill the audience even more with his exciting flying escapades with more fuel to the fire that ignited him, an undertaking that sent him flying—yes, he did. He flew totally out of the big tent!

His lifeless body was found facedown three weeks later, his head still pressed against the big tree that he had apparently come in contact with during his final, incredible, history-making flight.

The newspaper reported that the "man in the canon" act was the highlight of the circus that night and that Uncle Batiste had indeed "soared magnificently through the air for the delight of both adult and child."

Needless to say, the family was again devastated but agreed that, at the very least, they did have the opportunity to share many years with Uncle Batiste and that he certainly had passed on to the ancestors in the next world doing what he loved to do the most and that he had, for that matter, passed on while wearing his circus boots, his circus helmet, and with a huge circus grin still on his face.

Oh my! Have I not digressed again! Time is truly becoming short, and there is so much more to tell the family stories, and so back to the final day of my family's reunions and to my remaining lovable old uncles.

Chapter 22

SUNDAY BREAKFAST PRIOR to the Sunday morning services during our family reunions was very important and joyful, not only for the delicious food being served, but also because it brought the opportunity for my uncle Gaston's second time to tell a family story, this one about just how the LaPierre-Menard family reunion came about in the first place.

It might have been Mon Claire LaPierre, the firstborn daughter of Jean Pierre and Evelina, that was instrumental in bringing religion, or 'ligion as she called it, to Mon Village, but it was the joy of Dolice Marie LaPierre-Menard's and Mr. Bernard Menard's heart, that is, their sweet Monique Aimee Elizabeth LaPierre-Menard, that was instrumental in bringing the family reunion to Mon Village.

Uncle Gaston would cross one leg over the other, take a long but slow sip of his strong Louisiana coffee, and lean back to a comfortable position in his chair after enjoying his Sunday breakfast. The young boys would respond by taking a long but slow sip of their coffee-milk and lean back to a comfortable position in their chairs to listen to the old man tell the story of how the family reunion began.

The Menards of New York

It had taken some time, but Madam Dolice Marie LaPierre-Menard had, with the gentle, mysterious, and most kindly attention given to her from her new friend and confidante, Kip Salma, finally adjusted to her charming new home in Upstate New York. Her beloved husband, the ever-debonair Mr. Bernard Menard, continually showered her with love and understanding, never expecting or insisting upon more than she was able to accept or give at any moment, following her lead until she felt truly comfortable away from the land of her birth and those familiar surroundings.

Madam Menard, as her new and indeed much friendlier community now addressed her, and so shall I, also had developed a wonderfully warm relationship with her mother-in-law and father-in-law, Lord and Lady Menard of Toronto, Canada, who were both quite pleased that there was finally some color in the Menard bloodline, which, as both agreed, had been far too white for far too long.

In fact, the younger Menard family had traveled most frequently to the elder Menard's home in Toronto, Canada, to enjoy not only extended holiday family visits, to spend time with Mr. Bernard Menard's best friend and fine Canadian attorney, Wilhelm, but also for Mr. Bernard Menard to enjoy his favorite sport, ice hockey.

Whether enjoying the sport as a spectator or actually participating in a friendly game with Wilhelm and their other chums that could be dressed for the sport in just a matter of minutes, Mr. Bernard Menard was truly a profound ice hockey fan.

Madam Menard, on the other hand, considering the fact that her tiny bones were created in the heat of America's Deep South, kept far away from the icy rinks of Canada's and her husband's favorite pastime but was always gracious enough to listen to the delights of both her husband and their daughter as they both raved on and on about what fun they had in the freezing cold of the ice hockey season.

It would be the delightful Lady Menard that truly empathized with her daughter-in-law and always chose to plan a shopping trip for the two of them to the many stores that lined the city streets of Toronto during those times that the Menard men indulged themselves in their favorite fancy, even though she, too, thoroughly enjoyed the excitement and competition of the game.

The unselfish act on the part of Lady Menard was an easy exchange, indeed, for the smiles, bright eyes, and giggles exploding from her beloved daughter-in-law as she leafed through bolt after bolt of beautiful fabric to choose just the right ones, fabrics that would be made into dresses for her own beloved daughter, for herself, and for fabric that the Menard seamstress would be able to create into matching outfits that simply elated the two of them as they gazed in the mirror at the finished products.

(I might also interject here that there were those times spent clandestinely with Minnie Menard, Lord and Lady Menard's ex-niece, that had been ostracized from the Menard family years before due to an accident that had occurred at a state dinner that caused an emergency visit to the local hospital for the elder Menards, where both Minnie and Mr. Bernard Menard laughed uncontrollably at the cause of the accident, which I dare not repeat at this present time.)

During the holiday seasons, Madam Menard would also search the shops that lined the city streets of Toronto both patiently and tirelessly for just the perfect gifts that she would bring back home to the staff of the Menard household in Upstate New York, who, too, waited patiently and tirelessly to see what bounty they would receive when the family returned home.

And indeed, there would be plenty to "Ooooh" and "Aaahhh" over for Wilhelmina the Cook, Maggie, Edward, and of course, Kuya and his wife, Kip, all who had truly become Madam Menard's surrogate family, not only taking perfect care of her every need, but also genuinely caring for her as well.

Madam Menard and the Menard child would clap their hands with delight as each would open a gift that had, year after year, been chosen with serene and loving care, especially for each one of those special people on their list of loved ones.

But there were also those gift boxes and bags, filled to the brim with life's essentials, that were brought home year after year and would be given to those less fortunate than the Menards of Toronto and the great state of New York—heavy winter coats, boots, gloves, woolen caps, and leggings—which Mr. Bernard Menard and Edward would deliver with holiday vigor every day after Christmas, the feast of St. Stephen, or Boxing Day, as it has been known since 1871, the custom in the country of our Canadian family, a custom that Madam

Menard was always so very eager to spread to the realms of her own home in the great state of New York.

These were the times that molded the heart of the Menard child, and although she simply loved new clothes, gifts, the sharing on Boxing Day, and all the other electrifying times of the holiday season, it would be at her father's and her grandfather's side that she truly enjoyed the most.

By the time she could steady her sweet little legs on the earth, the beloved men in her life, along with her uncle Wilhelm, had already bundled her up and taught her how to ice-skate, and it was truly apparent that she was not in the least bit affected by the icy Canadian winds.

The darling Menard child delighted at being sandwiched between her father and grandfather, squealing with delight each time she would lose her footing and fall to the ice, immediately being scooped up by her two guardians, who lifted her by her arms high in the air only to land her safely back down on the ice.

"Two things are important in life," Lord Menard would always tell his dear granddaughter, "family…and ice hockey!" Lord Menard always had plenty of stories of his own to share with his only grandchild as he helped her warm up and defrost in front of one of the many warm fireplaces in Menard Manor, stories of her father's shenanigans throughout his school days with his best friend, Wilhelm, and the rest of their chums, which included stories about his son's frostbitten ears, nose, and feet, his broken bones, the many times he had sneaked out of Menard Manor without his parents' approval, and all just to find a game of ice hockey!

The Menard child always delighted in her grandfather's stories, and her beautiful hazel-green eyes were as bright as her smile while she listened without any interruption to her grandfather's every single word, and even though her grandmother always saw his stories as "poppycock," she would smile sweetly as she brushed the Menard child's golden brown hair that fell down her back in large ringlets, even if just to see her beautiful granddaughter smile and to hear her laughter.

Hannah

The very first time that Dolice Marie had ever heard of the child called Hannah would be while all the signs of a budding springtime were beginning to appear everywhere, especially all around the lovely Menard cottage in the upstate area of the great state of New York. It was that time of the year that Monique Aimee Elizabeth LaPierre-Menard loved the best, and even though her birthday was still months away in late September, she enjoyed the springtime so much that she even celebrated an early birthday with lemonade with Wilhelmina the Cook's delicious lemon tea cakes whenever the buds started to appear on the trees and on the many bushes that encircled the lovely Menard cottage.

The years had flown by quickly for the beautiful Menard child, like a flock of birds returning from their winter homes in the warmer climates to find their way back to their summer homes where snow was now melting. Lizzie, as her best friend, Patima Salma, daughter of Kuya and Kip Salma, liked to call the Menard child, was as content as any child would be while living in the lap of such fineries that were always available at the Menard home and yet still being taught to always be aware of the needs of the less fortunate.

The Menard child attended a private school that was located within walking distance in their neighborhood, where she was taught all the basic lessons of reading, writing, and arithmetic by the nuns, as well as being taught those social graces such as manners and etiquette certainly necessary for a young lady growing up during her particular time in history, I might also add.

The child was truly loved by all her teachers and was especially delighted to wear the school's uniform, which consisted of crisp white blouses with large round collars, a sweet little red bow tie, and skirts made from the plaid of the Scottish clans.

Of course, her mother, Madam Menard, would always decorate the child's long golden-brown locks with matching silk ribbons, or hair barrettes, which she had fashioned from delicate pearls and ivory from Mr. Bernard Menard's import-export company.

But even with all the fuss, there was yet another side to the Menard child, a side that also loved being a tomboy, sneaking away to climb trees, scrape up her knees, or tear a hole in one of her beautiful dresses. But rather than insist that the child remain prissy at all times, both Madam Menard and Mr. Bernard Menard realized that their precious child was rather exceptional with her ability to fit into whichever role required of her at any given minute and so insisted that those times that required her to run, jump, or climb also required her to wear playclothes and not her dress-up clothes.

Madam Menard was always dressed quite well and always carried a delicate parasol and was so very proud to walk with her daughter to school every morning and to be there, in the exact same spot, patiently waiting to pick her beloved daughter up directly after her classes were finished for the day. In case of inclement weather, Edward would be already ready to drive the two of them to their destination in the fancy Menard carriage and to bring Madam Menard back to the school to wait for the Menard child.

She was indeed surrounded by a loving family, Monique Aimee Elizabeth LaPierre-Menard—a staff of loyal employees that not only took very good care of her every need but also loved her as if they, too, were her real family.

And then there was that clothes closet, filled with beautiful, handmade fashions that would surely speak to everyone who knew the younger Madam Dolice Marie that this was her child, indeed. Each outfit was complete with a matching hat and shoes, of course, for every occasion imaginable, including fashions to wear while having a tea party outside on a budding spring day.

Monique Aimee Elizabeth LaPierre-Menard seemed to be bursting out all over, through the seams, of absolutely every piece of clothing she owned, that is, from her undergarments to the lovely dresses that both the older Lady Menard and the younger Madam Dolice Marie Menard always had created for her by the finest dressmakers in the great city of New York and in Toronto, Canada.

Even the larger garments that had been created and placed in reserve for her next size had suddenly become smaller as well, letting

Madam Menard know that it would truly soon be time for a day trip in the fancy Menard carriage to the great city of New York.

Yes, the signs of spring were all around, but the signs that the Menard child was also growing like a weed and was most assuredly sprouting the same very long legs that supported her beloved father, Mr. Bernard Menard, were everywhere as well.

As Madam Menard began to surf through the mound of little-girl dresses, each adorned with silk ribbons and delicate eyelet trim in the most beautiful colors of the rainbow, she immediately made the decision to gather them all into a bundle and ask Edward to deliver everything to their family church; they would be given to those who had far less than her precious little girl.

"Aimee [as her mother loved to call her], dear one," Madam Menard said aloud, "Edward will make a trip today to the church to leave these fine dresses for other little girls that can still wear them and would certainly appreciate having them."

"Why, Mommy?" the dear Menard child unexpectedly replied to her mother's announcement. "Hannah would look just wonderful in any of these dresses. And as you already know, she's much smaller than I am, even though she is older than me."

"Hannah?" Madam Menard responded quizzically while busying herself with the task at hand. "And who is Hannah, my dear Aimee?"

"How could you forget Hannah, Mommy? She is always here."

Madam Menard stood in her daughter's bedroom, pondering for just a moment or two, trying to remember ever having met any friend of her daughter's friends other than Patima Salma. She discreetly motioned for Wilhelmina the Cook to join her and the Menard child in the bedroom and, after repeating her daughter's suggestion, scanned her eyes for answers before she realized that her own dear Aimee was more than likely speaking of an imaginary friend.

"Well, of course, I remember her, dear one," Madam Menard replied. "And we'll just keep these dresses in a safe place until Hannah comes for another visit. Why not keep them here, in the window seat?"

"Oh, what a wonderful idea, Mommy!"

Madam Menard planned at that very moment to have Wilhelmina the Cook and Maggie sneak into the child's bedroom while she was busy doing her childhood things outside the lovely Menard cottage and then have Edward deliver the clothes to their family church in their Upstate New York neighborhood, where other blossoming little girls could certainly use them. It appeared to all of them to be a good idea. But was it?

Yes, it was truly an excellent plan, and one that would be extremely helpful to those little girls who were not as fortunate as the Menard's Aimee, but when Wilhelmina the Cook and Maggie returned to the child's room and opened the top of the window seat to remove the dresses and undergarments, they were extremely surprised to find that everything was already gone!

"Missus!" Wilhelmina the Cook screamed for Madam Menard, who was just as surprised when she, too, looked into the empty window seat.

A perplexed Madam Menard caught sight through the window of her little Aimee playing what certainly appeared to be alone outside in the backyard of the cottage, with her playthings, no sign of a real little girl who could possibly be named Hannah, to whom she could have given her clothing.

Madam Menard and Wilhelmina the Cook stared out of the window for several minutes as though waiting for Hannah to appear, or for the perfect solution to pop into one of their heads to answer the question, "Is there really a Hannah?"

"Ah, missus," Wilhelmina the Cook finally stated, "I doubt there's very much to worry about here. Children have their imaginary friends, you know, and for a child to hide her clothing would just be a way to keep the fantasy going, I would say. Why, Mr. Menard himself had an imaginary friend, several, to be exact, as he was growing up, as I recall. Perhaps a little talk with him would give you some direction about the situation. Perhaps he has even seen the child Hannah."

"Yes," Madam Menard answered, nodding. "I agree with you, but perhaps a little talk with both Aimee and Monsieur Menard when he returns from work this evening."

"Well, that would be that," my dear uncle Gaston would always say, and my other sweet uncles always agreed quite matter-of-factly, for the moment, anyway.

Mr. Bernard Menard returned home from work that evening with the usual sweet smile on his face, happily looking for the members of his little family and greeting each one of the members of his household staff with a grateful smile and his usual pleasant response to their pleasant "Hellos." Aimee, as Mr. Bernard Menard also liked to call his sweet daughter, ran to his side, as she always did, and hugged him as if she had not seen him for a very long time, as she always did. It was truly a happy homecoming for everyone, every day, when Mr. Bernard Menard came home from work.

Today, however, Mr. Bernard Menard's beautiful wife would greet him with a troubled look upon her face, a look suggesting that there might be a problem that needed his immediate attention, and as usual, when there was an issue that required his attention, he was always ready to give it.

"Monsieur," Madam Menard greeted Mr. Bernard Menard with a soft kiss on his cheek, "it appears that Aimee has created a friend that no one else can see but herself."

"Oh, an imaginary friend," Mr. Bernard Menard responded in his usual charming manner. "I do believe that I had a few myself growing up. It shows that she has a great imagination. But why so sad, dear heart?" he asked.

"I thought perhaps we could, all three of us, discuss her friend that no one else can see at dinner this evening," Madam Menard answered. "It appears that Aimee has given her beautiful clothing that she no longer can wear to her…imaginary friend. She has even given her a name, Hannah."

"What a lovely name!" Mr. Bernard Menard said with a big smile but soon realized that Madam Menard was not in the least bit amused. He nodded to acknowledge what his dear wife was saying and, with a wink of his eye, assured her that he would, indeed, discuss the missing clothes with his beloved Aimee.

But even before Mr. Bernard Menard and Madam Menard could bring the missing clothes to Aimee's attention, Maggie tiptoed into the parlor, where the two were sitting, and whispered that the situation had seemingly taken care of itself. "Missus," Maggie whispered, "our sweet Monique is putting her clothes back in the window seat!"

"The household staff always called the Menard child Monique," my sweet uncle Gaston would always clarify to the young boys. "In fact," he would add, "seems as though everyone had a special name for the child! I always like to call the child MAE, an acronym for Monique Aimee Elizabeth—at least after all her 'little names' have been introduced."

Mr. Bernard Menard and Madam Menard followed Maggie to the dear child's room, and sure enough, Monique, or Aimee, was indeed putting the clothes back in the window seat in her room, and as she turned to exit the room, she smiled as she came face-to-face with Maggie and her parents.

"Hannah cannot wear the dresses," she said quite matter-of-factly, staring up at her parents. "She did ask me to thank you for being so kind as to offer them to her, but she said she is quite happy with what she is wearing now. I think she only has that one dress, poor thing."

Monique Aimee Elizabeth LaPierre-Menard, MAE, as my dear uncles called her, skipped happily away, leaving her parents and Maggie quite confused but also quite happy that the situation had truly rectified itself without any interference from any of the adults.

"But that would only be the first encounter that the adult Menards would have with their daughter's imaginary friend," Uncle Gaston would say as he looked each young boy in the eye to bring even more mystery to the mystery of Monique Aimee Elizabeth's imaginary friend.

"Hi, Lizzie," Patima's voice rang from the back door of the Menard cottage, where she and her mother, Kip, were standing. Patima, who was almost two years older than her little Menard friend, would always accompany her mother when Kip came to give Madam Menard her weekly massage. Madam Menard and Kip Salma had also become good friends, solid friends that enjoyed sharing time together even away from the weekly massage.

Lizzie, or Monique, or Aimee, could not be happier when her friend came to visit, and the two would always find some wonderful adventure upon which to embark, spending hours together pretending to be the kinds of people and the occupations that only the boys were supposed to be, like a policeman chasing the bad man all around the backyard of the Menard cottage, or a fancy carriage driver with his distinguished male passenger, and sometimes even hiding away up in the trees and throwing apples or acorns down upon Edward or Kuya as they went about their daily duties. It was certainly apparent that the two had great imaginations, whether together or apart, as each dreamed up the next game to play when they would be together again.

On this particular spring day, Patima returned shortly after leaving to the back porch, where Madam Menard and her mother, Kip, were sipping tea while sharing some serious conversation that suddenly ended when Patima appeared in front of them.

"Oh! And where might Aimee be?" Madam Menard quickly asked.

"She is standing by the gate," Patima answered quite politely, "on the inside, of course, talking to some invisible person again."

"Invisible person, Patima, are you sure?" asked Kip.

"Yes, Mother, she's always talking to some little girl that I cannot see, even though she insists that I can."

"What little girl?" Madam Menard asked quite sternly as she stood up quickly. "Did she call her Hannah?"

"Do you see Hannah, too, Madam Menard? Come with me, madam," Patima answered, "and I'll show you where Lizzie is."

Madam Menard, followed by Kip, paraded from the back of the lovely Menard cottage, led by Patima, past Kuya, who was working in the yard, straight to the front gate, where, lo and behold, Lizzie was standing, all alone, waving her arms around like she was indeed having a joyful conversation with no one.

"Aimee, my darling," Madam Menard said softly as she carefully approached her. "Whom are you talking to?"

"To Hannah, Mommy. Do you not see her, again?"

"Hannah?" she answered. "No, my darling, I do not see her."

"Oh, no, now she's gone!" Aimee answered sadly, while pouting her lips, folding her arms and thrusting her head downward. "You scared her away!"

"I did not mean to scare her away," Madam Menard said as she kneeled down to comfort her child. "I want to know all your friends, whether I can see them or not."

Madam Menard looked sheepishly at Kip, desperately seeking some sort of reasonable explanation from her friend about the situation, while Aimee stomped away, closely followed by Patima.

"There is no need to worry, Dolice," Kip said, touching her friend's hand. "You will have another opportunity to meet this Hannah. With our children, there is always another opportunity."

Madam Menard would have several more encounters, indeed, with the mysterious child that her beloved Aimee called Hannah, but it would be bright and early on a Sunday morning, while preparing MAE for services at the family's local church, that Hannah would finally explain her presence, indeed.

"Mommy," MAE said as Madam Menard combed her long golden-brown locks, "do you know how to put 'qwets' in my hair?"

Madam Menard dropped the comb from her hand and stared at her daughter with a look of sheer shock on her face. That was truly a word that she had not heard in a very, very long time.

"Where did you hear that word, Aimee?" Madam Menard was finally able to ask her daughter, after sitting down and finally catching her breath.

"Why, Hannah, of course," Aimee answered in her usual loving manner. "She always wears her hair in qwets."

In an instant, the proper Madam Dolice LaPierre-Menard, wife of Mr. Bernard Menard, import-export extraordinaire, was transported back in time to the boundaries of Mon Village, a place and time nearly forgotten—her life as a young slave, the big house, her beloved Jean Pierre, the New Orleans House, and everything in between. Tears swelled in her eyes, and one tear dared to escape and roll down her cheek.

"Aimee," she said, kneeling down to come eye to eye with her daughter while trying desperately not to shed a tremendous amount of tears in front of her, "do you think it would be possible for me to speak with your friend Hannah?"

"Of course, Mommy," Aimee answered with great excitement. "I would love that, and I know Hannah would love that too. Come with me, Mommy, and we will find her."

MAE gleefully extended her hand to her mother, and once Madam Menard accepted the child's hand, the two embarked on a journey to the past that neither one would ever forget.

"There she is!" MAE shouted while pointing and running toward a large tree in the backyard of the lovely Menard cottage. She began talking toward the tree as if there truly were another child standing there, while Madam Menard tried desperately not to let on that she had no idea where the invisible child was standing.

"This is my mother, Hannah, Madam Dolice Marie LaPierre-Menard," MAE said proudly to the invisible child. "Mommy, this is my friend, Hannah."

"I am certainly happy to meet you," Madam Menard responded, still trying to hold back her tears while staring at the tip of her daughter's finger, where she could only assume the invisible child was supposed to be standing.

Madam Menard had so many questions for the invisible child, but before she could even begin to ask one of them, MAE jerked her arm to gain her attention.

"Hannah just said that you are very beautiful, Mommy," MAE said proudly. "Did you not hear her?"

"Oh, yes, I did," a confused but truly determined Madam Menard responded, finding it quite difficult to pretend to be having the conversation with someone that could see her but that she could not see.

"Who is Mozelle?" MAE asked quite innocently. "Hannah said that you are just as beautiful as Mozelle."

"Mama!" Madam Menard whispered quietly as she swooned into a genteel faint—yes, she did—and landed at the invisible feet of the invisible Hannah, whose lovely, childish smile glowed brightly, so brightly that Madam Menard was truly able to see Hannah, and also her beloved ancestors, whom she had not seen or thought deeply about in such a long time.

There was her own dear mother, Mama Mozelle, smiling sweetly, the strong African-with-No-Name, later known as Jean Pierre I, standing beside Mama Del, the old voodoo priestess, who was always there between the earth and the other world, and the child Hannah, standing with hands behind her back, qwets decorating her hair, all reminding Madam Menard of that special promise that she and Jean Pierre had made to Mama Mozelle so many years before while sitting together under the huge magnolia tree.

Madam Menard began to weep, and as she did, she began to awaken, finding herself in her own bed, being watched by a distraught Mr. Bernard Menard, Maggie, Wilhelmina the Cook, Edward, and of course, her own sweet child, Aimee.

My dear, sweet uncles were filled with the same loving connection to our ancestors and this so very special meeting that was, indeed, precipitated by an invisible child named Hannah. Uncle Gaston always paused again at this portion of the stories and reached for that noteworthy handkerchief of his that was never too far away from his reach to wipe away his tears of accolade for the early family. Those young boys were truly filled with pride by now and seemed to puff up just a bit in the presence of these dear old men.

"Mommy, are you all right?" MAE asked with a quiver in her voice, laying her head softly on her mother's chest. "I was so worried."

Mr. Bernard Menard, who was standing beside her, bent down to kiss her gently on her forehead and wiped the tears away from her eyes.

"I am fine," Madam Menard answered, reaching out to MAE and then holding her ever so closely. "I am so very sorry that I made you worry, all of you," she continued, "but we have work to do, Monsieur Menard. We are going to Mon Village to make a family reunion."

"I have always wanted to go there, Mommy," MAE said, smiling, "to see the place where I was born, to see my family that I have never seen but have heard so much about. Father, will you come too?"

"Of course I will, Aimee," Mr. Bernard Menard responded. "I would not miss this journey for anything! Oh, and we will ask Uncle Wilhelm if he would join us for this adventure as well, what do you think?"

MAE was thrilled at the possibility of her beloved uncle Wilhelm visiting Mon Village with the entire family, and Madam Menard was also very happy that her husband would share this time with his best friend as she spent time with her family and best friend, Jean Pierre.

Before Madam Menard could say another word, the staff of the Menard household began to scurry throughout the lovely Menard cottage, preparing for a journey, a delightful journey, one that was certainly long overdue, to say the very least. Both Maggie and Wilhelmina the Cook worked diligently picking and choosing the necessary items for the journey, with tears in their own eyes, while Edward made ready the Menard carriage and horse that would take the Menards to the train station in the upstate area in the great state of New York.

"Oh, Mommy," MAE began with such excitement, "can Patima come with us, please?"

Madam Menard slowly raised her eyes to meet those of her husband, who nodded subtly, giving affirmation to the request from his beloved daughter. Madam Menard smiled, having received the answer that she was truly searching for, and immediately asked Mr. Bernard Menard to ask Edward to find Kuya and ask him if he, too, would approve. The kindly man kissed his wife one more time on her forehead and escaped through the bedroom door to perform the tasks at hand.

Now that she was alone with her beloved daughter, Madam Menard assured MAE that the family would soon be embarking on a magnificent adventure, one that would certainly bring change to her own life forever.

"But for now," Madam Menard continued, "we have a journey to plan, dresses and shoes to pack…oh, yes, and plenty of presents to purchase for everyone at Mon Village."

Several moments later, Mr. Bernard Menard returned with both Kuya and Kip, who seemed quite delighted about the possibility of their little girl, Patima, traveling with the Menards to the great state of Louisiana. Kip, however, did have her reservations about her little girl being so far away from home and parents, and certainly for an unknown period, reservations that she boldly voiced before Madam Menard, who listened quite closely.

"Perhaps you, too, could come with us," Madam Menard said with her bright eyes opened wide, as though she had just stepped into a wonderful world filled with all her very favorite things.

"I have not been away from you for one day since I came to this place that you helped me to love," she continued, reaching out to hold Kip's tiny hands with her own, "so for you to come with us would be as much for me as for you to feel comfortable about Patima coming with us."

Kuya and Kip turned toward each other as if in shock and, for several moments to follow, began to speak in their native Filipino language, Kip's face being filled with smiles and excitement, while Kuya seemed quite the opposite. MAE, Mr. Bernard Menard, and Madam Menard quietly turned from Kip to Kuya and back again as the two continued with their conversation, Kip's voice rising above Kuya's several times, and then Kuya's voice rising above Kip's as each one expressed their own feelings about the situation. Suddenly, it was completely quiet, and then a moment later, Kuya spoke out. "We are very pleased to accept the kind offer for Kip and Patima to travel with you to Madam Menard's hometown." He bowed briefly, excused himself with a quick smile, and disappeared through the bedroom door, followed by a smiling Kip.

"Well," Mr. Bernard Menard said quietly after several moments of absolute quiet, "it seems as though everyone is going to Mon Village!"

But the next thing to be done on Mr. Bernard Menard's list was to send a wire to Jean Pierre at Mon Village to tell him and the rest of the Mon Village family that the Menards were on their way to Mon Village to plan and implement the very first family reunion.

Next, there would be a wire to his best friend, Wilhelm, to ask him if it would be possible for him to meet the Menards of Upstate

New York at the train station in the great city of New York at the scheduled time for a journey to the great state of Louisiana.

It would be yet another day before the Menards, along with Kip and Patima, and possibly Wilhelm, would all meet at the train station in the great city of New York. It was a time of great happiness, a time of great expectation, and most of all, it was the time for a family reunion.

Chapter 23

BACK IN THAT great city of New Orleans, the activities at the New Orleans House were now becoming a faded memory of the past for the lovely ladies that resided there, as well as the guests, who now spent their coins on entertainment of a different kind.

From a deep bowl of spicy gumbo served with steaming rice to a quiet seat on a divan in the main parlor to listen to the piano music being played by the strange Madeleine Dubois-Chachere while a spirited Angeline kicked her heels up to entertain them all, the New Orleans House was there, in one fashion or another, to stay.

Madeleine Dubois-Chachere

Miss BB always had a comment to make about Madeleine Dubois-Chachere—a very loud comment, I might also add—as she peered peculiarly at the lady behind the piano on those special Saturday nights that Obadiah would accompany her, holding herself back from simply asking her who she really was and where she did go every night and every weekend when she quickly left the New Orleans House. "Stop that, Aunt BB," Angeline would always whisper to her as Miss BB actually opened her opera glasses to get a much closer look at Madeleine. "Madeleine will see you! That is very rude!"

"Poppycock!" Miss BB would always answer Angeline sharply while continuing, of course, to use her opera glasses to spy on the beautiful yet outlandish Lady Madeleine. "I would say that it is better to safely pursue the truth than to have the truth hit you smack-dab in the face when you least expect it!" Miss BB would always say with that slow Southern drawl of hers and then motion to Obadiah that she was ready, indeed, for a sip of her smooth Kentucky bourbon from her silver flask that he had hidden away for her in his coat pocket.

Although Madeleine had come to the New Orleans House during that period when the activities were truly transitioning, she had certainly made it perfectly clear that she was only there to play the piano and to sing, and that she had no reason ever to go up the stairs to the pleasure palace with the other ladies of the New Orleans House. The bizarre woman also declared to Angeline that her salary should be put in an envelope and placed on the top of the piano each week and that she would retrieve it once she appeared, whenever that would be.

Since Madeleine was certainly making all the major decisions about her employment at the New Orleans House for herself, by herself, no one disputed her decisions, not Angeline or Miss BB, but everyone wondered, most of the time verbally, where she came from and where she went when she was not entertaining at the New Orleans House.

Perhaps it was that aggressive nature of Madeleine Dubois-Chachere and the fact that she would suddenly appear at the New Orleans House just in time to delight the guests, or the certainty that at some time during the night she would disappear, that brought such attention upon her from Miss BB and the other ladies and the household staff as well. It became apparent after her very first night at the New Orleans House that she was truly talented and certainly enjoyed playing the piano and singing and that everyone truly enjoyed when she did.

The money was flooding into the New Orleans House like the waters from a torrential downpour, and much of it was due to Madeleine Dubois-Chachere, even though that fact seemed not to impress her at all.

It would be one of those exciting Saturday nights that Miss BB announced to Angeline that she had been working on a plan to find out all the answers to all the questions she, and everybody else, had about her newest employee.

"Aunt BB," Angeline answered her, "why is it so important for you to know everything about Madeleine? Perhaps she would prefer no one knowing all there is to know about her!"

"Perhaps," Miss BB replied, "but we may have a villain harboring here, just biding her time before she pulls out a weapon and kills us all!"

"Oh my goodness!" Angeline answered. "Now, why would she want to do that?"

"Well, I think we need to find out all about her before she does that!"

In spite of Angeline's concerns, Miss BB was determined to find out everything there was to know about Madeleine Dubois-Chachere, and even as she peered through her opera glasses at the woman, her mind was turning like wheels while she continued to talk to her niece.

"You need to have more fun, Angeline, more than just dancing in this house! Come with me!"

"I will not be a party to this…thing…Aunt BB," Angeline answered. "You go and have enough fun for both of us!"

And that Miss BB did! It seemed as though Miss BB had hired someone, a young man to be exact, to spy on the mysterious woman during every minute of her day. Of course, this person was yet another one of Miss BB's "friends" that owed her a favor or two, and he was all too eager to assist the Lady Beatrice Carson Declouette in her plan to find out everything there was to know about her. Besides, Miss BB had never been known to give in to a good fight or accept that she could be wrong until she could prove she certainly was not.

The plan, or might I just call it by its accurate name, scheme, began on Saturday evening after Miss BB and Obadiah had entered the New Orleans House to enjoy the entertainment. Miss BB spied the young man that she had hired through her opera glasses as he cunningly approached Madeleine Dubois-Chachere while she was playing a lovely tune on the piano.

He was well-dressed in a gray suit trimmed with black, a fashionable, matching black tie of the era around his neck, holding a tall silk hat in his hand. He smiled as he came near, but Madeleine Dubois-Chachere completely ignored the young man and continued to entertain the crowd of people that were there to listen to her. The young man came a little closer and put some coins in the brandy snifter that sat on top of the piano for tips, but Madeleine Dubois-Chachere simply tipped her head slightly in gratitude, continued to play the piano, and gave no true never mind to his person.

An impatient Miss BB squirmed in her seat on the divan as the scene slowly played itself out between the young man and Madeleine Dubois-Chachere.

When the pianist finally stopped playing, the young man began to compliment her talent, but she still gave no never mind to him and simply responded "Thank you" to his accolades. When it became quite obvious that Madeleine Dubois-Chachere had absolutely no interest in the young man, he bade her a good night and moved slowly away from the piano and found a seat on a divan near Miss BB and Obadiah.

The young man repeated the exact same scene with Madeleine Dubois-Chachere over the course of several Saturdays, each time assuring Miss BB that he, too, had a plan and asked her to just be patient with him.

It would be on a breezy fall evening that the young man decided to play out his own plan and waited until Madeleine Dubois-Chachere had completed her final set and began to gather her belongings together in order to leave the New Orleans House. Wearing all black, the young man blended in with the dark of night and leaned against an outside light pole as he waited for Madeleine Dubois-Chachere to walk out of the New Orleans House, and that she finally did, at the exact moment when a city carriage appeared, stopping directly in front of her as if the city carriage driver had been cued when to arrive. As the mysterious woman escaped into the city carriage, the young man realized that there was yet another person inside, but whether or not that person was a male or a female was difficult to determine in the darkness of the night.

MINT JULEP

The young man quickly retrieved his own horse and began to follow the city carriage at a comfortable distance to keep the passengers unaware that they were being followed. On and on the city carriage traveled through the great city of New Orleans, past the great river, all the way to that "other side of town" where the not-so-fortunate lived.

The city carriage parked in the front of one of those unfortunate houses, where a woman with long dark hair and a plain dress emerged from the one side while what appeared now to be a man in every sense of the word emerged from the other side of the city carriage, the same side that Madeleine Dubois-Chachere had entered.

The young man who was now inhaling the scene found his eyes nearly popping out of his head.

Where is Madeleine Dubois-Chachere, he thought to himself.

There had been no stops on the way to this house, and if this "man" had been in the carriage as well, where would Madeleine Dubois-Chachere be?

Miss BB's young spy quietly dismounted from his horse in the darkest of night and surfaced just a little closer, just close enough to see the city driver jump down from the top seat of the carriage and tie the horse to a pole near the carriage. Still no Madeleine Dubois-Chachere, or so he thought.

My crazy uncles would laugh and laugh and laugh until they could laugh no more while those young boys that were being initiated sat virtually stupefied, wondering the exact same thing as the young spy.

"Where is Madeleine Dubois-Chachere?"

The next day, the young man reported his findings to Miss BB, who was just as perplexed as her young spy, citing every possible scenario that might have confused the situation, but there was a practical answer to every single suggestion she recommended.

"No, ma'am, there was only one stop, at the house."

"No, ma'am, there was no one else in the city carriage."

"No, ma'am, the carriage was parked in front of the house and the driver went inside of the house as well."

Determined to find out the truth and nothing but the truth, Miss BB instructed her young spy to repeat the scenario as many times as it required until the case could be solved, and that he did, week after week after week, with the exact same results, until, almost giving up in despair, the young man came up with another plan, to simply knock on the door and ask, "Where is Madeleine Dubois-Chachere?"

With his heart thumping quite loudly, the young man watched as the scene played out as it had so many times before, but this time, as the door to the house closed, he emerged from the darkness where he had been hiding and bravely walked to the door and knocked loudly. Apparently, those inside were quite startled, and for a moment or two, everything seemed to just freeze in time. He knocked again, and finally, a man's voice asked, "Who is it?"

"I am looking for Madeleine Dubois-Chachere, sir. Can you assist me with my search?"

"No, sir, I am sorry. There is no Madeleine Dubois-Chachere here. Now please leave us alone," the man behind the door quickly answered.

"I beg to differ with you, sir, since I have been following you week after week, watching Madeleine Dubois-Chachere being driven here, to this address, but a man exiting from the city carriage instead of her."

"And why would that be of any concern to you, sir?" the voice inside the house asked.

"I have been detained by Miss Beatrice Carson Declouette of the Declouette Mansion and the New Orleans House to locate a Madeleine Dubois-Chachere that is in her employ, and my search has led me here."

There was a long pause and then, finally, the sound of the door being unlatched, and there, standing in the doorway, was a man whose resemblance to Madeleine Dubois-Chachere was quite uncanny, an appearance that suggested that this man was certainly related to the strange woman in question.

"And what would Miss Declouette have of this Madeleine Dubois-Chachere?"

"Perhaps just the matter of curiosity, sir, but one that could cost her the job that she profits from at the New Orleans House."

The young man was gaining such strength in his voice that the man standing in the doorway began to think hard before he answered any further questions.

"It is rather late, sir," the man in the doorway responded. "Perhaps we could have this conversation at a later time. There are children here, asleep, and as you already know, we have just arrived ourselves and were preparing to go to bed when you knocked on the door."

"I understand, sir. However, I must report to my employer in the morning and feel that a short answer would make it possible for all of us to go to bed this night. Can you tell me where Madeleine Dubois-Chachere is at this moment?"

The man in the doorway excused himself for a moment and began a quiet conversation with the woman that had emerged from the city carriage night after night with him. After several minutes, he returned to the doorway and, after several deep breaths, admitted that *he*, indeed, was Madeleine Dubois-Chachere.

The young spy was taken aback and, after taking several deep breaths himself, began to laugh hysterically.

"My real name is Marcel Dubois, and the Chachere is my wife's maiden name."

"May I ask you why, sir, would you continue such a charade?"

"My wife and I are entertainers, sir. As you have already witnessed, I play the piano and sing, as does my wife. It was extremely difficult to find work here in New Orleans as a man, so I—"

"So you decided to dress like a woman!" The young spy began to laugh again.

"And quite successfully, sir!"

"Yes," Miss BB's young spy added, "and quite successfully."

"What will you tell Miss Declouette?"

"The truth."

"If you do that, I will surely lose my job, sir, and I cannot afford to do so. You must admit that Madeleine has brought a fair share of the money that comes into the New Orleans House."

"I understand," the young spy responded. "And yes, she has certainly brought in money to the business. I will think on this during the night to find the best solution for all of us involved. For now, it is a real pleasure meeting you and your family. In fact, now I am extremely happy that you did not accept my attempted advances!"

"You were not my type, sir."

After climbing upon his horse and tipping his hat to the family inside the house, Miss BB's young spy made his way in the dark toward his own home, all the while contemplating what he would tell Miss BB to calm her down and yet help Madeleine Dubois-Chachere as well.

When day finally arrived, Miss BB's young spy had come up with an excellent plan, one that would be beneficial for all involved, and after quickly dressing and securing a city carriage, he headed toward the other end of town, that end of town where Madeleine—er, Marcel—lived.

After finally waking someone in the house and being led to Marcel's bedroom, the young spy began to rattle off his plan with eagerness and excitement.

"Now hurry and get dressed, please. I will be waiting for you in my carriage."

A short time later, Marcel emerged, dressed as what he truly was, a man. He hopped inside the carriage where the young spy was, and the two began to talk about the plan as they rode to the Declouette Mansion. After being greeted by Obadiah, the two were led to the main parlor, where they awaited Miss BB's arrival, which came rather quickly and pleasantly.

"Well," she said, "and whom do we have here?"

"This is Marcel Dubois," the young spy answered. "He is an entertainer, one with a very unique act. He would like to audition for you on this fine day."

"Oh, so now you are in the entertainment business!"

"You might say that," the young spy answered.

Marcel proceeded to the piano, but it would be Madeleine that began to play and sing. Miss BB seemed confused as she continued to listen and peer intensely at Marcel but said nothing even though her jaw began to drop open. After the first two songs were played, Marcel excused himself for a few moments, and when he returned, he was wearing the makeup, the hair decorations, and the earrings of—yes, Marcel Dubois truly was—Madeleine Dubois-Chachere!

"Well, I never!" Miss BB said as she fell, limp, against the back of the divan, weak in her arms and legs.

No one said anything for the longest time, but when the silence was finally broken, it would be by Miss BB, who began to laugh uncontrollably, so much so that she began to cough, loudly, I might also add, and so fiercely that Obadiah ran into the parlor, followed closely by FiFi and GiGi, and he lifted Miss BB into the air, holding her upside down until she was breathing easily again.

"Now, *that* is what I call entertainment!" Miss BB quirked as she fanned herself with a handkerchief that Obadiah gave to her to wipe her face.

"You know, that had to be a scene," Uncle Clovis would pipe in.

Once everything quieted down in the parlor of the Declouette Mansion, it became quite obvious that Miss BB was concocting a brand-new plan, one that would certainly be advantageous for everyone involved.

Well, why not take advantage of the extremely talented Marcel Dubois as well as the extremely talented Madeleine Dubois-Chachere? Why not introduce the customers of the New Orleans House to both Marcel Dubois and Madeleine Dubois-Chachere during a well-planned evening of entertainment, one that would be well advertised throughout the great city of New Orleans? Why not arrange for Marcel to evolve into Madeleine Dubois-Chachere right there, in front of the very eyes of the guests, during one of the Saturday evening concerts, just as he had done for Miss BB? Yes, why not?

"Shall we get started?" Miss BB asked, summing up the entire plan, which, within just a matter of a few short weeks, proved to be one of the most exciting evenings in the entire history of the New Orleans House and, do I dare say, the entire history of entertainment ever in the great city of New Orleans.

And what about the young man that Miss BB had hired to spy on and uncover all there was to know about Madeleine Dubois-Chachere? He was accordingly rewarded for a job well done, so much so that he was able to open his own office of private investigations that served the great city of New Orleans for years to come.

Chapter 24

JUST AS I observed the light of life being snuffed out from each of my sweet old uncles as they passed on to the other world to be with the ancestors as I was growing up, so it was as well in the stories that they told to the young boys as they were being initiated into our family.

Our history was filled with its hysterical events, those moments that triggered a roar of laughter from the old storytellers that vibrated throughout Mon Village like an earthquake. But like all family histories, ours had its sad times as well, its time of loss and sadness, stories that were hard, indeed, to tell. But these were the stories that must be passed on as well.

Miss Beatrice Carson Declouette

It would be during the late morning hours in the great city of New Orleans that the pride of Savannah, Georgia, that is Miss BB Carson Declouette, awakened to find Obadiah, Angeline, and several of the lovely ladies from the New Orleans House who had been visiting her standing over her with watery eyes, sad faces, with her beloved FiFi and GiGi positioned beside her in her big bed in the master bedroom in the beautiful Declouette Mansion. She took a long, deep breath, and after slowly exhaling, Miss BB frowned and began to look from one to the other of her loved ones before commenting.

"My, my, my!" she said in that slow Southern drawl of hers. "You all look like somebody has just died!"

After a brief pause, and after looking from one to the other once again, she realized that she had obviously amused only herself.

"Oh, I see," she said, commenting calmly, "I guess you must have thought it was me!"

"You scared me so much!" Angeline said with that thick French accent of hers, falling softly across Miss BB's body, weeping while trying to wrap her arms around the gentle woman's neck.

Obadiah quietly wiped the tears from his eyes, first the left eye, and then the right eye, with a white handkerchief that he pulled from the inside pocket of his long black coat.

"Well," Miss BB commented as she raised herself upon her elbows to lean against the lace-covered pillows, fluffing them both, and then her hair, "I certainly must have given you all a big scare. It is not very often that Obadiah gets that emotional!" She chuckled, but when no one chuckled along with her, Miss BB began to feel the seriousness of the present situation.

"Your breathing was so slow," Angeline said as she wiped her own eyes again. "You had not come down from your daily nap, so I came up here to look in on you. You were not moving, and there was a deep, gurgling sound coming from your throat, and I was afraid that you were—"

"Dead?" Miss BB asked quite calmly. "You do realize that I am going to die one day..."

There was a loud chorus of gasps and great sadness from those gathered around the beloved lady of the Declouette Mansion, each person expressing their desire not to hear the dear lady speak of her own death.

"Well," she continued, "I am now alive, awake, and am now ready to resume my life among the living, so if all of you would not mind, I would like to freshen up. Rest assured, I will be down in just a few moments."

As Miss BB attempted to lift herself up to place her feet on the floor, her hand suddenly grabbed her head as if she had just developed a terrible headache, her eyes squinted, and she fell back on the bed, breathing rapidly.

"Obadiah!" Angeline screamed for him as she leaned over Miss BB to listen for her heartbeat. "Please, get the doctor, get the doctor!"

One of the ladies of the New Orleans House ran quickly to get a cold towel to put across Miss BB's brow, while Obadiah ran quickly down the stairs and out into the street toward Dr. Blanchard's office. By the time Obadiah returned with the doctor to the Declouette Mansion and up the stairs to the master bedroom, Miss BB was lying flat, perfectly still, on her back, with her eyes closed, again breathing very, very slowly.

The eyes of everyone in the room were filling again with tears as each person, in the quiet of their own hearts, began preparing themselves now for the impossible and most certainly the inevitable.

Dr. Blanchard, who had been Miss BB's regular doctor for many years now, examined the beloved lady for several minutes and, after directing everyone into the hallway, quietly informed Angeline, Obadiah, and those ladies of the New Orleans House of his findings.

"Beatrice is very tired," he began.

"So you are going to put Aunt BB into the hospital for a rest?" Angeline asked with great hope in her voice.

"No, Angeline," he answered quite sadly, patting her hand with his own. "Her body and her mind are tired, my dear. After all, she is more than eighty years old, closer to ninety, as a matter of fact. She has lived a very long, happy, and very busy life, always surrounded by the people who love her and that she loves. And now she is happily ready to pass on to the next world."

Everyone in the room became frozen in time, completely taken aback by the fact that this lovely lady was more than eighty years old, closer to ninety, a fact that no one knew and everyone was now finding extremely difficult to believe.

"How long?" Angeline was finally able to ask the doctor.

"A day, a week, two weeks," Dr. Blanchard answered. "It depends on her, how long she feels she needs, but I do suggest that you begin to make the arrangements."

"She made those herself, years ago," a brokenhearted Obadiah responded. "The papers are in the armoire over there, in the corner." He pointed toward the beautiful piece of furniture in the corner of the master bedroom.

Dr. Blanchard smiled sadly yet reassuringly and told both Angeline and Obadiah to be sure to let him know if and when he would be needed, and then he slowly slipped down the stairway.

In the meantime, time slowly marked time for everyone that adored the kindly Miss BB, and all waited for the time if and when Dr. Blanchard would be needed.

Chapter 25

Dolice Marie LaPierre-Menard awakened to the familiar sounds of her youth, birds chirping, a bobwhite singing his familiar song, a whippoorwill proudly welcoming the dawn with his song while a nocturnal owl bade a good night to the sun with a quiet hoot, and in the distance, the sounds of farming machines and other farm equipment, while the residents of Mon Village awakened as well to a familiar routine that had certainly kept the former plantation flourishing, even while she had been so far away for so very long.

It had been an exciting train ride for her family and friends to this place, and Dolice stretched her arms high over her head, closed her eyes, and smiled; she was at home, lying beside her devoted husband, Mr. Bernard Menard, and yet being here in the home of her beloved Jean Pierre, with him and his wife being just a few yards away from her, and his children with their child MAE, who, with her best friend, Patima, were quietly sleeping together in one of the children's bedrooms and getting to know one another throughout the night.

Mr. Bernard Menard's best friend, Wilhelm, had been waiting at the train station in that great city of New York just as the train schedule had required him to be, just as excited as everyone else was about the journey, and even though he had spent his life just a short distance from the Canadian side of the beautiful Niagara Falls, he found himself just as overwhelmed with the sight of the mighty

Mississippi River as anyone else who had ever seen it for the very first time.

Jean Pierre and Evelina were also very happy to finally meet Wilhelm, the man that they had so often heard about and who was now peacefully sleeping in one of the children's bedrooMiss. Their warm welcome was a glad tiding for the young man who was truly more family than friend, having shared every good and every not-so-good moment of his best friend's life from the time they both learned what the word *friend* actually meant.

The smell of fresh Louisiana coffee and the sound of bacon sizzling on the stove drew Dolice Marie toward the kitchen, where she was greeted by the welcoming embraces of her beautiful sister-in-law, or would that be cousin-in-law, Evelina. Surprisingly, Kip was already awake as well and sharing conversation with Evelina while sipping on her coffee by the time Dolice Marie found her way to the kitchen. It was quite obvious that Kip and Evelina had already become fast friends, if not already family.

"How 'bout a nice cuppa coffee and some catch-up talkin' while everyone is still sleepin'?" Evelina invited Dolice with a huge smile as she pulled back a chair at the dining room table.

Dolice immediately recognized the familiar drawl of the land of the plantations as differing from the diction of the proper-speaking people of the great state of New York, to which she had become so very accustomed. But even though the now very proper Madam LaPierre-Menard had developed a truly notable knack for the queen's English, it took but a very short while for her to fall back into the routine of the old Dolice Marie, the former slave girl with the broken English who had become the mistress of all that the LaPierre eye could see.

"Oh, yeah, chère," Dolice Marie responded with a big laugh, making fun of her own self. "I sho' could use that cuppa' strong coffee!"

After a long period of family hugs, again, coupled with grins, smiles, and those old familiar girlie giggles, Dolice Marie ran quickly from the kitchen and back into the guest bedroom, where her beloved husband was sleeping, and quietly searched through the train cases for something special that she had brought all the distance from the great state of New York to Mon Village, a gift, just for her beautiful Evelina.

Returning to the kitchen with as much fervor as she had exited, Dolice Marie suddenly stopped in her tracks and handed Evelina a package carefully wrapped in brown wrapping paper and tied neatly with course string.

"Open it," Dolice Marie said with such excitement that one might think she would explode at any minute if Evelina did not do as she had instructed.

"Open it!"

Evelina slowly and methodically began to untie the course string and very neatly unwrap the gift inside the brown paper wrapping. It was a lovely dress, made of silk, yellow, just like the color of the sun, with plenty of buttons in a darker yellow and lace around the high collar. This dress was certainly one that Dolice Marie herself would wear at such an occasion as this, where lots of family could see it and inhale its beauty, a dress that came from the very closet of Madam Dolice Marie LaPierre-Menard. It was a very thoughtful gift, indeed.

"Oh, my, my, my!" Evelina said with sheer and utter gratitude as she inspected every single inch of the beautiful dress. "It is beautiful!"

"I thought you would like it," Dolice Marie answered with such pride. "I had it made for myself several months ago and still have not worn it, so it really is brand-new."

"I will wear it to the family reunion," Evelina said as she held the dress against her and twirled around and around as if she were already wearing it.

"I brought more fabric to sew clothes for the children," Dolice continued. "There was not much time to go shopping for gifts, and I know how much Miss Penelope and you love to sew, once upon a time, anyway."

Uncle Gaston would always add at this point of his stories that the ladies all began to dance around the room again as if they were silly little teenaged girls. "You know what I'm talking 'bout," he would say to the young boys, who would always agree with him by nodding.

The sound of their laughter resonated throughout the house as each woman recalled to the other what had been happening since the Menard wedding several years before in the great city of New Orleans, the very last time that Dolice Marie and Evelina had been together until this very moment. Both remembered how very loud Evelina had announced to the wedding party that she was, indeed, about to give birth to her youngest child, her sweet Jean Pierre III.

It was a time for joyful remembrance, a time to talk about children, spouses, and close friends; it was a time for family, and most of all, it was a time to plan for a family reunion.

It was jointly decided upon by Dolice Marie and Evelina, while everyone else was asleep, that the very first LaPierre-Menard family reunion would be held in the middle of the residential area, just like in the old days, when everyone met together for the music of the La La, good food, and just to pass a good time together.

As usual, everyone would have their own job to do, a job that would be based upon each one's special talent, whether cooking, decorating, playing music, or running all the necessary errands. Everyone would have something special to do. But of course, everyone would be in charge of cleaning up and putting everything back in the order that it needed to be.

My sweet uncles would always agree that some things just never changed, and cleanup was one of them. "Cleanup is everybody's business!"

The laughter and the aroma of breakfast food cooking on the stove in Jean Pierre and Evelina's house sent an unmistakable invitation to those still sleeping in the other rooMiss. One by one the children made their way into the kitchen, swapping hugs and kisses for deep plates of hotcakes, bacon, eggs, and freshly squeezed orange juice.

Mon Claire had recently become a young teenager with a family history of her own, already a fine horsewoman who spent much of her time with Jubil in the stables, grooming as well as treating the ailments of the horses that were boarded at the LaPierre stables, and the other portion of her time split between her daily chores, her education in the schoolhouse, and encouraging the other residents to join her at the church house the following Sabbath. Evelina always bragged about how helpful the eldest LaPierre child was with her siblings, and with the housework, and that was usually when she found the time to allow her steady steed, her best friend, Ti-Garçon, to rest a bit.

The eldest child of Jean Pierre and Evelina stood medium height, with long muscular legs and equally long dark-brown hair, hazel eyes, and an extremely quiet nature that was only ruffled when her siblings failed to adhere to their daily chores and responsibilities.

Petois and Pecous, those chubby little twins, would soon be eleven years old and had put their love for food to work for themselves and the family by cooking and delivering food to the older residents at Mon Village that were now living alone. Even at their tender age, the twins had been invited to the big house, which had been the temporary church house while the permanent one was being constructed, to assist the cook in preparing food for special guests and special events. It was obvious, indeed, that the twins were a favorite pair at Mon Village, and when they were not eating a dish that they had created for themselves or someone else, they were taking a taste of something delicious that someone else had cooked in order to impress them.

Standing at just medium height as well, the identical twins were distinguishable only by a slight difference in the structure of their faces, Pecous having higher cheekbones with some hollowing just underneath, while Petois's face was as round as a full moon. Both were devoted to their family and loved to play practical jokes on each other as well as their siblings, and occasionally even on Jean Pierre or Evelina.

And then there was Labelle Jelee, who had stolen Dolice Marie's heart when she was still a sweet baby being carried on her mother's hip, now soon to celebrate her ninth birthday. In fact, it was actually Dolice that had given Jelee the name Labelle when she first held the child in her arms, whispering in the sweet baby's ear the name Labelle.

Evelina was already "havin' a time with that girl," as she put it, who spent too much of her time primpin' herself in the mirror.

Evelina had all too often found her digging through garbage around Mon Village to find scraps of fabric that she would use to create dresses for herself that exposed a tad too much skin, if you know what I mean! Evelina had expressed her concern to her beloved husband, Jean Pierre, that Labelle Jelee was just "a little too grown for her own britches!" But Jean Pierre, on the other hand, had only praise for his youngest daughter and tried hard to console his beloved wife by pointing out that the child had talent, indeed.

Short by stature and developed far before her time, Jelee was the true replica of Dolice Marie LaPierre, including the flair for fashion, fun, and self. She did, however, have a heart as big as the great state of Texas and would indeed give her right hand for family or friend.

"Jelee's day was yet to come," as my sweet old uncle Michele would always say. "And it was coming with a force!" Uncle Michele would always emphasize his words by balling up his fist and shaking it hard, with a force.

Patima Salma, the Menard child's best friend, who had journeyed with her mother, Kip, and the Menards from the great state of New York to Mon Village, was just a couple of years older than her Lizzie and had already celebrated her eleventh birthday just a few months before. Dolice Marie and Evelina certainly already had family reunion plans for the Salmas' child as well.

Even Jean Pierre III, the very last of the LaPierre children, had already turned nine years old during the early fall season, and the only Menard child, the Menard's own beloved Aimee, had already turned nine years old during the late summer season the year before. Jean Pierre III had long legs and the handsome face of his father, Jean Pierre II, while Aimee had long legs and had the appearance of a striking combination of both of her parents, the beautiful and petite Dolice Marie and the tall and slender Bernard Menard.

This reunion of the children would be their first union, although all of them quickly became more than just family—they were all instant friends, and it was obvious that they intended to remain that way forever.

Time had truly flown by, and it was indeed time for the entire family of Mon Village to get to know one another, just as Mama

Mozelle had said when most of these children had not even been born. Everyone at the former plantation, now known as Mon Village, carried the surname LaPierre, and just that very fact had worried Mama Mozelle, the fact that unless all the LaPierres knew whom they were related to, there could unknowingly and unfortunately be some very regrettable relationships with a family member. It had truly been one of her dying wishes that a family reunion be held occasionally to introduce family members to one another to ensure that those regrettable relationships with a family member did not happen, or at least not very often.

A knock on the door turned everyone's attention toward Jubil, who was standing on the porch, smiling that same old familiar smile, but this time, and for Dolice Marie's first time ever meeting her, Jubil was accompanied by his lovely bride, Miss Sylvia, who had a smile just as big as her husband's. Dolice Marie was truly overwhelmed with joy as she ran to the door and opened it to hug both Jubil and Miss Sylvia at the same time.

A short time later, while all were enjoying a delicious breakfast, a still-sleepy Jean Pierre, Mr. Bernard Menard, and Wilhelm appeared at the dining room table with plenty of hugs to give away and even more smiles. It was truly obvious that the LaPierre-Menard family reunion was already well on its way.

It was Mr. Bernard Menard's turn to disappear from the dining room and swiftly return with gifts from the Menard cottage in Upstate New York—two packages, both wrapped in brown wrapping paper, tied neatly with course string, one of which he gave to Jean Pierre, the other to Jubil. Both were pleasantly surprised and quite anxious, I might also add, to open their gifts, and just as Dolice Marie encouraged Evelina to quickly open hers, Mr. Bernard Menard cheered on as the two opened and admired their gifts, white dress shirts, one for Jean Pierre and one for Jubil, with fancy cuff links to close the cuffs at the end of both sleeves.

Tucked sweetly within the folds of Jubil's shirt was another small package wrapped exactly the same and labeled "For Sylvia LaPierre." Jubil smiled as he gave the gift to his beloved wife, who was both surprised and deeply appreciative. While Jean Pierre and Jubil "Oohed" and "Aahed" over their gifts from the Menards of Upstate New York, Miss Sylvia was duly excited about the lovely silk scarf she found wrapped in the brown paper.

"Oh, my, my, my!" Miss Sylvia echoed Evelina's words as she draped the lovely silk scarf around her neck, allowing one end to softly fall down her neckline while grabbing the other end with her right hand to bring the fabric to her face, where she gently rubbed the feeling of silk against her cheek.

"It is absolutely fine!" Miss Sylvia responded. "Just absolutely fine! I have a lovely hat that will match it perfectly."

"Her smile said it all," my dear, sweet uncle Gaston would always say to the young boys, and as usual, my other uncles would nod in agreement with him.

Dolice Marie and Mr. Bernard Menard were certainly pleased that these loved ones enjoyed and appreciated their gifts, and that first breakfast together lingered on and on while the family laughed with and listened to one another's family stories of childish antics and very fond memories of those that had already gone on to the other world. Wilhelm was certainly enjoying hearing all about the family antics and laughed just as jubilantly as did his best friend, Mr. Bernard Menard.

But even though talk was truly wonderful, it was already far later than the family needed it to be in order to plan and implement that first family reunion, and so everyone began to scurry and hurry to dress and then tend to their own particular set of tasks at hand.

As Miss Sylvia excused herself to open the mint shop for the day's business, Mr. Bernard Menard, Jean Pierre, Jubil, and Wilhelm proceeded to inspect the grounds of Mon Village, from one end to the other, for more modern improvements that could be made by the Menard import-export company.

Jean Pierre was truly proud to introduce the tall redheaded Canadian who had married his sister (er, cousin) to the residents of Mon Village, who welcomed him with a handshake and a broad smile. (Several residents quietly mentioned to Jean Pierre that Mr. Bernard Menard and his best friend, Wilhelm, were undoubtedly the whitest white men that they had ever seen!)

MAE could hardly wait to join them and to visit every single inch of Mon Village, and so after quickly dressing, the darling child approached her mother, with the support of the remaining children in the household, with a splendid idea. "Mommy, can we please take a walk around Mon Village, please? We could tell everyone about the family reunion as we walk around. Can we, Mommy, please?"

Dolice Marie needed no encouragement, and after reaching for a lovely white parasol to match her very feminine white-laced sundress with pale-yellow ribbons, she gathered Evelina, Kip, and all the children (that is, except for Mon Claire LaPierre, who was already sitting atop her best friend, Ti-Garçon, and accompanying the men), and everyone was off for the visit.

Jean Pierre and Jubil, along with Mr. Bernard Menard and Wilhelm, made their way through the business district of the huge Mon Village, surveying and assessing the growth as well as the many improvements that had been made with the assistance of the Menard import-export company. Jean Pierre could not help but beam with pride when the small entourage approached the buildings where those beautiful silver cups and other products of silver were being manufactured.

From the schoolhouse to all the many shops that lined the streets of the business district they traveled, meeting and shaking hands with the many residents that owned their own businesses that provided valuable merchandise to the other residents as well as to the public that still visited from the surrounding towns and left a hefty income for the owners.

Mr. Bernard Menard was especially impressed with the construction that had been done to the bank that he had suggested for all the money that had been hidden all over Mon Village. Jean Pierre had named the bank the LaPierre Bank of Mon Village, and over the years, most of the residents had become acquainted with the operation of the bank and had begun to trust that their money was indeed safe while stored in it.

But it was Miss Sylvia's mint shop, the shop that sold and provided numerous ways in which to use the abundance of that pesky mint that grew all over Mon Village, that most fascinated Mr. Bernard

Menard, and Miss Sylvia was truly pleased to give him the grand tour of her shop, complete with a complimentary bag of mint stuffed in one of Jean Pierre's beautiful silver cups for both he and Wilhelm to take home with them.

From the stables, where the men caught up with Mon Claire and Ti-Garçon, to the big house, which was now the temporary church house, it was a truly fascinating journey, even for Jean Pierre and Jubil, who made the exact same trek every single day.

Wilhelm found his favorite spot, with Mon Claire and the horses that were either owned by the residents of Mon Village, or just being boarded by citizens outside Mon Village for Jubil's veterinary services and while their owners were out of town. Mon Claire chose a gentle-natured horse for her new uncle Wilhelm, who admitted that he had never ridden a horse and needed one that would certainly stop when he said "Stop!"

Dolice Marie and her entourage, on the other hand, strolled quite leisurely throughout the residential area, holding hands with one another and gathering people with familiar faces, and some with not-so-familiar faces, along the way as she hugged each one and introduced them to her sweet daughter as they came out of their houses to greet her.

"It looked like the Pied Piper of Hamelin leading the rats into the river," Uncle Gaston would always say, and then as usual, he would laugh, making my other sweet uncles begin to do the same. Isn't that something!

But it was MAE, reminiscent, without a doubt, of the child Dolice Marie LaPierre, who enjoyed the stroll more than anyone else as she held her mother's hand while inhaling all the unfamiliar sights and sounds of the Mon Village residential area.

There were those that were older and remembered the young child Dolice Marie, and they ran from their homes to extend their arms to her for a warm hug; some even shed tears as they remembered her dear mother, Mozelle, while the younger residents who had heard all about Dolice extended their hand for a warm handshake. But all were excited to meet her offspring, Monique Aimee Elizabeth

LaPierre-Menard, and she was just as excited to meet each one of them.

"Mommy," she whispered to Dolice Marie as they walked along, "this is where I want to live when I grow up!"

Dolice Marie smiled and simply dismissed the statement as a mere childhood thought and continued the visit, even dismissing the fact that Patima agreed with her friend Lizzie that she, too, would simply love to live at Mon Village (and maybe even marry a boy from the residential area). Indeed!

For the very first time in all these years, since her passing on to be with the ancestors, Dolice Marie finally realized what her mother, Mama Mozelle, meant when she said that it was truly important to know everyone in the family—everyone in the residential area's last name was LaPierre, with the exception of a few, when the slaves were freed, that had come to the old plantation carrying their old master's surname from other plantations, which meant that in one way or another, everyone was related, everyone was family.

It had now become understandable to Dolice Marie why this subject had been extremely close to Mama Mozelle's heart; it was because she, too, had come to the LaPierre Plantation as a Castille from the Castille Plantation and was carrying that name in between her first name, Mozelle, and her new last name, LaPierre, when she passed on to the other world.

As Dolice Marie continued her trek throughout the familiar grounds of Mon Village, she found herself lost in thought about her own childhood and all the events that had led to her unbelievable new life with a husband, child, and more wealth than she could have ever deemed possible for herself. She glanced down at her sweet Aimee and wondered just how much she could know about her own mother, her family, and what Dolice Marie's life had been like before freedom came to the slaves.

She had lately become quite grateful to the child Hannah for giving some insight to her daughter but was sure that Hannah could not have given her all the details, those details that most people would have hidden away in the deep recesses of their mind. Dolice Marie suddenly smiled as she found herself near the huge magnolia tree that had often brought shade to her and her beloved Jean Pierre, that place where Mama Mozelle had fallen asleep and never woken up. She caught a tear with her fingertip and placed it on her daughter's forehead just as the child looked up.

"Why did you do that, Mommy?" she asked.

"So you'll never be without me, Aimee!" Dolice answered. "You will always remember me just as I have always remembered my own Mama Mozelle."

By the time Dolice Marie and Mr. Bernard Menard returned to Jean Pierre's and Evelina's house, it was truly obvious that both were on a mission—Dolice to create a perfect family reunion, and her beloved husband to secure the items necessary to bring Mon Village up to par with the latest inventions. (Mr. Bernard Menard mentioned to Jean Pierre that he had recently heard talk about a motorized carriage in the making that would retire that old horse and buggy. He was sure that Mon Village could use at least one.) But for now, it was time to get to work since time was quickly passing by.

It was agreed upon by Dolice Marie and Jean Pierre that the LaPierre family reunion would have to most assuredly be held the day after the very next day, and throughout the entirety of Mon Village, from the residential area, where everyone lived, and the business area, where almost everyone worked, to the big house, where all the food would be prepared and everyone would eat, just like in those early days when the former slaves had sneaked in and eaten once the sun had gone down.

Preparation for the family reunion began almost immediately, and that meant gathering up vegetables from the vegetable gardens, readying the chicken and the beef to cook with powerful seasonings that made the eye tear and the tongue burn, the purchase of fresh crawfish from the nearby town, and of course, filling up the liquor jugs with homemade spirits and apple wine.

Even that pesky mint would have a place at the family reunion. Miss Sylvia would be in charge of just how it would be used and where it would be; after all, even that pesky mint had a place in the traditional telling of the family stories.

That first LaPierre family reunion was nothing less than phenomenal, and all my sweet old uncles agreed, at every family reunion thereafter, that every family reunion was truly based on what had happened during that very first one. Even the traditional telling of the family stories began with Dolice Marie, Jean Pierre, and those that made up the very first LaPierre family, including those that were too young to even understand what was going on.

A plan was developed by Dolice Marie and Jean Pierre, a plan that would find the older residents of Mon Village, the ones that remembered the life that was, gathered in one place, in the very center of the residential area, where Jean Pierre and Jubil would build a temporary shelter from the elements and where everyone else could sit in a shaded spot to listen to the stories about when Mon Village was known and operated as the LaPierre Plantation. Jean Pierre, Jubil, Mr. Bernard Menard, and Wilhelm would assist the older residents to the temporary shelter, led by Miss Penelope, who was still delivering babies and patching up their boo-boos.

Uncle Gaston would always point toward the outside shelter that had been delegated as the gathering place for all the family when they arrived for the family reunions, that place where dances and modern-day talent shows would be held, sometimes that blessed place where libations would be exalted to the ancestors after the Sunday services in the church house. "The shelter is important to every family reunion, and it has been reconstructed several times to make sure it is here with all generations, just as it is now." Uncle Simon always reminded the young boys of this fact at every family reunion.

Although Mama Del never, ever came out of her comfortable home, she was indeed present, standing with a very pleased Mama Mozelle and the African-with-No-Name and with all the other ancestors from the other world, invisibly giving direction to Dolice Marie and Jean Pierre about the preparations being made in honor of each and every one of them.

Uncle Clovis would always smile at this point of the stories and tell the young boys, "Music was always a big part of every family reunion, just as it is now."

And then he would begin to tap on the breakfast table with his silverware, close his eyes, and hum a festive tune that would just pop into his head at that very moment. My other uncles would begin to sway with the beat, encouraging the young boys to do the same, until everyone was swaying and clapping their hands. What a wonderful moment it always was, indeed!

Cook from the big house would do all the cooking for that first family reunion, assisted by those chubby little twins of Jean Pierre and Evelina, Petois and Pecous, who would also help her plan the menu, do all the fetching, and even help serve. My old uncles would laugh hysterically and again remind the young boys, "Cleanup is everybody's responsibility!"

When all the preparations had finally been made, with even less than twenty-four hours before the reunion was scheduled to begin, there was barely enough time to breathe, let alone enough time to have a good night's sleep, but it was also agreed upon by the entire LaPierre family, which now included the Menards and the Salmas, that sleep was truly unimportant, indeed, at least for the night before the very first family reunion.

Just as Dolice Marie began to drift off into the world of sleep, she was overcome with a heaviness in her chest, the forgotten feeling of labored breathing of a soul leaving the earth, the sad feeling that she had not felt since the loss of a loved one, and she gasped. Just as the feeling had come upon her, it began to leave, but certainly not dismissed, and she began to settle herself gently in the safe and warm arms of her beloved husband. Soon Dolice was asleep.

Chapter 26

THE FORGOTTEN AND unexpected sound of the old African drums that had been hidden away for many years began to echo throughout the entirety of Mon Village, calling its citizens to awaken and come together to celebrate their lives.

Dolice Marie leaped from her bed and sprang toward the window, peering out to see residents from all directions of Mon Village being beckoned toward the sound of the druMiss. Dolice Marie smiled as she realized that some of the older residents had actually taken it upon themselves to begin the new day with the sound of the days that were now long gone.

It was indeed a joyful moment, and everyone in Jean Pierre's and Evelina's house began to scurry to get dressed and assume his or her assigned post in the very first LaPierre family reunion. The children giggled as they shared their anticipation with one another, while the rhythmic sound of the African drums continued until everyone at Mon Village was standing, and dancing, in the center of the residential area.

Mr. Bernard Menard, along with his best friend, Wilhelm, and Dolice Marie's best friend, Kip, were simply delighted to be a part of this historic event in Mr. Bernard Menard's beloved wife's family, both overseeing the children's progress and then shooing them off to assist the adults.

Petois and Pecous, Jean Pierre's and Evelina's chubby little twins, wearing huge chef's hats, rushed off to the big house to help

Cook with the crawfish boil and to add their expertise to the rest of the menu that would be filled with Creole delicacies from the past. Even Cook had a special task during this first family reunion; she would give the history of the preparation of the foods that the early slaves consumed and that are now considered delicacies to the outside world, and overpriced as such, I might also add.

Mon Claire quickly made her way to meet Jubil at the stables, where she would help groom and decorate the horses in their finest fashion for the day, for they, too, had a history at Mon Village that would be celebrated on this day.

Labelle Jelee, Jean Pierre III, Patima, and MAE were content to walk with Dolice Marie, Evelina, Kip, Jean Pierre, Wilhelm, and Mr. Bernard Menard to the site of the reunion and to assist the older residents into the temporary shelter that had been built for them. As their small entourage reached the shelter, it became apparent just where the sound of the African drums was coming from.

All were dressed in their finest fineries, I might also add—Evelina in her beautiful, new yellow sundress; Miss Sylvia wearing her lovely silk scarf to accent her outfit for the day; Jean Pierre and Jubil wearing their handsome white shirts and manly cuff links; while Dolice Marie sported a precious pastel-blue dress with plenty of lace, a straw hat with a pastel-blue band, and a chic white parasol. Oh, but I digress for just the moment.

Several elderly men, truly African by descent, were sitting in the shelter, beating methodically on drums that were worn and torn by years and abuse, just as the men were, but the sound was as pure as it had been when these drums were first created. Even in the fragility of their later lives, these men seemed to have gained the strength that was definitely needed to drum and bring the quality and tone to this life for all to hear and never forget.

As the residents ventured closer and closer to the shelter where the drums were being played, a very elderly man that Dolice Marie remembered from her childhood as Amos LaPierre stood with the assistance of two of Miss Annabelle's ladies who had made their way from the big house to enjoy the day. The elderly man began to speak, and when he finished, another man began to speak, and then another, and as they did, the entire population of the residents of Mon Village became quiet and turned their complete attention to them as they began to tell the story of the LaPierre family, from the legend of the infamous Master and Mistress LaPierre to the beloved family that came after them, Mama Mozelle, her brother, the African-with-No-Name, who would later be named Jean Pierre, all the way to the descendants of the true master and mistress of Mon Village, Jean Pierre and Dolice Marie LaPierre.

"Mommy," MAE said as she tried to get her mother's attention, "you and Uncle Jean Pierre are famous here!"

Dolice Marie smiled with the child and assured her that she and Jean Pierre were simply part of the history that seemingly had to happen in order for everyone to have that special moment in history. MAE was satisfied with her answer and ran off to be with the other children.

The traditional telling of the family stories began at this very first family reunion, truly unexpected by either Jean Pierre or Dolice Marie, who were delighted and consumed by tears that flowed freely down their cheeks, but sharing these stories with everyone was certainly appropriate and truly quite sad, I might also add, because the memories of the older residents included their own personal walk, their story about their own lives as slaves. But then, they spoke of their own lives as freed men and women of color who owned their own now and had made a home for themselves and those that would come after them.

Some elders, even though just a very few remained, proudly shared their special memories about their true home in the villages of Africa, and there were even one or two remnants of precious African artifacts from the motherland, simple pottery cups and beautiful combs for the African hair, that the elders brought forth on this day to share with the entire population, those of the next generation who were born here in this land, truly the hybrids of the world, created right here in Mon Village, and in the many other plantations of the Deep South, by the masters and, in the case of Jean Pierre's parentage, a mistress or two. If you know what I mean!

At one point of the traditional telling of the family stories, MAE excitedly tugged at her mother's dress, her bright eyes glowing even more than ever, and when Dolice Marie bent down to listen to her, she whispered that Hannah had already shared her story about the African village where she was born, how hard it had been for her to leave her family, and how she had been brought to the plantation where she lived, here in America. Dolice Marie stared at her daughter with great sadness in her eyes, realizing that the two of them were now sharing the story of Dolice Marie's life, a story that she certainly regretted not sharing with her beloved daughter many years before. It was obvious that Mr. Bernard Menard felt his wife's pride and regret as he reached for her hand and held it close to his heart.

"But of course there were those moments that caused everyone to laugh, and even blush," my sweet uncle Gaston would say with a wink. "The forbidden stories of those bodies buried in the gardens that no one ever spoke of anymore, and the countless stories of the events at the big house! There was even a small mention of that ever-present, ever-pesky mint!"

"Mommy," MAE again whispered to her mother, "I really do want to live here when I grow up!"

Again Dolice Marie smiled as she bent down to caress her beloved daughter, but just as before, she simply dismissed the comment as the dream of a sweet child, nodding as she directed the smile toward Mr. Bernard Menard, who returned her smile and dismissed the comment as well, but this time the comment was echoed"

"Lizzie," Patima said aloud from a short distance ahead of her friend, "I want to live here too!"

The two girls giggled and, after encouraging the other children to join them, quickly ran off together, holding hands, to get a closer look at the elders in the temporary shelter, and to enjoy the family reunion while Dolice Marie, Mr. Bernard Menard simply beamed and took great pleasure in the sight of it all.

As the sound of the African drums began to diminish, the sound of the La La, the zydeco beat, began to vibrate throughout the center of the residential area, and the tears of those who were listening to the stories were soon traded in for smiles and the movement of the dance. Modern-day instruments replaced the tin tub used for a drum, the washboard was still used to scrape with two spoons, and the old squeeze-box and fiddle were replaced with brand-new ones, but the distinct sound of the zydeco was still there to enjoy, and enjoy everyone certainly did!

Both Patima and MAE, as well as Kip and Wilhelm, and Mr. Bernard Menard, were simply captivated by the excitement of it all, including taking several turns dancing with Jean Pierre and Jubil, and anybody else, for that matter, that felt like "cuttin' a rug."

There was plenty of wonderful food for everyone to eat their bellies full, the kind of food that "sticks to your ribs," as my old uncles would say as they themselves munched on their own breakfast foods. From the simple foods that were created from the leftovers of the masters' pots to the cuisines created from the fresh fruit, fresh vegetables, rice, fresh chickens, seafood, and fresh beef as well as delicious desserts created with pure sugarcane—all grown or produced right there at Mon Village! It was truly a feast!

That first family reunion went on and on well into the night, and even the youngest of the young children celebrated without tiring a bit, and when it was time to say good night for the night, everyone spent yet another hour just hugging one another, staring into one another's eyes to clearly create a picture in the mind of a relative, someone off-limits to another relative!

Mr. Bernard Menard leaned over to whisper in Jean Pierre's ear that he was quite anxious to say hello to Mama Del, whom, it appeared, no one had made any effort to invite to the family reunion. The kindly Canadian gentleman had become intrigued with the Mon Village matron when his beloved Aimee was born and was brought to Mama Del for the secret ceremony that was held directly after the children of Mon Village were born. Mr. Bernard Menard had expected to certainly see her at some point during the family celebration. "She would never have attended anyway," Jean Pierre answered. "Mama Del likes to be alone, but we can always stop by her house on the way home to say hello, and perhaps even bring a plate of food. She is very picky about her company, but I am sure she would just love to see you."

And that they did, a short visit to Mama Del's house with a plate piled high with a taste of virtually everything that had "hit the spot" with everyone that had attended that first family reunion. And yes, Mama Del was happy, indeed, to see Mr. Bernard Menard and even asked about his little girl, Monique Aimee Elizabeth LaPierre-Menard, and, of course, his beautiful wife, her sweet Dolice Marie.

"We are all just fine," Mr. Bernard Menard answered. "Just fine, indeed."

Just before bidding each other farewell, Mama Del reached into her bag of goodies and created a charm that would tell his fortune when the contents of the bag were thrown on the table. Mama Del laughed that eerie laugh of hers and, after a suck on her corncob pipe that still hung between her missing front teeth, described a journey that he and his wife, her sweet Dolice Marie, would be taking on a cruise ship sometime in the future. Mr. Bernard Menard laughed with delight with the old woman and, after thanking her profusely, walked out of the old Greis Greis's house and preceded to join the rest of the family.

"A journey on a cruise ship," Mr. Bernard Menard repeated. "How wonderful! I cannot wait to tell Madam Menard!"

"But what did that truly mean?" Uncle Gaston would ask the young boys as he scanned their eyes, one boy after another, who all stared back at him with absolutely no idea at all what it meant, and neither did Mr. Bernard Menard, I might also add.

As the LaPierre-Menard family, with Wilhelm, Kip, and Patima Salma in tow, slowly made their way back to Jean Pierre's and Evelina's home in the residential area of Mon Village, deeply touched by the celebration of family, MAE felt a strong tug at the tail of her beautiful dress. Slowly turning around, she discovered a small gold-colored puppy with big floppy ears playing tug-of-war with her dress, and she began to giggle, spinning around and around as she tried to capture it, causing everyone to follow her around and around in a circle in an attempt to try to capture the happy little dog as well.

"Stand still, Aimee," Mr. Bernard Menard said lovingly. "He will stop turning around and around if we all stand still, then one of us can grab him."

"Oh, please do not hurt it, Father," MAE said.

"Never, beloved," he said, chuckling. "I sort of like it too!"

Sure enough, when MAE stood still, the little gold-colored puppy continued his fascination with her dress but stood in one place, playing his tug-of-war game, and therefore allowed Mr. Bernard Menard to gently pick it up, remove the dress from its sharp teeth, and cuddle it against his own neck. Once the little puppy had finally settled down, Mr. Bernard Menard put it in his daughter's waiting, outstretched arMiss.

"Please, Father, can we keep it?"

It was most obvious that the kindly Mr. Bernard Menard had already fallen prey to his beautiful little daughter and the little gold-colored puppy with the big floppy ears as well and was already finding it difficult to say no, and after receiving absolutely no help from his beloved wife, Dolice Marie, the poor man found himself the proud owner of a feisty, sharp-toothed, gold-colored puppy with big floppy ears. And when the puppy was caught chewing, quite vigorously, I might also add, on a sweet piece of sugarcane in Evelina's kitchen that night, MAE giggled again and informed her family that the puppy would forever be known as Sugar—how appropriate, since it was a little girl puppy, indeed!

That night, after Dolice Marie and Mr. Bernard Menard reviewed the activities of the very first family reunion, Dolice Marie again felt the strong feeling of a labored breath from a soul leaving the earth and, after catching her own breath, informed Mr. Bernard Menard that it was truly time to leave Mon Village and travel toward home. But first, there needed to be a short visit to the great city of New Orleans.

Chapter 27

At the Declouette Mansion, where the beloved Miss BB remained the same, peacefully and quietly lying on her bed with her eyes closed, her breathing shallow, and now surrounded by her entire household staff, all the lovely ladies of the New Orleans House, and even a few of the neighbors that had stopped by after having seen Dr. Latolais coming to and leaving the Declouette Mansion, it became apparent that these were the final days for their beloved friend and loved one.

Shirley, one of the lovely ladies of the New Orleans House, and the apple of Obadiah's eyes, had inched herself closer and closer to him, to comfort him, and in her own need for comfort. "Oh, chère," she said sadly in his ear, "we will face this together."

Ever the proper gentleman, Obadiah simply nodded in agreement while keeping his eyes directed at the lady lying in the bed. Quite discreetly, Obadiah extended his hand toward Shirley, who placed her own hand in his, and the two intertwined their fingers together. It was apparent, at this somber moment, that they had committed themselves, one to the other.

Moments later, following the instructions from Dr. Latolais to begin to make the arrangements as soon as possible, Angeline and Obadiah forced themselves to approach the armoire in the corner of Miss BB's room to begin the heartbreaking search for the arrangements that the dear lady had already made for herself when that sad time would finally come. Both spied the same stack of papers on one of the shelves of the armoire, delicately tied together with a satin ribbon, probably one that Miss BB had once upon a time used for her own hair. Both hesitated, seemingly waiting for the other one to seize the stack of papers, but eventually, both reached out and took the papers in their possession, Obadiah relinquishing his hold as the two walked from the room that was now dimly lit and where the sobs were now constant.

Angeline and Obadiah entered one of the beautiful parlors of the Declouette Mansion and sadly sat down together on a divan in front of a large window to review the written arrangements made by the lovely Miss BB on the occasion of her passing on to the other world.

"Certainly, Aunt BB has planned a solemn Catholic Requiem Mass," Angeline said as she leafed through the pages of the stack that had been taken from the armoire. "Yes," she continued. "Here is the request for a Mass at the cathedral in the French Quarter—oh, to be celebrated by the same Jesuit priest that married Dolice Marie and Bernard!"

"That does not surprise me at all," Obadiah added quietly. "She knows everybody in the entire city!"

"Oh!" Angeline said and suddenly began to cry, dabbing her eyes with a small handkerchief that she pulled from the sleeve of her dress. "Here is the order for the casket, already paid to Ardoin Brothers Funeral Horne."

Both began to weep, clinging onto each other for a brief moment before coming back to the reality that this business needed to be completed as quickly as possible and that there would be plenty of time to mourn at a later time. Angeline wiped her eyes again with the small handkerchief and then pulled another document from the stack of papers and began to read.

"Mrs. Beatrice Carson Declouette, formerly Beatrice Adeline Carson, of Savannah, Georgia, known as Miss BB by her friends, family, and..."

"Well," Uncle Gaston would always say, "it looks as though Miss BB had even written her own obituary for the local newspaper."

MINT JULEP

The obituary for the local newspaper in the great city of New Orleans also listed Miss BB's next of kin as "Angeline Toussaint-Marie, her niece from Paris, France; her son and faithful companion, Obadiah; and her niece from the Bayou Frou-Frous, Dolice Marie LaPierre-Menard."

The autobiographical obituary continued with the mention of her beloved father, Harrison Carson, and Monsieur Daniel Declouette, her husband, described by Miss BB as "my one true love." Miss BB even mentioned her furry babies, FiFi and GiGi, as her only children, her dearly loved members of the family.

There were several receipts for flowers, lovely calla lilies, to be exact, instructions for the Declouette cook describing what foods should be served at the Declouette Mansion after the funeral, several suggestions for the dress she had chosen to be buried in (the final choice to be decided between Angeline and Dolice when the proper time came), and finally, another document that was sealed in a separate envelope; the writing on the outside the envelope read, "Will: not to be opened by anyone other than my attorney, Patrick LeDeau, upon the occasion of my death."

Angeline put the envelope aside, stating that she would be sure to give it to Miss BB's attorney as soon as possible, while Obadiah agreed, assuring her that he would be ready to fetch the funeral director with the carriage whenever that time came.

On the other side of the mighty Mississippi River, on the front porch of Jean Pierre's and Evelina's house, stood solemnly the Menard and LaPierre families with their friend Wilhelm, along with Kip and Patima of the Salma family, all sobbing uncontrollably in a heart-rending scene that my sweet old uncles simply described as "sad, just so very sad."

From the adults to the children and the feisty little pooch, Sugar, saying goodbye was indeed a memorable, poignant recollection.

Each and every time those dear old men shared this portion of the traditional telling of the family stories, it became obvious that they, too, were genuinely brokenhearted for the families on the porch and all that they were about to experience just down the railroad track in the great city of New Orleans.

Jean Pierre tenderly handed a box filled with his signature silver cups to his beloved Dolice Marie, who accepted the box in her trembling hands and held it tightly to her chest as if she were holding on for dear life.

"Come to New York," Dolice Marie whispered in Jean Pierre's ear as she reached to hug him with one arm and then sobbed deeply from within her heart. "Please, Jean Pierre, promise me that you and Evelina will take the children to New York!"

"I promise," Jean Pierre answered as he hugged her even tighter. "We will plan a journey."

There were great cheers of approval from the children standing on the front porch of Jean Pierre and Evelina's house, cheers that soon gave way to tears as everyone noticed the familiar, fancy LaPierre carriage approaching, which would soon separate them until their own journey to the great state of New York became a reality.

A teary-eyed Jubil, with his beloved wife, Miss Sylvia, signaled the horse pulling the fancy LaPierre carriage to halt in front of the house. Jubil wiped his eyes before he jumped down from the top seat to join his own sorrow with that of the others.

After several moments of hugs and promises to be together again soon, and this time in the great state of New York, the Menards, including the feisty little puppy Sugar, along with Patima and Kip Salma, walked down the stairs from Jean Pierre's and Evelina's porch and proceeded into the fancy LaPierre carriage, while Wilhelm chose to stay behind on the porch to privately share his goodbyes with his new friends, thanking them for their kindness and reiterating the invitation to plan a journey to New York and, even farther, to plan a journey to Canada. He hugged Jean Pierre and Evelina tightly, gave smiles and hugs to the children, and then joined Jubil on the top bench seat of the fancy LaPierre carriage to begin the somber journey toward the Atchafalaya River station.

Nestled in the loving arms of her husband, Mr. Bernard Menard, Dolice Marie again felt the labored breath of a soul leaving the earth and fought hard to catch her own as she realized that the trip to the great city of New Orleans could certainly not be quick enough.

The journey was somber, indeed, and even the sight of the mighty Mississippi as it rolled in the opposite direction of the train barely caught the attention of the young woman who had always been mesmerized by the very sight of its awesome splendor. However, MAE and her best friend, Patima, were overjoyed and could barely catch their breath.

"Oh, Lizzie!" Patima squealed. "I really want to live here!"

"I do, too," MAE answered with her nose pressed against the window of the train. "I do too!"

The Big Easy

Mr. Bernard Menard stepped onto the street adjacent to the train station in the great city of New Orleans, smack-dab in the midst of a ferocious rainstorm, to hail a carriage to drive him, his family, and his friends that were accompanying them directly to the Declouette Mansion. When a city carriage finally did stop, an amalgamation of people of all different colors, ages, cultures, and even species piled inside the city carriage with their train cases before the driver could object to anyone (or any furry little puppy) in particular.

"Good day," Mr. Bernard Menard said as he flashed that charming and debonair smile of his, tipping his hat after hopping aboard the top seat of the city carriage before the driver could object, seating himself directly beside the driver.

"Bloody weather, I say," he continued talking with the driver while pulling at his coat and hat to shield himself from the storm beneath the cover directly above the top seat of the carriage. The driver simply looked straight ahead, even as he asked for directions.

"And where are you *all* going today?" he asked in a sarcastic and distinct Southern drawl.

"To the Declouette Mansion, please, not far from the river," Mr. Bernard Menard answered nonchalantly with his usual friendly flair, certainly and apparently not giving in to the driver's arrogance, and certainly not to his insularity. "I am certain that you know exactly where that is, sir."

The driver clicked his teeth and jiggled the rein to signal the horse that it was time to move, and move the city carriage it did, quite quickly, I might also add, so much so that the passengers inside were tossed around, back and forth, then up and down, and finally landed upon one another when the city carriage came to a sudden stop at its required location. All the while, MAE clung steadily to her new friend, Sugar, who was barking and growling quite loudly, and with her lifelong friend, Patima, the two giggling uncontrollably throughout the whole ordeal.

Mr. Bernard Menard hopped down from the top seat of the city carriage and quickly opened the door to climb in to attend to those inside that were well shaken. Wilhelm jumped out first to assist his best friend, Mr. Bernard Menard, now drenched from the rain, assist the passengers (including the furry little Sugar) from the city carriage, and direct them to scurry to the front porch of the Declouette Mansion, where they would be safe from the torrential downpour.

Dolice Marie was the final passenger to exit the city carriage, but instead of following the lead of those who were now standing on the front porch of the Declouette Mansion, being sheltered from the rain, she opened her parasol, adjusted her fancy traveling hat, walked around the city carriage to the front, where she was completely visible to the driver, smacked the horse with all her might on his backside to make him rear, and when he did, the driver popped up high in the air and fell to the ground at the feet of Mr. Bernard Menard and his beautiful wife, the feisty petite Dolice Marie, who still remembered how to exact a modest retribution when a situation required it.

"Oh, pardon mois!" she insisted, and quite sweetly, I might also add, as she leaned down through the pouring rain to assist the city driver to his feet.

"I would say that it was the lightning that spooked your horse, sir," Mr. Bernard Menard retorted, raising an eyebrow as he peered down at the man stretched out on the wet ground in the pouring rain.

Dolice Marie extended her hand toward the city carriage driver as Mr. Bernard Menard reached into his pocket for money to pay him, and after some obvious reservation, the man unwillingly met her hand with his own. For a brief moment, Dolice Marie contemplated hitting the horse again to make him stir and to drag the evil man all around the great city of New Orleans, but she thought again.

"I have learned many things, monsieur," Dolice Marie began while staring deep into the man's eyes, still holding the city carriage driver's hand, with him still on the wet ground in the pouring rain. "I have learned so many things since I have been living in my new home in New York, especially that I should treat people the way that I want to be treated. Well, it is obvious that you will never treat me good, the way I deserve to be treated, and knowing that, I have allowed myself to be bitter. And so now, monsieur, we are even. I apologize to you for being bitter about what you did to me and to my family in this carriage. When I help you to get up off this wet ground, and I mostly will, I feel I can expect an apology from you as well, and then we can start all over again."

Perhaps it was Dolice Marie's sincerity, or perhaps it was the fact that Mr. Bernard Menard was standing behind her, ready to...

"Give the city carriage driver the kind of justice he really needed!" my uncle Alexandre would always interrupt to say to the young boys, and he also balled up his fist and bashed it into the palm of his other hand at this point of the stories.

Well, whatever the reason was, truly, the city carriage driver allowed the tug of Dolice's hand to assist him to get off the wet ground, and when he did, he apologized.

Preparation

By the time the two adult Menards reached the porch of the Declouette Mansion, a distraught Angeline was standing in the doorway, completely overcome with tears, while Obadiah and the grieving ladies of the New Orleans House attended to Wilhelm, Kip, and the children, who were completely drenched from the rainstorm. As Dolice Marie reached for Angeline, she, too, became overcome with tears.

"I knew you would know to come, I knew it in my heart," Angeline was able to finally say as she gasped through her tears.

"I have missed you so much, Angeline!" Dolice Marie responded as the two remained in each other's arms for what seemed as long as they had been apart. "Where is she?"

The two best friends held on to each other for physical as well as emotional support while Angeline led the way up the stairs and to the bedroom where Miss BB was breathing short, deep breaths with a whistling sound as she breathed inward. Dolice Marie knelt down beside the bed and gently reached for Miss BB's hand, which she kissed numerous times as her tears fell upon the dear woman's flesh, just like the torrential rainfall from which she had just escaped.

"Please, Angeline, you must tell Obadiah and the household staff, and all the ladies, to come quickly to say their goodbyes," Dolice whispered, "and please ask Monsieur Bernard Menard to come also, and please ask him to bring Aimee."

Angeline quickly left the bedroom and headed toward the parlor, where she relayed the message to Obadiah, Miss BB's household staff, Mr. Bernard Menard, and the lovely ladies of the New Orleans House. All quietly and quickly made the trek up the stairs to the bedroom where Miss BB was lying almost lifeless, all surrounding the bed from the headboard on one side to the headboard on the other side, and all sadly preparing themselves to bid their farewells.

My dear Uncle Gaston never hesitated to ask the young boys if they thought Miss BB had been waiting for Dolice Marie to arrive, to be with her just one more time before the sweet lady surrendered her spirit to the other world, and then without even waiting for their response, he would give them his own answer. "Well, she most definitely had been waiting for Dolice Marie," he would say with exaggerated animation, waving his hands in the air and searching their eyes from one to the other, and of course my other uncles would agree without hesitation.

"Miss BB opened her eyes the very moment she felt Dolice Marie's tears fall softly on her hand," he would continue. "But just long enough to gaze into the eyes of those of her loved ones, but just for a moment, and then a moment later, she slowly released a very long breath as her spirit escaped to the other world."

MINT JULEP

My uncles would pause for a few short moments while they bowed their heads in respect before they continued with the traditional telling of the family stories.

"Miss BB was not a blood relative," Uncle Gaston would say, "but sometimes family crosses all lines, even blood, and that was exactly what the relationship between Dolice Marie, Angeline, and Miss BB had always been, across all lines to be family."

But now Miss BB was gone. Mr. Bernard Menard wrapped his beloved wife and daughter gently in his arMiss.

"Mommy," MAE whispered as she looked up to her mother's sad face, "why is everyone crying?"

"Because someone we love very much has passed on to the other world," she forced herself to reply as she bent down to come eye to eye with her beloved Aimee.

"But Hannah said that when we die, we meet our ancestors and become happy like we have never been before!"

"And she is absolutely right, Aimee," Dolice Marie replied, wrapping her arms around her daughter. "We are sad because she will not be with us for now."

The sobs and screams of great sorrow from the bedroom rose to unbelievable heights as grief overcame everyone standing around Miss BB, who now lay lifeless, with an expression of great peace upon her face. But just as quickly as the sounds echoed from the master bedroom of the Declouette Mansion, they suddenly diminished and were overcome by the sounds of a sad and heart-penetrating gospel song that was being sung, and hummed, by the lovely ladies of the New Orleans House.

But once the singing had ended, Dolice Marie, Angeline, and Obadiah knew that the task at hand was now more important than their own personal loss and grief, for which there would be plenty of time, once their dearly loved Miss BB was laid to rest.

Obadiah hurried to the office of the coroner for the great city of New Orleans and informed him that Miss BB's lifeless body was ready to be transported to the Ardoin Funeral Home, according to her own prepared wishes. It was a very sad task, indeed, and Obadiah fought hard not to completely fall apart prior to its completion.

Once Obadiah returned to the Declouette Mansion, he joined Angeline and Dolice as they searched through the plans that had already been made by the sweet lady herself and agreed that the funeral should be held as soon as possible, for more reasons than one, the first being that the Menards of New York needed to return to their home because of Mr. Bernard Menard's import-export business, Wilhelm needed to return to Toronto because of his law practice, and of course, MAE and her best friend, Patima Salma, were due back to school.

"Monsieur Wilhelm, I have not had one moment to welcome you to New Orleans," Angeline said to Wilhelm as she wiped away her tears and brushed back her hair with her hand. She forced a smile and gave her hand to him. He accepted her hand with his own and politely kissed it.

"I am so very sorry for the loss of your aunt," Wilhelm replied. "I have heard so much about her from Bernard and Dolice Marie, who loved her as well. But please think nothing of such formalities at this time," he continued. "If I can be of any help at all, please let me know. I do, however, hope that you and I will have some time to talk before we must leave."

"I would like that," Angeline responded and excused herself to begin scribbling the words to a message that would be wired to several friends that lived outside the great city of New Orleans but, who most assuredly, needed to be informed that Miss BB would very soon be laid to rest, old friends that had once or twice joined her for a spirited bal masque in the Declouette Mansion, or one that shared a quiet sip of smooth Kentucky bourbon on the back porch of the Declouette Mansion to toast a budding friendship—all needed to know.

"Please send this message as soon as possible to Mr. Monte Leonard of Kentucky," Angeline instructed Obadiah. "You know how much she enjoyed his company on the back porch."

Mr. Bernard Menard volunteered to accompany Obadiah to the local train station, where the wires would be sent to MIS BB's friends, even though the final arrangements would not be made until the following day. Certainly there would be plenty of rooms available for those who chose to come to the Declouette Mansion and share their grief before the funeral.

And as the New Orleans sky began to give way to nightfall, it became obvious to those that were now in charge of assuring that Miss BB's final wishes were honored that their work would begin again in the morning, when the New Orleans sky welcomed the sun of a new day and the businesses that needed to be contacted would be opened.

No one was able to sleep that night, and eventually, everyone found themselves meeting downstairs in the main parlor to simply share their fondest memories of Miss BB or to just simply grieve until it was time to get dressed and begin the sad task that was ahead of them.

As the day began to break in the great city of New Orleans, the Menard child and her best friend, Patima, both being led by Kip, found their way downstairs, where the adults were sitting together with eyes puffed and red, apparently having been awake and crying throughout the entire night. Angeline was the first to notice the two children as they approached Dolice Marie, who had both arms stretched out to greet them.

"Good morning," Dolice Marie said, hugging both of the girls at one time. But before she could introduce the three of them to Angeline, MAE continued toward Angeline.

"Are you my aunt Angeline?" she asked quite sweetly, to Angeline's great surprise.

"Why, yes, I am, you beautiful little girl," Angeline responded, and even before MAE could introduce her aunt to her best friend, Angeline reached out to hug the Menard child. "We did not have the opportunity to be introduced yesterday. I am so very happy to finally meet you."

"This is Monique Aimee Elizabeth LaPierre-Menard," Dolice Marie said proudly, "but Monsieur Menard and I call her Aimee."

"You are so very beautiful, little one," Angeline responded as she hugged MAE again, swelling again with tears of great sadness.

"And such a…long…but beautiful…name as well!" she added.

"I call her Lizzie," Patima chimed in.

"Then I shall have to find my own small name for her as well," Angeline replied, forcing herself to smile just a little. "Perhaps I shall simply call you Monique. What do you think?"

"Oh, I would like that," the Menard child answered. "I love all my special names!"

This would be the very first time that Angeline actually had the pleasure of meeting the Menard child that had been born in Mon Village but was whisked away to Upstate New York without a trip to the great city of New Orleans. Needless to say, Angeline was quite moved at the sight of her dear "niece," and even during the introductions of Kip and Patima to everyone in the Declouette Mansion, Angeline continued to smile and, I might also add, keep her eyes on her sweet Monique, quite taken by the beautiful little girl with the long golden-brown hair and hazel-green eyes.

Unfortunately, the first meeting between the two would be interrupted when the reality of the day became first and foremost for the adults in the parlor of the Declouette Mansion. Hurrying after freshening up, Angeline, Dolice Marie, Obadiah, and Mr. Bernard Menard met back downstairs in the parlor, Angeline with the clothing that Miss BB had chosen for her funeral, Obadiah with the receipts for the flowers and the casket, the will for the attorney, and the obituary for the newspaper, all those places that would be visited by them this, the day after Miss BB's passing.

Angeline and Dolice Marie quickly climbed into the fancy Declouette carriage, while Obadiah and Mr. Bernard Menard had already climbed atop the carriage onto the driver's bench. The day was just as gloomy and somber after the torrential rains the day and night before as these grieving people were, adding even more sadness to the current situation at hand.

Wilhelm and Kip volunteered, of course, to stay with the girls to assist Miss BB's household staff and the lovely ladies of the New Orleans with preparations and to greet people as they began to arrive.

The first stop on the agenda was the funeral home, to view the casket and to drop off the clothing that the body of Miss BB would wear. After several minutes of discussion, it was decided that the wake should be held beginning the following morning, throughout the night, and until the funeral began, which would be the day following that next day, in order to accommodate those visitors that would surely be coming to the Declouette Mansion from outside the great city of New Orleans.

The funeral director volunteered to contact Miss BB's priest to have him officiate at the solemn Catholic Requiem Mass, which would be held at the cathedral, and to deliver a homily on behalf of her family and friends.

With that task sadly completed, it was on to the local newspaper office, with the obituary that Miss BB had handwritten for herself, to have the date and time of the funeral listed in the very next edition to ensure the locals the opportunity to attend the funeral as well.

Next, on to the florist shop, where lovely calla lilies had already been paid for and simply waited for the day when they would adorn the funeral of one of the shop's favorite customers.

"They will be delivered to the funeral home before evening," the florist said sadly as she patted her chest softly. "Miss BB was certainly one of our favorite customers, and she will surely be missed."

The final stop was at the office of Patrick LeDeau, Miss BB's faithful attorney, where Mr. Bernard Menard hopped down from the driver's bench of the Declouette carriage to enter the front door. Moments later, he emerged and reclaimed his seat next to Obadiah and exclaimed quite softly, "The reading of the will has been scheduled for one hour after the funeral and burial, at the Declouette Mansion, my dear Obadiah."

"Very good, sir," Obadiah responded, looking straight ahead in a failed attempt to keep his tears inside his eyes and not let them drop down his sad face.

The quiet journey back to the Declouette Mansion allowed everyone their own realization of just how tired each one was and how very much each desperately needed to rest before people began to arrive to pay their respects. The small group of four was met at the entrance by Miss BB's staff, still performing their own duties with their puffy red eyes and holding on to their handkerchiefs to dab their runny noses. Angeline, Obadiah, Dolice Marie, and Mr. Bernard Menard found Wilhelm, Kip, and the two girls in the kitchen with Cook, who was preparing lunch while catching her own tears in her apron.

"Mommy," MAE said as she hugged her mother and father. "Is there anything that Patima and I can do to help you? We've been in the kitchen with Cook, helping her to prepare the foods, and we will help serve everything after the funeral, but if you need us…"

Dolice Marie was quick to answer that after lunch she would be taking a short nap to prepare for the events and people that were to come. Angeline did have a great suggestion that gave the girls something to look forward to during these strained times. "You can help me and Obadiah as well," she said, "but only after we, too, take a short nap. I would love to spend some time with you before you and your family must leave to go back home to New York."

Hugs were exchanged with Cook as well while she began to serve deep bowls of steamed rice with shrimp étouffée piled high, which Kip found to be quite tasty.

"Filipinos eat plenty of rice as well as seafood," Kip explained, "but this red gravy with the shrimp is especially delicious. Perhaps you can give me the recipe for this dish to bring home with me."

The short verbal exchange gave a break to the grieving cook and those that were seated together in her kitchen, but it would soon be apparent that rest was a necessary commodity that was taking over mind and body.

As Angeline and Obadiah, along with Mr. Bernard Menard and Dolice Marie, found themselves heading off in different directions toward their respective bedrooms, Wilhelm and Angeline spontaneously locked eyes with each other. Although the temptation to share yet more of these moments together was overwhelming, both gave way to Angeline's complete exhaustion and the current set of circumstances but again reiterated the desire to share some time together when the time was appropriate.

The news quickly spread by the words of the obituary in the local newspaper and by word of mouth throughout the great city of New Orleans and throughout those places that had been informed by wire that Miss BB was now with her ancestors.

MINT JULEP

Word of the great lady's demise quickly reached an exhausted Mr. Monte Leonard of the noble Commonwealth of Kentucky, who was sitting alone on the front porch of his own home, after a long day of work, with a flask filled with smooth Kentucky bourbon, when the wire arrived. In the midst of his preparation for a quick journey to the great state of Louisiana, particularly the great city of New Orleans, Monte Leonard allowed his mind to wander back to his friendship with the beloved Miss BB and voluntarily allowed his tears to flow freely down his cheeks.

Within just a few hours, Monte Leonard was atop his horse and following the path that had been created by his friend, Jubil, who had dropped pieces of the wretched mint to remember his way home when he was working with the horses in the noble Commonwealth of Kentucky. Jubil's actions resulted in bush after bush after bush of that pesky mint lining either side of the path to and from Monte Leonard's house and served as a quiet reminder of one of his favorite people in the entire world, Jubilation LaPierre, who was still, at the time of Miss BB's passing, traveling back and forth himself.

Monte Leonard knew that he might not make the long journey in time to share time with Miss BB at the wake, but he was truly determined to be there before the funeral ended, whenever that would be.

Within hours, local residents began to arrive at the Declouette Mansion, bringing with them their deepest regrets—flowers and trays of delicious foods to feed the masses that were expected prior to the funeral. Messengers were coming and going to the Declouette Mansion, delivering wires in response to those that had been sent to friends outside the local area of the great city of New Orleans, some confirming their arrival and others offering their condolences and their apologies for being unable to attend.

All the activity became much too much for the household staff of the Declouette Manor, and thus it became quite necessary to interrupt Angeline, Obadiah, and the Menards as they attempted to rest for just a little while.

Obadiah was the first to be awakened by the clatter and, after quickly dressing, joined the household staff and assumed his role as the master of organization, meeting, greeting, and directing the people and things that were now descending upon the Declouette Mansion. Angeline, who had found it rather difficult, indeed, to rest at all as the visions of her beloved aunt continued to creep in and out of her mind, soon joined Obadiah.

The lovely ladies of the New Orleans House that had stayed the night at the Declouette Mansion prepared to return to their dwelling by carriages driven by members of the Declouette staff to prepare for the long wake at the funeral home. Everyone and everything began to move along like a well-oiled machine, an abundance of action with very few words being spoken by anyone.

In the meantime, on the other side of the great city of New Orleans, at the Ardoin Funeral Horne, the funeral director and his staff were busily preparing Miss BB's body in time for the wake that would begin in just a few hours, dressing the body in the dress chosen by Angeline from Miss BB's chosen two, an ivory silk long-sleeved dress covered in ivory lace, gathered high at the neck with a pearl button, and gathered at the waistline, allowing the material to fall in delicate pleats to the ankle. High-buttoned shoes were covered by the hem of the dress, and even though the casket would cover that area of the body, Angeline had insisted that Miss BB would have wanted to be completely dressed on this day as she would have been if she were about to take her sweet babies, FiFi and GiGi, for a walk throughout the neighborhood.

Both hands were dressed in lovely ivory lace gloves and crossed just at the chest, her favorite everyday rosary intertwined throughout her fingers and the crucifix at the end allowed to fall from the hands, with the figure of Jesus facing the spectator.

Miss BB's hair was gently tucked under a lovely wide-brimmed hat, covered in rolls of silk, with delicate violets hemmed between the silk pleats that coordinated quite nicely with the lining of the casket. Wisps of her hair softly framed her face down to her closed eyes and just over the pearl button earrings that adorned her ears, while a very light blush gave a final color to her cheeks, and a dab of her favorite lipstick created a charming replica of the dear lady when she was alive.

Once the preliminaries had all been complete, Miss BB's body was placed in the casket and rolled into one of the family rooms in the funeral home, where family, friends, and neighbors would be able to pay their final respects.

A barrage of flowers from family, friends, and neighbors had already been delivered to the funeral home and placed affectionately in the family room, just waiting for someone to admire them, and the wait was not very long. And yes, people began to arrive; in fact, they began to arrive almost immediately after Miss BB's body was placed in the family room, even before the scheduled wake was to begin.

"I know over half the city of New Orleans came to pay their respects to Miss BB and to her life," my uncle Simon would always sadly add.

Also arriving at the Ardoin Funeral Home were the reporters from the local newspaper, fully prepared to find some really juicy gossip throughout the proceedings, but they found themselves saddened as well and connecting with the demise of the dear one being honored.

The Menards of New York were now awakened by the sounds and smells of the Declouette Mansion on this day of mourning and, as with everyone else, quickly dressed themselves and made their way downstairs to the parlor, where they were truly surprised to see the number of people that had already arrived. Just the sight of so many people, in the midst of such a sad day, I might also add, again caused Dolice Marie to break down in tears.

"You look so tired, my sweet sister," Angeline said as she hugged Dolice Marie. "Why not rest some more and meet us at the funeral home later?"

"No," Dolice Marie answered. "She would have wanted us to be there with her, all of us."

Within the span of just a couple of hours, the Menards, along with Angeline and Obadiah, had boarded one of the Declouette carriages and led the long cavalcade of carriages to the Ardoin Funeral Home on the other side of the great city of New Orleans. Kip was very happy to stay at the Declouette Mansion with Patima and MAE, because she was convinced that children should not be exposed to such things, she had said to Dolice. "Besides, you and Bernard should have your time to grieve without scaring your Aimee and Patima with such great sadness."

Dolice Marie and Mr. Bernard Menard agreed and bade their loving goodbyes to their daughter, assuring her that they would be back in her presence as soon as the funeral was over.

Wilhelm, too, had volunteered to remain at the Declouette Mansion with Kip to serve in the capacity of the household staff as they, too, attended Miss BB's final goodbyes.

Chapter 28

As everyone sadly traveled the route from the Declouette Mansion to the funeral home, Wilhelm fought his overpowering feelings for the grief-stricken Angeline and tried desperately to distract his sudden feelings until another, more appropriate time came. The household staff had been extremely happy to have Wilhelm's assistance while MAE and Patima giggled at all the ladies of the New Orleans House while each of them put on their very best show to gain his attention. Shameful!

In the meantime, Angeline fought the feelings as well that she was beginning to feel erupting inside herself for Wilhelm, while all the while questioning why Henri de Marquis had never again tried to contact her throughout all these years.

Perhaps he is dead, she thought to herself. After all, he was much older than she was.

As the carriage rode along the streets of that great city of New Orleans, Angeline questioned herself, wondering why no one had actually pursued her with a vengeance to woo her; not at Miss BB's house, or the New Orleans House, had anyone even so much as commented about her fancy dancing or anything about her personage. She shook her head to bring her back to this moment, that moment that truly belonged to Miss BB and no one else.

The Funeral

People were lined up all the way around the corner in every direction of the Ardoin Funeral Horne, all dressed in their greatest fineries, and most clutching a handkerchief to catch their tears. All were silent, some carrying flowers, but not one was complaining about the wait, I might also add.

"Miss BB would have certainly been grateful and just a tad surprised with all the falderal!" my uncle Simon would always add, and of course, my sweet uncles would nod in agreement.

Obadiah led the way to the door, where the family would be welcomed in, and, once inside, drew in a very deep breath before continuing to lead the others to the room where Miss BB's body lay peacefully, actually appearing to be waiting for her company to come and sit with her on her front porch.

"Angeline!" Dolice Marie declared excitedly after peering inside the casket. "Miss BB is dressed just the way she was dressed on my wedding day, the day the photograph was taken of all of us. Do you remember?"

"I do, and that is why she is dressed the way she is," Angeline replied with a forced smile. "We will never forget the way she looks right now, because we have the photograph of her on one of the happiest days she ever had."

After saying their final goodbyes to Miss BB, the family took its place in the reserved seats in front of the room, near the casket, where they each received hugs and thought-filled commiseration from those coming in and out of the room, also saying their final goodbyes. For the family, emotions ran high and low as they recognized neighbors, friends, and a few former customers of the New Orleans House—ah-hem!

The lines of people continued to come and go throughout the night, and when it became apparent that the lines contained fewer people and people came less often, the family said a final, quiet prayer together, proceeded together past the casket one final time, and then escaped through the family door from which they had entered. The journey to the various places called home was extremely quiet as well, as each person came to the same conclusion in their own private way that Miss BB was truly gone.

The hours flew by, and day emerged over the great city of New Orleans, and just as quickly as the family and friends of Miss BB had given way to sleep, the sun beamed brightly to quickly awaken them to the new day and to the current circumstances at hand. It was an extremely quiet and somber journey to the cathedral in the French Quarter of the great city of New Orleans, with carriage after carriage leading the way and groups of people walking on the streets, heading in the same direction.

The family of Miss BB had already been seated in the front rows of the cathedral on either side of the casket that sat elongated in the center aisle, one end pointing toward the altar, and the other toward the front door. Grief had given way to final acceptance as well as that peace that passes all human understanding; it was now over and time now to celebrate the life of everyone's beloved Miss BB.

The solemn Requiem Mass began and continued as it should have, with Miss BB's priest leading the celebration of life, while family, friends, and neighbors quietly expressed their grief in their own particular manner.

In his homily, the priest spoke of Miss BB's generous donations to the church and the church community, to the people outside the church that were searching for their way back, or those that needed just a "lift" in their lives to get started again.

"She was always there, with a ready smile, a listening ear, and a purse that never seemed to empty when it came to her fellow man."

Of course, the priest also spoke dearly of her humorous nature, and he smiled when he referred to her fun-loving attitude that made her a favorite guest at any occasion.

"We will miss you, Beatrice," the priest concluded after descending from the altar, where he paused for a long moment after placing his hand on the casket.

After the final blessing, there was an explosion of applause that resonated throughout the huge cathedral, and then, row by row, one by one, the congregation, encompassing family, friends, neighbors, and citizens of the great city of New Orleans, slowly processioned out of the cathedral and into the streets of the French Quarter.

To the surprise of those who knew him and knew just how much he meant to Miss BB, Monte Leonard from the noble Commonwealth of Kentucky was standing at the foot of the cathedral steps, tipping his hat to all those that walked past him, whether they knew him or not. Angeline and Dolice Marie were simply delighted that the young man had arrived, just in time, and although it was obvious that he was extremely exhausted, Monte Leonard volunteered to replace the elderly Declouette Mansion maintenance man who had been with Miss BB for more than thirty years as one of the pallbearers, joining Obadiah, Mr. Bernard Menard, the Declouette gardener, Attorney Patrick LeDeau, and the tearful young man that had taken the "family" photograph at the Menard wedding, who requested this opportunity to bid his farewell to Miss BB.

Once everyone was outside the cathedral and standing staggered on the concrete steps, the casket was carried and placed in the elongated carriage.

"Lord, have mercy. What a sad sight that must have been!" Uncle Simon said as he, yes, as he began to cry. And yes, my other sweet uncles teased him for a very long time for being so very sensitive.

As the huge crowd of people following the elongated carriage began the extremely slow walk to the cemetery that was located approximately two city blocks from the cathedral in the French Quarter, the sound of music behind them began to overtake the sounds of silence. Dolice Marie and Angeline glanced back and noticed a second line coming up the street toward them, complete with at least fifty men with musical instruments, black suits, white shirts and ties, waving white handkerchiefs, and a leader wearing a top hat and carrying an umbrella.

The music was slow, sad, and seemed to be tugging the heart straight out of the chests of the people walking ahead of them, and they began to cry uncontrollably, and quite loudly, I must also add.

"Oh, when the saints go marching in. Oh, when the saints go marching in, Lord, how I want to be in that number. When the saints go marching in."

Uncle Clovis began to slowly tap on the table to demonstrate to the young boys the beat that was now almost deafening to those following the casket.

For the almost two-city-block stretch to the cemetery, the mourning could be heard louder and even louder, causing people along the route to begin to come out of their homes to wave their own handkerchiefs and yell "Au revoir!" as the casket passed them by. Dolice Marie, Angeline, and Obadiah, who had their arms stretched out to touch the back end of the elongated carriage, turned swiftly to evaluate the music coming from behind them and found themselves clapping—yes, I said *clapping*!

The clapping grew louder and caused the other people following the casket to clap as well, until all the mourners were clapping their hands or waving their white handkerchiefs while wearing a smile in the midst of their own tears, pausing briefly in their slow funeral walk to allow the second line to catch up with them. Once they did, the tempo of the funeral walk began to quicken, to develop into a funeral march, as demonstrated again by my dear uncle Clovis.

"That second line began to speed the beat of the music up, just a little," Uncle Clovis would say as he tapped out the new beat with his hands on the breakfast table, "so that the leader could show off his high-stepping moves, his way to grieve."

Once the elongated carriage entered the cemetery, everything became silent in respect for all those resting in coffins above the ground or in one of the beautiful mausoleums that adorned the cemetery.

The carriage found its way to the place in the cemetery where Miss BB's body would be buried, in the same vault and right next to her beloved husband, Carson. The six pallbearers assumed their positions to lift the casket out, amorously placing it in the vault, and once the people, including the second line, had quietly found a place around that area, the priest led a short prayer for the dead, followed by all reciting the Lord's Prayer.

With tears streaming down their faces, Angeline, Obadiah, Monte Leonard, and the Menards of New York surrounded the casket and were the first to say their final goodbyes before they began their long journey back to the Declouette Mansion, where people from the funeral or people from outside the great city of New Orleans had already begun to arrive before them.

This time, the second line went first, quietly leading the way from the cemetery, but once outside the confines of the sleeping departed, they lifted their musical instruments again and began a spirited march toward the French Quarter, where they bade their farewell to Miss BB's family, friends, and neighbors.

The Declouette Mansion came alive and was quite busy again once the Declouette Mansion household staff arrived, from Cook in the kitchen preparing the meal that Miss BB had requested for those that came to extend their condolences, to greeting the people from the funeral that had come to pay their respects to those that remained on the earth.

A saddened Monte Leonard was greeted at the front door of the Declouette Mansion by one of the household staff, who led him to a comfortable divan in the parlor, and after being asked if there was anything that he needed at the moment, he simply replied with a smile and a tip of his head as he reached in his coat pocket for a small bottle of smooth Kentucky bourbon, "Just a glass would be sufficient at the moment, ma'am, and I sincerely thank you."

Patima and MAE ran toward Dolice Marie and Mr. Bernard Menard, followed closely by Kip and Wilhelm, when they came through the door to the Declouette Mansion, clinging to them tightly as though the two alone could make everything on earth so much better.

"Is Miss BB in heaven?" MAE asked.

"She could be nowhere else, my darling," Dolice responded.

"Good!" the innocent child said with an enormous smile. "Then Patima and I can go and play outside in the backyard, right?"

"Of course," Mr. Bernard Menard said, kissing them both on top of their heads. "Just be very careful and go no farther than the backyard."

Within the moments after the girls left to play outside in the backyard of the Declouette Mansion, Miss BB's attorney, Patrick LeDeau, approached Dolice Marie and quietly whispered in her ear that now was the appropriate time to read Miss BB's will and asked if there was a place that they would be comfortable doing so. Dolice Marie quickly found Angeline and relayed the message that it was time for the reading of the will and suggested that she use Miss BB's upstairs parlor, where they would find the privacy they needed.

As Dolice excused herself and began to walk off to join Mr. Bernard Menard, Attorney Patrick LeDeau quietly let her know that she as well as Obadiah would be needed at the reading of the will. Dolice was taken aback, indeed, and totally speechless, but after catching her breath, she smiled to her beloved husband and then adhered to Attorney Patrick LeDeau's request to join him, while Angeline went off to find Obadiah, who was equally surprised that he would be needed as well.

Once everyone was in one place, Patrick LeDeau led the way to the upstairs parlor, where the official reading of Miss BB's will began.

The Reading of the Will

"Miss BB was very adamant about this will and extremely specific about what she wanted to do with her money, her property, and her personal possessions. With the exception of her household staff, you are listed as her family and loved ones and the heirs to the estate of Mrs. Beatrice Carson Declouette."

After her formal declaration that she was indeed of sound body and mind at the time of the writing of her will, Attorney Patrick LeDeau began with, "For each of those faithful people that have served me well over these many years, I can assure a permanent position for you with the new owner of the Declouette Mansion, for as long as each desires one."

"New owner?" Angeline said, surprised. "Who is the new owner?"

"We will get to that shortly, Miss Toussaint-Marie," the attorney said. "Now, where was I?"

Then he continued, "I bequeath the sum of $1,000 to each one of you, the wonderful persons that were in my employ at the time of my death. I also give my permission for you to choose what you would have from my clothing, shoes, hats, and accessories. Thank you for your service, and your friendship.

"I bequeath the sum of $1,500 to each one of the young women that reside and work at the New Orleans House. You have been a great source of joy to me as well as the source of a great business enterprise. I also give my permission for you as well to choose what you would have from my clothing, shoes, hats, and accessories."

Attorney Patrick LeDeau removed a stack of envelopes from his briefcase and explained that these were the checks that Miss BB had instructed him to make ready to distribute to the aforementioned persons.

"When this meeting is over, we shall do so together," he said. "And now for specific items of her person and her possessions.

"To my new and dear friend from Kentucky, Monte Leonard, I leave my sterling silver flask from which I have enjoyed sipping smooth Kentucky bourbon. You do the same! And have one for me. You have been a good friend, and I will miss you terribly.

"To my beautiful Dolice Marie LaPierre-Menard…"

Dolice lowered her head and began to cry.

"You remind me so very much of myself as a young woman, strong, tenacious, and most definitely fearless. I leave you no money, for I know that Bernard is taking good care of you and money has never been important to you anyway—you would only give it away! I will, however, leave $10,000 to your daughter, for her education, and my beloved Daniel's pocket watch to Bernard. I would not have anyone else have it. He is such a gentleman, as was my Daniel, and every true gentleman should have a pocket watch.

"I leave to you, my dear Dolice Marie, the portrait that was made from the photograph of all the ladies in your life that was taken on your wedding day here at the Declouette Mansion, hanging in the downstairs parlor. I hope it will always remind you of how very much I love you.

"Also, I leave to you the entire china tea set, the one with which we enjoyed that first brunch together so many years ago, and the lovely lace tablecloth and napkins. It would please me that you keep it for your daughter and that she pass it on to hers. It was very important to me, as it was given to me by my husband, Daniel, from one of his many trips abroad."

Dolice Marie was certainly overwhelmed to have been remembered by Miss BB in this extraordinary way, and held Angeline tightly in her arms to keep her from swooning into a genteel faint and then falling upon the hardwood floor, as she certainly had been known to do on various occasions.

"My beloved niece, Angeline…"

The two young women continued to hold onto each other as Attorney Patrick LeDeau continued to perform the task that had been left to him.

"I could not love you more if you were my own sweet daughter. For years now, since your arrival from Paris, I have been preparing a surprise for you, a lovely furnished country home on the outside of New Orleans, complete with everything you will ever need to be happy and comfortable. The stipulation was that the keys would be given to you upon the occasion of my death."

Attorney Patrick LeDeau again reached inside his briefcase for an envelope containing two keys. Angeline became so overcome with disbelief and grief that she had to be consoled by both Dolice Marie and Obadiah.

"You will be, I am sure, given permission by the new owner of the Declouette Mansion to choose paintings, furnishings, and other items of your choosing for your new home."

Dolice Marie, Angeline, and Obadiah again looked up and asked the question, "What new owner?"

"We are almost there," Attorney Patrick LeDeau said, "I assure you, so please, if you would, let us refrain from any more interruptions."

Then he continued, "Ah, $25,000 was placed in a separate bank account at the Bank of New Orleans several years ago, which means with the interest made during these years, you will have no need to worry about money. Perhaps you will consider taking those dancing lessons you wanted to many years ago.

"I also leave to you my share of the New Orleans House. Manage it carefully! Lead fairly and always share your earnings with those that are less fortunate than you are. May you always be healthy and happy."

The attorney paused. "There is just one last item, outside of the money bequeathed to her favorite charities and incidentals for all of you, such as specific articles of clothing, jewelry, and other fineries, and that would be the Declouette Mansion."

Then he continued reading, "To my beloved son, Obadiah, I leave the Declouette Mansion and everything that is both inside and outside of it, all other interests such as the household staff, and most of all, my precious FiFi and GiGi."

"When Obadiah came to," as my crazy uncle Clovis would say, "that is, after faintin' and fallin' straight out on to the floor, he was sweating and his heart was pumping so fast it could be heard outside of his chest!"

Oh, how my wonderful uncles laughed, but deep inside, all of them truly knew that this gift was also one of those stepping-stones throughout our history, if you know what I mean.

It was certainly Dolice Marie or Angeline that put a cold towel over his sweating forehead, and both were standing over him, calling his name and dropping their tears on his face.

"Now, Obadiah," Attorney Patrick LeDeau said, "there is more, young man, and I would appreciate it if we can get this done so that I can go home to be with my own family."

Dolice Marie and Angeline quickly assisted Obadiah to the divan, where he sat in complete and total shock, sweating and wiping his forehead with the cold towel.

"Are we ready?" Attorney Patrick LeDeau asked, raising one eyebrow to assure everyone that he was serious, indeed. He reached for a final time in his briefcase to bring out a final envelope with the keys to the Declouette Mansion.

"Yes, sir," Obadiah answered.

"I am also leaving $25,000 to you, my dear Obadiah. Consider it operating expenses for the Declouette Mansion. Manage it well. Always be fair to your employees, and most of all, be good to yourself. Of course, your regular salary will continue to be paid monthly from the proceeds of my beloved Daniel's import-export business, which, as you already know, has been turned over to his family.

"And please take good care of mon bébés, FiFi and GiGi, as I already know that you will. My husband, Daniel, loved you as much as I do, as our own son, so I am sure you will enjoy certain articles of his clothing, his hats, and his jewelry, which I give to you. Please allow Angeline and Dolice Marie to choose articles of my clothing and jewelry before giving them to the staff or to charity. Please do not cling to these things from which to remember me but quickly disperse of them.

"I hope you will find a wonderful girl to marry, Obadiah, perhaps that lovely little Shirley will be the one and the two of you can fill this big house of yours with the laughter of many children."

"Well, there you go!" one of my dear old uncles would say. "The reading of Miss BB's will was now another part of history for the LaPierre and Menard families. But…there is more, much more to come!"

By the time the dazed recipients of Miss BB's will descended the stairs to the parlor, Monte Leonard was already bidding his good-byes to the household staff. The young Kentuckian was overwhelmed when presented with Miss BB's silver flask, and he smiled a quick smile as he accepted the treasure, tipped his hat, and disappeared through the door to make the journey back to the Commonwealth of Kentucky.

Chapter 29

Miss BB had been laid to rest, and time simply marched on without any assistance at all. Wilhelm and Angeline had begun to communicate with each other regularly, even contemplating, I might also add, a visit between the two, perhaps even a visit to Wilhelm's home in Toronto, Canada.

The lovely little house that Miss BB had prepared for Angeline was now an absolutely charming home, that place where Angeline spent her time in the gardens, in the kitchen, or in the parlor, still practicing the art of the piano and the dance. She had not yet hired any help for either the inside or the outside the charming little cottage, choosing instead to do it all herself.

She was quite happy, indeed, except for those few times that allowed her loneliness to creep into her mind, and she would wonder again whatever happened to Henri de Marquis or why no one ever seemed to long for her company. But that feeling would only last for a fleeting moment, and eventually she would remember just how very happy she really was.

Obadiah, on the other hand, was still finding it rather difficult to transition into being the master of the Declouette Mansion and having the Declouette household staff work for him instead of him working with them, as it had been for so very long.

He was still being so very careful of the possessions of the Declouette Mansion, such as the crystal and the dinnerware that Cook would set for him, and he found it difficult to find his way to the formal dining room instead of eating with Cook in her kitchen. Eventually, the poor man realized that since the Declouette Mansion was now his, indeed, he could eat and sleep wherever his heart led him, and most of the time that meant eating in Cook's kitchen and sleeping in his old bedroom.

Both Marcel Dubois and Madeleine Dubois-Chachere, enjoying their newfound fame and fortune, had moved from the other side of town to a very nice cottage at the foot of the mighty Mississippi River, providing a solid home for his family and a steady income for the owners and operators of the New Orleans House.

Word quickly spread about the talented young man who successfully impersonated a young woman, and Saturday nights brought hundreds of visitors, so many so that Marcel and Madeleine had to perform twice each evening, well into the night, in order to accommodate the numbers. Well, it was truly worth it for everyone. Miss BB would have been so very proud.

Across the great state of Louisiana at Mon Village, Jean Pierre and Evelina continued to enjoy their family and home as time delivered both old age and a new age that would soon be managing the affairs of the former LaPierre Plantation.

Mon Claire LaPierre eventually began to travel with Jubil to the noble Commonwealth of Kentucky on horseback, following the trail of that pesky mint all the way there and back. Jubil would make sure that Mon Claire had everything she would need during their visits for both the spring and fall Kentucky Derby meets, placing her safely in a boardinghouse just a few miles from where he would rest his head with the young boys in the bunkhouse.

Mon Claire was now, without a doubt, a fine horsewoman in every sense of the word, from grooming the horses to riding them fiercely down the dirt track in front of buyers from all over the entire world. Once the horses were safely in their own stalls for the night, she would spend yet another hour or two visiting each one and talking with them as if they were human, offering suggestions to them for an even better ride the next time.

There were plenty of young men who rivaled for her attention, young men of color and those without color; those who rode the horses and those that did not. But for the moment anyway, Mon Claire's heart belonged to her very special friends, the horses.

Once back home from the Kentucky meets, Mon Claire would spend that first night in the barn with her best friend, Ti-Garçon, seemingly sharing with him her experiences in the noble Commonwealth of Kentucky.

It was, of course, extremely difficult for Jean Pierre and Evelina to see their firstborn child slowly but consistently leaving the nest, and although they tried to no avail to keep her from exploding into adulthood, Mon Claire assured her parents that she would always be near them, in one way or another.

Those chubby little twins of Jean Pierre and Evelina, Petois and Pecous, were growing older as well, taller and less chubby, but they were still quite well-known for their culinary expertise, and eventually Jean Pierre had a restaurant built where the two could provide meals for the residents who were just simply too tired to prepare their own meals, for the elderly who were quite tired of cooking for themselves, and for the visitors who shopped at Mon Village and who might find themselves hungry before they journeyed back to their own homes.

Once the new church house was up and running, a small kitchen was built in the lower portion of the building, where Petois and Pecous could prepare meals for people attending the Sunday services and who became hungry after a very, very, very long sermon or homily.

When the two young boys became men, they were truly favorites of the young girls growing into womanhood at Mon Village and often found themselves being flirted with as they served food either in the restaurant, the church house, or when delivering to the elderly in the residential area. Of course they smiled and even once or twice found themselves flirting back, but neither one was truly ready to settle down—not yet, anyway.

Labelle Jelee was already contemplating the easiest manner in which to escape the confines of both her parents and Mon Village. By the time she was in her early teens, the protégé of Dolice Marie LaPierre-Menard was already making plans for her future, a future that would include the big lights and the big-city happenings of places like the Big Apple (New York City) or perhaps Chicago, the place with plenty of excitement, or so she had heard or read about.

Jelee loved designing dresses for herself and for others with the fabric scraps she found while traveling throughout Mon Village or fabric that Evelina would purchase for herself to create beautiful dresses for herself and her two girls. Jelee dreamed of being paid for her designs and even having her own business, but certainly not at Mon Village, which she considered to be just too "country."

And Labelle Jelee also had an alternative plan, just in case her desires to leave Mon Village could not be attained in the shortest amount of time possible. She knew, as well as anybody at Mon Village, the stories of the big house and the sultry women that had worked there, making their money with their bodies and wearing scanty clothes that showed off much of their bodies. All this was truly fascinating to the young girl, who often was seen by Evelina peering at herself in a mirror while dancing or blowing kisses to herself. Shameful little thing!

She was just so sure that Mon Village would one day belong to herself and her siblings, so why not transform the big house back into "the business," if you know what I mean, if and when she could get out from under her parents' control? After all, it was that business that had brought plenty of money to all the residents at one time, now, was it not?

Any parent would feel blessed to have a son such as Jean Pierre III, as he now wrote his name, the baby boy and baby of the family, I might also add, because he was always ready to share a hug or give Jean Pierre or Evelina a kiss, always ready to lend a helping hand, especially when it came to keeping Mon Village the successful home that it was.

As much as Labelle Jelee was ready to leave Mon Village, it was that much and more that Jean Pierre wanted to stay and live his life right there at home. Jean Pierre was satisfied in both his head and his heart that it would be Jean Pierre III, most certainly, that would replace himself as master of all that the LaPierre eye could see.

Although the handsome young man Jean Pierre III had been the apple of many of the young ladies' eyes at Mon Village, he found it quite difficult to settle down with one or even imagine a future with any of them. He did, however, have his mind set upon furthering his education once he had finished his schooling at the Mon Village schoolhouse, and Jean Pierre vowed to make that happen for him.

The Menards of Upstate New York continued with life as it had been for them prior to Miss BB's passing onto the ancestors, even though she remained in Madam Menard's heart and in conversations with her best friend Kip, or Mr. Bernard Menard's mom, Lady Menard.

Throughout those years, Monique Aimee Elizabeth LaPierre-Menard had grown into a lovely young lady with proper etiquette and social graces; in fact, the child had celebrated her sixteenth birthday with a lively cotillion that her parents had planned for her, complete with all her friends from school and her best friend, Patima, of course.

Both girls were very popular at school, both intelligent and both attracted the boys at school as well; however, both Mr. Bernard Menard and Kuya Salma tried their best to steer them away from any extracurricular activities until they had completed college.

"There should be no unnecessary interruptions until you have created a future for yourselves," both fathers would agree. "The young men that were created for you both are on a parallel path with yours, and one day, when the time is appropriate, your paths will cross with theirs and there will be no question about it. They will have the same desires, the same goals, and the same hopes for their future as you both will have for yourselves. There is plenty of time yet, so in the meantime, study, study, study!"

Both the Menard child and the Salma child listened intensely, and when their fathers' lectures were complete, the two girls smiled a sweet smile, agreed with them, and once alone, complained to each other about their boredom and just how much they wanted to do something totally different, something absolutely exciting, something that would probably get them into big trouble.

Wilhelm and Angeline

Angeline stepped out on the front porch of her lovely home just as the postman was passing through his daily route, delivering letters, magazines, and catalogs from all over the world. She smiled with him as he handed her the mail that was addressed to her, which included a letter from Toronto, Canada, a letter that must have been from Wilhelm. Angeline smiled and held the letter to her chest as she walked back into the house and sat down at the dining room table, where she had been enjoying a delightful cup of tea.

"My dear Angeline," the letter began. "I hope all has been well with you since our last letters. I will be traveling to New Orleans sometime during the coming spring with regard to a legal matter for one of my clients and would be most honored if you would allow me to plan a visit with you during that time." Angeline's heart began to thump loudly, and she smiled broadly at the words written on the lovely stationery.

"I would appreciate hearing from you as soon as possible so that I can plan my itinerary for the journey," the letter continued. "And would it also be possible for me to secure a few nights at the New Orleans House while I am in New Orleans? I have no knowledge of any other boardinghouses in the city, and being able to reserve a room at your establishment would give me a definite place to stay while I am there."

Angeline closed her eyes and twirled around the room as if she were dancing a spirited dance at the New Orleans House, kicking up her heels and spinning first left, and then right. But just as quickly as she had allowed herself to twirl and spin, Angeline persuaded herself to stop, not only to stop the dance, but also to stop the thoughts that were rising within her heart.

Angeline reached again for the letter from Wilhelm and read the last few lines.

"I look forward to seeing you again, and perhaps you will consider having dinner with me in one of New Orleans's fine restaurants. Until then, I remain your faithful friend, Wilhelm."

It would be several weeks later that Wilhelm appeared at the front door of the New Orleans House with train cases in his hands, asking the lovely lady that answered the door for Angeline Toussaint-Marie, who was simply delighted at the mere sight of the handsome young man. The lovely lady of the New Orleans House remembered the handsome young Wilhelm from Miss BB's funeral and was extremely excited about telling Angeline that he had traveled all the distance from Toronto, Canada, to see her.

After a warm embrace, Angeline showed Wilhelm upstairs to his room, where she left him to freshen up. After closing the door, Angeline quietly leaned against it, smiled as she closed her eyes, and took a deep breath.

On the other side of the closed door, Wilhelm smiled as he also closed his eyes and took a deep breath.

"There was more to this story!" Uncle Simon would yell out. "I have a feeling that the boy had an ulterior motive of sorts!" And what an *ulterior motive* of sorts it was! Angeline would soon find out that there truly was no urgent legal matter that required the handsome young Wilhelm to journey to the great city of New Orleans; in fact, the only matter he had outside Toronto, Canada, was Angeline.

It would be over a delicious bowl of chicken and sausage gumbo over steaming white rice that Wilhelm made that confession to Angeline.

"I am most certain that a lady such as yourself would never have traveled as far as Canada to visit a man that she knows very little about, and therefore, I made a reason to travel to see you." Angeline blushed, but she was extremely pleased and excited about the fact that Wilhelm was there for her from such a great distance, and for her alone. She blushed again as Wilhelm moved his chair and his bowl of gumbo from his position directly across Angeline to being right next to her. It was a true sign of promise of what was to come between the two of them, but for now, just sharing a dinner in the formal dining room of the New Orleans House was enough to be considered a beginning.

H. Sophie Newcomb Memorial College

"Have you decided what you will do now that you have finished with your lower classes, Aimee?"

It was approximately 1893. The nineteen-year-old Menard child, who had definitely inherited her father's very long legs and could virtually read his mind, knew very well that the question had been coming, sooner than later, and she had prepared several responses to soothe her father's worries.

"Well, Father," she began as the two sat in the sun on the back porch of the Menard cottage while Dolice Marie and Kip went through their daily routine that kept Madam Menard calm. As the scent of warm Jasmine circled around the entire porch, the discussion between father and daughter continued.

"I had considered taking a year off to travel. Perhaps I could visit Paris and London, or maybe Italy."

Mr. Bernard Menard raised an eyebrow but maintained his concerned smile as he listened for that which he was truly listening for.

"Of course I had considered finding a nice job, either here in New York, or perhaps with Grandmom and Granddaddy in Toronto. I could work with the children. Perhaps I could watch after children while their parents are working."

Again, Mr. Bernard Menard raised an eyebrow, and his smile began to fade as he carefully listened for that which he was truly listening for, but instead, Aimee paused as though she was in deep thought about her future.

"School…yes…college," MAE finally gave in with a deep sigh. "If I just plunge myself into college right away, I have a better chance of finishing college without losing interest. Is that not what you always say? Is that not what you were hoping that I would say?"

"Yes, dear Aimee!" Mr. Bernard Menard answered excitedly, throwing his hand up in the air. "But the good news is, you can attend any school that you care to attend."

"Can I go to school in Paris?"

"No," Mr. Bernard Menard answered quickly. "Maybe after one or two years in a college here in the United States," he continued.

"Your mother and I must know that you are serious about college before we send you anywhere else for school."

"I understand," MAE answered. "But I eventually want to live in Louisiana anyway, at Mon Village, so if going to college is the answer you were waiting to hear from me, perhaps admittance to one of the colleges there, somewhere in the state of Louisiana."

"Ah, my beloved Aimee," Mr. Bernard Menard began. "*College* is the word that I was waiting to hear you say, and now we will begin the search for an appropriate college…in Louisiana, if you are sure that Louisiana is the place you want to be."

"And you are sure that you and Mom would not even consider—"

"Not for a moment," Mr. Bernard Menard interrupted. The doting father kissed his sweet daughter on the top of her head and left the Menard child to ponder over the conversation. She sighed deeply in her disgruntlement regarding her father's decision and, just a moment later, said her goodbyes to her mother and Kip and then exited the porch of the Menard cottage to find her best friend, Patima.

Over the next few weeks, Mr. Bernard Menard and his beloved daughter searched for and asked others to obtain any and all information about the colleges available for women or where women were allowed to attend in the great state of Louisiana, and one such cottage certainly met the Menard interest and requirements, the new H. Sophie Newcomb College at Tulane University, New Orleans, in the great state of Louisiana.

One of Mr. Bernard Menard's associates in the import-export business had recently read that a Mrs. Josephine Louise Newcomb had established a college for women, having opened in 1886. The college, in coordination with Tulane University, was opened in honor of Mrs. Newcomb's beloved daughter, Sophie, who had died in 1870 at the tender age of fifteen. According to the information that was gathered, Newcomb College was considered "the nation's first successful, self-sufficient women's college connected with a men's college," specializing in, as requested by Mrs. Newcomb, education looking "to the practical side of life as well as to literary excellence."

MINT JULEP

MAE and her loving father, Mr. Bernard Menard, were both thrilled at the possibility of her attending this very fine college in the great state of Louisiana, situating her quite close to the place where she had already made the decision that she wanted to live.

Everyone was excited, with the exception of Madam Menard, whose reservations were erupting from a place deep within her spirit, that place inside her that remembered the days of her youth when people of color were enslaved in the very land that her sweet child craved to be.

Madam Menard also knew firsthand that even though enslaving people of color was against the law now, the heart of mankind could still harbor hate toward another simply because of the color of their skin. Even in the midst of this celebration, Madam Menard could not stop her heart from anguishing over the possibility of her own daughter feeling such pain, and once alone with her husband, she expressed her concerns.

"I have considered the same, beloved, many times," he responded to his loving wife, "but I have also recalled the many times that we have together overcome such ignorance, as we will again. Aimee is strong and iron-willed, just like her beautiful mother, capable of handling herself in such situations should they arise." He sighed. "Besides," he continued, "Aimee will always be under the watchful eye of Jean Pierre and Jubil, and then there is Obadiah and Angeline, right there in New Orleans. Aimee will be in good hands."

Mr. Bernard Menard hugged his petite wife and kissed her on top of her head as she allowed her tears to fall down her cheeks, satisfied with her husband's understanding and thoughtfulness.

Within a month of locating the college of his daughter's dreams, Mr. Bernard Menard was able to secure an entrance appointment during one of the summer months, just prior to the opening of the school year, with the registrar of Newcomb College. And within that month, Madam Menard was able to arrange for Jean Pierre and Evelina, as well as Jubil and Miss Sylvia, to meet them in the great city of New Orleans, at Obadiah's house to be exact, to spend some valuable time together.

She was also extremely excited about being able to see Angeline, her very best friend, whom she had not seen since the death of their beloved Miss BB. It was these things that captured her mind and filled her with some semblance of peace as she anticipated what she felt to be obvious at this meeting at Newcomb College.

MAE was beginning to get extremely excited herself, I might also add, since she would be seeing some of her family and Patima had agreed to come with her since it would be just for a few days this time. Her beloved grandmother had been ailing for months, and Patima had already begun to prepare herself for living life without the dear woman that she had been with all her life.

Soon everything and everyone was in place. Edward drove the Menard carriage with Mr. Menard and Madam Menard, MAE, and her best friend, Patima, to the upstate train station, and once the train made its way to the great city of New Orleans, the excitement began to heighten.

From the sight of the massive, rolling Mississippi River and the discernible temperature change, to the sight of the Menards' beloved Obadiah standing beside his fancy Declouette carriage in that great city of New Orleans, it was apparent that this was not a dream.

Unfortunately, there would be just enough time to get to the Newcomb College from the train station in the great city of New Orleans to meet the appointed time scheduled with the registrar. Obadiah quickly drove toward the Newcomb College and, once arrived at the campus, steered the huge horse pulling the Declouette carriage into the designated parking space for visitors and then took his familiar position beside the carriage, preparing himself for the wait.

"Obadiah, my friend," Mr. Bernard Menard addressed him, "you are no longer a chauffeur, my good man. You own this carriage, you own your own home, and you have been invited to join us, not to simply drive us here. Please."

It was quite apparent, indeed, that the gentleman was still somewhat uncomfortable in his new role, but with a little encouragement from Patima, who offered him her arm, Obadiah became a little more comfortable as the small entourage approached the main building on the Newcomb College campus.

The grounds of the small campus were lined with lovely oak trees and a water fountain that truly enhanced the appearance of America's Deep South, including the familiar wooden chapel with a huge cross on its steeple and several other buildings that were unfamiliar at the moment.

Mr. Bernard Menard opened the door to the main building and allowed Madam Menard, MAE, Patima, and Obadiah to enter the large room just inside the door, where a woman, dressed in a proper gray business suit, was sitting behind a desk. She appeared to be stunned at the sight of the five people that had entered the room.

"Good day, madam," Mr. Bernard Menard said with his usual smile, removing his hat and running his fingers through his long red hair. "We are the Menards of New York, here with our daughter, Monique Aimee Elizabeth, and we have an appointment to meet with the registrar this morning. Could you kindly inform the registrar that we are here?"

The woman stood frozen behind her desk.

"Is there a problem, madam?" Mr. Bernard Menard asked.

"No, no, monsieur," she finally answered, forcing a smile. "I shall return in just one moment."

Dolice Marie stepped closer toward Mr. Bernard Menard, who intertwined her arm within his own to assure her that he would let nothing happen to her, their child, or their friends.

Just as she had said, the lady that was sitting behind the desk returned with another woman who was also dressed in a proper business suit.

"May I help you?" the second woman asked.

"Yes," Mr. Bernard Menard began. "As I have already told this nice lady, we are the Menards of New York, here to register our daughter for the coming semester."

"I am the registrar," the second lady said.

"Wonderful," Mr. Bernard Menard said, extending his hand to shake hers. "This is my beautiful wife, Madam Menard; our beloved daughter, Monique Aimee Elizabeth; her best friend, Patima; and our friend, Obadiah. It is truly a pleasure to meet you."

"My…pleasure," she responded hesitantly. "I do apologize for the delay, monsieur, but we have never registered a—"

"Canadian?" Mr. Bernard Menard interrupted quickly. "I assure you that once we finish here today, registering our dear Aimee, I will spread the good news about this lovely college, and there will be many, many more…uh-um, Canadians…registering to attend."

"And there you go again!" Uncle Alexandre would say with a slap to his own knee, followed by the usual guffaw from his crazy brothers.

Once they were inside the office, the registrar introduced herself and began a short history of the campus, quite stoically, I might also add, much of the same information that Mr. Bernard Menard had already heard, not leaving any time between sentences for the family to ask questions.

"Newcomb College is located approximately three miles from Tulane, which is an all-male university, but we have no direct contact with them at all," the registrar added and then began to ask the pertinent questions.

"Did you bring the records of your daughter's completion of her schooling in New York?"

"Is your daughter considering staying on campus, in the dormitory?"

"What made your family choose Newcomb College for your daughter's education?"

On and on the questions came at Mr. Bernard Menard in what seemed to truly be an attempt to discourage the Menards from placing their child in the Newcomb College.

Suddenly, MAE stood up from her chair, much to the concern of her mother, who turned toward her beloved daughter and attempted to stop her, but it was Mr. Bernard Menard who quite subtly touched his wife's hand to let her know that she could certainly handle herself in this current set of circumstances.

And handle herself she most certainly did, indeed, in an extremely intelligent manner, and with plenty of poise as well. "Here are my records, madam," she said, extending her arm over the desk to give them to the registrar, and after sitting back down, she cleared her throat and then continued to answer the questions that had been directed to her parents.

"Yes, I intend to stay in the dormitory. I came here from New York. I cannot go back and forth every single day.

"And yes, madam, we are a loving family of many different colors, many nationalities, as you can certainly see. And in response to the questions that you are not asking, yes, my father is Canadian, from Toronto, where my grandparents are still living. So I am one-half Canadian. My father owns a very prosperous import-export company and is very kind to everyone whose path he has the occasion to cross. Certainly, he has already considered extending his financial kindness to your school, should I chose to register."

"My parents are legally married, and this is my beautiful mother," MAE continued as she stood again to come face-to-face with the registrar. "Madam Dolice Marie LaPierre-Menard was born into slavery, yes, owned by other human beings, to be exact, owned by Madam and Monsieur LaPierre from France. Actually, my mother lived right down the road from here, on the Bayou Frou-Frous, where I, too, was born. The master of the plantation, Philippe LaPierre, a Frenchman, was her father, and her mother was the woman he truly loved, Mama Mozelle, half-African and half-Spanish. Thus, from my mother's side of the family, I have inherited my deeply respected African, French, and Spanish ancestry."

"And here," the Menard child continued, pointing to her best friend, Patima, "this is my very best friend, Patima, who is a first-generation American from the Philippine islands. And next to her is Monsieur Obadiah Declouette, a name that was given to him because he was loved, not because he was owned, a man of color to whom I show respect by calling uncle, a dear man that inherited an entire mansion from Beatrice Carson Declouette, who called him her son. You do remember, Miss BB, do you not, madam?"

"I chose Newcomb College because I want to study academics in order to become a good teacher and to bring my skills to my mother's home, right here in Louisiana, where I intend to teach the children at the former LaPierre Plantation, where the color of one's skin is as many as the stars in the sky that blankets the Bayou Frou-Frous. This is who we are, madam, and all of us here are extremely proud of everything that is."

Then she added, "Oh, and by the way, madam, did I mention to you that we own the LaPierre Plantation, which is now called Mon Village du LaPierre en Bayou Frou-Frous, Mon Village for a short name, and have owned it since long before I was born? My family owns everything surrounding the LaPierre Plantation for miles, and miles, and miles around, including the Bayou Frou-Frous itself, and all the land almost to the Atchafalaya River. In fact, all that the human eye can see."

Dolice Marie was so overwhelmed with extreme admiration for her daughter that she allowed her tears that had swelled in her eyes to fall freely down her cheek as Mr. Bernard Menard gently caressed her. MAE paused for a moment and, after taking a deep breath, began again speaking to the registrar.

"With all that said, madam, and with all due respect, I sincerely hope that Newcomb College will consider admitting me for your fall semester. I can assure you that I will study hard and obey all the rules of the school, for this is the manner in which I have been raised."

After yet after another pause, MAE took yet another deep breath and, after a slight bow of her head, said, "Thank you, madam." She sat back down in her seat next to her father.

After an extremely uncomfortable few moments of silence while the registrar completed writing her notes on a pad, she stood slowly, scanning from MAE to her parents, to Patima, to Obadiah, and back again. Finally, she cleared her throat. "Young lady," the registrar said, and then paused another brief moment, "if it were my decision alone to register you as a student here at Newcomb College, I would do it without hesitation. However, I am only one voice. But I can assure you that I will personally pass along your application and school records as well as my observations of your passion, your intelligence, and your commitment, all the characteristics we look for when looking for girls to become students here."

"Unfortunately," the registrar continued, "the Newcomb College Board will not convene for another few weeks to review applications, but you will receive a letter in the mail with their decision. Thank you all for coming." She concluded with an extremely subtle smile extended toward MAE, who returned the smile with her own, while Mr. Bernard Menard escorted his wife, Patima, and Obadiah back to the large room where the lady was sitting behind the desk. No one spoke a single word until everyone had seated themselves in the Declouette carriage.

"You were so great in there," Patima said to her Lizzie with a smile of pride. "I am so very proud of you!"

MAE simply smiled back at her best friend but placed her hand upon her mother's hand. "And you, Mom, what did you think?"

But Dolice was too choked up with pride to even speak. She simply placed her other hand on top of her daughter's and smiled while closing her eyes. A few moments later, she complimented her daughter freely and commented that it was truly obvious that…

"You are certainly my daughter, and I am so very proud of you!"

MAE simply smiled again and hugged her mother tightly.

"I had no idea that you knew as much about our history as you do, my sweet Aimee," Dolice Marie said. "I know we have discussed some of these things, but where—"

"Oh, Mom," MAE answered with a casual smile, "Hannah has been telling me all that for years!"

Chapter 30

Up top of the carriage, where the two men were seated on the driver's bench, Mr. Bernard Menard and Obadiah quietly reviewed the events of the previous hour or so and simply smiled to themselves and with each other in great delight.

Once the carriage arrived in front of the Obadiah Declouette Mansion, Dolice Marie placed her arm around her daughter's waist and held her tightly as they walked toward the porch. She suddenly stopped in her tracks and began to run toward the front porch of the mansion. There, standing on the porch, was Dolice Marie's beloved Jean Pierre with Evelina, Jubil with Miss Sylvia, another man who looked unfamiliar and quite young, and her best friend, Angeline. She continued to run until she was wrapped in between all the people that had come to visit her, her family from Mon Village, and her very best friend in the entire world.

"I am so happy to see you all!" she said, hugging each one individually. "And who is this young man?" Dolice asked without letting go of him.

"Why, this is Jean Pierre III," Evelina answered in her deep Southern drawl. "This is the baby of our family."

Dolice Marie was very moved at the very sight of her nephew (or cousin, but by now, who really cares?) and hugged him tightly. "You remind me of your father when he was young, my dear," Dolice said as she stroked the side of his face with her hand.

But there was another whose eye had been captured by the young Jean Pierre III.

"You may not remember me, Jean Pierre III, because we were so young, but—"

"Oh, but I do remember you, Patima Salma," the young man answered flirtatiously. "And now I will never forget you!"

Patima smiled a smile that glowed so brightly it could only be compared to a twinkling star in the heavens, certainly a sign that she approved of his interest, and after a hug that made it apparent to everyone else and a loud "Uh-hum" from Evelina, the two quickly parted from each other to share their hellos with everyone else.

Once inside the Obadiah Declouette Mansion, the Menards from Upstate New York were again surprised, indeed, by the presence of the lovely ladies of the New Orleans House. More hugs and tears filled the air as each welcomed Dolice, Mr. Bernard Menard, Patima, and MAE, who, even though extremely happy to be in the great state of Louisiana, had so much more on her mind.

"You have made your mother and me so very proud," Mr. Bernard Menard whispered to his beloved daughter. "Now rest your mind and enjoy your family. There is nothing more you can do, and if the Newcomb College fails to recognize what a gift they have been handed in you, then it will be forever their loss!"

MAE smiled broadly and nestled herself in the arms of her father, who, at that moment, realized how very tall she had become, with him not needing to bend over quite as far to kiss his beloved daughter upon her head anymore, but standing without bending over to kiss her on her forehead. Could this have been the very moment in time that the Menard child's future would be sealed in providence? Who could know?

In the midst of the homecoming, Cook's voice resounded throughout the large dining room as she called everyone to a hearty meal of okra gumbo with chicken and seafood, steamed rice, corn bread, a crisp green salad, and plenty of ice-cold lemonade to drink. Across the huge dining room table, the conversations were as exciting and filling as the delicious meal.

First of all, Obadiah and Shirley, one of the lovely ladies of the New Orleans House, had recently been married in a quiet ceremony there at the mansion and officiated by Miss BB's priest. From shock and awe to tears, to "Congratulations," and back again, it was apparent, indeed, that everyone was truly happy for the two.

The second order of business was why Jean Pierre III was there, in the great city of New Orleans, with his parents, but not the other children. Coached by his mother, Evelina, Jean Pierre III was told to stand up and stand up straight whenever he was speaking to any adult, which he did when he began to address his uncle and aunt.

"Uncle Bernard and Aunt Dolice Marie," he began, "I will be finishing with my education at Mon Village this coming year and would ask that you help me find a college, like you found one for Monique Aimee Elizabeth. I, however, would like to go to college in Canada."

Mr. Bernard Menard was the very first to stand and applaud the young man's request and answered quite happily that both he and his wife would do their very best to help him attain his goal.

"Excellent choice, my boy! My mother and father will be happy as well to help you apply for a college in Toronto. In fact, I am very sure you can stay in my old bedroom in their house!"

Jean Pierre III was frozen still for a moment and finally cleared his throat to respond to his uncle. "Thank you so much, Uncle Bernard, but I would much rather stay in the dormitory—that is, if you and my parents would approve."

"We need to get you into college first, and then we will talk about the dormitory."

And finally, the discussion was opened regarding MAE's application to the Newcomb College, and it would be Dolice Marie that responded first.

"Aimee was wonderful, but now we must wait. We were assured that a letter would come to New York before the fall semester to tell us whether or not she will be able to attend. We have great faith that she will."

Dolice Marie and Angeline would find a few moments alone to chat, giggle as they did when they were young, and confide in each other as best friends often do. Angeline explained to Dolice Marie that Wilhelm had recently been for a visit with her, all about the imaginary legal matter that he had used as an excuse to see her, and the journey that the two had planned to see each other again, but this time in his home, in Toronto, Canada. Dolice Marie was absolutely shocked since Wilhelm had not even told his best friend, Mr. Bernard Menard, but was most delighted for her best friend.

"Wilhelm is a good man," Dolice Marie replied. "I could not be happier for both of you! I will let you in on a little secret, though," Dolice Marie continued. "Wilhelm loves Canadian ice hockey, and Canada is much too cold!"

Acceptance

Just as the registrar had said, a legal-size stamped envelope was delivered by a messenger to the Menard cottage in Upstate New York just two short weeks before the fall semester would begin from H. Sophie Newcomb College in the great state of Louisiana. Maggie happily accepted the letter and concentrated on only thinking very positive thoughts as she quickly delivered it to Madam Menard, who was outside on the porch with Kip.

"Oh my goodness!" Madam Dolice Marie squealed as she jumped up from her seat on the back porch of the Menard cottage. "It is from Newcomb College! Where is Aimee? Has anyone seen Aimee?"

"She and Patima have gone shopping in the city with Edward," Maggie said. "They have been gone a while, so I would say that they should be home soon, missus."

The following hour or so felt more like the longest period ever felt for Madam Menard and those on the back porch of the Menard cottage eagerly awaiting MAE's return to find out what decision the Newcomb College had rendered regarding her admittance to the fall semester. The excitement was becoming entirely too much to bear when suddenly Edward appeared on the back porch with several boxes wrapped in brown paper and tied with string.

"Edward!" Madam Menard exclaimed. "Where is Aimee?"

"She and Patima are in the cottage, missus, in the kitchen, looking for something to eat. You know how growing girls are…"

Madam Menard grabbed his arm to drag him along with everyone else to find her daughter so that everyone else could hear the final verdict. Both MAE and Patima were found in the kitchen with Cook, each having a cool glass of lemonade and a very large piece of pound cake topped with fresh fruit.

"It is here!" Madam Menard squealed. "Your letter from Newcomb College is here!"

"Oh my," MAE said as she sucked in her breath and grabbed at her chest with her hand. "Oh my!"

"Open it, dear heart, open it!" Madam Menard demanded.

"Should we not wait for Father, Mom?"

"Well, Aimee, that would be your decision to make," Madam Menard responded, even though she was hoping all the while that the child would simply choose to tell him what the letter said once her father had come home that evening. And that was exactly what she decided to do.

MAE took a deep breath and slowly let it out. Carefully opening the envelope to expose the letter, she gently pulled it out and unfolded it to read the words. However, another letter fell out first, on smaller stationery.

"Your brief visit to the Newcomb College this past summer was quite enlightening, and I am convinced now that no one is too young to teach, and none too old to learn. Your message was well taken, and I have passed it on to the Newcomb College Board of Directors, and I have explained to them that you would certainly be a loss to the student body should you not be accepted. Please give my best to your parents and friends, and do stop by for a visit when you arrive at Newcomb College." The letter continued, "I can assure you that you will have no troubles whatsoever throughout your years of study." (And it was signed by the registrar, I might also add!)

Well! Even before MAE had the opportunity to read the official letter of acceptance that was in the envelope, it had become apparent that she was now, indeed, an officially registered student at the college of her choice, in the great state of her choice.

Mr. Bernard Menard was met at the doorway that evening before he could get completely inside the Menard cottage by Madam Menard, MAE, and the entire Menard household staff, each one speaking at the very same time, telling the very same story—his beloved daughter, Aimee, was on her way to H. Sophie Newcomb College!

During that first week of the two weeks remaining before MAE was due to begin her studies at the Newcomb College, Madam Menard and her beloved daughter shopped for all the necessary items for a college student—new bedsheets and cases for her pillow, extra bath towels, toothbrushes, hairbrushes and combs, appropriate clothing, hats, shoes, and whatever else caught their fancy at that moment. It was certainly a bittersweet week, one filled with the excitement of MAE going to college, the other being the sadness of her leaving home for the very first time.

Higher Learning

MAE exited the train with a train case under one arm while juggling a larger train trunk filled with her school necessities with the other arm. She paused at the bottom of the steps and thought how wonderful it would be if someone would be there waiting for her to drive her to the dormitory at Newcomb College, but since there would not be anyone, she adjusted herself and her belongings again and then proceeded to the ticket agent, where she awaited a city carriage. While waiting, the sweet child fought back the tears that strained to fall from her eyes as she reflected on what could be ahead once she arrived. Once inside the city carriage, she allowed her tears to flow, and flow they did, reddening her eyes and leaving telltale streaks on both of her cheeks. But by the time the city carriage arrived at the H. Sophie Newcomb College dormitory, she had truly settled herself, washed her face with her tears, sucked in a long, deep breath, and was now ready to meet whatever came her way.

The dormitory was filled with girls searching for the room that had been assigned to each one of them, young ladies that seemed just as lost and lonely as MAE did. She sighed when she found her room, but once she walked in, she was surprised to see that her roommate was already in the room, sitting on one of the two beds in the small room, crying her heart out. The scene upset MAE so much that she, too, sat on the other bed and began to cry her heart out as well.

After several minutes of this particular scenario, the young lady on the other bed began to sniff and wipe her nose with a handkerchief; MAE did the same. When both young ladies had completed their crying spell as well as the drying-up process, there was that uncomfortable moment of silence before the two could gather their emotions together to introduce themselves to each other.

"Hello," the young lady on the other bed said, reaching out to shake MAE's hand. "How do you do?" she said. "My name is Margaret McPherson, from New Bedford, Massachusetts. My family originally came here from Scotland. I guess you think I am just a big baby."

It was amazingly obvious that Margaret McPherson was Scottish, certainly because of her name, but more so because of her delightful, thick brogue accent that simply thrilled her new roommate.

"Well," MAE answered in her own East Coast American accent, "I guess the people in charge knew what they were doing when they matched us together. I am a big baby, too, from Upstate New York. My father is from Canada, my mother from the Bayou Frou-Frous right here in Louisiana. Oh, and by the way, my name is Monique… uh, just Monique Menard is enough for now."

The two girls laughed at themselves, and at each other, quickly bonding while unpacking and putting their own personal touches on their own personal side of the room. That night, after dinner with other new students in the cafeteria, and even more talk, the two climbed into their own bed and slept quite comfortably, until they were awakened by a loud knock on the wooden door by an upper-class student just looking for any excuse to make their lives sheer hell, as tradition always had it.

That first year at the Newcomb College flew by, and other than the constant hazing from the upper-class students and learning to conform to the strict rules set forth by the college for new students, Monique, as she now liked to be called, found herself quite content and looking forward to the years ahead. Monique had made it her personal business to visit the registrar when she first arrived to personally thank her for her kindness and the help she had set forth to help the Menard child gain entrance at the college.

"I simply passed along your own words, my dear," the registrar had responded. "I was just the messenger."

The registrar was also very clear to let Monique know that she would be there to help her throughout her college years, if there was ever a time that she needed help, of any proportion.

Monique loved everything about the academic program at Newcomb College but was especially excited about the talk going around about a new game called basketball, a game created for men by Dr. James Naismith, a Canadian, who eventually became a physical education instructor in Springfield, Massachusetts.

The very first game of Dr. Naismith's basketball was played on January 20, 1892, and required the players to throw the ball into a "peach basket" in order to score a point. Also in that same year, 1892, physical education teacher Senda Berenson of Smith College in North Hampton, Massachusetts, became extremely interested in modifying the game created for men into a game for women as well, and the very first women's game was played on March 21, 1893 (around the same year Monique Menard turned twenty years old), and was held between the Smith freshmen and the Smith sophomores.

Serious interest in the popular game made its way to H. Sophie Newcomb College around the year 1893, when Clara Gregory Baer, who specialized in physical education at Newcomb College, began to show her students the fundamentals of the game. By 1895, Newcomb College was in the rotation to play basketball with other colleges for women, such as Smith, Mount Holyoke of South Hadley, Massachusetts; Wellesley of Wellesley, Massachusetts; Vassar, located in the Hudson River area of Poughkeepsie, New York; and Bryn Mawr, located at Bryn Mawr, in Pennsylvania.

During the early days of the women's game, only certain parts of the female body could be shown to the public: the hands and head (of course) and the area between the head and the shoulders, which meant that the women could actually trip over their own clothing while running up and down the court.

Clara Gregory Baer solved that problem around the year 1896 when she introduced bloomers, or what could be called a skirt that was split down the middle, which gave the women the freedom and ease to run harder, spread their legs farther, and still meet the strict rules of the college as well as the fashion sense of the era.

Many parents of the young women of Newcomb College that had shown an interest in the game were concerned about their daughter's physical health because they were running and jumping so much during such a rigorous game. To eliminate their concerns, as well as her own, Dr. Baer introduced the fifteen-minute half that required the women to play two halves with a rest period in between the two.

The game became so popular that Dr. Baer created the "Basketball Rules for Women and Girls," which was published and distributed throughout the women's colleges that had adopted the new game as part of their physical education curriculum. The journal also described the one-handed and the jump shot that she described as Newcomb ball.

Monique Menard had always known that she had inherited her beloved father's long, long legs and knew that one day they would come in handy for something, and while watching a demonstration of the game during her physical education class, she quickly realized that the new game would certainly be one of those handy things, indeed. She became absolutely fascinated, and after discussing the game with her parents, who insisted that the game not interfere with her academic education, Monique proudly stepped onto the court to learn more about Newcomb ball. Monique Menard was truly a natural, with her natural ability to run fast and far and to jump high, which certainly caught the absolute attention of the Physical Education Department of Newcomb College. Monique Menard became one of the top players of the Newcomb College team until her final season, which ended just before her graduation in 1897.

"I'll bet there were more catfights and name-calling during those early years of women's basketball than fights between real cats and dogs," my sweet uncle Michele would always say. "We all know you can't put that many women together at one time without something going wrong!"

Of course, my dear old uncles would agree to that statement, especially since they were all worried about what their wives were saying about them at that exact time!

Newcomb ball might have been Monique's choice as an extra-curricular activity, but Margaret McPherson, who now enjoyed being called Maggie, on the other hand, found her fascination in Newcomb pottery, which was also introduced to the students of Newcomb College around 1895 by Ellsworth Woodward, director of art instruction.

Interest in the pottery class quickly grew as well, and Mary Sheerer was soon added to the new class as assistant director. Her pottery designs were introduced to Joseph Meyer, who served the college as the potter, creating beautiful, quality pieces of pottery that were decorated by the students during their art classes. Unlike Newcomb ball, Newcomb pottery provided a skill for its graduates that could easily provide a way for making a living in the outside world.

Monique Menard would return to her dormitory room each evening thoroughly exhausted and sweaty, while Maggie McPherson returned to the dormitory thoroughly exhausted and covered in paint. After washing up and redressing, the two young women would walk across campus to have dinner with classmates in the cafeteria, and then, after evening study, the two would climb into their respective beds and easily fall asleep. The routine would begin again in the early morning, when some upper classmate would ring the loud school bells for an extended period, just to seemingly aggravate the newcomers.

Newcomb College was also known for the caliber of its academic studies, the teaching of reading, writing, and arithmetic as well as world history, art, and music history. Monique Menard was particularly interested and excelled in her studies of arithmetic, which, of course, surprised her parents and even herself. Arithmetic came just as easy for Monique as basketball did; perhaps the two had some sort of connection in her brain that helped her to outshine everyone in her arithmetic class, and almost everyone on the basketball court.

Monique also loved to write, to express herself on paper with pencil, in a manner that she sometimes found difficult to articulate within the boundaries of the classroom. From her very first encounter with Newcomb College through her experience with the registrar, Monique had been taking notes of her feelings about everything, a journal of emotions that was much better expressed on paper than aloud; after all, this was the child of Dolice Marie LaPierre-Menard, who truly knew how to express herself.

By the time Monique completed her first year of college, Jean Pierre III was being admitted to the University of Toronto in Canada with the assistance of Lord and Lady Menard. There he found his own academic and physical education passions, law and Canadian ice hockey! Patima Salma, on the other hand, would be one year ahead of her best friend, Lizzie in her education at the local college for women in New York.

By this time, Wilhelm and Angeline had journeyed across state and international lines to visit each other several times, and it was becoming quite apparent to both of them, and those that knew them, that the two were most definitely committed to each other. The adorable Frenchwoman had finally found the man of her dreams, one that would love her, one that would never leave her, and she was now at peace.

Angeline had also become quite accustomed to the fact that Wilhelm was absolutely enchanted with Canadian ice hockey, and she found herself enjoying the sport herself; however, she was having just a little trouble becoming accustomed to the Canadian cold. Wilhelm would just hold the petite Angeline just a little closer when she began to shiver. My dear old uncle Gaston would ask the young boys what they thought would happen with Wilhelm and Angeline, and their response was that they would certainly date and eventually marry, and that they did!

It would be during one of Angeline's visits to Toronto, Canada, that Wilhelm would finally set the stage for a long and happy future together with the woman he simply cherished. A local ballet troupe was scheduled to perform the Russian ballet *Swan Lake* by Tchaikovsky at the local Canadian opera house during one of Angeline's visits to Toronto.

Tchaikovsky's *Swan Lake* was the very first ballet that had ever been set to a score written by a symphonic composer and was Wilhelm's very favorite ballet; he, therefore, made sure that he had tickets for the event prior to Angeline's visit.

It would be during act II of the ballet, when the prince himself is frozen while witnessing a delicate swan as it is being transformed into a lovely young woman, a woman who identifies herself as the swan queen, Odette, one of many that had been placed under a spell by the evil Von Rothbart. According to the ballet, the spell turned the young women into swans during the day and back to human form at night.

And while Odette explained that the tears of her own grieving mother had created the waters of the lake and that the spell could only be broken if a man that had never been in love vowed his eternal love to her and married her, Wilhelm leaned over to Angeline and vowed his eternal love to her and asked her to marry him.

Angeline eventually moved to Toronto, Canada, to marry and live with Wilhelm, leaving her interest in the New Orleans House to the lovely lady Gloria, the one that had simply charmed Lord Menard during the younger Menard's wedding at Miss BB's mansion. The lovely little cottage that Miss BB had built for Angeline became their winter home, allowing Wilhelm and Angeline to live the best of both worlds throughout their entire lives.

Chapter 31

EVERYTHING AS WELL as everyone in our family has a story, and the stories of the big house are just as important, eventful, and worthy of being mentioned in the traditional telling of the family stories, as well as the people who found themselves walking in and out of its doors at some time or another.

From the personal quarters of the former Master and Mistress LaPierre during the days of slavery, to a…uh-hum, a house of ill repute; from a church house to a boardinghouse for former, need I say, ladies of the night; from a party house to its final blueprint plan as a nursing home, the big house had seen its share of stories, and Lord, if those walls could only talk, there would probably be even more stories than could ever be told!

The very final reconstruction of the big house at Mon Village on the Bayou Frou-Frous was actually created due to demand by the Menards' beloved daughter, Monique Aimee Elizabeth LaPierre-Menard. I might also add that this final reconstruction of the big house was a peek into the final installment in the history of the Menard and LaPierre family.

But I shared with Miss Gracie that I truly thought that we should dabble just a tad into the historical contributions that Labelle Jelee brought to the family, as well as to the big house, before we charted any more waters of LaPierre and Menard stories.

Labelle Jelee and her House of Entertainment

My uncle Simon was always the one that volunteered to tell the story of Labelle Jelee and the big house of Mon Village. He always cleared his throat and shook his head with just the slight presence of a mischievous smile and began.

"What a little spitfire," he would always say. "No one could ever put anything past that little girl!"

Absolutely no academic goals, no future academic goals, and certainly her marks reflected that fact. Her only true interest was in designing clothes, and especially clothes that exposed lots and lots of flesh, to the dismay of her mother, Evelina.

"Chile, go put some clothes on!" Evelina could be heard throughout the residential area saying to her youngest daughter.

"I do have clothes on, Mama," she would answer. "Just not the kind of clothes *you* would wear."

The two would go on and on and on, arguing over the clothes that Jelee chose to wear, the designs in which she styled her hair, the amount of face powder she chose to put on her cheeks, and the amount of red lipstick she put on her lips. It was a never-ending argument, but Jean Pierre, on the other hand, believed that Evelina should work with the child, not against her, to teach her to sew properly and to help her with her creations instead of "pickin' on her," as he would always say.

After contemplating on the latter, Evelina finally decided to heed her husband's words and set up a time for the two to work together to create the fashion designs that were in her daughter's head, a special time the two could share together as mother and daughter.

Jelee believed that women should wear their bloomers outside, without a skirt or dress covering them, and that they should be gathered around the bottom, which should fall just below the knee, and topped with a camisole created out of some smooth fabric that would feel especially good when run through the fingers. Jelee also believed that clothing should be created out of brightly colored fabrics, not just white, the dark grays, navy blues, and blacks that she was accustomed to not only wearing but also seeing other women wearing as well.

Evelina was having a difficult time accepting any of her daughter's thoughts but was most against her clothing designs that exposed the entire leg below the knees. Jelee assured her that this was definitely the style in places like Chicago and New York that she would find depicted in the catalogs she ordered and received from all over the world.

"Besides," Jelee would say with a snap in her voice and a flip of her head, "there are going to be even shorter skirts and dresses in the very near future, Mama. You just wait and see!"

"Well, child," Evelina would snap back, "jest as long as you ain't wearin' them, I could care less what everybody else is wearin'!"

Jelee made her intentions quite clear to her mother that her designs were going to sell in those big cities that she wanted to visit, and even perhaps where she might even live one day. Fashion was changing, and Jelee was not going to remain a "country bumpkin" wearing dark long oversize clothing!

After many discussions with Jean Pierre, Miss Sylvia, and even the elderly Miss Penelope, who actually thought Jelee's designs were quite pretty and very stylish, Evelina compromised and assisted her daughter's designing process but still would not agree to let her wear them, not where she or anybody else could see her wearing them anyway.

"Well, then," Uncle Simon would say, "that meant that Jelee had to find a place to model her new fashions, the ones that her mother said she did not want to see her in. So guess where she decided to wear them?"

Why, where, indeed?

Jelee, who already had made big plans for the big house for some time to come in the future if she could not find a way out of Mon Village, began to sneak out of her parents' home in the darkness of night while her parents and her siblings were still asleep and run like a fury to the big house, where she would sneak in with her own designer clothes, a hairbrush, and plenty of makeup.

Since the church house had already been constructed, and Jubil's construction crew had already created new homes for Miss Annabelle and the ladies that once did business at the big house, there would be no one at all there but Jelee and her vivid imagination. But Jelee would not be alone for too very long.

Something else began to happen in the big house while Jean Pierre and Evelina were sleeping, something that Jean Pierre and Evelina had no idea was happening; in fact, only Jelee and the small group of people that she had let into her inner circle of trusted friends knew exactly what was happening at the big house.

"Ya'll know something, if that was my child," Uncle Simon would say, "I would have ripped her a new one when I found out what she was doing!"

Well, it would, however, be a long time before Jean Pierre and Evelina, and the other parents of the other young people that were following Jelee, I might also add, found out exactly what was going on at the big house while they were sound asleep. And just what were they doing so late at night? Why, they were having themselves a ball!

The truly brave Jelee had convinced a few of her friends, those her own age and some a little older, all the female persuasion (thank goodness!), to join her at the big house during the night of the last day of school for the week, after their families had fallen asleep. Once inside, the young people would do just what their own parents had done before them when the Master and the Mistress LaPierre had gone off into the Bayou Frou-Frous. They would have themselves an extremely good time!

Jelee had transformed the main parlor of the big house into a party, complete with velvet-covered divans and heavy velvet curtains to hide the inside from the outside (covers and curtains that she had designed herself, I might also add), stocked it with plenty of food and apple wine that she would sneak into the big house as well, and of course, there would be several new clothes designs that she had created during the week for her friends to view and eventually enough for the other young girls to wear. And of course, there was plenty of face powder to color the cheeks, dark pencil to outline the eyes, and of course, plenty of red lipstick for the lips.

After partying heartily for several hours, the young people would sneak back into their own homes and climb into their own beds as if they had never escaped.

Months and months after the very first time Jelee and her friends had their party time in the big house, there began to be rumors throughout the residential area that someone or something was making noise in one of the rooMiss. Occasionally, dim candlelight would be seen, seemingly spinning around and around and then suddenly disappearing from sight, only to reappear again later in the night.

There were also reports of eerie sounds coming from the big house, and sometimes even loud thumps came from what appeared to be the porch, and since nothing and no one could be seen, some residents began to report that there were spirits, indeed, taking over the big house, again, and eventually they would take over the residential area! Some residents even discussed that this could be the possible return of some of the spirits that Preacher Bubba McKnight had expelled so many years ago from the big house.

Jean Pierre and Jubil made plenty of excuses at first for the strange activity at the big house, but the residents of Mon Village insisted upon an investigation to find out the truth, and they would not accept anything but the truth, so Jean Pierre and Jubil planned to do just that, investigate.

It would be in the middle of the night that Jean Pierre instructed Evelina to make sure that their children were safe throughout the remainder of the night by bolting the door to their house behind him as he disappeared from the front porch. Jubil met Jean Pierre in the middle of the residential area, and the two slowly walked the distance toward the big house, and once there, the two set up their surveillance behind a row of bushes. There they sat, for hours and hours, waiting for something to happen, but during this first night, nothing did—no sights, no scenes, no nothing!

Jean Pierre and Jubil would repeat this same scenario for days, to no avail, but it would be the night of the day that marked the end of the school week that success was finally achieved.

Again, in the middle of the night, Jean Pierre and Jubil made their way to the bushes that were just a few yards from the big house, and there they began their wait. Because Jean Pierre and Jubil were spending most of their nights waiting in the bushes for something strange to happen and then working all day long, the two found themselves falling sound asleep and actually missed Jelee and her friends as they made their own way to the big house.

Yet again, Jean Pierre and Jubil missed their opportunity to see the root of the eerie happenings at the big house of Mon Village, but that would be the very last time that they did.

After several weekdays of surveillance without success, Jean Pierre and Jubil would set themselves up for their very last attempt! This time the two fought their sleep; in fact, they fought sleep for hours until they caught a glimpse of someone running toward the big house, followed by a group of people in the rear.

"Who could that be?" Jubil asked.

"I surely do not know," Jean Pierre answered, "but I am surely going to find out."

Just as the door to the big house opened, it abruptly closed, and just as the residents had reported seeing, there was candlelight, virtually spinning around and around, and then the light disappeared. The two men slowly walked up the steps to the big house and stood on the porch, crouching down so that they could not be seen through the windows from the inside as they approached the front door. Slowly turning the doorknob to the front door of the big house, Jean Pierre was certainly not surprised that the door was locked.

He immediately began to knock loudly on the door, and when there was no answer, he knocked again, and this time even louder, then he saw the curtain on the window facing him move as if someone was looking out. Jean Pierre knocked again, and this time he heard a muffled conversation just as the door opened and several young girls began to run out from the door, onto the porch, down the steps, and toward the residential area and into the darkness; however, there would be one young girl left standing on the porch of the big house, and that someone would be his own dear youngest daughter.

"Papa!" she squealed. "What are you doing here?"

"No, Jelee," he answered in anger, "what the hell are you doing here?"

Jean Pierre bent down and stared at his daughter straight in the eyes. He held his hands on his hips so as not to give her the biggest whooping she would ever hear of before he took the time to hear her explanation.

"Look at you!" he said. "All that face powder on you, and those short little bloomers, and is that apple wine I smell on your breath?"

Jean Pierre grabbed the child by her arm and began the trek back to the residential area of Mon Village, dragging a screaming Jelee behind him.

"Just close the door for tonight, Jubil!" Jean Pierre yelled out over his shoulder. "I want to get a good look at what is inside, in the light of day!"

After Evelina washed her daughter's face, tapped her several times on her gluteus maximums, threw her in her bed, and slammed the door to her room shut, she met Jean Pierre in the kitchen for some serious conversation about their youngest daughter.

(Oh, by the way, the other children? Those that were with Jelee in the big house? They, too, got the tar whooped out of them and were put on punishment until they were ready to move out of their parents' houses!)

"What was goin' on in the big house?"

"I have no idea, not yet, anyway," Jean Pierre answered his wife soberly.

"Do you think there were boys in there?"

"Jubil and me only saw little girls runnin' outta' there. I sho' hope not, for their sake as well as hers!"

As the conversation between the two parents continued throughout the remainder of the night, it became the general consensus that they were indeed dealing with something that they were not accustomed to dealing with. None of their children, not the older three or the youngest, had ever given them such things to deal with, and the two were definitely at a loss for a solution. And then it happened.

"What are you doing up so early, Mon Claire?" Evelina asked.

The eldest LaPierre child poured a cup of coffee for herself, yawned, and sat down at the kitchen table between her mother and father. "I heard the two of you talking, so instead of just turning over and going back to sleep, I thought I would spend some time with my parents," Mon Claire answered her mother quite matter-of-factly.

"Your sister has been carousin' in the big house, and she has brought other chirren from the residential area over there to carouse with her," Evelina said with a very angry tone.

"This is all new to us," Jean Pierre joined in. "I have to admit, we really have no idea what to do, even how to punish her!"

Jean Pierre and Evelina continued their conversation with their eldest daughter, describing what Jean Pierre and Jubil had found at the big house and the fact that Jelee smelled just like apple wine when she stood directly in her father's face on the front porch.

"Were there are any boys with them?"

"I really think it was jest girls, at least that was all me and Jubil saw runnin' outta the big house."

"Mama, Papa," Mon Claire said as she began to address her parents, "Jelee is a young woman, not a child. You need to stop treating her like a little girl. I think Jelee is trying to get your attention, even the attention you gave to her butt! Think about it for a minute. All of us have some sort of "thing" that we like to do, or be. I like horses, the twins are chefs, Jean Pierre III likes education, and Jelee really has never shown any great love for anything except clothes, shoes, makeup, and fancy hairstyles. Perhaps you should think about the best way to help her to be the best woman she can be. Did you ever think of sending her to school for designing clothes?"

Jean Pierre and Evelina turned toward each other as if a light bulb had suddenly gone off in both of their heads at the exact same time.

"And where would that be? Where would we find such a school?"

"Oh, I guess I could try to find out for you," Mon Claire answered. "Perhaps Chicago, New York, or even places outside of America. I can find out for you, if you would like."

Mon Claire stood up after finishing her coffee.

"Oh, and as far as the apple wine is concerned," she said as she looked over her shoulder and began to walk away from the kitchen. "I keep a jug in my room, in the armoire, right behind my books. And Petois and Pecous? They keep their jug under the front porch. Jean Pierre III has been known to have a sip or two on occasion as well."

Jean Pierre and Evelina sat with their mouths hanging almost down to the floor, perhaps finally realizing that Mon Claire had already become a young woman with goals for a life of her own, that she was indeed making her own way even though she still lived at home, when she was at home, and not with Jubil in the noble Commonwealth of Kentucky.

Mon Claire was right. Petois and Pecous were businessmen in their own right, making their own way with their own money, and were at home only when it was time to go to sleep, while even the baby, Jean Pierre III, was on his way to finishing his studies at the Mon Village schoolhouse and beginning a life of his own as well.

Jelee was nearly twenty years old and was truly ready to face the world, her world, whatever world she would choose for herself, apple wine and all. It was time for Jean Pierre and Evelina to let go and let their children create their own lives.

Within a couple of weeks, Mon Claire was able to find plenty of valuable information about schools that specialized in teaching potential students about designing clothes as well as interior design, which included creating lovely chair and divan coverings and window curtains. Jelee was ecstatic, and after choosing a school in Chicago, she began to make arrangements for the journey, where she would make her own application and meet with the registrar, all by herself.

Jelee would make it to Chicago all right, and she would study all there was to learn about design, and she would eventually become quite successful after graduating, opening her own design shop right there in the middle of downtown Chicago. Upon the occasion of her rare visits home, both Jean Pierre and Evelina would only share their nice comments about her talent, her beautiful designs, and join in her success, even though they still had their own reservations about her style.

It would be approximately twenty years later, during the inception of the Roaring Twenties, that Jelee's designs really took off, during that period when women became more bold, smoking cigarettes in public, when ladies' legs would be shown without any reservation at all, and when men sneaked gin into a speakeasy and drank it out of a woman's slipper, or even from her bathtub.

Yes, Jelee had truly found her place in life, created her own world, and happily lived up to the name that had been given to her by her aunt Dolice Marie LaPierre-Menard, Labelle Jelee LaPierre!

Chapter 32

THE MENARD CHILD's deep love and desire for education, coupled with her fondness for the game of basketball, meant that either she or her parents were seemingly always traveling between Upstate New York and the great city of New Orleans.

Although Mr. Bernard Menard's passion was truly ice hockey, Canadian ice hockey, to be exact, he had become increasingly more fascinated with the women's basketball game that was being taught, as well as being played, at Newcomb College, Tulane University, where his darling daughter was a student and an athlete. The doting father was always prepared to visit the college and spend time with his precious child, even if for just one day at a time.

Madam Menard, on the other hand, had not yet developed that insatiable desire for either of the two sports, but it was apparent that she would truly walk to either destination just to be with her beloved husband and daughter.

MAE's holiday breaks, and semester breaks from school, afforded her ample opportunity to visit her home at the Menard cottage in the great state of New York, where she romped with her sweethearts, Sugar's two babies, Tea and Crumpets, and to spend time with the household staff, especially Wilhelmina the Cook, who had virtually helped raise her.

MAE's constant companion, Sugar, had gone on to wherever pets go to wait for their masters in the grand scheme of things, after giving birth to her two babies, Tea and Crumpets. Sugar just could not handle the stress from the birth of her babies and quietly gave way to her own demise, while being held in Mr. Bernard Menard's arMiss. It was a very difficult time for not only MAE but also Mr. Bernard Menard, Madam Menard, and the Menard household staff. Being at Newcomb College and playing a rigorous game of basketball always helped MAE put that great loss to her in the depths of her heart, where Sugar would live on forever.

MAE always smiled broadly, from ear to ear, I might also add, whenever she saw the Menard carriage parked at the Upstate New York train station, with Edward standing beside the horse and her eager parents rushing toward her as though they had not seen her in forever. The scene might have always been expected but was always truly appreciated.

Patima Salma, Kip, and Kuya were always there as well when MAE reached her home, standing in the doorway of the Menard cottage. Patima always stood there waiting for her best friend's return, and when she saw the Menard carriage driving up, she would begin to run toward it to welcome her Lizzie back home. The two would hug and giggle for what seemed to be forever, trying hard to catch up with each other before they had to share each other with other members of the family.

Patima had accepted the position as one of the teachers at a local private school for girls so that she could always be near her parents, Kip and Kuya, especially after the sad passing away of her beloved grandmother several years before. She always had countless stories about her girls, as she referred to her students, and seemed to bubble over with pride while she spoke about them, and seemed to be quite settled in her decision to stay in the great state of New York.

Jean Pierre III, Jean Pierre and Evelina's sweet baby boy, lived in a dormitory at the University of Toronto in the great city of Toronto, Canada, which had accepted him with the help of Lord and Lady Menard (who just simply adored him, I might also add).

Jean Pierre III was especially happy when the Menards of Upstate New York would visit because he had the opportunity to be with his family, and with Patima Salma, when she chanced to visit with them. In fact, Lizzie had begun to notice a few stolen glances from her cousin Jean Pierre III and her best friend, Patima, while they were all together. Even though MAE had asked questions about the two, neither Jean Pierre III nor Patima had ever answered her questions; both would simply wear a silly grin on their faces.

"Now, you know MAE knew that something was happening there!" Uncle Alexandre would say, as if he had been there himself to see it happening.

"Oh, Alexandre," one of my sweet uncles would always say, "we all know what was happening between the two of them, even way back then!"

And then there would be the laughter, as there always would be laughter with my sweet old uncles. Anyway, back the Menards.

MAE would always enjoy the many festivities that were planned in her honor, especially during her holiday visits with her family and friends, and she certainly delighted in the sights, smells, sounds, and gifts of the season. She especially enjoyed those short trips to the big city with Patima and Jean Pierre III—this, of course, was when they were older and he could also find the time to come for a visit.

Seasonal lights and choirs of angelic voices filled the air while the three savored a cinnamon stick dipped in a mug of hot chocolate or a fancy petit fours, all dressed up in holiday style. MAE could not be happier and never tired of the fanfare, but ever so subtly, ever so discreetly, times were changing and difficulties were on their way within the protected confines of the Menard household.

Perhaps it was MAE herself that began to notice those tiny hints that something was wrong with her parents, and at first, after a chat with the aging Wilhelmina, Maggie, or Edward, she was able to be consoled with their explanation that her parents were simply getting older and just beginning to develop their own special set of circumstances between themselves.

"It is to be expected," Edward always assured her. "Nothing for you to fear, my darling."

Always reassured by Edward's kindness, MAE would make her journey back to school, and then shortly after returning to her own school routines, she would allow her daughterly concerns to fade—that is, until her next visit home.

MINT JULEP

MAE began to notice that sometimes, only sometimes at first, her parents seemed to stop talking to her right in the middle of a sentence, only to stare at her as if they suddenly had no idea who she was. It would be only after hearing their child's sweet young voice again that they seemed to snap out of it. Again, the reassurance of Edward and the other members of the Menard household staff that her parents were indeed just experiencing the journey toward old age comforted the child, and she simply dismissed her parents' actions once again.

It would be during one particular visit at home, however, that MAE saw the journey of old age manifesting itself right before her very eyes. While the child was in her bedroom, freshening up for dinner, she noticed her parents strolling past her doorway, laughing, holding onto each other and peering deep into each other's eyes as if they were young lovers again. Just as they passed her door, the two suddenly backed up and stood directly in the doorway, paused, and began to stare at her for a moment. It was truly an awkward moment.

"Hello," her father finally said with a curious smile. "Is this your first voyage?"

MAE was thoroughly shocked and confused, but before she could even attempt to answer his question, her mother chimed m.

"What a lovely stateroom you have here, my dear." Madam Menard stuck her head in the room and began to survey the contents of the room as she smiled. "Perhaps we will have the opportunity to talk together at dinner," Madam Menard said. "Will we see you there?"

MAE was finally able to catch her breath to answer, "Why, yes, dinner. I will see you there."

The two continued their stroll just as they had been enjoying before their brief encounter with their daughter, and she found herself sitting on the side of her bed, mouth open, completely unable to move until she heard Maggie calling her for dinner.

MAE quietly entered the formal dining room, where her parents were already seated. She sat in her chair, staring with great anticipation at her parents while waiting for what was to come next.

"Are you okay, Aimee?" her father asked with true concern. "Is something wrong?"

"Are you not feeling well, darling?" her mother asked, reaching over to touch her hand.

Realizing that they were truly "back to normal," MAE answered her parents, but still quite apprehensively, "Oh, no, I am just fine." She said this while forcing a smile. "And how are you two?" she bravely asked, searching their eyes as if she might be able to see deep within them to find the answers she certainly wanted and so desperately needed.

"We could not be better," Mr. Bernard Menard answered. "What could make us happier than to have you home, my darling?"

But MAE was not convinced that her parents "could not be better," and thus, after dinner, she settled herself for the night with a decision to investigate the situation more with Patima, the members of the Menard household staff, and to have a little chat with Kip and Kuya when the sun welcomed the new day.

After a night of tossing and turning, MAE awakened early the next morning to the delightful smells of Cook's kitchen and the realization that she had lots of work to do on this, her last full day at home before traveling back to school in the great state of Louisiana. She began to go over her mental list of people to see and questions to ask, resolving to get to the bottom of the present set of circumstances with regard to her beloved parents within the short time that was still remaining during this visit home. She quickly made a path to Patima's house and heard her say the exact same thing that everyone else was saying: "They're just getting older, Lizzie, nothing to worry about."

MAE convinced Patima to come with her to the Menard cottage to see for herself. She knew eventually she would need a witness, so why not a witness that had known them for years and years?

Once inside the Menard cottage, MAE and Patima entered the kitchen to discuss the situation a little further with Wilhelmina the Cook, but she quickly caught sight of her parents first, both fully clad in formal attire, her mother sporting a lovely two-piece white-and-navy-blue pinstriped suit, her hair swept up under a fashionable white hat with a navy-blue band, cocked to one side, and she was holding a lovely silk-covered parasol.

Her father, Mr. Bernard Menard, on the other hand, was quite debonair in an eggshell-colored suit with matching navy-blue tie. Both were sitting at the informal kitchen table with their backs to her, exactly where she and Patima had once sat with Wilhelmina for breakfast or lunch, or just a quick snack when they were much younger children.

MAE could see by the look of sheer confusion in Wilhelmina's eyes that something, something just not right, was going on between her and Mr. Menard and the Madam Menard. She stopped, frozen in her tracks in the doorway, where she could not be seen, to observe and listen.

"Well, then," Mr. Bernard Menard was saying to Wilhelmina, "we would certainly appreciate it if you could find out just what time the stagecoach leaves for the falls once the ship docks at Niagara. We will be celebrating our anniversary tomorrow and could not think of a single place more charming to do so than Niagara Falls—the Canadian side, of course, the Horseshoe Falls."

"Of course," Wilhelmina answered, slowly raising her eyes to meet those of the Menard child.

"Wonderful!" he exclaimed, raising his hand in the air and smiling broadly. "I would say we have enough time for a short nap," he continued, offering his arm to a blushing Madam Menard.

She giggled, accepted his arm, and twirled her parasol with the other hand. As the two of them turned to exit the kitchen, they came face-to-face with MAE and Patima, who were utterly shaken, indeed.

"Hello, my dear," Madam Menard said with a big smile. "I hope you are enjoying your cruise."

"Cruise?" Patima repeated the Madam Menard's word while looking at MAE with an air of bewilderment.

"Yes, yes, I am," MAE answered her parents, totally bewildered herself and yet forcing a smile, after giving Patima the signal not to say anything.

Mr. Bernard Menard tipped his hat to Patima, smiled as well, and then the two slowly strolled away, arm in arm, beneath Madam Menard's parasol.

MAE plopped herself down on one of the chairs in the informal kitchen, buried her head in her hands, took a deep breath, and then, while resting her jaw upon her hand, began to question Wilhelmina, who was quite taken aback herself about what she had just witnessed.

"Have you ever seen them like this before?" MAE asked Wilhelmina when she was finally able to speak.

"Not this bad," Wilhelmina answered casually. "I thought they were just teasing with each other, you know, when they get that way. This was the worst I have ever seen them, though, almost oblivious to reality!"

"I understand," MAE said as she stood up. "This is far greater than the two of them just growing older." She turned to face Patima. "And it is far greater than just me or any of the rest of us."

While Mr. Menard and the Madam Menard enjoyed their nap, their sweet daughter, dragging her best friend, Patima, with her as usual, took that time to ask questions of all the household staff, Kuya, the groundskeeper, and Kip, who always had the cure for whatever ailed her friend, Madam Menard, along with Maggie and Edward.

Both Kuya and Kip maintained that the mister and the missus were growing older, indeed, but lately both had begun to notice that the Menards had been more isolated from other people, and yes, sometimes even detached from their common surroundings.

"We did not want to worry you unnecessarily if it was simply the two of them growing older," Kuya tried to assure MAE. "I, too, had noticed the situation becoming somewhat more obvious but had chosen to wait to see if my observation was correct or not."

"Both the mister and the missus are in such good hands here," Kip said as she gently touched MAE's hand. "They are truly loved and well cared for by all of us. No need for you to worry so far away from home."

MAE listened carefully with both her head and her heart, struggling to keep her tears from flowing down her cheeks, but it was Wilhelmina, Maggie, and Edward that encouraged her to shed her tears and helped her decide what her next move should be in order to properly care for her parents.

"Come on, Lizzie," Patima said, "are you not a student in college where access to all the resources are available to you? Why not bring your concerns to one of your professors?"

Why not, indeed?

"Great idea," she answered. "As soon as I get back to school, I will make an appointment with someone that can help me to sort through some of this, or perhaps lead me in the right direction."

Well, it seemed as though MAE now had a plan, and what a plan it would prove to be, if you know what I mean!

The vastness of the magnificent Mississippi River as it thundered in the opposite direction of the speeding train that was headed toward the great city of New Orleans was of no consequence to MAE, whose mind was consumed solely with the disposition of her parents. The trip from the great state of New York to her temporary home at the Newcomb College dormitory was usually grueling and left her exhausted for several days after, but this particular trip seemed to fly by without notice, without time, without thought, except the thought of a conversation she would most assuredly have with one of her professors as soon as it could be arranged.

Since the invention of the telephone in the recent years, most of the colleges on the eastern coast of the United States were now equipped with at least one telephone per dormitory, and so MAE also planned to call her cousin Jean Pierre III, who had become as close to her as any brother could be. Perhaps he might also have an idea as to what might be done about her beloved parents; after all, Madam Menard was Jean Pierre III's aunt, or cousin, whichever; they were most definitely close family.

(She also made a mental note to ask Jean Pierre III about the secret glances and smiles between himself and her best friend, Patima.)

MAE gave no never mind to the friends and classmates that she encountered on her way to her room in the campus dormitory, where her roommate was already asleep, and after strategically placing her train cases in her closet, the Menard child removed her high-top lace-up shoes, climbed on top of the covers of her bed, fully clad, I might also add, and drifted off to a sound sleep.

The sound of the headmistress's whistle announcing the early-morning wake-up did its job, and within seconds, all the girls in Newcomb Hall dormitory could be heard scurrying around their respective rooms to get dressed and face the new day. With no regard to Maggie McPherson, who expressed her concern about her new friend, MAE simply slipped back into her high-top lace-up shoes, raked her fingers through her golden-brown hair, and stuffed it under a casual hat, then she slipped through the hallway, virtually unseen, and walked out of the door toward the office of the dean of student affairs, Dr. Gabby—which sounded like a nickname for Gabrielle—Latolais, whose office was located on the other side of the campus.

"Why not just start at the top?" MAE asked herself after finally making a decision.

A young woman who identified herself as an assistant to the dean of student affairs met MAE just inside the door to the dean's office and asked why she needed an audience with Dr. Latolais.

"A personal matter," MAE answered. "Nothing to do with school."

After a brief wait in the outer office, she removed her casual hat and was escorted into the office, where she was introduced to a tiny lady that appeared entirely too small for the big desk behind which she was seated in an equally big chair that seemed too big for her as well. Her salt-and-pepper hair was piled high on top of her head, rolled neatly in a bun, while her circular black glasses appeared to cover almost all her face. She was dressed in a neatly starched and ironed dark-colored dress with a white choirboy collar that boasted the Newcomb College faculty pin.

MAE was already aware of Dr. Latolais's impressive qualifications, as were outlined in her public curriculum vitae, and on any other day but this day, she would most probably be shaking in her high-top lace-up shoes in her presence, but there was no time for those childish reservations; there was adult business to address.

"Dr. Latolais," she began, extending her hand to greet the dean. "My name is Monique Menard. My father is—"

"I know who both you and your father are," Dr. Latolais interrupted with a genuine, quite-thick French accent, standing to accept her hand. "Not only are you a good student here, but a favorable athlete on the school's basketball team as well. Your father has been extremely kind to Newcomb College, and I am personally grateful. However, in a matter of moments," she continued, focusing her attention on a large clock in the corner of the office, "both of us will be late for class, and so I would suggest we get down to business."

"Yes, madam," MAE answered and then began, with her usual poise, an emotional description of the goings-on in the Menard household in Upstate New York with regard to her parents.

She repeated what she had witnessed firsthand while at home for this latest visit and the findings of the people most involved with both her father and her mother, while Dr. Latolais listened attentively for several minutes.

"I need your help," MAE concluded. "If not from you, madam, then please direct me to someone that can help."

"It is certainly true that your parents are experiencing some sort of problem that causes them to act and react the way they do," Dr. Latolais explained, "but there are two concerns that came to my mind as you were speaking. If this is truly senility or dementia, why are both experiencing the exact same symptoms at the exact same time? And why do they assume that the two of them are on a cruise ship?"

MAE listened carefully to Dr. Latolais's every word, but her attention stayed on the words *senility* or *dementia*.

"Miss Menard!" Dr. Latolais's voice sounded throughout the office of the dean of student affairs, bringing her back to the reality of the moment.

"Did you hear what I said?"

"Yes, madam, I am so sorry," she answered Dr. Latolais with all due courtesy. "But unfortunately, I cannot seem to get past your diagnosis of *senility* and *dementia*."

"It is not a diagnosis, young lady, it is simply an opinion," Dr. Latolais continued. "After all, I am a doctor of education, not of medicine. But my suggestion to you is that you wait a little longer to see how this situation progresses. From your own observation, your parents have a loving, attentive family in New York that will care for them and keep you well-informed."

"Yes, madam," MAE answered with a slight bow of her head, a courtesy taught to the students in their etiquette class. "You have been most helpful."

"One more thing," Dr. Latolais said as she stood and walked around the big desk to come almost eye to chest with MAE. "It would be a great loss to Newcomb College, for many reasons, if you were to leave school before completing your education, my dear, if that is what you are contemplating at the present time. I do suggest that you give much thought before you feel the overwhelming need to leave school, your education, your future, to care for your parents."

After a few moments of silence, MAE smiled and, with another slight bow of her head, excused herself. Once outside the office of the dean of student affairs, she popped her casual hat back upon her head and began the walk back to Newcomb dormitory.

"I am sure Newcomb College would miss the Menard money much more than the Menard child!"

Chapter 33

Jubil stood frozen in his tracks for a moment while brushing a horse that was being boarded at the LaPierre stables; once moving again, he led the horse into its stall and raced to the front of the stables, where the fancy LaPierre carriage was waiting. Hitching another horse to the carriage, Jubil jumped aboard the carriage with the reins in his hands and headed quickly toward his own house, where Miss Sylvia was waiting for him on the porch. "Someone is coming!" he yelled from the carriage. "I do not know who it is this time, but I am on my way to the Atchafalaya River train station to pick him or her up!"

Miss Sylvia waved her hand and smiled. "Be careful!"

Jubil had traveled countless of times to the Atchafalaya River train station, but this time toward the unknown.

The huge train was just pulling into the Atchafalaya River train station when Jubil tied the horse and carriage to a pole, looking all around himself for a clue to the unknown visitor. He slowly neared himself toward the train as the passengers began to disembark, still quite ignorant as to the reason he was even there.

Suddenly his eyes stopped and focused upon a beautiful young girl with long golden-brown curls hanging beneath a fashionable hat that was the same shade of color as her two-piece traveling suit, with a train case in each hand. If he did not know that his lifelong friend Dolice Marie was in the great state of New York, he would stake his very life that this lovely vision was truly her.

As the young woman stepped off the last train step, she cupped her lovely hazel-green eyes from the sun, and suddenly Jubil's smile met her own and he recognized the lovely lady as the Menard child, Monique Aimee Elizabeth LaPierre-Menard, whom he had not seen since she had fallen in love with the horses at the LaPierre stables many years before.

"Uncle Jubil!" she squealed and began to run toward him as he ran toward her, the two finally meeting in a warm embrace.

"Well, look at you," Jubil said as he pulled her away from himself to get a good look at the young woman who was no longer a child. "So you are the one I had to fetch here from the Atchafalaya River train station!" he continued. "It is about time you decided to come visit your family at Mon Village!"

"I know, Uncle Jubil," she said as the two held onto each other and walked toward the carriage. "But unfortunately, I must also tend to some unfortunate business while I am here, and I hope you, Aunt Sylvia, Uncle Jean Pierre, and Aunt Evelina will be able to help me."

MAE put the two train cases inside the fancy LaPierre carriage and, holding on tightly to her fancy hat, climbed upon the top seat to sit beside Jubil as they made the short journey to Mon Village.

"I am so happy that you still know when someone is coming, Uncle Jubil." MAE smiled. "I could have been here all night long!"

During their time together as they journeyed toward Mon Village, MAE had the opportunity to share a portion of the story with her beloved uncle Jubil, who, by the time the two arrived at Jean Pierre's house, was flooded with tears and heartbreak for both MAE and her beloved parents.

By the time MAE retold the story to her uncle Jean Pierre, her aunt Evelina, and her aunt Sylvia, there were probably enough tears to fill the two large barrels on the back porch that caught drops of rainwater for laundry and head washings, and it was apparent that something had to be done to help Dolice Marie and Mr. Bernard Menard during their time of illness.

Evelina was extremely quiet and thoughtful and, sometime during the family discussion, lifted her head and proclaimed to the family that she had an idea.

"Why not bring the two of them to Mon Village?"

At first, no one commented about Evelina's suggestion, and then MAE dared to ask questions about their current lifestyle. "Where would they live?" she asked. "What about Edward? Maggie? Wilhelmina, their cook? They have been family to Mommy, Dad, and me for many years and even worked at Menard Manor in Toronto, Canada, for my grandparents before that. And what about Kuya and Kip? They have taken care of my parents, the house, the gardens, and the yard. Kip has become Mom's very best friend!"

"Well, they could come too," Evelina responded, as if the answer were as simple as that.

"We would have to build a very big house," Jubil replied.

"Or," Jean Pierre interrupted, "reconstruct what we already have! The big house has been so many other things. Why not a place for older people to stay when they are sick or too old to care for themselves?"

"A hospital?" MAE asked while everyone else listened intently.

"No, not a hospital, more like a home, a really nice home with people there to care for those who are not able to care for themselves," Jean Pierre continued with his suggestion. "We are all getting older. In fact, we are all as old as Dolice and just a few years younger than Mr. Bernard Menard, so a nice place like that would be very useful to all of us in the future, the not-so-far-away future. We could still live together, but there would be other people there to help us take care of ourselves."

"I think it is a wonderful idea," Jubil retorted. "The big house has twelve bedrooms, two kitchens, and several parlors, more than enough room for everyone."

"There is just one problem," MAE said after taking a deep breath. "Mommy and Dad think they are on a cruise ship, traveling around the world, and we are all there with them, including a captain, a stewardess, and lots of deckhands taking care of their every need. Much of the time, they have no idea who anyone is, except themselves."

"Well, I never!" Evelina said, patting herself on her chest. "My, my, my! A cruise ship! I would imagine that does not have to change either," Evelina said with a huge smile. "We can turn the big house into a cruise ship! Dolice owns as much of Mon Village as we do, and the least we can do for her and the man she loves is to make them as comfortable as possible. I say we turn that old big house into a cruise ship!"

After several moments of quiet thought, it would be Dolice's beloved Jean Pierre that ended the discussion and gave his executive approval to the idea.

"Jubil," he began, "we will first need to fix whatever is broken at the big house and make sure it will be ready before the Menards get here."

Jubil quickly responded that he would gather a group of men into a construction crew that would be capable of making the major repairs to the big house, from replacing shingles on the roof to replacing boards in the wood floors, painting the big house with bright colors, and ensuring that it would again be the strong, lasting symbol of the history of the residents of Mon Village.

After questioning many sources and investigating many ideas about the disposition of her parents, MAE was finally feeling more assured and more at peace now than she had been in the preceding months, and she smiled broadly as she announced that she would ask Edward to find out how the Menard import-export company could help make the big house even more efficient and modern.

Evelina and Miss Sylvia agreed that the big house could certainly use new curtains and other new fineries that would make it look even more beautiful, more appealing to the new tenants, and even suggested that pictures of the family should hang on the walls.

"Sort of like a history of our family lined all along the walls of the big house."

Everyone agreed.

Evelina stated that she would contact Jelee in Chicago to ask her to design some lovely covers for the divans and chairs in the big house and to create lovely curtains that could be hung all throughout, all the things that a proper cruise ship would have.

All my sweet uncles agreed that our early family members were always at their very best when they were together, planning something special, and planning to convert the big house into a cruise ship that would meet the needs of the Menards of Upstate New York became everyone's priority.

The Mon Village family agreed with MAE that she should leave everything to them now and head back to school for the last couple of weeks before graduation, with sincere hope that her parents would be in touch with the world and could attend this extremely prestigious event in their daughter's life and be able to enjoy it.

This was MAE's thought throughout her entire journey back to Newcomb College, where she was able to at least concentrate on her final examinations and all those other preparations for graduation, fittings for graduation caps and gowns and rehearsals for walking across the stage of the auditorium as well as how to sit as a lady of refinement would sit for a long period on a hard wooden chair.

Graduation

Maggie McPherson proved to be a great friend to Monique Menard, and after hearing all about Monsieur and Madam Menard and the malady that so concerned her roommate over the past four years, Maggie McPherson offered the exact same advice that she had been getting from everyone else.

"Your parents are evidently in good hands, Monique. You should just be grateful that there are such loving people that surround them and care for them and have cared for you as well. I know someone in New York will send a wire to you if you are needed. What can you do that they cannot?"

"What could she do?" my old uncles would ask.

MAE finally succumbed, not only to Maggie McPherson's suggestion, but also to the suggestion that had been given to her by virtually everyone else that she chose to speak to about her parents' situation. In between academic classes, basketball, and visits to Upstate New York to check on her parents, the last two years of MAE's education at Newcomb College seemed to fly by, and yes, Monsieur and Madam Menard maintained themselves, just as everyone had suggested to her, with the help of all those loving people who did just what they said they would do.

Suddenly, graduation was upon all the graduating class at Newcomb College and their instructors. It was terribly difficult for any of the girls at the Newcomb dormitory to realize that graduation was just a few weeks away, and the excitement was simply thrilling, but it was most difficult for MAE, who had so much more on her mind during the entire last portion of her college life.

Basketball seemed to have been the only thing that had kept her parents' dilemma from creeping into her mind, but she had already played the last basketball game of her life and would soon be awarded her license to teach, and then she would begin her own life and fulfill her own dreaMiss. But just prior to graduation, MAE felt the great need to pay a visit to Mon Village, where she would discuss the disposition of her parents with the only people in the world that would truly be able to understand and give her the help she so desperately needed at this time and for that time in the not-so-distant future.

From the icy environs of Toronto, Canada, to the chilly regions of Upstate New York, to the warmth and mugginess of the Bayou Frou-Frous and that great city of New Orleans, MAE expected and awaited her personal entourage of family, loved ones, and best friends to attend her final graduation. Although she was certainly elated that she would truly be represented by a number of people on her graduation day, MAE also realized that she would be absolutely ecstatic and even more than that if her parents would recognize her and her accomplishments, even if they were the only guests she would have.

Graduation day arrived without a single hitch, and the twenty-six young ladies of MAE's senior class rose to the occasion with the greatest of ease. When the signal was given from one of the professors standing on one side of the stage, the sound of the young women collectively inhaling could be heard just prior to the sounds of the school's song, which instructed the young women to begin their procession to their proper places for the ceremony. With eyes straight ahead, singing loudly and beautifully, and marching in perfect cadence, the procession continued until the final graduate was in her proper place.

Being seated upon the stage in the auditorium to be honored because of her success as a Newcomb College basketball player, along with several other members of her team and still others that would be receiving special accolades for academia, made it much easier to locate those that were there to celebrate with her, so she took advantage of the current set of circumstances, indeed, and scanned the massive audience of relatives and friends to locate hers. And there they were.

Uncle Jean Pierre and Aunt Evelina along from Mon Village; her beloved uncle Obadiah and his wife, Aunt Shirley, from right there in the great city of New Orleans; her uncle Wilhelm and aunt Angeline with Jean Pierre III, from Toronto, Canada; and from her own home in Upstate New York, her beloved Edward, Maggie, Wilhelmina, her best friend Patima, and yes, her beloved parents, Mr. Bernard and Madam Dolice Menard.

The young Menard woman could hardly contain her emotions as she allowed her eyes to settle on her parents' eyes, which seemed connected to hers as well; they smiled and quietly blew kisses to her.

"Well," my uncle Alexandre would always say at this portion of the family stories, "this would be the very last time that the young Menard woman would have such a moment with her parents. But fear not—there are many more fun times with them before they go on to the other world to meet the ancestors!"

After several long speeches by administrators and faculty, the awards ceremony began, which included awards being given to students that had accomplished extremely high marks in their education, those that had excelled in the art and the creation of the now-famous Newcomb College pottery (including MAE's roommate, Maggie McPherson) and, finally, to those that excelled in the athletic department, particularly in basketball.

There would be a sudden burst of applause when the latter was mentioned and continued throughout the entire list of names, including Monique Aimee Elizabeth LaPierre-Menard, the beautiful young woman that fought her way into and captured the hearts of virtually everyone at Newcomb College.

Another long round of applause could be heard as each individual young woman proudly walked across the stage to receive her diploma; even the staff of professors and teachers seemed to boast their pride for both their students and the college itself.

Once the last of the twenty-six graduates had received her diploma and was seated in her particular place, all were instructed to stand, and at the signal from that same professor standing at the side of the stage, the graduates stood in unison and began to procession out of the auditorium in the manner in which they had entered it, but this time to the sounds of *Pomp and Circumstance*.

It was a most beautiful ceremony, to say the very least, after which everyone was invited to attend the graduation reception that was being held in the student atrium of Newcomb Hall, where cake and punch were served.

The LaPierre-Menard families settled themselves at one of the very large tables that had been reserved for them, tables decorated in the school colors with beautiful pieces of Newcomb pottery, balloons, fancy plates, napkins, and silverware, and before long, everyone enjoyed being served by the incoming class of young ladies who would now begin their journey into the future.

Jean Pierre III inhaled every moment of the wonderful day, imagining that it was his own graduation day, which was actually yet another year away, and as his eyes scanned every morsel of the celebration, they fell on a sight from which he could not diverge. There, sitting at another end of the long table next to her best friend, Lizzie, was Patima, whom he felt he was seeing for the very first time.

The strikingly beautiful young woman was sitting next to his uncle Wilhelm and aunt Angeline, with whom he had traveled from Toronto, Canada, attentively listening to them, smiling, and at times appearing to be a delicately sculpted statue. Patima was clothed in a lovely pale-orange dress with see-through sleeves that was gently gathered at the neckline, with sweet little rhinestones covering the bodice. Her long dark hair had been swept up in a perfect bun on top of her head; her dark almond-shaped eyes were enchanting to him, and for the very first time, he realized how very small she was, a tiny angel that he realized at this moment had captured his heart long ago.

"Why not tell her how you feel?" Evelina's voice brought Jean Pierre III back to reality as she whispered in his ear, causing him to jump almost to the ceiling.

"I have no idea what you are talking about, Mother," he calmly answered, but his eyes found their way back to Patima, and eventually their eyes met. Patima smiled and lowered her head to one side, causing Jean Pierre III to smile as well, and then, lo and behold—yes, he did—Jean Pierre III excused himself, walked over to where Patima was sitting, bent over, and in a whisper, told her for the first time in all these years just how he felt about her.

"I think I am in love with you, Patima Salma," he whispered.

Lo and behold, he received a response that he certainly did not expect.

"I know you are, Jean Pierre III," Patima answered with a sweet smile of confidence in that sweet, quiet voice of hers, "as I am with you."

"Now what?" my uncle Rene would always ask. "What do you think is going to happen to Jean Pierre III and Patima?"

The young boys would always answer shyly, "They're going to get married," or "They're going to start dating." Well, actually, both were correct. Jean Pierre III had finally spoken his true feelings to Patima, and she had responded favorably. And yes, they would start "dating," and yes, they would eventually get married.

While Jean Pierre III and Patima sealed their future together with a simple hug that afternoon, MAE snuggled closely with her parents while giggling with the other graduates whose families were now being served by the incoming class of young ladies. What a perfect ending to a perfect beginning!

There were many "Congratulations!" that day, many handshakes, hugs, and the promise of new lives as the graduates and their families said their goodbyes to their professors, one another, and to their times at H. Sophie Newcomb College. But just before leaving the college that had been her home for the past four years, MAE found her way to the kind registrar who had helped her gain entrance into Newcomb College.

"Thank you, again," MAE said. "I will never forget you and what you did for me."

"As I shall never forget you and what you did for me and Newcomb College."

Jean Pierre III and Patima Salma

The story of Jean Pierre III and Patima Salma is one of great love, great love and family devotion, for their own parents and friends, each other's parents and friends, and a truly deep love and devotion for each other.

With Patima teaching in Upstate New York and with Jean Pierre III completing his own education in Toronto, Canada, dating was a little difficult, but the two were obviously committed, and as my old uncle Michele would always say to the young boys, "LaPierre men always find a way, remember that, young men!"

The two would visit whenever it was possible during the final year of Jean Pierre III's education, whether it was Jean Pierre III journeying to Upstate New York to visit with Patima and the Menards or Patima journeying with Monique to visit her grandparents in Toronto, Canada. As the medical condition of Mr. Bernard Menard and his beautiful wife, Madam Dolice Marie Menard, began to progress, it became obvious that it would not be long before MAE would be compelled to take her parents to Mon Village, and that meant that Kuya and Kip would be leaving as well to help care for them.

It would be during one of those visits to Upstate New York, probably just at the turn of the century, to assist with the particulars for the transfer to Mon Village that Jean Pierre III finally sealed the fate between himself and Patima.

"Lizzie has always said that you want to live at Mon Village. Is that true?" Jean Pierre III carefully began.

"Ever since we visited there for the family reunion, when I met you for the first time, I have wanted to live there, as well as teach in the schoolhouse," Patima answered in that sweet voice of hers. "But why do you ask?"

"Your parents and your best friend will be moving there shortly, and other than your students here, you will have no one with you."

"There will be you," she answered, "whenever you can be here."

"But how often will that be?" Jean Pierre III continued. "I can only come to visit so often, with school, so you will be alone much of the time until I graduate."

"Well," Patima answered, "your graduation is just a few months away. I certainly can be alone until then."

"I think you should consider going to Mon Village with Lizzie and the family," he said quickly, "and I can come to meet you there when I have completed my education."

"But what about my students?" Patima asked.

There was a long pause as the two seemed to contemplate the current set of circumstances, and then, as if a bubble suddenly exploded in Jean Pierre III's brain, he gently took Patima's hand in his own, knelt down on one knee, and proceeded to ask the young woman to marry him.

"When?" she asked.

"Now," he answered.

"Yes!" she countered.

"I will ask my father to have my uncle Jubil and a construction crew build a new home for us, and you can stay there until I can meet you there."

Patima stared deeply into Jean Pierre III's eyes, smiled, and then softly touched his cheek with her hand; he met her lips with his own, and then the two embraced.

"We can talk to your mother and father about a small wedding here, and we can have another big ceremony for my parents and the rest of the family when we both get to Mon Village," Jean Pierre III continued with great excitement. "What do you think?"

"I think you love me!" Patima answered. "Just as I love you. But I will not leave here until my own students complete this year. Besides, I intend to attend your graduation!"

Kuya and Kip were delighted to hear that Jean Pierre III had finally asked their daughter to marry him, and after giving the two their blessings, Kuya and Kip immediately began to make plans for the small wedding they wanted.

Jean Pierre III wired his father to let his parents know that he had asked Patima to marry him, about the construction of the new house, and about another ceremony once everyone was there together. Needless to say, both Jean Pierre and Evelina were certainly in agreement that Patima was the perfect person for their beloved son to marry.

Well, there certainly was an enormous amount of activity going on for the LaPierre-Menard family. Jean Pierre was in the midst of overseeing the progress of the conversion of the big house into a pseudo cruise ship to accommodate the needs of his sister and her husband, an overhaul that had certainly taken more time than anyone would have guessed.

There were plenty of new creations by Labelle Jelee, personally brought to Mon Village by Jelee herself, along with other designs that she brought home to her siblings as well as her mother and father, who still could not bring themselves to wear such profound articles of clothing.

The construction of a brand-new house at Mon Village for Jean Pierre III and Patima was just as forthcoming, and taking just as long, unfortunately. Jubil was recognizing the fact that he and Jean Pierre were getting older, and to find younger people that would want to work as hard and as long of a day as the two had always worked was extremely difficult. Many of the young people at Mon Village were more concerned about finding a way out of the peaceful life at Mon Village than they were at being a part of a construction crew that built houses, even if it was just a temporary means of employment.

The entire Menard household as well as Kuya and Kip were preparing to move from Upstate New York to Mon Village in the great state of Louisiana as soon as all was ready for them, and now plans for a small wedding had been added to the long list, which indeed proved to be the easiest of all.

Once Patima and Jean Pierre III had come to their agreements, Patima quickly kissed Jean Pierre III on his cheek and ran off to tell her best friend, Lizzie, that she was, indeed, getting married. Lizzie, in turn, quickly joined Kuya and Kip (after loud screams and big hugs) in their arrangements for a quick small wedding, which had to be within the next few days, since the groom-to-be was due back at school.

Mr. Bernard Menard and Madam Menard were still happily spending their time strolling on what they believed to be a cruise ship, and even though they were with their beloved Aimee every single day of the week, they were still convinced that she was just another passenger during one of their honeymoon cruises, a very nice passenger, albeit, that they truly enjoyed when they happened to encounter her.

"As long as they connect with me in some way, I am grateful," MAE said to the Menard household staff, and after another episode of tears shed for them, everyone went on about their personal business to make the journey to Mon Village as trouble-free as possible.

But even in the midst of all the great activity that was going on all around them, the Menard family priest from the school where both MAE and Patima had attended joined Jean Pierre III and Patima in holy matrimony. It was a lovely ceremony, celebrated in the backyard of the Menard cottage, where both Kuya and Kip had spent so much of their time with Mr. Bernard Menard and Madam Menard. The yard was filled with neighbors and school friends that brought packages wrapped up in pretty wrapping paper and tied with brightly colored string and placed strategically on a table on the patio.

The scent of jasmine filled the air, and beautiful orchids adorned the patio where the ceremony was held. The mystic of the Philippine islands was in the air as well as in the kitchen, where Kip had prepared traditional Filipino dishes for the reception—plenty of seafood and rice, vegetables, and special sauces and gravies that just could not be resisted.

Jean Pierre III was as handsome as his father was when he married Evelina, his mother, so many years before and wore a gray suit with a fashionable ascot and white shirt. The beautiful Patima captured him all over again in her charming white dress with a low-cut, gathered empire bodice with a flowing skirt that fell to the floor. She wore multicolored flowers from Kuya's garden in her upswept hair, a small borrowed comb from her mother to keep it all together, and she carried a bouquet of bluebells that Kuya was able to purchase for his daughter before the wedding.

Madam Menard, who had so graciously accepted the invitation from the "captain" for herself and her husband to attend the wedding, gazed intensely at the young Jean Pierre III throughout the entire event and even seemed to recognize him for a moment or two when she closed her eyes and softly touched his cheek at the reception. He, in turn, reached out and held her tightly for a moment or two before she turned to walk away, looking back several times at him before she joined her husband.

"I just bet she was remembering her Jean Pierre," my uncle Clovis would say, and then, as usual, swelled up with tears.

Within a matter of less than an hour, and after the priest pronounced them as such, Jean Pierre III and Patima had become man and wife, under the watchful eyes of God, and under the legal issues of the great state of New York, amid applause and tears of joy.

It was a wonderful day filled with hope, love, and promise.

After the nuptials and congratulatory hugs and kisses from the family and guests in attendance, Patima readied herself to throw her bouquet into the small group of single female attendees, which included her best friend, Lizzie, who had absolutely no desire to "catch" the thing! But just as she made that point perfectly clear and began to walk away from the group, Patima threw the bouquet, and after it flew into the air over the heads of the other ladies, it landed directly in Lizzie's hands, leaving Patima to laugh hysterically.

"Hey, Lizzie!" Patima yelled out to her best friend. "Did you think it was a basketball?"

After a chuckle or two from my dear sweet old uncles, Uncle Michele would tell the young boys that after Lizzie caught the bouquet, which meant traditionally that she would be the next bride, she stared at it for a moment or two, and contrary to what many of the guests would have believed…

"She kept it!" Uncle Michele would always say. "Perhaps the young woman had a brief thought about herself, her own future, things she had not thought of for so long, and not at all during her parents' illness."

The happy couple, that is, Jean Pierre III and Patima, was whisked off to the great city of New York for the night, and the next day, by a city carriage being drawn by a horse adorned in ribbons and a driver decked out in a tuxedo to commemorate the event, but not before Kip began to cry and cry and cry, so much so that Kuya began to swell with tears as well as he attempted to console her, and then the classmates that were there allowed their tears to flow from their eyes, and finally, Lizzie began to weep with a vengeance, a weep likened only to her sweet mom, Dolice Marie.

What had begun as a joyful occasion was now giving way to the sights and sounds of a funeral. Jean Pierre III and Patima's wedding day was about to fall apart with emotion. But it would be the happy couple that would provide the answer to the current set of circumstances; the two simply climbed into the city carriage and disappeared down the road to the great city of New York!

Alone again, after the reception, with just the Menard household staff and her parents, MAE bade her good nights to everyone and then proceeded to climb the stairs to her room, where, once inside, she cried some more, much more. In fact, she cried herself to sleep.

Chapter 34

TIME SEEMS TO bring with it its own irony, and so it was for the LaPierre-Menard family during the time of such transition, an irony of such sadness in the midst of time.

Jean Pierre III had spent all the free time he could find caring for and enjoying the company of his relatives in Toronto, Canada, Lord and Lady Menard, during his four years in college. The exploitation of his time was even more thinly spread once he and Patima had married, which now included visits to Upstate New York as his priority. The presence of his uncle Wilhelm and aunt Angeline, who cared for and spent time with the elder Menards during those times that Jean Pierre III could not be there, became invaluable, and thus, it was Wilhelm and Angeline that found Lord Menard in his bed, just after his spirit had passed on into the other world to be with his ancestors.

Lady Menard had passed on to the other world just a few years before, during a time when MAE's parents were still capable of recognizing her and Madam Menard's husband's parents and capable of deeply mourning for Lady Menard's passing as well, and soon it became very obvious that Lord Menard was grieving himself so much for his beloved wife that he began to isolate himself from virtually all his friends and the activities that he had once enjoyed so much, including Canadian ice hockey.

Everyone that knew and loved the two elder Menards knew it would not be very long before Lord Menard would go on to where he truly wanted to be, to meet the only love of his life in the other world. It was a bittersweet passing for just that reason.

MAE sadly attended both funerals in the icy regions of Toronto, Canada, where representatives of the highest posts in England and certain members of Canadian royalty came to pay their final respects to both Lord Menard and his only granddaughter. It was always wonderful to spend time with her uncle Wilhelm and aunt Angeline, who had traveled many times to Upstate New York to visit with Mr. Bernard Menard and Madam Menard until it was impossible to absorb the depth of their terrible illness, which was taking the two away from all who loved them. This time her visit to their home would certainly be much shorter than usual as she traveled back to Upstate New York to care for her parents, on the train by herself, alone, with the loss of both of her grandparents now and the illness of her parents.

While journeying back to her home, a home that was in such a disarray with all the packing for the move to Mon Village, MAE wrote hastily in her journal of her memories of both of her grandparents, and her parents, as if she would surely forget what life had been with all of them, for all of them as well, when life for everyone was warm and wonderful.

By this time the dear child had filled several bound booklets of empty pages with her words regarding her experiences with those that she loved, specific events where she had even taken the time to describe what their smile looked like and just how their eyes flickered when they did. Serious events, sad events, and the most hilarious events were included in her journal, and because her mind was remembering so much quicker than her hand could journal her thoughts, she found herself laughing and then crying and then laughing again, and as the train neared the Upstate New York terminal, MAE prepared herself for whatever was waiting for her at home. An aging Edward met MAE at the train station, and the two made the short journey to the Menard cottage, where an aging Wilhelmina the Cook had created a delicious evening meal for her that she enjoyed with the household staff in the kitchen where she had eaten many meals. This was her life now, and after seeing her beloved parents pass the kitchen again, arm in arm, smiling only with each other, she realized that it was certainly time to begin the move, ready or not.

Bon Voyage

The beautiful Menard cottage appeared uncharacteristically vacant of any and all personal effects that had given it life throughout MAE's life, and she sighed a deep sigh of sadness as she closed and locked the door for the final time. Wilhelmina and Maggie, who were also aging, had already taken the journey by train with her parents, thus leaving Sugar's babies, Tea and Crumpets, for company and only Edward to assist her in turning the cottage over to her father's import-export business, the thriving business in which she now had controlling interest with her father's illness. The Menard child had chosen to present the cottage to some other family that would certainly enjoy living there as much as she, and everyone else, had.

Wilhelmina sobbed tears of sadness, so much so that she had to actually be pulled from her kitchen and out of the door by both Maggie, who was also sobbing, and Edward to join the Menards in the carriage, and she sobbed the entire journey to the train station in the great city of New York. Both Wilhelmina and Maggie forced themselves to control themselves as they explained to the Menards that they all would be traveling to another state to board yet another cruise ship that was soon to board for yet another fantastic voyage.

"Will you be traveling with us?" Mr. Bernard Menard said to his daughter. "We always seem to be traveling in the same direction, the three of us!"

"Yes, sir," MAE responded. "I am truly delighted to say that I will be along shortly and am very happy to be traveling in the same direction."

She smiled at her father, and after closing the door to the carriage, Edward gave the signal to the horse to begin his journey to the train station.

Both Jean Pierre and Jubil would be there at the Atchafalaya River train station, waiting to greet the Menards and their party of Wilhelmina and Maggie, who were all too happy to finally get off the uncomfortable seats of the train. There would be several train cases and train trunks for each, and in order to accommodate all those departing the train from the great city of New York, both Jean Pierre and Jubil had driven separate carriages.

Mr. Menard and the Madam Menard kindly chose to be assisted by Jean Pierre to his carriage, which nearly broke his heart into two separate pieces as he stared deeply into his sister's empty eyes and vacant smile. Several times during the walk to his carriage, Madam Menard seemed to recognize him, placing her hand on his arm and staring deeply into his sad eyes, smiling sweetly just as she did when she truly knew who he was.

In the other carriage, Jubil listened quite attentively to Wilhelmina and Maggie as they described what life had been like during the previous few years with the Menards, while their tears fell like waterfalls down their cheeks.

Jubil listened to every word and was especially proud of hearing just how strong Monique (MAE) had been throughout the entire ordeal and how responsive she had been to her parents' every wish. Now, it was time for everyone to be in one place again, and as MAE joined Edward in the Menard carriage just one more time, she suddenly gave way to a smile as she remembered that on this day, she would once again be with her parents as well as her best friends, Jean Pierre III and Patima.

Even the mighty Mississippi River, rolling along without a care in the world, brought that hidden pleasure back to MAE's mind as she pointed out its surrealistic beauty to Edward, who had already become simply mesmerized just as everyone else had been during their first journey toward the great city of New Orleans.

It would be Jean Pierre and his youngest child, Jean Pierre III, that were waiting at the Atchafalaya River train station for MAE and Edward and assisted both with their train cases and train trunks. The short drive to the Mon Village home for the ill offered just enough time for MAE to hear just how everyone was adjusting to their new lives in that place that had, with the exception of herself and her mother, always been such a mystery.

Once the fancy LaPierre carriage passed through the secret entrance to Mon Village, MAE could see the giant flag that sat atop what was once called the big house, and she smiled broadly when she also saw the round windows of a cruise ship that had been created just for her parents by her cousin Labelle Jelee.

The carriage pulled in front of the house and allowed the men to remove the luggage and place it on the porch, where Wilhelmina and Maggie met Edward and Monique. It was a wonderful reunion.

"Mr. Menard and the Madam Menard are sunning themselves on the back porch," Wilhelmina the Cook said to MAE. "Perhaps you would want to say hello to them first, and then we will show you around the house and to your room."

MAE agreed, and after being recognized as the young woman they had traveled with before, she found her way back to the main parlor, where everyone, including her aunt Evelina, uncle Jubil, and aunt Sylvia, was now sitting and enjoying an afternoon cup of tea, a new luxury they had acquired from Wilhelmina.

MAE was quite pleased with the reconstruction and simply adored her new bedroom, which had been personally decorated by Labelle Jelee for her cousin, with beautiful pastel colors, soft thick pillows, and "plenty of lace for the properly poised Miss Menard," as Jelee chose to describe her with a fond laugh.

There would be a pleasant surprise that no one had shared with MAE, definitely for a purpose, but the surprise would show itself when Patima came uncomfortably through the front door of the house: Patima was with child, and by the looks of her, MAE considered the possibility of twins.

"Lizzie!" Patima squealed. "Lizzie!"

"My goodness, Patima!" she answered with all due concern. "Are you about to have this baby or what?"

"I still have about two more months until the baby is born, Lizzie," Patima answered. "I may look like I swallowed one of your basketballs, but the way this baby kicks me, I feel like the entire team is in there!"

MAE had not been able to attend the big wedding ceremony of Jean Pierre III and Patima but was now about to hear all about it.

The two young women hugged each other as carefully as they could, considering the present set of circumstances, and then both walked off to talk, and talk they did, and giggled like when they were both just two little girls again, for hours and hours, until Wilhelmina called for everyone to meet in the dining room for dinner.

Shortly after everyone had sat down at the dining room table, Maggie entered the room with Mr. Menard and the Madam Menard, who were both dressed in their formal fineries for dinner. Both smiled and extended their hellos to everyone at the table, and for some unforeseen reason, MAE felt quite comfortable talking with her parents, on their terms, and found herself finally at peace about the entire situation.

Living at Mon Village proved to be everything MAE had expected it to be, and as soon as the summer months would be over, she would have her opportunity to find out what she could do in the schoolhouse, which seemed to be calling her name.

Although she had been raised in the tradition of the English Catholic Church, MAE had lately become quite intrigued by the Protestant profession of faith and, I might also add, found herself attending the Mass and the Protestant service every Sabbath with her cousin Mon Claire, whenever she was at home from the noble Commonwealth of Kentucky, and most of the other members of the LaPierre family.

MAE, in fact, found it quite hard to wait until the following Sabbath to hear the sermon preached by the handsome young pastor Benjamin Broussard, who found himself enjoying the Sabbath for the exact same reason, to see the beautiful new member of his congregation.

Patima spotted the attraction right away and began to urge her best friend to pursue such a fine man as the pastor Benjamin Broussard, but MAE's mind was deeply rooted in caring for her parents, pursuing her goal of teaching at Mon Village, and enjoying being there with family and friends, just as she had always wanted to be.

"The attraction was definitely there, between both the pastor and MAE," my uncle Alexandre would always say. "And who better than a man of the cloth to be both forthright and understanding?"

Jean Paul III and Patima

It would be during that time of the year when the days steamed with the heat of a Louisiana summer but the early mornings and nights brought a chill to the bone that Jean Pierre III and Patima's baby chose to come into the world.

The residents of Mon Village had become accustomed to seeing the two young people walking hand in hand throughout the residential area in the cool of every evening as they sat on their porches, and many commented lightheartedly about the rise in Patima's belly and the measured gait of her step during the months before the birth of their baby. She would smile that beautiful smile of hers while he seemed to stand a little taller and raised his head a little higher while he bade his "Good evening" as they passed each house.

"Now you know all LaPierre men have a certain arrogance about themselves when it comes to their offspring," Uncle Simon always liked to point out to the young boys.

"Yeah, you right," one of my other uncles would chime in, and then all of them would agree and sit up a little taller and raise their heads a little higher, just like our ancestor did before us.

Anyway, back to Jean Pierre II and Patima!

It would be during one of those pleasant evening strolls throughout the residential area of Mon Village that Patima felt that very first twinge of a labor pain, and she stopped in her tracks, put her hand under her belly, and leaned on her husband. He, of course, nearly panicked.

"Are you all right?" he asked.

"Yes," she answered softly. "I think it was either an elbow or a foot that just punched me!" she teased him, and he immediately felt calmer, but just for the moment.

"Oh!" Patima squealed minutes later. "That one really hurt!"

"Maybe we should head on over to my parents' house," Jean Pierre III said as he covered her shoulders with his arms and led the way to Jean Pierre and Evelina's house in the residential area.

Jean Pierre and Evelina were comfortably sitting in rocking chairs on their porch when Jean Pierre III and Patima made their way up the steps to their house.

"I think something is wrong," Jean Pierre III said to his father as Evelina assisted Patima onto a bed in one of the rooMiss.

"Son," Jean Pierre said with his hand on his son's shoulder. "Raisin' a baby is the most right thing there is!"

"So you think Patima is about to have the baby?"

"Could be!" Jean Pierre answered. "But there is nothing you can do now, son, but stay out of the way!"

Hours passed on by without the sound of a whimper from Patima, nor had Evelina come out of the room to give the two men a progress report. Jean Pierre finally stood up and began to walk toward the front door.

"Are you leaving me, Papa?" Jean Pierre III asked quite timidly. "Where are you going?"

"No, son," Jean Pierre answered. "Not leavin', just going out to get the necessary reinforcements!"

Jean Pierre's laughter could be heard all the way down the road to Jubil's house. Jubil joined in the laughter while Miss Sylvia grabbed her shawl and quickly headed in the direction of the big house to inform Kip and Kuya as the two men made their way to the big house as well, where they awakened Patima's best friend, Lizzie, who had just gotten comfortable in her bed.

"But is it time yet?" MAE asked, leaning up on one elbow. "Patima thought that the baby would be born sometime next month."

"Babies have their own time clock," Jean Pierre answered.

The Menard child quickly dressed and informed Wilhelmina that she would be with Patima at her uncle Jean Pierre's house should she be needed at any time, and then the three quickly made their way toward the residential area of Mon Village.

By the time the small group of family members arrived at Jean Pierre's house, the door to the bedroom was opened and Miss

Penelope, along with Kip, could be seen just inside the door, one holding her hand and the latter wiping Patima's brow with a cold, wet towel. Kuya was waiting for the men in the parlor.

"Her water has broken," Evelina said quietly. "She will be havin' this child today!"

Jean Pierre III almost had a heart attack after hearing his mother tell him that Patima's water has broken.

"Oh, but is Jean Pierre III going to get the surprise of his life!" my crazy uncle Clovis would say. "Time for him to…"

And my other uncles would chime in, "Run!"

Moments later, Patima let loose with a horrifying screech, a sound that resounded throughout the household, a screech that caused both Petois and Pecous to run into the house as they were returning from the big house, where they had been working all day. Petois grabbed his little brother, Jean Pierre III, by the arm and suggested that he make himself quite scarce now before Patima got any further with her labor.

"Why would I want to leave my wife while she is bringing our child into the world?" Jean Pierre III asked nervously. "I know she wants me here."

Petois smiled and stared at his baby brother as he remembered the day Jean Pierre III was born, the screaming, the throwing of items through the air, and the running.

"Well, then," Petois said as he sat down on a divan in his parents' house. "Shall we have a seat?"

MAE stood beside her best friend's birthing bed while Patima held tightly to her hand, which she clenched tighter with each labor pain, and with each labor pain, MAE seemingly went into shock. In between labor pains, Patima breathed deeply and even seemed to drift off to sleep until the next labor pain began to grow to great heights, and MAE would begin to breathe harder and virtually faint.

"Why are you so upset?" Patima asked her best friend quite loudly. "You are not the one in labor!"

Patima's tone seemed quite disturbing to MAE, and she backed away from the bed until the next labor pain, when Patima screamed out for her to hold her hand.

"Well, which one do you want, Patima? My hand or my absence?"

Several more hours went by, and Patima's labor pains became more intense, more frequent, and so did the screaming. "Where is Jean Pierre III?" Patima finally said, softly, in between a labor pain and her moment of rest. "Please tell him to come in here."

Both Evelina and Miss Penelope stood frozen in their tracks as both realized that the time had come, and Evelina quietly, and bravely, I might also add, suggested that she wait until the baby was born.

"I...want...Jean Pierre III...right...this...minute!"

Patima screamed, right in the middle of an intense labor pain, and it would be her Lizzie that volunteered to announce to her cousin that his wife needed him, before Miss Penelope could suggest that she wait. But Jean Pierre III walked into the bedroom, where he was welcomed pleasantly by his beautiful wife, who, at the moment, was in the middle of a moment of rest between labor pains. She reached her arms out to her beloved husband, and he carefully bent down to tenderly hug her, and then it happened. Patima transformed into the wicked witch of the south, digging her fingernails into Jean Pierre III's back as she screamed at him.

"Jean Pierre III!" she screamed with all her might. "You will never touch me again, do you hear me?" And then she pushed him away from her as hard as she could, and he flew backward, toward her mother, Evelina, who reached out to catch him.

"What happened, Mama," he asked. "Who is that woman?"

Jean Pierre was certainly confused by the sudden change in Patima's behavior, especially within just that matter of moments. Evelina tried to console her baby boy, who was completely traumatized by the sudden change in his beloved Patima's attitude with him, and explained that this was just the mind-set of a woman in labor, and most definitely a LaPierre woman in labor to bear a child.

"Aw, chère," Evelina said while stroking her son's head. "You might as well go to the gardens now and wait until I call you when the baby is born. Oh, and take your daddy with you. He should know the way for sure, by heart!"

But the devoted Jean Pierre III was also hardheaded and refused to leave, especially at this time, but when Patima threw the water pitcher toward him, he made a dash for the front door, where his father, Jean Pierre, was already waiting for him with the door already opened, ready to run.

"This is nothing like I expected it to be, Papa," the poor child said to his dad as they sat in the gardens. "I suppose this will have to be the only child we have."

"Why?" Jean Pierre asked. "This is just a part of life, son! Raisin' a baby is never easy for a woman. All you have to do is stay out of her way!"

But Jean Pierre was not sure if either one of them could go through such an experience again, and as he contemplated what that would mean for himself and the woman he so greatly loved, he heard the sound of his mother's voice ringing through the gardens. Patima had given birth, and it was now safe for him to come home and welcome his new child into the world.

As the two men entered Jean Pierre's house, Miss Penelope, who echoed the words of Evelina that it was *safe* to come back to the house, met them. Miss Sylvia opened the door to the house and hugged Jean Pierre III tightly, and there were more hugs as he walked through the house toward the bedroom where Patima was holding the tiniest thing he had ever seen in his life. He paused at the door to the bedroom, virtually shaking in his boots, until Patima caught sight of him.

"Jean Pierre III!" she said quite excitedly. "Why are you standing there at the door? Come quickly and see your new…son!"

A son! Even those words did not give him the courage he needed to approach the young woman who, just a few hours before, had vowed to kill him, but not only did Patima beckon him nearer her and the baby, but Kuya, Kip, Lizzie, and everyone else in the house encouraged him as well.

"What is wrong, Jean Pierre III?" Patima asked. "Come and hold the baby! I have a wonderful name for him. Do you not want to hear it?"

"Of course I do," Jean Pierre III answered. "I just want to make sure you are who you are supposed to be right now!"

"I have no idea what you are talking about," Patima answered. "Now, come here!"

Jean Pierre finally made his way to the bed, where Patima was holding a tiny baby with a head full of dark-colored hair and skin the color of buttermilk. He smiled as he reached down for his son and, after lifting the baby from Patima's arms, finally exhaled.

"I think we should name him Jean Pierre IV," Patima said with a huge smile on her face. "What do you think?"

Mama Del's words to Jean Pierre when his youngest child was born rang in Jean Pierre's head, and he quickly made his way to his son's side.

"Are you sure you want to name him Jean Pierre IV?" he asked.

"Why, yes, Papa," he said. "I was named after you. It could only be as appropriate that the child be named after me."

"Yes," Jean Pierre said cautiously. "Have you noticed that I am an only son and you are the last son and both of us are named Jean Pierre?"

"Then it is settled," Patima chimed in. "This baby boy's name is Jean Pierre IV."

The fate of the family had been sealed; Jean Pierre IV would be the only child that Jean Pierre III and Patima Salma LaPierre would ever bring into the world. But oh, my, Jean Pierre III would become the father of my father, the father of my entire uncles and aunts, yes. He would become my own dear granddaddy!

Once Patima had given way to sleep, Evelina carefully removed the sweet baby boy from her arms and gave him to her husband, Jean Pierre, who led their son Jean Pierre III out of the house, toward Mama Del's house, for the secret ceremony.

Chapter 35

Perhaps the most exciting and self-satisfying portion of the LaPierre-Menard family reunions would be the Sunday services, rich in nostalgia, blessed with devotion to the higher power, flavored with emotion-charged music, and certainly chockfull of people, both present and those who made their presence known from the other world.

Uncle Gaston would glance down at his watch and inform all my other sweet uncles and the young boys being initiated into the family that it was indeed time to make their way to the church house for the Sunday services. There would be just enough time for the young boys to make a pit stop, if you know what I mean, before rushing to meet their parents, who proudly welcomed them as though they had just gone through the old African ritual that made a boy a man.

As I was growing up, I am proud to say that my own dear daddy led the congregation of family in their worship of the higher power and their tribute to the ancestors that had come before them. And what a joyous celebration it always was, that third day of the family reunion, when everyone was dressed in their finest finery, complete with hats, jewels, shiny shoes, and heads held so high, as if their noses would surely touch the ceiling of the church house.

When it was time for the Sunday service to begin, Big Daddy would signal the choir, which was made up of several families that Uncle Clovis had already chosen from local family members and had rehearsed throughout the year, to sing an explosive gospel song that he, of course, had written.

"Welcome home, you have family in this place. Welcome home, we are gathered by God's grace, to honor him, those who came before, to honor family, evermore!"

The huge bells that were located at the very top of the steeple of the church house began to ring proudly with no apparent assistance from human hands. Uncle Simon would often and so innocently tell the young boys that, "I often wondered if there might be an ancestor or two up there in the steeple pulling the ropes that caused the huge bells to ring, but I never went up there to check it out or asked anyone in the family if they knew, 'cause I really didn't want to know!"

It was quite obvious by the look on the faces of the young boys that they, too, would rather not know if one or two of the ancestors might be up there in the church steeple, pulling the ropes to make the big bells ring during the Sunday services on the third day of our family reunions. I would always chuckle to myself as I recalled how very afraid I was of the very same thing while I was growing up.

Soon hands would begin to clap, and the rhythmic clapping would beckon the other family members that were still standing outside, chatting with other family members, to meander into the church house, as they always did, while clapping their hands as well, as they searched the pews to find a seat.

"Welcome home, where our family first began. Welcome home, to every child, to every woman and every man."

The music would go on and on for what felt like an hour, the choir swaying to the rhythmic beat as directed by my sweet uncle Clovis, while the congregation of family members simply enjoyed being together again, while some enjoyed being together for the very first time.

There were plenty of "Amens" from the congregation, there were many nods in agreement with the lyrics of the gospel songs, and there were lots of hands waving in the air as the music, the singing, and the clapping of the hands created an electrifying atmosphere.

The beautiful flower arrangements that the women of our family had picked from the Mon Village gardens and had prepared early every Sunday morning of our family reunions filled the air with the aroma of their various blossoms, they, too, seeming to sway with the rhythm being created in the church house.

And during our family reunions, when God had the occasion to peek beneath the clouds to see what all the racket was about, he surely got a good glimpse of the garden, of lovely hats that the women of our family styled, with matching gloves, belts, and fancy shoes. I might also add that Miss Sylvia must truly have had the loveliest of the lovely hats, since her sweet husband, Jubil, made sure she had a wardrobe of derby hats in every color of the rainbow, direct from the noble Commonwealth of Kentucky.

Once Big Daddy pulled out his handkerchief from his lapel pocket to wipe his brow, Uncle Clovis would instantly wave his hands into the air to signal the choir that it was time for the rousing gospel climax, and oh, how exciting it was! Once the music, the hand-clapping, and the "Amens" had finally stopped, my own dear daddy stood tall and handsome at the podium in the church house, where he would deliver an equally rousing and inspirational message to eagerly awaiting family ears. I was truly blessed while growing up to have my own dear daddy serve as our spiritual leader at the family reunions when my other uncles retired or expired, one after another, and I might also add, how very proud of him I was.

I especially loved to hear Big Daddy speak about the history of our ancestors, those that had been brought to this place as slaves, to live and work on the plantations in the deepest recesses of the South, those whose very lives made it possible for every other generation to exist and certainly live much better than they had ever lived. It was always a positive message of love and hope, a message of truth directed to those whose time was now and to those whose lives were to come, with a strong voice that resonated throughout the church house.

The middle portion of Big Daddy's message was always different at every family reunion as he addressed the troubles and the successes of the day, but he always managed to end his sermon with the same strong tribute to our ancestors, their history, the history of slavery, a history that made it possible for my family to have something to unite about in this place, something to celebrate. Just as my family immortalized the thundering words of Jubilation LaPierre as he wrote them in his diary, Big Daddy's positive history of our ancestors boldly hangs on a wall in the big house, where everyone can inhale as they walk in the steps of my own sweet daddy.

"Those sure are appropriate words for today, Clovis," my daddy would say as he turned toward his big brother Clovis, who acknowledged his comment with a tear trailing down his cheek and a nod.

"Welcome home, brothers and sisters!"

The congregation of LaPierres exploded in applause and shouts of "Hallelujah!" while hands were raised high in the air in full agreement. Big Daddy waited until it was quiet again, and then he began.

"God sure chose the right people when he chose the slaves to walk the walk of slavery with him," he would say with such a force that the congregation would begin to shout a loud "Amen!" Some would agree loudly, "That's right!"

"He knew I couldn't do it. He knew you couldn't do it. So he chose his children that would do it, a proud people, and he Graced them all with his own strength, his own courage, and he showered them with his love. We must never forget their sacrifice, their struggle, or the contributions that our ancestors made to this great country of ours."

The entire congregation of the LaPierre family that had gathered together in the church house at Mon Village became so still now that it was truly possible to even hear the sound of someone breathing, and even though the older relatives had most probably heard the history stories time and again, they, too, listened with anticipation and all due respect.

"In order to be successful in our journey together as a people, to the future, it is essential that we remember and honor the past, and especially that we pay homage to those that forged the way for all of us to be gathered together here in this place. And what an appropriate place it is, here beneath the beautiful magnolia blossoms, where our ancestors made history, our history, and so it is here, during every family reunion, that we pause to remember with this historical tribute."

My dear old uncles would always nod in agreement when Uncle Gaston repeated the words of my own Big Daddy on this, the third day of our family reunion.

"Aw, yeah," he would say, agreeing with what Big Daddy would be saying at that very moment.

"Brothers and sisters, you already know the story of how they got here, our ancestors, that is, shackled together and stuffed in the bottom of those great big ships that carried human cargo. You already know, don't you?"

The entire congregation would always shout out, "Amen!"

"You already know how they suffered."

"Yes, we do," the congregation would say.

"How they must have struggled to understand what was going on, struggled to survive, struggled to even understand one another while being chained together for months in the bottom of a ship until they reached their destination.

"You already know that they must have had nervous breakdowns…

"Lost their minds…

"Gone completely crazy…

"Not knowing, not understanding *why*!

"I don't even want to hear myself repeat the horror of the journey of the slaves to their new lands!"

Big Daddy would always pause here for a brief moment as he tried to calm his own emotions before he began to relay the history of slavery to our family. Uncle Gaston would pause as well as he tried to calm his own emotions before he could continue with his portion of the traditional telling of the family stories to the young boys.

"But let us hear of it one more time," Big Daddy would say quietly, and after taking a deep breath and raising his head high, he would begin.

"Brothers and sisters, the history of slavery, our history, begins all the way back in the year 1564, when Sir John Hawkins, the very first English slave trader, captured 1,200 Africans from the west coast of Africa and sold them to Spanish settlers in the Caribbean. Hawkins would make four journeys to the Sierra Leone River on the west coast of Africa to capture Africans and make slaves of them during the next four years.

"During the 1600s, Jamaica and Barbados became English colonies, and the Caribbean began to swell with the number of Africans being brought there as slaves. And then, in 1698, the slave trade became legal to anybody in the business of trading, making the business of capturing and enslaving human beings of color both popular and extremely prosperous.

"Even before the pilgrims steered their vessel, the *Mayflower*, toward the coast of Massachusetts in 1620, a Dutch ship had already brought two thousand African slaves that had been stolen from their own home country to the colonies at Jamestown, Virginia. In 1705, the Virginia General Assembly declared that 'all Negro, Mulatto, and Indian slaves shall be held to be real estate. If any slave resists his master while correcting such slave and shall happen to be killed in such correction, the master shall be free of all punishment.'

"Well, it seems only natural to me that any enslaved people would rebel against their captors. Everybody's history talks about such rebellions, those that ended in the massacre of countless human beings of many colors, and those that guaranteed freedom for an oppressed people.

"Such a slave rebellion occurred in Jamaica in 1760, to no avail, but another such slave revolt occurred in St. Dominique in 1791, ending in 1804, when Haiti became a free and independent place, the only other independent black state at that time outside the continent of Africa.

"The American Revolutionary War for Independence was fought in the colonies between 1775 and 1783, while France conquered Grenada, Tobago, and St. Kitts from the English.

"All those countries, brothers and sisters, all those powerful nations freely involved in the business of slavery!"

Big Daddy would pause again, bow his head, and close his eyes before continuing. Uncle Gaston always shook his own head as well while my other sweet uncles stared ahead as if they were all in great thought.

"Powerful people, brothers and sisters, have powerful appetites!" Big Daddy would say quite quietly while the congregation agreed to the statement with an "Amen" or "That's right."

"Enslaved people have no rights, not even over their own bodies," Big Daddy would say, looking deeply into everyone's eyes as he made contact with each and every one in the congregation of family.

"Flowing throughout our very being is the blood of those powerful people, those who exercised their authority over the women of color to produce the next generation of African slaves, now mixed with the blood of those powerful people, the English, the French, the Dutch, the Spanish, and later, the Cubans and the South Americans.

"You've all heard that old expression 'Nothing, nothing is pure.'

"Well, somewhere along these dates in time, England gained a conscience and began the mighty task of abolishing the slave trade throughout the Caribbean. The Society for the Abolition of the Slave Trade was established in 1787.

"In 1788, the United States Constitution was adopted, and included within it was the clause that declared that the slaves would be counted as only 'three-fifths' of a white person. The reason for this, of course, was to balance congressional representation.

"In the year 1794, France abolished slavery and freed all enslaved people in her colonies. During that same time, the United States Congress passed legislation preventing any and all US vessels from being used in the business of the slave trade.

"Between 1807 and 1888, the known world began an honest attempt to correct the evil committed by the human slave trade. Both Britain and America abolished the Transatlantic Slave Trade, and Britain declared Sierra Leone in West Africa as a Crown colony.

"In 1810, Britain negotiated with Portugal to also abolish slavery under the terms of the South Atlantic Slave Trade.

"In 1817, a treaty was signed between Spain and England that immediately ended the Spanish slave trade north of the equator, and then in 1820, the treaty expanded to include the Spanish slave trade south of the equator. The slave registration was also put into effect in 1817, which required all slave owners to provide a list of all their slaves every two years.

"In 1820, the United States lawmakers ended the slave trade and made it a crime equal to piracy and punishable by death.

"In August of 1834, Britain officially abolished slavery under the Abolition of Slavery Act, which gave freedom to all enslaved people in the British West Indies.

"Perhaps it was the incident aboard the Spanish schooner slave ship known as *La Amistad* that brought the brutality and inhumanness of slavery to the consciousness of the slave traders, if not to the entire world.

"On June 28, 1839, *La Amistad*, a Spanish ship that had been built in America, began its journey from Havana, Cuba, toward another part of the island with fifty-three shackled Africans that had been illegally abducted from West Africa and sold to Cuba, in violation of the international law, by the Spaniards.

"After just a few days at sea, the Africans, led by twenty-five-year-old Mende rice farmer Sengbe Pieh, revolted and took charge of the ship, ordering their captors to 'follow the rising sun back to Africa.' But their captors outsmarted the Africans and brought them to the New London Harbor instead, where they were taken into custody and held in a New Haven, Connecticut, jail on charges of murder.

"The *La Amistad* incident became the first human rights case ever to be argued in an American court on behalf of Africans when American abolitionists represented them and former president John Quincy Adams, then seventy-three years old, successfully argued on their behalf before the Supreme Court to uphold their freedom even while Spain was demanding their return. Adams's argument lasted over eight hours during a two-day period. During a portion of his narrative, Adams cited, 'The words *slave* and *slavery* are studiously excluded from the Constitution. Circumlocutions are the fig leaves under which these parts of the body politic are decently concealed. Slaves, therefore, in the Constitution of the United States, are recognized only as persons, enjoying rights and held to the performance of duties... What have the Southern states to do with this case, or what has this case to do with the Southern states? It is a question of slavery and freedom between foreigners, of the lawfulness or unlawfulness of the African slave trade, and has not, when properly considered, the remotest connection with the interests of the Southern states.'

"After nearly two years, the Africans, only thirty-five of them surviving the ordeal, were returned to their homes in Africa. Slavery was officially abolished in Cuba in 1886. Two years later, in 1888, Brazil abolished slavery as well.

"The abducting, buying, and selling of human beings from the west coast of Africa, throughout virtually the entire known world, was at its end within the international community, and although the United States Congress banned the importation of slaves from Africa in 1808, there were already hundreds of thousands of enslaved persons with their children, their children's children, and even their children's children's children, all being born and living in slavery within the boundaries of America.

"African slave labor had been used to develop the plantations in Britain and was now being imported to the New World in America to develop the new land. The invention of the cotton gin in 1793 led to the expansion of slavery in the plantation-laden South, which was able to get around the international slave laws by buying and selling slaves within states and from state to state.

"I assure you, brothers and sisters, that it was by the blood and the sweat of their human backs that the deep recesses of the South is allowed to still boast about its production of rice, sugarcane, tobacco, cotton, and so much more.

"It would be in 1865 that the American Congress would pass the Thirteenth Amendment to the Constitution of the United States, which would officially and legally end the horror of slavery. Despite the atrocities of the American Civil War, the Emancipation Proclamation, and the assassination of President Abraham Lincoln, it would be not be until December 18, 1865, with twelve generations as direct descendants of the nearly five hundred thousand enslaved Africans that were imported to North America by the European traders, that the American Congress would pass the Thirteenth Amendment to the Constitution of the United States of America to officially and legally end slavery.

"Now, we can safely assume that our ancestors were brought to Louisiana somewhere between 1717 and 1721. In fact, during that time, there were approximately five thousand slaves brought to the settlements along the Mississippi River from the west coast of Africa. That great and wonderful city of ours, New Orleans, that sits quite prettily on the banks of the Mississippi River, was already famous and very important for the import and the export of agricultural goods such as dairy products, tobacco, flour, lard, etc., so it was not that surprising that it also became important to the slave trade market.

"Certainly, our own ancestors were purchased by the plantation masters and taken to their new homes in Louisiana, homes like right here on the banks of the Bayou Frou-Frous, once owned by a crazy woman who lusted after her African male slaves and a French master who had an unquenchable lust for his female slaves, and whose last name was LaPierre, a name with French roots that was given to all the 'property' owned by the LaPierre Plantation, including its slaves, listed with the belongings of the plantation alongside the land, the house, the furniture, and the cattle."

Big Daddy, always filled with great emotion at this portion of his telling of the family story of slavery, would pause and allow his sad eyes to swell with tears.

"This is our history, brothers and sisters, our story, and an inheritance that we are ordained to continue to pass along to each new generation, not just so that this mayhem never happens again, but to pass along this tribute for the people that were known as slaves, our people, our ancestors.

"We are able to be gathered here today, brothers and sisters, in freedom, because of them. Please don't forget that, especially you, young people. When you become lazy about accomplishing anything within your life or get stuck in the negative, complacent about the struggle that got you here, self-centered and expecting anything without hard work, when you disrespect your parents or any other adults in your world with your inappropriate speech, your disobedience, or your ill treatment of them, and most of all, when you disrespect yourselves by not being the very best that you can be, you disrespect every moment of every slave that lived and died so that you would never have to suffer their consequences."

A thundering roar of applause would resound throughout the entire church house as Big Daddy finished his history of slavery, everyone standing to acknowledge his words and, indeed, the manner in which he had delivered them. The thunder would continue for several more minutes, and I remember how big and strong my sweet daddy would look at this moment, during every single family reunion.

Uncle Clovis would keep his kind eyes on Big Daddy, waiting for his signal to prepare the choir to stand and sing one more time.

"Ah, yes, brothers and sisters, I'd say God made the right decision when he chose our ancestors to walk the walk of slavery! He knew I couldn't do it. He knew you couldn't do it. But God was certain he knew exactly who could and would do it! And look at us, their descendants, blessed, blessed, my brothers and sisters, blessed! Because God's in the blessin' business. God's business is blessings!"

Uncle Clovis would raise his hands high up in the air to signal the choir to stand, and stand tall they always truly did! The first notes of the piano would begin as the choir members began to sway to the rhythm.

"God is in the blessing business. His business is blessings. So don't you fret, 'cause you will get all that God has in his store."

I particularly loved it when Big Daddy would use his words like that to lead the choir into a song, and I especially loved the fact that Uncle Clovis was always ready to lead the choir at just the right time, with just the right songs.

"God is in the blessing business. His business is blessings. So don't despair, our God is always there, 'cause God is in the blessing business. His business is blessings."

What a more appropriate time for our family to give homage to those of our present generation that had passed on to the other world to be with the ancestors than during our Sunday services.

During his lifetime, it would be my dear, dear uncle Gaston, and after his passing on, it was my sweet uncle Simon, uncle Clovis, and so forth, in accordance with age, until it was my own Big Daddy's turn. I truly believe that it was certainly because of this portion of our family reunions that we were always able to keep track of our loved ones, our history, and our traditions.

By the time I was a young woman, I knew all about the family that preceded me and could most probably have passed it on to those that came before Miss Gracie. But of course, everything comes in its own time, and in its own manner.

Chapter 36

THE YEARS WENT by, at their own pace, and afforded everyone at Mon Village, in the great state of Louisiana, their own rites of passage. It is truly amazing how the mind and the body begin to subtly reject the very things that were once the very most important things in our lives, and so it was with virtually all the older LaPierres.

For Jean Pierre, it meant to willingly relinquish his responsibility as owner and master of Mon Village, of all that the LaPierre eye could see, the role he had cherished since the time of his youth, to his and Evelina's offspring, their baby boy Jean Pierre III, who accepted the role with the vigor with which Jean Pierre had once ruled. Along with Patima and their beloved baby boy, Jean Pierre IV, the younger LaPierre family was now the head of the entire LaPierre family and ruled with fairness, love, and an open heart.

The eldest of Jean Pierre and Evelina's children, Mon Claire, finally and permanently moved to the noble Commonwealth of Kentucky around the turn of the century, after finally accepting the position as a buyer for the horse farms for which she had worked with Jubil. Certainly, the job was an important reason to move, but Mon Claire had also fallen in love with a Kentucky boy who had won her heart after winning a horse race between the two during a demonstration for a potential buyer. No one had charmed her the way this young man did, and after receiving her parents' blessings over the telephone, she and the young man were married in a simple ceremony by the justice of the peace. Her visits home now were few and far between.

Petois and Pecous remained at Mon Village after each having their own home constructed in the residential area, where they could keep an eye on their parents, but have their own lives as well. The twins married twins, two young women who were employed at their restaurant in the capacity of bookkeeper and concierge, respectively.

Labelle Jelee remained in Chicago, dividing her time between her design shop and the nightlife that was so popular during the early 1900s. Rumor had it that Jelee had a propensity for bad boys and was said to have even entertained certain Chicago Prohibition bigwigs, if you know whom I mean.

Monique Aimee Elizabeth LaPierre-Menard was hired by the Mon Village schoolhouse to teach physical education and health, a position at which she both enjoyed and excelled. It would be during her second year at the school that she introduced basketball to her female students and was even able to schedule games between the Mon Village basketball team and those from schools outside the confines of the Bayou Frou-Frous. Patima Salma LaPierre would remain MAE's very best friend throughout their entire lives, and the child Jean Pierre IV was both her adored and cherished nephew.

MAE's relationship with Pastor Benjamin Broussard continued to grow more serious over the years; however, MAE kept the young man at a close distance as she continued to devote her life to her parents, who were beginning to need more and more attention from her, as well as from the nurses and other professionals who provided assistance to the home.

Edward was the first of the former Menard household staff to pass away from the earth to the other world to be with his ancestors. It was truly a peaceful passing. He was buried in the LaPierre-Menard family cemetery with all the ceremony afforded any LaPierre.

Wilhelmina the Cook was the last of the former Menard household staff to pass on to the other world to be with her ancestors, shortly after Maggie had passed on. Both ladies had been tremendously important to both MAE and Patima during their formative years, and memories of lunches together in the cook's kitchen would always be the special memories of the two ladies.

The years also gave way to age for Jubil, who finally shared his veterinary skills with a young man that he had hired to work with him after Mon Claire moved permanently to the noble Commonwealth of Kentucky. Even though Jubil hesitantly relinquished his knowledge to the young man, Miss Sylvia was delighted to be able to spend more time with her beloved husband, and eventually, Jubil, as well, began to enjoy his retirement.

Kuya continued to bring extraordinary beauty to the grounds of Mon Village, while Kip remained the mysterious, beautiful woman that she had been all along, even in her older years. The two remained faithful to Mr. Menard and the Madam Menard, but it was obvious that the time would soon come when they, too, would need that special care given at the home for the ill, the former big house.

Even the ever-beautiful, ever-expanding Mon Village itself began to experience its own change, with the railroad challenging its growth through the residential area, bringing the perimeter inward, toward the center of Mon Village, where the La Las had once been held. The older homes, those built first so many years ago, were the first homes to be demolished, but the railroad company chose a slight detour once it neared Mama Del's house!

Farewell

With the passing of the former Menard household staff, MAE had the sad task of locating a few new staff members to give the special attention to her parents that Edward, Wilhelmina, and Maggie had given them, even in light of the home's own medical staff. MAE needed someone to literally live with them while she was away teaching at the schoolhouse, to understand their special needs, and to truly care about them. All those requirements and more came in the person of Miss Annabelle, the former madam of the big house during its former life. Miss Annabelle would prove to be one of the most important people in the lives of Monsieur and Madam Menard during their final days on the earth, and she gave them all the love she could possibly muster.

It had become Jean Pierre III's sad task to move both his father and his mother into the home for the ill once the railroad tore down the houses on the outer perimeter of Mon Village, and even though LaPierre pockets were filled with cash for the inconvenience, it meant that the move for Jean Pierre's parents came much earlier than he anticipated. The two were happy just to be with each other and spent much of their time with Mr. Menard and the Madam Menard on the back porch of the former big house, listening to the two tell of their many journeys on the cruise ships on which they had had the pleasure of sailing.

It would be on a bright and sunny Louisiana summer day that the ancestors came to claim their own.

Jean Pierre was sitting on the front porch with his youngest son, Jean Pierre III, discussing the events of the day as they watched the sun slowly begin its daily routine. It had been an especially warm day, and Jean Pierre III had been sweating hard when he climbed the stairs to the former big house to join his father. He wiped the sweat from his brow with a handkerchief and politely accepted a cool glass of sweet lemonade from one of the staff members of the house that saw him as he climbed the stairs.

Evelina was with Patima at her home in the residential area, talking to her sweet grandbaby Jean Pierre IV, while Patima was chatting away about something that had happened at the schoolhouse with her students. She had now been teaching for a few years, English classes to be exact, and just as her Lizzie did, Patima enjoyed both her students and her classes.

Jean Pierre IV was now a young boy who loved his granny and enjoyed those moments he had to share with and learn from the old woman. He was tall and muscular from working with his dad, Jean Pierre III, his hair was deep brown, and his almond-shaped dark-brown eyes were just like his mother's.

Mr. Bernard Menard and his beautiful wife, Madam Dolice Marie LaPierre-Menard, were sitting on the back porch of the former big house with Miss Annabelle, enjoying their late-afternoon tea. Miss Annabelle loved to listen to the two wonderful people tell about the stories of their travels, but most of all, she enjoyed watching them hold hands, hug each other, and smile at each other as though they were still newlyweds.

Everything became quiet, a quiet that everyone at Mon Village could hear and feel, the kind of quiet that caused people to begin to expect something to happen. The kind of quiet that could not be ignored.

"Evelina was most probably the first," my dear old uncle Gaston would always say, "the first to begin 'the walk.'" Yes, she was the first to begin the walk toward the big magnolia tree, and then it would be Jean Pierre II who stood up on the front porch to tell his son that he needed to take the walk. Jean Pierre III was sure that he meant to say a walk and stood as well to accompany him.

The Menards on the back porch also felt the need to take a walk, as Miss Annabelle had heard it, and proceeded to stand up to accompany them as well.

MAE met her uncle Jean Pierre II and her cousin Jean Pierre III as they were leaving the former big house to go for a walk, as her cousin repeated. Realizing that something was amiss, she quickly made her way through the house and onto the back porch just in time to see her parents preparing to take a walk as well with Miss Annabelle. As she approached them, she suddenly realized what was happening and she did all she could do to avert the inevitable.

"Wait!" MAE screamed. "Please stay here. Please do not go!"

The young woman made a quick dash to Patima's house, and breathing quite hard, she explained to Patima what she thought was happening. With Jean Pierre IV behind her, Patima joined her best friend, her Lizzie, to find their parents, who, by now, were walking together toward the magnolia tree. They would meet Jean Pierre III and Jean Pierre II just as they, too, reached the big magnolia tree.

Yes, they were all walking together, taking "the walk" toward the magnolia tree, Jean Pierre with his beloved Evelina, Mr. Bernard Menard and his beloved Dolice, and they were all smiling and all holding hands, as if they were playing a childhood game.

"Please, Mom, Daddy, stay with me!" MAE yelled out.

Dolice Marie turned her head toward her daughter and stared for a moment and then blew a kiss to her, and then smiled. Mr. Bernard Menard did the same, and for just a brief moment, MAE knew that they recognized exactly who she was. She was their daughter, their beloved Aimee.

"What is it?" Jean Pierre III asked. "Where are they all going?"

"To the ancestors," MAE said as she wiped away her tears. "They are all leaving us, together!"

The young Menard woman caught sight of her mother, who was looking directly at her, smiling and pointing at her own forehead. At first, MAE was quite unsure of what her mother was trying to tell her, but Dolice Marie continued to point at her own forehead until, finally, MAE realized that her mother was reminding her of the day that she had caught her own tear and put it on her sweet Aimee's forehead, when she was a young girl, and told her that she would be with her forever. MAE smiled, touched her own forehead, and shook her head to let her mother know that she did, indeed, understood.

Jean Pierre III began to cry. Both Patima and her Lizzie tried their best to comfort him, but he was inconsolable.

Uncle Clovis told the young boys, "You must also remember that real men cry." Then he wiped his own tears away. "It takes a man to cry!"

"Mama, Daddy!" he cried out, but after blowing kisses to them as well, Jean Pierre II and Evelina sat down under the magnolia tree and were soon joined by the Menards.

Jubil felt all of them leaving him, and he began to walk as quickly as he could to say his goodbyes, Miss Sylvia joining with him, and as they approached the scene under the magnolia tree, Jubil began to cry.

"Jean Pierre! Dolice Marie!" Jubil yelled. "Wait! Wait!"

Again, Dolice Marie appeared to recognize them all as she and her beloved husband stared toward the people that were staring at them, begging them not to leave, and then suddenly, for all eyes to see, the ancestors appeared behind them—Mama Mozelle and the African-with-No-Name, who later became known as Jean Pierre I, with Mama Del, who would leave the earth for every appearance of the ancestors, and behind them were others that were not recognizable, ancestors from Africa that had come to show them the way home in the other world. Within moments, the vision faded, and left behind was only the lifeless bodies of the loved ones.

By the time the residents of Mon Village had made their way from the residential area, the shops, the gardens, and the former big house, their loved ones, as they had been known on earth, were gone. There were tears—oh, yes, there were plenty of tears—but once the crying had ended, there was a time of celebration and a time for remembrance.

The Menards and the LaPierres were laid to rest in the LaPierre cemetery alongside those that had gone on before them to the other world to be with the ancestors. A solemn church service was held in the LaPierre church house, officiated by Pastor Benjamin Broussard of the Mon Village Protestant Church, which MAE had arranged in honor of the entire family. "We are reminded by the Holy Scriptures that there will always be 'a time to weep, and a time to laugh; a time to mourn, and a time to dance,'" Pastor Benjamin Broussard said to the many attending the service, repeating the words from Ecclesiastes. "Let us take our time to weep and mourn, but let us be sure to laugh and dance."

Following the service, a rousing march led the way to the site where the four would be buried, and after prayers, tears, and kind words from those who knew them best, a second line consisting of all the residents marched the entire distance around the perimeter of Mon Village to honor the former slaves that became the master and mistress of all that the LaPierre eye could see, and the spouses that they loved.

That night, there was plenty of corn liquor and apple wine to go around, and the residents of Mon Village danced!

Chapter 37

"Adieu, Miss Gracie, Adieu"

Monday was not actually a day included in our family reunions, but the Mondays after the family reunions were always the same, indeed—that unfathomable drop in emotions that always follows a huge event when loved ones get together, like right after celebrating Christmas or the Fourth of July. The human body seems to be left too heavy to add even one more feeling, so it just shuts down for a while to allow the mind to rest before it experiences the loss of celebration, or as it always was for the LaPierre-Menard family, the loss of the excitement of reunion.

For some reason, this particular Monday after the family reunion felt extremely void of emotion, so very void that the feeling could certainly be likened to that dreaded feeling of depression when there becomes nothing at all to look forward to. I tried desperately to describe that feeling to Miss Gracie, fine writer that she is, when she finally showed up at the big house for our final conversation about the LaPierre-Menard family reunions.

We were, even now, both having been later than we had planned to be in order to meet back at the big house on this Monday morning, but I was terribly happy when I finally saw her racing across the meadow toward the big house for what would prove to be the very last time that Miss Gracie and I would meet.

This day was reserved for the final goodbyes, until the next time, for the members of the LaPierre and Menard families.

It was a time for parting, the parting of ways for all those that attended our family reunions every five years. The cars that were parked throughout the areas of Mon Village were already thinned out before Monday mornings, because some of our relatives and loved ones would leave to return to their own homes on Sunday evenings, after Sunday dinner, which brought us together just one more time. This time the men, headed by my sweet uncle Gaston until he was no longer able to participate, would cook a wonderful meal for the women of the family and serve them as though everyone were in a fancy restaurant.

It became a tradition long before I came along, perhaps as far back as when my ancestors Petois and Pecous did the cooking for such wonderful and exciting events and, I am sure, a tradition that was enjoyed and anticipated by everyone that could participate.

Those family members that lived the farthest distance would leave the earliest, while those that either lived here at Mon Village or within driving distance would stay later or, in some cases, until the next morning. These fortunate ones would enjoy one more zydeco, one more spin around the dance floor, but unfortunately, many more moments of tearful goodbyes as family bade one another adieu.

The young boys had been initiated and were now with their parents, either leaving the old uncles that they had spent the weekend with or still here with their parents, enjoying one more day together with the family.

It was also a final time to talk about what happened to our family members after Mr. Bernard Menard, Dolice, Evelina, and Jean Pierre passed on to the other world to be with the ancestors.

Jubil and Miss Sylvia carried on the memories of their beloved Dolice and Jean Pierre for years after they passed on, telling the stories to the children of Mon Village who sat for hours listening to their stories about Jean Pierre and Dolice Marie LaPierre.

Jubil passed on first, right there in his stable, while caring for a horse with his new assistant. Some say it was a heart attack; others say that Jean Pierre and Evelina simply came to get him on a cold winter's day.

Miss Sylvia's mint shop was the last business to be torn down, because there was still so much of that pesky mint growing in the gardens and, of course, between the noble Commonwealth of Kentucky and Mon Village. She processed and sold mint for years and years after her husband passed on, and she, too, lived in the big house until she passed on to meet her husband. Rumor had it that Miss Sylvia was found in the gardens, picking mint, just like she had been doing when she first met her wonderful husband, Jubilation LaPierre.

Jean Pierre III, Patima, and Jean Pierre IV continued to live and work at Mon Village throughout their entire lives; in fact, they lived right here in the big house during their old age, being cared for by their devoted son and the household staff. They were extremely happy all their lives and never once neglected from time to time to visit the old magnolia tree with MAE, that place where their parents had lain down and gone to sleep, a sleep that took them to the other world to be with the ancestors.

MAE and Pastor Benjamin Broussard eventually did get married, and they, too, lived at Mon Village until it was their turn to pass on. MAE continued to teach physical education and health at the schoolhouse until her retirement. The two never had any children, but the children that MAE taught deeply loved her and the pastor, leaving them never without the love for and of a child.

After her parents passed on, Monique Aimee LaPierre-Menard Broussard gathered all her notes together from all her lifelong journals and sent them off to a publishing company to be considered for a book. Months later, she would receive a large box with several copies of her new book, which she had simply entitled *Mom and Dad*.

MAE and her husband, Pastor Benjamin Broussard, were eventually moved into the big house, where they spent their last days in peace and happiness.

As far as Mon Village is concerned, what the human eye can see is all that remains of the former plantation; the railroad took over much of it as well as modern developers that built skyscrapers and big businesses that stand all around the Bayou Frou-Frous, the gardens, and of course this big old house. Mama Del's house still stands, of course, and so does she, after all these years, still looking out for the very last of the LaPierre-Menard family. And that would be me.

Well, Miss Gracie, that about does it. Now you know every single thing that I do about my own family, the LaPierre-Menard family, and I hope that you will pass it on without prejudice, and perhaps you could even find it in your heart to add a few words about me when you do.

My name is Alexandra LaPierre-Menard, an African European Asian American and heiress to the LaPierre dynasty of manufacturing companies that, at one time in history, provided this fine country of ours with luxurious mint julep cups.

I met Miss Gracie, fine writer that she is, when I was 114 years old and had outlived every single one of my family members, including the most recent ones. Unfortunately, my own mother and father passed on to the other world to meet the ancestors many, many years before, and I, having been their only child, was left with no one here but those who care for me here in the Mon Village Nursing Home, that place where my sweet ancestors Madam Dolice Marie LaPierre-Menard and her beloved husband, Mr. Bernard Menard, once resided. Although it no longer has the appearance of a cruise ship, this old house still has many memories of them, and so many that came after them, their portraits, and items of clothing, diaries, and yes, even this old woman.

I never married, never had any children, although I was asked several times for my hand by some very sporty men who had eyes not only for me but also for the fortune of Mon Village that had been passed down to me. Perhaps I found it more feasible to protect this wonderful place than to share it with someone that would outlive me. After all, I am a genuine LaPierre. Can you imagine Mon Village being willed to someone whose surname had not a drop of Bayou Frou-Frous bloodline? Perish that thought!

Mon Village was a thriving city to its own self when I was a young child, full of life, full of people, my family as well as those that visited here for one reason or another, if you know what I mean. Ha ha! This place was the pride and joy of the LaPierre family, of the great state of Louisiana itself, from the residential area to the business district, where all the shops stood tall and proud, to the schoolhouse, to the church house, and yes, this place that has been everything imaginable!

Oh, and by the way, Miss Gracie, even though all those treasured belongings are all gone, replaced by those fancy bridges and pavement, that ever-present, ever-pesky mint still sits there in the gardens like a royal king on a throne, still growing, still providing the locals with its fresh foliage. If it could talk, I can only imagine what kinds of stories it would tell about the people that picked it for their own special requirements, or those that lay on top of it, not to mention those that are still lying underneath it!

Well, Miss Gracie, I feel for sure now that I have only a few moments remaining with you, as I can feel my own life slipping away from this earth and expect that the ancestors will soon come to take me to the other world with them and all those that I love tremendously.

Please remember, Miss Gracie, it is now up to you, and you alone, to continue to carry on the traditional telling of the family stories of the LaPierre family, my little friend! Come quickly and let me hold and pet you just one more time, my fine, furry little feline friend! Who would ever have dreamed that I would tell the stories of my precious family to you, Miss Gracie, you beautiful stray cat in your beautiful calico colors that stole my heart! Thank you for being such a good friend, for being such a good listener, and for being such good company to a lonely old woman!

The staff here at the nursing home has already been informed that they are to make sure you have your strong Louisiana coffee with plenty of milk every single day, just as if I were still here with you. I have asked them all to cater to your every need, just as if I were still here with you, and I believe that they will, for I am sure that they know that I will be watching over you, and over them, to make sure. I am certain that you have your own ancestors that will come to take you to the other world someday, but for now, it is my turn, and I bid you goodbye.

Adieu, Miss Gracie, adieu!

The LaPierre Family Tree

Madam Frou-Frous LaPierre + African-with-No-Name (later, Jean Pierre I)= Jean Pierre II
Philippe LaPierre + Mozelle Castille = Dolice Marie
Jean Pierre II and Evelina
Dolice Marie and Bernard Menard
Mon Claire
Monique Aimee Elizabeth
Petois and Pecous
LaBelle Jelee
Jean Pierre III and Patima Salma
Jean Pierre IV and Ma-Elsie
Gaston Menard and his wife, Kathleen
Dominique Eduard and his wife, Philamena
Simon and his wife, Stella
Cecile and her husband, Dobb
Sophia and her husband, Tomas
Marie and her multiple personalities
Clovis and his wife, Gertie
Jean Pierre V and Momo-Belle
Batiste (died from accident on a swing)
Michele and his wife, Mercedes
Rene and his wife, Lucia
Alexandre (never married)
Jean Pierre VI and Zothra
Alexandra LaPierre-Menard

About the Author

A NATIVE OF THE bayous of Opelousas, Louisiana, Creole-bred Nita Clarke currently resides in Lexington, Kentucky, where she spends her highly anticipated and enjoyable retirement from the public workforce since 2006. She has two children, Michael and Michele; ten grandchildren and two great grandchildren. Nita attended the University of Southwestern Louisiana in Lafayette, where she studied English and Journalism. She also attended the Lexington Theological Seminary in Kentucky, where she graduated in 2013. She is a disabled veteran of the US Navy, having served during the Vietnam era as a journalist and in public affairs. Nita spent nearly ten years in radio as a talk show announcer at KSLO/KOGM Radio in Opelousas, Louisiana, and at KJAE/KLLA Radio in Leesville, Louisiana. Her favorite pastimes are writing, volunteering at her church, St. Peter Claver, and spending time with her family and friends.

CPSIA information can be obtained
at www.ICGtesting.com
Printed in the USA
LVHW091155130520
655430LV00001BA/16